Saving Magdalene

a novel

Also by Michael-Patrick Harrington

Deep Autumn

I See No Angels

www.michaelpatrickharrington.com

Saving Magdalene

Michael-Patrick Harrington

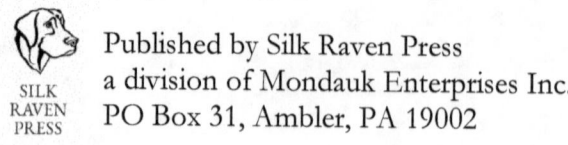
Published by Silk Raven Press
a division of Mondauk Enterprises Inc.
PO Box 31, Ambler, PA 19002

(SRP-003)

Saving Magdalene and *A Lab's Ears Are Made of* SILK © 2013 by
Mondauk Enterprises Inc. & Michael-Patrick Harrington
All rights reserved.
ISBN: 0615849369
ISBN-13: 978-0615849362

stubble, his breath pungent, his tie askew) had patted her head and told her it was truly not.

After Magdalene had spent a few days in self-imposed exile, dodging phone calls from the principal (Christina had taken Magdalene's cue, cutting once to spend an afternoon shopping), Christina's father convened a private conference on Sister Rita and her falling face for his daughter and her best friend. Dr. Fuller was a pediatrician, and he offered Magdalene a kind, open smile, his oval head bouncing slightly as he chewed his ever-present piece of gum; Dr. Fuller's breath was always spearmint-fresh.

"Girls, there is no leprosy in our part of the globe," Dr. Fuller said, his words coming fast between bursts of mint. "Besides, leprosy is so contagious, if Sister Rita did have it, they wouldn't let her teach."

Magdalene felt a generosity in the way Dr. Fuller looked at her, as if he knew that her father was on leave from work and spent most of his days inside one bar or another—McCullough's Inn usually—his head in his hands, eyeballs upward, glued to a silent ballgame, his sport jacket sleeves pushed up, his hairy knuckles gripping a Camel. But if Dr. Fuller knew this (and, honestly, how couldn't he?—ADA Barrows had become one of the town drunks), he had given no obvious sign to Magdalene, just a gripping handshake upon her arrival. Magdalene was grateful nonetheless. Not that she thought she would *really* catch leprosy (one couldn't be too careful though; there were better ways to go)—she usually left the hysteria to Christina, who could be counted upon for more traditional girl behavior: notes to boys, high-pitched giggling, absurd hugging of the other girls each morning in school, as if they hadn't seen each other in decades—but it was comforting to know that an adult, other than principal Sister Mary Joseph, had noticed her absence. Magdalene's father usually didn't wake up until long after noon and didn't seem to notice her until late in the day. She'd gone through the charade anyway, staying in her room until 3:15, then going downstairs to slam the door and announce her presence, a pointless ruse, as her father had been awake only one morning during her three day vacation.

Dr. Fuller chewed his spearmint gum and opened several books, showing Magdalene and Christina what leprosy victims really looked like, and although the girls agreed some of the photographs bore a passing resemblance to Sister Rita's sagging globe, the nun evidenced none of the open sores and general demeanor of a person being eaten alive. Magdalene secretly thought her father looked to be in more dire straits than Sister Rita.

Dr. Fuller offered a series of possible explanations for Sister Rita's deformity and frequent absences, but finally settled on poor medical care in the face of a possible childhood neurological disorder. "It's more than likely, girls, that no one took Sister Rita to the doctor's when she was little. No one took care of her," Dr. Fuller said. Christina paid scant attention to her father; she seemed entranced by the dyed blonde bangs that fell into her eyes, and she employed a number of methods to halt their descent—blowing her breath upward, tossing back her hair, shaking her head like a dog— Christina was bored; Magdalene knew these rituals from eight years together at Assumption of Our Lady Elementary School. Magdalene, however, basked in just being near an adult of some authority other than a nun or a lay teacher. While Christina paged through a human sexuality text, Magdalene left her chair to sit on the floor and lean against Dr. Fuller's crossed legs, a neurological book open on his lap.

Magdalene didn't hear Mrs. Fuller enter the room. She just seemed to appear, a mass of frosted hair and clumpy, pale red lipstick, flicking a duster.

"Out, girls—now!" Mrs. Fuller demanded in a voice—clipped bursts followed by a long, drawn out final syllable—perfected in Assumption Faith Board meetings.

Christina was up, slinking past her mother before Magdalene could drag herself from the lulling intensity of Dr. Fuller's voice. He snapped the book shut and Magdalene jumped. If there was a sound worse than a book closing, Magdalene didn't want to know. She wondered briefly what Dr. Fuller would think of *her* book; her own father was too soused to read the back of a cereal box.

"Really, Samuel. The girls should be outside. I have cleaning to do."

Mrs. Fuller's eyes rested on Magdalene's blushing face.

Dr. Fuller flipped the book open again; he had kept his finger on the page.

"What do we pay Mrs. Bochdan for?" he asked, his voice trailing off, his eyes already lost in some diagram or figure.

Mrs. Fuller pointed the duster at Magdalene who was already heading towards the door. Magdalene averted her eyes from Mrs. Fuller's, wishing for a secret trap door or a revolving bookcase, like the ones the Hardy Boys were always stumbling through—there were an awful lot of bookcases in Dr. Fuller's den—anything to not walk past Mrs. Fuller's sour perfume.

"Go back to school, Magdalene," the doctor called after her.

"Really, Samuel, this is for her father to…"

Magdalene blocked the rest out. Her father was probably in McCullough's now. The mantle of respect Dr. Fuller wore with casual ease was buried beneath mountains of cigarette ash on Assistant District Attorney Gregory Barrows.

So Magdalene returned to school. She also swore off after-school catnaps, convinced the puffy way her face presented the pattern of the sofa when she looked in the mirror was a prologue to the kind of later destruction evidenced by Sister Rita. School wasn't so bad—better, at least, than being home most days, if she was honest with herself. Magdalene was a bright girl, precocious even (according to several teachers). Her black bob haircut framed a face brimming with equal amounts of curiosity and defiance (an opinion also held by many of her instructors). School came easy to Magdalene, too easy; she could perform basic algebra in her head in the fourth grade and had read *Romeo and Juliet* by the end of fifth grade (though for Magdalene's money, it was hard to beat the Hardy Boys), so her current deportment was beginning to alarm not only her teachers and principal Sister Mary Joseph, but, at least today, in the confines of Sister Rita's stuffy classroom, Magdalene herself. Still, Magdalene knew the pendulum swung quickly in the mind's eye (especially hers), so she was not surprised, less than a week after promising Dr. Fuller she'd return to her schoolwork, to find herself once again in the emergency room at Holy Redeemer, having a slimy tube forced down her throat while nurses slapped her face, doctors yelled orders, and Magdalene counted the swirling holiday lights that had stamped themselves into the canvases of her eyelids during the brief ambulance ride.

In retrospect, Magdalene suspected Sister Rita's interpretation of the Nun's Story to have been the spark, the catalyst, the proverbial straw, but that was too easy. She had tried once—not that her father had noticed much, but Aunt Tiddy had been appropriately upset—so it stood to reason that she could either have sworn off suicide altogether or have found herself drawn into its uneasy comfort again.

It was near the end of the school day when Sister Rita began the tale; there had been an unexpected rain storm during recess, and many of Magdalene's schoolmates had removed their shoes. (Her mother's face slid into her thoughts that drowsy afternoon, the light perfume that always clung around her mother's neck snaked behind the smell of white chalk and anxious feet.) If nothing else, the Nun's Story was proof enough to Magdalene that while some people were clearly too good for this world, others of lesser stock were only waiting for a moment when they would be given a chance to ascend. Such was the case of Sister Mary Magdalene de Rosa.

Sister Rita wasn't telling it right though, Magdalene thought. Her version was *too* immersed in the fire and brimstone. Sister Edna had had the right tone. Sister Edna had been frightened not by the details of the story as much as by its possibilities. (Magdalene knew this was a rather adult observation for an eighth grader; she was proud of the way her mind worked.) Sister Edna heard what Magdalene heard in the story: possibility. Would one scale the fiery ladder to greatness, thus earning the right to the epitaph: *too good for this world*, or would one cower, shriveling from every sort of saintliness or genius? Magdalene was sure chunky Sister Edna, with her thick, too-hairy arms and fuzzy moustache, experienced the query posed by the Nun's Story purely in spiritual terms: would Sister Edna have the right stuff? Did she have the stuff of her Saviour? Magdalene was confident that Sister Edna, in fact, did not, and was even more sure—shit sure, as Michael would say—that Sister Rita didn't have a single clue, much less the wherewithal to recognize a potential moment of greatness, even if one unveiled itself the way it had in the Nun's Story. Sister Rita's thought process seemed as muddled as her face.

It was the incident with the yardstick that melted away any authority, spiritual or otherwise, from Sister Rita's Halloween mask. As usual, skinny, freckled Jerry Eves was entertaining in the back of math class. Jerry was the author of a series of rudely drawn cartoon panels detailing the adventures of Stick Man who, in the grand tradition of much eighth grade comedy, fought against not only arch villains and filthy nuns, but also his own gaseous tendencies. (Stick Man tended to fart away his enemies, his distinct odor his secret weapon.) Jerry was in the midst of revealing his latest masterwork to his loyal, captive cadre when Sister Rita, spittle escaping her crooked mouth (her lips drooped and hung open on the right), snagged him by the back of his hair (all the Eves boys—there were four of them— had a cowlick and a little hair tag dead center on their necklines; plenty of places for nuns to latch onto), and dragged him to a desk in the front row—the desk Sister Rita kept empty for just such displays of punishment and power.

Magdalene was familiar with Stick Man—although she was not considered part of the cool crowd (too weird, the kids said; too distant; a real gay bird), despite having connections through Christina (and Michael). Christina was a member in good standing of the Bod Squad, the all-girl upper echelon treated as schoolyard royalty by a majority of students. (Christina had french kissed two boys in the seventh grade, lending an increased air of sophistication to her dyed blonde halo.) Dr. Fuller attended to many of his daughter's classmates; Christina never held this over anyone's head, but the other kids granted her a mantle of respect—there was a distinct possibility that Christina could be privy to any number of embarrassing incidents (puberty, menstruation, bed wetting, nightly emissions), so her membership in the elite was assured. (Behind their backs, the self-named Bod Squad were referred to as the Jesus Sluts, and if the name was an undesirable sobriquet, Magdalene never heard one squeal of protest.) But despite not being cool (and being a girl), Magdalene had read many of the past adventures of Stick Man, albeit only after they had made the rounds in the boys' circles but before they were ensconced in what Jerry referred to as the Vault: the green three ring binder on which he had inscribed the names of several rock'n'roll bands Magdalene was sure he had never listened to but whose posters most likely hung in his older brother Mick's room. Stick Man was funny in that boys' way: bodily functions that Magdalene would have otherwise kept to herself were badges of honor among the boys. Not even menstruation escaped their consciousness; Stick Man had several run-ins with tampons, but his (and the author's—and by extension, the male audience's) lack of comprehension of their true use was revealed in the way the slightly drawn superhero used them more like diapers (and had once used four of them as suction cups to scale a building). Magdalene forgave Jerry and the boys their ignorance (at thirteen, she was still waiting for her first period) and secretly applauded their toilet humor even if she didn't find all of it particularly humorous. (She had made a mental note, however, to include some gaseous emissions in her own, possibly posthumously published book to perhaps widen her audience to include boys.)

Sister Rita didn't see *any* humor in Stick Man. Magdalene was sure the nun didn't even know humor was involved. Other teachers had caught Jerry practicing his art and had punished him for it; Stick Man was notorious in teachers' circles, and several panels of work had to be redone by the artist—a notation at the bottom of a page would list the dates of the original's conception and subsequent confiscations. But Sister Rita seemed to not know exactly what Jerry was up to that day and neither impounded the comic strips nor even gave them a second glance until after it was all over.

Instead, Sister Rita produced her yardstick, and, in front of the class, proceeded to whack the gnarled blue stick upon Jerry's knuckles, the blue shimmering in the air like a bug's antenna after each smack. This was not unheard-of behavior for Sister Rita. She'd sworn to Magdalene's class that she would rather beat Jesus into their hearts then let their organs "*grrrrow* black with the *ffffungussss* of *Sssatan*." To Magdalene, Sister Rita didn't appear to be in the throes of any great religious revelation while she beat Jerry Eves. Sister Rita was a wobbler. Her gait was shifty and unsteady, and as she teetered to and fro between hits, each step revealed log-like legs ensconced in ancient pantyhose. The old nun twisted her face so it resembled a hoary prune, and her wandering eye kept a close guard upon the rest of the class. It didn't matter where one sat in the classroom; there was no escape from Sister Rita's eye—or her spittle; getting splashed was a daily experience. She beat the children when they misbehaved, Magdalene hypothesized, because she was full of anger: at God for making her this way or at her parents for being too poor to afford her proper medical attention as a child (Dr. Fuller's explanation) or both. Whatever the root cause, when Sister Rita struck Jerry's knuckles with the yardstick, it was with considerable force; Magdalene could feel the air part and *whoosh* in her face each time the yardstick met Jerry's knuckles.

All of this would have proceeded as previous beatings had: Jerry would be remanded to his front row seat for the remainder of the day (not that there was much time left on the clock, and maybe that explained Jerry's response) or, even worse, be sent to Mrs. Peitzman's office (Mrs. Peitzman was school secretary *and* disciplinarian, and while she never used a ruler or a yardstick, she was renowned for doling out extreme essays, due the next day, on proper Catholic behavior)—but Jerry laughed. Actually, if Magdalene had really thought about it at the time, Jerry *cackled*. Still, it was barely rousing; the air in the room was stifling on this late spring day, Magdalene's head was heavy, and her eyes burned like they'd been underwater for long periods of time. The beating of Jerry Eves aroused just a distanced alacrity; only the Nun's Story could have sufficiently stirred her from her somnolence.

"P*rrrr*epa*rrr*e fo*rrr* you*rrr* puni*shhhh*ment," Sister Rita said.

The words slid out of Sister Rita's mouth like applesauce; it was as if the nun's tongue was thick like a cow's, and her words had to navigate the opening on the right side of her mouth in order to escape. There was no telling which consonants or vowels would be slaughtered.

Jerry seemed to point at Sister Rita, although his hands never left their place on the desk where he'd folded them as instructed.

"Thi*sss* is no time for lau*ghhhh*te*rrr*," Sister Rita told Jerry, her final syllable accompanying a glob of spit that landed on a habit already stained with a variety of yellow splotches.

Jerry threw his head back. Magdalene winced. The yardstick bounced against Jerry's knuckles again.

"Let me kno*wwww whhhh*en you'*vvvv*e had enou*ghhhh*," Sister Rita said, her left eye wobbling around quick enough to catch Megan Riley stuffing a Jolly Rancher into her mouth.

"Out!" Sister Rita said.

Megan Riley spit the Jolly Rancher into Sister Rita's outstretched hand.

Jerry grabbed the business end of the yardstick and hit his own knuckles, braying like a donkey.

Whap went the yardstick.

Sister Rita stashed the candy in the folds of her habit.

"Sister, Sister!" said Mary O'Brien.

"Sha*rrrr*up!" Sister Rita demanded; the room was unhinging in a rather noisy fashion.

Magdalene watched Christina pass a note to Megan Riley, but she felt no jealousy, just a late afternoon hunger. Magdalene couldn't remember the last time she and Christina had shared a secret.

Jerry stuck a finger up his nose and winked at Joseph Connelly. Sister Rita snorted—and cracked the yardstick against Jerry's nose. Megan Riley covered her mouth with her hand. A couple of girls gasped, then the room went dully quiet. Jerry withdrew his finger from his nose. Blood appeared on the boogies he'd unearthed. He stared at the end of his finger.

"Go to the o*ffffccccc*e," Sister Rita grumbled, and Jerry looked ready to cry—not that he hadn't been to the office before—hell,

Magdalene had seen him sitting in one of the chairs outside of Mrs. Peitzman's door just this morning—but to be hit in the nose by a nun—in front of everyone—even Jerry Eves recognized the gravity of the situation dripping down his face.

Jerry wasn't the only one in the classroom dripping. Drool navigated its way through Sister Rita's stubby chin whiskers. Her left eye rolled into her skull, and the raw redness of her triple chins spread to her exaggerated chipmunk cheeks.

"Go to the *offfficcccœ*!" Sister Rita gargled, and Jerry lifted his shaking body from the chair and shuffled to the door.

"Wait till I tell my mom…you…" Jerry said, "…you…"

Magdalene closed her eyes.

"…nun!"

Magdalene opened her eyes when she heard the door click shut. Goodbye Jerry Eves.

Sister Rita crumbled the remaining comic strips in her sweaty fist.

"Sister, Sister!" Mary O'Brien implored, breaking the students' silence. "Ooh, Sister!"

"Sha*rrrr*up," Sister Rita said quietly, staring at a cartoon that had drifted to the floor, and Magdalene was close enough to the front to catch a glimpse of Stick Man drawing a comic himself—a figure of a fat nun with a movie monster face melting from his cartoon pencil.

"Sister, Sister," Mary O'Brien whispered.

Sister Rita pulled herself to her full height, which wasn't much, but her weight and bearing and turkey-sized fists and straining belly made her seem like a giant. A drop of sweat escaped from beneath her wimple.

And this was when Sister Rita told *her* version of the Nun's Story.

All versions of the story—even Sister Rita's—had the same basic details. It came down to the accent, the slant. Father Dave, the pastor, told it like he was imparting bad news; his tone turned soft and gentle; he touched heads as he walked around the classroom; he caught the children's eyes in his—Magdalene felt that the nun in the story had been a personal friend of Father Dave's. Old Father Vincent, his bald head an extreme exclamation point, his almost wrinkle-free face moving like a cartoon character's, all jaw and eyebrows, painted the most extreme version of Sister Mary Magdalene's sacrifice. To Father Vincent (who began his seventh grade Matrimony Class by scrawling "LEAVE ROOM FOR THE HOLY GHOST" on the blackboard in huge letters), the important part of the story wasn't the children or even the fire—it was Sister Mary Magdalene's consciousness those few moments before her skin peeled away from her bones. Sister Mary Magdalene had gotten a taste of hell according to Father Vincent, a free preview. Sister Edna's version was a ghost story whispered around the campfire; Sister Edna seemed as wide-eyed as the rest of the class, as if she couldn't possibly comprehend the level of faith confirmed by the martyred nun.

The yardstick incident had given Sister Rita enough gravitas to properly imbue the Nun's Story with all the accoutrements of horror. Magdalene thought Sister Rita was doing a terrific job setting the tone, Jerry's knuckles notwithstanding. It was like watching a thriller on the late show those nights when their father allowed Magdalene and Michael to stay up for Hitchcock or *Laura*. Then it had been considered a treat—now her father wouldn't notice if she *never* went to bed; Magdalene kept proper hours if only to compensate for the lack of parental direction. Not that she'd watched those types of movies since Michael disappeared. It had been bad enough watching them with him! There had been no telling when Michael would take advantage of her fictionally induced terror. Horror movies kept her awake at night; thrillers had her checking behind the shower curtain. Raven afforded her little comfort; the dog's affection for her brother transcended any instinctual need to protect the baby of the family. She'd be just as apt to trip over Raven as she warded off the ghouls as to be strangled by that English necktie murderer from *Frenzy*. But Sister Rita's version of the Nun's Story was scarier than *The Brute Man* (there *was* a physical resemblance between the nun and actor Rondo Hatton) and more unsettling than *Rosemary's Baby*.

(Magdalene allowed herself a smile at her vocabulary: *accoutrements of horror*. Afterwards, in a fit of dramatics when she was dying again, she would think of it as her last *real* smile. Her father—the father she and Michael had had before their mother passed away, the father who'd taught them to skip stones, who'd played stickball with half the neighborhood in the summer and practiced spirals with Michael every night until it was too dark for either of them to see, who'd smelled like a mixture of aftershave and sharp cheese: a comforting, familiar smell, one that would linger on their pillows long after he had tucked them into bed—that father would have been proud of her vocabulary. Back before Michael had gone missing, before Gregory Barrows' drinking had graduated from a pastime into a full-blown excuse to dirty some glasses, Magdalene's father would quiz her with vocabulary words. They'd press their heads together, squinting into a dictionary whenever Magdalene stumbled upon a word she couldn't put into recognizable context. She thought they must have looked funny—their two heads—Magdalene's pageboy bob and her father's structured sweep, a crest like a wave, riding his forehead. At bedtime, her father quizzed her until she fell asleep, awash in nouns and gerunds and adverbs and words ending in –ion. It was the only physical link Magdalene felt with her father—Michael had football and their father was the head coach of the Assumption Knights and everyone knew, everyone, that football was a boys' game—but Magdalene had her words.)

It appeared to Magdalene, however, that Sister Rita had momentarily lost her footing with the English language altogether. Her words tipped and stuttered and skipped, stones across a polluted stream.

"A*rrrr*," said Sister Rita, but Magdalene knew what she meant. She suspected a few of the other kids did too. The mood in the room had changed; Magdalene imagined a Bernard Herrmann score rising up behind Sister Rita.

"*Whhhh*en you li*vvvv*e you*rrrr* li*ffff*e for Je*ssssu.ssss*," Sister Rita said, "*whhhh*en you gi*vvvv*e you*rrrrsssss*elf to him, you don't ha*vvvv*e time to play game*ssss*. Je*ssssu.ssss* i*ssss*n't going to wait; you ha*vvvv*e to an*sssswerrrr* in a hea*rrrr*tbeat."

"The fire started in the girls' lavatory…" Magdalene whispered; she knew the Nun's Story by heart.

"The *ffffirrrre sssstarrrr*ted in the gi*rrrr*ls' la*vvvv*ato*rrrr*y…" Sister Rita began.

"In the old school building," Magdalene continued to herself.

"…the one do*wwww*n the hall."

Magdalene sat up in her chair. She had peed in that bathroom, the one just down the hall, at least once every school day; it was a place she hated. Knowing the other girls could hear her splashing water bothered her, not because they could hear, but because it all sounded pretty much the same behind closed doors, and until the girl emerged, she couldn't tell if the splasher in the adjacent stall had been her best friend Christina or sloppy Donna Gaynor or lonely, big-boned Bridget Boyle. Peeing was the great equalizer, and Magdalene felt nothing if not disdain for anything that brought everyone down to the same level when, clearly, the world was not built that way, no matter what the priests and nuns and lay teachers had taught her. Catholic school, with its uniforms and monotonous ritual prayers represented to Magdalene a faith of the lowest common denominator. The Apostles and other Saints surely hadn't subscribed to this mediocrity and had suffered in spectacular ways, as illustrated in *Butler's Lives of the Saints*—arrows for Saint Sebastian, boiling oil for Saint John—making a point that there were those who chose to rise above. Catholic school preached one thing and practiced another, Magdalene thought; she felt removed from greatness.

And here, yet again, was proof: after years of hearing the Nun's Story set in another building—the mostly-abandoned structure to which the new school had been clumsily attached, removing the tale even further into the past—the truth was out. Sister Rita, in her haste to use Jerry Eves as a cautionary tale (against what, Magdalene wasn't sure; artistic complacency maybe) had brought the Nun's Story home to roost: right here in the girls' bathroom on the third floor of Assumption of Our Lady Elementary School's new yellow building.

Magdalene looked around to see if anyone else had caught the change of locale, but most of her classmates were busy staring at the clock or else at the back of the person sitting in front of them. Christina was smiling into the clip of her pen, checking her teeth. Megan Riley was trying to adjust her unnecessary bra. Only Mary O'Brien had a look other than boredom on her face; Mary O'Brien looked ready to burst.

"Playing with mat*ch-ch-ch-ch*es," Sister Rita growled, her lower lip reaching past her upper lip to kiss her runny nostrils.

"*Sss*omeone wa*sss sss*moking in the gi*rrrl*s*ss*' lavvvvato*rrrr*y. E*xxxx*haling God out of her li*ffff*e."

Nobody knew who'd thrown the lit cigarette into the trash can. But Magdalene wasn't sure which part of the tale was fact (there'd been a fire, and Sister Mary Magdalene de Rosa had died in that fire—there was a little plaque commemorating her death outside Mrs. Peitzman's office) and which part was fable (like chopping down the cherry tree, Magdalene was sure the cigarette smoking details were added for maximum effect: see, smocking *is* bad for you). Still, to find out that the bathroom down the hall had been the bathroom in question—Magdalene shuddered.

"*Sss*i*sss*s*ss*te*rrrr* Ma*rrrr*y Magdalene *wwww*a*sss sss*tanding by the doo*rrrr*. The *chhhh*ild*rrrr*en *wwww*ere all *sss*econd g*rrrr*ade*rrrr*s*ss* and couldn't be le*ffff*t un*sss*upe*rrrr*vvv*i*ss*s*ed. *Sss*i*sss*s*ss*te*rrrr* Ma*rrrr*y

Magdalene didn't kno*wwww* the*rrrr*e *wwwwassss* a *ffffrrrr*e until *shhhh*e opened the doo*rrrr* and *ssss*aw the *ffff*lame*ssss*."

Magdalene doubted this part of the story—always had—it was good theater, as Aunt Tiddy would say, for the flames to just suddenly *appear*. More likely, the good sister was helping one of the girls hike up her skirt or reach the sink to wash her hands. Magdalene always imagined her partially-namesake'd nun to be wonderful with children—more friendly baby-sitter than teacher.

"They *ffff*illed the doo*rrrrwwww*ay!" Sister Rita said, her chubby hands tracing a crescent moon above her head before landing on the gelatinous sides of her stomach. The cross all Good Sisters of the Order of Saint Joseph wore around their necks lay horizontal on the shelf of Sister Rita's massive boobs, the late afternoon sun glinting off its surface into the nun's squinty eyes.

"The *ffff*lame*ssss wwwwe*rrrr*e evvvve*rrrr*ywhhhhe*rrrr*e!" Sister Rita shouted, her hands fanning the stuffy classroom air.

Magdalene looked around again. With the exception of Christina, who appeared to be surreptitiously attempting to extract something from between her teeth, the rest of the class was now riveted, glued to a story they had heard more times than any childhood fairy tale or Dr. Seuss book. This was the *good* part, Jerry Eves would have said. This was the gooey part, the part with teeth.

"*Ssss*isss*ste*rrrr Ma*rrrr*y Magdalene kne*wwww* shhhhe *wwwwassss* God'*ssss vvvve*ssss*el," Sister Rita said. "*Shhhh*e kne*wwww wwww*hat *shhhh*e had to do*ooo* to *ssss*a*vvvv*e the *chhhh*ild*rrrr*en. *Shhhh*e ne*vvvve*rrrr he*ssss*itated, not on*cccc*e. *Ssss*isss*ste*rrrr *ssss*aid a p*rrrr*aye*rrrr*. *Shhhh*e told the *chhhh*ild*rrrr*en *wwww*hat to do*ooo* and d*rrrr*opped *ffff*ac*cccc*e *ffff*i*rrrrssss*t into the doo*rrrrwwww*ay, *ssss*mothe*rrrr*ing the flame*ssss wwww*ith he*rrrr* body, he*rrrr* body cat*chhhh*ing *ffff*i*rrrr*e, and the *chhhh*ild*rrrr*en *wwww*alked o*vvvv*er her like a b*rrrr*idge and e*ssss*caped the *ffff*lame*ssss* of hell."

"Forever gone forever," bulky Bridget Boyle whispered into her trembling fist.

The bell rang for the end of school. No one moved, except Christina who stopped picking her teeth, grabbed her bag, and made for the door. When the rest of the class stayed put, she sat down noisily, looking over to Magdalene. Christina breathed through her nose in frustration. Magdalene ignored her.

"*Whhhh*at *wwww*ill you do*ooo whhhh*en you*rrrr* time come*ssss*?" Sister Rita asked, and Magdalene could see the nun's yellow, crooked teeth.

"*Wwww*ill you be *wwwworrrr*thy? D*oooo* you ha*vvvv*e *whhhh*at it take*ssss* to be a *ssssavvvviourrrr*? I*ssss* you*rrrr ssss*oul clean? I*ssss* you*rrrr* mind empty o*ffff* impu*rrrr*e thought*ssss*? D*oooo* you ha*vvvv*e *whhhh*at it take*ssss* to *ssssavvvv*e the *chhhh*ild*rrrr*en? D*oooo* you ha*vvvv*e *whhhh*at it take*ssss*?"

Magdalene knew for a fact that she herself did not. All of life's tests so far administered: she had flunked miserably. And Magdalene knew that although she had failed the last big test, if nothing else, she would not fail her upcoming final task. There was nothing worse than not being ready when it was your time, and Magdalene was tired of living like a ghost. Her father was a ghost now too, and Aunt Tiddy, dear old Aunt Tiddy would be one soon enough. Though still breathing, Aunt Tiddy qualified as a shadow of a shadow, living her life, according to Magdalene's father, in the wake of his mother's— Tiddy's sister's—extraordinary one: first female County Council member, married at eighteen, sending her only son to an Ivy League school. Magdalene felt surrounded by ghosts and quite comfortable in their company in as far as being able to slip in and out of their lives as she pleased—she just didn't like being invisible *all* the time. Granted, Aunt Tiddy was difficult to avoid—she always seemed to appear peripherally with a fist full of apple-butter sandwiches and *Reader's Digest* advice—but for the most part, Magdalene was as free as any adult—more free in fact: no taxes, no bills, just a large hanging stone of unbearable, immeasurable weight dragging her neck down. When her head hit the pillow at night, it was with sheer exhaustion, although she rarely slept. Michael was always there when she did, and although she missed him greatly, more than she thought she would have even though she adored him to no end (in love with him, some would say, and they wouldn't be entirely wrong), Michael had also been endlessly annoying, always bossing her around, always daring her to—*well, push that thought right out of your head, Magdalene Harper Barrows*. Michael had been no ghost. He'd been quite corporeal, loud and smelly—all boys were sort of loud and smelly though, Magdalene thought—and he'd lived his life like a Fourth of July firework: in midair for half a heartbeat, then plunging spectacularly down, down, down.

"Sister, sister," Mary O'Brien whispered again.

"*Whhhh*at Mi*ssss* O'B*rrrr*ien, *whhhh*at?" asked Sister Rita—finally— as the class gathered their belongings in silence.

Magdalene could see the small puddle at Mary O'Brien's feet and was thankful the rest of the class was preoccupied with escape. Mary O'Brien's time had apparently come.

When Sister Rita released the class into the warm afternoon, Magdalene avoided Christina. It had to be tonight, Magdalene thought; putting it off any longer wasn't getting her anywhere different. She was pretending. Pretending her father's time away from the DA's office was a leave of absence. (There was little evidence to suggest he hadn't permanently left.) Pretending that she wasn't responsible for everything that had happened. Pretending that her therapist knew anything other than how to push pills. Pretending to feel the same way about Raven—or about anyone. But Raven was the key—his runny black nose would poke into her side when he walked into her room at night, and Magdalene felt no need to reach over and comfort the dog, despite knowing that the mourning process was as far from over for Raven as it was for her father.

Magdalene pressed home, a knot growing in her stomach, knowing Raven's greeting at the door would be over-celebratory and a bit sad: *at least you're home, at least you're home,* his butt shaking in the opposite direction of his tail, eager to be petted and cooed to and fed cookies of comfort. Raven was still waiting for Michael to come home, and Magdalene hadn't the courage to even whisper to her dog that Michael might never be coming home. Michael might be forever gone forever.

+

Magdalene could easily have walked home from Assumption with her eyes closed; she had never been out of Mondauk County (let alone to Philadelphia just to the south or New York City). Other than the less-than-exciting exceptions of Bard's butcher shop in neighboring Spring House across Pennypack Creek (the muddy stream that everyone called the Puddle) and forced window-shopping on the Avenue in Rhawnhurst, Magdalene had rarely been outside the town of Mondauk Proper. Mondauk County had seven townships or boroughs: four on the western side of the Puddle (Anchor Hop, Warminster, New Hope, and Spring House), bordered by the larger, river-like Neshaminy Creek, which in the spring was filled with boats, and three on the eastern side (Mondauk Proper, Rhawnhurst, and Fox Chase). Magdalene had been to four.

Mondauk Proper (which folks called the County Seat) was the largest of the townships and home to the local government. The town had grown up around an asbestos factory that had finally closed in 1962. The derelict factory and smokestack provided an ominous backdrop to the Mondauk Proper Train Station in the northwest section. The mysterious Dr. Mattison, the egotistical eccentric who'd built the asbestos company in Mondauk Proper (which had been a "dry" town until the factory's workforce arrived), had erected Lindenwold Estate (which included a statue of himself and a stagnant man-made lake, Loch Linden) in the northern part of town. When the factory waned, most of the town did not—but Dr. Mattison did. He ended his days living in a small apartment across the street from Lindenwold Estate, strapped into a wheelchair, playing checkers with himself on the front lawn or just simply staring at the iron gates of his former Xanadu. Asbestos, found to be harmful to the health, had been especially dangerous to Dr. Mattison's mental bearings when its toxicity ended his empire. The large gates of Lindenwold now hid a small monastic retreat as well as a shelter for abandoned, neglected, and abused children and an orphanage with a school.

Rhawnhurst, the second largest and most urban of the towns, was to the northeast. There were lots of row houses and twins and concrete playgrounds and a small Jewish community that conducted itself with a willful obliviousness to the county's internecine Christian rumbles. The tiny range of hills that constituted Mondauk County's eastern border began in an elevated neighborhood in the southeastern section of Mondauk Proper (called the Heights), flattened out in Rhawnhurst, and began again north of Fox Chase. Fox Chase, north of Rhawnhurst, was the smallest of the three boroughs on the eastern side of the Puddle. Its northern border was a massive, old graveyard from the eighteenth century. According to Michael, while there were plenty of foxes in Fox Chase (referring to the town's all-girl prep school), the actual animals were pretty scarce. "Snipes? Yes," Michael had told her. "Red foxes? No."

The four towns on the western side of the Puddle were more scattered, separated by large swaths of Pennypack Woods. (Pennypack Woods surrounded the whole of Mondauk County. Spring House was the least populated. It sat adjacent to Mondauk Proper (across the Puddle but connected by Olde Bridge). Spring House consisted of one long highway dotted with tiny shopping centers. New Hope, huddled against the banks of Neshaminy Creek in the westernmost part of the county, was a town torn between Jersey shore gaudiness and art school hipness. Warminster was the biggest borough on the western side of the Puddle. To the north of Spring House, it was all townhouse communities and like-minded construction. From the car, each house resembled the next. The smallest town, Anchor Hop, tucked northwest of Warminster, was also the home of some of the county's wealthiest families, although they seemed to regard their wealth as something to count rather than something to use. The Roman Catholic upper-middle class of Mondauk Proper had long ago assumed the mantles of power.

(There were also several hamlets dotting the map—Blue Bell, Waganer, Quakertown, among others—which belonged legally to none of the seven boroughs, which claimed them anyway. These communities had failed, in the heady days of Dr. Mattison or before, to incorporate, thus robbing their citizens of the full opportunity to participate in the democratic process. They could vote, of course, but they had no local representatives of their own. What was good for the surrounding town or the one it bordered was good for the hamlet. This did not sit well with the inhabitants of these villages, especially the non-Roman-Catholic population. It was like they were illegally adopted. " 'The genius and the mortal instruments are then in council,' " Aunt Tiddy had quoted, " 'and the state of man, like to a little kingdom, suffers then the nature of an insurrection.' ")

When Magdalene's father's mother had died, the funeral required a trip tiny New Hope, nestled on the Neshaminy. (They couldn't imagine their father growing up there.) Michael whispered to Magdalene in the car that she belonged in New Hope, amid the hippies and artists. The idea made her nauseous; kidding or not, she had little desire to leave Michael's side. Their father had just begun his descent (his wife's headstone hadn't even been ordered and now this); Michael *was* Magdalene's family. The dead woman in the big, black funeral car was Aunt Tiddy's sister, their paternal grandmother, only Magdalene and Michael had met her just a handful of times and found it hard to get their mouths around the word "grandmother." Magdalene believed relationships were often nothing more than assignments: visiting Grandmother Barrows (when she'd been serving on the County Council in Mondauk Proper) was necessary to maintain some semblance of order, she supposed, even though Grandmother Barrows, perfectly capable, rarely left New Hope or the Council office to visit them.

Magdalene found the distance between her father and his mother odd. After all, Grandmother Barrows had been a distinguished woman in Mondauk's local government. She had surely sacrificed to send her only son to an Ivy League school. It was well known that she had a grudge against the Catholics; Magdalene's father likewise had little time for religion, only tolerance (a lot more tolerance than his wife). Grandmother Barrows' first husband, Peck Barrows, Magdalene's grandfather, had died in a bizarre confluence of lightning and a sudden, unavoidable Crohn's attack during a walk home from church (he'd been using a tree for support when emptying his bowels)—an act of an angry God, Grandmother Barrows had said. Her second husband became (after their marriage) a drinker of some renown, and this feisty, independent woman found it the height of absurdity that the Church would frown upon her departure from the marriage bed. Aunt Tiddy said that her sister's second husband only strayed from the barstool long enough to pass out—on the couch, in the front yard, and, once, on the steps of the church. Aunt Tiddy said that was where her sister wanted to leave him: on the church steps. But instead, she packed her things and moved into her own apartment and a few months later ran for a seat on the County Council. It was with no small amount of indignation that Magdalene's grandmother found herself in a Catholic hospital when a lump in her breast turned out to be just the harbinger of the indignations to come. She desired no visitors, allowing only her son to pay his respects while she was dying—and him only once. Magdalene guessed Grandmother Barrows was proud of her son's law school record and his rapid career trajectory, but the woman had kept her distance, claiming, according to Tiddy, that the worst thing she could do for his developing mind was mother him. Tiddy always claimed an affinity for Magdalene's father, if only for the sole reason of having together survived her sister's developmental indifference.

Aunt Tiddy's real name was Tiberius Wheelwright. Tiddy's father had wanted a boy after his wife gave birth to Tiddy's sister (Veronica—a resolutely Catholic name that Magdalene's grandmother resented to no end near the twilight of her life) and so, in a pique of rebelliousness (Tiddy's father was a watchmaker, and he knew, biologically, he'd already lost his struggle against time in his quest for a son), he named his second daughter Tiberius after the Roman Emperor Tiberius Caesar Augustus. According to legend (Magdalene's great-grandfather had been a man of certain education),

Emperor Tiberius, after recalling Pontius Pilate to Rome, insisted the Roman Senate install Jesus among the gods; the Senate refused, and Tiberius was said to have died in seclusion, mired in debauchery. Magdalene's great-grandmother, a staunch supporter of the Church, found her husband's choice for a name neither alarming nor particularly damning, as did many of her fellow parishioners. Magdalene's great-grandmother was said to have bucked the system, unheard of in their little Catholic enclave. Her love of God was not tied to her wallet or her politics, and she frequently championed the causes of other denominations, going so far as to assist the Methodists in establishing their own fund-raising carnival in Mondauk Proper. The town elders, who'd been pleased at the Methodist migration to the trailer parks that clung to the Puddle downstream from the asbestos factory, had what principal Sister Mary Joseph called a bird. ("They went ape shit," Michael said.) Resurrection of Our Lord, the Roman Catholic church and school in Rhawnhurst had their own carnival too. Assumption's lay church board in Mondauk Proper (the powerful Faith Board) didn't appreciate another carnival, especially a Methodist one, competing with their own lucrative corner on the Christian carnival fund-raising market. "There's no place for God in the voting booth or the bread line," Tiddy often liked to say. (Many of Mondauk Proper's Methodists lived on or below the poverty line; the Faith Board members were more affluent, like Mrs. Fuller.) Thus the seeds were sown, Magdalene liked to think, not only for her grandmother's repudiation of the Church when she opted to leave her besotted husband for her own questing nature, but also for Magdalene's own theological difficulties.

It wasn't that Magdalene didn't believe in God and Jesus and the Holy Ghost, but she found it hard to believe that her family's religion was the only true religion. (Aunt Tiddy referred to herself as agnostic, and Magdalene was fairly certain that she and Tiddy did not belong in the same category.) Surely, Magdalene felt, God would have come to different cultures in different guises—whatever guise would best fit the situation. Magdalene understood that the Church would consider this heretical and equally understood that not a single one of her classmates—especially Christina (despite being raised in proximity to the hothouse of Dr. Fuller's superior mind)—thought the same way if they thought about it all. And forget about her teachers. An awful lot of Magdalene's instructors were nuns and made pains to avoid even controversial words. Sister Edna asked "Does anyone have to make?" rather than "Does anyone have to use the bathroom?" (Nuns, Michael had said, do not poop.) What Magdalene *did* believe was that God administered tests of faith—well, not of faith, exactly, but of mettle. Sister Rita's hissing taunt ("*Whhhh*at *wwww*ill you d*oooo whhhh*en you*rrrr* time come*ssss*?") was quite real to Magdalene, and she knew, with a certainty that eclipsed, she was sure, even the religious conviction of the nuns responsible for her education, that she had failed her last test and that the failure had made the world around her a miserable place—not just for her, but for everyone.

Magdalene crossed the stony driveway of the Calvary United Methodist Church to cut through their cemetery, careful not to stray too far from the edge near the woods. No sense raising the ire of Mrs. Nicholas, who tended the grounds with a nun-like vigilance. Neighborhood kids called Mrs. Nicholas "Good Saint Dick," and the groundskeeper waged a private war against Catholic kids traipsing through the cemetery to reach the northern part of town. The Methodists accounted for a small percentage of the town's population; they were squeezed between the Catholic majority and the black, Baptist population that lived in the poorer (but not poor) part of town along the creek banks in the southwest. Magdalene and Michael had peeked into a Baptist service once and found it rousing—the dancing, the singing—thrilling even, when compared to the austere, ritual mumblings of the Catholic Church. The Methodists were even more austere, in Magdalene's opinion—just cutting through their sterile cemetery with its neat ordered rows of stones made Magdalene aware of the subtle differences. The Catholic cemeteries dotting the landscape were filled with haphazardly-shaped stones and drunken-soldier lines, as if death had been an utter surprise to each and every one of the interred. But what was subtle in a small town? Just seeing the few Jewish residents walking to synagogue on Saturdays in their yarmulkes made drivers of various Christian denominations slow down their cars to stare.

The Methodist pastor was Earl Mockingbird, and his bearing was more improbable than his surname: short, skinny legs supporting a massive tractor-trailer tire that circled all the way around his waist. His multiple chins rested on his crisp, black collar. Magdalene found him a bit intense—his eyes squinted in suspicion behind chunky glasses when he spoke, and his tone brooked not a bit of doubt at God's terrible greatness and Man's trembling evil. His heavenly

Father was nothing like gentle Father Dave's, whose God was less a severe taskmaster (Saturday student detentions aside) than a kindly, doting uncle. When Father Dave initiated the guest lecture series, Pastor Mockingbird gave a sermon to Magdalene's class (and a smattering of transplanted Methodists) in Assumption's basement chapel. Pastor Mockingbird had a speech disorder which rendered everything he said slightly comic (especially to Jerry Eves), but when elderly Father Demetrius, the retired monsignor and former pastor of Assumption, began (inexplicably) dousing the tall liturgical candles—the main source of light in the basement chapel—Pastor Mockingbird finished his sermon in the dark, where his speech disorder grew from a humorous impediment into a serpent's hiss. More disturbing to Magdalene, Pastor Mockingbird never acknowledged that he spoke in almost complete darkness as if to do so would be to give in to the Morning Star or, worse, become complicit in some Catholic contrivance. His voice struck at the darkness like a hammer striking an anvil. Many of the visiting Methodist faithful were from Paradise Lakes Trailer Park, and despite the gloom, Magdalene could still make out their tattoos and motorcycle boots and stained t-shirts as they nodded at Pastor Mockingbird's words and bent their heads in shame. Still, despite the obvious financial decline of its congregation, the seriousness of the Methodists (and Pastor Mockingbird) earned Magdalene's respect. She found Sister Rita's "Don't X Christ out of Christmas" campaign and Father Dave's popular all-singing mass mildly reprehensible—or, at least, the opposite of sensible. How were crack-ups like Jerry Eves supposed to learn the mysteries of faith singing dirges like "Faith of our Fathers" or making Christmas propaganda posters for scary Sister Rita?

In the unmown back field of the cemetery, the sun was still high in the sky, haloed by little bugs and specks of flying wishes. Magdalene stopped at her favorite Methodist gravestone (after making certain Mrs. Nicholas wasn't lurking along the underbrush). Rosewood Seton, born 1848–died 1944. Rosewood Seton never got to see one hundred, but she'd seen two world wars, and judging by the lack of any further engraving on the stone and any further Setons in proximity, she'd died unmarried. In Magdalene's mind, she had died untethered and untangled too. For sure, Rosewood Seton, in her long life, would have made connections—surely she had had relatives and parents and maybe siblings and hopefully a few close friends to see her through, but Magdalene liked to think of Rosewood Seton the way she thought of her paternal grandmother: aloof and independent. Magdalene thought if she herself could have achieved that level of aloofness, that stage of independence, she wouldn't have to die on this late spring day. If she could sever connections as incisively as Grandmother Barrows had done with her second husband (and her son, when it came down to it), Magdalene could live with Michael's disappearance. But the Mondauk County Seat was a small town in a sea of small towns (even now, Magdalene had already crossed the back field, counting the cracks in the pavement that led to her house, dead in the center of Candy Lane), and Magdalene couldn't breathe for all its ghosts; there was no other way to escape.

From the corner of Candy Lane and Hendricks Road, on its slight hill, Mondauk Proper laid itself out: the Heights to the east, the Puddle and Paradise Lakes Trailer Park bordering the west boundary, Pennypack Woods sealing the town off from its nearest county neighbors. She imagined she could see the blinking sign above McCullough's Inn several blocks away—it had shorted out some years ago, and neither the late Mr. McCullough nor his daughter Zooey had bothered to fix it; Magdalene thought its blinking neon was like a trashy hooker's sidelong wink. If Magdalene squinted hard enough, she'd see her father, slumped on a barstool, the mantle of ASSISTANT DISTRICT ATTORNEY—a title Magdalene always saw in capital letters—hung in the corner with the forgotten coats and caps. Candy Lane was empty, but soon kids would finish their after school snacks and the little ones would finish watching *Star Blazers* or *Scooby-Doo*, and the street would be filled until dinner or practice or homework time.

She heard Raven's bark echo down the narrow street; it was like he could tell time. Magdalene rarely dawdled on the way home from school (except for lingering in the Methodist cemetery from time to time) or stopped at a friend's house. She knew Christina's mom didn't appreciate her presence, especially after the self-laceration incident last year, and Magdalene's friendship with Christina was now, for the most part, conducted during official school hours or on the weekends. But even the weekends had become problematic, as Magdalene's father sometimes slid off the stool to lurch home for a catnap or a sandwich or to throw up in his own toilet before returning to the bar to see the evening through to its end. Christina had borne witness to one of these intermittent homecomings, and

Magdalene had rushed her out to the backyard and together they'd hopped fences until they reached third grader Katie McAllister's house on Orchard Street, where they threw pennies at Katie's window. They helped the little girl make cakes in her bake-oven and oversaw hermit crab races in her driveway until an unshaven, grumpy Mr. McAllister shooed them home. Raven had been barking then too, when Magdalene and Christina sulked back to Candy Lane. Magdalene's father had vomited on a kitchen chair before leaving for the bar, and Magdalene heard the black Lab's warning yelps a block and a half away. She abandoned Christina to sprint home, guilty that she'd left Raven with the acidy contents of the ADA's stomach. (Christina, as a rule, never ran anywhere and was annoyed at all the rushing about.)

Katie McAllister was the only person Magdalene thought she'd actually miss—Raven wasn't a person, after all. Katie was Magdalene's baby-sitting charge, but the baby-sitting assignments were further and further apart. Mr. McAllister said he was working fewer nights, but Magdalene doubted it. After Magdalene had tried to die the first time, everyone treated her like a deviant—why would Mr. McAllister be any different? Aunt Tiddy and the kids at school were the worst, but in opposite ways. Her classmates treated her with delicate reverence and left the stage-whispered comments to echo in cupped hands. Aunt Tiddy poured it on and became ubiquitous (the old woman just about moved to Mondauk Proper)—forget the ghosts (as if!), Magdalene couldn't breathe for all the administered hugs and bowls of chicken broth and entreaties to go shopping on the Avenue. Magdalene studiously avoided Aunt Tiddy, even once ducking behind the mailbox on the corner when she saw old Tiberius scanning the landscape from the front porch on Candy Lane, her wrinkled hand shielding her eyes against the sun. Everyone treated Magdalene with what Sister Mary Joseph had called kid gloves. (Whatever *that* meant: kids' gloves were cumbersome; had the principal meant to imply, during one of the good sister's interminable one-on-one sessions, post-Magdalene's-first-suicide attempt, that Miss Barrows was too hard and difficult to peg?) Everyone except her father, that is; he seemed not to notice. He cried to himself a little when she came home from the hospital, stirring a splash of soda into his scotch with his finger, and slumped back into his chair after trying (unsuccessfully) to extract himself to hug his daughter. (Aunt Tiddy had brought her home from the hospital.) Magdalene was convinced that if it wasn't for Aunt Tiddy, Magdalene's body could decompose in her room all through the coming summer.

There was Raven to consider though; the poor dog had been through so much for being only eight-years-old. Magdalene's disappearance would be a mystery to the dog, one more in a series of mysteries. Magdalene suspected that Raven thought people were made of air and that occasionally they returned to it, leaving Raven in the hands of new owners. Even Raven's arrival into her and Michael's lives had been tinged with death: their mother's. Patricia Archer Rumsey Barrows had not been two months in the ground when their father adopted the Labrador retriever from Brookline Rescue. Raven was black and his snout was gray. He had a little white spot on his chest to mark his heart. Raven was adopted to fill a void—to replace their mother (their father had just started tossing them back with vigor)—such was Raven's insurmountable first mission in the Barrows Bungalow. Their father explained to them that Raven had been turned over to Brookline Rescue by his original owners who felt they couldn't give him enough attention. (They had two babies and twins on the way.) Raven had then been neglected by his second owner, a local musician known to the ADA (the guitar player being a fellow patron of McCullough's), and was stolen by a concerned neighbor (the malnourished dog had been left tied to a rope outside overnight) and delivered back to Brookline. Raven was needy, and so were Magdalene and Michael; Raven fit right in— except that Magdalene found herself needing less and less. Michael was the dog's hero. Raven slept with Michael most nights, his warm belly against the top of Michael's head. Their mother would have had a bird had she been alive! Their mother had been conspicuously clean, and she considered pets—especially hyper, slobbering ones— superfluous to the family unit. Not that she didn't have a soft heart for a warm puppy, but somewhere in her upbringing, of which Magdalene knew little, cleanliness had been drilled into her like nails into a coffin. After her death, Michael found it increasingly impossible not to push at the boundaries, sometimes only to see if anyone—their father in particular—was paying attention. No physical challenge impeded his momentum. No dead tree was too tall (or too dead) to leap from. No parent (dead or otherwise) could prevent serial repetition of less than sanitary behavioral activities.

Sleeping with Raven on his head had been Michael's continuing (silly) rebellion against a mother two months gone. It was a wasted rebellion, Magdalene thought. Not only because their mother was dead, but because their mother, when she was alive, despite a rather pronounced cleaning fetish, allowed her children to pretty much do whatever they wanted. This was due at least partially to the lies; their mother was a constant and imaginative liar. Patricia Archer Rumsey Barrows had been too wound within alternative, barely interior monologues to follow-up on promised punishments for deeds of dirt. Lying was their mother's most pronounced gift and quite possibly her own method of escape—from either the quiet existence of Mondauk or plain old domesticity or both. Magdalene was never sure.

Magdalene's mother not only dusted the Barrows Bungalow (as Michael called it) twice a day, but had also once crossed the street, uninvited, to dust the old Russian lady's house, an event that brought the police to the home of the ADA. Mrs. Nedya had died in her bed not minutes before Patricia Barrows, uninvited, let herself into the elderly, sickly woman's abode—both facts (the breaking and entering and the death of Mrs. Nedya) unknown to Mrs. Nedya's caretaker daughter, who emerged from the bathroom to find Mrs. Barrows chatting away, dusting around the old woman's newly lifeless body. Magdalene's mother's statement to the apologetic police (she was the Assistant District Attorney's wife after all) was a whopper, a Patricia Barrows Special.

"Mrs. Nedya asked if I could execute a handstand, and I did, but Mrs. Nedya, well, let's just say she became a little gassy. I went back to my dusting. I didn't want to embarrass her."

Magdalene knew Michael found his mother dizzying, intoxicating even. Her lies did nothing to diminish his worship; in fact, if anything, her willingness to scale the required absurdities without cracking so much as a smile in the process (and this from a woman whose frequently furnished smiles navigated the clichéd passage from ear to ear) filled Michael with such hubris (now there was a fifty-cent word!) that Magdalene cowered in advance of whatever new bullying techniques might emerge from her brother's mother-addled brain. Magdalene watched their mother-son relationship from the last row, her back to the wall, her eyes open wide: if the truth existed, Magdalene had to be awake enough to find it; if her brother turned bully, she had to be aware enough to absorb his blows—for with the bullying came his dares.

And after their mother's passing, it just got worse: the hubris became carelessness. The heights of the dares increased. The Rules of the Dare were codified. Magdalene dangled: Michael's marionette. There was no escape from a dare. Michael needed more than a friendly, sloppy dog; he needed parental guidance, and as their father increased his libations, Magdalene felt she only needed Michael.

Raven exploded in a fresh barking barrage when Magdalene reached her front stoop. The Barrows Bungalow was one of many small, single, whitewashed homes on Candy Lane with only the colors of the faux shutters or a particular lawn ornament distinguishing one house from the next—except Magdalene's. Raven was loud. How Raven already knew she'd reached the top of the block, Magdalene could never figure out—they didn't have a fenced front yard for the dog to romp in, and no one was home during the day to let him into the backyard; it had to be an internal clock. But she heard him the moment her black and white saddle shoes touched the corner—Raven barked like no other dog. His barking was rarely joyful—it was filled with nervous remorse for imagined bad behavior, a needy, full-throated, imitation Mondauk Yawp. Raven knew he was adopted, Magdalene was sure. How else to explain the way he couldn't wait for Magdalene (or Michael, before he went missing) to come home or how he wouldn't stay alone in the backyard even two seconds after relieving himself? When Aunt Tiddy tried to tell Magdalene that all dogs acted like this, that it was just pack mentality, that dogs had no true sense of time passing, Magdalene ignored her—just another senseless round of yammering from her good intentioned, but ultimately clueless aunt.

And there he was: sixty-five pounds of black fur, thumping runaway heart, cold runny nose, and humid breath. Raven's penis was sprouting from its spicket, and Magdalene turned her head to avoid its slimy, insistent presence. Magdalene didn't quite know from penises, but despite her innate curiosity (not about Raven's), she felt, considering that this was going to be her last day on earth, that she should just ignore any thoughts about boys. Raven licked her kneecaps and presented her with his stuffed monkey. Its fur was ragged and gnarly. The monkey was missing an eye. Magdalene fingered the empty socket and tossed the monkey into the kitchen, slipping up the stairs as Raven tore after it, careful to slide out of her saddle shoes to make her ascent quiet—in case her father had found his way home. She could have bet her life—oh, the humanity!—that he was planted square in the middle of a barstool, leaning for his life into a half-drained glass of some potent potion—a potion strong enough to tear a man away from his career and his family and his last remaining child. She heard Raven clamber up the stairs, breathing heavy around the monkey crammed into his mouth. She pushed her bedroom door closed.

The panda was on her bed. It wasn't the first time—the first time had been when she'd returned from the hospital last year. Aunt Tiddy, if she was around (and she usually was), corralled Raven's stuffed animals into a corner if she found them in her way or picked them up using two fingers if they'd been deposited on the furniture. But after tidying up her room (Aunt Tiddy made sure to tell Magdalene, exhausted, scared, embarrassed upon her return from the hospital, every detail of the cleaning), Tiddy had left the panda where it was. Even Aunt Tiddy knew: the depth of Raven's sorrow was measurable in the manner and frequency with which the panda disappeared and reappeared. It was Raven's way of mourning the loss of Michael, even though the dog could never fully comprehend Michael's absence. Raven still sniffed at Michael's closed bedroom door, still tried to climb into his bed if the door had been left open—which was rarely—and on one occasion, Magdalene had found her father, in a soiled dress shirt and ripped boxer shorts, asleep on Michael's bed, the dog's stomach resting on the ADA's crown.

When their father had first brought Raven home from Brookline Rescue, he took Magdalene and Michael (with Raven in tow) to buy the pooch one toy apiece. Michael picked the panda, which he named Monien (pronounced mō' nĭ ən—short for pandemonium). Magdalene didn't like the way the name sounded—the hard M made her think of words like: *M*om, *M*ommy, *M*umsy, *M*other. Michael claimed he named the panda after their new used dog who'd spent the length of the car trip to the store in a state of low moaning. Their father had been afraid Raven would pee in the car, so Magdalene and Michael never let go of his coat, never stopped petting him, purring into his *SILK* ears, kissing his quivering snout, playing peek-a-boo by covering his fluttering eyelids. At the pet store, Magdalene picked out the large stuffed monkey. The monkey's face reminded her of Raven's; they sort of had the same nose and the same puffy cheeks. Once they got Raven home, he seemed to favor the monkey (named simply Monkey) until he squeezed it too hard between his powerful jaws, and Monkey emitted a jungle cry. Raven hid beneath the sofa, a tight fit because of Raven's considerable size, and as Magdalene knew from playing Freedom with Michael (the house looked exactly the same as when their mother had been alive, only not as clean, with various pieces of furniture, the sofa included, in slight disrepair: a tear here, a puff of stuffing there), even if Raven had been a little girl nursing a bruise, hiding from her bully brother, it would have been uncomfortable. Only Raven's nose emerged from beneath the sofa, sniffing furiously for any sign of the monkey.

But the panda: Monien the panda sang a song when its stomach was pressed, that made Raven tremble—and made Magdalene feel as if someone had scraped a finger bone down her spine. Michael ignored it—or tried to; he pretended he didn't recognize the song, but whenever Monien struck up its tune, Michael's shoulders hunched and his nose crinkled before his face assumed its practiced insouciance, cooler than cool. It was a song Magdalene and Michael had heard maybe a thousand times before, but never quite the way Monien the panda sang it—besides, Magdalene and her brother were used to hearing it *whistled*. But coming from Monien's belly, the melody sounded older than the songs the trees played with the wind—even older than those of the dogwoods that populated just about every backyard in Mondauk Proper and Rhawnhurst (except the Barrows'). The tempo appeared irrelevant: the song slowed down and sped up at will, creaky and petulant. The panda sang reluctantly and with great effort and even greater grace, for when the panda's song finished, even Raven, who'd been shaking like the last leaf of autumn, lowered his graying snout to the floor in a show of servitude. The monkey's screaming was scary—but not quite as scary as the panda's song. When the panda sang, Magdalene thought even the ghosts stopped rattling their chains to listen. Raven's original owners had had back-to-back babies, and maybe Raven recognized the melody from listening at the children's door at bedtime. (Magdalene had heard the song performed more than once as a children's number.) Or maybe Raven, like Michael and Magdalene, recognized the panda's song as something pure—even in its creaky, time-addled lethargy—in a house where purity often involved fermentation and the wisps of lies still hung in the air just beneath traces of their dead mother's perfume.

Magdalene sat on her bed and picked up the panda. The stuffed animal smelled a little like Raven. Raven used to carry the panda everywhere—even outside when he had to relieve himself. He'd hold Monien in his mouth while he squatted. The monkey lay ignored wherever Raven last tussled with him, wherever the monkey last screamed. At best, Magdalene thought, using one of her favorite vocabulary words, carefully counting out the syllables, Raven had a *contentious* relationship with the monkey. As much as he seemed to loathe setting the simian off, her used dog could not resist attacking Monkey almost every day, tossing it with his jaws until it jungle-screamed once more, sending Raven scampering for cover under anything other than the sofa. (Once Raven had settled into his new home, he'd gained substantial weight.) But he only squeezed the belly of the panda when completely necessary—and thank God. If Magdalene and Michael had been fighting or if they had just witnessed their father falling into the house (an increasingly regular occurrence then), Raven would snatch the panda and make him sing.

Example, mid-Indian-burn:

"Jesus, Lil," Michael winced, his hands over his ears, sister-torture momentarily forgotten. "Make it stop.

"Go away," Michael said to their dog. "Go away."

Magdalene tried to hum along with the melody. It was familiar *and* elusive—like raindrops tracing numbers on a windowpane.

"She whistled that song every single day," Magdalene said to Raven later that night, as the dog slunk off to Michael's room from the darkness of hers, "but I never remember how it goes until Monien sings."

Then one afternoon—the day before Michael slipped away, the day before their father found himself stuck in the bottle he had previously, it seemed, only been trying on for size, the panda stopped singing. Nothing Raven did brought the song back. He pounced. He pummeled. Little bits of fluff and fur flew about the house. Michael tried to get him to stop—they both did, and Magdalene had to admit it *was* a little like laughing at a funeral. Maybe Michael wasn't trying that hard, but it didn't matter: the panda was silent. After much circling and huffing, Raven left Monien still and retrieved his monkey; its screaming had no effect on Raven this time. The dog settled into his daybed next to the sofa and munched softly on the simian.

"He loves Monkey after all," Michael said, his hair falling into his eyes. "A comfort monkey!"

Magdalene said nothing. The monkey *was* scary—not all that different from herself, she thought: dark, brooding, ever ready to howl. A comfort monkey? Second fiddle to the grace and glory of the panda's tragic song was more like it! Like she was second banana to

Michael. She'd been secretly hurt that Raven had such a troublesome relationship with the stuffed, screaming simian, but she was used to troublesome relationships. It her belief that their father—not quite the drunk he would become but nevertheless inebriated a little more each day—preferred Michael to her. The alcohol hindered his attempts to hide it. It seemed fitting, then, that Raven would favor her brother (and thus Monien as well). Football was a big part of the problem. Hell, even Raven liked to run around Michael as her brother practiced throwing spirals through the old tire hung from the sycamore in the backyard. Raven would retrieve the ball and deliver it, slimy, back to Michael, who never seemed to mind the drool. But their father's preferences couldn't be explained by just football.

"C'mon, it's funny," her brother said, and it was—sort of. Raven remained on his daybed with Monkey, his head cocked at Monien the panda. The stuffed bear stared at the ceiling, obstinately mute. Every few seconds, Raven would look back at the siblings. Magdalene found herself smiling too, *damn it all to hell.*

"See, Lil, he needs the monkey after all," Michael said. "Come out and play catch."

"Dad'll be home soon."

"He's not going to be mad 'cause you're playing catch. He just thinks football is a boy thing. It's nothing against you."

"Except I'm not a boy. Daughters don't play football."

"C'mon, I'll teach you the Yawp."

"I already know about the Yawp."

Magdalene kicked at the panda. Raven glanced at Monien and gently released a little belly gas. Magdalene waved at the air.

"He'll be toast when he comes home," Michael said. "You coming or not?"

He tossed the football to the ceiling and caught it behind his back. He was a tease, her brother. He faked a pass. She wondered if she flinched.

Raven ignored the ball and stared at Monkey, as if Monkey had been responsible for the smelly gaseous emissions. He took a swat at the panda with his paw, but the panda still refused to sing. Raven abandoned his daybed, circled the panda, and sat on its head.

"Can't we go down to the dock or walk to Sol's? I don't want to listen to Dad slur his way through a gender dissertation."

"Count them syllables, Lil," Michael said, shaking his head. "Big words, little boobs."

Magdalene crossed her arms.

"Tomorrow," her brother said. "The Puddle's too shallow anyway. It's going to rain tonight, pour. We'll go to the Puddle tomorrow, you and me, okay? Play catch with me now. I don't want to just throw this thing through the tire anymore, Lil."

"Stop calling me that."

"Pretty please with cherries on top?"

Raven lifted his bottom from the panda and batted it away with a paw. The panda sang nothing; Raven whimpered.

"Okay, as long as tomorrow you take me to the dock."

"What's the big deal about the Puddle all of a sudden? You never jump anyway."

"This year is my year," Magdalene lied. She wanted to skip stones or chase frogs.

"You doin' it just so you can write about it in your diary?" Michael taunted. "You gonna put the experience down in the never-ending tome?" He executed a phantom pirouette catch. "What's it called, Lil? *Dance of the Chickenshit?*"

Had he been looking at her journal? *Brush it off, brush it off.* She couldn't show Michael any fear. She really did just want to skip stones across the Puddle's scummy surface, count the bounces, and watch the stones trace weird little patterns like wet astronomic charts. She didn't want to Puddle Jump. She just wanted to be near her brother.

"As long as it rains tonight, I'll take you tomorrow," Michael said. "But if you don't jump, I'll dare you."

He raised a fist, and Magdalene turned her face away.

"Lil…"

Magdalene spun around to stare at her brother. Michael punched her twice in the shoulder.

"Two for flinching."

And Michael *did* take her to the dock at Finch's Landing the next day, but she'd pushed it out of her mind. She didn't remember much about that day at the Puddle. She vaguely recalled being questioned by people of authority but not about what. She thought a flock of priests had been there too, holding her hand. It was easier to count. It was easier to hold her breath than break the surface of her own damp memories. She counted her way through most things these days—held her breath and counted. Sometimes she counted her own breaths; other times, her brain recited nursery rhymes or children's songs—the ones involving numbers. She gave herself credit for being aware of the counting, or at least aware of the times when the numbers dared to surface from the recesses of her brain. Magdalene suspected her brain counted without her.

Jumping in the Puddle had been the last time she'd seen Michael before…well, before whatever happened *happened*. Before whoever had taken him took him. Magdalene squeezed the panda and started to cry, the tears dripping down on Monien's worn, chomped-upon face. Raven whined in the hall. Magdalene forced herself from the bed and opened the door wide enough to place Monien in the narrow hallway. Raven scrambled to squeeze through; Magdalene blocked him with her knees. It was best if the dog didn't witness this; it was best, thought Magdalene, if the dog didn't associate Monien with yet another loss. She wedged her chair against the knob.

Raven continued to paw at her door as Magdalene climbed back into her bed, curling her body around her journal. The journal had a black cover and large white pages. Aunt Tiddy had bought it for her for Christmas of 2000, the year Magdalene's mother had died. (Magdalene had been allowed to pick it out herself; it was a year of many presents.) Magdalene didn't use the blank book as a diary though, despite what Michael thought. Not that real life didn't need to be documented, Lord knew, but writing fiction was detective work (to quote her fifth grade teacher Sister Theresa). Her silly, little novella—which made up most of her journal—was not much of a novel, but it was too long to be called a short story. It was a children's book, begun that Christmas as a present for their recently adopted dog—as if she needed proof that she was as crazy as her classmates believed.

The Nun's Story: now there was a woman (and a story) with a purpose. Magdalene had neither. Sister Mary Magdalene de Rosa had been a person whose life was important to others—Magdalene was a sorry second prize to both her father and to her dog, she believed. If her mother's death had been the motivational push behind her father's first step into decline (the uncorking of the bottle), then Michael's disappearance had been the cause of his full immersion. Raven's worship of her brother was the frost on the glass, the icing on the cake.

Magdalene had been encouraged not to grow attached to football; she'd been encouraged to do girl-things—as if Magdalene had any idea exactly what those things were. If they were anything like what

Christina did in her spare time—paint her fingernails, dye her hair, page through catalogs, circling a cardigan here or a pair of pumps there, only to dress like a vampire (death was in vogue) and revolve her free time around boys—then Magdalene wanted no part of it. She'd rather study the stars or write in her journal. But she loved one extracurricular activity, even above her Hardy Boys books. (Nancy Drew was a priss, Magdalene thought; Magdalene would rather solve mysteries with Scooby-Doo than Nancy Drew. The Hardy Boys may have been a little stiff—never as realistic or funny as Alfred Hitchcock's Three Investigators—heck, Joe and Frank Hardy never even seemed to go to the bathroom, and they called their friend Chet their "chum," which Magdalene knew from *Jaws* was chopped up fish guts shark hunters tossed overboard to attract the shark—but at least they weren't concerned with makeup or baking or anything that Aunt Tiddy found amusing or interesting in the pages of *Good Housekeeping*.) Leave fingernail painting to Christina (who never cracked a book for pleasure, unless *Cosmopolitan* counted)— Magdalene loved football. And even that was denied her. Magdalene adored just about everything about the game. Not watching it on television or from the bleachers though; she wanted to immerse herself in its muddy glory. Football was messy and painful and difficult, but there was a glorious lack of mystery about the game—it was all strategy. She didn't want to make a career of football; the game was her public passion (as opposed to writing or stargazing) forced private. Her career choices (writer and detective) would have kept her busy enough if she wasn't planning on checking out, punching her own ticket, taking that long black train back home— wherever that was. Sure, other kids had it much worse: parents who abused them or neglected them—there were starving pagan babies in Africa, their stomachs distended like they'd swallowed a football— but Magdalene felt there was little room on the team Jesus had drafted her for, just the moribund roles of Lil and Maddie, the brownie-baking dutiful daughter. And now that Michael was gone and her father just about, Magdalene knew those positions had long been cut from the roster.

The first attempt had gone awry. She never knew who had found her. All Magdalene remembered was Aunt Tiddy's hot breath on her face at Holy Redeemer (the old woman had spent the evening at the Barrows Bungalow, eating pepperoni from Bard's) and the space her father created in his absence while he "convalesced" (another nifty vocabulary word) in a "special hospital." But cutting her wrists had been harder than she'd guessed. This time (tonight), she'd narrow the margin for error: in addition to cutting herself, she'd prepare an overdose to hasten her departure.

Magdalene pulled out the razor she'd stashed between her mattress and bedspring. She had broken her father's disposable that she'd lifted from the bathroom wastebasket. Wrapped in a tissue were twenty-two children's aspirins and one fuzzy-looking cold capsule she had found in the cabinet under the sink.

Magdalene grimaced: everything before was merely prologue; she was going to die in chapter one.

Raven scratched at her door.

Magdalene took a volume of Funk and Wagnalls encyclopedia from the shelves above her desk and found a diagram of human veins. She propped herself on her pillows and carefully considered the drawing. It was like the map in *Treasure Island*. She had to make sure she followed the right path or she would be brought back to life again. With a magic marker, she traced the veins on her left wrist and, satisfied, drew a large X on the inner part of her arm. ("Don't X Christ out of Christmas" indeed!) Magdalene opened the tissue and counted out the children's aspirin, aligning them across the bedspread like little soldiers, the fuzzy red cold capsule at the lead.

Twenty-three little Indians, and they all fall down.

FOCUS.

Ignore the numbers.

No counting.

She had forgotten to get a glass of water, but if she opened the door, Raven would bound in, and she might look into his huge, wet eyes; she might even see Michael staring back, and Magdalene knew she could never bear that. She still wasn't sure how everything had gotten to this point exactly, but she didn't want to experience it over and over again like the Nun's Story. Enough was certainly enough. She could dry swallow the pills if she had to.

Whhhhat wwwwill you doooo whhhhen yourrrr time comessss?

The important thing now was to at least finish the first draft of her book before she began her leaving. She owed that much to Raven. The book had been a long time coming—as much a present now for smart little Katie McAllister as for her morose dog, a last will and testament for her father to find. She needed to leave *something* in her wake. When Michael went *poof* and, like magic, disappeared, all he'd really left behind was Magdalene and their dog. And somehow, it was her fault. All of it.

First: the pen. Good, Magdalene. Don't be afraid. It's only fiction.

Now: take the plunge. Swallow the pills.

Jump.

Float float float.

When she awoke some time later, Raven was still out in the hall crying, and she realized she hadn't cut her wrists yet. Everything was slightly out of focus, but she found the razor and followed the pirate's map, found the little ropes that tied her heart to her skin, and began to release herself from this world, Raven's crying now a reverberation from a muddy past, hollow echoes of an endless prologue.

Michael always said that to hold somebody by the wrists was to save their life.

So Magdalene let go.

Chapter Two

The Summarizing

As soon as someone is gone, the summarizing begins. She heard it at funerals and at wakes and the one time she sat shivah when a public school friend's grandmother died. All the disparate, unique parts of the departed, all their peccadilloes, their hard won preferences were narrowed down to a couple of inches of newsprint, then decimated even smaller by the summarizing.

Stacy always loved children.

Marcus was a wiz at numbers.

Magdalene knew this summarizing was instinctive and, just as instinctively, knew that she was not, in fact, gone.

Sheldon adored hard-boiled eggs.

Mickey once caught a fifteen and a half inch pickerel in the Puddle.

Magdalene wanted to open her eyes but could not. They were glued shut, she was sure of it. Behind her eyelids, she listened for the summarizing; she listened for her life read back to her by Saint Peter or the angel Gabriel. She sniffed about for the smell of sulfur.

Your brother loved you unconditionally.

I've never seen anything like it.

Your great aunt on your mother's side, Aunt Theresa—the one who played her nose at your First Communion party, remember?—well, she said she'd never seen a brother love a sister like Michael loved you. That's the truth.

Aunt Tiddy?

Yes?

Aunt Tiddy?

Open your eyes, Magdalene. Open your eyes.

And she did, and Tiddy was there all right. Her aunt's reading glasses swung over a nonexistent bosom. Her nose was dotted with newsprint. She wore a flower print frock that had faded over time and now resembled an old dishrag—except it was spotless and pressed just so. Aunt Tiddy liked things just so.

Tiddy raised her pointed chin and swung her reading glasses onto her hawk nose, the ends of the glasses disappearing into what Michael always swore was a wig of silver gray, each hair in perfect position despite whatever chores occupied Tiddy's body. A few years back (a lifetime ago), Magdalene had tried to pull on Aunt Tiddy's hair (on a dare from Michael). She could no more ignore Michael's dares than she could Tiddy's cooking, although both often ended up with Magdalene deeper in Dutch than she expected—and she expected quite a bit.

Keep them open, Magdalene.

Look at me.

Open your eyes.

Tiddy's visits to the Barrows Bungalow had been a constant reminder that Magdalene and Michael lived in a one-parent house.

"Do it," Michael had whispered.

"Michael..."

"Do it."

Michael pinched Magdalene's bottom to egg her on.

Magdalene reached for Tiddy's hair. The old woman never turned from the stove. One arm swung around, and Tiddy boxed Magdalene's ear with an oven mitten emblazoned with the Bard's Meats logo: a pig with reading glasses and a bloody apron, holding, inexplicably, a quill pen. The dinner was wrapped and shoved into the refrigerator, and Michael and Magdalene spent the remainder of the evening being served (force-fed!) cold peppers (two dozen!) that made them pass wind like a couple of uncorked cows (as Michael had put it). The mystery of Tiddy's hair would remain unsolved.

Mysteries.

Michael...

Aunt Tiddy?

Open your eyes.

"Well, I guess you've gone and done it again. Why I'll never know. I want to know, but I won't ask."

Magdalene was surprised to see Tiddy crying, the tears collecting in the lenses of her glasses, which had slid down the not inconsiderable length of her nose.

Had Magdalene tried to pull Aunt Tiddy's hair again?

"Says here that one Mickey Hatfield of the 1700 block of Zaentz Street was arrested for fishing in Pennypack Creek without a license."

"Tiddy?"

"Do you know Mickey from school? Is he as big a dope in school as he is outside of it? The gamesmen are all over the Puddle anymore; fish floating up..."

Tiddy stopped and pushed her glasses back over her tears.

"Stacy Whitaker. Now there's a brainiac for you, Magdalene. Adopted a lion cub. Found him on the computer it says. This computer business will come to no good. Still, you think Stacy Whitaker would know a lion from a tabby, don't you suspect?"

The slightest tinge of southern accent lingered in Tiddy's voice; Aunt Tiddy felt it made her more genteel—at least that's what Michael had said their mother had told him.

"Tiddy?"

"Yes, dear?"

"Where am I?"

"Don't be silly."

Tiddy laid the newspaper in her lap and her fingers curled its edges.

"You know exactly where you are and what has been done, and I'm here to bring you home. This has got to end. All of it. 'The course of true love never did run smooth.' Shakespeare said that."

Magdalene located a small piece of a smile.

"You say that about everything, Tiddy."

Magdalene's voice cracked. She shivered like a thin piece of string stretched across a broken button. The hospital blankets were thin, and the air conditioning unit thundered somewhere behind her.

"Well, if he didn't, he should've. Our Bill said a great many things, and I'll be damned if I remember every single one of them."

The newspaper flapped up to her face again, but her reading glasses dangled on her chest.

"Where's Daddy, Tiddy?"

The ceiling undulated.

"He'll be here shortly, I expect, but it's my shift now."

Magdalene stared at the ceiling, and the ceiling became a wave. She closed her eyes against its crashing.

Her father was there in the wave, and he smelled like he'd smelled before he started drinking: hair tonic and shoe polish and light aftershave. His whiskers were little, almost invisible dots on his chin and cheeks. His breath smelled like Wrigley's gum, and his briefcase was full of briefs.

"Underwear!" Michael and Magdalene had chimed.

"Legal briefs," their father always replied.

"Objection," Michael said.

"Overruled," their father would decide.

"Boxers!" Magdalene screamed, as she tried to tackle their father, and somewhere behind the father-smells, the scent of their mother's baking wafted out from the kitchen—but their mother didn't bake, she burned. It was a family joke: Mother was good at everything except food. She even ate like a bird, their father said.

"Eat," Aunt Tiddy said, and she was pushing Magdalene up against her pillows and all the hospital smells came back. A television was secured to the upper corner of the far wall, silently playing cartoons of unfathomable violence.

"Raven?" asked Magdalene between mouthfuls of almost tasteless Jell-O.

"I'm not one for dogs or pets in general, mind you," Tiddy said, stirring the soup with a straw. It smelled like chicken noodle. "But you owe that hound a cookie or two."

"Labbie. He's a Labbie."

Tiddy ladled some lukewarm soup toward Magdalene's mouth.

"I know damn well what he is. Who do you think has been taking care of him and letting him out for his constitutions thrice a day?"

Raven's graying snout floated down from the ceiling. Magdalene could smell his sour mash breath.

"I'm sorry, Tiddy. I really am."

Tiddy wrapped her arms around her grandniece's body.

"I know you are, my dear. I know. We're all sorry, and we're all going to get through this. My sister—your grandmother—didn't have much in the common sense department (too smart for that!), but she didn't raise a fool. Your father's going to come around, clean as a whistle soon too. All we have is each other now—you, me, and your father."

Magdalene wiped her snot on Tiddy's sleeve.

"And Raven."

Tiddy's eyes filled up again too, and she hugged Magdalene tighter.

"And that hound dog of yours too."

"He's a Labbie."

"I know, Magdalene, I know."

"He misses Michael."

Tiddy's body stiffened for a second and then a spoonful of soup was heading towards Magdalene's mouth.

"We all do, dear."

"Does Daddy?"

"Of course," Tiddy scoffed.

"He never mentions him."

Tiddy regarded the soup with a wary eye and plucked out an errant hair.

"And neither do you. Until now."

"I think about him every day."

"As do I. Now eat your soup. Don't slurp. I've got pepperoni from Bard's in my bag for later."

Magdalene found it hard to swallow with the spoon in her mouth.

"I just want to keep it to myself."

"What's that, dear?"

"The Puddle," Magdalene said, but soon she was asleep, and in her dreams dying stars searched for their reflections in the dirty water of Pennypack Creek.

+

Raven had rescued her. Sort of. It was Aunt Tiddy who had forced the bedroom door open, jammed a finger down Magdalene's throat, and called 911, all within thirty seconds; Aunt Tiddy was nothing if not efficient with her time. Tiddy had been dropping off food. She was aware the situation at the Barrows Bungalow was becoming untenable, and she was unsure of when and where to jump in, although she said later she was also aware it was just a matter of time before she had to act—Mondauk Social Services would be at the door soon. So when Raven went bonkers, just crazy, pawing at Magdalene's bedroom door, Tiddy, already on the alert, rammed her skinny, muscular arms against the wood (muscles earned from years and years of washing the dishes of men who deserved little more, Tiddy had once said, although who these men were remained a mystery to Magdalene) until the chair Magdalene had wedged against the knob gave way—and there was her grandniece, serene as a nightingale except for a puddle of vomit in the crook of her neck.

Magdalene heard all of this—it was repeated for each nurse as the shifts changed around Magdalene by an apparently sleepless Tiddy.

On the sixth day, when Magdalene opened her eyes, it was not Tiddy with her glasses and her newspapers and her opinions sitting on the chair next to the bed, but a stranger with a strong chin and steady eyes and prematurely graying hair. The stranger's hand was wrapped around her wrist. Magdalene tried to keep her eyes open but failed miserably. The waves in the ceiling lapped at the corners of her eyes. Her nose and mouth filled with water, and she counted backwards until the tide receded.

"Nibble on the biscuit, dear. Get something inside you at least."

Magdalene was sitting up in bed, and Tiddy was buttering a biscuit. Magdalene wolfed it down.

"You were moaning in your sleep, dear. Bad dreams?"

"I was dreaming of the Puddle. I don't know why."

Tiddy looked over her glasses at Magdalene and continued to butter the last piece of biscuit.

"You're going home tomorrow."

"Is Daddy coming to pick me up?"

"No, he has to work. I'll be taking you home."

Magdalene swung her legs off the bed and collided with the meal tray. A little container of milk bounced and spilled on the floor.

"He went back to work?"

"Eat your bread."

Magdalene put her hands on Tiddy's shoulders.

"Daddy went back to work? Tiddy, you have to tell me."

Tiddy looked as if she wanted to grin but wouldn't allow herself.

"It's just the first step. There'll be many more, Magdalene, many more. It's a first step for all of us."

Magdalene hopped out of bed, and her legs buckled beneath her. Tiddy caught her under her arms and led her back to her pillow.

"One *small* step at a time, Magdalene. That's how we get to where we have to go, dear. One foot in front of the other, leaning against each other for support. Shakespeare…"

"…said that. I know. Oh, Tiddy, I can't believe it, I can't believe it."

Tiddy tucked Magdalene back into her blankets.

"It doesn't solve everything. But it's a start, dear. A start."

"Why hasn't he come up to see me?"

Tiddy's face changed; it was almost a smile. Magdalene's chest grew hot.

"He was here this morning," Aunt Tiddy said.

"I knew it, I knew it! I thought at first he was a doctor. I didn't even recognize him. But somehow, I knew it was him too."

"Get some sleep, dear. Tomorrow we go home, and then we get the house settled for the summer."

"Are you visiting for a while, Tiddy?"

"Visit? Why, my dear, I'm moving the hell in!"

Magdalene's eyes grew wide, but she shut them before Tiddy could see. *Thud thud thud* went her heart. Tiddy was moving in! Her father was back at work; perhaps some part of life at the Barrows Bungalow would return to normal, if he was really sober. But Tiddy moving in? Magdalene lost herself in the ceiling as she pictured endless hours of chores and baking.

And somewhere among the aquatic images the ceiling offered, Magdalene saw her own face shimmering in the Puddle. She almost didn't recognize herself amid the sun sparkles and dragonfly blurs. The water's muddy surface was littered with spiral helicopter leaves forced down during a recent rain. She bent closer to the creek, searching for a second face, red mud on her legs, splinters from the dock at Finch's Landing stabbing her knees, and only when her own eyes stared back did she twist away, frightened not by what she saw, Magdalene remembered later, but by what was missing.

Then Tiddy was there, and Magdalene realized she was awake. They were still in the hospital.

"The Puddle—I don't—"

Tiddy pressed a cold washcloth against her forehead.

"You will, my dear, you will."

+

When Magdalene opened her eyes, she screamed. Father Dave stood at the edge of her hospital bed.

"I felt the same way when I looked in the mirror this morning," Father Dave said.

Magdalene clutched at her chest to catch her heart.

Father Dave scratched at his red beard.

"That's why I don't shave much. Father Vincent, he doesn't like my beard, but he's just jealous," the priest said, tapping the top of his head. "I have more hair than I know what to do with."

When Father Dave leaned closer. Magdalene saw little red stalks jutting from his white collar.

"Now, I'll anoint your head and bless you, but God helps those, Magdalene Barrows, who help themselves. When the going gets tough, the tough go to…"

"…God," Magdalene finished. How many times had she heard Father Dave recite his stock clichés during class or in a homily?

Father Dave stepped back, and his smile drained away—but not from his eyes. His eyes were still smiling.

"Nobody needs to be alone, Magdalene," Father Dave said. "You come see me anytime you want. If I'm not in the rectory, one of the volunteers from the Faith Board works the reception desk, and they can tell you when I'll be back."

Father Dave rolled his eyes when he said "Faith Board."

"Or you can just call the rectory and make an appointment. We can meet outside the rectory too, if you like. No one has to know."

Father Dave's smile reemerged. "I usually have several of your fellow students as guests on Saturday afternoon, cleaning and whatnot, working off detention. I believe you're in class with Mr. Eves, a *frequent* guest of mine. Hate to see a Saturday go by without him. A fan of Stick Man, are you?"

Magdalene turned her head away; she hated it when adults were condescending.

A fan of Stick Man, are you?

A hand framed in red fur reached for her shoulder and squeezed it.

A fan of torturing eighth graders by making them scrub the floors or clean your undies at the rectory, Father?

Warm oil was traced on her forehead, eyelids, and lips.

Magdalene kept her mouth shut. She heard the hospital's PA system echo in the busy hallway: an unintelligible name, repeated twice, then a series of numbers.

Prime numbers.

Magdalene continued the sequence in her head until Father Dave backed out of the room.

Two, three, five, seven, and done! Got no factor 'cept myself and one!

Prime numbers don't need anything else to exist. They just need themselves to make sense. Prime numbers don't require a mother or miss a brother or wonder what brand of whiskey their father drinks.

+

The morning she was to be discharged, Magdalene gathered all the things Tiddy had brought her—Hardy Boys books, puzzle magazines, a photograph of Raven the day they adopted him, the dog grinning and more than a little nervous—and stuffed them into the laundry bag Tiddy had given her.

After three days of sleep followed by four days of bad television (observational purposes), Magdalene's thinking was sharper, less muddied. She knew she would stand trial for what she had attempted, unsuccessfully, a second time. Let the summarizing begin, Magdalene thought. She remembered returning to school after her first attempt and the looks she'd endured: awe, pity, revulsion. She couldn't really blame them. How many eighth graders had had a brush with a genuine resurrection? That the one resurrected was the sister of the missing boy made the story that much juicier.

She'd counted her way through her classmates' derision. She'd counted the syllables in their insults. She'd multiplied and divided and subtracted in her head while they gossiped. She had little idea how the counting had started; Magdalene disliked mathematics as a rule, although her grades were always decent. She understood people in terms of numbers. Some people were negatives, others positives. A great many were merely fractions. Very, very few people were perfect. A perfect number was a whole number (and how many people were whole?) greater than zero that equaled the sum of all its positive factors.

$$1 + 2 + 3 = 6$$
$$1 + 2 + 4 + 7 + 14 = 28$$

She climbed back into bed and closed her eyes. If she had to define herself in terms in numbers, she was a prime, divisible only by one and itself.

Magdalene smelled his aftershave even before his hairy knuckles brushed her face; the low-pitched gravel tones of his voice thundered through the underbrush of prime numbers tiptoeing in her busy, busy brain.

Perfect people were as rare as perfect numbers. Everyone she'd thought of as perfect didn't add up.

"Can I help the young lady with her bags?"

"Daddy!"

Magdalene pushed her face into his stomach. How soft it had become in the bars! No longer was it the hard stomach of a father who used to start each morning with fifty push-ups and fifty sit-ups, creaking floorboards the family alarm clock—of course, that had been when there'd *been* a family to wake. But Magdalene still recognized his smell—his aftershave, that awful hair tonic; he smelled like home.

(Michael had once done two hundred naked sit-ups on a dare.

Magdalene had kept count. All the summarizing in the world wouldn't bring Michael home.)

Magdalene ran through a series of primes and pulled away from the soft stomach.

Her father pulled her back, murmuring…*something*. Nurses bustled back and forth past the door. A frizzy-haired nurse stuck her head in, seemed to see through the two Barrows clinging to each other in the middle of the hospital room, and continued on.

Her father had told her once lawyers were all about bending words, taking them apart like a mechanic does a car engine, seeing if they could fit in a keyhole or slip out of a tight knot. His words brought justice, Michael had said, and Magdalene, too little at the time to understand what Michael had meant (and suspecting Michael was just repeating something he'd heard on television), asked her father to show her justice, and the next day, he did just that. As she walked the halls of Mondauk County Hall, her hand in the firm, dry grip of her father's, she could see the deference with which everyone—including the mayor!—treated her father.

"I brought Michael here last year," he said. "Now it's your turn." He stood her upon his desk and mouthed the words with her as she recited Edward Lear's "The Owl and the Pussycat" for his staff. (She loved the image of the "beautiful pea green boat"!) Even the mayor stopped by to give her a lollipop. (To Magdalene, the mayor looked as if he should make a habit of giving away *all* his snacks; he'd barely brokered his way into his suit vest!) The District Attorney was there too. "My *other* boss," her father said, winking at the gaunt, older man who told her that her father would someday stand in his shoes and that then she would dance on *his* desk—but it was all over Magdalene's head. She knew only that her father was an important man to more than just her and Michael and their mother.

"Mommy," Magdalene said, and the name was swept away in the competing tide of PA announcements.

Justice was gone. This was a hospital.

Her father let go and wiped the tears from her eyes.

"We'll have plenty of time to talk about Mommy too. I promise. No more secrets. No more dark places."

He tilted Magdalene's face with his fingers.

"Understand? We're going to find all the pieces and make them fit. And Aunt Tiddy's going to help us."

"Does she have to move in?"

Her father laughed.

"That was more Tiddy's idea than mine, but it's a good one. We all need an extra pair of eyes or hands once in a while. You, me, and Raven too, okay?

"Besides," her father added, "it'll keep her off the road."

"The Baby Blue Cadillac of Doom," Magdalene whispered.

"You know, she's been be driving here every day."

But Magdalene wasn't really listening. She was counting. She didn't want to let go of her father; she was afraid he would fall in the whirlpool forming in the ceiling.

+

In the car on the ride home: "It was all I could do for you not to have to go into Friends again."

Magdalene avoided her father's eyes in the rear view mirror.

"Dr. Meade again? Okay, Maddie?"

Magdalene stared past her own reflection in the window. Two teens with greasy hair flicked their cigarette butts into the street at the same time.

"Okay, Maddie?" her father repeated, his eyes searching along the rear view mirror.

Magdalene sucked on her upper lip.

"Fine."

"She's a good doctor. She recommended someone for me to see, and he's been great." Her father cleared his throat. "The law requires we do something here."

Magdalene doubted the law took an interest in her failed suicide attempts, but if seeing Willa Meade was the cost she paid for having her father back, then she was prepared to pay it in spades.

They'd been driving west toward Pennypack Woods, and when they reached the Basin, the drained pond near the Puddle, her father pulled over by the picnic area. Although it was early in the day, a few families and their dogs huddled around the picnic tables, having claimed the ones parked in the shade of the sycamores and magnolias. Magdalene marveled how each family seemed to move as if they were one organism, separate tendrils emanating from a central heart—even their dogs seemed to belong to something bigger than what was visible except to someone far enough away to see the entire picture: there, the obstinate preteen daughter, too much makeup caking her face even though the heat of the day had not begun to rise; the older brother, home from college perhaps, eager to appear adult-like in his actions, almost setting his untucked dress shirt on fire lighting the grill; the younger brother, just plain eager, too old to sit aside and too little to take part; the mother, harried but pleased to have everyone in one place without having to scrub the kitchen afterwards; and, finally, the father, his cheeks puffed out, grin plastered on his face, the can of Budweiser (his wife had frowned when he'd taken it out of the Styrofoam cooler; it was hardly noon) forgotten on the picnic table.

"I should have told you, Maddie. I didn't even tell Aunt Tiddy. It was something I had to do, and I figured that you were already somehow dealing with me not being around, so a few more days wouldn't hurt. I wasn't thinking straight."

Magdalene continued staring at the picnic family. The daughter had removed herself from the scene to lean her back against an elm a short distance away. Magdalene watched as she pulled a piece of notebook paper from the back pocket of her too-tight turquoise shorts. The girl appeared disconcerted, disturbed, in trouble. She had what appeared to be a teardrop tattoo under her left eye.

Magdalene's father continued: "I'd checked myself into EPPI. Seems funny now. How many times had I remanded someone to the state's care there? How many times had I directed a young person through its doors, knowing the parents could afford nothing more? It was Karl who came to see me, Maddie, found me in the corner at McCullough's. Bought himself a club soda and lime. Just sat there for maybe a half hour or more before I even noticed it was him. Then I wasn't even sure he had recognized me, until I tried to slink away and fell off my stool. Karl just reached over, helped me back up, and told me to stay until I felt like leaving. Told me he wasn't here to force me to do anything I wasn't ready to do. Then he took his teeth out and laid them on a cocktail napkin."

Magdalene watched the girl in the turquoise shorts read the notebook page. They seemed roughly the same age. The girl shook her head from side to side as she read, occasionally looking up to the leaves. Magdalene doubted it was homework and wondered what school she went to, if she was from the County Seat or down from Warminster or Rhawnhurst. The whore-shorts aside (Christina wore tighter, and Magdalene knew Christina's had cost what Tiddy called a pretty penny), she looked too healthy to be from Paradise Lakes—

there was too much color in her cheeks (but maybe that was from the girl's crying). Still—not everyone who lived in Paradise Lakes Trailer Park subsisted on junk food and illegal pharmaceuticals, and plenty of Bod Squaders dressed provocatively. Magdalene grimaced. She had to work on her writer's eye. Too many suppositions; too much summarizing.

Her father had grown quiet. Magdalene knew she had missed what her brother used to call a cue: if their father thought they weren't paying attention, he would throw a one-eyed one-horned flying purple people eater or a lime green loon into the story. Michael had no problem keeping his attention on more than one thing, even during a parental lecture. Magdalene had trouble focusing even on *one* thing some days. (Of course, the counting wasn't helping.) She felt the hope that had sprung when she'd first seen her father this morning evaporate in the growing, late spring heat.

Her father cleared his throat again. He was forever clearing his throat.

"Then Karl took his teeth out and laid them on a cocktail napkin," he repeated.

Magdalene glanced at her father—"His teeth? Mr. Matthews took his teeth out?"—and when she looked back out of the car window, the girl in the turquoise shorts was gone. A torn piece of the notebook paper floated in the light breeze, landing and taking off in the tall weeds.

"Thought Zooey McCullough was going to have a bird, but she didn't say a thing, just went on watching the game, drying the beer mugs."

Her father took off his black frames and cleaned the lenses with his tie. She didn't want to look straight at him, but Magdalene could see the dark circles under his eyes, the shaky way his hands replaced the glasses on his face. (He couldn't see past his nose without them.) From the corner of her eye, Magdalene searched the landscape outside the car window for the girl in the turquoise shorts. Other picnickers wandered in and out of view; the girl was not among them.

"Karl starts telling me about the years after Marietta died. That was his first wife, Marietta—Spanish, I guess. I knew he was married before, but I was so far in my cups, it took me a second or two to figure out what he was talking about, to remember that his first wife had died when he was a young lawyer."

Her father chuckled softly to himself.

"And that was a hell of a long time ago. For all of us."

There she was—the girl in the turquoise shorts—near the edge of the picnic area where a small tendril of the Puddle cried itself into a quick running stream. The girl peered into the distance, towards the Puddle, her left leg quaking, her thigh quivering.

"Said it took three years—three and a *half* years—to extract himself from the bottle. Said he still goes to AA meetings. Not often—just to give back. Karl said he hasn't even wanted a drink in over fifteen years. He told me he knew a few good programs, a few good counselors, but I just kept looking at his teeth sitting there on the napkin. Karl's not young—hell, I'm the youngest one in the DA's office and I'm no spring chicken—so it's not out of the question that he could have had dentures, but I couldn't figure out for the life of me why they were sitting on a cocktail napkin next to bowl of mixed nuts and cigarette ash."

The picnic father yelled something towards the clump of elms, and the girl in the turquoise shorts turned her head. The mother jumped, startled, and a little spoonful of potato salad flung off a big spoon. The little brother pointed and laughed. The mother smiled nervously and fussed with her mussy hair. The father barked a few syllables in his son's direction, and the boy stopped laughing. The older brother came up behind the little brother and tickled his armpits. The picnic father placed his fists on his lumpy sides and scowled at the elms just as the girl in the turquoise shorts emerged, wiping her eyes, and walked towards her family. The family relaxed into their previous activities: the brothers wrestled, the father unsuccessfully tried to relight the grill, and the mother steadied her trembling hand as she doled out the potato salad and coleslaw.

"Karl said it only took a couple of years for his teeth to rot away. He wasn't eating right—nothing nutritious. The drink just ate his gums away. Bloody stubs, he said. Black teeth and bloody stubs. The dapper gentleman in top hat and tails who'd exchanged vows with his Spanish Marietta became a guy in a dirty suit who would just *point* to his brand of cigarettes at Sol's rather than expose his rot. I couldn't take my eyes off his teeth. I couldn't stop thinking about your mother and Michael. And you know what's funny, Maddie? I thought that was all I'd been thinking about for the past two years: your mother, and then after last year, your brother. I thought that's what I was doing: mourning them. But I realized in McCullough's, staring at Karl Matthews's teeth, that I hadn't thought of them, not really, not since

I started hitting the sauce. I couldn't even remember what Michael was wearing that day."

Michael was naked that day, Daddy, Magdalene thought—and then chased the image from her head with a few choice numbers.

The girl in the turquoise shorts was back by the edge of the Puddle's stream. Something in the girl's hand caught the late spring sun and glinted into Magdalene's eyes, something silver, shiny.

"When your mother was dying, when the cancer was just eating her away, her gums seemed to pull back; her teeth were huge, long. It just seemed to happen one day. You know how they say the light goes out of someone's eyes? Well, it's true. You could just about hear the light bulbs being ground into ashes. Your mother fought hard, Maddie, but it just gnawed at her, ravaged her. She had stopped looking in the mirror even. She knew whatever was coming for her was coming soon, she told me. Now it was up to me to make sure the world revolved around you and your brother. She'd sewn herself into our lives and wanted to tie up the loose ends, get the story right for once."

Her father tried to catch her eyes, but Magdalene ignored his gaze. The girl in the turquoise shorts had squatted beside a huge dead tree, her back to the trunk. The silver object glimmered again from her hand.

"When I had to...when I had to identify..."

Magdalene thought: *it's a knife*. The girl was going to cut herself at the edge of the Puddle's stream—the Trickle, Michael had called it. Magdalene placed her hand on the door handle. This was the countdown. Somewhere, in another car, in another park, on another street, her father was drying his tears with his tie, his glasses on the dashboard.

...*seven, six, five*...

Raindrops on the windshield.

"...they first ID'd...dental records...that was all I could think of..."

...*four, three, two*...

Raindrops on the windshield: lonely, lost globular star clusters.

"And that was it. Just sitting there looking at Karl's teeth, I knew it was time to do what your mother had asked me to do. In my grief, I had failed Michael, but I couldn't fail you. After what happened to you last year, I knew it was up to me. Tiddy was forever appearing in McCullough's, tugging at my sleeves, filling my ears with warnings and curses, but I couldn't hear her. It all seemed too much. But the thought of having to identify you like—the thought of not having you anymore—well, you probably thought I had forgotten all about you, but I didn't. I thought of you every day. I did, Maddie, and looking at Karl's teeth, I knew I couldn't continue living the way I'd been living, or I'd lose you too. That night at the Puddle—"

Magdalene pushed the door handle and tripped out of the car.

"Don't!" Magdalene screamed towards the girl in the turquoise shorts. "Don't!"

The girl in the turquoise shorts lowered her lighter and stubbed out her cigarette. Rain fell quick and hard. The girl looked back towards her family in the picnic area, but they were busy staring at the girl who had fallen out of the back of a parked car; they seemed to have taken no notice of the covert smoking.

"Don't," Magdalene whispered, and her father bundled her into the back of the car, retuned his glasses to his stately nose, and turned the engine. As they pulled away, Magdalene watched the picnic father dress down the girl in the turquoise shorts (the rain had revealed that the girl had not bothered wearing underwear), and then the sketchy-gray sky, suddenly swollen with fat rain clouds, descended. It was like a dense cluster of stars, overcome with grief, had covered Magdalene's eyes, submerging her head until her teeth felt like they were floating in her skull.

+

Raven beat Aunt Tiddy to the front door. The house smelled like soup—chicken noodle soup. Magdalene hated chicken noodle soup. Even the dog (whose fur normally smelled like stale popcorn) smelled vaguely of chicken noodle soup when Magdalene hugged him.

"I'm sorry, thank you," Magdalene whispered to her dog. "I'm sorry."

Aunt Tiddy had set the table, and salad preceded the soup. Magdalene could barely keep her head from falling in her plate.

Tiddy placed a cup of steaming tea in front of her.

"Let her go to bed if she's tired," Magdalene's father said.

"And then we'll have to wake her for her meds. No—she only needs to stay up a little while longer," Tiddy said, her long chicken neck craning to look at the kitchen clock.

Tiddy rolled her eyes slowly.

"Jesus, Gregory, can't you get a proper clock? That thing makes me buggy."

Magdalene managed a smile. The clock's numbers were backwards and opposite. A backwards six was where the three normally resided and so on.

"Patricia bought that clock. She loved it."

Magdalene loved it too.

"Well," Aunt Tiddy said, clearing the dishes from the table in one swoop without looking at Magdalene's father, "she was always a strange bird, that wife of yours."

Magdalene's father laughed into his coffee cup. Tiddy pulled a pocket watch from her apron (Tiddy's father had left her the watch in his will), shook her head, and replaced it. Good, bad, or indifferent: Tiddy shook her head at everything. It took Magdalene very little effort to make Aunt Tiddy roll her eyes or shake her head.

"That she was, Tiddy, that she was. Your mom would have loved her."

"*Your* mother would have loathed her, if my sister ever bothered to acquaint herself—and *then* been melted away, if she'd anything to melt."

"Patricia had that effect on people. Passive-aggressive."

"Fruit Loops," Tiddy said.

"A smile as wide as the Puddle is wet," Magdalene's father said. He tilted Magdalene's chin so it wouldn't land in the soup. "Shakespeare said that." Tiddy muttered something to herself that sounded to Magdalene's exhausted ears suspiciously like "horse shit."

"What say we give Maddie her medication now? It's not going to hurt anything. Just a few hours early."

"Fine, fine," Tiddy said, rummaging through the shopping bags on the counter. Raven poked around under the table, happy to be near the noise of the family. Magdalene watched the dog through the slits in her eyes.

"Christ, Tiddy. How many light bulbs did you buy?"

"Gregory, this house is as dark as a tomb. Time to brighten things up. I brought a couple of lamps from home too. There can never be too much light."

"Here Maddie, swallow these," her father said. "Now the water. Good girl. Okay, we'll take care of the dishes, sweetie. Get thee to bed."

Magdalene smiled wanly.

"Shakespeare, right?" she asked.

Tiddy scowled and turned her attention to the remaining shopping bags.

"Right as rain," her father said as he led her to the stairs, Raven close behind, the monkey drooping from the Labrador's jaws. Magdalene could barely hear the simian screaming.

+

Upstairs, Magdalene paused by Michael's door. It was slightly ajar. Her father and Tiddy were cleaning up in the kitchen. Raven was sitting in the hallway licking his privates. She pushed the door open.

Michael's room always seemed to be filled to the breaking point: football pennants, posters, shoulder pads, sweat socks, records, programs from professional sporting events, football cards, baseball cards, hockey cards, a basketball, and buried somewhere, hidden until minutes before they had to leave for school, his textbooks. Their mother—Mumsy had been what Michael called her—was forever on Michael to pick up his room (although she did little to back up her breezy exhortations). Magdalene had been in sixth grade (and Michael in seventh) when their mother died, which was not that terribly long ago, though at times, her mother was nothing more than a distant memory, like an old Disney movie she'd seen with Michael at the decrepit drive-in, huddled in the warmth of the fuzzy blankets their parents had placed in the backseat, struggling to stay awake, the dancing animals and silly rhymes all jumbled in her head afterwards. The prevalent memories of her mother were not dissimilar: just the trace of her huge, toothy smile, the wisps of her lies, the insouciant way she regarded her maternal responsibilities—as if her mother was waiting for the end credits to roll so she could return to whatever incongruities bubbled in the deepest creases of her mind. Being a mother surely hadn't been Patricia Archer Rumsey's life calling (Magdalene, going by Tiddy's hints, wasn't even sure being married to Gregory Barrows was high up on the list), but she discharged her duties with panache, and, having been blessed with well-behaved children, she generally left them on their own unless her expertise, opinion, or referee skills were needed.

Their father had been the disciplinarian, despite coming home late for dinner almost every night, apologetic, explaining the details of some case or other to their mother while he made himself a cocktail he rarely finished. Their mother defined carefree. She stayed on Michael about his room, Magdalene supposed, because that's what she felt she was supposed to do. Magdalene sometimes tossed her socks or underwear on her bedroom floor to see if she could raise a reaction, but their mother would just add her own delicates to the pile, as if making an offering to the laundry gods—or, in the case of the Barrows Bungalow, the laundry goddess. Magdalene found herself in charge of the washer and dryer, and their father often came home with a couple of new dress shirts still in their wrappers, never saying a word, as his wife floated around the house in the shrunken results of Magdalene's best efforts. Only Aunt Tiddy's ubiquitous presence saved the surviving Barrows wardrobe from further decimation. (U•biq•ui•tous—*a-ha!*: now there was a vocabulary word worthy of dropping around her father; she liked the ominous image of Tiddy motoring in her Baby Blue Cadillac of Doom towards omnipresence.) The household under Patricia Archer Rumsey Barrows was always in a state of disarray—never messy, just scattered. Their mother always had her long slender hands in two or three projects at a time: sand bowls, her vegetable garden, sewing mittens for Magdalene in the summertime, or knitting a wool hat with a pink, fuzzy ball on top for Michael.

Michael's room was pretty much the way he left it the day he disappeared—which was a much better way of putting it than *gone missing* (although she'd put it both ways). Disappeared was like—*poof*—magic; *gone missing* sounded like he'd wandered off, a stray dog, a lone sock lodged behind the dryer, something one could find at a later date. She knew Tiddy had tried to straighten up afterwards, but Magdalene remembered her father, dripping wet, barely able to stand from drink, slamming Michael's bedroom door shut, muttering, "Boys will be boys," and a few seconds later, in a much softer, but still slurred voice: "Goddamn it, Tiddy, goddamn it."

Some of Michael's sweat socks were piled in the corner. An abandoned pair of underwear—tighty whities!—peeked from beneath the bed. Shin guards leaned against his bureau. Two of its drawers were open, one overloaded with more socks, the other with...well, just about everything. Magdalene had stared at the drawer on many occasions, trying to remember what had become of her brother, where he had made off to, thinking for a nanosecond that he had gone to the Ambler for a movie without her or had run down to the

Fields with his football and some of the boys, leaving her behind. The drawer contained their whole childhood; it was his keepsake drawer, his junk drawer: ticket stubs to films Magdalene knew she had seen but no longer remembered; a trinket from a Crystal Caves tour; a key chain from the Franklin Institute with a little Benjamin flying his kite made almost invisible from rubbing against Michael's other mementoes (Michael went on a school trip to Philadelphia, and Magdalene fought her jealousy by immersing herself in Franklin's autobiography); a couple of comic books (*Legion of Super-Heroes*, *Green Lantern*, *The Mighty Thor*); a potpourri of electronic football-shaped games; birthdays cards; little miniature helmet replicas (the Eagles, the Steelers, the dreaded Cowboys). Magdalene also knew at the back of the drawer, safe for the moment because of her father's apparent commitment to keeping the room as Michael had left it (*had left*—as if!), were a couple of pages torn from a lingerie catalog, stashed under some college football programs, each wrinkled page presenting a pretty brunette modeling a series of lavender see-through camisoles.

And between his mattress and bedspring, if she looked, she knew she'd find Michael's stash—his newspaper money and birthday and Christmas money.

Raven's gray muzzle whimpered at her knees. Magdalene shushed him and rubbed his ears—no sense getting in trouble during her first day home. She was wide-awake again. She felt so close to *everything* in Michael's room. That was the problem, wasn't it, Magdalene thought, because this room was a museum, and its exhibits, artifacts, fossils even. And it was her fault. Magdalene wasn't sure how; she couldn't even remember what had happened, but she was sure the blame was somehow hers.

Magdalene stepped out of the room (and over the mute panda; Raven had placed Monien by Michael's doorframe) and closed the door. Raven stretched out at the top of the stairs, his shiny black nose hanging over the top step. Magdalene sat next to him, and the dog's tail wagged furiously. The monkey hung from his jaws.

She had always felt for sure that if her father ever came back to life, that if he left McCullough's behind, then everything would make sense, that the puzzle, the mystery would be solved in one bold reveal. And there was a moment, when she'd realized the handsome, older gentleman sitting next to her hospital bed—there was no mistaking the hair tonic and aftershave!—had been her father, all the waves had swept away, and the waters in her head were calm, drifting easily in the wind. And when he'd picked her up, the whirlpool had gone still. But it had crept back, tickling her toes, the Mystery of the Puddle—an undertow!—and the tickling turned into throbbing, tootsies into stubbed toes.

She had made Michael disappear. She had made the house dark.

From the top of the stairs, she could see her father bend over her mother's old stereo atop the liquor cabinet, and Frank tumbled out of the speakers, his voice like the well-worn leather of Magdalene's church shoes. Troubled Frank, her father called this voice—*In the Wee Small Hours, September of My Years*, and other albums with raincoat titles. Her father stood before the stereo and watched the vinyl spin. He looked small, vulnerable, and Magdalene realized that he wasn't going to be the hero; he wasn't going to save the day. Raven growled in his sleep, and the monkey slipped out of his mouth and fell a few steps. Magdalene stretched to reach it; she hoped it wouldn't scream. Her father turned away from the turntable and stepped out of view.

"Of course I'm coaching Summer Camp. I've been doing it for fifteen years, Tiddy—give or take a year or two there."

"Give or take. Don't you think you should be spending this time with Magdalene?"

"Tiddy, what Magdalene needs is normalcy. She needs to have things level out, and it's my job to maintain that level. She and I— and you—we need to get back to *living*. I'm back at the office, and I should be back on the sidelines too."

Sidelines. Borders. Outside the parentheses. Magdalene knew the intimacies of marginalia. Tiddy should just leave it alone. No one can drag anyone from the margin.

One has to jump.

"You owe Karl Matthews for holding your job," Tiddy said, her voice not as sure as it sounded, the tone nowhere as mean as intended. Magdalene knew Tiddy was arguing for argument's sake and realizing it as the words left her mouth.

"I do, Tiddy, I do. Karl came through for me again, and I'm going to come through for him and the office. And I'm going to come through for the kids at Summer Camp. I mean, can you see Frankie Bean's kid filling in for me?" He chuckled. "He means well, he's good natured, Frankie Junior, but he doesn't have two peas to rub together."

Tiddy managed a sound between a laugh and a wheeze. "I'm just worried about my grandniece is all. She doesn't even talk about it."

Talk about what?

In sixth grade, Sister Fatima had told the class that eavesdropping broke both the ninth and tenth commandments. But in eighth grade, Mr. Day, the science teacher, and mustachioed Mr. Peitzman, the disciplinarian's son and history teacher, eavesdropped on Sister Rita's meltdowns all the time. It seemed to be a major form of entertainment for Messrs. Day and Peitzman.

"I don't think she even knows what happened to..."

Her father breathed heavily through his mouth.

"Willa will help that, Tiddy. She's good, the best."

Doesn't know what happened?

Eavesdropping was a clichéd plot device—but Jesus, Mary, and Joseph!

"Hah!" Tiddy said, and Magdalene jumped as Raven scrambled to attention. Magdalene clamped his mouth shut with her hand.

"Damn lot of good she's done Magdalene so far."

"How many times did she see Willa, Tiddy? Hell, I was so out of it, I didn't even know she was still going."

"She was supposed to go twice a week," Tiddy said (with a tone of moral superiority Magdalene knew well), "but she stopped on her own, erased Willa's messages from the answering machine."

"Good thing Willa didn't prescribe anything yet then."

Tiddy cleared her throat: "They knew what her home life was like so they were dispensing the pills at school."

"God," her father groaned. "The other kids must have given her hell."

"Didn't say," Tiddy replied. "She didn't say."

"Oh, no one, really," Magdalene whispered into Raven's trapped snout.

Just the bullies.

The Bod Squad.

The Nuns of Deformity.

"Well, Willa helped *me*," Magdalene's father said, regaining his stride, "and she's testified in court for us a number of times. She's a good doctor. She's knows her business."

Magdalene heard her father's bad knee crack.

"Willa's as gay as the day is long, Gregory—no, don't interrupt me, because you know I don't give a good goddamn who she sleeps with. But you said it yourself: normalcy. Our Magdalene needs things to be normal, and..."

Willa: A lesbian! Who knew? Magdalene was impressed. She no more wanted to see Willa Meade than she wanted to return to Assumption for makeup exams—a subject that had yet to be broached; the school year had ended during her convalescence—but Willa being gay gave the therapist a flavor other than hippie, and as far as Magdalene was concerned, anything was better than hippie-dippie doo-dah love-you-too.

Raven's nose ran between Magdalene's fingers.

"She's going to see Willa, and that's that. She's the best children's therapist in the county, and if she could help *me* find help, she can help my daughter. No—not another word. That's it. Just please make sure she goes, Tiddy. Twice now. Twice. If I hadn't—"

Tiddy snorted.

Might be time to scram.

Doo-dah. Doo-dah.

"Now it's my turn: what's past is past. You put down the drink. You're back in the office (maybe too soon, but who am I to say?), and Magdalene is safe—for now. And it's our job to make sure she *stays* safe. You've only been sober for six days."

"Seven, Tiddy," her father said, and Magdalene could imagine his jaw tighten around the words like the way they did the one time he'd let Magdalene and Michael watch him in court. She'd thought his jaw was going to explode any second then! She'd actually felt sorry for the defendant, having to face this jaw—the jawbone she believed, until this morning, had crumbled like the red, polluted shore of the Puddle after a thunderstorm, a dying star reduced to dust-encrusted fingerprints on a bottle of booze.

Whhhh*at* wwww*ill you d*oooo whhhh*en you*rrrr *time come*ssss*?*

"Seven. And you're back at work already, and your daughter *just* tried to kill herself again, and you want to coach Summer Camp football, *and* you still have counseling sessions yourself, do you not?"

Seven: seven is a prime number. Seven doesn't need. Seven: divisible by itself and one.

Seven stands alone. Seven stands alone.

Hi-ho-the-derry-o: seven stands alone.

Magdalene watched Raven's snot dry on her fingers.

"Yes, ma'am. I'm due back at EPPI tomorrow. I'm going on my lunch break to a meeting."

"You can afford better than the Eastern Pennsylvania Psychiatric Institute, Gregory. For God's sake, that place is a hell hole."

Raven blinked once, twice, three times.

"Not quite, Tiddy, but it's not pretty and I deserve what I dole out, and that's where our office remands the disadvantaged."

"If they're so disadvantaged, where are they getting the money for the drugs?"

"Tiddy…"

"Fine, fine. EPPI for you. Hip-hip-hooray! My point is this: you need me if you're going to do all this and still be a father. You need to let me run this house. I can't be taking orders from someone who insists on doing six things at once."

Six: a perfect number. One plus two plus three equals six. Equal to the sum of all its positive factors—excluding itself. A summarizing.

Better to be a prime.

"I just want things to be normal, Tiddy."

"I know, I heard you. I'm not saying anything more."

"Good."

"Except this."

Magdalene heard her father groan beneath Nelson Riddle's string arrangement.

"Let her play football," Aunt Tiddy said.

Magdalene tightened her grip on the dog's snout. Raven rolled his sugar-brown eyes and went back to sleep.

"You know she's listening, Gregory," Tiddy whispered, "and if she isn't, she should be. She needs to be involved in her own redemption—no, don't look at me like that. There's a time and a place for Jesus and Mary and all God's saints in heaven, but we're not vying for her carnival ticket. Our girl needs a better head, not a perfect play. We can help, but she's got to find her own path out of this mess. She loves the game. Let her play. Other girls play at Summer Camp at least."

Perfect play.

Magdalene counted Raven's whiskers.

Why would anyone want to be perfect? What was perfect about having to be the sum of all that came before? What was perfect about needing an exact sequence (a path) of numbers to reach full potential?

The prime stands alone.

Nothing else can even touch it.

"Touch. They play touch," Magdalene's father said quietly. "I coach football, Tiddy, not touch."

"Gregory—"

"Tiddy, football is for boys—and I know that's old fashioned, fine, then it is. Let someone else coach her."

"Where? In Spring House? Rhawnhurst? Should I just toss her the keys to my Caddy?"

"I've seen you drive, Tiddy. It's not a bad idea."

"Hogwash, Gregory Barrows. She doesn't even have baby-sitting anymore."

Magdalene squeaked and pinched her chapped lips. Raven kept his eyes shut but wagged his tail.

She doesn't even have baby-sitting anymore?

Onetwothreefourfivesixseveneightnineten.

Her father was in front of the stereo again, turning the record over.

"I haven't told her."

"Gregory!"

"She just got out of the hospital, for Christ's sake. McAllister's an angry, vengeful man."

"And whose fault is that?" Tiddy asked.

"Mine? He broke the law. He's lucky I didn't put him away."

"Still paying off that fine, I understand."

"He put his house up, Tiddy. The county doesn't put people on payment plans for damages."

She doesn't even have baby-sitting anymore?

"The man lost his wife, Gregory," Tiddy snapped. "He's suddenly a widower. He was drunk."

"Nancy McAllister died three years ago."

"Ned O'Neill needed a new newsstand anyway."

"That's not the point."

"Damn right, it's not. You're dead on the money. McAllister stopped living when his wife passed, started drinking, rammed into O'Neill's newsstand—while Ned was in it—and God knows what else he's done, and now he's got to pay. Fine. Understood. But when are *you* going to pay, Gregory?"

"I'm doing everything I can here, Tiddy!"

Raven's drool dripped from Magdalene's fingers, and her hand slipped from his snout. Maybe she should just jump, she thought. If she stood up and tossed her body down the stairs, all her bones and every drop of blood would spill from her sausage casing—and everyone would see, but no one would be able to find the sum. Only the head cheese would survive, lumpy, silent, probably still counting.

The cheese stands alone.

"Too much, if you ask me, way too much. You should extend your leave, take care of your daughter, and let her tackle the boys if she wants to. You should allow your system more than a few days rest before you jump into something as big as the Bochdan boy's case. I'm here, Gregory, and I'll do everything and anything to help you, but it's going to be a long, hot one this summer, and you've a debt to pay to your family—the family that's here. The family that's left."

"Tiddy—"

"Don't start."

Her father had his back to the stereo now. Magdalene saw the strong shoulders that had borne her and Michael, piggyback-style, to bed when they'd fallen asleep watching old black and white movies on television (she rarely, if ever, made it to the end credits; Michael spent the mornings after filling in the blanks), the taut arms that had lifted her brother from the field the time he'd sprained his ankle in his first game as starting quarterback, and the spine that had been curved like a broken question mark in McCullough's, now ramrod straight, as if trying to hold an entire house of ghosts upon its muscles. Sister Mary Magdalene had had a back like that, a bridge across a fire. How could Magdalene ever measure up after what happened at the Puddle?

The Puddle?

What happened at the Puddle?

Raven woke up and licked her face; he gripped Monkey between his teeth and curled up behind Magdalene's back.

"You have to let me pay you."

"Gregory Barrows," Tiddy started, " 'what a piece of work is man!' "

"Tiddy, just going back to work and coaching, not to mention AA, is going take a hell of a lot of my time. I quit smoking again too. I'll have to watch my temper."

"You don't have a temper."

"...but this case—the Bochdan boy—"

"It's what's wrong with our time. When I was a little girl—"

"God was still young," her father said, laughing. "This time is no different than your time. We just hear about it more. Cable, Internet, more newspapers than you can shake a stick at."

Magdalene stood up to her full height (which was a quite respectable four feet ten inches) and turned around, her back to the stairs. Best not to look, she thought. Heights and all.

Under her breath, she recited one of Michael's taunting rhymes:
Divide, conjugate, bag o' stones;
Next sound you'll hear is the rattling of bones.

"You're going to leave the boy's mother alone, right?" Tiddy asked.

"The father's gone. We're looking for him because the gun was hot and before the shooting, apparently in his possession, which is a violation of his parole. But Andriy Bochdan hightailed it out of town. Hugh wants to go after the mother. 'An act of responsibility,' I believe he said. I think he was looking at me when he said it."

The story could end right now. The final summation trapped forever in her head cheese. Was there a rule against daring herself? Magdalene knew the Rules of the Dare intimately.

I. Dare. You.

There: it's done.

Fall back on three.

"Hugh Greene!" Tiddy cried. "Can't this town ever vote for somebody else? I knew Hugh Greene when he couldn't wipe his ass with all three of his clueless kids *and* his dopey wife on their knees wearing pith helmets. The only thing Hugh should be in charge of is his belly. That man could use some sit-ups."

ONE!

"Regardless, Tiddy, he's the mayor. It's his call."

"What does Mr. Matthews have to say?"

"Karl's the DA. In the end, he's going to have to do whatever the mayor wants."

TWO!

"I'm not saying that it's not the parents' fault—something went wrong for the Bochdan boy to pull the trigger," Tiddy said, "but I'll be damned if that poor woman can face this brunt alone. Hell of a sorry state, I have to tell you."

"Hugh wants us to charge Mrs. Bochdan—someone to feed the carrion crows of the fourth estate, it seems—at least until we find the husband. Parental responsibility—Kuhns v. Brugger, which is normally reserved for civil proceedings. But that's what Hugh is pressuring Karl to pursue in regards to criminal prosecution"

"More hogwash. Muddy hogwash of a terrible sort."

"I can only imagine what great English Renaissance play that's from, Tiddy."

TWO AND A HALF!

Muddy?

Her father sighed. "We can't go after the boy. We're talking about second graders. But that's not entirely up to me. I have a voice, of course, but the decision making power lies with Karl and the mayor."

Sinatra skipped on a phrase, and Magdalene didn't hear the weariness in Frank's voice, just the cold hard fact that he was trapped, doomed—if her father didn't lift the needle, Ol' Blue Eyes would forever repeat himself.

The Bochdan boy? Little Joseph Bochdan?

"That poor woman. The Cabots too. These are sorry times, Gregory, sorry times."

Magdalene could hear Aunt Tiddy leave the sofa, her creaky back harmonizing with the old sofa springs.

Magdalene, under her breath again:

Divide, conjugate, bag o' stones;
Next sound you'll hear is the rattling of bones.
Diverge, gin mill, Daddy's dive bar;
Next sound you'll hear is the falling of stars.

THREE!

Raven yawned audibly and sniffed Magdalene's bottom.

"Fix the record, Gregory, and then put your daughter to bed. I think she's heard enough for one night."

Magdalene hit the sheets before her father lifted the phonograph needle, Raven beating her by a nose. She'd forgotten to brush her teeth.

+

When he entered her room, she realized that his old bar odors were completely gone: the burnt match and sticky beer scents. Magdalene could only smell perspiration beneath his hair tonic and aftershave. She shoved her journal beneath her pillow.

He was in his shirtsleeves still, and Magdalene remembered how when her father, before the days of the drink, immersed himself in a case, the back of his dress shirts would soak through, and she'd have to scrub them, like her mother used to (before she'd yielded the duties to her daughter), in the old wash basin that sat between the dryer and the washing machine in the basement. Magdalene knew she could never earn those kinds of stains.

"Listen, Maddie, about school—"

"I'll catch up, Daddy, I'll—"

"No, I spoke to Sister Mary Joseph this morning. You can take a week or two, then hit the books, and she'll administer the final exams to you in her office."

"Summer school!"

"No, no. You can study at home. Sister had the teachers mark the chapters and photocopy notes for what you missed. There was only a week left before exams, so it's not much. And you decide what you want to do about high school."

"Not go?"

"Well, no, you have to go, but maybe we can defer it for a year or six months if you don't feel up to it. I don't want to pressure you," her father said. "Maybe you could do some volunteer work with the senior citizens at Artman's."

Magdalene decided not to ask about baby-sitting Katie McAllister. Just thinking about taking all her exams in Sister Mary Joseph's office was scary enough for one night.

"Now, you start back in a few days with Willa."

"Daddy, I don't want to."

"Please don't fight me. I know I haven't been around like I should have been, but I'm here now, and we have to move forward together. We can't forget them: your mother and Michael, but we have to live like they would have expected us to. Willa's going to help you with whatever you need help with, Maddie. Tiddy will remind you of your appointments and either give you bus fare or—God help us all—take you there herself. Whatever you like. I know you used to like to ride the bus by yourself."

Her father kissed her forehead, stood up, then leaned down to kiss it again.

"I love you. You're my Maddie Monkey. We're going to be okay. We're going to be just fine."

Magdalene wiped her forehead.

"Do you want Raven to stay here with you tonight."

Magdalene wasn't sure but answered yes anyway.

Her father flicked off the light.

"I'm right downstairs if you need me. Good night."

Raven climbed up into her bed, and his hot breath filled her nostrils. He was warm and needy, and he curled up as close to her as he could. Raven was going to be a problem, Magdalene thought as she surrendered to the choppy waters in her head. What was she going to do about her dog?

Chapter Three

The Dead Boy

Grandparents, Magdalene thought, prepared you for life in ways parents never could. They were the first glimpse for most kids, when they were wrinkled and small, of how small and wrinkled they'd eventually become. Grandparents had already accomplished what parents were just setting out to do. They'd fought wars and survived market crashes and fell in love and buried loved ones and experienced tragedy first hand. Unlike babies, grandparents had earned their wrinkles, every one of them. And grandparents often taught their children's children their first lesson about death by dying first.

But Magdalene's theory was flawed, she knew, for although her grandmother, like Magdalene's mother, had died of breast cancer, it wasn't like Grandmother Barrows had been around every day for treats and admonishments, teaching her grandchildren songs while they perched on her knee. Those had been Aunt Tiddy's jobs, and Magdalene was quite sure Tiddy was never going to die.

Only twice in her eight years of formal schooling (nine years if Magdalene counted kindergarten) had a fellow student's *parent* died. Those were unspeakable tragedies. A strong hug or a shoulder to cry upon might be offered if a grandmother or grandfather passed away (though there seemed to be a paucity of grandfathers in Mondauk; "The war," was Tiddy's tight-lipped response when Magdalene had asked her), but when Lisa Singer's dad died or when the mother of that boy in the grade below her died in a horrible wreck—Magdalene's father had prosecuted the drunk driver, so Magdalene at least felt she had done *something*, if only by extension—there was nothing anyone could say or do. The normal course of events had been circumvented: the bird hadn't flown south, the cock crowed at midnight instead of at dawn, the Puddle drained away after the summer rains. A heavy crown of clouds settled in. Lisa Singer became the class whore (although Magdalene was sure she never did much more than french kiss a lot of boys; she didn't think Lisa Singer was smart enough to know what to do next); she wore heavy makeup that the nuns washed off with old sponges in the rusty faculty sink;

she wore black rock'n'roll t-shirts beneath her navy blue school blouse. The boy in the grade below Magdalene just looked like he'd lost something, like he'd never find it ever.

Magdalene's grandmother hadn't been around enough for her death to teach anything of value, but Magdalene doubted very much that even if Grandmother Barrows had been sticking her nose into everyday family matters, like her sister Tiddy did, that she could have laid the groundwork for Magdalene to handle both the passing of her mother and the vanishing of Michael.

Magdalene knew her own case history was something her classmates shared in whispers—but at least not in any circles where Magdalene could feel their whispers tickle her neck. Not that it mattered: Magdalene no longer ran in (school) circles. With the sole exception of Christina, with whom she had maintained at least the façade of friendship (and Magdalene was keenly aware of the subtle differences in Christina's behavior during the past school year, as if Magdalene were cursed and the curse contagious), Magdalene had never had what she would have qualified as a close friend at Assumption. She had never been a member of the Bod Squad or any other clique. Not that she had needed a huge social life when Michael had been here; Michael had been more than enough to handle.

School, of course, didn't get any easier after the first suicide attempt. How word got around, she didn't know. (Christina, despite her almost complete aversion to discussing the event with Magdalene, was suspect number one; Christina's *only* complete aversion was to keeping her mouth shut.) Mondauk Proper was a small town in a small county but neither were that small. Still—it seemed as if suicides were rare. Magdalene had looked through the obituaries in the library—there was barely a single reference to someone taking his or her own life, just more summarizing.

Passed away suddenly…

Survived by…

After a long struggle…

In lieu of flowers…

There was that old drunk, Avery Finster, who had tried to gas himself in his car, parking it just inside a neighbor's lean-to adjacent to the Puddle, but he failed to actually put the car in park, so when the carbon monoxide started to fill the interior, his foot slipped from the brake, and the car and its passenger slid rather noiselessly into the water; Finster was able to escape through the window as the car began to sink. It had been a dry summer that year; the Puddle was shallow. The car ceased its decline when the water reached the door handles, but that fact never stopped Finster from suing his neighbor for maintaining such unsafe grounds—as if, her father had said when it happened, the Puddle had lured the car into its gaping maw.

A high school girl had slit her wrists the year prior to Magdalene's first suicide attempt, but no one (except Magdalene) even remembered her name, let alone the actual circumstances (which Magdalene had never discovered) that had led Michelle Byrd to her bloodletting. Everyone agreed the attempt had been due to poor grades and a recalcitrant boyfriend and overbearing parents and teachers who didn't understand. Everyone agreed it was hardly the poor girl's fault.

Magdalene's first suicide attempt had made her a celebrity—notorious, like she'd risen from the dead. At first, Christina didn't treat her any differently. Suicide, Magdalene was convinced, was the providence and curse of the enlightened and the aware (Avery Finster excepted). Christina Fuller was not a deep thinker, or perhaps Magdalene had grown too advanced intellectually for her friend. Christina wouldn't know the adjective "recalcitrant" if it ran away from her, screaming. Christina concerned herself with boys mostly—flirting, passing notes, and screaming loudly for their favor and attention when congregating in circles with the other Bod Squaders. (So much screaming in fact, that Magdalene had come to believe that it was part of the dating ritual.) Christina had only mentioned the first suicide attempt once, during a tense sleepover. Tense, for Mrs. Fuller wouldn't leave them be, forcing diet snacks and carrot sticks, recommending that evening's television programs, and trying to enforce a bedtime, as if, under the careful scrutiny of a good, Christian soul like Mrs. Fuller's, Magdalene couldn't possibly pull off a sleepover suicide.

(Mrs. Fuller, who served on Assumption's Faith Board, never missed a church function or charity event and always sang the loudest, even at funerals; Magdalene had secretly hoped, before both attempts, that her funeral could be kept secret from Mrs. Fuller; Magdalene wanted potential mourners spared the woman's off-key caterwauling at the most solemn end of a short, unhappy life.)

Snuggled up in front of the television at the foot of Christina's bed, Christina had asked what it was like—not *are you okay?* or *how are you feeling?* or even *are you feeling better?* (as if suicide was a nasty bout of the flu)—but just: *what was it like?*

"Like slicing bread."

Christina gasped and covered her mouth with her hand. Christina had recently had her nails done and spent a considerable amount of time that evening running her nails through her dyed blonde hair; Magdalene wasn't sure if Christina was truly shocked or had merely discovered another way to show off her fingernails.

Magdalene ran a quick finger over her scar.

"Bread."

Christina never asked her to sleep over again.

Finishing her exams in the presence of principal Sister Mary Joseph would be creepy enough, but Magdalene knew it was better than if she had been released from the hospital early and forced to take the exams during the final couple days of school. Her second resurrection would surely have taken the school by storm. (She considered it a shame, really, that she didn't attend Resurrection of Our Lord Elementary School in Rhawnhurst instead of Assumption!) Regardless, Magdalene's neighborhood fame would now rival that of James Orienti's, who had never lived down that he had not only peed his pants twice in the second grade, but he had also pooped himself during a rather strenuous (for a second grader) gym class. Due to the caste system firmly in place at Assumption, James Orienti had developed into the class scumbag—not a geek (too slow, mentally), not a stoner (or even a stoner-in-waiting), and not a dweeb (a designation that Magdalene heard never left grade school; a dweeb put his or her gloves on backwards and answered when someone else's name was called in class); James Orienti became someone even the geeks and the stoners (although not the dweebs; the dweebs were very self-involved) made fun of. In the eighth grade, James Orienti was *still* dealing with having peed and pooped his pants in the second, and his behavior bore this out: he picked up dog excrement in the schoolyard and chased girls with it; he kissed other boys on the cheek and ran away; he stuck his hand down the back of his pants, farted on it, then smelled his fingers. Magdalene understood that her second suicide attempt would raise her to James Orienti's unique pariah status. Even bullies like Stevie Rich and John-John Hagarty left James Orienti alone, and they picked on *everyone*. Magdalene never understood how Michael could have been on the same team as those two animals.

High school might be better. Most of her classmates would be attending Hoskins High in Spring House too, but the boys and girls were separated there. The summer would suck some of the sting out of what she had done; the shock value wouldn't be as high.

Magdalene mulled all of this while she dressed. (She made sure to wear her silver bracelets to hide the scars and the magic marker lines on her wrists.) She couldn't picture herself in the Hoskins High navy blue girls' uniform. This reinforced what Magdalene had begun to suspect the morning after returning home from the hospital (the first time): *everything has a place and the world has a place for everything—except for her.* It was as if, by trying to murder herself, she had lost her place, moved the bookmark. Her part had played out, and like Judas in the New Testament (what choice did *he* have?; his behavior had been predicted by *God*), she'd essayed her part well. Her role—in what?; *The Mystery of the Puddle?*; she could almost hear Frank and Joe Hardy licking their chops—had been written specifically for her, and she'd written herself out.

When Magdalene woke this morning, the first person she'd thought of was Katie McAllister. Had she dreamt it, or had Tiddy said to her father the night before: *she doesn't even have baby-sitting anymore?* No—that hadn't been a dream; the pain in her belly was too real. Another goddamn investigation. And Tiddy knew she'd been eavesdropping. Magdalene started the morning annoyed—and it just grew worse. Raven wasn't in her room when she climbed out of bed—which meant someone had opened her door in the night to check on her. Magdalene poked her head into the hallway and was shocked to see Aunt Tiddy emerging from her father's bedroom in her nightgown.

"Close your mouth," Tiddy said. "You'll catch flies."

"Where's Daddy?"

"He slept on the sofa. Breakfast's been waiting for you."

In the living room, two pillows sat upon a pile of neatly folded sheets. The sofa looked too small for her father. He was trying hard to fit. Magdalene could feel her eyes sinking in salt water.

"Your father insisted I stay in his room," Aunt Tiddy said, shoveling scrambled eggs onto Magdalene's plate. "It was all I could do to not have him put me in the shed."

Tiddy winked at Magdalene. Magdalene ignored her. The house was settling. Magdalene, at least, had slept in her own bed—it hadn't occurred to her until this morning that she had tried to leave this earth twice from that very bed and had failed. Magdalene wanted to switch bedrooms too, but her sense of privacy—already trespassed by *someone* during the night; Raven hadn't opened the bedroom door by himself—prevented her from asking.

There were ten in the bed,
And the little one said,
"Roll over, roll over!"
So they all rolled over,
And one fell out.

Magdalene thought she understood Raven's dilemma: the dog might not remember specifics of previous owners (the way they smelled, their favorite sleeping positions, the timbre of their voices), but, Magdalene was sure, Raven knew there was *something* he'd forgotten to remember, that despite having a found yet another new home, he didn't quite belong to any of them. Raven was going to be a problem in the grand scheme of things, a clog in the master plan. Magdalene caught a tear in her throat: Raven would have to go too. The dog would never survive the grief of *another* disappearance; Raven was still looking for Michael.

Magdalene pushed at the eggs with her fork; thinking of what she would have to do to Raven had made her lose her appetite.

"Well, we need a plan," Tiddy said, sitting across from Magdalene, "for the day." Tiddy took a marker and a little pad out of her apron. "I figured we could go shopping, get you some new summer clothes, maybe a bathing suit—"

"I'm going to visit Katie and leave a note for Mr. McAllister, see when he needs me to baby-sit."

Aunt Tiddy's nose twitched and her painted-on eyebrows arched higher than usual.

"Your father didn't...no, of course, he didn't."

Magdalene concealed her glee at tripping up her aunt. Had Tiddy forgotten that Magdalene had been privy to last night's discussion?

"Didn't what?" Magdalene asked.

"We—your father thinks it's best for you to take it easy for a little while."

"Swimming is taking it easy?"

"Swimming, dear?" Tiddy's eyebrows threatened to jump off her forehead.

"You said we're buying a bathing suit. Are we going to the pool or wading in the Puddle?"

Aunt Tiddy stared at Magdalene and Magdalene stared back.

Magdalene didn't know what waited for her at the Puddle (something did), and she didn't necessarily want to explore this topic with Aunt Tiddy, but she knew Tiddy wasn't ready for this discussion either—or maybe Tiddy didn't know.

"I told Michael that," Magdalene said.

"Told him what, dear?"

"Told him I'm starting to believe that nothing connects."

"Maybe you could help me set up house."

"I'm going for a walk," Magdalene said. Tiddy said nothing, but the force with which her aunt piled the dishes next to the sink was response enough.

Raven was waiting for her by the door, sitting pretty, holding Monkey. The Labrador's tail wagged at top speed. Magdalene didn't dare wonder where Monien the silent panda was—probably sitting on Michael's bed or inside one of his football helmets, just waiting for Michael to find it and chase the dog around the kitchen table or toss it in the air for Raven to leap and catch with increased excitement and decreased accuracy.

"No, Raven, go lie down," Magdalene said.

Raven continued looking at her with his huge, brown eyes wide with anticipation.

"Raven, go lie down, boy. Take a nap. I'll be back later."

The dog was having none of it; he dropped the monkey and leapt, his front paw striking her hard in the chest. Raven ducked his head under the end table near the door and gripped his leash between his teeth.

"No, Raven. I have to go," Magdalene said. Raven tried another tack. He dropped the leash, picked up Monkey, and forced it into Magdalene's stomach.

Magdalene heard the tap in the kitchen turn off; she knew Tiddy was listening. Magdalene's chest grew hot; her neck and ears started burning. All she wanted was to be by herself. Everyone else seemed to be able to do what they wanted—a week ago, her father was drunk in McCullough's, and now he was preparing rhetoric for court and plays for the field; Tiddy had moved to Candy Lane and proclaimed herself boss—why couldn't she go for a goddamn walk alone?

"Raven!" Magdalene screamed, pushing the dog away with more force than she knew was necessary.

"Go away. Get! Go lie down! Now!"

Raven butted her leg with his head.

"This isn't a goddamn game, Raven—GO *AWAY*! *NOW*! GET *AWAY* FROM ME!"

Raven sat on his tail (which continued to wag furiously), barked once, then scampered under the dining room table.

Magdalene stepped outside. The late spring-early summer breeze smeared tears across her cheeks. There could be only one outright goodbye when it came down to it. She couldn't continue contributing to Raven's misery. Raven might have to say goodbye before Magdalene did.

+

Magdalene circled the streets, working up the nerve to knock on Mr. McAllister's door. Magdalene had been baby-sitting Katie since the fifth grade, after Katie's mother passed. Katie had been in kindergarten. There had been interruptions in service however. Michael's disappearance had led to a long chunk of unemployment, culminating in her first failed suicide. Magdalene was aware that Mr. McAllister had hired other girls in her absence, but she knew that Katie liked her best. They were old souls, she and Katie. Magdalene suspected Katie to be even smarter than she was.

The berry bushes on the corner property opposite Mr. McAllister's house, which was two from the end, provided perfect cover, and Magdalene untied and tied her shoes, gazing across the street at the two story whitewashed twin. Mr. McAllister's blue Chevy was in the driveway, but Magdalene knew he hadn't driven it since his accident—she wasn't even sure it still ran. Mr. McAllister spent his Saturday mornings under the car, his greasy hands occasionally creeping out to grip a forgotten tool or land on a filthy rag. Magdalene didn't like seeing Mr. McAllister's feet sticking out from beneath the blue Chevy; she always imagined the jack giving way, and the car separating Mr. McAllister from his feet and creeping hands, or the bumper severing him at the neck, his angry head rolling away like the unfortunate orb in the story of Lou's Head, a recently minted tale that fascinated Jerry Eves and his cronies (and Michael). Magdalene massaged her temples and stretched the muscles in her calves—no sense scaring herself. Mr. McAllister was scary enough himself, thank you very much, without replaying the story of Lou's Head. Besides— knowing Jerry and her brother, it was just made up. Heads don't sing Neil Diamond songs after they've been separated from their bodies.

Shiver.

Magdalene decided to confront Mr. McAllister another day; there was no telling if he was even home. She had already broken her nerve by waiting so long in the berry bushes (and conjuring Lou's Head), blowing almost a half an hour fiddling with her shoelaces and flicking away squashed red berries. She could always come back tomorrow. Aunt Tiddy would become harder and harder to avoid, but Magdalene figured that she had a day or two before the severe schedule of fun Tiddy had in mind commenced. By then, Magdalene thought, maybe this would all be over.

Magdalene felt inside her pocket for her library card. Mrs. Stanley didn't like kids hanging around the library unless they were researching a paper; then she wanted to know what the topic was, like she was going to verify it, as if the kids could possibly be lying and were researching "Tippecanoe and Tyler Too" or Sacco and Vanzetti for kicks. But when her pocket came up empty, Magdalene decided she'd risk it.

The air in the library was cool. Mrs. Stanley seemed distracted, beating the insides of books with her stamp, looking for late returns. Magdalene swore Mrs. Stanley lived for late returns, and once, when Magdalene had tried to read *Gone with the Wind* over a Christmas vacation, Michael had to lend her some of his newspaper money to pay the late fees. She hadn't wanted Mrs. Stanley to go to the Assistant District Attorney about her fines. (Magdalene wouldn't have put it past her.) The ADA's drinking had just begun around then; a library fine might result in the purchase of an extra fifth.

(Quick thought: Michael's mattress stash could come in handy during her final days, especially since it appeared she was now unemployed. Of course, Michael would kill her for stealing from him if he ever came back...)

But Magdalene wasn't in the library to borrow books; she wanted to research suicides. How could so many people have killed themselves, and yet she herself was a two-time loser? Magdalene knew Mrs. Stanley frowned on kids using microfilm to look at old newspapers without school supervision (John-John Hagarty and Stevie Rich had once raced to see who could rewind the microfilm faster and busted a machine), but Magdalene already had a cover story: summer school! If Mrs. Stanley had heard about Magdalene's second suicidal endeavor—and why wouldn't she have?—then the old lady would know Magdalene had makeup work to do.

It was even cooler in the microfilm/microfiche room. It was dark too, and Magdalene had to fight sleep as she scanned obituaries from the *Mondauk Common*, going back two years. Mrs. Stanley had scowled when Magdalene had gone to the microfilm cabinets, but maybe thought better than to mess with a victim of recent psychological trauma. Magdalene grinned: *victim*. Maybe they'd take her away from Tiddy and put her in a holding cage or stick her in the drunk tank with ol' Avery Finster.

Magdalene pinched her leg to keep her eyes open and let the machine's knob spin in her hand.

Terrorists…

Congress…

The President…

Magdalene let these headlines fly over her head. What did those people have to do with Mondauk County? What did the President of the United States know from a missing brother and having to decide how to handle an adopted dog's demise?

Black and white faces and bold headlines blurred into a thousand exploding stars.

Investment Tycoon Dies at 84.

Ice Cream Lady, 72, Lived Full Life, Friends Say.

Grade School Football Hero Dies in—

Magdalene opened her eyes and was surprised to feel the microfilm canister pressing into her face; she had fallen asleep on the desk. The microfilm was rewinding with a backwards whistle, and when it clicked off, Mrs. Stanley, her breath sour like she hadn't brushed her teeth for centuries, leaned her face into Magdalene's. The librarian's gaudy, gold, costume necklace brushed Magdalene's cheek.

"Young lady, this room is not, I assure you, a flophouse."

Flophouse? One of Aunt Tiddy's favorite descriptions for when Magdalene and Michael would drag their toys and books and records into the living room on a rainy Sunday. Magdalene looked around the dark room; she was alone except for Mrs. Stanley.

"I wasn't making a mess, I swear."

"Get out, Miss Barrows, before I have to call your father."

Magdalene cringed. She knew by now what was coming next.

"If I can find him."

Magdalene didn't bother to correct her, didn't bother to inform stinky, old, cranky Mrs. Stanley that the Assistant District Attorney was back on the case, stalking the halls of justice. It had sounded like what Tiddy and her father had been discussing—a case involving elementary school boys—would land her father's name on the front page of the *Common* again, like cases had so many times when she was little. (Their mother clipped the headlines and hung them from the fridge with magnets so Magdalene and Michael could see their father in action every time they went for some iced tea or a piece of fruit.) Mrs. Stanley would see soon enough. In fact, Mrs. Stanley would see it before Magdalene did if Magdalene could just get around to formulating an exit plan. Magdalene almost wished she'd be alive to see Mrs. Stanley's face and the faces of the rest of the Assumption Faith Board (especially Mrs. Fuller's) when Gregory Barrows made his comeback, but she wouldn't be, and neither would her dog. They were soon to be just two of the thousand stars exploding.

+

The sun outside the library was blinding. Magdalene walked a few feet without seeing. When her sight returned, she found herself headed towards Assumption. Her head was heavy, full, and even though she wanted to go home and lie down, she wasn't sure how that would go over with Aunt Tiddy. She was supposed to check in with principal Sister Mary Joseph before starting her private final exams. Now was as good a time as any to meet with Sister, she guessed. Magdalene doubted it was past one in the afternoon. Her stomach wasn't rumbling, even though she had barely eaten Tiddy's scrambled eggs, but then again her appetite, which she knew would soon be a subject of much debate under her aunt's vigilant eyes, wasn't what it had been before. It was affecting the way her face looked. Oh, it was still round, there was nothing she could do about that. She had her mother's dimples (and the same half-moon baggage carriers under her eyes) but her father's angles when it came to her nose and chin and cheekbones. Lately though, her cheekbones seemed to push towards her eyes, and her chin appeared to stick out even further from her chapped lips and sunken, pale cheeks. Magdalene knew she must look like a little ghost, blinking sluggishly in the sunlight of the coming summer.

Assumption of Our Lady Church had been constructed from large, gray stones; it looked almost medieval to Magdalene. The old school building, constructed sometime during the early '40s, was fashioned with ugly, pale yellow bricks. The new school building (the one housing most of the classrooms) was built after the lavatory fire and was set at a right angle to the older building, attached by a dusty, iron stairwell. The stones of the newer school building were an even uglier shade of yellow. It was as if one of the saints had peed on it, Jerry Eves had said; Sister Edna had called the color unfortunate.

The convent had thankfully (Sister Edna had agreed) been made of material similar to the stones used to build the church. It was a squat, one floor building that looked for all the world like a Nazi pillbox, and it sat on the east side of the crumbling, black asphalt that was designated as the playground for recess and lunch. Magdalene often wondered how the nuns ever slept in if they were sick: the north side of the convent was adjacent to a large expanse of lawn, the west and south sides faced the playground's L. Each morning, Christina and her *other* friends screamed greetings to one another in the recess area, and boys hollered challenges or rock'n'roll lyrics or football chants. The Corridor, as the bottom part of the L was called, was a noisy, festive place. During the summer, kids often played street hockey there. The windows facing the playground had bars over them, and the nuns didn't seem to mind as long as the noise didn't exceed expected levels; the Good Sisters of the Order of Saint Joseph did not allow boom boxes.

Magdalene entered the schoolyard from the northern side (not across the grass; no need to disturb the penguins) and slowed her pace as she turned left at the southern end of the convent. There were a group of kids gathered on the pavement near the opening of the Corridor. They were up to no good, Magdalene was sure. The nuns didn't allow kids to just hang out during the summer months— maybe they were the first wave of summer school students on recess, taking a break between periods. Magdalene hoped they hadn't seen her. She had just about reached the wheelchair ramp that led to the side doors of the school (Magdalene didn't want to approach Sister Mary Joseph's office head-on), when the flowers caught her eye peripherally: there seemed to be an explosion of flowers, all sizes and colors, along the convent wall.

Magdalene heard a squeal of laughter, then an admonishment from an open school window, and then Michael was there (*here*), teasing her as she walked in line to her first grade classroom, winking as he passed her in the hall. But the embarrassment of her brother calling out to her had morphed into pride over time, hadn't it? When

Michael became Assumption's starting quarterback, Magdalene tried to ignore those who said he had made the varsity first string because their father was the coach. Tiddy had told her the brunt of the muttering came from parents—Faith Board members in particular. Very few kids said anything to Magdalene's face, and the ones that did never went out for a sport anyway. Michael's teammates knew his sense of the game was innate, and they wrote off any nepotism to coincidence. (*Criminy*—if her final exams focused solely on vocabulary, she'd have them sewn up!) He had been chosen simply because he was the best boy for the position. Michael had a little strut in his walk, especially after a win (and even after his sprained ankle). Magdalene had begun to call out to *him* in the halls, and the grin he'd flash before ducking into a classroom never failed to set her chest on fire.

But even then the story of Sister Mary Magdalene de Rosa extinguishing herself in the flames to make a bridge for the children wouldn't leave her mind. Magdalene was already obsessed with the story by the second grade; the tale, like the one of Lou's Head a few years later, made the rounds (embellished, of course) long before the nuns co-opted its lesson of unselfish Christian bravery. Partially to allay her fears (but mostly because it was a good dare), Michael had helped her sneak into the old school building. It was rarely used for classes and served more as an adjunct auditorium, albeit one without a stage. Aunt Tiddy said that various self-help groups met there on a weekly basis: alcoholics, smokers, cancer victims, the abused. Magdalene imagined the abused gathering in the gloom of the old school building, plotting their revenge like an angry mob in a monster movie, exiting into the cool air of Mondauk, eager to act on their emotions—whereas the cancer victims hobbled out, leaning on each other, perhaps looking up at the spires of the church, silently cursing God for their crumbling bodies and bald heads. (She couldn't imagine the substance abusers at all; she could only picture her father.) And there, among the ghosts of the dying and the walking wounded, she and Michael had run the halls in their socks, skidding down the dusty hallways, looking for evidence of the long ago fire— Frank and Joe Hardy—and when they found none, Michael declared Sister Mary Magdalene's immolation a myth, a legend, like Lord's Finger or those astronomical gods his sister so admired. But Magdalene couldn't stop the tears that raced to meet the snot painting her chin: if Sister Mary Magdalene *had* died here, there wasn't a plaque or a marker—the little one in the new school building didn't count, and, besides, it was curiously absent of any information about cause of death. (Michael had said this was a clue.) There had been nothing, and now even the knowledge, gained a week ago from the frothing Sister Rita, specifically that the fire had taken place in the newer of the two buildings, did not begin to alleviate the fears that the real Sister Mary Magdalene had been forgotten, that she had become an old wives' tale—an old nuns' tale—her sacrifice now simply a warning, a scary story told to keep students in line.

Magdalene cleared Michael from her head. (*As if!*) She abandoned the wheelchair ramp and walked towards the convent. Normally she'd be able to see the wads of gum stretched along the cement lines of the gray stones or the black streaks left by street hockey pucks, but now leaning against the convent wall were large white poster boards festooned with pictures and scribbling alongside various pieces of cardboard of every imaginable size from a variety of sources (delivery boxes, beer cases, cereal boxes). And in front of all this cardboard: flowers—loose, wrapped in professional florist cellophane, bunches of dandelions stuck in Styrofoam cups, the cups covered in magic marker graffiti.

One word, one picture dominated the display, its accompanying image repeated on each board, on the back of each cereal box, until the word became a name and the picture a photograph.

Henry, Henry, Henry.

As Magdalene neared the wall, the photograph came into focus. She assumed the towheaded boy with the big head in the picture was the boy whose name was plastered on every available writing surface. His missing two front teeth did nothing to dampen his grin. Perhaps the sweater he wore over his dress shirt made him feel sharp; maybe the photographer had made him laugh. Either way, Henry had been happy when this photograph was taken; he had been in a good mood.

Magdalene blinked. He looked familiar. Had she seen him in the halls? Had Henry ever unleashed his toothless smile in her direction? Older kids were often called to accompany younger students—first graders, second graders, third graders even—to and from the principal's office or the nurse's. During the last school year, she'd rarely been asked to walk anyone. She supposed the nuns were afraid she would kill herself in the hallways on the way back, but prior to her first stab at suicide, Magdalene had looked forward to "walking safety," as it was called. Had she walked Henry at some point? Some of the little ones were chatty, others were strangely silent. Magdalene guessed Henry to be the former type. Even the sweep of his hair across his forehead seemed casual, carefree. And if kids were like puppies, then Henry was going to be an Einstein—his head was that big!

There was another photograph: Henry Richard Cabot—his full name was on quite a number of newspaper clippings glued to the poster boards—wrestling with a chocolate Labrador on his front lawn. The Lab's mouth was open wide, like he was smiling, and Magdalene's stomach felt like it had been kicked. She stumbled, and one of the kids lounging near the opening of the Corridor laughed and said something to his pals; Magdalene knew it was directed at her. One of them threw a pebble.

The poster board in the center of the display was covered in handwritten notes surrounding the largest of Henry's school photographs.

May God open His arms to you, Henry.

We love you Henry and will miss you forever.

God bless you, Henry.

I miss you Henry (written in a child's scrawl).

Rest in peace, Henry.

Whoever did this should burn in HELL.

(This was written in ballpoint pen—everything else was done with magic markers—and had been scribbled out, then colored over, but was still visible beneath the scratches and grooves.)

Rest in peace?

Another pebble—no, it was a balled-up hamburger wrapper—landed at her feet. Someone said her name and someone else said, "Shush!"

She found an article taped to a piece of cardboard. The newsprint was smeared, but Magdalene knew it was from the *Common*—and not from the obituary section, although it wouldn't have been out of place there. A french fry hit her shoes and bounced into a bunch of daises.

COUNTY SEAT—On the last day of the school year, Henry Richard Cabot, 8, of Mondauk Proper, was shot and killed by classmate Joseph Bochdan in their Assumption of Our Lady Elementary School second grade classroom. Students say that Bochdan pulled the gun out of his book bag during an indoor recess, and the gun went off while showing it to Cabot and other friends. Reports put the teacher, Sister Agnes Ynez, in the classroom at the time, but Chief of

Police Cutter Hagen refused to elaborate. Cabot and Bochdan were said to be best friends, and classmates say the two were not involved in an argument prior to the incident. Bochdan attended Assumption despite being Orthodox Catholic. Authorities say recent tensions between the Roman Catholic community and other denominations were not a factor in the shooting.

Magdalene felt the blood on her knees before she felt the pain of falling to them. Her head rested on a bent piece of white cardboard, and her eyes opened to little slits. She could just make out the words written near the fold:

Sometimes you can love too much.

Magdalene opened her eyes all the way—the words had no reference to anything else scribbled on any of the poster boards and cardboard scraps. Had the Bochdan boy loved Henry Cabot so much he had to *kill* him? Had he been trying to impress his friend? Boys could be so macho. Or had he been defending Henry and shot him by accident—Lord knows even the second grade had its share of bullies—and then there were the *professional* bullies like Stevie Rich and John-John Hagarty to consider.

"It's Magdalene the prostitute," said a voice to her left, and a french fry hit her head.

"Gonna to try to raise him from the dead?" a second voice asked.

The first voice laughed and said, "The resurrection girl."

That was it, Magdalene decided: the Bochdan boy had brought the gun to defend his friend from the bullies and the jerks like the summer school boys hurling the fries. Joseph Bochdan had been afraid enough for Henry Richard Cabot's safety to steal a gun. But something had gone wrong. In Magdalene's experience, something *always* went wrong.

Magdalene lifted her head and faced Henry Richard Cabot. Her eyes caressed the place where his two front teeth should have been. She gently patted down his cowlick with a couple of wet fingers. She tickled his laugh lines with a knock-knock joke and a limerick. Henry, despite all his apparent charm, Magdalene thought, had been in need of rescuing, and his best friend had tried to scare away what he'd believed would chase the boys for the rest of their lives if they didn't make a stand. The Bochdan boy had saved Henry, maybe by accident, maybe in the only possible way. Good people, kids who knew the best jokes, the coolest tricks, friends who would give you the last lick of their ice cream cone or do your homework for you if you were sick, they always left first, they were always among the missing as you climbed the grades; the bullies, Magdalene knew, never left.

Magdalene bent her head. The taunting behind her faded behind the squeal of a second grader, a gunshot, a distant door slamming, the sound of Henry's body falling to the ground. And somewhere—she wasn't sure where—the Puddle?—Michael was falling too, and he would keep falling, trapped in her brain, over and over like a repeating formula, and when she tried to pray aloud for the souls of Henry Richard Cabot and Joseph Bochdan, the only word she could say, amid a fresh rain of french fries, was: Michael.

Michael. Michael. Michael. Michael. Michael. Michael. Michael.

Magdalene continued to pray long after the boys had dumped the rest of the french fries into her hair and stuck ice from their sodas down the back of her shirt, well after they'd backed away in whispers from the girl who prayed out loud for the dead with the name of the missing.

A Lab's Ears Are Made of *SILK*
by
Magdalene Harper Barrows

Episode I

What Happened

Finn's mother was a Goner.

Finn wasn't sure how he knew his mother was a Goner, but he was sure of this much: she was gone. He remembered climbing on top of her and how warm she was and how he had to wrestle his brothers and sisters for some of her milk. They lived on a farm, or at least Finn thought it was a farm: lots of straw, lots of puppies. What Finn remembered best was sleeping against his mother's belly and how it went up and down, up and down as she slept too and how safe sleeping against her belly made him feel.

Then she was gone.

Or, rather, he was.

Finn didn't remember much about his First House, where he'd lived after being taken from the farm and from his mother, but sometimes little glimpses came to him and he'd become confused. Why would he have had a First House? Why wasn't he there now? Had he done something wrong? Had he been a Bad Dog?

Whenever Finn got confused, he would go and find the Boy. If the Boy was too busy for him, Finn would lie down as close as he could to the Boy, close enough to smell his feet. And then Finn's Little White Tie would slow down, and his eyes would grow heavy, and he'd fall into his ninth nap of the day.

And what did Finn look like?

Finn was black like a raven's wing except for a little white spot at the top center of his barrel chest—Little White Tie!—that marked where his heart was. In fact, Finn thought Little White Tie *was* his heart (at least that's what the Boy had told him many, many times), and most days, Little White Tie pounded out a jubilant beat, but Finn knew the rhythm wasn't always thus, and he was afraid of the beats that had come before.

But life with the Big Uns helped muffle any ominous tempos. The Boy loved to tickle Finn's Little White Tie, and Finn loved to be tickled; it was one of his favorite spots—there and right above his tail where Finn couldn't reach. The Boy would rub his knuckles on Finn's tailbone—and *oooh, doggie,* did that feel good! The Big Uns were always saying Finn had a good heart and that he wore his heart on his sleeve. Finn didn't know if the sleeve part was true (Little White Tie was on his chest, after all), but when the Boy was away at a Sleepover, it was Little White Tie that ached like a flower someone had trod upon. If nothing else, Finn was glad his heart was marked by Little White Tie, so that he could never forget he had one—a heart that is. It seemed like such an easy thing to forget. Though, to be honest, he wasn't sure what a heart was of what its purpose was, but it seemed pretty important.

The Boy and the Big Uns called him Finn, but he didn't know if that was his *real* name. Sometimes they called him Huckleberry, which was a mouthful, but he didn't know if Huckleberry was his real name either. The Boy said Finn was named after a Literary Lion, and though Finn did nothing to disavow the Boy of this noble notion, Finn was certain he was a Labrador retriever.

In the First House, he thought he had a different name, but he couldn't remember what it was. The First House was a house of Yellers. He sort of remembered hearing some names that didn't sound so nice shouted to him from the other side of closed doors. But these thoughts and shouts made his thick body tremble, and whenever they came, Finn would seek out the Boy.

In the end, he was Finn and that was good enough for him. Old Finn, they called him once in a while, although he didn't feel old. Forty-two in dog years, they said, but Finn wasn't very good at math, and that embarrassed him, so he would just wag his tail and accept the Big Uns' ear tickles and belly rubs.

But just lately, Finn had noticed a few changes in himself. He slept more, for one. Finn enjoyed sleeping. He liked dreaming too— just not of squirrels. See, Finn loved to chase squirrels when he was awake. But a squirrel had doubled back on him once, and Finn ran away, his tail tickling his undersides. Imagine! A squirrel chasing a black Labrador retriever! Finn had nightmares of squirrels—and of that squirrel in particular—but mostly he dreamed of the Boy and of cookies. Finn loved cookies; he was a cookie connoisseur. Sleeping more meant more dreams about cookies!

Sleeping more wasn't the only change he'd noticed. Finn found his legs slower, his joints achy, and his vision wonky. These were most noticeable when he and the Boy played basketball. The orange and blue striped basketball (it wasn't regulation size) had come with Finn to the Second House—the Big Uns' house. Finn could just about hold the ball between his jaws. During a game, it would eventually it would become covered in drool, and Finn would have trouble picking it up. Then the Boy would rub his ears and feed him a cookie, and Finn would fall asleep with his big head in the Boy's lap. If this was getting older, Finn thought, it wasn't so bad.

Basketball was Finn's favorite extracurricular activity. The game was not without its issues however. He couldn't dribble because dogs can't dribble. Finn couldn't pass either, but not because black Labrador retrievers don't like to share—black Labs are a friendly sort, by and large—but simply because he was a dog. The lack of an opposable thumb was at the center of many of his sports-related issues, but Finn worried not a lick about them. If the Boy or one of the Big Uns threw the ball, Finn would retrieve it. Almost any ball would do, but the little basketball—well, that required a *unique* skill. See, it's rare that black Labrador retrievers (or any dogs, to be up front about it) are involved in basketball. Finn was unaware of this distinction (among others) that separated him from his breed (and other dogs); Finn just loved the basketball. He thought of it as an extension of himself—literally—just orange and blue and round rather than fuzzy and black and round.

Every night, Finn followed the Boy up to his room and watched the Big Uns tuck the Boy in and read him stories from the Blue Books. Sometimes they'd clasp their hands together and stare at the ceiling. Finn stayed very quiet during these times, but as soon as the Big Uns left, Finn clambered into the Boy's bed and licked the Boy's face once or twice before snuggling up next to him. The Boy was warm when Finn was cold. He let Finn sleep on top of the cool sheets when Finn was hot.

And every single night—except those terrible, terrible times when the Boy went to Sleepovers and Finn had to stay in the Boy's room by himself (it was so scary those nights, that Finn would sneak down the hall to see if the Big Uns would let him in their bed, but even if

Finn managed to climb in, one of the Big Uns would eventually ask him to leave)—every single night, the Boy brought his soft Boy hands to Finn's noggin and slowly run his fingers down Finn's very soft ear flaps. And every night the Boy would whisper the same words into Finn's ears.

"A Lab's ears are made of silk."

Finn took this to be a Truth, up there with "Basketball is Fun" or "Cookies are Good Eating."

"A Lab's ears are made of silk," the Boy whispered.

Finn didn't know what silk was exactly, but it sure sounded like something special.

Silk.

Actually, Finn imagined the word in capital letters: *SILK.*

SILK was precious.

SILK was important.

SILK was a necessity.

Finn didn't actually think of those big words—precious, important, necessity—as much as he felt them inside his big barrel chest, and the words would fill him up, and he would sleep the best sleep there was, and Finn would dream of the Boy.

He was just an average Boy: dirty-blonde hair, little round face, a laugh like a belly full of cookies. The Boy liked to laugh. Finn believed the Boy liked throwing the little basketball more than Finn liked retrieving it! The Boy sang into his hairbrush (and Finn's tail) and splashed Finn from the bathtub and stared really, really hard at books Finn couldn't read. Once in a while, the Boy would read to him, and although Finn didn't understand most of it, he liked to hear the Boy master the big words and swagger his way through the little ones. Finn would lie next to the Boy, and when the story was finished, the Boy would remind Finn that his ears were made of *SILK.* It was a struggle, but Finn tried to stay awake until the Boy was asleep. Finn considered it part of his job, and he was happy to do it.

Now the Boy wasn't much of a Boy anymore though, if you know what I mean. He had grown into someone you would like too—like someone you will grow into. Finn was beyond fond of the Boy—Finn loved him so much that the days when the Boy came home later than usual (or when he went to the dreaded Sleepovers), Finn's chest hurt so bad he thought it would burst and all the cookies he had ever eaten would be revealed to all the Wold.

As for the Big Uns: they were nice people too. Mommy Big Un

was pretty and always smelled like you'd think a tickle would smell like. She didn't pet Finn very often, but she always made sure Finn had his cereal and his water, and she took the Boy to buy Finn a new toy now and again. Sure, she'd yell at Finn to stop chasing Alley Cat whenever Alley Cat crept into the backyard, but Finn got the idea that Mommy Big Un didn't really like cats all that much, and that all the yelling was to scare Alley Cat, who'd jump to the top of the fence and preen and pout well out of Finn's reach. Daddy Big Un liked to roughhouse with Finn. Finn would growl and howl and bounce and pounce until Daddy Big Un rubbed Finn's belly and, in a gulping breath (his chest going up and down), declare the game over and Finn the winner. Finn liked the Big Uns: Mommy Big Un looked after Finn (and the Boy), and Daddy Big Un kept Finn occupied when the Boy wasn't home. But Finn loved the Boy most of all. He loved the Boy more than basketball, more than cookies, more than anything in the whole wide Wold.

"A Lab's ears are made of *SILK*," the Boy said every night before falling asleep (unless the Boy was stuck in a Sleepover), and then one dark, dark night: the Boy didn't say it.

Finn paced the floor. He sniffed the Boy's socks for signs of sickness. He climbed on the bed and sat next to the Boy. The Boy didn't look sick. Sure, he looked older—the Boy smelled more and more like Daddy Big Un every day, but that wasn't a bad thing. Something *had* to be wrong though. Finn chewed on his fur and nibbled on the ear of a stuffed animal. He wandered downstairs to the family room and stared at the fish aquarium and the cage with the guinea pig. He poked his nose into the turtle's tank. Back upstairs, Finn pushed open the door at the end of the hall with his nose and stared at the Big Uns, but Daddy Big Un was snoring so loudly (he sounded like he had swallowed a cow!) that Mommy Big Un was clinging to the edge of the bed. Her mouth was open, and drool dripped to a puddle on the floor. The Big Uns wouldn't be able to help him.

Finn crawled to go back to the Boy's room, but he couldn't make himself climb next to the Boy. Finn curled into a ball on the floor at the foot of the bed instead. When he woke the next morning, the night's unpleasantness dissipated instantly like the nightmares he had sometimes about Alley Cat chasing *him* like the dream-squirrel had. It wasn't until after the Boy had left for school that Finn remembered what had happened—and only because something else occurred: the

Boy left without saying goodbye to Finn. The Boy *always* rubbed Finn's noggin before he left for school. "For luck," the Boy used to say, but he hadn't said that in quite some time. (It took Finn a while to get used to the phrase's absence, until Finn just started saying it to himself whenever the Boy rubbed his noggin.) Finn stationed himself near the door in case the Boy remembered that he had forgotten. He had been sitting there for a good long time when Mommy Big Un came swooping by, heading up the stairs.

"He's gone already, Finn," Mommy Big Un said. "I have to vacuum, so skedaddle."

Finn bunkered beneath the kitchen table where he nibbled on a few stray Cheerios, trying to ignore Vacuum's noise. The only sound uglier than Vacuum's sucking *whoosh* was Alley Cat's singing. And if there was a sound uglier than Alley Cat's singing, Finn hoped he'd never hear it.

Finn lay low most of the day. Minutes were hours. At the appropriate time, Finn positioned himself by the front door (Finn couldn't really tell time as much as *feel* it), and Mommy Big Un chattered at him in words he didn't completely understand other than this: the Boy wasn't coming home directly from school.

Now Finn went through something like this at the end of every summer. He knew it was coming—the end of summer—just like you know school starts again on Monday, and thoughts of Monday drape a cloak over almost all of Sunday. It was like that. Every fall, Finn had to get used to a new routine and a day without the Boy running around in wet shorts and bare feet. This wasn't like fall though. This was different. During the school year, the Boy always came right home after school. Finn's brain couldn't stop thinking of all the horrible things that could have befallen the Boy. Cars were fun to ride in, but they sometimes squished creatures just because they could; cars weren't completely domesticated. Maybe the Boy had been hunted down by a car. One time, last summer, some kids from around the corner chased the Boy and tripped him and the Boy fell on his face and cried and the tears made designs in the dirt that had caked on his face. Finn made sure to snuggle up extra close that night. "Bullies," Mommy Big Un had said. Maybe the Bullies had trapped the Boy and were making him kiss the dirt *this very second!*

Finn didn't nap at all the rest of the afternoon. Every time he drifted off—about every fifteen minutes or so—he was jolted awake by images of the Boy in some sort of danger. Finn couldn't eat; he didn't want to pee. Mommy Big Un let him into the yard, and Finn stayed near the door, listening for the return of the Boy. When Alley Cat jumped on the top of the fence and sang in his trembling soprano, Finn covered his ears with his paws.

"Are you dying, Dog?" Alley Cat asked from a safe distance atop the wooden fence. Alley Cat looked like most of the other cats in the Wold to Finn: a fuzzy porridge mixture of gray and black and silver with jewels for eyes and switchblades for toes—except Alley Cat, although full grown, was only half the size of every other cat Finn had ever seen.

"What's 'dying'?" Finn asked back, his head flat on the patio pavement.

"Buying the farm. Biting the dust. Pushing up daisies."

Finn didn't like the sound of these choices—especially the one about the farm. Finn thought that one was especially cruel-sounding.

"Are you sick then, Dog?" Alley Cat asked.

"I don't think so," Finn replied, flicking his tongue to his nose.

"Depressed?"

Finn shook his head and sighed.

"Debilitated?"

Finn shrugged as best as a dog could shrug.

"Destroyed?"

Finn was getting annoyed, but not so much at Alley Cat—Alley Cat was *supposed* to be annoying. Finn was annoyed with himself. He had to have done something wrong to make the Boy stay away so long, to make the Boy forget about Finn's *SILK* and neglect Finn's noggin.

"Defeated," Alley Cat said as he sauntered away. "Disgusting."

And disgusting, Finn thought, just about summed up how he felt. In truth, all of Alley Cat's D words seemed to describe perfectly the hollowed-out sensation filling Finn's barrel chest. When Daddy Big Un came home—Finn knew it was Daddy Big Un because the Boy didn't drive a car—the Big Uns sat down at the table and ate together—no Boy! No one sneaked a piece of bread or a slice of apple under the table for Finn. No one rubbed his back with their toes.

When the Boy (finally) arrived home, Finn forgot all of his despair—there's a D word Alley Cat had left out!—and leapt on him, smacking him with his wagging tail, licking his hands and his face when the Boy leaned down to untie his shoelaces.

"Hey Finn," the Boy said before heading upstairs.

Finn bounded after him.

The Boy walked into his room—and closed the door.

Finn was devastated. Finn was demolished. Finn was dismissed.

Later, when Mommy Big Un yelled up the stairs that "the phone's for you—it's a *girrrrrlllll*," the Boy opened the door, stepped over Finn, and stood in the Big Uns' room talking into the receiver.

"...he was *so* mean...I know!...can't read all those chapters in one week..."

Finn crept into the Boy's room and sniffed the blankets on the bed. Nope—Finn hadn't peed there by accident. He poked his head under the Boy's desk—the Boy must have been sitting there because books were open and the seat of his chair smelled warm—no, no pee or poop there either. Not that Finn really thought he'd peed or pooped in the Boy's room. Finn never had any accidents. But he had to have done *something*.

"...right...and then the pop quiz on top of that..."

Maybe if Finn brought the Boy his shoes. For some reason, Daddy Big Un had once spent an entire day trying to get Finn to bring him a pair of slippers. Finn fetched them all day long and everyone seemed pretty happy. They gave Finn lots of cookies, but no one ever asked him to fetch the slippers again. Finn thought maybe he was supposed to fetch them on his own, but soon the whole slipper incident was a just a little memory in his big noggin.

Maybe that was it! Maybe the Boy wanted Finn to get his shoes!

"...sure, that would be cool...I'll ask my mom..."

Finn snatched the Boy's shoes—the ones the Boy wore to school—and stood in the hallway. He wanted to peek in the Big Uns' room, but in the end, Finn decided that surprise was best. The Boy would be so happy!

"...yeah, no, well, I like you too..."

Of course, what happened next would haunt Finn for a long, long time. You know the cliché: the straw that broke the camel's back? Well, Finn had never seen a camel was or a cliché was completely foreign, but deep beneath his black fur, inside Little White Tie, camels were breaking down into tiny little pieces, and as Finn well knew from listening to the Boy read aloud, all the king's horses and all the king's men could never put the broken camel together again. Or something like that.

The Boy hung up the phone, and Finn noticed that the Boy's face was pink, and Finn could smell that the Boy was sweaty—not sweaty like he'd been running around the backyard playing basketball with Finn; this was a different kind of sweaty. It wasn't a sick sweaty either. The Boy was smiling. And Finn thought the smiles were for him. He let the shoes drop from his mouth, wagged his tail like he was trying to sweep the floor, and waited for the Boy to notice.

And, *woo wee!*, did the Boy notice. At first Finn couldn't figure out why the Boy's face went from sweaty pink to angry red. Finn had seen the Big Uns paint their faces this color often, but not the Boy, not often anyway, and *never* directed at Finn.

"BAD DOG!" the Boy yelled.

Debased.

Degenerate.

Dead weight.

Finn looked down. Where there had been shoes, there were only two piles of crunchy black leather. Finn flicked his tongue around his mouth and spit out another little piece.

D words crowded inside his slowly diminishing chest.

The Boy yelled again.

Mommy Big Un yelled more.

Daddy Big Un didn't yell, but he ignored Finn, and Finn crept behind the sofa and stayed there until after lights-out, licking his paws, crying softly to himself.

Disgusted.

The next day, Finn was determined to be on his best behavior. Daddy Big Un stepped over Finn with a barely a grunt, but that was nothing unusual for morning time. Mommy Big Un let Finn out for his morning pee, then gave him a cookie when he came in. All normal. Finn didn't want the cookie—he didn't feel he deserved a cookie. But he ate it anyway. It had been a long night behind the sofa.

Finn didn't quite remember what he'd done to feel so bad—it is the peculiar curse of dogs: to be unable to let go of the emotion, but to not always recall *exactly* how they got that way. One thing was for sure: when the Boy came down for breakfast, Finn would be ready for him.

It took Finn a minute or two to rustle up his basketball. He found it behind Daddy Big Un's chair, and a spider had started spinning a web from the surface of the ball to the back of the chair. Just pushing at the basketball with his nose—which was running, by the way; running like it was in a hurry but had no place to go—made

Finn's Little White Tie heavy and sad. When the tiny web stretched and snapped and broke apart, Finn thought he understood what the spider might feel when he returned home and found it gone.

Finn set himself up at the bottom of the stairs, sat straight up so the Boy would see Little White Tie, and held the basketball between his big jaws. There was little time to reflect on pettings past, but if ever a dog needed...

The Boy came down the stairs—and walked *around* Finn.

This wasn't good. No noggin rubs. No, "Morning, Finn!" Finn ran after the Boy and dropped the basketball at his moving feet.

"Not now, Finn," the Boy said, kicking the basketball into the living room.

Ahh! Here we go! Finn tore after the basketball. The Boy would be so happy to see how fast Finn retrieved the ball!

But when he returned, the Boy was already sitting in the kitchen with the Big Uns, concentrating on a bowl of crunchies. Finn sat in the kitchen doorway, tail wagging, drool gathering around the ball.

Nothing.

Finn dropped the ball and pushed it towards the Boy with his black nose.

Absolutely nothing.

Finally, in a move that Finn would later severely chastise himself for, Finn opened up his huge, huge mouth and let it all out: the frustration and the sadness and the confusion and the D words, but most of all: the love—Finn's crushing love for the Boy.

WOOF!

WOOF!

WOOF!

WOOF!

WOOF!

WOOF!

WOOF!

And the Boy was woofing back! Little White Tie leapt like a cold frog on a hot stone.

"Out, Finn! Now! Get out!"

Get out?

"That was a fifty dollar pair of shoes," said Mommy Big Un.

And then Finn remembered what he had done.

That night, the Boy was late coming home again, but the Big Uns didn't seem worried. Finn did all the worrying, thank you. Finn paced and cried a little (to himself) and gnawed his way through a bone that should have lasted him a month. When the Boy finally walked through the door, Mommy Big Un was already in bed reading a book. (Finn had checked on her several times to make sure she hadn't sneaked out to pick up the Boy.) Daddy Big Un, who'd been lounging downstairs in his pajamas, patted the Boy on the back and told him to get some rest.

Finn followed the Boy upstairs and lay outside the bathroom peeking. The Boy was staring at himself in the mirror. The Boy ran a finger over his upper lip and then pursed both lips—that's when Finn noticed the Boy's lips were redder than usual. The Boy kissed the mirror. Finn buried his noggin in his paws.

When he lifted his noggin again, the bathroom light was out and the Boy's bedroom door was closed.

No bedtime stories.

No sharing a pillow with Finn.

No reminders about Finn's *SILK* ears.

Finn crept back behind the sofa.

When the next day was a repeat of the day before, Finn knew it was time to go. Although he didn't recall much about his First House, home of the Yellers, Finn knew at least that there had *been* a First House. So there could be a Third House somewhere.

How could this have happened if my ears are made of SILK, Finn wanted to know. How?

Finn thought he would die, just buy the farm, packing his things—especially when he realized he didn't have many *things*. The food and water bowls were his, of course, but they proved too wieldy to bring along. There were his stuffed animals too. Finn loved his stuffed animals. He used to pretend *he* was the Boy and that the monkey or the frog or the elephant or the panda was him! Finn knew he'd miss those games and miss his guys, monkey and frog and elephant and panda, but in the end, the orange and blue striped basketball was the only thing Finn took with him.

How come no one remembers that my ears are made of SILK?

Finn walked around the house one last time, avoiding any reflections. He didn't want to know what Devastation looked like. It was bad enough to feel it. It was bad enough that D words were inside of him, settling in, getting comfortable, muffling Little White Tie.

What if the Boy had lied?

What if my ears aren't *made of* SILK *after all?*

Finn took one look behind him and scooped the ball up.

He'd find out. He'd seek out the wise and the learned. If his ears were truly made of *SILK*, Finn thought, then he would be worth more than a fifty dollar pair of shoes. And if that was true, then maybe he could sell his ears and buy the Boy new shoes and once again be allowed to fall asleep next to the Boy, counting all of the Boy's heartbeats, waking each morning with his noggin buried beneath the Boy's blankets.

And if my ears aren't *made of* SILK?

He had to find the answer.

Finn shuddered and took the first of many steps into the outside Wold.

Chapter Four

The Baby-sitter

Aunt Tiddy believed the world was a scarier place now than it had been when she was a child.

"It's worse," Tiddy said, as she stood over the stove, shaking her head. "Nobody thought to rape and pillage the way these kids do now."

"Rape and pillage?" Magdalene asked.

She'd run home and was a little breathless. Tiddy had looked at Magdalene's hair, still damp from the bullies' attack, and had handed her a towel.

"When I was growing up—well!—you just didn't hear all this nonsense about terrorists or WMD or kidney burglars or—"

"Kidney burglars?" Magdalene asked.

"It was a different time. People aren't *together* now. Back then, yes, yes, the blacks weren't *really* free, and neither were a whole bunch of other people, but they started banding together, working together: blacks, Italians, even the Irish, if they could pry themselves from the tap room."

Aunt Tiddy shook her head again. Magdalene watched a bobby pin escape and land an inch shy of Raven's nose. Raven sniffed at it, seemed to judge it inedible, and went back to sleep. Magdalene thought Raven was lucky. She'd give anything to sleep.

"Today, no one's together! No one! Sure, after 9/11 or Columbine or the Space Shuttle blowing up, everyone flew their little flags and hugged and made speeches at the dinner table. That feeling, Magdalene? That feeling lasts less and less each time something bad happens. The terrorists? *They're* together! Not us. Not for long. Just little pieces."

"I'm going upstairs," Magdalene said.

Her father came home from work early and ate and showered while Magdalene worked on her book. When she heard the bathroom door open, she tiptoed down the hall and perched on the closed toilet lid; it was the only to place to get him alone for a few minutes. She watched him comb his hair. She studied the way he ducked so he could see his reflection in the clear patches of the foggy bathroom mirror. Downstairs, Tiddy banged away in the kitchen, cleaning up after her father and preparing Magdalene's dinner.

"Did you pick Michael to be quarterback?"

Her father stopped fussing with his hair and stared at the mirror.

"Why do you ask?"

"Just curious. Was he as good as they say?"

"As who says?" her father asked. He resumed fixing his hair.

"I don't know."

"You watched him play, Maddie. You rarely missed a game."

"People say, I guess."

"People." Her father knelt down next to the toilet. "I bet people say a lot of things, Maddie, and sometimes they say things that aren't even remotely true just to hurt somebody else. They'll talk trash to get other people not to like somebody else too—like politicians do."

Magdalene stared over his head. Michael was too big, too cool to have ever been bullied like she'd been today. He was the quarterback—he called the shots: for Magdalene, and his friends as well. He was rarely bossy (with anyone other than her)—just sure of himself.

"I asked the assistant coaches to make the decision. I recused myself from making the final cut. I'm too close to some of the boys."

The bathroom air was thick with the scent of her father's aftershave. Magdalene wondered when her mother's smells had left the Barrows Bungalow. She wondered when Michael's smells would.

"Was he good?"

Her father rinsed his comb in the sink and parted his hair again. His voice was husky.

"The best, Maddie. He was the best quarterback I ever coached. If he hadn't been my son, I would have thought the same thing. And if he weren't already, I would have wanted him to be my son. That's how much I loved him, Maddie."

Her father left the bathroom, and Magdalene closed the door behind him; she had learned that closing the bathroom door was the only way to get true privacy. Her father (drunk or sober) never barged in when she was using the bathroom. He seemed embarrassed even handling her underwear if he did the wash. Not that he'd be rushing in to continue their conversation: tonight was the start of Summer Camp football at Lawndale Fields behind Assumption. Her father was the Master Coach, which meant he not only coached the high school kids looking to stay in shape during summer vacation, but also oversaw all the other coaches who ran teams ranging from second graders to eighth graders. (Sober, he coached the Assumption Knights to three championship trophies.)

The steam left over from her father's shower clouded the mirror again, and Magdalene wrote Henry Richard Cabot's name with her finger. She had checked today's *Mondauk Common*. There'd been no new information about the shooting—nothing exculpatory, to steal a word of her father's, or illuminating—just the facts, Jack. And the facts were a load of horse hockey, to steal another phrase, this time from Aunt Tiddy. There was more to the shooting than was apparent to the naked, untrained eye—that much was obvious to Magdalene. Random acts of violence were rarely *that* random—original sin and all that hoot and holler. And what about the note? *Sometimes you can love too much.* It was almost too bad she had to die soon—for here was a case for a writer *and* a sleuth. Magdalene erased Henry's name with her hand.

"She doesn't even have baby-sitting anymore," Aunt Tiddy had said the night before.

Now, what did that mean, Magdalene wondered. Her father hadn't broached the subject of baby-sitting Katie McAllister, and Magdalene had decided not to bring it up. Who knows where *that* conversation would lead?

After another reconnaissance mission on her way home from Assumption, Magdalene had come to the conclusion that Mr. McAllister was out of work or worked part-time. It certainly seemed to be an odd time of the day to be home. Mr. McAllister had come out of his house and tossed his still-smoking cigarette into the street; Magdalene stamped it out when he went back in and considered bagging it for evidence, but she hadn't brought any baggies and wasn't sure what she'd need the evidence for. (She did note the brand: Marlboro.) She knew Mr. McAllister wasn't allowed to drive for a specified period of time after the incident with O'Neill's News, and perhaps that had led to his current employment situation. Of course looking roguish and sinister, as Mr. McAllister certainly did with his sloped forehead, wary eyes and pockmarked nose, probably didn't help. (Aunt Tiddy had once called him a Bog Trotter; Magdalene had no idea what it meant; it sounded like something out of *The Hound of the Baskervilles*.)

Magdalene sat on the toilet for a few minutes more before she noticed Monien leaning just inside the door. *One two, buckle my shoe.*

She squeezed the panda's stomach—nothing, not a peep. The panda had no song left in it. *Three four, knock at the door.* Her heart hurt thinking of Raven sneaking in to drop the panda off while she'd been quizzing her father. *Five six, pick up sticks.* She couldn't leave Raven hanging. Everyone needed a voice. And Raven's sorrow surely seemed insurmountable to the Lab. Who would be the voice for Henry Richard Cabot and Joseph Bochdan if she was right about the bullies? Who would even think to look past the murky surface? *Seven eight, lay them straight.* The town had long ago stopped searching for Michael. Magdalene knew from her books that clues were best found in the first twenty-four hours, or soon after, while the trail was still warm. Magdalene stared in the mirror at the dark circles beneath her eyes. So that was it: continue to plan her suicide while solving the Cabot Case. Once Raven was gone, the game would be up; she would have to go through with it. It was for the best, really. The guilty had to pay. *Nine ten, a good fat hen.* Magdalene scooped Monien up and opened the bathroom door. *Eleven twelve, dig and delve.*

Raven was sitting in the hallway, his mouth open in his peculiar smile. With one paw on the monkey, he searched the air for a handshake with the other. Raven loved to shake hands. It was pretty much his only trick. Magdalene lowered herself to the floor and scratched Raven's chest, stroked his nose, whispered in his ear; his tail thumped against the hardwood floor. (Magdalene heard Tiddy downstairs: "Jesus Lord in a bucket!") Raven munched on the monkey, and a little *whoosh* of air escaped from Monkey's natty fur. Raven took a few more chomps then deposited the monkey in Magdalene's lap. Magdalene offered Raven the panda, but the dog nudged the monkey with his black nose.

"I think you broke him too, Raven. You broke Monkey."

(She could poison him.)

The dog wagged his tail and looked from the monkey to Magdalene's face and back to Monkey again. Tiddy started the vacuum in the living room.

"You loved him too much. You loved him too hard, Raven."

(It would have to be painless.)

The dog glanced at the panda and whined.

"I don't know what happened to Michael."

(She couldn't drown him or strangle him like John-John Hagarty supposedly did to stray cats.)

The vacuum cleaner stopped.

"Magdalene? Who are you talking to? Are you talking to that dog?"

That dog?

Raven moaned and licked the monkey.

"Get down here please, and help me move the sofa. Your father's left for camp, and that dog's hair is everywhere."

(Poison or something that would take him in his sleep.)

Magdalene stood up and left the panda where it was. Raven pushed the monkey into her leg.

(Just don't look into his eyes.)

"Not now, Raven. You heard. I have to help Tiddy."

(If she looked into his eyes, he'd know.)

Raven followed her down the stairs.

"There," Tiddy said, "take the other side. Good. Just move it out."

Raven leapt on the sofa.

"Goddamn it, dog."

(And she knew: if he knew, he'd let her.)

"Raven. Get down," Magdalene said. Raven didn't belong anywhere either.

The task done, the sofa back against the wall, Tiddy pulled a piece of paper from her apron, but Magdalene walked back upstairs. Tiddy could wait until tomorrow. Magdalene's head throbbed, and she went to bed early, plotting the murder of her dog.

+

"No one escapes Tiddy for long," Michael had said.

"Here's the plan for today," Tiddy said. "First, run down to Sol's and pick me up some flour. If Mrs. Bochdan didn't open...never you mind...just go—and buy skim milk too, for your father."

It was morning, and Magdalene watched Raven through the kitchen windows chasing squirrels in the backyard. Although she preferred jeans to shorts, it was going to be shorts weather today, and she had dressed accordingly.

Snap fizz whirr.

"Found my old instant camera! How 'bout that, girlie-girl!"

Tiddy slid a Polaroid photograph across the table. Magdalene barely recognized herself. The girl coming into focus looked like a silent movie star: dark circles around the eyes, theatrically pale skin.

"Girlie-girl," Magdalene said.

"I made a list. We're gonna clean out the basement, then after lunch—oh, I picked up some pears at the Farmer's Market—we'll go over to Morrone's and see if they have any nice fish. 'Course we'll pick up some pepperoni and cheese at Bard's. What do you say?"

Magdalene stared at the photograph: here was the face of a failed murderer; here was the face of one who'd blinked when her time had come. She pushed the Polaroid away.

"I have to take a test today, Aunt Tiddy."

Tiddy's forehead creased, and she glanced down her list.

"I thought your father said you were supposed to let Sister know when you were ready, that you didn't have to take…"

Here comes the counting: *five ten fifteen twenty twenty-five thirty thirty-five forty forty-five fifty…*

"He was wrong. I have to start now."

Magdalene was a terrible liar (but a terrific counter). A writer or a detective: both trafficked in lies; she wasn't sure she had what it took. Her mother had always known when Magdalene was fibbing; Magdalene always left out an important detail or forgot the point of the lie altogether. Of course, her mother had been the grand marshal of all liars and not particularly adept at it herself—although the lies were wondrous in their constructions and audacity. Her mother had only been good at one thing: whistling—and then only one song. The same song Monien the panda refused to sing.

Tiddy could easily investigate this lie, but now that it was out there, Magdalene decided to run with it.

"History."

Magdalene let Raven back into the house and smiled when he left muddy paw prints across the shiny kitchen linoleum.

"History? You have your History final today?"

"Yes," Magdalene said. She wished Tiddy would just let her go; Magdalene was bound to trip up sooner or later.

"And Religion," Magdalene added, wincing inwardly. She should have saved that for another day. She would be dead by the time Sister called the house to see why Magdalene hadn't stopped by to schedule the exams. Magdalene needed to use the tests sparingly.

"Okay, okay," Aunt Tiddy said, eyeing her grandniece over her glasses, "we'll go over to Spring House another day. Now don't forget you have to see Willa this afternoon. And pick up some flour at Sol's on your way home. Do you have an exam tomorrow?"

But Magdalene had already bounded out to the front porch. Raven, who'd fallen asleep on Monkey during the exchange, ran after her, pushing the screen door open with his big head. (Her father had broken the latch during his drinking days after he'd locked himself out.) Magdalene grabbed her sneakers from their space next to the milk box and plopped herself down on the stoop. Raven's head disappeared from the doorway, and the screen door slammed shut. Magdalene cringed; Tiddy hated slammed doors. Magdalene was halfway down the block, her left heel still not fully in her sneaker, when she heard the screen door squeak open again. If she stopped and acknowledged whatever Tiddy had to say, she would never have the chance to solve the mystery before she tried to die again. Glancing back, her feet still moving, Magdalene watched the screen door close (*one Mississippi two Mississippi three Mississippi four...*)—but no Tiddy. When she reached the corner, Magdalene dared a full look. Monien was perched on the top porch step.

+

Magdalene had begun writing her children's novella, *A Lab's Ears Are Made of* SILK, as a present for Raven (the dog's relationship with Monkey, her first gift to her him, had long since turned bellicose), but since he would be a somewhat unappreciative audience, she'd planned to give it to Katie McAllister. Suicide attempts had thus far scuttled planned completion and release dates, and Katie McAllister had since outgrown Dr. Seuss books. (Magdalene wasn't exactly sure how to write a book for children anyhow; she now thought of her effort as perhaps more of a young adult fable.) But no matter who the intended audience had been, Magdalene suspected she was writing for her father. When he became a fixture at McCullough's, she wrote it for a dead man, a father in absentia. Now the book would be an addendum to a suicide note, she supposed. At least her father would appreciate her vocabulary; Magdalene was right proud (as Tiddy would say) of her vocabulary.

Father Dave had once said in a homily that perhaps hundreds of thousands of people had the first chapter of a novel tucked in a drawer, but that the truly faithful were like those that pulled the chapter out and saw the tale to its end. Magdalene wanted to finish her novella before she died. She didn't want to be in the First Chapter Crowd. So what if it was a children's book? Before she had moved on to more advanced reading material (at an earlier age than most of her peers), her literary diet had consisted of Dr. Seuss and Encyclopedia Brown. The hero of Magdalene's book was a black Labrador retriever named Finn. Not a very original name, she knew, but ol' Huckleberry had been adopted too. Father Dave had also said that the best writers wrote what they knew, and Magdalene knew black Labrador retrievers—or at least one. She knew they smelled like slightly burnt popcorn. She knew their husky breath, the patter of their nails on hard surfaces, their rough and ready kisses. And she knew the most important thing of all: Magdalene knew that a Lab's ears were made of *SILK.*

Magdalene walked south, towards the little convenience store on the corner of Butler and Loretta Avenues. Tiddy's need for flour tugged at the back of Magdalene's mind for a second, but she remembered something else too; something Aunt Tiddy said had triggered it: Sol's was owned by a *Bochdan.* Two of them. A Mr. and a Mrs. Bochdan.

Little school shooter Joseph Bochdan's parents?

Flo's had been the store's original name, but when Flo retired to Florida, old Sol bought it (he already had a store in Rhawnhurst) and then died in it. He had a heart attack right behind the register, falling face-forward onto the little counter, spilling Bazooka Joes and packs of Topps baseball cards everywhere. The Bochdans had owned Sol's since Sol hit the counter; they had never changed the name of the store, or at least they hadn't changed the sign. Everyone still called it Sol's, from the kids buying Baby Ruths to the men covered in soot, trudging home to the Heights, who stopped to buy lottery tickets.

Tiddy, during one of her countless soliloquies, had given Magdalene another clue. Her aunt, who claimed no special affinity for the Roman Catholic Church but could not resist a swipe at *any* organized religion, had sniffed: "All the Eastern Europeans, the ones that don't bow to Mecca, go Orthodox."

"Something about the way the Ukies paint their eggs," Tiddy had added.

Magdalene knew, from the newspaper account of the shooting, that the Bochdans (at least *Joseph's* Bochdans) were Orthodox Catholic—and thus probably Ukrainian. In Mondauk County, church affiliation, if not actual faith, was often the demarcating line—even more than race. Magdalene rarely, if ever, heard a disparaging word said against black people; rather, they were scorned as "those

Baptists," a far worse designation in a fiercely (at least socially) Roman Catholic community. The closest Orthodox Catholic church, Immaculate Conception, was in Philadelphia. It made sense for the Bochdans to send Joseph to a local school with the closest approximation of their own faith—Assumption of Our Lady. Magdalene imagined the Faith Board having a tizzy, but not Father Dave—and he was the pastor. Religious intolerance, Father Dave had said, was the curse of Mondauk.

Religion in general, Magdalene's father had told her, had *always* been a problem in Mondauk County.

"Dr. Mattison was a Presbyterian," her father had said. "Most of his workforce was Irish Catholic. When Dr. Mattison began to lose his marbles and his asbestos empire tumbled, he left Lindenwold Estate to the Catholic Church. The Protestants never forgave him. There are eight churches in Mondauk Proper alone and one synagogue. They're all competing for the same souls and the same dollars. There are bound to be conflicts. When I was young, the best private school in the county was run by an offshoot Seventh-day Adventist group—one couple, actually. They believed the messiah would come from their congregation—from their classrooms. A school for geniuses, they called it: the Remnants School. They were constantly at odds with the community. It finally closed when one of its founders was discovered dead in the school. The papers said the body had been laid out on a dining room table for three days before being found. The Faith Board held a private party to celebrate its closure. You didn't know whether to laugh or cry or just hang your head in shame."

Magdalene considered researching Ukrainian Easter eggs in the library but remembered Mrs. Stanley's breath and thought better of it. How many times had Magdalene heard someone making a crack (she laughed to herself) hoping that Mr. or Mrs. Bochdan didn't plunge to their deaths on Sol's counter too and crush all those eggs—those exquisitely painted eggs? The eggs were kept on display year round, but Easter was especially festive: painted eggs were everywhere, coddled in tiny gold tripods—always out of reach—squeezed on every shelf and even inside the old cold cut display case (which housed boxes upon boxes of candy; Magdalene guessed the Bochdans didn't want to compete with Bard's, even though Bard's was in the next town). Magdalene hadn't put it together until now that the eggs were Ukrainian. The eggs had just been part of the background: something she expected and admired whenever she went in Sol's, never thinking about what they represented or who had painted them.

If Magdalene's hunch was correct, the owners of Sol's were *the* Bochdans, the parents of the boy who had killed his best friend, Henry Richard Cabot, possibly while defending Henry from the bullies. Magdalene wanted proof. She wanted to talk to Joseph Bochdan, but seeing how he was in protective custody, according to her father, she'd settle for his parents—or just Joseph's mother if the authorities hadn't located his father yet. If the bullies were at fault, then the real mystery of what had happened in the second grade Assumption classroom would be solved. She needed information—social behavior information—and she wanted to know how Joseph had gotten the gun. Not she expected anyone to spill the beans easily.

Despite how unusual the name Bochdan had struck Magdalene's ears, it had taken the length of her walk to realize that Dr. and Mrs. Fuller's maid was *also* a Bochdan. Maybe it was just the word *maid* that had thrown her off; who needed a maid in Mondauk Proper? Even the biggest houses weren't much more than double the size of the Barrows Bungalow. Magdalene wracked her brain to recall what the Fullers' maid looked like, but all she conjured was the image of a woman in a hairnet bent over an enormous porcelain bathtub, suffering in silence under Mrs. Fuller's shrill admonishments. (Magdalene swore Mrs. Fuller went to bed in a suit of armor; there could be no cuddling up to Mrs. Bernadette Fuller for warmth; one had to only look at Christina's desperate dalliances with the boys of Assumption—and Paradise Lakes most likely, if Magdalene believed some of the snipe talk in the hallways—to see the effectiveness of Mrs. Fuller's ramparts.) Perhaps Sol's wasn't as lucrative as the Bochdans had hoped; maybe Mrs. Bochdan didn't like being home with Mr. Bochdan—Magdalene's father had made him out to be a scoundrel. Or it could also be as simple as this: Mrs. Bochdan wanted more for her son than was available selling quarts of milk and scratch-off lottery tickets.

Sol's was a small white stucco corner building, with a little backyard visible from Loretta Avenue. Stubby towers of milk crates were stacked against the low fence, but otherwise the yard was empty. Magdalene sat on the brick wall across Loretta from Sol's. She was casing the joint, she thought; she was on surveillance detail. But neither Bochdan so much as stuck a toe out of the door.

Magdalene decided extreme situations called for extreme measures—she had heard that somewhere, anyway—and strode across the road into Sol's. She would just sniff around until they asked her if she needed help, and then—*whamo!*—let the interrogations begin. There was only one customer in the store, thank heavens—an old man with slicked-back hair murmuring to himself. The woman behind the counter was bigger than Magdalene had remembered—not big as in heavy, but tall. She looked as if she could carry all the milk crates in from the milk truck by herself. The woman kept her shoulders unnaturally hunched and avoided eye contact. Magdalene still couldn't place her as the Fullers' maid, but the hunch was familiar. Mrs. Bochdan's skin was slightly darker than Magdalene's. Were Ukrainian people darker, Magdalene wondered.

The floor space in Sol's was only a tiny bit bigger than Magdalene's bedroom; there wasn't much room to be surreptitious. Magdalene fingered a candy bar. Mrs. Bochdan handed the whispering old man his change. "Thank you, Mr. Quayle." (What kind of accent was that?) Then Magdalene was alone with Mrs. Bochdan. And there were the eggs! The woman produced a rag and gently lifted the exquisite eggs and their little gold stands, wiping the counter down. Magdalene wrapped her fist around the candy bar. Mrs. Bochdan never looked up. Magdalene stood on one foot and hopped a couple of times. Mrs. Bochdan finished with the counter and started on the metal snack rack on top of the old deli display case. Magdalene pocketed the candy bar. Mrs. Bochdan walked around the counter—Magdalene's heart tried to exit through her throat—and sprayed the front of the display case with Windex. Magdalene tried to not inhale any stray Windex fumes (her heart was busy choking her anyway), and she mumbled something about asking her father for money and left, the little bell over the door signaling the end of the first round. She tried not to notice how shaky her hands had become and assumed her position on the brick wall across the street. Her fist bloomed open—an Almond Joy. *Good God*—it was a poor choice for a first theft; she didn't particularly care for either coconut or almonds. Still: if that was Mrs. Bochdan—*the* Mrs. Bochdan—Magdalene knew she could have stolen the deli case without much effort; the woman seemed quite distracted.

Magdalene sighed. The sun was high in the cloud-stained sky. There was nothing more she could do here, not without a plan. Even though she only had a few days left to live—a couple of weeks tops (*seesaw*)—she was going to need money now to facilitate the Raven situation. Her father would surely give her a few dollars if she asked, but that would make him an accessory, and asking Aunt Tiddy for money was like trying to squeeze lemonade from a watermelon. Magdalene didn't have much cash; a few dollars at the most. She didn't want to spend it frivolously (on candy bars, for example), and she only wanted to use Michael's stash if she had to (assuming it was still under his mattress). She was going to have to brave it and make an appeal to Mr. McAllister soon for her job (a temporary position, of course; *seesaw, seesaw*). Besides: she missed Katie.

Magdalene walked northwest to the McAllister house, avoiding those streets that were filled with kids playing street hockey or Wiffle ball. There was no need to expose herself to more abuse if she could help it; she knew she was a pariah. (Though no one had blinked twice at her at Summer Camp, but surely that had to do more with the boys' fear of her father than any inherent likeability on her part.) The Bod Squad would spit on her as soon as shake her hand. Magdalene knew a bully's strength and safety came from belonging: to cliques, to sports teams, even to gangs (with silly names like the Stars and the Fuller Street Gang) that hung on corners and shared the few cigarettes they'd been able to snatch from their parents. Magdalene had never smoked and didn't want to; some people would do anything to fit in. Magdalene prided herself in always having been less concerned about wanting to belong than with the reasons why she didn't.

Behind the berry bushes on Orchard Street, across from the McAllister place, Magdalene nervously flicked red berries. She squished a few between her fingers. She didn't like to admit it, but she was more than a little frightened of Mr. McAllister, and it wasn't just his drinking or the episode with O'Neill's News. Mr. McAllister had always looked like a ruffian to Magdalene. Emerging from beneath his car on Saturday mornings, the huge, pale arms jutting out from his cutoff t-shirt were splotchy with patches of red, and she could always see red tufts of hair exploding from his armpits. Magdalene didn't know if Mr. McAllister owned any t-shirts with sleeves; he either wore white wife-beaters, invariably stained with spaghetti sauce or Salisbury steak gravy, or else he had cut the sleeves off a college t-shirt from a college he couldn't possibly have attended.

For the first time since before the second suicide attempt, Magdalene wished she had a Xanax or an equivalent. She'd sworn off all her previous psychiatric medications and had convinced Willa of the same. After the first suicide go-round, Willa had asked the school nurse to dispense the medicine. (Magdalene's father had had to scribble his suddenly limp signature on a permission paper, and hadn't that been a fun little trip to McCullough's?) The Xanax made her slightly loopy; twice she'd fallen asleep in class. Once she walked home the wrong way—not because she'd forgotten where she lived, but because the sun had dazzled her eyes. Sleepwalking, self-hypnosis, Willa had said, but Magdalene hadn't told her where she had walked to: the Puddle. Even now, Magdalene felt the pull of the Puddle, as if it was calling her. Maybe if she had a Xanax, she could force the same thing to happen again; maybe it would help her solve the Mystery of the Puddle.

Magdalene squashed a berry beneath her sneakers. The berries were beautiful: an orangey red, like the sun during the few minutes it had to say goodbye before it died yet another day. Their shiny, almost translucent skin rose to form a perfect lip that revealed the tops of the little black pits inside. Magdalene squashed another one.

Enough.

When she knocked on Mr. McAllister's door, Magdalene knew he wasn't home. The television inside was blaring soaps—Aunt Tiddy called them "her stories." Katie didn't watch soap operas or any other adult daytime television. Mr. McAllister? No, Magdalene thought, giggling; she could never picture Mr. McAllister wrapped up in the heartaches of the daytime set. The thought almost made Mr. McAllister soften a bit in Magdalene's head.

It took Magdalene a few seconds to adjust her eyes and kill the giggles when the door opened.

"Magdalene," Valerie Plum said.

"What are...?" Magdalene asked. She could barely find her voice.

"Magdalene! Magdalene! Magdalene!" Katie cried from behind Valerie.

Katie's arms jutted out past Valerie Plum and pulled Magdalene, stunned, into the house. Katie never stopped talking.

"I have to show you my lizards. There were three, but now there are only two. I have to tell you all about them. You haven't seen my turtle in a while. You have to see my turtle. My turtle has this new spot on his shell now. Not one I painted—not the same color anyway. I looked it up on the Internet, but I couldn't find anything about turtle spots. Do turtles change the color of their shells,

Magdalene? I don't think so. Turtles aren't chameleons. There's been a tabby cat hanging around here. He's fat. I don't know if he's got a home, but I think he must because he scratches at the back door like he wants to get in. I gave him milk today, but Valerie had a fit. Do you know Valerie? Well, you do now. I'd like to take the cat in, but I'd have to ask Daddy first, and, well, he's been kind of busy. Plus, I've seen what I think are some *new* stars. I'm so glad you're back, Magdalene. Nothing against ol' Valerie here, but you haven't even seen my lizards."

Valerie and Magdalene stared at each other, lost for a moment in the silence that followed Katie's speech. There it was: Magdalene's chest actually *ached*. Raven wasn't the only one who could do that: constrict what was left into a tight little ball, a dying star, an object to obsess over. She was going to miss Katie—she *had* missed her—and her crazy speeches. For an eight-year-old, Katie was fond of forensics. Magdalene made a mental note: perhaps Katie could join the debate team when she entered high school; she should plant the suggestion while there was still time.

"You shouldn't be here," Valerie Plum said.

Magdalene peeked over Valerie's shoulder. The house looked the same: a hodgepodge that included beanbag chairs and television snack stands. Magdalene's chest loosened; nothing had changed. It was still just Mr. McAllister and Katie living here. For half a second, when Valerie had opened the door, Magdalene thought that maybe Katie had moved, and that this was the big story Tiddy and her father were keeping from her.

"I…I need to talk to Mr. McAllister," Magdalene said.

Valerie Plum was one of the schoolyard screamers, a model Bod Squad member, greeting her girlfriends each morning with a shriek and a screech. Sometimes Valerie hung out with Christina. Magdalene wasn't invited when the two of them did whatever acquaintances do when they get together after school. Valerie had shiny black hair, very straight, and tremendous boobs for an eighth grader. They weren't massive like Christina's; they were prominent and shapely. Magdalene envied Valerie's tremendous boobs. The rumors in school were that Valerie had let Kevin Meany see them or touch them or draw on them with a magic marker at one of Megan Riley's make-out parties. Magdalene knew she couldn't believe everything she heard, but that last one seemed like Valerie's speed; Valerie wasn't the sharpest tack in the box.

"And then my grandma bought me this book on bugs," Katie said.

A large hardback book was shoved into Magdalene's hands.

"Every single kind of bug is in there. Look at 'em all. I think Daddy stepped on this one last week in the backyard. He's forever stepping on bugs. Daddy said this book was a menu for the lizards, but the lizards don't seem to pay any attention to the pictures. I thought they would be scared. Oh my God! I have to tell you what happened to Billy the baby lizard. He was so cute, but I think they ate him. Look at this bug. It looks like a sand crab. Maybe it's in the same family. Sister Jezebel said that I can't understand this book, so I shouldn't be reading it, but Daddy said this one time I could ignore her, so I did and read it anyway. Did you know that some spiders devour their young? Devour means eat, Magdalene. Did you know that? The black widow devours her husband after they make babies. Sister Jezebel said I'm too young to talk about making babies, and this time Daddy agreed with her, but he let me keep the book. What's the big deal about making babies, Magdalene? Ol' Valerie here, she doesn't seem to know anything unless it's about stinky Paul Stern or her stupid soaps."

"Shut up, Katie," Valerie said.

"I'll tell my daddy about Paul," Katie said without looking up from the bug book Magdalene held open in her hands.

Valerie closed her mouth.

"Come on upstairs, Magdalene. I want to show you my lizards."

"Katie, your father said—" Valerie started.

"Paul Stern," Katie said quickly.

" 'He's *my ill-made knight*,' " Katie said, mimicking Valerie's *uh-huh*, breathy voice. Valerie closed the front door and slumped on the sofa, focusing on the television. Katie took the bug book from Magdalene's sweaty palms and led Magdalene up the stairs.

"Why is Valerie here, Katie?"

Katie pushed opened her bedroom door.

"I have to keep it closed. I don't want Valerie creeping in. She pokes around too much. It's like I'm invisible."

"You just finished the third grade, Katie. No one pays much attention to third graders (or fourth graders, for that matter), unless they're your parents, your teachers, or some kid in the second grade."

Katie's room was a zoo: models of the human body sat atop a fish aquarium filled with what looked like tiny baby sharks. A round-mouthed algae eater clung to the side of the glass. Books were everywhere. Like Magdalene at the same age, Katie McAllister had graduated from Encyclopedia Brown to Robert Louis Stevenson and astronomy books. Two rabbits bounced around in a large cage they shared with a startled guinea pig. Minnie the turtle sat on a flat rock in a Tupperware bowl full of water in another aquarium. Magdalene knew Minnie well; many a summer day had been spent searching for Minnie. Minnie was the Houdini of turtles, and she never let speed deter her from making a break if she saw an opportunity. No matter what color Katie painted her shell (which she did, endlessly), Minnie could be right in front of their eyes, inches away from a big toe, and still, they wouldn't see her.

Katie's room smelled a little like the Quakertown Petting Zoo outside New Hope. All that was missing were the dispensers filled with turd-shaped pellets to feed the goats. It was amazing, Magdalene thought, how two rabbits, a turtle, a guinea pig, and a couple of lizards kind of smelled like a goat in a closed room. She wanted to light the prayer candles gathered on Katie's windowsill.

Katie's tongue was fixed in the corner of her mouth, and she had pulled her straight, blonde hair behind her ears while she attempted to catch one of the lizards running away from her fingers inside a glass aquarium filled with colored pebbles and fake trees nicked from the fish tank.

"Katie, what is Valerie—?"

Katie didn't take her eyes off the lizards; one was a light sandy-yellow; the other was long and dark green.

"She's dumb, just plain dumb, Magdalene. I asked her for some chocolate peanut butter. Do you know what she did, Magdalene, do you? She mixed Quik in the peanut butter! But right next to the regular peanut butter was the chocolate peanut butter! What I wouldn't give for a few more inches. Then I could get my own darn peanut butter."

From the stairs: "Shut up, Katie!"

Magdalene jumped back; she would never dare tell Katie to shut up. "Shut up" shouldn't be in a baby-sitter's vocabulary.

Was Valerie Plum baby-sitting?

"If you keep snooping, Valerie, I swear I'm telling Daddy about Paul Stern."

"What about Paul Stern?" Magdalene whispered.

"I'll tell you later," Katie stage whispered.

"Go watch your stupid stories!" Katie screamed, her fingers still chasing the lizards.

The little girl smiled.

"I told Angela about Billy."

"Your aunt?" Magdalene asked.

"Yep. I told you about her, didn't I? She's only twenty-two, but she's my aunt. She lives in New Hope. She's smart and funny and pretty like you. I hadn't seen you in a while, and I couldn't find anything on the Internet or in the Funk and Wagnalls about it. So I asked Angela. You want a Cherry Coke?"

"Asked her about what?"

Magdalene's temples throbbed. Her brain was counting again.

"Billy! You see, there were three lizards to begin with. Got one!"

The lizard stopped squirming as soon as Katie's fingers curled around its slender stomach; she caressed its emerald head with her thumb.

"This is David. That one in there: that's Sarah. They're married. Well, when I got them, they came with a baby—like me and Daddy and Mommy before Mommy got sick—and his name was Billy. He was tiny, real little with funny spots, as if he hadn't chosen whether he was going to be his dad's color or his mom's. He was cute."

Magdalene nodded. Was Valerie Plum the new baby-sitter?

"Then one day, Magdalene, one day, Billy was gone! I had the lid on tight. It has holes, but it goes on tight, and he was little, but there's no way he escaped. Do you want to know what happened? Do you?"

Magdalene realized she was staring out the window into the backyard below. A dogwood tree stood in the center of the backyard. One long, horizontal branch reached almost to the side fence. It reminded Magdalene of—she wasn't sure. The Puddle? A small breeze shook the dogwood, and the shadow beneath the long branch shimmered. Everything seemed caught up in the Mystery of the Puddle: nothing seemed the way it should be. What was Mrs. Bochdan looking at right now? Would Mrs. Cabot forever see Henry where he wasn't?

"I'm sorry, Katie. What happened?"

"They ate him! They ate their baby!"

The down of Katie's blonde eyebrows punctuated the details of the tale; her pixie face—the kind of face, Magdalene thought, that could grace magazine covers if Katie wasn't destined to be a veterinarian or a surgeon or a professor—was animated and pulsing; Katie's discoveries came alive on her face.

"They ate him?" Magdalene asked slowly. Words were stuck between her teeth.

"I tried to look it up, but, yep, they ate him. Here's my theory—"

"Hypothesis."

"Hypo—say it again. What's it mean?"

"Hy-poth-e-sis," Magdalene said. "It means educated guess. You didn't just make up what you thought happened. You did some research first, so your guess is educated."

"Hy-poth-e-sis. Yep, I did some research, but you know what? I think they just loved him too much."

"They...?" Magdalene could feel the color leave her face.

"My Uncle Larry caught the lizards in the woods, and maybe Sarah just gave birth to Billy when he caught them, and maybe David and Sarah didn't want their only baby to grow up in an enclosed environment. (Did I say that right?) Maybe they loved him too much, so they decided to take him out of his misery. And the only way they could do it, I guess, was to eat him. They ate their son."

Magdalene stared at the sedate lizard in Katie's little fist. She was nauseous. Her nose was filled with the smell of Raven's stuffed animals, Monkey and silent Monien, their matted fur and chewed-upon ears and loose stuffing. They all smelled like Raven's breath, his sour mash, hot, friendly breath. And Raven's breath smelled like Michael's bed.

"Katie, why is Valerie Plum here?"

Katie lowered David the lizard back into the aquarium. She slapped both hands together.

"Now, you haven't seen the bunnies and the pig in a while!" Katie cried. "The boys!"

Magdalene raised her voice. The television volume downstairs was lowered.

"Katie! Stop!"

Katie released the top of the rabbit cage but didn't turn around. The television returned to its original volume, but Magdalene whispered anyway.

"Why is Valerie here?"

"I think Daddy has a girlfriend."

"What?"

Katie didn't turn around.

"I think he has a girlfriend. See, first he told me you didn't want to baby-sit me anymore. He told me he went to talk to you, and that your decision was final. I didn't believe him. I was so upset, Magdalene. I looked up your phone number, but I'd left Daddy's phone book open, so he knew before I called—I was going to wait until he left—and then he told me the truth. He said that things— things!—were very busy. He said he got a new job, but I don't know what it is. He takes the bus somewhere at night too, so I asked him what was so busy at night, and he said he met a new friend—a lady friend!—and that he was taking the bus to see her."

Katie's shoulders hitched, but Magdalene couldn't move.

"Daddy told me he needed someone more…reliable—I think that's the word—like Valerie to babysit, and that your summer was going to be pretty busy too because you were sick like Mommy was sick, and you had to go to the doctors a lot. Are you sick, Magdalene? Like Mommy was sick?"

When Katie turned around, her face glowed red.

Magdalene pulled the bedroom door open and ran down the stairs, through the living room, past a startled Valerie Plum, and hit the street, her lungs searching for air, her throat and chest hot like she had fallen asleep in front of the little space heater her mother had used to warm her feet.

The prime numbers less than 100 are: 2, 3, 5, 7, 11, 13, 17, 19, 23, 29, 31, 37, 41, 43, 47, 53, 59, 61, 67, 71, 73, 79, 83, and 97.

Someone had taken this from her—baby-sitting Katie McAllister. Everything, really: Christina, Assumption, Raven, her father, her mother, Michael. Was it God? Lucifer? What had she done to deserve these afflictions?

The prime factorization of 160 is: $160 = 2 \times 2 \times 2 \times 2 \times 2 \times 5$.

The prime factorization of 1,368 is: $1,368 = 2 \times 2 \times 2 \times 3 \times 3 \times 19$.

When she tripped by the mailbox at the corner of Orchard Street, a joke dislodged itself from the march of the primes, and laughter plotted its course between what she could only assume were baby ulcers. As she limped home, dabbing at the large circular cuts on her knees, the laughter reached her mouth. She got the joke: she was the turtle! She was Minnie the escape artist, the turtle whose shell changed colors without ever knowing why, too darn slow to comprehend or ever really escape, too self-aware to do anything less.

And Michael? Why, Michael was Billy the lizard, of course—the lizard devoured by those who loved him.

Gone. Washed away. Swallowed whole. We don't speak of it. The turtle stands alone.

+

Tiddy was pissed Magdalene had forgotten the flour. Her aunt launched into a litany of literary declamations the second Magdalene walked in the door. Magdalene listened for a few minutes before escaping to the bathroom.

"How many cans of shaving cream does one man need?" Magdalene asked Raven. She was on her hands and knees on the bathroom floor. The dog picked up the monkey and placed it behind her feet. Magdalene ducked her head into the cabinet under the sink.

To hell with solving the Cabot Case, to hell with the Mystery of the Puddle—it was time to check out. Raven had to go first, Magdalene thought, as she scrambled through cotton balls and scouring pads and Q-tips and old cans of hairspray that must have belonged to her mother. The dog was just about ready to explode with all the love he'd stored up. Magdalene sniffed at the nozzles; nothing smelled familiar. Raven deposited Monkey on the lip of the cabinet and panted expectantly.

There weren't any pills in the medicine cabinet, not even aspirin. The linen closet, which held precious few linens but quite a few bars of soap, contained nothing even remotely potable or sharp. She returned to looking under the sink. Magdalene needed to silence the turtle; she could hear its screams of frustration: why am I always the last one to know? Why am I the one incapable of hiding? Why am I the one left sitting out, everything that is burning inside me a bright, obvious target on my back?

Raven nudged the monkey with his nose. She could feel his warm breath on her backside. Magdalene pushed aside another bag of cotton balls. She still didn't know how she was going to "do" Raven—just nothing to actually cause him pain. She loved Raven to bits. If she could find some medicine, she could split it with him and hide it in his food. Maybe she could search her father's old bedroom—Tiddy's room—for medicine. Magdalene had once seen the painter's palette contents of Tiddy's pillbox. Aunt Tiddy was old; surely, she had to be on *something* that would kill her grandniece and her grandniece's pooch.

Her father cleared his throat and said: "I moved everything."

Magdalene remained kneeling and kept her head inside the cabinet under the sink. What was her father doing home?

"I was just looking for some hairspray," Magdalene said.

"Well, I think your mother left some cans under there."

His voice sounded odd: cracked, broken, or perhaps just on the mend from a fierce cold.

"Mommy didn't *leave* anything," Magdalene said. "She died."

She could feel the turtle slow down, confused, unsure of even where it had meant to run. If she could just crawl inside…

"I threw out anything that might be harmful," her father said. He cleared his throat again. "Like my razors, headache medicine, stuff like that. I can use my electric razor to shave. I mean, we don't want Aunt Tiddy to hurt herself now, do we?"

Magdalene sensed the weight of the turtle shell crushing down on her neck. How heavy it must be to carry everything on your back! Magdalene pulled her head out of the cabinet.

"Katie said that Mr. McAllister told her I couldn't baby-sit anymore. Said it was because I was sick."

"Maybe Mr. McAllister thought it would be too much for you to handle right now. He was probably just thinking of your welfare."

"You knew."

It was the first time she could ever remember confronting him. Even when he smelled like the gunk on the bottom of her shoes and drank every meal, she'd never faced him like this.

"You knew. You and Tiddy. You both knew I wasn't *allowed* to baby-sit Katie anymore, and you never told me. You knew I'd been *fired.*"

Her father reached for her, but Magdalene ducked, hip-checking Raven into the side of the tub, and escaped to the hallway.

"Why don't you go back to the bar?" she screamed. Raven's ears jumped. "At least you knew what to do there! I'll get my own job back, thank you very much."

Magdalene reached her bedroom and kicked the panda from the doorway, locking the door behind her. She heard her father breathing in the hallway beneath Raven's energetic huffing and puffing. Part of her wanted to open the door and run to her father. Here was a man who had lost so much and was desperately trying to hold onto what little was left (her?), but Magdalene couldn't help but think he'd lost the wrong child: the football hero was missing, and the would-be writer, the junior detective, was digging through the bathroom cabinet, had mined into her veins, ingested suicide pills into her stomach. She didn't even fit into her shell. There was little left for her to do, she thought; she couldn't hide, couldn't help, couldn't hurt herself anymore than she was already hurt.

Of course he loved Michael more than her. That didn't hurt as much as the fact that he couldn't see that she'd been the only one trying to *find* Michael! Her father and Tiddy didn't even see the Mystery of the Puddle for the mystery it was! At least Frank and Joe Hardy's father was a detective. *Her* father was lost in words the same way he'd been lost in drink: a lawyer! His arguments were too careful. A mouthpiece was what Megan Riley once called him. (Megan's father had been in trouble with the county for digging behind his yard without a permit.) But Magdalene had caught the drift: her father was just interpreting someone else's words—old words, ancient laws. His job was to entangle or untangle (depending upon the needs of the DA's office) those words and phrases and syllables into something Mondauk County could hang its hat on. Why couldn't he see Magdalene had been trying to the same thing for Michael?

She fell asleep to the sound of running water. Her hand reached into a swiftly moving darkness but grasped nothing but damp air. When she pulled her hand back, the skin on her wrist was smooth and white like bone; the scars were gone. When she woke, it was dark out. An owl hooted its hunting call from Pennypack Woods. She listened for the splash of the Puddle.

Raven was in her bed. She curled her body around his and prayed the way the nuns had taught her. She prayed for the mysteries to be taken away or for at least the strength to solve them if her first request was too much to ask. Then she prayed for a plan to die. That couldn't be too much to ask for now, could it?

A zero is neither positive nor negative, neither a prime number nor a composite. Zero isn't the starting point; it's the end zone. In multiplication, if a zero is a factor, the sum returns to zero. Zero doesn't count.

" *'Two drifters off to see the world,'* " she sang to Raven, " *'there's such a lot of world to see.'* "

She'd try to solve the cases first, she promised God or Mary or Baby Jesus. She'd do the best she could anyway. And she'd wait until she finished her book. Waiting would give her time to steal Tiddy's medication. She'd write Michael a letter explaining everything in case he came back. She'd lay out any evidence she found for her father.

Magdalene whispered into her doomed dog's *SILK* ears:

" *'We're after the same rainbow's end / Waitin' 'round the bend...'*"

Her eighth grade algebra textbook warned students to exercise caution when zero was involved in division. If Mondauk was about to be turned upside down, who better for the job of fixer than the least valued among its population? After all, Magdalene thought, every dog has its day, and every good Judas deserves to die. Mondauk County would finally see how much zero doesn't count.

" *'...my Huckleberry friend, Moon River, and me.'*"

Chapter Five

The Yawp

Dr. Willa Meade's office was always darker and warmer than was comfortable. Magdalene supposed (congratulating herself for such an insightful, adult thought) it was meant to be womb-like, but she thought it felt like one of those haunted house rides at the summer carnivals (either one, Catholic or Methodist): too gaudy to be truly scary, too hot (*Donna fainted, you guys!*) to worry about ghosts and vampires jumping out, too dark to be anything but annoying—the older kids playing the monsters seemed to bump into walls and doors as often as their dehydrated victims. When the ride ended, the faithful always exited, panting, with a look of relief, sweat beading on their upper lips: perfect advertisements for anyone waiting in line or those younger ones too scared to line up, watching from the side. Such was Willa's office. Magdalene imagined that the kids in the waiting room would think Magdalene cured after a prolonged workout inside a tunnel when she emerged from Willa's office squinting and sweaty.

"Art therapy is therapeutic because sometimes issues—thoughts, ideas, past events—that the patient can't or won't speak out loud can be revealed in a piece of art," Willa said. "It can help ease survivor's guilt."

Magdalene sat on the floor before a low, oval-shaped, wooden table covered in crayons and magic markers and colored pencils. Willa had encouraged Magdalene to abandoned the "safety of the chair" for the "adventure of the floor." As if to demonstrate, the therapist had gathered her multicolored skirt and sat Indian-style on the rug. Magdalene thought this was such a load of shit that she said it aloud to see how it sounded.

"This is such a load of shit," Magdalene said.

It hadn't sounded so bad, but it seemed to have zero effect. Willa just adjusted her skirt and dumped a box of thirty-two assorted colors on the table.

Willa looked at Magdalene over her glasses like Aunt Tiddy did, and Magdalene pushed herself from the floor to take a tour of the office. She'd been here a few times, but she'd always been so wound up that she never really took everything in.

There were a pile of toys in the corner. Magdalene remembered some of these: Strawberry Shortcake, Smurfs, a baby that pooped and peed. Michael had had that robot-boy, the one with the remote control.

"Anything there you'd like to play with, Maddie?" Willa asked.

Magdalene walked away from the toys; better to not let Willa see her interest in anything. She would find herself playing on the floor like all the younger kids twitching in the waiting room.

"You don't have to be little to play with toys," Willa said.

"How old are you?" Magdalene asked, as she looked at the artwork neatly hung on the walls with colored thumbtacks. Here was a daddy in violet Crayola beating a mommy in a periwinkle housedress. Above and to the right was a little baby in sea green escaping the red slashes of a yellow-orange mommy. In another, a man in navy blue was jumping from a tall stack of gray into a raging lawn of flickering red and yellow. There were no artists' signatures; the pictures hung in total anonymity.

"I'm in my fifties. Fifty-five to be exact. Do you think that's old, Maddie?" Willa asked.

"Do you?" Magdalene asked as she squinted a mauve jumble of baby doll parts drowning in a sea of fire engine red and scorched yellow. "It's older than me. My dad is fifty-four and that's pretty old, but not old like Aunt Tiddy."

"Do you want to talk about your book, Maddie?"

"MY NAME IS MAGDALENE!"

Her voice didn't echo in the room but fell swiftly. She'd noticed the double doors when she'd came here after the first suicide attempt. She decided the room must be soundproof.

"SHIT!" Magdalene yelled. She sounded like the boys playing touch football in the schoolyard at recess. "GODDAMN!"

Willa remained on the floor. Her face was twisted into that half-smile—a smirk really—that adults flashed when confronted with what Father Dave had called "the indulgent behavior of youth." Magdalene wanted to smack her one.

"You want me to try?" Willa asked. "It's okay; no one can hear you out there. Alright, here goes: BASTARD!"

Adults cursing always startled Magdalene a little, and hearing I'm-a-hippie-let's-love-everyone-and-listen-to-crap-music-with-fiddles-so-we-feel-all-earthy-Willa cursing was, in the very least, disturbing.

"Okay, here's another one," Willa yelled. "SUCKER!"

"That's not a curse word," Magdalene said, turning back to the wall of art. She couldn't take her eyes off the navy blue man falling into the raging red and yellow blanket of—flames? It hung next to another Crayola masterpiece: a black dog and a tiny silver cat.

Flames?

"Do you like that picture?" Willa asked, gesturing from her position on the floor. "Which one, Magdalene? The one with the dog or the man flying?"

"He's not flying. He's jumping."

"Do you want to draw something?" Willa asked.

"This is for little kids," Magdalene said, but still, there was the man falling, it seemed, from a great height. Not waiting to jump, not burning in the flames below, but captured midair, in the act of *doing*. Magdalene knew how far she had drifted from the act of doing and how far she had to go to accomplish what she needed to before her blessed moment.

Why did this man look familiar, Magdalene asked herself, this falling man?

"Little kids often me tell me stories they are unable to express otherwise by drawing me pictures. Self-identification. Is there something you would like to draw, Magdalene?"

"FUCK YOU!" Magdalene screamed.

"DOODIE HEAD!" cried Willa.

"FUCK YOU!"

"Sometimes it's the only way children—not just little kids—can talk about the horrific events in their lives. They have no other tools. They've dissociated from the bad things. Dissociation. Sometimes they make up stories, and they tell them to me, and then we figure them out together."

"FUCK YOU!" Magdalene screamed a third time.

Willa's particular madness—healing via coloring, story time redemption—made sense, as much as Magdalene hated to admit it to herself. Had Katie been trying to tell Magdalene a secret with the story of the lizards' suspected filial cannibalism? Katie hadn't seemed incredibly upset at Billy's disappearance however. Dissociation? And what about Minnie the escape turtle with her constantly changing painted spots? Magdalene had identified with the turtle (slow, incapable of true escape)—but what if Minnie the turtle and Billy the lizard had been Katie's method of communicating the unspeakable? The Turtle Theory! As much as she thought Willa was full of doodie, there might be some validity to this sort of therapy.

"POOP!" screamed Willa. The therapist grabbed a bunch of crayons and markers and offered them to Magdalene.

"Fuck you," whispered Magdalene.

Katie hadn't seemed hurt or scared, but maybe her nonstop talking had been covering up a darker color. Had Billy really existed or had Katie just been trying to communicate to Magdalene something she couldn't express any other way?

"Maddie?" asked Willa, but Magdalene had already opened the second of the two doors.

Magdalene is my name, Magdalene thought, what do I have to do? Draw you a picture?

+

Magdalene skipped the bus and walked home, enjoying the sound of her sneakers flapping against the warm sidewalk. There was much to figure out: Mrs. Bochdan, Raven, and now Katie. When she reached home, Raven was waiting at the screen door, barking.

"Shhh, boy. Come on, Raven, shush!"

"Dog?" Aunt Tiddy yelled from inside the house. "What is it, dog?"

Magdalene hid alongside the house as Tiddy reached the screen door.

"What the hell are you wagging your tail for? Her highness isn't home yet, dog. Taking her first exam today, then her doctor's appointment. Math, she said."

Her highness?

Magdalene had hoped Tiddy would be shopping at Bard's or Morrone's so she could sneak in and retrieve her journal. The mysteries were growing tendrils, and she needed to write them all down.

Her highness?

Magdalene thought: *to hell with Aunt Tiddy*, and, hunched over, she crept up the porch steps. Aunt Tiddy was nowhere in sight. Raven watched her through the screen, strangely silent, as if he was aware of his impending great escape. Magdalene put a finger to her mouth and eased the screen door open. Raven clambered past her, knocking the door out of Magdalene's hand. It slammed shut and bounced open a fraction before slamming again.

From the kitchen: "You stay away from that door. You hear me, dog?"

Magdalene pulled the screen door open again, knelt down, and snaked her hand in, her fingers feeling along until they reached the low shelf of the end table. Raven barked at a passing car from the porch and took off.

"Jesus wept! What's the matter now?" Tiddy yelled from the kitchen. "I think it's time for your backyard constitution."

Over her shoulder, Magdalene saw Raven in the middle of the street chasing a boy on a silver bike. The kid had playing cards clipped to his tire spokes with clothespins. She heard their *click-clock, click-clock* (one, two, one, two)—and something heavier rumbling in the background. A truck? A bus? Then Raven was out of her sight line. She could tell he'd changed direction by his barking.

Not now. Not today.

Her fingers discarded newspapers and *Alfred Hitchcock's Mystery Magazines* and something that felt like an old Christmas cookie, a gingerbread man with glittery sprinkles on top. How had Raven missed that?

Magdalene heard Tiddy shut a drawer.

"Where the devil are you, dog?"

Magdalene craned her neck. It *was* a truck—a trash truck. Was it trash day? Magdalene stuck her head through the doorway and spied the leash on the floor behind the table; only the loopy handle was lying atop the magazines. She grabbed it and whipped her body back out through the door.

"Dog?" Tiddy asked.

Magdalene lay perfectly still on her stomach; the business end of the leash was caught in the door. The truck rumbled into its next gear. Raven's barking intensified. He was having fun; it was his fun bark, his I'm-raring-to-go-Michael bark.

Leave it alone, Raven. Let the truck be.

No dares, Raven.

Not again.

Not again?

"Did I put you in the yard already?" Tiddy mused. "I can hear you."

Tiddy was walking into the living room.

Magdalene yanked the leash through the door and ran down to the street. Raven was running towards the truck.

Not now, Raven. Not today.

Not unless I go with you.

Magdalene's sneaker slipped in the remains of a chocolate éclair. Good Humor. She grabbed the bumper of a parked car—there he was!—and then hurled herself towards Raven, who was sprinting *ahead* of the truck.

When the dog caught sight of Magdalene, rolling in the street, he ran to her and licked her face. His breath tasted like chocolate éclair. Magdalene sat with her back against the bumper and held Raven's collar as the truck lumbered by. The driver waved at her.

"Dog!" Aunt Tiddy was on the porch. Magdalene cupped Raven's snout and waited.

"Damn it, dog!" Aunt Tiddy screeched.

The screen door slammed shut. Magdalene peered over the car in front of her. The coast was clear.

"Ready for an adventure, Raven?"

The dog started to bark, but Magdalene clamped down on his snout again. Raven looked up at her (*what did I do wrong?*), but his tail swept the air.

"First, Raven, the Cabot Case. Come on!"

Magdalene whispered in his ear: "A Lab's ears are made of *SILK*."

She clipped the leash to his collar, and together the two detectives ran towards the sun. At the end of the block, Magdalene took a backward glance, and there was Tiddy, sitting on the porch swing, waving goodbye, but then the biggest star of all flooded Magdalene's eyes and dragged Tiddy beneath its rays.

+

Mrs. Bochdan was struggling with a trash can lid. Trash was strewn about the little store's backyard. Other trash cans lay on their sides in the middle of Loretta Avenue. A soft wind carried more trash down to the corner. Magdalene sat on the low brick wall across the street; Raven was asleep at her feet. Some detective, Magdalene thought.

Mrs. Bochdan pulled at the lid and then kicked the can over, leaving the garbage bag where she had dropped it. The woman covered her face with her hands and uttered something Magdalene assumed was in Ukrainian and shook her fist like the oppressed often did in the movies.

When Mrs. Bochdan went back inside the store, Magdalene hopped off the wall, and Raven, fully awake, ran in a circle. *How did dogs do that—go from a dead sleep to a bounce in a heartbeat?* Magdalene found each day more exhausting than the last; she'd nap all day long if it weren't for the ever-present Aunt Tiddy. Magdalene opened the tiny gate to Sol's backyard and cringed when it squeaked. She used all of her weight to pull the lid off the trash can; the remains of cracked eggs and old soda made her gag. Raven nibbled on a stale biscuit.

"No, don't," Magdalene said absently. Someone had spray painted KILLER'S MOTHER on Sol's back screen door. Eggshells and condom wrappers were everywhere. Magdalene left Raven in the backyard nosing at some stale Twizzlers, while she collected two trash cans and one of their lids from the middle of Loretta Avenue.

Back in the yard, Magdalene knelt down and scooped up garbage using a pair of stained paper bags. She didn't hear the screen door swing open. But Raven did—he jumped up and lost his grip on a snowy white doughnut. Mrs. Bochdan smacked Magdalene's cheek (her hand smelled like exotic spices) and kicked at her stomach.

"Get out of my yard!" Mrs. Bochdan screamed. "I called police. Leave! Now!" Magdalene covered her head with her hands. Raven was in between them now, the low gurgle in his throat threatening escalation.

"No, Raven, no," Magdalene croaked. The fur on Raven's back had risen like a black wave, seconds away from crashing. He does love me, she thought.

Mrs. Bochdan backed into the store and returned seconds later wielding a broom. She swatted at Raven. Magdalene lost sight of him in the sudden dust clouds. Raven sneezed.

"You think this is joke? You think this funny?" Mrs. Bochdan asked. "I piss on you. I tell your parents."

Mrs. Bochdan's hands went to her chest. Magdalene moved towards her. (Was Mrs. Bochdan winded? Having a heart attack?) Mrs. Bochdan lowered the broom and spat at Magdalene.

"Get! Out!" Mrs. Bochdan wheezed.

Raven, in a disturbing lack of instinct, seemed to disregard their imminent danger as soon as the broom stopped swinging (and he stopped sneezing) and snatched up the crusty doughnut with his teeth. Magdalene grabbed Raven's leash, and the detectives left the scene of their attempted good deed and didn't stop until they reached the edge of the woods near the school. Magdalene could hear the Puddle trickling in the distance, beyond the tree line, its dirty water slipping over slimy, green rocks.

Magdalene sat with her back against a tree and rubbed Raven's head as he munched on the doughnut.

"I don't know how we're gonna talk to her now. You think she knows who I am? If she tells Daddy, the whole operation will be in jeopardy. Raven, don't eat that."

Raven ignored her and finished the doughnut in one swallow.

"Maybe that's how we'll handle the goodbye, Raven. I could hide something in your food. I don't think you'd ever notice."

The dog wagged his tail in approval, licking his snout clean of crumbs.

It was important that she speak with Mrs. Bochdan to get her side of the story and find out the names of the bullies who'd picked on Henry Richard Cabot and maybe even her own son. If the police and the judge (and Magdalene's father) knew the whole incident had been the result of a bullying—that Joseph Bochdan had (somehow) gotten the gun to defend his best friend, or perhaps to put his best friend out of his misery (although it was probably best not to mention the latter theory)—then maybe the authorities could see their way to releasing Joseph from wherever they were holding him.

Michael would have known what to do. Nobody had ever picked on Michael, and he'd picked on no one—except her, but that was part of the package that came with being a younger sibling (especially a sister). Older brothers—even younger ones sometimes—tormented their sisters, teasing them, planning sneak attacks, tossing their underwear into the trees, even trying to get their sisters to pee in their beds by placing their hands in cereal bowls full of warm water (which hadn't worked on her). On the whole, Michael hadn't been too bad. He did declare war on her once and used masking tape to mark the boundary line between their bedrooms, proclaiming each section its own country and assaulting her with his dirty football socks (which smelled amazingly like week-old Easter ham). No, Michael was no worse than any other older brother she'd ever heard about—except for the dares.

Everything to Michael was worthy of a dare—exploring the old school building was the least of it as far as Magdalene was concerned.

Their father was of the "boys will be boys" school—which meant, essentially, that Michael was rarely, if ever, in trouble for anything he did, particularly after their mother died. Their mother had been a soft-spoken, fun woman with a smile like a secret; she took nothing in the way of sibling rivalry seriously. Before she died, when the cancer seemed to be eating her right before their stunned eyes, their mother pulled Michael next to her on the bed, wet her fingers in an attempt to tame his cowlick, and asked him why he always picked on his sister. Michael just blushed and pushed his face into her neck. He was in the seventh grade. No amount of sibling torment or dangerous dares could get Michael in hot water. Magdalene was the baby, but Michael was the anointed one.

Her father called her Maddie, which was annoying enough, but Michael insisted on calling her Lil—as in Little. At first, it was just Lil Sis or Lil Mags. During the last year of their life together, it had become Lil Boobs. Magdalene didn't much care for the last one; her boobs *were* little and seemed to be in no hurry to grow beyond the nickname. And even though Magdalene acquainted boobs with breast cancer (the cancer that had devoured her mother's easy laughter, until she became nothing more than a dimly lit home movie memory, had taken root in her breasts), Magdalene still wanted bigger boobs. (Maybe they'd arrive when her period did.) Her mother possessed a prominent, adequate bosom, not too large, but more significant than Magdalene's mosquito bites. She was a sweater girl, Magdalene's father had said of the laughing stranger he'd fallen in love with and married. And even the slight traces of her light perfume, which clung to almost everything the first few weeks after she'd left for the hospital never to return, dissipated like the way Aunt Tiddy's old 8mm home movies had deteriorated: slowly at first, then one hole leading to another and then another. Only their mother's sweaters still held any firm indication of her existence. Their father had given most of his wife's clothing to Good Will after she'd died, but not her sweaters. Magdalene and Michael had stood before her open sweater drawer often, moving the backs of their hands gently over the woolen indentations.

In the months between Magdalene's first and second suicide attempts, there was a moment when she'd wished she had her mother's classic bosom (or even Christina's massive globes) for the sole purpose of catching cancer. Breast cancer seemed an easier way out than the one she had chosen. Suicide was proving elusive. Cancer was the great eraser—and not just of breasts and lungs and skin, but of memories too.

Suicide, Sister Edna had said, was nothing more than a shortcut to hell. Michael had been all about shortcuts. He'd spend half an afternoon trying to find a faster way to Sol's (cut through the Russian apartment complex, down the hill beside Hairy McGill's house—provided ol' Hairy didn't hear him and chase him back up the hill; despite, or maybe because of, the enormous amount of hair clumped like black celery stalks in either ear, Hairy McGill could hear a pubic hair fall off a nun's ass, as Michael was fond of saying—and then a quick hop over the brick wall); he loved mapping out a route to *anywhere* so long as it involved hopping at least one fence or cutting through someone's backyard. A nickname was just another form of a shortcut to Michael. Eventually, he even found a shortcut in her nickname, and Magdalene became just Lil (as opposed to the dreaded Lil Boobs). Michael was a master nomenclator (another word of specific dollar value, Magdalene noted); he gave everyone a nickname of some sort, and even if few rarely stuck, to be granted a nickname by Michael was considered an honor. Example: Michael insisted upon calling Jimmy Lonergan the Big Log, which somehow didn't float with Mrs. Lonergan, a recently un-lapsed Catholic who handed out scented, plastic rosary beads at Halloween and sprinkled masks or makeup from a shot glass of holy water. Michael didn't attend school along the normal dividing lines; he bestowed nicknames on the geeks and the gawds (another favorite expression of Michael's). Sometimes the nicknames were whatever rolled from his tongue, but more often they had rather elaborate origins, like comic book superheroes.

Poor adopted Raven became Boo—as in Boo Radley, the mildly creepy shut-in who lived down the road from Scout and Jem in *To Kill a Mockingbird*. That made sense to Magdalene in a way: Raven hoarded and hid his stuffed animals; Boo Radley left gum and clues in a tree knot for Jem and Scout. Plus, their father (pre-booze) was every bit Gregory Peck in the movie version: staid, graying, obstinate, gravel-voiced, and good looking. Harper Lee's *To Kill a Mockingbird* was their father's favorite book. It was the family book; they'd all read it multiple times. Magdalene had the book to thank for her middle name—Harper. So Boo Radley became Boo Raven—or rather, Raven became Boo Raven—then Boo Bear, and finally just plain Boo. But mutating nicknames wasn't enough for Michael; there was also the snatch of a song Michael sang to Raven at breakfast every morning in an almost insufferable falsetto. *Every morning.* Raven's theme song, he said. Magdalene once tried to stuff toast in her ears to block out Michael's voice.

" *'Boo Raven, wider than the sea—my Huckleberry friend, you'll see...'* "

Her last clear memory of Michael involved a dare—although she couldn't recall the exact details of the dare, so maybe *clear* wasn't the correct adjective. She was sure it was somehow tied to the Mystery of the Puddle, but the Cabot Case and Katie's situation were wearing her out. (All these incidents were capitalized in Magdalene's head; she had read somewhere that the best detectives were able to compartmentalize; Magdalene also had the added skill of being able to capitalize with panache!) Her synapses were so much chewed-upon string. (Synapses: now *there* was a goddamn two-bit word, Lil, her brother would have said, but he was gone, and she still didn't have a *goddamn* clue what had happened there.) She had asked Michael to take her to the dock on the Puddle, Finch's Landing—suggested, really—the day of the last dare, the last day she'd seen him, that much she was sure of. And she had lied about possibly Puddle Jumping, she remembered. Everything else was jumbled up. Why hadn't they just played football or street hockey or walked to Sol's for water ice? Why had they taken the risk and pushed their luck? With Puddle Jumping, there was always the chance of getting caught or hurt or worse. What the hell had she been thinking?

She closed her eyes and leaned back against the tree.

"Like my head to a gun, Lil," Michael said, tossing the football.

Raven ran in between the siblings, hoping for an incomplete pass.

"That doesn't even make sense."

Magdalene caught the pass deftly and threw a spiral back.

"Shakespeare said that," Michael said, grinning.

"Oh right, that's rich."

She dove for Michael's pass and just missed simultaneously tackling Raven and falling into Raven's baby pool.

"The Dead Injun Tree!" Michael cried. "The old sycamore!"

"I just don't get it. Why even try?"

"It's like Russian roulette."

"That's sick," Magdalene said—and as she replayed this scene now, the tree digging into her back, poking and prodding the memories of her brother, her stomach turned panicky. It was as if when Michael had said "Russian roulette," there had been no going back.

"No, it's not like that," Michael said, laughing. "It's more like Lou's Head singing. Sometimes you do things just because you can, just because it makes you feel alive. That's what I love about football. Gives me a rush to call an audible, to escape the blitz, to see the receiver catch the pass and run into the end zone. The Dead Injun Tree is a challenge. I've never jumped from the Dead Injun Tree. The guys always Puddle Jump from the mimosa. It's the rush, Lil. It's all about the rush. It's all connected."

Magdalene spit deftly to her side.

"I'm beginning to think *nothing's* connected," she said.

"Besides," she continued, "Lou's Head is an urban myth. Like Mom's hot dog in the ginny story."

"Ask Jerry Eves about Lou's Head, Lil."

"He wasn't there," Magdalene said. "Was he?"

"No, but it's a good excuse to talk to him, no?"

Magdalene threw the football at Michael's head and made a face.

Michael laughed, imitating their father's gravelly voice: "Football is for boys, Maddie."

"Cut it out."

Raven chased after the football and managed to fit it into his mouth. Magdalene watched her brother adjust himself below the waist. The football popped out of Raven's mouth from the pressure of his jaws and the copious amount of dog saliva.

"Lil, I've Puddle Jumped a million times. Besides, I told you I'd talk to Dad about football."

Magdalene shook her head.

"It was your idea to go," he said. And it had been. Summer would end soon; school would start, then football season and high school for Michael. She wanted to spend as much time as possible with her brother before he slipped away. And no one would interrupt them at the dock—no alcoholic father, no teammates slapping backs and exchanging stale Playboy jokes, no other girls—at least not likely; Finch's Landing was more popular as a nighttime hangout spot than a daytime one.

Raven whined at the football and batted it with his paw. It was too slimy for him to pick up.

"Don't say it," she said, knowing it was pointless. Both of them knew any dare Michael offered would be accepted.

Raven tried to sit on the football and slid sideways into a lounging position. His big head followed their conversation.

"I will."

"Goddamn it, Michael. Jesus."

"You in, then?"

"Poop, Michael. Poop!"

"Are ya? Lou's Head! Don't go losin' Lou's Head!"

"I'm in," Magdalene said. "Lou's Head.

"But just from the Jumping Tree," she added. "Please."

" '*Boo Raven, wider than the sea...* '" her brother sang.

"Moon River": Raven's theme song. Raven wagged his tail and panted.

" '*Wider than a mile,*'" she corrected.

It was that simple: she had accepted his silent dare. She had placed the proverbial gun to her head. And even though silent dares weren't specifically mentioned in the Rules of the Dare, she had to steel herself since she couldn't be sure there wasn't a loophole. She'd watched Michael jump from the mimosa, the Jumping Tree, a million times. She knew how it was done. Still her knees trembled. And she wanted no part of jumping from the ancient sycamore, the Dead Injun Tree.

" '*Boo Raven, wider than a mile...*'" her brother sang and it was awful and she'd never hear him sing it again.

Yelling and grunting pierced her gauze of sleep.

Michael? Bullies?

Raven was up and was barking like mad.

No one. No dares here. No Michael. Just a tree drilling into her back like it had been planning to lay roots.

Raven's barking increased in ferocity as the shouting in the distance swelled.

Magdalene used the back of her hand to wipe the sweat from her forehead. She scratched Raven's neck.

"It's just kids playing football," Magdalene told her dog. "Summer Camp football."

Mondauk Summer Camp wasn't a camp in the traditional sense; the kids didn't sleep over; everyone went home at the end of the day. But everything else was pretty much the same as the sleepover camps Magdalene had heard about. It was the best the Catholic community had to offer; Mondauk Proper, being smack up against a muddy, flood-prone creek, didn't offer much in the way of a campground. The neighborhoods to the west and north of the school, built in the '50s, tapered off, in the far northwest, into almost a mini ghost town, a huge cul-de-sac really, bordered by the train tracks and the old asbestos factory. Beyond the abandoned factory, Bethlehem Pike, which ran through the town, curved westward out of Mondauk Proper into Spring House. The old three-story stone houses in the cul-de-sac were now subsidized housing. Magdalene's father had told her Dr. Mattison's company had built the houses during the halcyon days. "A case of too much, too fast," her father had said. Whereas similarly constructed homes in the neighborhoods surrounding the Barrows Bungalow were well tended and sold for insane amounts, this area had fallen on hard times when the factory closed. And squeezed between the ghost town and the Puddle, in the extreme northwest of Mondauk Proper, was Paradise Lakes Trailer Park. The water from the Puddle frequently rose after the summer rains, and the land sloped in such a way that the banks of the Puddle often smelled like raw sewage (especially Paradise Lakes, which had the added complication of an ancient septic system). The run off had, at one time, fed into the Basin Pond, now a frequently muddy picnic area. Despite abutting the woods, Lawndale Fields, to the east of the drained pond, were far from ideal camping grounds.

Lawndale Fields was home to the Mondauk Summer Camp. The Fields ran east from the Basin to the concrete ramps in front of Keasbey Public Elementary School and south from behind Assumption all the way to the hospital. Father Ronald R. Hoskins High, the Catholic high school in Spring House, called the football field home. Assumption claimed the soccer field. Keasbey had its own carefully manicured sports fields. Between the school territories was a large swath of no-man's-land maintained by the county (with significant meddling by the Faith Board). For all the squabbling, Lawndale Fields was carefully tended, the only negative being the flooding from the Puddle, for which no side accepted the blame. In town meetings, the Faith Board chastised Mayor Greene and the County Council for cheaping out the floodwalls. Privately, according to Magdalene's father, the county wished the Faith Board would pray harder. In the middle of the often swampy, but neatly cut grass was a little outhouse of a building that served as headquarters for the Mondauk Summer Camp. All county-endorsed sports (as opposed to Catholic school related extracurricular activities) emanated from this building, and it was from there that Magdalene's father ran Mondauk Proper's football program (including Summer Camp football). It was open to kids of all faiths and schools. Girls played soccer or softball or basketball, touch football even—but not real football. Not under Coach Barrows. Football was for boys.

Magdalene was on the edge of the Fields, her sneakers just beginning to crunch the yellowed grass. She made sure to keep Raven on a tight leash; the dog was salivating at the chance to filch a football. She heard her father before she saw him. There were rows of boys, intent on the coach's—her father's—speech, oblivious to the skinny girl with the chubby dog. By the time she turned the corner of the outhouse headquarters and saw her father addressing the troops, his tie loosened, a clipboard behind his back, his three assistant coaches standing in a tight line behind him, their hands folded behind their backs, Magdalene was unaware of the boys as well. Her father was as captivating in front of ten- to thirteen-year-olds as he was in front of a jury.

(She suddenly remembered watching her father and brother from her bedroom window playing catch, her father still wearing the dual mantle of savior and buddy with only the occasional gin fume polluting the air, Michael making passes, practicing handoffs, the two of them analyzing Michael's footwork, her brother's positioning a perfect series of split-second Polaroids.)

"This is not one of those speeches where an adult tells you how different it was when they were a kid. This is not a speech where I tell you how important it is to be 'involved,'" Coach Barrows said, "and how good it will look on your college application, or how it will make you a better man, or that learning how to lose is as important as learning how to savor a victory. None of these things, gentlemen, not a one, amounts to a hill of beans."

Some boys in the audience tittered; Magdalene saw Jerry Eves' shoulders shake. Beans equaled gas. Sometimes boys never knew when a joke needed to be retired.

"You may think the only reason you're in Summer Camp is because your parents wanted you to have something constructive to do during the summer—which may be true—or that this camp will improve your game, which it will, if you apply yourself. But the real reason, gentlemen, the real reason you are here is because you want to answer the bell that your life has rung; you want a chance to ring that bell for yourself."

Magdalene snorted. Here were these gangly, pimply boys playing *her* game. What she wouldn't give to ring the bell!

"Football—like life—offers you opportunities; it presents

chances—not so much to *win* as to *play*; not so much to *participate* as to *excel*. We can teach you the fundamentals. We'll show you the plays and run your body until it collapses—I'm talking to you, Jerry," her father said suppressing a smile; the other kids poked and punched Jerry Eves who grinned back at her father. Magdalene suppressed a grin of her own; she'd heard this speech a hundred times when she and Michael were little. Magdalene thought Jerry liked her father's attention; in the least, it had to be a relief from the nuns and the rulers; Jerry was used to a different, less positive notice.

"But it's not *what* you do on the field so much—hell, we can *teach* you *everything*—but *how* you do it, *how* you meet your moments head on. Everything you need, gentlemen, is deep inside your souls, buried in the pits of your stomachs, itching from the inner recesses of your muscles, pulsing from your brain cells. You just need to grab hold of these things and say: YES, I'M IN! When your time comes, gentlemen, when your time comes to ring the bell, what will you do? The question always is: *how bad do you want it?*"

The assistant coaches huddled together. It was hard to tell them apart (although Magdalene thought one of them was Frankie Bean, Jr.); they were all more than a little paunchy, their faces oddly misshapen from all the fast food they must have used to buff away their high school football muscles. One of them stepped forward and extended his arm to reveal to the boys a large silver bell hung from a shiny piece of wood. The other two assistant coaches stood on either side of the bell, both holding little metal sticks with black rubber tips. The kids who had attended previous Mondauk Summer Camps knew the drill and formed two lines, their quiet forcing a calm among the neophytes. Two by two, the kids approached the assistants, took the mallets, and struck the bell, yelling to the sky.

"YAWP!" they screamed. "YAWP!"

Her father called the bell the Bell of the Yawp. It had become a Mondauk tradition—so much so, that when Old Man McCullough used to ring the last call bell, all the patrons would yawp at the top of their lungs. (After his death, his daughter Zooey led the yawps herself.) Sporting events of all types were consumed in yawps. Mayor Greene even tried to use the yawp as a part of his campaign slogan during the last election. (Response was negative—yawping belonged to the people—but he was reelected anyway.)

The yawp scared the enemies of the Lawndale Fields' football teams. Opposing teams didn't know if the boys were yelling to God for assistance or if they were just plain crazy, for the players yelled it amongst themselves constantly during a game. They didn't growl or show their teeth. They yawped. It was a form of playing possum—a noisier form. Magdalene used to imagine the drunks in McCullough's staring at their father—the originator of the Mondauk Yawp—slumped over an ashtray and a shot glass.

Magdalene tugged on Raven's leash and got in line on the left. When it was her turn, the assistant coach closest to her—there was simply no distinguishing them; they were all so pudgy; when had *they* stopped ringing the bell?—pulled the mallet away from Magdalene's reach, then relented, eyeballing the other assistants. Magdalene gonged the bell. Raven's breath was warm on her arm. The assistant coach holding the bell was stuffed into a pair of ill-fitting shorts and his socks were pulled up to his knees. When Magdalene yawped into the early summer air, the assistant appeared about ready to vacate his outfit. All the boys stopped and stared too. Magdalene avoided her father's eyes.

"YAWP!" cried Magdalene.

Raven answered her and began twisting himself in his leash, barking and howling.

"YAWP!" screamed Magdalene.

The assistant coaches backed up—the boys too. Except Jerry Eves. He stood in front of her—far enough away to avoid Raven's lunges—and smiled like he knew a secret, a really good secret.

Magdalene faltered. It was her mother's smile—Jerry Eves smiled at her like her mother had.

"YAWP!" Magdalene's voice loosened, then fell flat.

"Yawp!" Magdalene squeaked; her voice was hoarse; her throat felt like sandpaper.

"Okay, that's enough, everyone back—" her father began.

"YAWP!" Jerry Eves screamed, his head tossed back, helmet in his hands, the cords on his neck like liquid steel beams.

"Okay, okay," her father said.

"YAWP!" Jerry Eves repeated, and Magdalene realized with a jump that *if* she liked boys (she didn't, not really; not yet) *and* if she wasn't planning on being dead within a week (give or take a few days; she still had mysteries to solve and her dog to murder), she *might* like Jerry Eves, despite his constant fart jokes—or maybe because of them. Anyone who could squeeze so much humor from such an exhausted subject matter was worthy of a second look. True, she didn't find much humor in Stick Man or in any of Jerry's other extracurricular comedic routines, but still, here he was, yawping his lungs out, taking up her cause—a cause of which she was only dimly aware. She renewed her vow to add a flatulence reference or two into her book.

The other boys murmured to each other and nodded. Jimmy Lonergan belched: "YAWP!" and the rest of the camp fell in. The assistant coaches continued to back up and look at one another, as if the others' pimply faces and fat deposits held any answers.

"YAWP!" cried the boys to a man; even the rookies were yawping. Jerry howled with glee and stared at Magdalene. Magdalene's skin color had baked into a deep Crayola red.

"*Hup, hup, hup!*" her father said. "Lonergan—take the rooks out to the west field and punt to them. Eves, you and Connelly lead the rest in laps, then take 'em out to the tackle dummies."

The assistant coaches had finally halted their retreat and were busy looking down at their stomachs. Her father had broken up the yawping circle by delegating to the kids, not to the lumpy assistants. If this is what happened when you gave up on living but continued to breathe, Magdalene thought, looking at the three clueless men eyeballing her father, then maybe it was better to follow her course of action, no matter how extreme.

Her father pointed and the assistants jogged (sort of) after their charges.

"How did the first of the exams go?" her father asked; it was as if the yawps had never happened.

"Exams?" Magdalene asked, her mind painting big red targets on the jiggling behinds of the assistant coaches, and a big, red Valentine heart (*what the heck?*) on the lanky figure of Jerry Eves in the far left field—only on his helmet, not his bottom.

"Exams. You remember those, Maddie," her father said. "Pencils. Paper. Nuns."

"Good," she lied. "Good."

"What did you take today?"

"Religion," Magdalene said. "Religion."

Watching Jerry Eves and Jim Lonergan and the other boys work off their yawps in the Fields, Magdalene realized that she could yawp all she wanted, but even if her voice held out, she could never convince herself. She had missed her one, real chance at ringing the bell; that much was for sure. She just couldn't remember when or how.

Two, three, five, seven, eleven, thirteen, seventeen...

Her father grabbed her shoulders and shook her. Magdalene jumped back and stepped on Raven's paw. The dog hid behind her father.

"I'm sorry, Maddie. Jesus, I'm sorry," her father said.

Magdalene looked into his face; he had never touched her like that before. Her father had never been physical with either her or Michael. He'd punished by taking away what they loved the most—unplugging Michael's stereo for the weekend or telling Magdalene she couldn't read the Hardy Boys for three days. He'd doled out punishments that worked, Magdalene thought, because they interrupted the normal pattern of things. His hands shaking her shoulders seemed obscene.

"I'm sorry," he said again. "Quitting smoking is harder the second time around."

"Can I run laps with the team?" Magdalene asked. She wanted the subject to end; seeing her father's angry face had scared her, and she'd been frightened enough today.

"You know you can't, Maddie. I can't allow you to join practice when I don't allow girls on the tackle team. It would set a precedent."

"Prec-e-dent," Magdalene said, sounding out the syllables for no discernible reason. "I'm not asking to play; I just want to run laps."

"And then what's our boy Raven going to do?" her father asked, rubbing the dog's ears.

A Lab's ears are made of *SILK*, Magdalene thought. She could do with a little *SILK* herself right now: something precious and valuable and unique. Michael had had *SILK*.

"He could just watch," Magdalene said, almost whispering. She knew she had lost the opportunity.

"Where are you headed now?" her father asked; he knew the discussion was over too.

Magdalene thought for a moment: Sol's to see Mrs. Bochdan and explain about the trash cans? Katie's to see if the Turtle Theory was correct?

"The library," Magdalene lied.

"Well, mind Mrs. Stanley. She's a doozy."

Her father kicked at the yellowed grass.

"If we could just get the town to invest more in the program—not just football—but the whole thing. Lawndale Fields. Assumption's too poor to invest—at least that's what Father Dave said. Who knows? I've talked to Hugh a million times, but it's really up to the County Council; they hold the purse strings, and getting a dime out of them is like…

"Separation of church and state," he sighed. "Everyone's so geared up for a fight over the old asbestos factory, no one wants to upset the apple cart. But you watch when the carnival weekend hits. Money will be flying and so will the fur." He shook his head. "I have to get back to the office."

Magdalene followed little of what her father said—Jerry Eves was back and putting his head in the water fountain; the younger kids followed his lead.

"Lonergan," her father said, walking away, "round up the rooks and bring 'em over here."

Jerry Eves stood close enough to Magdalene for her to smell his sweat. Raven sniffed at his cleats. Magdalene seriously wondered if Jerry could read her thoughts—that smile on his face; she had never seen him wearing that particular smile before. She turned her head to watch her father, trailed by the fumbling assistants, run drills.

"Was that for your brother?" Jerry Eves asked."The yawp?"

Magdalene jerked her head around, and her eyes met Jerry's.

God, they are so *blue*, Magdalene thought. And twinkling. Like stars. It didn't just happen in the movies.

"He was great, you know," Jerry said. "Not just football, but yeah, he was great at football too."

Then where is he, Magdalene wanted to ask.

"I didn't know you were friends," Magdalene said. She found that Jerry was shrinking away from her eyes now. Was this how the boy-girl thing worked? Back and forth?

Nineteen, twenty-three, twenty-nine, thirty-one, thirty-seven, forty-one, forty-three…

"We were. School friends, right? Teammates. Geeks and gawds."

"Eves!" her father yelled from inside a huddle.

Magdalene couldn't stop looking at Jerry's face. How hadn't she noticed before that his face, festooned with freckles, resembled a star map?

"That's why *I* did it, Tonto," Jerry Eves said, snapping on his helmet. "I did it for Michael."

As she watched Jerry run towards her father, Magdalene thought: *I did it for me. I've lost my brother. I don't know where he is. I did it for me.*

+

Magdalene walked back to Sol's. Raven lagged a step behind her; he was beat from the adventuring. She knew she should have cleaned up all the trash and righted the trash cans before she'd run to the Fields. Mrs. Bochdan would have known then that she was a serious girl, not a girl to be taken lightly. It's what one of Michael's Legion of Super-Heroes members would have done. Frank and Joe Hardy? For sure!

But when she reached the corner, the trash cans were back in the little yard, tied to the fence with rope. All the trash on the street had either been blown away or picked up; Magdalene figured the latter: someone had swept the sidewalk around Sol's with a broom recently too; the street dust was neatly lined. She'd dillydallied at Summer Camp too long. She would have to be careful with her time if she expected to accomplish all of her missions before she died, she thought. Stupid boys. What did Jerry Eves have to do with any of this anyway?

Raven peed on the weeds growing along Sol's fence. Magdalene pulled him back and led him to a lot a block and a half away to poop. Seeing the fluid broom lines in the dust had been a showstopper. She didn't feel up to facing Mrs. Bochdan a second time today. She decided to brave Mr. McAllister's again. Besides, she had to fill Katie in. Plus, Magdalene thought, if the Turtle Theory had any validity, then it was her duty to do what she could for Katie. Maybe the little girl was in real trouble. Lord knows Mr. McAllister was a dirty, vile man. Magdalene could tell what he had for dinner just by looking at his t-shirt! If he was willing to forbid Magdalene from baby-sitting Katie because of a couple of suicide attempts and then lie about it, what else was he capable of?

Katie's house was northwest of Sol's, but Magdalene took the longer route so that she could stop by the Methodist cemetery. Rosewood Seton wouldn't have entangled herself in this mess like Magdalene had; Magdalene was sure the woman had died without tying herself to any one person or situation. If one couldn't pass the tests with flying colors, then maybe one could live to a ripe old age by simply avoiding them altogether. Magdalene wondered where Aunt

Tiddy fit in the this particular theory; Aunt Tiddy was perpetually cranky, she cursed like a sailor, yet she'd moved to the Barrows Bungalow for the singular purpose of helping out with Magdalene as ADA Barrows rediscovered sobriety. Maybe Magdalene was Tiddy's test.

While Raven grazed in the grass nearby, dragging his leash, Magdalene fell asleep (again) leaning against Rosewood Seton's stone; When she woke, the sun had moved from one side of the sky to the other. If Mrs. Nicholas had seen her... Magdalene banished the thought from her head. (Were those *numbers* hiding back there?—it wasn't unusual for her to wake already counting.) She was stretching her achy legs when she realized Raven was gone. He had been wearing his blue collar with identification tags. But still—how could she have been so stupid, so careless? If anything happened to Raven, it would be her fault. If Raven went missing like Michael...

Raven shook himself awake and yawned from the other side of Rosewood Seton's gravestone. He stopped to scratch himself. Magdalene hoped it wasn't fleas. Fleas hid themselves in the tall grass that bracketed the back end of the cemetery.

"Good boy," she said, taking hold of Raven's leash. "I thought something had happened to you."

Raven wagged his tail and yawned again. Magdalene rubbed his ears, and Raven growled low in his throat.

Magdalene thought: *a Lab's ears*...but couldn't finish.

Magdalene scratched Raven's tummy, and he rolled over in the grass in front of Rosewood Seton's headstone. Raven was the harbinger: she had to take care of him before she took care of herself. (*Take care.*) There was no way she could let him suffer her disappearance if she was actually capable of pulling off her own magic act.

Magdalene looked at the sun again. There would be time enough to mull this over later. She had to reach Katie's before Mr. McAllister came home from work or wherever he was.

Magdalene walked Raven west towards Katie's, trying to avoid, unsuccessfully, the streets that seemed filled with kids. How they stared! Magdalene could see them whispering behind cupped hands; she could see them move out of her way—as if she were a leper from Dr. Fuller's book. The boys played wire ball and touch football and street hockey and stickball. The girls were gathered on steps to watch the boys. How pathetic, Magdalene thought, too disgusted at the girls to realize she was counting under her breath. There was Donna Gaynor, sitting on a stoop, pretending Magdalene wasn't passing her murder of crows walking a large black dog. There was Lila Lillianfield, cheering the boys along in their game, her shorts too tight, her thighs bruised, her eyelids painted a startling fuchsia. Someone laughed (was that Megan Riley?—Megan couldn't even perform long division!) and Magdalene had to pull a growling Raven away from their gaggle.

Bullies.

Two, four, six, eight, ten, twelve pairs of eyes.

"Resurrection girl," someone said.

Was that Donna Gaynor's voice? Boy, Christina was going to be pissed when she heard about *this*, Magdalene whispered to herself. Christina didn't like it when the Bod Squad picked on her best friend.

How had she become a pariah? Because she had tried to die— twice? Because her brother was missing and her mother was dead and her father just recently dragged himself away from his Camels and his scotch and waters and whatever else came in large plastic bottles with Russian names? Someone had taken all of this from her: her friends, her brother. She felt like Job—except she didn't have much of a relationship with God to begin with. She believed God was there, in the heavens, but she was beginning to wonder how *involved* He actually was. Why had He abandoned her? Why had He allowed Michael to disappear? What kind of God would put the test of fire before poor Sister Mary Magdalene de Rosa? And what kind of God would put a sweet dog like Raven through the same hell as her? Either one who didn't care all that much or no God at all. Magdalene wondered how far away she was from believing that: no God at all.

Magdalene and Raven took up their point of surveillance in the berry bushes across from Mr. McAllister's house. The Chevy was in the driveway, of course, which meant nothing; there was way of telling if Mr. McAllister was home. Magdalene didn't want to confront Valerie Plum again either; just thinking of Valerie doing the job that had been Magdalene's for three summers and odd weekends made her sick to her stomach.

Magdalene felt in her pocket, and her fingers touched her last few coins. She looked both ways before crossing the street and held her breath like she was jumping into the Puddle. (There it was *again*: the Puddle. What about the goddamn Puddle?) She shushed Raven and eased open the gate to Mr. McAllister's backyard. They hid themselves beneath the dogwood tree for a few minutes. When Katie's shadow crossed by the double back room windows, Magdalene tossed a penny.

The screen rattled, and Katie stuck out her head.

"Sure making a racket out there!"

"Can you come down?" Magdalene stage whispered.

"Sure. The witchy-witch is here though. Hi Raven!"

Katie left the window. Magdalene struggled with Raven's leash.

"What are you sniffing at, Boo?"

Raven dragged Magdalene to the holly bush in the far left corner of the yard.

"You're gonna get your nose pricked by those leaves, Raven."

Katie tiptoed across the yard in her bare feet. She was in her pajamas.

"I pulled the kitchen curtains closed, just in case," Katie said. "Do you want to see my new hermit crab?"

"I have to tell you about my mission," Magdalene said.

A long, thin, red cut ran down the right side of Katie's snowy cheek.

"Katie, did you cut yourself shaving?"

"I don't shave! No, I was climbing the tree and I fell. Got in trouble. I'm not allowed to climb anymore. Valerie got in *worse* trouble. Daddy went to her house and talked to her dad."

Magdalene ran a finger down the length of Katie's cheek.

"A branch did this?"

"Yep. Hey, that cat's been—"

"A branch?"

"Yep. Did I show you my hermit crab? He has to live in a shell, and when he grows too big for the one he has, he searches for another one that's bigger and then moves in! Just backs up! That's what the book says anyway."

"So if the first one is too..." Magdalene paused, "dangerous?...then he moves to a new one?"

"No, silly," Katie said, "they just get too *big*. The crabs."

"For their home? They outgrow their home?"

"Their shell. Magdalene, you okay? You look sad."

"Do you know what happened in school last week?"

Katie crossed herself.

"Joseph and Henry," Katie said. She bowed her head when she said each name.

Magdalene nodded.

"I've been following Mrs. Bochdan."

"The mom—"

"The mom of the shooter? Yeah, but Katie, I think I know why Joseph did it. I mean, I think I know why it happened. Oh, it's confusing."

Magdalene sat on the ground and put her head in her hands. Raven pulled on the leash. Katie walked over to the dog and rubbed his chest and tummy while he sat pretty and licked the cut on her face.

"Did you know a dog's saliva has a healing agent?" Katie asked.

From a tangle of arms and hair: "What do you mean by healing agent?"

"Not sure," Katie said, "but I read it in the Funk and Wagnalls, I think. Dogs can help in the healing process."

"And who helps dogs in theirs?"

"I don't know," Katie said. She stopped petting Raven. "Why are you following Mrs. Bochdan?"

Magdalene lifted her head; Raven pawed at Katie to continue.

"I was looking for clues."

"Clues?" Katie's voice twisted into a higher register.

"You sound like the nuns, Katie," Magdalene said, and Katie belly-laughed, covering her mouth with her hands.

"If Joseph shot Henry by accident, Katie, then Joseph won't have to go to jail. Henry was his best friend. He didn't just shoot his best friend. It would be like me shooting you. I would never shoot anyone I loved, even if I was really mad at them. I mean, I used to get so mad at Michael."

Katie's eyes went wide. Raven sat up at attention.

Magdalene continued: "I think the bullies were after Henry—not like chasing him—but sort of. Making his life hell."

Katie covered her mouth again.

"Sorry, but it's the truth, I think. And Joseph was just trying to protect his friend. He stole the gun from wherever to scare the bullies away."

Magdalene thought it best to not mention her shadow theory: that Joseph may have stolen the gun to take Henry out of his misery; that maybe Joseph had a very mature flash-forward and saw Henry suffering his way through the Mondauk Catholic school system and wanted to remove the misery from the boy's life by removing him.

"They were picking on Henry?"

"I don't know for sure, but I bet Mrs. Bochdan knows. She's the lady who runs Sol's, right? She sees how kids act. She would know. Maybe Joseph told his mom that he and Henry were getting picked on."

"I think his mom would have told by now," Katie said. Her hands caressed Raven's ears.

A Lab's ears are made of *SILK*, Magdalene thought, unless the Lab is dead.

"Maybe, maybe not. Maybe she hasn't thought of it yet. Or maybe she doesn't even know her son was trying to be a hero. But if I talk to her, maybe she'll give me some more information, tell me something that would help bring the pieces together. It's Joseph's only hope. They'll send him to jail."

"They don't send kids to jail, silly."

"They send them to kids' jail, and that's bad enough. We can't let the bullies get away with this. This whole world..." Magdalene said, not aware that she was crying, barely conscious of Katie staring at her.

Katie placed her lithe arms around Raven. Raven tried to lick Magdalene's face while keeping one eye focused on the holly bush.

"...this whole damn world—sorry, Katie, but that's what it is— it's all about bullies and dares, I swear to God. No one is happy with the way things are. Everyone wants to be either on top of everyone else, or they want to make everyone else do things they shouldn't do."

"Dares?" Katie asked. "Like 'I double-dare you'?"

Magdalene grabbed Katie's hands. The leash went slack, and Raven crept towards the holly bush.

"Don't ever say that," Magdalene whispered. "Swear to me you won't ever say the D word."

Katie's eyes were ovals, and she swore—to God and Minnie the turtle and the lizards and the bunnies and the guinea pig and her dad—that she would never, ever make a dare.

"It's a mystery, Katie. But if I can find out who was picking on Henry, then maybe Joseph won't have to go to jail or juvenile hall. He won't have to leave his mom."

Katie let go of the leash and hugged Magdalene. Raven lunged for the holly bush. A fat tabby cat bounced like a ball to the top of the fence and leapt into to the next yard. Raven released his most ferocious bark (which, in Magdalene's opinion, was never that ferocious or vicious, but rather just loud and boastful, like Jerry Eves telling a dirty joke during History class) and ran headlong into the prickly holly bush.

"Raven!" Katie cried and ran after the dog.

Magdalene leaned her head back in the grass. Katie didn't have a dog; guinea pigs and lizards didn't chase after anything except maybe bugs. Raven had spent last spring howling and chasing a tailless tabby that had been hanging out on the Barrows' property. This tabby was fatter (and had a tail), but Raven had developed a tabby-chasing disposition.

"Oscar Sceebers!" Katie cried. "Oscar Sceebers!"

Magdalene closed her eyes. Her entire body was tired—she felt like she hadn't had real sleep in weeks. Why couldn't every day be like this one, Magdalene asked herself: baby-sitting Katie, feeling the warmth of the sun, knowing the rest of the day promised the pleasures of summer. Freeze Tag, Freedom, Puddle Jumping with Michael, touch football.

Except she didn't like Puddle Jumping, now did she?

The truth, the truth: two minus one equals one. And one stands alone.

A shadow fell across Magdalene's skinny frame.

"What the *hell* are you doing here?" Valerie Plum asked. Her eyes were heavy slashes of mascara.

Magdalene jumped to her feet. Her mouth was open, but she couldn't locate any words. (Was she about to yawp in Valerie Plum's face?) Katie ran back with Raven's leash, a whimpering dog behind her, a holly leaf stuck to his hose.

And a one and a two and a three and a four...

"She was just leaving, Val," Katie said. "She stopped by to show me Raven."

At the mention of his name, Raven attempted a bark, then whined and groveled.

Magdalene knelt and pulled the prickly holly leaf from her dog's nose. Raven licked her hand.

"You know what your dad said," Valerie huffed. "I'm telling."

Katie grimaced: "I saw you with Paul Stern."

Valerie flipped her carefully feathered hair and put a hand on her hip.

"You saw nothing. You don't know crap, Katie McAllister. Mind your own beeswax."

"I saw you in the driveway in Daddy's car," Katie said, "and Paul Stern had his hand on your boobie. I saw *that*. I might even have taken pictures with my camera. Daddy gave me a camera last year for Christmas, and he told me to take lots of pictures."

"You wouldn't dare."

"I wouldn't risk it, Val," Magdalene said without looking up from Raven.

"I'm *supposed* to tell," Valerie said weakly.

"Go ahead and tell," Katie said. "But your face sure is red."

"I'm sure Mr. McAllister wouldn't mind you making out in his car with Paul Stern," Magdalene said as Katie turned her back.

"I'm supposed to tell," Valerie repeated, but she was already walking into the house.

"Paul dumped me," she added before slamming the screen door.

Magdalene collapsed on the grass. Raven, who had managed to fall asleep, opened his eyes, licked her cheek, and went back to his nap. Katie danced around Magdalene and Raven.

"That'll teach ol' Valerie Plum," Katie cried.

Here it comes again: Magdalene squeezed her eyes shut and let herself ascend. She was leaving her body, reaching for the trees, the smell of dirty water strong in her nostrils, the leaves on the low hanging branches tickling the top of her head.

She held her breath: *one two three four five six seven...*

Katie stood over her and released a tiny fistful of dogwood blossoms onto Magdalene's face. Magdalene opened her eyes, took a breath, and watched the petals float (*float float float*) down over her eyes.

"Don't be sad, Magdalene. You've got a mystery to solve," Katie said. "Like Scooby-Doo. You have a dog and everything!"

"Except friends."

"What?"

"Shaggy had friends," Magdalene said, "to help."

"I'm your friend," Katie said. She danced in a circle, tossing dogwood blossoms into the air. Raven opened his eyes and followed a single blossom as it floated down to Magdalene's face.

Katie slid into Magdalene's side like she was sliding into third base.

"Magdalene, Magdalene, maybe if you solve the mystery and help save Joseph Bochdan, Daddy will let you come back and baby-sit me for the rest of the summer."

"That's wishful thinking."

"Now's a good time for wishes," Katie said, and she picked up a few dogwood blossoms and laid their soft petals on Magdalene's cheeks and forehead and lips.

"Do you know the Legend of the Dogwood, Magdalene?"

Do you know the Mystery of the Puddle, Magdalene asked inside her head.

"Well, I have this book, *Everything's Coming Up Jesus*. It's not Catholic, Daddy said." Katie frowned as she worked out her thoughts. "There's all kinds of stories in there that aren't in the Bible exactly."

"Exactly?"

"Exactly! That's why they're legends. Sister Jezebel said legends are stories that probably didn't happen but have a kernel of truth. Popcorn!"

"Third grade, huh?" Magdalene asked from beneath her blanket of dogwood petals. Something about being buried, even if only by several dogwood blossoms, was familiar, comforting in the way that counting out the sleeping pills had been.

"What does that mean?" Katie looked a little hurt; Magdalene could just make out her face between the pink-purples of the petals. "You know I'm going to start fourth grade in the fall."

"I was kidding," Magdalene said. The dogwood petals smelled like the Puddle.

Katie kissed Raven on his nose. Magdalene remembered Michael giving a confused Raven Eskimo kisses—nose to nose—before they'd climb into bed.

"Well, in this book," Katie began, "there's a whole chapter on the Legend of the Dogwood. You see, dogwoods used to grow big and tall like oak trees. This was back in the days of the Bible. And the Romans, they cut down a dogwood to get wood to make the cross for Jesus 'cause it was such a strong tree. But the dogwood grew distressed—that means upset; I looked it up!—and Jesus on the cross had mercy for the dogwood and forgave the tree."

Katie knitted her eyebrows.

"Actually, the book said 'absolved.' It's weird: the dogwood didn't *choose* to be cut down and made into a cross. Anyhow, Jesus changed the tree's shape so that it would forever grow skinny and twisted. The Romans would never be able to use the dogwood for making crosses again. And He formed the blossoms into a cross with four petals and a crown of thorns in the middle. Did you ever notice how the tips of the petals are stained with blood? Jesus' blood! Or maybe it's the tears of the dogwood. I forget. But anyway, the dogwood is supposed to remind us that Jesus loved us even though He was suffering. All the dogwood had to do was remain strong, and Jesus took care of it."

Magdalene peeked through the purple of Jesus' blood. Katie had paused and composed her face into the most serious face Magdalene had ever seen her wear—and Katie was pretty serious for someone in the third grade…er, fourth grade. Magdalene brushed the petals from her face and sat up.

"That's what you have to do, Magdalene. Be like the dogwood. Jesus will see you through."

Was Jesus deaf to the yawp, Magdalene wondered. This strong and silent stance sounded like horse hockey.

The little girl handed Magdalene a fistful of dogwood blossoms. Magdalene stuffed them into her pocket. Katie looked close to tears, and Magdalene stroked her friend's face, tracing the long, thin cut on her cheek.

"Is there something you want to tell me?" Magdalene asked. This was someone Willa should have drawing pictures, Magdalene thought, not her. Katie was someone bursting with hurt.

Katie threw her arms around Magdalene, and Magdalene knew her hunch was right: she needed to rescue Katie too. So much to accomplish before she died! Magdalene's bones were weary. Just knowing she needed *another* plan—this time for Katie—was exhausting. She couldn't "take care" of Katie like she could Raven.

There was a rustle near the dead little garden that ran the length of the back of the house. Raven saw it too. Magdalene put one hand on his collar.

"Katie?" Magdalene asked; the girl was holding tight to Magdalene's neck, but she wasn't crying—not yet. Poor thing, Magdalene thought. "Katie?"

Raven scrambled to a sitting position and watched a turtle attempt a left turn in the loose dirt. Raven's head cocked to the side, his tail swept the grass, and his mouth hung open, tongue lolling, in a smile. Magdalene tried to smile back: this was what Raven had looked like when he was a puppy, she was sure.

"Katie, is that Minnie?"

Katie ran towards the turtle and scooped it up as Raven barked and shivered with excitement. Magdalene stepped on his leash.

"I didn't even know she was missing!" Katie cried. Minnie pulled her head and appendages into her shell of ever-shifting colors. A mood shell, Magdalene thought.

"How did she get out, Katie? She couldn't have climbed out."

There was the thought again: was the turtle Katie's way of saying things she could never dare speak aloud—just like the little kids who drew sobbing self-portraits and pictures of bleeding mommies and smoking daddies and people falling from buildings into blankets of flame.

Magdalene kissed the top of Katie's head.

"I'll think of something," Magdalene told her. She jogged towards the gate, tugging on Raven's leash. "I'll come back when I do. Just hang on."

Raven took a couple of final sniffs of Minnie and licked Katie's protective fingers.

Magdalene pulled her reluctant, doomed dog to the street and plotted her course home through the badlands of the cupped whispers and averted eyes of her classmates and neighbors. She needed a lie or two for Aunt Tiddy. As Magdalene swiftly crossed corners and cut through backyards, she thought: *I'm barely going to have time enough to die!*

+

Snap fizz whirr.

The silent movie star hid behind her hands. Her nails were chewed and ragged. The Polaroids came into focus like the Puddle after a rainstorm.

Magdalene shook the photograph. The silent movie star melted in the Technicolor rain. Magdalene tossed the picture on a stack of other Polaroids. Aunt Tiddy had gotten into her head that what Magdalene needed to fill her time (and shield her from unhealthy thoughts) was a hobby—a scrapbook specifically. A scrapbook of Polaroids taken by Aunt Tiddy. Magdalene, Raven, even ADA Barrows had suffered the *snap fizz whirr* indignity of Aunt Tiddy's instant camera.

A half of a toasted cheese sandwich was thrust under Magdalene's nose. A halo of glistening potato chips surrounded a wet slice of pickle.

"And how was your exam?" Aunt Tiddy asked, turning away to face the stove.

Magdalene knew Tiddy was disappointed just from her tone. Magdalene glanced down at the blurred Polaroid to make sure LIAR wasn't painted across her forehead.

"Fine. Good," Magdalene answered. In her pockets: one, two, three, four dogwood blossoms.

"Science, was it?"

Magdalene couldn't remember her lie. "Yep, that was it," she answered. "Science."

One, two, three…

"Raven help you with your studies?"

Magdalene choked on a piece of toast and waved away Tiddy's silent offer of a glass of tap water.

"He was…he was running around outside, so I brought him to school. No one seemed to mind."

A crumb of toast migrated to Magdalene's nose.

"Oh, that's good. Well, if Sister Mary Joseph calls me back, I can let her know you were home safe and sound by…" Tiddy stared at the backwards clock, "a quarter after five, and she can tell me all about how the dog did in school."

Magdalene closed her eyes. Maybe Tiddy was bluffing. Raven slept by Magdalene's feet, his head resting on Monkey, his eyes squinted in somnolent concentration—and yet, he was vigilant, sensitive to every movement, bouncing awake when she shifted her legs. The trick was not to get distracted from the mysteries at hand, Magdalene decided. She blew her nose into a tissue and peeked at the results.

(Michael had always asked her: "What color is it?" It was a running joke—a nose running joke.)

Tiddy pulled out the old, silver pocket watch, twisted the crown, shook her head, and returned it down the ugly red and purple checkered apron she insisted upon wearing all day long. The pocket watch went with every wardrobe ensemble; its disinterment (Magdalene's father would have smiled at that word!) was followed by much squinting, winding, and slow shakes of her aunt's head, as if to say: in my day, time was precious; a twenty-four hour day was a luxury.

"Your father called me from the office and said you were down by camp today."

"During a break in school."

Tiddy poured the water down the sink and washed the glass.

"You sign up for camp?"

Magdalene looked at Tiddy's back.

"You know Daddy won't let me."

"Did you try?"

Magdalene tore the crust from her toast.

"You try talking to him."

"I did," Tiddy said, turning to face Magdalene; Magdalene looked away. "Right before he left for his AA meeting last night. And I'll talk to him again tonight and the night after that and the one that falls after that one. Your father is trying something that no one thought he'd be able to do after your mother passed and your brother...but he's doing it. Goes to reason he shouldn't stand in *your* way, and I won't let him, not on my watch."

Magdalene felt a passing hope warm her hands and throat—the exact place on her throat where the autumn wind would catch when she played football during any of the innumerable touch games she and Michael organized among the kids in the schoolyard, the street, the backyard, the same kids that avoided her company now that Michael was gone.

...four, five, six...

What was with the counting, anyway?

Magdalene brushed it off. The mysteries needed all her attention. Tiddy had gone back to the stove. What good would football do her now, Magdalene thought.

Assistant District Attorney Gregory Barrows came through the back door in a rush of air (bus exhaust, Wrigley's gum, sweat) and laid his briefcase on the kitchen table, kissing the top of Magdalene's head as he passed.

"How are my girls?" he asked.

"You're late," Tiddy said.

"We're working overtime on the Cabot Case," her father said; Magdalene blushed. "We need to come to a consensus on how we're going to handle it—hell, a decision hasn't even been made on what we're going to charge the boy with, let alone the mother."

"The poor woman."

...seven, eight, nine...

"I know, I know. We have a warrant out for the father, but he's gone, left town, hightailed it out of here."

Tiddy scowled.

"He's not in Mondauk County anyway," her father said. "How was your religion exam, Maddie?"

Magdalene blushed even harder if that was possible; Tiddy ignored her and prepared a plate for her father.

"Fine, Daddy. Good."

"What do you have tomorrow?"

"Science," Magdalene said; she was befuddled now.

"We're going to hit the books tonight," Aunt Tiddy said as she set the table, "aren't we, Magdalene?"

Her father focused on his plate.

Is this how adults really talk? Tuning each other out and then tuning back in when they felt like it?

Magdalene threw a Hail Mary pass. "Daddy, can I go play at Christina's tonight. I'll be home by dark."

Tiddy rapped her knuckles against a pot.

"Sure, Maddie. Tell her I said hi. Her father too. I haven't seen Dr. Fuller in a dog's age."

"She's got to study," Aunt Tiddy said.

...ten, eleven, twelve...

The numbers danced in her head until they assembled themselves into a melody she recognized—the ladybug song!

"She's got to enjoy her summer, too, Tiddy. No harm in that. You're ready for the test, right Maddie?"

"Yep!"

"Science was it?" Tiddy asked, but Magdalene was already halfway through the back door, humming now:

...and they all played games at the ladybugs' picnic.

+

She had never felt so alive! The irony was not lost on Magdalene. She understood that sometimes things simply didn't add up. How could she be days away from dying, and yet so filled with excitement? God, Magdalene thought, wouldn't it be great if she didn't have to die? Still, she was smart enough to know that everything that was happening was conditional; all the mysteries were there for her to make up for failing to solve the biggest mystery of all, the Mystery of the Puddle, and thus she had to unravel them all.

Instead of walking to Christina's, she turned west towards Katie's house again, though she had no real destination; she just wanted space to think it all out: Katie and Mr. McAllister; Mrs. Bochdan and Joseph; Raven. Besides, Magdalene didn't know if she could stomach Christina right now—let alone Mrs. Fuller.

The good news was that Christina's goth phase, which had lasted all through the fall and winter, had appeared to subside just before Magdalene's second suicide attempt. Christina was too enamored with the Bod Squad's top tastemakers and too easily swayed by their peer pressure to join the punk and goth kids who hung out at the fountain in the Common. Christina simply liked to wear black and apply heavy eyeliner; she said she was goth, so Magdalene had shrugged and agreed—at least it had been a conversation. Around the time of the leper investigation with Dr. Fuller, Christina had taken her Gucci shoes out of the closet, and her late spring attire had consisted of a variety of pastels. Summer would be the death knell of goth. (Magdalene bet Christina was glad the Fullers had forbidden their daughter to dye her hair black!)

"Goth is all about how you feel on the inside," Christina had said to her. "We all carry a darkness." But Christina had shut up almost as soon as she had begun; after all, she had been talking to the Resurrection Girl.

Between hospitalizations, their friendship had maintained a cordial if distant connection. Christina's well-practiced (and frequently misplaced) cynicism found no purchase in Magdalene; Magdalene's worry-stones were worn smooth, and the dark circles around her eyes had not come from a makeup counter. Still, Magdalene missed Christina's goofy nonchalance and the ease with which she slipped off one mask to don another: nothing original in Christina (Magdalene felt Christina should be thankful goth was the current trend and not clown noses), but it beat being stuck with the same dour face and excessive eye luggage.

When they were younger—before Christina's ascension within the ranks of the Bod Squad—Christina had told Magdalene that she thought that the two of them would rule the school: the daughters of a doctor and a lawyer! Magdalene thought her absurd. The bullies ruled the school; everyone knew that. The bullies had been part of the scholastic makeup of Assumption since the first grade. The popular crowd had always surrounded itself with its share of bullies, like bodyguards, and the jocks were too busy with sports to worry about bullies at all. Hell, some of them were part-time bullies in the off-season. Magdalene wanted nothing to do with bullies; she had her share of bullying at home.

Christina had had a crush on Michael; everyone had known it, Michael included. Magdalene had found this mildly annoying, but understandable. Her brother *was* good-looking in a raffish way. His black hair flopped in his green eyes, eyes that Magdalene always thought were too big and when combined with his contagious grin often meant Magdalene would end the day at the bottom of a compost pile or dangling from a dogwood. Michael's hands were big too, like a puppy's paws. Their father said he could have played wide receiver just as easily as quarterback, his hands were that big. But Michael's brain ran on its own steam and quarterback was where he belonged. He liked calling the plays or making one up on the spot (a practice that had annoyed their father to no end, at least on the field, but Magdalene thought him secretly proud of his son's leadership prowess). If their father made the team run laps, Michael always ran one extra—and more than half the boys followed his lead. Michael liked to push everything just a little bit further if for no other reason than because he could. He called it lighting fires.

He was the same way with the dares.

The Truth or Dare game had emerged in the summer of 2001.

It was late summer, just before Michael went missing. They'd been playing indoors. The rain had been drumming intricate, lulling patterns on the roof, and the Barrows Bungalow smelled damp. The basement smelled the worst; the basement smelled like feet. They had exhausted every indoor game possible. Christina was there—so were nascent Bod Squader tramps Megan Riley and Peggy Runyon.

Their father had been at work, and Magdalene and Michael knew he would stop by McCullough's on the way home; there was no escaping that place then, not for their father, not since their mother had died the year before.

"What now?" Peggy asked.

Michael removed his shirt. Peggy and Megan pretended not to notice his muscles. Christina stared at his hairless chest.

"Truth or dare," Michael said.

"I'll go first," said Christina.

Magdalene sat in the corner, her back to the wall. The last game—a rather physical game that required them to keep a sweat sock filled with dog cookies away from Raven—had wiped her out. She had hit her head twice on the low overhang by the top of the basement stairs. The Bod Squaders were annoyed by her presence, and Magdalene was tired of watching them fawn over her brother. Just the year before they had all been on a somewhat equal social standing. Then, BANG!: Christina and Megan and Peggy, Valerie Plum even, just about the entire sixth grade class of Assumption of Our Lady (well, the girls anyway) started developing breasts—nothing too breathtaking, although Christina was easily ahead of the pack, but breasts nonetheless. Magdalene? Flat as a board and easy to screw, Michael teased. And now, in the reeking basement, Michael was (suddenly) a god. The girls hung on his every word; they *ooohed* and *ahhhed* over stories of his athletic accomplishments. They brushed up against him like a pack of starving alley cats. Magdalene was disgusted and jealous.

"Have you ever wet your bed?" Michael asked Christina.

Magdalene snorted. Christina sat on the floor and crossed her legs Indian-style.

This was an unfortunate game. Christina had, in fact, wet her bed, and rather recently. Furthermore, Magdalene knew that Christina, who hadn't looked at Magdalene yet, would suspect she'd told her brother although she hadn't. Christina would suspect Magdalene because Magdalene had been in Christina's bed when the latest incontinence incident occurred.

Christina bit her lower lip.

"She did!" squealed Megan Riley with her usual amount of viciousness. Magdalene hung her head. Unless Christina had told her, which Magdalene highly doubted (Megan Riley leaked secrets like a sieve), Megan was playing off Christina's obvious body language.

"Yeah, when I was like four years old," Christina said, but now even Peggy Runyon, normally a good little Catholic girl, was contorting her face into a joker mask, covering her mouth, and pointing at Christina.

"Dare," Christina said, launching a grenade of a look towards Magdalene.

"You already answered the question," Magdalene said, hoping to help her. "You said you did it when you were four."

Christina ignored her. "Dare me."

Michael smiled at his sister and stretched, showing off his muscles.

"Kiss me," Michael said to Christina, "for thirty seconds."

Megan squealed again. Peggy, finally caught up in her

Catholicism, cringed and gasped. Magdalene stared at the floor. Michael was lighting fires again.

Christina crawled towards Michael and placed her hands on his bare shoulders.

"Here." Christina handed her gum to Megan.

Michael turned his head and grinned at his sister. Magdalene whistled softly for Raven, napping in the opposite corner.

Christina closed her eyes and pursed her lips and tilted her head.

"*Psych!*" Michael cried as he jerked his face away, and, oh, how Peggy and Megan laughed. Christina lowered her head, pushed herself to her feet, and after another grenade glance towards Magdalene (was it *fuck-you-very-much* or a request for empathy?; Magdalene hoped it was the former), ran for the back door.

"Nice," Magdalene said.

"I was just kidding around," Michael said.

Megan whooped it up, dancing with one hand on her waist: "Taken down a notch!"

Peggy, her Catholicism flooding her cheeks, looked ashamed, as if *she'd* french kissed Michael and had enjoyed it.

Michael's grin deflated. Magdalene called Raven again, and when the dog pretended not to hear, she started up the steps.

"Okay, who's next?" Michael asked, and Peggy and Megan sprinted up the stairs past Magdalene, squeaking like pigs in a slaughterhouse, Peggy with true fear and Megan with a tone of regret.

"That's wasn't nice, Michael," Magdalene said. "Christina's embarrassed."

"I was just playing."

"Fix it," Magdalene said, leaving her brother on the steps. "Please."

Later that night—not two weeks before he'd disappeared (*splash*)—Michael pushed open Magdalene's bedroom door.

"I took care of it. She hadn't gotten too far. She was by the cemetery."

"You just get in?" Magdalene yawned and closed *Treasure Island*. The night was cool; her bed was cozy warm. "Is Dad home?"

"No, not yet," Michael answered; they both knew where their father was. "I told her I was sorry. She was pissed at you about the bedwetting thing, but I didn't know what she was talking about. I told her I just picked the question out of the air."

Magdalene studied her brother's face: it was the same face she saw in the mirror, but someone—God?—had polished the edges. Where her face was round and her cheeks were dimpled, his face was square and his cheeks were smooth, clean plains. (They both had prominent cheekbones.) Whereas she squinted in an effort to avoid having to get glasses, Michael's eyes were wide and sparkling, as if always in the aftermath of a laugh.

"I kissed her," Michael said. "I felt bad, so I kissed her."

"Was it nice?"

"I don't know. I never kissed anyone before," Michael said as he eased out of her room and closed the door. "It was okay."

Magdalene turned off her reading lamp and stared at the shadows the sycamore splashed on her ceiling. They undulated like waves lapping up the beach. She could hear the whistle of the train as it left the station in the shadow of the old asbestos factory. There was the volunteer fire bell too—so familiar a sound, it was like hearing a kettle boil. An owl called out in the night and another owl answered—or maybe it was just an echo, and the owl was talking to himself. The night was as quiet as a yawp. Why was she jealous of her brother kissing Christina Fuller? Magdalene covered her head with the sheet. The crazy owl continued his conversation. She didn't want to kiss her brother, she was pretty sure, nor did she want to kiss Christina. She wasn't jealous about Michael beating her to the first kiss either; despite a certain warmth in her tummy whenever Jerry Eves cut up in class, she didn't feel the urge to kiss anyone just yet—certainly not Jerry Eves.

Magdalene sat up in bed and pushed the sheets from her body. Anger rose in that slow, creeping way she'd grown accustomed to since their mother had died; sometimes she wouldn't even know she was angry until she found herself in the bathroom, pulling at her hair or making faces in the mirror, her cheeks and forehead drowning in purple.

Michael was going to leave her.

This thought raced past all others and took the lead.

Michael was going to leave her.

A Lab's ears are made of *SILK*.

In September, Michael would start high school, and by the time she made it there, he would be firmly ensconced: league football, dances, dates. Magdalene would be forced to play catch up, as always. They would become separated by more than just the year that separated their birth dates.

Of course, all this had changed. She was the oldest sibling now. The end of the Barrows line—at least until Michael was found.

"A Lab's ears are made of *SILK*."

Magdalene mouthed the words, as she crushed little red berries between her fingers in the bushes across from the McAllister house. The past, though clouded by numbers, seemed closer than ever— pregnant cumuli awaiting a wink from Zeus to begin their shit storm. For a brief period after Michael went missing, Christina gained notoriety as the last girl he kissed. No one, except Magdalene, knew that Christina had been the *only* girl he'd kissed. The goth overtones may have had their genesis in Michael's Houdini act, but Christina could only play the widow for so long—after all, her best friend was the missing boy's sister, and there were so many other boys to kiss and with whom to unburden her heavy, busty heart. Magdalene squashed another berry. The red, juicy outer part of the berry stained her fingers, but the hard little core was impervious to the crushing. It shot from her fingers whole.

Impervious.

The kissing game, Truth or Dare. Magdalene spit. Her mouth tasted sour. Everyone and everything had revolved around Michael like satellites—the Bod Squad, the football team, their father's affections—so why wasn't anyone still looking for him? Or rather: why did everyone act like he was past saving? Her father had stopped drinking this very week like it was as simple as switching a off light. Aunt Tiddy busied herself with Barrows Bungalow maintenance and tried to fill Magdalene's days with activities. (God, Magdalene hated that word—*activities*; it reminded her of activity time in kindergarten and first grade.) Everyone was moving on. Everyone except her. Once again, she didn't fit in.

And with Mondauk County drowning in mysteries, how could anyone heal? (They all needed dog saliva!) And it *was* just about everyone that needed healing. Henry Richard Cabot's death was the biggest story to hit Mondauk since the towers fell in New York. Lots of fall out. And if her interpretation of Willa's psychobabble was correct, Katie McAllister needed rescuing too. Sometimes a turtle is just a turtle, Magdalene reminded herself, but little girls (even Katie) often didn't have the vocabulary to express how dark it was in their skulls. And little girls didn't often have long, skinny scratches cascading down their faces.

Magdalene's mind wandered to the soft, red mud of the Puddle's banks; she inhaled the creek scum, the breath of frogs, heard the *whirr* of a thousand dragonflies gazing at their own distorted reflections in the polluted water, sure of their beauty in the early, hazy steam of summer.

Mr. McAllister emerged from the house and slammed the door behind him. Magdalene pushed herself further back into the berry bushes. The sky was almost completely burnt orange. How long had she been sitting across from the McAllister house? Mr. McAllister lit a cigarette and stood on the steps smoking. He was dressed in a brown pullover shirt that was too tight; Magdalene could see his belly protruding. The shirt did show off his muscles though; whatever Mr. McAllister currently did for a living certainly kept him in shape— except for his stomach; his stomach was a doughy, oversized basketball. But it was his face, silhouetted in the flickering outside house light, which truly frightened her. His smoke drifted like a nightmare overtaking a safety blanket, hiding his mouth, then his nose, then his eyes, until only his red hair hovered above his shifting features. He had always looked like Dickens' Scrooge to Magdalene: a younger, huskier Scrooge. His nose was long and crooked like Alastair Sim's in the movie, but it was planted on a round, plump face, so that it resembled a carrot on a snowman. His hands were old man's hands: long, slender, wrinkled fingers that naturally seemed to cup themselves into a claw. Magdalene always pictured them curled around the handle of a cane. His fingernails were long and usually dirty. Were those hands the hands that could hurt a child, a little girl? Had those fingers curled around Katie's neck? Had those fingernails scratched Katie's porcelain face?

Mr. McAllister descended the steps, ran his hand across the Chevy the county (personified by ADA Gregory Barrows, Magdalene realized) had denied him the privilege of driving, and started towards the curb. Magdalene froze. Had he seen her in the berry bushes? Was the cigarette just a bluff? Had he been giving her an opportunity to leave before her presence forced his hand? Magdalene willed herself not to pee—that was the one thing that Magdalene thought could possibly prevent her from being a detective (besides suicide; can't forget that!): her bladder felt ready to surrender at the slightest whiff of danger. Magdalene cupped her hands between her legs. Better for Mr. McAllister to find her squatting in the berry bushes, holding herself, than to be found soaking wet.

Mr. McAllister pitched his cigarette into the street, turned right, and walked away, his scary hands—his claws!—in his pockets, a tuneless whistle on his lips. Magdalene was torn. Surely, Mr. McAllister hadn't left Katie alone. Valerie Plum was baby-sitting, no doubt. Valerie could be dealt with, but Magdalene wasn't sure how to get Katie to talk about her abuse. She couldn't just make like Dr. Willa Meade and hand the girl some crayons and gesture towards the turtle's shell. Tailing Mr. McAllister could shed some light on his behavior. What would Sister Mary Magdalene de Rosa have done?

Magdalene flicked a final berry. Follow him. Sister Mary Magdalene de Rosa would have followed Mr. McAllister. But if he wasn't working nights, where was he going? To McCullough's? Better men than he, Magdalene knew, lost themselves there on a regular basis, leaving their families to mire in liquor and darts, losing their reflections in the dusty television that hung in a corner. If, in following Mr. McAllister, she discovered the motives behind why he'd attack his own daughter (and fire Magdalene), then she'd be forewarned. And to be forewarned, as Aunt Tiddy had said, is to be forearmed.

Magdalene stayed on her side of the street after taking a quick glance at the cigarette butt—Marlboro. To avoid the streetlamps, she skipped between the halos, careful to stay a few feet behind her mark, just like Frank and Joe Hardy. As advanced as her reading tastes had become (Tolkien and Mark Twain and, thanks to Tiddy, Bill Shakespeare), she knew the wisdom of the Hardy Boys would come in handy in situations such as this. Okay: splitting up to search a haunted house did not seem to define logical behavior, but in most other areas—surveillance, the trailing of suspects, the gathering and interpretation of clues—their skill was unparalleled. Sherlock Holmes may have been more pragmatic in his reasoning, but Frank and Joe got by on pure gumshoe gumption. The Hardy Boys were doing more than just trying to please their father (although that was certainly part of their makeup): they were trying to carve out their own identities—white bread and wholesome, but their own—even if their own wasn't all that removed from their father's. (The Three Investigators acted more like the boys she knew.) The Hardy Boys didn't wait to ask to belong; they knew what to do when their time came.

Magdalene had read just about every one of the original Hardy Boys books. *The Tower Treasure*, *What Happened at Midnight*, and *The Hooded Hawk Mystery* were her favorites. She had used her baby-sitting money last year to buy *The Missing Chums* and the invaluable *Hardy Boys Detective Handbook*. She knew to keep a safe distance from the person she was following—close enough to jump in if need be and far enough away to blend back into a shadow if the mark suspected a tail.

Mr. McAllister thumbed his nose twice and dug into his back pocket for a handkerchief. He stood on the corner, looking west. Magdalene crouched near a trash barrel. Was the nose thumbing a signal? Had he seen her?

When the bus appeared in the distance, Magdalene figured she had about ten seconds. The bus came to a hissing stop like a wheezing dragon, and she watched Mr. McAllister deposit his fare through a cloudy window. As the bus idled, Magdalene ran through the fumes emitting from its rear. *What would Frank and Joe Hardy do? What would Frank and Joe do?* Magdalene peered around the back of the bus; Mr. McAllister had already found a seat. If she didn't get on now, she would have to either bang on the closed door or give up the chase. Wouldn't McAllister see her either way? She sprinted for the door, Sister Rita's destroyed voice echoing in her ears: "*Whhhh*at *wwww*ill you d*oooo whhhh*en you*rrrr* time come*ssss*? *Wwww*ill you be *wwwwworrrr*thy? D*oooo* you ha*vvvv*e *whhhh*at it take*ssss*?"

Magdalene leapt up the bus steps just before the doors closed and stood with her back to the rest of the bus, slowly depositing her change, inspecting each coin. (She hoped she had enough.) The driver, an elderly black man with gray, kinky hair and a big fuzzy gray moustache nodded and reached for the door handle, the skin on his arms raw and leathery like corned beef. Magdalene hated corned beef. She was fifteen cents away from making the fare. Her mind danced all over the damn place. *Maybe I'll be a vegetarian. I'll never have corned beef arms. I'll be dead in three days. Four, tops.*

One two three four five six seven eight nine ten eleven twelve thirteen fourteen fifteen.

Magdalene spilled her remaining coins on the floor of the bus as it lurched forward.

"Missy, Missy," the driver said.

"Oh, I'm okay. I can get it," Magdalene said. "There's one."

The bus turned and headed south. Soon they would pass Sol's. Magdalene kept her head low, but her eyes were on the passing landscape, except for when she was playing with the coins. She found one of her nickels next to a piece of ancient gum, and she flicked it with her finger so it rolled towards the front of the bus.

"I'm so clumsy," Magdalene said.

Frank and Joe, eat your heart out!

Magdalene peeked out of the window as she bent for the coin. Sol's looked closed. Was it that late already? *Criminy!* What the hell was she doing following ol' Scrooge McAllister? She should have waited for Mrs. Bochdan to close Sol's and talked with her about the possibility of bullies—or knowing that Mr. McAllister had boarded the bus, knocked past Valerie Plum and grilled Katie McAllister (assuming Katie hadn't been left to fend for herself). But then again, it didn't seem like Katie was going to spill much of anything, let alone confess that her father was responsible for the cut on her little face. Magdalene kicked at a penny.

"Missy, take a seat," the driver pleaded. "You have to be behind the yellow line. Sit down, Missy."

The bus turned east and slowed as it climbed a hill on the outer rim of town. Everyone called this neighborhood the Heights because from the houses on the edge of the hill, one could look down at the rest of Mondauk Proper. Aunt Tiddy said the Heights was just a bourgeois name to make the lower middle class residents feel above the trailer trash, but Magdalene wasn't sure that hadn't been a bit of Wheelwright blue blood bubbling to the surface. Most of the houses here were connected, little rows of the exact same building with only various flashes of color or an accoutrement distinguishing one house from another: a lawn gnome, a ribbon on a door, a yellow awning instead of a green one—pretty much the same as Magdalene's neighborhood except that these were row homes or twins. One house had a Wanted: Dead or Alive poster in a window. A few had tiny stone porches. Some doors were painted, some were unfinished wood, almost all were open to the evening air, and all the aluminum screen doors had wavy screens. Each house had a thin strip of grass that sloped from the door to the cracked pavement. Many had small faded flags stuck in the ground. Lower middle class, Magdalene thought, didn't look all that different from upper middle class—or whatever social strata the Barrows inhabited. Working stiffs, Christina called them. But these weren't the shanties and shacks and trailers of the people who clung to the banks of the Puddle and lived in the shadow of the asbestos factory smokestack. They weren't living in nice, old single homes like the Barrows Bungalow either. These people lived in between.

A little boy waved at Magdalene as the bus blew past him, unsettling his hair.

In between didn't look so bad.

Magdalene kept her back to the other riders and held on to the silver pole behind the driver. If Mr. McAllister headed towards the front exit, she could jump off ahead of him. The bus pulled towards a corner stop. Magdalene scanned the area: residential. Nowhere to hide if Mr. McAllister got off now. A young girl in a Mondauk Summer Camp t-shirt got on the bus and wriggled her way around Magdalene.

The bus lurched to a stop, and Magdalene stumbled into the driver.

"Missy, sit down now, please," the driver shouted, and Magdalene did as she was told, her bottom hovering over the plastic seat.

As the bus pulled away, Magdalene watched Mr. McAllister comb his hair with his fingers in the reflection of a newspaper box. She'd forgotten to watch the side exit!

Ten nine eight seven six...

The bus was already halfway up the next block when Magdalene grabbed the fat, gray wire that ran above the window and yanked down.

"I'm sorry. I missed my stop," she cried. "Could you please let me off, mister?"

"Missy, I'm not allowed to stop this bus between designated—"

"PLEASE, MISTER, I CAN'T BE LATE OR MY DAD WILL BE PISSED OFF AND I CAN'T GET IN TROUBLE AGAIN. HE'LL SMACK ME ONE!"

...five four three two one...

The driver hit the brakes and threw open the door. Magdalene bounced down the steps and ducked behind a parked car. Mr. McAllister wasn't in sight. She ran towards the side street. The world slowed down as she sped up. *Blurry, blurry.* The air cut into her nose, burning her nostrils. Her body had forgotten how to run since Michael had disappeared—barely half a block, and she was already winded. *Blurry, blurry.*

She collided into a pair of legs.

"You lookin' for me?" the owner of the legs asked.

Magdalene twisted on her heels. The man grabbed her arms in his tight, hairy fists. Magdalene was suddenly sure she was going pee her corduroys.

"Magdalene, Magdalene," the man said, releasing her. Magdalene swung a fist and connected with his belt buckle.

"Oh man, oh man," Magdalene said. Her knuckles were on fire.

Police Chief Cutter Hagen knelt down and held her hands in his. His bulbous nose was crisscrossed with veins that had broken through his scarlet skin, and his white hair had a slight yellow tint. His breath smelled like whiskey.

"You alright there, Magdalene?" he asked. "I scare you?"

"Chief Hagen. I, I—"

"What are you doin' on this side of town this time of night?" Chief Hagen asked.

One vein two veins three veins four.

How could she not have noticed Cutter Hagen, in full police uniform, standing on the corner? Magdalene was beginning to think she was going to make a lousy detective—then reminded herself that she was going to die soon. Somehow that made everything a little better.

"Study group," Magdalene said. Despite her less-than-stellar sleuthing, Magdalene was proud of her quick thinking. It was like when she used vocabulary words in the right context. It *was* almost too bad she had to die; she had an idea that perhaps she might be brilliant—or brilliant enough.

Chief Hagen looked her up and down.

"I just went out for some fresh air," Magdalene said.

"And where's this study group of yours?"

He looked over her head. Mr. McAllister?

"Bridget's house."

She risked a look behind her. The street was empty.

"Bridget who? And where are your books?"

Magdalene's face grew red. Unless she came up with something better than an imaginary pal, her father's friend, the police chief of Mondauk County, would haul her in for a curfew violation or some other trumped up charge. He was squeezing her hands in the same authoritative way Father Dave had squeezed her shoulder in the hospital.

"I was already at Bridget's house. Took a breather, ran around the block."

This might work; she was still out of breath.

"Where does this Bridget live?" Chief Hagen asked. "Bridget who? This is my neighborhood."

One vein two veins three veins four.

"I have to catch up with my schoolwork because I was in the *hospital*," Magdalene emphasized, and that did it: Police Chief Cutter Hagen—Cutty Shark to his friends—looked like he'd swallowed a bug. *The hospital.* He stepped back, let go of her hands, and mumbled an apology.

"It's okay, Chief Hagen. I'm sorry I ran you over," Magdalene yelled, as she broke into a jog. "Bye!"

The side street was empty. Magdalene ran the length of the block, down one side and up the other. Mr. McAllister was probably already inside one of these houses. Maybe not even one on this block. She'd missed him.

She walked back towards the bus stop, her eyes on her sneakers. And there, by the curb, halfway down the block: a smoldering cigarette butt. Magdalene paused; it was a Marlboro. She would earn her detective shield yet.

The house before her was nondescript. The only difference between this house and the rest on the block was that the porch was enclosed; the other porches were open (and thankfully devoid of any porch-sitters). It had to be past nine; it was quite dark now. Televisions glowed from just about every front window.

Instead of row homes, twin houses populated this block. Magdalene walked down the driveway that separated one set of twins from the next. There was a wooden sign above the mailbox on the house on her left. Burned into the wood, with what Magdalene guessed was a wood burning hobby kit: *The Tidwells.* The porch light was on; she heard music playing faintly from inside the house. Magdalene walked in the shadows of the shared driveway, careful to not step on twigs or anything crunchy. Lights were on in every window of the house—even the ones on the second floor.

The trash cans were in an alcove halfway down the driveway, below a pair of open windows. At the end of the drive was a little side stoop. Beyond the stoop was a low wooden gate. The backyard was untended; the grass was high and weeds scaled the fence. Inside the house, a woman laughed. Maybe this was the wrong house, Magdalene thought; a lot of people smoked Marlboros.

She moved the trash can back and forth—it was full—and climbed on top, careful to distribute her weight so the aluminum lid wouldn't cave in. She could just see into the middle of the house— the dining room?—and the woman who'd been laughing sat in a chair facing the windows. She waved at Magdalene, and Magdalene tried to duck her head below the ledge, but the woman kept on waving. Magdalene's heart raced, and her head filled with numbers. *Wait*—she wasn't waving—the woman was fussing her hair in the reflection of the window. Magdalene lifted her head so just her right eyeball cased the room. The woman sat at an octagonal table with a half-empty glass of wine in front of her. There was an old-looking breakfront on the woman's left, a china cabinet, but with only three dishes on display on the middle shelf. The woman was all dolled up. She wore a white dress that had blue polka dots. Her hair was mousy brown and thin—poor hair, Aunt Tiddy would have called it—done up with hairspray in absurd swoops across her forehead. She wore too much makeup—there were huge lipstick smudges on the woman's wine glass—but not in the way that Mrs. Stanley at the library did, with her disturbing blue swashes of eye shadow, or even in the way the ladies that hung out at McCullough's wore it, like they were trying to hide something important about themselves. This woman was trying to feel pretty.

Magdalene raised her head a little bit more. Even though the woman was smiling, the smile on her face looked like something she was trying on—it didn't quite fit her and she knew it. She kept turning her wine glass around and around in her hands; her nails were chewed to the bone.

Magdalene glanced down and adjusted her footing. She heard a male voice clear his throat. When she looked up, a shadow shifted, and Mr. McAllister's body suddenly blocked Magdalene's view. She ducked below the window ledge.

One two, buckle my shoe.

Three four, knock at the door.

"Can't ruin the dining room table now, can we?" Mr. McAllister said in a dulcet voice that Magdalene found both threatening and sickeningly sweet. The Tidwell woman—Magdalene assumed that she was a Tidwell, going by the sign on the front door—tilted her head and barked a choppy laugh, wiping her lips with the back of a shaking hand. The laugh ended abruptly. She made to push back her chair.

"No, no. I know where the coasters are. Sit yourself," Mr. McAllister said, and the Tidwell woman giggled like a member of the Body Squad.

Mr. McAllister opened a drawer on the breakfront. He *did* know where to go for the coasters! He was familiar with the house,

Magdalene noted. Was the lady a relative? Magdalene doubted it. The Tidwell woman was acting like Christina and the other girls in school did whenever boys were around: silly, self-conscious, jumpy. Was this Katie's Aunt Angela? No, Katie's aunt lived in New Hope, and although this woman wasn't old, she was too old to be Aunt Angela—and too old to flirt like a schoolgirl. Magdalene knew that's what the Tidwell woman was doing: she was flirting with Mr. McAllister.

The woman covered her mouth and nervously ran her fingers over her lips. She was wearing a wedding band! When she reached for her glass, she tipped it off the coaster. Mr. McAllister snatched the glass up like he was yanking a rabbit from its hole. His laugh sounded like a car engine that refused to turn.

"I know where the napkins are too, Beth," Mr. McAllister said as he walked into the kitchen.

"Sunday night, Jack, I'm making *you* dinner for a change."

From the kitchen: "No need, I think I'm doing just fine."

The Tidwell woman smiled into her fist.

"Well, I'm doing it anyway, Jack McAllister. In fact, why don't you invite…"

Magdalene shifted her weight; her left leg was cramping up. The trash can lid creased with a shriek, and when Magdalene tried to lower one leg from the lid, the can wobbled and crashed. Magdalene's body slammed to the driveway. A bag of trash spilled from the can and split open. Her cheek rested on a banana peel. The garbage reeked of coffee grinds and wine and cigarette butts.

A light flickered above the back door. The screen door hinges squeaked.

"Jack, what was that?" The Tidwell woman's voice was shaky, unsure, peeking at ghosts. But Magdalene could barely hear her; she didn't know what was louder: the *thud-thud-thud* in her heaving chest or the echoes of the trash can's fall.

Or the numbers lining up inside her head.

Mr. McAllister was on the back stoop. His husky, winded breathing rose above the sound of her racing heart. Magdalene lay on her side, her back to the yard. Magdalene hoped there was enough shadow cover. She didn't dare lift her head even when she heard Mr. McAllister walk down the three steps to the driveway. If she ran, there was a chance she'd slip on a banana peel (how classic!) or some other piece of garbage.

She heard movement by her sneakers and tuneless whistling. Something soft trotted by her head. Magdalene held her breath, closed her eyes tight, and counted.

"Found you!" Mr. McAllister said, and Magdalene curled herself into a ball to ward off the expected blows. If Mr. McAllister was capable to cutting his own daughter's face, what would he do to a former baby-sitter snooping around his girlfriend's house?

"Come on home now," Mr. McAllister said, and a cat purred in response. Magdalene risked turning her head and peeked through her eyelashes. It was the fat tabby.

"Your mom's been worried sick about you," Mr. McAllister said to the cat.

More footsteps, and the screen door squeaked and slammed shut.

From inside the house, a muffled Mr. McAllister said: "He was hanging' around outside. Knocked over the trash cans. You know, Katie said a tabby's been hanging' around our house too. You think old' Oscar here could have made it there and back?"

"Followed you, you mean?" the Tidwell woman asked.

"Cats do that," Mr. McAllister said. "They know their way around. I saw a TV show about it once."

Magdalene was lulled by the soft way their voices tiptoed around each other. All the fear and curiosity and adrenaline had left her body. She felt like a warm strand of overcooked spaghetti, which wasn't a surprise; she was laying on a fair amount of discarded pasta.

"I'll have to remember to clean those cans up in the morning," the Tidwell woman said.

"Don't worry. I'll do it now."

"But you're in your slacks."

"I'll take care of it, Beth," Mr. McAllister said. "It's no trouble."

"You should really call Katie."

"Don't worry about Katie either," Mr. McAllister said. "I'll take care of the Katie situation too."

The back door squeaked open again. Magdalene counted his footsteps; she matched her breathing with his strangled inhalations and exaltations.

"What the hell?" Mr. McAllister said, and Magdalene's heart jump-started her sluggish body. Blood rushed to her head and fingers and toes. Her feet remembered how to run—they recalled football games in the backyard with Michael; they remembered the cold of the Puddle in the teasing weeks of early summer—and Magdalene was halfway down the block before she realized she had finally wet herself.

Chapter Six

The Reveal

Although there had been hell to pay for coming in so late—she had never had a curfew before, but she would have one now, by God!—neither her father nor Aunt Tiddy had called her on her lies about taking exams, nor had they tried to reach her at Christina's house. They just wanted her to respect the rules, they said.

Where had she heard that before?

"Home before dark, no matter what, unless you call first. It's ten o'clock!" Aunt Tiddy said. She nervously squeezed a long stick of pepperoni. The pocket watch bounced in her lap.

"Don't make us worry, Maddie," her father said, but he didn't appear worried; he let Tiddy do all the yelling. Maybe he didn't care, Magdalene thought; maybe he was just going through the motions. He wouldn't stop staring at her face, as if he'd never seen his daughter before. Take a good look, Magdalene thought. Take a look while you have time.

"You should be home studying," Tiddy said. "Hitting the books, head out of the stars. Sharpen your pencil and you'll sharpen your mind. Shakespeare said that."

Only Raven—her future murder victim—seemed glad to see her. For a brief moment, she thought it might have been better if Mr. McAllister had caught her. Better to be slain by your enemies than to be smothered by your friends. (Shakespeare, eat your heart out!)

"Go to bed, Maddie," her father said. He looked quizzical, suspicious. Had he been drinking? "Do you have a test tomorrow?"

Magdalene decided not to risk it and answered no.

"Alright, go to bed then."

Snap fizz whirr.

"Tiddy—" Magdalene's father said.

"Sometimes the best way to see yourself clearly is to *really* see yourself and everything around you. Shakespeare—"

"Don't," Magdalene's father said.

Raven followed her up the stairs, his monkey in his mouth, and sat outside the bathroom while she brushed her teeth. Neither Tiddy nor her father had noticed the front of her pants were wet—she had tried to soak up the urine with a newspaper she'd found at the bus stop although she didn't take the bus: Magdalene had walked, hoping to dry her corduroys before she arrived home.

Raven dropped Monkey when she opened the bathroom door and trotted to Michael's bedroom. The dog whined once and pushed at the door with his nose.

"I still don't know what happened, Raven," Magdalene said. "I miss him too."

Raven stretched out in front of Michael's door and whined softly to himself.

"The parents are the focus of the case, Tiddy," Magdalene's father was saying.

"Well, I don't see the sense in that!" Tiddy replied.

Magdalene lowered herself to the floor next to Raven. The dog licked her cheek.

"You would rather the county prosecute the boy?"

"Well, no," Tiddy answered, less sure of herself.

"Well, then?"

"It's the father you're after. What does the mother have to do with it?" Aunt Tiddy was gaining steam again. Magdalene smiled; it was hard to beat Tiddy in an argument even when her aunt was wrong. "Mrs. Bochdan did nothing illegal. She's a hardworking citizen. Sends her boy to parochial school. She even works as a maid for the Fullers and their ilk on top of it all to make up the shortfall."

"Past tense, Tiddy. After the shooting, Mrs. Fuller forced Sam to let her go; everyone else on the Faith Board did the same. Mrs. Fuller wields considerable power amongst the wealthier housewives. Mrs. Bochdan is running Sol's by herself now, and it's her only source of income."

Mrs. Bochdan! They were talking about the Cabot Case! Magdalene crawled on her belly towards the top of the stairs. Nothing like a clichéd literary device to keep her up to date! Raven followed her, crawling too (he was so cool, so adorable!), dropping the monkey on her head. Drool slid from the monkey into Magdalene's ear.

"The gun was stolen property even before Joseph found it or took it," Tiddy said. "The father didn't even have a firearms license. Isn't that what you said?"

"Yes, true—all of it. Ballistics confirmed as much. The gun was used in previous crimes. Feargal's working the case. But Andriy

Bochdan is gone. And we're looking for him. State troopers too. Hugh even called the ATF because of an assault weapons cache found in Rhawnhurst. It appears a transaction was about to do down, and Andriy is a suspect, although the evidence is circumstantial. That's the ATF's headache now. But the weapons charge in our case will stick."

"The boy needs help," Tiddy said, "nothing else. You put Joseph Bochdan in the system, you can bet your ass to tin cups you'll be prosecuting him again by the time he's fifteen."

"Ass to tin cups. That Shakespeare or Marlowe?" her father asked, and Magdalene suppressed a giggle, glimpsing the father she used to have—before the cancer had eaten her mother, before Michael had disappeared into the ether. "Ben Jonson perhaps?"

Aunt Tiddy was not amused. "You know what I'm saying is the gospel truth, Gregory Barrows. Mrs. Bochdan is going through absolute hell. She can't even see her son."

"We're working on that. It's only supposed to be the first seventy-two hours, and then his mother at least is supposed to be able to see him. There have been complications. The criminal implicitly of his parents, for one. And the boy's not talking."

"Poppycock! You're expecting a confession? A whole classroom saw him shoot Henry."

"No, I mean he's not talking at all," Magdalene's father said. "To anyone. Not the doctors, nurses, no one. Henry Cabot was his best friend. The only thing we know—and we know this from interviewing all those poor kids; Tiddy, some of them even had blood stains on their shirts—is that Henry and Joseph were definitely *not* fighting or arguing before it happened. The best guess is that the Bochdan boy was showing off."

"It's the rap music," Tiddy said.

Her father ignored her; score one for her father, Magdalene thought. She hated it when the nuns blamed the decline of western civilization on rap music or punk rock or *Pulp Fiction*. Magdalene had watched *Pulp Fiction*. Sure, there'd been a heck of a lot of creative cursing and it was gory violent—*icky*, really—but it didn't make Magdalene want to go out and spray bullets over the schoolyard, no matter how rotten the other kids made her feel.

"Did anyone think to ask if the Bochdan boy—now you've got me saying it!" Aunt Tiddy yelled. "Did anyone think to ask *Joseph* if he'd brought the gun to school for protection? Was anyone picking on him? Or Henry?"

Magdalene was genuinely surprised. She hadn't come to expect that much *depth* from Tiddy's arguments. Her aunt always seemed content to coast upon what she called "common sense" (or in the case of William Shakespeare, rote memorization). The deductive reasoning and critical thinking taught in school and in books, the kind of methodical processing and analytical hypothesizing that the Hardy Boys seemed to have at their fingertips in spades, that elusive combination of guts *and* brains necessary to survive the mean streets of Mondauk—these were all poppycock to Aunt Tiddy.

"Tiddy, we're looking into everything," Magdalene's father said. "What was Andriy Bochdan doing with a stolen gun? Who did he get it from? Why? When? What did he use it for? And where did he keep it that the Bochdan boy—Joseph—could have gotten to it so easily? Hell, maybe the father *gave* his son the gun or hid it in the boy's room. We don't know. Mrs. Bochdan is pretty much in pieces and hasn't been much help. Joseph's not talking. The father's a fugitive."

"On the lam," Magdalene whispered to herself.

It was the bullies, Magdalene was sure; she knew it in her gut. She was behind on gathering clues. If she could just prove it, then Joseph Bochdan wouldn't have to go to jail.

"Let's not forget, Tiddy, that the Cabots have lost their son. Someone has to be held accountable."

"Tell me something Shakespeare *didn't* say," Tiddy scoffed. "But you told me the Cabots don't want to prosecute Joseph."

"No, they don't. They're not looking into a civil action either. The Cabots are good, God-fearing people. Mr. Cabot is a podiatrist. Has a practice over in Warminster. She's a homemaker. They're Methodists. Like the Bochdans, they sent their son to Assumption to keep him out of the public school system. Lot of good that did. The Cabots want to move on. They're ready to mourn their son. But Andriy Bochdan broke the law, and if he's at fault, they want him prosecuted to the fullest extent. Either way, the state wants *someone* brought to justice. It's complicated."

"Not to me," Aunt Tiddy said. "Get Joseph Bochdan the help he needs. Return him to his mother and leave her be. End of story. Curtain drop."

"I wish it were that simple," he sighed.

His voice betrayed his weariness. He wasn't drunk; he was bone tired. So was Magdalene. She crawled slowly past her dog back to her room.

"We need to know why Joseph did what he did. That's the real mystery here. Cutter's boys will find the father. Andriy will start using his credit cards. They'll catch him. Everything has an ending eventually."

"Not everything," Aunt Tiddy said, "and not always eventually."

Magdalene closed her bedroom door and opened her journal.

+

Friday morning, Magdalene tried to avoid Aunt Tiddy, but the old lady found her way into every nook and cranny, even going so far as to open the bathroom door and poke her head into the shower to ask Magdalene what she wanted for lunch. It was as if her aunt's barely suppressed anger at her grandniece's recent behavior manifested itself as ubiquity; Aunt Tiddy seemed determined to love Magdalene in her own peculiar, smothering way. She even snapped a picture of Magdalene through the shower curtain—*snap fizz whirr*—a skinny shadow, no boobs, hardly any curves—a boy's body.

The silhouette looked like a smaller version of Michael's.

"A picnic lunch is what I was thinking, or we could make brownies. Then we'll turn the rug over in the dining room, maybe pick up some meats at Bard's."

Magdalene and Tiddy made brownies.

They turned the rug.

They even sorted Magdalene's mother's Christmas ornament box though it was only June. Tiddy seemed particularly keen on pointing out which ornaments were Michael's. Magdalene didn't need Tiddy to tell her; Magdalene already knew.

When her father called just before dinner to let them know he would catch a bite at the office—the staff was working into the night on the Cabot Case, and he'd had a full day split between practicing the law and coaching Summer Camp—Magdalene saw her chance.

"You wore me out. I'm going to go to bed, Aunt Tiddy."

"Nonsense! I was just about the get out the Scrabble board. Keep you on your toes that game will."

"I'm tired, Tiddy. Can I just go to bed?" Magdalene asked in what she hoped was her most winsome voice.

"Of course, of course," Tiddy said, ushering her upstairs, the two of them stepping over Magdalene's doomed dog and his monkey. Tiddy took the dog's picture.

She'd have to do a better job at avoiding Tiddy on the weekend—especially if she wanted to get anywhere near Tiddy's pillbox. Magdalene still hadn't been able to find out why Tiddy took the pills—high blood pressure, allergies, simply being old; Tiddy appeared to be in bouncing good health. But her aunt took them before she went to bed, so Magdalene hypothesized that they made her sleepy. Magdalene grabbed her journal from her nightstand and settled in to wait and write.

When she woke, she cursed herself: she wasn't actually supposed to go to sleep. How could she keep losing time like this when there was so little time left? Magdalene dressed in the dark and stepped over Raven's mute panda sitting in the hallway. Her father's bedroom door was closed—Tiddy still slept there. Magdalene slid down the stairs, careful to avoid the creaky fourth step. She didn't think her father would be home yet. There was still a wink of light in the sky, so it couldn't be much past nine; when her father said he was working late during the past week, it usually meant after midnight, as if he were trying to avoid even the temptation of the hours before last call. And Magdalene was right: the sofa was empty. Tiddy had made it up, tucking a sheet into the cushions. The sheet was still untrammeled.

The problem, Magdalene knew, would be getting back in. When she returned from her reconnaissance, there was no way she could reach the stairs without going past her father on the sofa. And what if he looked in on her or locked the back door? Magdalene decided to risk it; she had to talk to Katie McAllister. If Katie was in trouble, it was up to Magdalene to douse the flames—or smother them. Whatever was going on between Mr. McAllister and the Tidwell woman (and something surely was), it was conspiratorial in nature. Hell, even the chubby tabby Katie wanted to take in belonged to Beth Tidwell.

Magdalene gave Raven a cookie, but the dog ignored it and stared at her as she slipped out of the back door.

In the berry bushes across from Katie's house, the old problem arose: how to be sure Mr. McAllister wasn't home. Throw pennies at Katie's window again? She contemplated a phony phone call when Valerie Plum burst from the front door, opened one of the trash cans alongside of the house (tossing the lid), and tore a piece of paper into confetti. Katie had Valerie over a barrel with whatever she had been doing in Mr. McAllister's car with Paul Stern. Maybe Magdalene could add another monkey to the barrel.

"Hey, Valerie," Magdalene said, jogging across the street, her face and neck red—even her arms were blushing. Valerie was just pulling the screen door open.

"Wait up!"

One two, buckle my shoe.

Valerie glanced at the trash can. "What do *you* want?" she sneered.

"Katie home?"

Magdalene was winded; if she didn't get some real sleep soon, she feared her whole body would just shut down.

"You shouldn't be here," Valerie said. "You're not allowed."

Three four, knock at the door.

Magdalene bit her lip and went for it: "Either is Paul Stern." Magdalene feigned a lunge in the direction of the trash can. "Was that from Paul?"

"Screw you, Magdalene Barrows! Screw you!" Valerie screamed, as she ran inside. The screen door slammed behind her.

Five six, pick up sticks.

Magdalene opened the door quietly and slipped into the house.

"Katie?" Magdalene whispered.

Valerie was on the sofa, curled up into a ball.

"Upstairs," Valerie said from inside the ball.

"She likes you better than me," she said around her thumb.

Seven eight, lay them straight.

Magdalene climbed the stairs and hesitated before Katie's door. At the other end of the hall, the door to what Magdalene assumed was Mr. McAllister's room was partially open. What clues would be found in there?

"Magdalene!" Katie cried, grabbing her hand and pulling her into her bedroom. "You have to see this book on the stars. Look, look on Atlas Chart 52: 'The Milky Way diminishes rapidly in intensity towards the southeast'. What does that mean?"

Katie shared Magdalene's fascination with astronomy. "Your head's always in the stars, dear," Magdalene's late, deceased, dead mother had said to her. "It's like you're looking upside down at the rest of us, wondering why our feet are still on the ground!"

Magdalene refocused on Katie—it had taken Katie a while to sound out all the words from the star book. The scar on Katie's cheek had settled into a deeper pink.

"I think it means that the further the galaxy is stretched out, the further it is away from the center, away from where it began, and that it starts to lose some of its brilliance, its shine, its…newness. It becomes less than what it was to begin with. Does that make sense? It's like it loses something as it grows."

"People do that sometimes," Katie said.

Magdalene looked at her sharply, then looked out the window into the night sky. The pollution from Philadelphia was creeping out towards the suburbs, but the stars here were still bright and steady. Magdalene couldn't imagine a part of the universe where the stars were shaky and the heavens were not firmly moored.

On Katie's windowsill was a silver tray—it appeared to be an antique—overloaded with a mass of prayer candles. Some of the candles had been melted down to little more than stubs; others were slanted severely in one direction or another. The bottom of the tray was almost completely covered in wax.

"Are these from the church?"

"Sister Jezebel said they were extra and gave us each a couple to have," Katie explained. "Some of the parents didn't want their kids to have candles—as if the candles were going to light themselves!—so they returned them, and Sister gave a couple more to me. I use them to pray. Then my dad saw them."

"He got upset too?"

"No. He said Mommy had kept a bunch of church candles herself, and he gave me some of hers."

Magdalene frowned. "Are these all of them?" she asked.

"Oh, no," Katie said. "I burned a lot of them up already. I've been praying a whole lot."

There's no end to praying, Magdalene thought. Don't get started, Katie-girl!

"I light them every time I pray. Sometimes I pray to Mommy. I ask her to watch Daddy. I prayed for you too, Magdalene, when you were in the hospital. Now, I light them and pray for the dead boy and his friend who shot him."

"Katie, do you know a woman named Tidwell?"

"I don't think so. I heard of a man named Frannie Tidwell, but Daddy says he's bad news."

"How do you mean?"

Katie lowered her voice to a whisper: "He's hooked on drugs. Daddy said Frannie Tidwell has to do drugs every day—a couple of times a day—or else something bad happens to him."

"I'm not sure what though," she added. "Daddy says he sells stuff called crystal meth and that's really bad. They call him Frannie Five Fingers 'cause Daddy says he steals anything that's not nailed down."

"Does Frannie Tidwell live in the Heights?"

"The Heights? Gosh, no. He lives in Paradise Lakes."

"He does?" Magdalene asked; it couldn't be the same Tidwell, but, then again, Mondauk Proper wasn't that big—maybe Frannie was the Tidwell woman's cousin.

"Did you talk with Mrs. Bochdan yet?" Katie asked.

Magdalene blushed. *No, I was following your father.*

"Tomorrow. I haven't done enough sleuthing to make the case to her yet."

"You're just like your dad! You can be a lawyer *and* a detective!" Katie yelled.

"Shhh," Magdalene said; she didn't want Valerie to have any reason to get off the sofa and climb the stairs.

"Oh, don't worry about ol' Valerie Plum. She's just sits by the phone and waits for Paul Stern. 'Paul, Paul, I'll give you my all!' That's what she sings. There's something wrong with ol' Val, Magdalene."

"You're not just whistling Dixie."

Katie laughed.

"I know your laughing at me!" Valerie screamed.

Shit—Valerie *was* eavesdropping.

"C'mon, Katie," Magdalene said, "let's go outside."

"But it's night time!"

"We can see the stars better that way. Get your telescope. Maybe we'll be able to see the end of the Milky Way."

Katie grabbed her telescope—a Newtonian reflector on a tripod—and the two of them navigated past Valerie, who was crouched in the middle of the stairs, still sucking her thumb. Valerie Plum looked ready to pop, Magdalene thought. Magdalene had seen that very look in the mirror more than once. Maybe Valerie's days were numbered too.

There was a breeze. The crickets were screaming. In the next yard, bed sheets swayed from a clothesline. Magdalene saw the cigarette smoke waft under the porch light before the smell hit her nose. Her legs turned to pudding.

Was Mr. McAllister home already?

The train whistle caught the breeze and rode it hard. Magdalene remembered a line from a Johnny Cash song: "*I hear that train a comin' / It's rollin' 'round the bend...*" A condemned man's voice, she'd always thought. Whenever she had to walk the sticky floor of McCullough's to retrieve her father, the same songs were always blaring from the jukebox, competing with the ballgames on the television that hung from the ceiling, and the Johnny Cash tune was one of them.

"*I shot a man in Reno just to watch him die.*"

Magdalene held her breath and counted to ten.

"Stinky," Katie said, waving at the air.

The smoker sat on his porch in the yard behind Katie's. Magdalene watched the firefly ember wink as he inhaled. When the man finished his cigarette, he crushed it underfoot and went inside.

"Daddy smells like sulfur sometimes when he smokes," Katie said as she aimed the telescope and adjusted a little knob on the side, "like that Black Snake experiment we did in Science."

Magdalene shivered. "Anything?" she asked, craning her neck to look at the sky, which appeared cloudy and nearly starless. Now that she was here, Magdalene had no idea how to bring up whatever abuse Katie was enduring. Her head was filled with numbers and there was no sum. She tried to think of Sister Mary Magdalene de Rosa.

"No," Katie said, and she started pointing the telescope on houses, trees, the swaying bed sheets, the ground.

"What's *that*?" Katie asked. She had the telescope pointed towards her feet at a little lump in the grass.

"I think it's a dead bird," Magdalene said.

Katie bent forward, tilting the tripod so that the lens of the telescope was right above the lump.

"It's a blurry—" Her eyes peeked over the eyepiece, and her shoulders slumped.

"It's a head," Katie said.

"A head?"

Lou's Head?

Magdalene knelt in the grass. It was a head, all right, but not a bird's. The head had been torn from the body: little pink and red strands sprouted from where its neck would have been. The field mouse's eyes were slits; from a certain angle, in the starlight, it looked like it was sleeping. Magdalene thought she could smell the rankness of the Puddle on the breeze. Was the mouse another clue? Magdalene steadied herself. Had Michael fallen asleep somewhere—on the dock or on the banks of the Puddle perhaps, or behind the Fields outhouse, like Rip Van Winkle, sleeping away his youth? She studied the mouse through half-closed eyes and tried to imitate its squinty visage. What did the mouse have to do with her brother? The mouse wasn't sleeping. The mouse looked more like the victim of the Headless Horseman than anything else.

"Stevie Rich!" Katie cried, poking at the head with a stick.

Magdalene jumped.

"What about Stevie Rich?"

Stevie Rich belonged to that special class of bullies who occasionally turned and picked fights with one other. Stevie and his pals even formed a gang in fifth grade, going so far as to wear matching t-shirts—if scribbling "Lakes Boys" in magic marker across the front could be considered matching. Jerry Eves said that Stevie Rich had wanted to call the gang "The Barbarians," but none of its members could spell it. Jerry had said that James Orienti got pummeled for calling them "The Barbies"—which was what a number of them had graffitied in the public school playground. The Lakes Boys proper had lasted all of a year; they were too stoned and too fractious to maintain a united front; now they were just an unruly pack of loosely confederated juvenile delinquents. But like all carnivorous canine packs, they still needed a leader.

"Stevie Rich likes to kill animals and take them apart."

This Magdalene had heard as well. Among other crimes, Stevie Rich, according to several schoolyard reports, had torn a wing from a wounded bird and stuffed it in his back pocket.

Katie looked ready to cry; Magdalene put an arm around Katie's shoulder. She could feel herself begin to well up too. The mouse is sleeping, Daddy, Magdalene repeated in her head, the mouse is sleeping.

"You know how the Joker in Batman always leaves a Joker card?" Katie asked. "Stevie Rich leaves dead animals. It's his calling card."

"His calling card?"

"For when he's going to kill you."

"Katie," Magdalene explained in the steadiest voice she could muster, "Stevie Rich probably doesn't even know who you are.

School's out. He's probably beating up kids in the Basin. Some animal did this. Maybe an owl. Owls eat mice."

"You mean the rest of the mouse is gone? Something ate the rest of the mouse?"

The little girl's eyes were wide with excitement, her tears forgotten.

"Katie, you have a zoo in your bedroom. You know sometimes animals eat other animals."

"Like Billy the lizard!"

"Right, like Billy."

"But maybe not, right?" Katie asked, looking around the backyard.

The mouse is sleeping, Daddy.

"Do you have a flashlight, Katie? We can search the yard and see if we can find the rest of the mouse."

"Another mystery!" Katie cried with as she ran into the house. Such exuberance! She returned with a flashlight *thirty-four thirty-five thirty-six* seconds later.

Magdalene turned it on and beat the flashlight into her palm like her father did when the beam flickered.

"Is that a tail?" Katie asked.

Magdalene got on her hands and knees. "No...oh, look—there's a little arm, I think."

A tiny red and gray arm was caught in a patch of onion grass.

"Go inside and get the microscope too if you want."

"Better not. Ol' Val's having a sniffle fit in there."

"Leave her be then," Magdalene said. There was a tiny drop of red on the pavement near the back stoop. Katie's breath on Magdalene's neck was hot and anxious.

"There's a little trail, right to the stoop," Katie said, taking Magdalene's hand into hers.

"Stevie Rich," the little girl whispered.

A twig snapped to their left—just like in the Hardy Boys—as their shadows fell across the back stoop. Magdalene was suddenly sure she was going to pee herself again.

"Oh my God, Magdalene!" Katie screamed. "Oh my God!"

There was a rustle in the driveway.

Magdalene pulled Katie close to her chest and retreated, huddling against the back of the house. When she peered around the corner, Magdalene couldn't see anything outside the circle of light. The shrubbery alongside the house was shrouded in darkness. A few bugs danced in delirium under the porch light.

"Your dad?" Magdalene asked.

"No," Katie whimpered, her eyes wide. "Oh my God!"

Ten nine eight seven six five four three two one.

Magdalene covered Katie's mouth with her hand. The little girl squirmed, and Magdalene held her tight until she stopped. Whoever was in the driveway moved in a deliberate pattern, as if he didn't want his approach heard—he was moving like a Pennypack Indian making his way through the woods.

"Shhh. Just whisper," Magdalene said. "Did you see who it is? Just nod your head—is it Stevie Rich?"

And Magdalene saw him. Magdalene saw the bully stalking the halls of Assumption. His lips were big and fat and protrusive; he had buck teeth; his forehead sloped down into the dead-end of his bushy uni-brow; he had a large skull, a jutting chin, and chunky but muscular arms; his belly was soft; his fingernails were dirty; his breath smelled like dead fish: the ultimate bully. How his family afforded a parochial school education was anyone's guess, but he was enrolled nonetheless. If Stevie Rich was snaking his way up the McAllister driveway, tearing up garden mice, she and Katie were dead meat; Magdalene had heard that he'd once broken a girl's nose in the Fields behind Assumption because the girl wouldn't kiss him.

"Katie, listen to me," Magdalene said, holding Katie's chin in her hands, but the little girl was already shaking her head. "Yes, yes, if he comes into the backyard, I'll distract him, and you hop the fence and run 'round the front and call the cops. Don't let Valerie stop you. She's a scardy-cat. Yes, you have to, Katie."

"No, no," Katie said, "he's not here."

"Who's not here?"

Tap-tap-tap.

Whoever it was had reached the concrete.

"Stevie Rich."

"How do you—?"

A lonesome whimper caught the wind. Magdalene didn't know if she could save whomever or whatever Stevie Rich was killing, but she sure as hell knew she couldn't listen to it being tortured. What will you do when your time comes, indeed?

"Just go!" she whispered in Katie's ear. Then Magdalene charged around the corner with a "YAWP!"—and tripped on the edge of the concrete. She tasted blood and dirt in her mouth. The fat tabby cat had jumped into the juniper bush alongside the McAllister house during the initial advance, but now it wound its way back to Magdalene, rubbing its body up against her face.

"Oscar Sceebers!" Katie cried and picked the cat up. It was the same cat Raven had chased in Katie's backyard the day before, the same cat cruising the Tidwell woman's driveway. Magdalene thought the cat must be used to seeing her splayed prone.

"I thought you said Stevie Rich was here, tearing up mice," Magdalene said, pushing herself to her knees.

"No, silly," Katie said. "That's his *mark*. If Stevie Rich killed that mouse, then he did it to scare us. A warning."

"Why would he want to scare us?" Magdalene asked, running her tongue over her teeth; they were all there, but it felt like she had taken out a chunk of her tongue. She was getting a headache.

"Maybe he knows you're snooping around. Maybe he has something to do with your case. Edie Killian told me Stevie brought a knife to school once."

"But why all the screaming? Who did you think was coming up the drive?"

Katie stroked the cat and held his stomach up to her ear.

"I was remembering," Katie said. "When we saw the little trail of blood, I remembered Stevie Rich beating up Henry Cabot. I wasn't there though. We went out for recess a little later than everyone else that day, but there were some spots of blood by the ramp door, and everyone said that Stevie Rich had beat up on a second grader."

"What grade is Stevie in?" It seemed like he was always older than everyone else in school.

"I'm not sure. He's been left back a *whole* lot."

"And he beat up Henry Cabot?"

"That's what Edie Killian said."

"You didn't actually see it? And Edie didn't see it either?"

Katie looked hurt. "No, Edie's in my grade, but all the older kids did. Didn't you hear about it?"

Magdalene was becoming more and more convinced that events just passed her by, that people and places, even birthdays, had little effect on her. *Float float float*. It was the same way that Michael's disappearance seemed to have affected no one else but her: no one was actively looking for him, no one really spoke of him, except maybe Tiddy, and she always used the past tense.

190 · *Saving Magdalene*

Jerry did, she thought, Jerry spoke of Michael.

"Alright, let's lay out the clues. Stevie Rich supposedly—"

Katie sighed and put her face into the cat's stomach.

"Okay, okay," Magdalene continued, "Stevie Rich beat up Henry—according to Edie Killian—and there's the rumor about him hitting a girl in the Fields. He certainly terrorizes the school. So, if Stevie Rich was bullying—"

"John-John was bullying too. John-John Hagarty," Katie said. "The boy with the pacifier."

Indeed, John-John Hagarty never went anywhere without his pacifier, but no one dared make fun of him. John-John was even taller than Stevie Rich: fatter too. John-John wore a trench coat that billowed around his thick torso and legs, so he looked like he'd eaten a thousand shadows; he barely fit behind the school desks. He had been in Magdalene's class at the start of her elementary education but had flunked the third grade; she had no idea what grade he was in now either. But if Stevie Rich was involved, then John-John wasn't far behind. Some kids even secretly joked that they showered together after gym class, but Magdalene didn't think much of secret jokes—she'd been the butt of more than her share, and besides: Michael would have told her if two boys had showered together under the same nozzle.

Magdalene bit her lip; she could hear Michael making fun of her for trying to solve the Cabot Case. Michael believed only in what was right in front of him. Even the dares followed a strict set of rules. "Life is like football, I figure," Michael had once said. "If a receiver doesn't catch the ball or, say, I can't make the pass, if I hesitate, the other team's gonna take advantage. That's it. That's the way the world is. The world and everything else." Magdalene, who rarely questioned her brother in worldly affairs, thought he was, in this matter, full of steaming dog poop. To Magdalene, the world was a place made up almost entirely of dark corners; *everything* was a mystery, their mother and suicide included.

"I need to talk to Stevie Rich," Magdalene said. This wasn't why she had come, but she couldn't ignore a clue or a suspect. Katie dropped a surprised Oscar Sceebers and clutched Magdalene's arm.

"He lives in the Lakes."

"All roads seem to lead to Paradise Lakes," Magdalene said, and, for the first time, she felt old. "And to the Puddle."

"You can't just go into the Lakes, Magdalene."

"Why not?"

"My dad says that everyone there is a 'goddamn Methodist.' "

Magdalene rubbed Katie's head. "They're just poor, that's all," she said. "I have to talk to Stevie Rich. If he was bullying Henry, then Joseph Bochdan may have been trying to just protect his friend. If I can prove it, Joseph won't have to go to jail or juvenile hall or wherever. He could be back with his mom, helping her paint more of those eggs and working with her at Sol's."

Katie smiled and hugged Magdalene around the waist.

"You're a real detective, Magdalene," Katie said, and as she reached up to touch Magdalene's face, the sleeves of her blouse slipped down her pale arms.

Magdalene jumped back a step and took both of Katie's hands into hers. A circle of oval bruises went around the circumference of Katie's left arm.

One two three four five.

"Who did this to you, Katie? Tell me. Tell me who did this."

Katie turned away.

"My dad says I can't keep the cat. Said he'd explain later. He said it was somebody else's cat. His name is right on his little tag, but no address, so how would he know for sure. See? Oscar Sceebers. What do you think that means—Sceebers? Minnie is named Minnie because she was the smallest box turtle I ever saw. The little turtles that live in water all the time, they're not box turtles. So Minnie is Minnie. Wonder why Oscar Sceebers is Oscar Sceebers? Maybe the owner's last name is Sceebers."

There were five ovals around Katie's arm. It was a handprint no doubt. From a big hand.

"Did your dad—?" Magdalene stopped. She knew Katie wasn't going to answer. All that was left was to help Katie escape. Of course, cluing Katie in to the plan would be a start, but if Willa's babbling had taught her anything (and Magdalene wasn't sure Willa Meade wasn't full of poop either), it was that little kids told things in their own ways. Like Katie and the story of Billy the lizard: the mommy and daddy lizards, David and Sarah, hadn't wanted Billy, so they ate him. Minnie the turtle—the turtle with the painted mood shell—was an escape artist. A turtle! Magdalene also knew from her sessions with Willa that little kids often needed help to get where they needed to go—some gentle but forceful manipulation. Securing the money situation was a top priority. Magdalene was becoming less and less sure that Michael's stash would cover all the expenses. And she'd need to talk with Katie's Aunt Angela (or at least call her when she'd gotten Katie on the Greyhound to New Hope.) There weren't many other options; she couldn't just drop Katie off at the shelter at Lindenwold.

How she was going to fit all of this in—the Cabot Case, saving Katie, and now Stevie Rich—she had no idea.

"Turn the tag over, Katie. Sometimes the owner's name and information are on the flipside. That's the way Raven's tag is."

Katie pulled her arms away, and Magdalene saw the circle of bruises hanging in the air, little puddles of fingerprints blinking the way flashbulb patterns did the first few seconds after the *snap fizz whirr.*

"Beth and Bobby Tidwell!" Katie screamed. Magdalene felt faint.

"Is this the same Tidwell lady you were talking about? Is it, Magdalene? It's a clue, isn't it?" Katie's face beamed.

Maybe Mr. McAllister had been angry with Katie because he wanted to be with Mrs. Tidwell. Magdalene forced herself not to count Oscar's whiskers. Where was Bobby Tidwell? Maybe Mr. McAllister and the Tidwell woman were going to elope, leaving Bobby Tidwell and Katie behind.

"Katie, I need you to keep Oscar Sceebers' tag a secret between us, okay? Don't tell anyone, not your dad, not Valerie."

"I wouldn't tell ol' Val anything. She's a gossip," Katie said. "You should hear her on the phone. She tells everyone everything about everybody."

Magdalene put on her best smile. "Good girl. I'm going to try to talk with Mrs. Bochdan tomorrow. I'm sure she told the police everything, but maybe they just didn't ask her about possible bullies, or maybe she didn't want to say anything, or maybe she doesn't even know. I have to find out. There's no way Joseph Bochdan killed his best friend for no reason; something happened, and if Mrs. Bochdan knows anything, I have to know it too."

"Are you going to tell *your* dad?" Katie asked.

"Only after I have all the clues figured out. My dad didn't mention anything about bullies to Aunt Tiddy. Joseph can't go to jail if he was trying to save his best friend, and his mom can't go to jail if Joseph stole the gun from his father—who'd maybe stolen it from someone else. Did I tell you Joseph's dad is on the lam? The police are looking for him. Maybe Mr. Bochdan was a bully too.

"Sometimes dads can be bullies," she added, watching Katie's face.

Katie rubbed the cat's belly again. Magdalene looked around the backyard. The moonlight threw the dogwood tree into silhouette, and for one brief second, Magdalene could almost imagine the Legend of the Dogwood being true; its longest bough stretched in supplication horizontally, almost at a right angle from its trunk, just like the trees along the Puddle, the ones closest to the old dock.

A slice of yellow light winked behind her, and Magdalene turned in time to see Valerie's face in the kitchen window—then it was gone.

"Katie, grab your telescope and go in. No, Oscar will be okay. He's an outside cat. I'll make sure he finds his way home." She kissed the top of Katie's head. "Be careful of Valerie. Don't say a word to anybody about what we talked about. It'll be our little secret. When I figure it all out, I'll report back."

Katie slipped into the house, and Magdalene picked up Oscar Seebers; the cat was purring like a vacuum cleaner.

"Okay, boy. I think you know your way home." Magdalene put the cat on the pavement in front of the house.

"Well, at least we learned how you got here. You're a smart kitty, Oscar Seebers. A detective! I bet Mr. McAllister is at your house right now. You better get gone."

Magdalene ducked as a bus hissed to a stop at the corner. She thought she could hear footsteps in the wake of the bus motor. Oscar Seebers sat in the middle of the pavement cleaning himself. Magdalene scurried across the street and dove into the berry bushes. She stuck her hand between her legs in an effort to halt her pee.

$1 + 2 + 3 + 4 + 5 + 6 + 7 + 8 + 9 = 45$

Mr. McAllister appeared in the halo of the street lamp and picked up the fat tabby.

"What are you doing all the way over here?" Mr. McAllister asked. "You been following me, cat? You better go home now. It's late."

He let Oscar down, and the cat curled around his legs. Mr. McAllister flicked his cigarette into the street and walked up the driveway. Oscar Seebers followed him.

Magdalene prayed Katie had jumped into bed and that Valerie would keep her mouth shut. She also hoped Aunt Tiddy and her father hadn't checked in on her or else he and Tiddy would initiate a manhunt—then again, maybe not. Still, she would have to navigate past her father once she returned home if he was sleeping on the sofa. And of course, there was Raven. How was she going to keep Raven from announcing her entrance? He would certainly smell Oscar Sceebers' scent on her. Magdalene sighed and crushed a red berry between her fingers, twirled its little, hard soul-pit, and wondered why she wasn't made of stronger stuff like the berry's soul. Her soul was as lost as her brother was. Maybe that wasn't such a bad thing: to be lost. Isn't that what detectives did all the time? Find things and people that were lost? And detectives solved their cases because they too had been lost and knew the darkness intimately— maybe not the cheery Hardy Boys, but Bogart's and Chandler's gumshoes for sure. If she could help Joseph Bochdan and his mother *and* Katie McAllister, then maybe she could stay lost; maybe she could stay lost and join Michael, and the two of them could play football or Freeze Tag until even the streetlamps winked out and the stars bade farewell to the sky. Maybe. She tossed the soul-pit into the bushes and made her way home.

+

Her father was on the sofa but lost in his own dreams—dreams of bailiffs and convicts, perhaps even dreams of Joseph Bochdan, his little frame swathed in prison stripes, for her father always got his man—with one exception, with one exception that gnashed at Magdalene's heart like the way the man at the Methodist carnival chewed upon a glass vase: in pieces, then all at once.

Magdalene climbed the stairs and stepped over Monien the panda as she entered her bedroom. She was surprised—startled even—to see that it wasn't much later than eleven o'clock; her father had obviously successfully navigated past the neon bar signs. Raven sniffed her all over; his ears were pinned back. He snorted once and retreated to the corner, as if he knew Magdalene had been consorting with that cat and hadn't bothered to invite or even notify him of the opportunity. Had she only been gone less than two hours? Her pillow smelled like dog. Burnt popcorn dog. Magdalene felt her entire world flicker like an unsteady minute hand.

And there they are: Magdalene and Michael, and it's late August and late in the day—summer has not quite surrendered the season, but there's still a ghost of a chill haunting the currents surrounding their bodies. Michael is nearly naked by the time they reach Finch's Landing. The dock is for babies, Michael said about four billion times, but he still likes to take his first leap from its worn and cracked wood. Magdalene is careful not to trip or stub her toe on one of the rusty nails sticking up from the wood like rotten teeth. It's August, and she's alone with her brother and everything is ugly and beautiful at the same time.

The sun is a marigold—a sinking, grand, somehow sad marigold, relinquishing its hold on the sky—and as Michael tears off the rest of his clothes, running silently towards the end of the dock, the Puddle and everything surrounding it—the huge overhanging trees, the little humpbacked frogs buried up to their eyeballs in red mud, the whirring dragonflies—shush themselves and bow their collective heads. Magdalene hears a golden oldie drifting from a passing car on Dirt Road—" 'Give me just a little more time / And our love will surely grow…' *" Magdalene hums under her breath.*

Michael's feet hit the pier—thunk thunk thunk—and there he is, suspended between the muck of the Puddle and the easy death of the sun. For half a heartbeat, his lithe body runs in the air, his arms pumping, his legs scissoring, chopping the air double-time—then the running boy sinks. She watches her brother but the dying sun blinds her eyes. Just the splash announces his submersion into the darkness of the Puddle.

Their conversation from their walk to the Puddle unspools. Magdalene listens in:

"But it'll be overflowed. It rained hard last night."

"That's the idea, Lil. This is the best time to Puddle Jump."

"But Dad said—"

"Yeah, yeah, I know, but as long as we watch each other, we'll be okay, right?"

"I don't want to take my clothes off."

"Then go swimming in your undies. Just don't complain to me on the way home that your butt's all squishy."

"Just from the dock."

"That's not Puddle Jumping and you know it. If I knew you were going to chicken out, I wouldn't have let you come. Shit, Lil, it was your goddamn idea to come here."

Michael emerges from the water and climbs back on the dock. Magdalene tries to will away the heavy oatmeal of hurt sinking into her stomach. She silences the replay in her head.

Michael points to the Jumping Tree.

"Just don't," she says. There is the tiniest of tremors traversing her voice.

"Don't what, Lil?"

"You know. Just don't."

"I…"

"*Michael*—"

"*...DARE YOU!*"

Michael's head slices the muck of the Puddle, then his arms, skinny and muscular, pull his body from the water again. Magdalene imagines even the sun would want to cease its descent to dry his athletic body. He is naked, and she tries not to look but she can't help it. Michael grins at her and points to another tree on the right of the dock, a gnarled old monster, its boughs (fingernails on a dead body) extended over the brackish water. The Dead Injun Tree. She wants to say, "Please don't." She wants to scream, "No goddamn way!" Michael shakes his head and smiles. No one Puddle Jumps from the Dead Injun Tree; the Jumping Tree is scary enough—he knows this; he's just fucking with her. He scales the Jumping Tree. Magdalene sheds her clothes; she swore to herself on the walk over that she wouldn't get naked in front of her brother. But Michael has never looked at her the way she looks at him—he couldn't. Maybe he's already seen other girls naked in magazines. Magdalene thinks she has the body of a twelve-year-old boy. But Michael doesn't care. A dare hangs in the air where Magdalene knows it will stay until it is satisfied. A dare respects nothing but the dare. She wonders how many times she or Michael have repeated that—a dare respects nothing but the dare—and as she runs naked towards her brother, who swings from limb to limb on the Jumping Tree like a monkey, the first finger of fall tickles her skin until goose bumps emerge and explode like popcorn in a sauce pan, goose bumps that will never leave her body, she thinks, not today, not ever. Far above her, Michael laughs, and his voice grows louder, increasing in volume until—

"This neighborhood's suffered enough, hasn't it, Barrows?"

Mr. McAllister!

Magdalene shook herself awake and was surprised to find that her hair was dry. She was in her pajamas. Raven stood by her closed bedroom door growling.

"Jack," her father said, and Magdalene recognized the lawyerly tone weaving its way into his voice. "Jack, she's going through a lot. She probably just misses Katie and wanted to visit. Is that so bad?"

"I'm tryin' to make everything normal, Barrows," Mr. McAllister shouted. "No offense, but your daughter is far from normal."

"Now, Jack, listen here."

"No, you listen, Barrows. We've been through enough, me and Katie. We gotta start our life over, and your daughter's not exactly a positive influence."

Magdalene couldn't hear her father sigh, but she knew he had; it was his way of buying time in a conversation, of holding back his reserves. She'd been witness to his practiced sighs innumerable times.

"How so, Jack?"

"Jesus, everyone knows she tried to buy it twice already. I mean, listen, I understand what your family's been through. Can lead a man to drink, I know."

"You're not still mad about the conviction, are you, Jack?" Magdalene's father asked in an even tone. "I was doing my job."

"Even if a man is broken, Barrows, it doesn't mean he's finished."

"True, Jack, true. Listen, why don't you come in? I'll make some coffee. Maybe we could go to a meeting together. There's one tomorrow night at EPPI."

"I'm not in AA, Barrows. Booze wasn't *my* problem, despite what happened with the newsstand."

"I wasn't accusing," Gregory Barrows said. "I was just asking."

"Well, I'm not asking. I'm telling: keep your daughter away from Katie. Things *need* to go back to normal. I'm seeing someone now, the first since Nancy—"

"Nancy was a very special woman, Jack." Magdalene's father's voice was steady, conciliatory.

Mr. McAllister exploded.

"Keep your kid away, Barrows, or I'll clip her pretty wings. I don't care what the goddamn law says. I gotta right to protect my family."

The screen door slammed, and Magdalene imagined her father standing in the frame for a while after, watching Mr. McAllister light a cigarette and disappear into the darkness between the streetlamp halos.

Raven whimpered at her feet, ready to fight for her honor, her Huckleberry friend. Hell, she thought, if Raven was willing to fight, maybe she should be too. Magdalene started to open the door, then shut it quickly as Aunt Tiddy, her face covered in green mud, her hair tortured back to her skull with rollers and pins and God knew what else, shrieked down the hallway.

"I heard everything!"

Tiddy pounded down the stairs.

"Shhh. Magdalene's asleep."

"Like a fox she is," Tiddy said. "She's Polonius!"

Magdalene resisted the urge to scramble back under the sheets.

"He threatened you!" Tiddy screeched. "He threatened Magdalene!"

"They were just words, Tiddy. No need to take the bait. If he doesn't want Magdalene to see Katie, then she shouldn't. It's his daughter."

"Like our Magdalene would ever do anything to hurt Katie McAllister!"

Her father sighed again. "I don't think that's his point. He's scared, Tiddy. After what happened with Nancy, he looks at what Magdalene did, and, I don't know, maybe he feels insulted by it somehow. He's scared of what she did. It unhinged him again. I think he just wants to forget."

"Made sure to tell you he had a new lady friend though, didn't he?" Tiddy said.

"Mrs. Tidwell."

Magdalene's ears burned.

"Who didn't know that?" Tiddy scoffed. "Men just have to tell other men anytime someone even glances at their pants."

"Beth Tidwell's a widow, Tiddy. I think her requisite mourning period has passed. She's allowed to date. It's a positive step."

"*Humpf!*"

"That doesn't sound like the Bard of Avon. Francis Bacon?"

"Stuff it, Gregory."

"Hmm. Bard the butcher say *that*?"

"She's from the wrong side of the tracks."

"No, Tiddy, her husband Bobby was."

"She's from the Lakes too, Gregory. She and McAllister deserve each other."

"Bobby brought her to the Heights. She's from Warminster, I believe," Magdalene's father said. "It doesn't matter. She's a good lady. Jack is right: he needs things to go back to normal. He sees Magdalene and he's reminded of what Nancy did. I don't know if he's an alcoholic, but he's not drinking now—that's the word around the courthouse anyway. I know his PO, Teddy Oteri, and Teddy tends, right or wrong, to tell tales out of school. Jack's even gotten involved with Big Brothers."

Magdalene didn't think Tiddy was buying any of it. Her aunt *humpfed* every time her father took a breath.

"I'll talk with Magdalene," he said, "straighten everything out. I should have just told her what happened to Nancy McAllister to begin with."

"Shoulda coulda woulda," Aunt Tiddy hissed. "What you need

to do is talk to her about *your* drinking, Gregory, about her schoolwork, and about what happened to Michael."

"One thing at a time, Tiddy. I think it's enough that I'm sober now. Let her finish her exams, enjoy her summer. We'll ease into everything else. She's all I have left, Tiddy."

"*Humpf!*"

+

It was all she could do to keep Raven from bounding down the steps to stake his claim in the discussion. She had to throw the monkey into her father's room (Tiddy's room now), and when Raven chased after it, Magdalene crawled in behind him and shook a small handful of purple pills from Tiddy's pillbox into her palm.

Downstairs, her father was saying something further about conciliatory gestures. " 'Et tu, Brute?' " Aunt Tiddy asked. " 'Then fall Caesar.' " Her father told Tiddy to keep her voice down. It was Magdalene's turn to scoff. If her father knew what Mr. McAllister had done or was doing to Katie, her father would lock him up, no ifs, ands, or buts about it, but Magdalene knew she had to be careful. No crying wolf. Love of the law held precedent over blood in the Barrows Bungalow.

No time for shoulda coulda woulda.

Her father's feet—still in his dress socks, she knew—hit the stairs, and the fourth step creaked. Magdalene tore down the hall and dove between the sheets, stuffing the pills beneath her pillow. Her journal fell from the bed with a loud crack, and Raven barked, announcing the presence of her father. She'd left her bedroom door open.

Magdalene rolled over on her side, offering her father only her back. He sat on the side of the bed. The bedsprings moaned like mud frogs. He leaned down to pick up her journal from the floor, and the mud frogs moaned again. Raven jumped on the bed and curled next to her.

"What are you writing?"

Magdalene panicked. She didn't want her father to read about Finn. He might find it alarming that his little girl was writing a story about running away for an audience of younger boys and girls. Magdalene was torn between tearing the journal from his hands and eating the pages or maintaining her silence and willing him to ignore it. Hell, he'd already done a bang-up job of ignoring her while he'd been drinking—what was a few more days?

Prime numbers that differ by 2 are called twin primes: 3 and 5; 5 and 7; 11 and 13; 17 and 19; 29 and 31; 41 and 43; 59 and 61; 71 and 73.

She heard her father moving her little alarm clock and shifting the stack of Hardy Boys books on her nightstand.

"I'll just leave it here, okay?" he asked. "Still reading the dictionary, Maddie?"

Maybe if she kept counting, he would go away. Why couldn't she visit Katie McAllister if she wanted to? What harm was there in that?

"Want me to read some words to you? I could do that," he said.

Magdalene kept her dictionaries on the shelves above her bed with the rest of her books. She was glad she hadn't hidden Tiddy's pills on her bookshelf.

"Here's one: 'ephemeral.' We'll sound it out: ĭ fĕm' ər əl. There are two definitions here. The first one: 'lasting one day only or lasting a very short time.' The second one is about flowers—didn't know this—'a plant that grows, flowers, and dies in a few days.' That doesn't sound very promising does it?"

Valerie Plum had dimed her out, that much she knew. (Mr. McAllister hadn't mentioned seeing the ADA's daughter fleeing the scene in the Heights.) She would get back at ol' Valerie one of these days—well, maybe not; she *was* running out of days.

"Okay, I'll pick another word at random. Here we go: 'palliate.' Three syllables: pal•li•ate. 'To reduce the violence of a disease, or to cover by excuses and apologies, or to moderate the intensity of, as in trying to palliate the boredom.' That's a good word. Palliate."

How was she going to find Stevie Rich? All that she knew was that he lived in the Lakes—at least she thought he did. Maybe Jerry Eves knew him. They ran in different crowds, but Stevie Rich had played some football. She would have to try to snag Jerry when he was on his way back from practice. She couldn't let her father see her cornering Jerry Eves.

"Mr. McAllister was just here, but I think you know that, and I think you know why. Or maybe you don't—not really."

Or was this just an excuse to see Jerry Eves again? She remembered Christina saying that different boys have different tastes when it came to kissing: some were like gum, some like bologna sandwiches, one—and Magdalene couldn't remember his name—had tasted like the underside of a turtle. Those had been her exact words; Christina had said it was the most disgusting thing she could think of. Magdalene imagined Jerry Eves would taste like peppermint—a peppermint candy stick, the kind Sol's sold for a nickel.

Damn it—she needed to concentrate. If she was going to accomplish everything she needed to do before she died, she'd have to push Jerry Eves out of her head.

"Mr. McAllister is...well, he's not a very pleasant man, let's say that," her father said. "I would categorize him as a bully."

Magdalene's body stiffened. A bully! Mondauk was infested with bullies!

"But he's cleaning up his act and taking good care of Katie, as I'm sure you know. It hasn't been easy for him, not after Nancy...Mrs. McAllister...passed away. He...well, he drank too much, and I don't think we have to get into that just now, but you and I both know that drinking doesn't solve any problems, it just makes more. It doesn't bring people back from the dead or make life any better. Now, I don't know that AA has all the answers. There's an awful lot of God in AA—hell, Maddie, there's an awful lot of God in Mondauk County—but whatever works, whatever gets people sober and helps them stay sober. For Mr. McAllister, it's anger. He's feeding off it, probably finding strength in it. His anger is keeping him alive. Now what I'm going to say is between you and me and old man Raven here, but I don't know if Mr. McAllister's drinking had anything to do with Nancy's death. I don't recall him being a drunk before that. But when Nancy took her own life, Jack McAllister went to hell in a hand basket, as Shakespeare should have said if he didn't."

Magdalene's counting froze: *took her own life?* Mr. McAllister's wife had killed herself? He lied, she thought, Atticus lied.

"No, it wasn't cancer. I told you that because...I was confused. Drunk. Jack—Mr. McAllister—feels threatened, I guess, by you, because of what happened to his wife. Now, I know we never talked much about any of this, about what you did, because I thought it best to let you get on with living, let Willa Meade sort out what needs sorting out, and then we would hack through whatever we needed to when the time was right. It's summertime, after all, and you should be enjoying yourself before high school—which we should talk about too. I want you in tip-top shape, but we can defer your freshman year if necessary. I was thinking maybe you could work in the file room a couple of days a week in my office. Mrs. Banniman could use the help. Karl Matthews' son worked there before he went to college, and you're at least as smart now as he was then. Grady Matthews isn't the brightest bulb in the batch, sorry to say."

Magdalene's stomach hitched and she sucked for air—quietly. It was as if someone had punched her in the stomach. Could she do *nothing* original? Nancy McAllister had committed suicide? Katie's mom had succeeded where Magdalene had failed? Magdalene didn't really remember her, but Nancy McAllister had probably hated her husband. He'd probably abused her too, and she'd just had to get out. But leaving Katie behind—that was unforgivable. Magdalene swore if she ran across Nancy McAllister in hell, she would punch her in the face. God—did Katie even know the truth?

Magdalene resisted the urge to ask how Nancy McAllister had done it.

"Katie's all he has left, Maddie, so he's a little overprotective. You didn't do anything wrong, and there's nothing wrong with you. I'm sure after a little time goes by, you can see Katie again. Mr. McAllister's a little—well, he's a little touchy right now. Had to try and bully me—you heard, I'm sure. That's what bullies do. They try to lord over people who are physically weaker—or at least people they *think* are physically weaker—but they're usually pretty weak themselves on the inside. Insecure. Mr. McAllister isn't going to hurt anybody. He's scared. Unsettled. It's nothing personal. The best way to deal with bullies, Maddie, is to not deal with them at all if possible, or, if that's not an option, confront them head on. I think the former choice is our best course of action. Their emotions always cloud their judgments. If you think like a bully thinks for a half a second, you can stay one step ahead."

Magdalene could stand it no longer. If her father knew about Katie's bruises, he'd be issuing warrants or whatever it was he did when someone broke the law. But if she told him, he wouldn't believe her. She'd sound like a whiny girl, like Megan Riley or any of the other Bod Squaders who'd swirled around Michael like Christmas lights. More discussions and lectures would follow. There'd be a chance Katie wouldn't be rescued—and Magdalene would lose all opportunity to do so. It was only because of Michael's mattress stash that Magdalene knew she could get Katie on a bus to her Aunt Angela in New Hope. There was no way to reach her father, throw herself on the mercy of the court, get him to see his daughter as more than a damaged egg.

"And what about Mrs. Tidwell?"

Her father didn't seem surprised when she asked; he merely laid his hand across her back.

"Well, that's a sticky situation. It's what I was just talking about. I'd heard rumors before tonight. And maybe it's good for both of them. Sometimes two people who've been decimated by tragic events can find solace in each other's arms."

"What's so tragic about Mrs. Tidwell?" Magdalene asked. "Tiddy said she's from Paradise Lakes. Is that the tragedy?"

"Well, no, Maddie. It's not tragic to live in the Lakes. Some parts of the Lakes are well kept, some not, but there are some good people living there. They just don't have the money to live anywhere else. It's sad, maybe, but not tragic. Some of the parents even send their kids to Assumption. If they didn't have the tuition, they could probably move to the Heights."

"That's where Mrs. Tidwell lives now."

Magdalene covered her mouth.

"There's nothing like eavesdropping to show you that the world outside your head is different from the world inside. But I'm not even sure Mrs. Tidwell ever lived in the Lakes. Her husband did, before they married. He was a fireman in New York City. Lived with a cousin up there so he had a city address. He had to be a resident of New York City in order to be a fireman, and Bobby Tidwell always wanted to be a fireman. The Mondauk County Fire Department is pretty much all volunteer. Bobby grew up in Paradise Lakes but escaped as soon as he could. Married a girl from Warminster. He stayed in the apartment in the city to keep his job and came home to Beth and a house in the Heights on his days off. He wanted to move to New York with Beth—there or Philadelphia—but his brother, his nephew, and his grandmother were still here, see. His brother's a junkie. The grandmother is handicapped. They live in two dilapidated trailers on a tiny plot of land in the Lakes. It's sad, Maddie. I knew Bobby a little. He used to come down to County Hall to help his brother out—bail him out mostly. I know his brother *very* well, I'm sorry to say. Assault, possession with intent to distribute, breaking and entering—tried to hold up Sol's with a homemade gun that exploded on the bus on his way home. Arson, even. I believe you go to school with his son, Steven. Every inch the bad egg in training. He's been in front of the court a number of times already."

Was Bobby Tidwell's criminally minded brother the Frannie

Tidwell Katie had mentioned? Magdalene didn't know a Steven Tidwell at Assumption, but she didn't know a lot of kids. She wanted to roll over and face her father, seek comfort in his neatly trimmed gray hair and steady eyes, check his breath for alcohol, study his fingers for nicotine stains, but she didn't dare; her poker face needed work.

"What happened to Bobby Tidwell?" Magdalene asked.

"Bobby died when the towers came down—the World Trade Center. He was off-duty, hanging around his apartment—packing for a few days back in Mondauk, actually. But like all the other firemen in the city, he suited up and was at the site within minutes. You see, Maddie, these men and women, the firemen and police officers who died on 9/11, didn't make the most money or have the most upwardly mobile jobs, but they're the ones watching over us at night—and that day, they did what was necessary without hesitation. Bobby Tidwell died doing what he loved to do—fighting fires. This time the fires won."

Her father cleared his throat.

"His brother tried to milk Bobby's death for all it was worth, as if there was money to be had in the wake of all this, as if that money—insurance, what-have-you—wouldn't go to straight to Bobby's widow. I don't know Beth Tidwell very well. I've met her a few times, of course—I think I've met everyone in this town a few times. She kept to herself. She never joined any of the widows' groups. She never spoke to the press. That's what I meant about finding solace in each other: Mrs. Tidwell and Mr. McAllister are both survivors. And both reacted in their own way: Beth Tidwell pulled back and locked the shutters. Mr. McAllister drank. If he's got an extra chip on his shoulder, it's easy enough to see where it comes from."

It only took a few seconds before the words clambered up her throat like vomit. She knew they were only the prologue, but she was able to suppress everything else, even if she didn't know exactly what she was holding down.

"WHY DID YOU LIE TO ME? WHY DIDN'T YOU TELL ME THE TRUTH?"

Her father didn't seem disturbed by the yelling; he rubbed Raven's head and told him to go back to sleep.

"There's a lot we haven't talked about, Magdalene. About you and me. The drinking—my drinking. Your brother. I just wanted us to spend the summer getting back to normal. I figured towards the end of the season, when we both are feeling a bit more like ourselves—"

"I'll never be normal," Magdalene said. "Not ever and not eventually. I'm not even sure I know what normal is."

Her father rubbed her back like he had Raven's head.

"I know. And I want to help you figure out why you feel that way. Some of that you're going to work on with Willa. But I thought we might get off on the wrong foot if we started in on everything right away. Maybe I was being selfish. I needed time to remember who I was before your mother got sick, before Michael...I needed to get back to work. I love what I do, and I needed to remember that. And I love you and your brother and Aunt Tiddy—what a godsend, her coming here to help us. We just need time to heal. Beth Tidwell didn't even want to talk to other 9/11 widows, and now she has a boyfriend. I would say that's a step in the right direction. You make those steps inch by inch, and that's what we're going to do. That's what tonight is. I'm sorry I didn't tell you the truth about how Nancy McAllister died. I won't lie to you again, Maddie Monkey, I promise."

Her father squeezed her shoulder. Magdalene pulled the sheet tighter and moved as far from her father as she could. Raven yelped in his sleep, and Magdalene knew that behind his soft little eyelids he chased the fat tabby cat.

"You probably heard—I should have just told you—I have this big case on my desk. The whole town has this case, I should say. It involves one little boy hurting—shooting—another little boy. It happened at Assumption when you were in the hospital. I'm sure you've put it all together, my little detective, just from going for your exams with Sister Mary Joseph. God, I'm so proud of you for plowing through those finals like you're doing."

Magdalene wondered if she could vomit her guilt too.

"This case is going to eat away at the heart of this town the same way the terrorist attacks did. It's going to require a lot of man-hours because...well, because there's no clear bad guy here. No one seems to know why the little boy shot his best friend—not even the little boy who pulled the trigger. But someone has to pay for the crime; someone has to figure out what went wrong that day in that second grade classroom. It's not Columbine, but a sweet little boy is dead, and real life has come to Mondauk County once again. But I'll be here for you, Maddie. If I seem distracted, it's just that I don't exactly know how to proceed with the case. I think we're both going to need to lean on Aunt Tiddy a little. I'd like to get my bed back though!"

He laughed a little and his laughter shook the bed. When Magdalene didn't laugh back, her father tucked the sheets tighter around her body and kissed her on the temple. His breath smelled tired—no booze, no Camel cigarettes, just bone-weariness. Magdalene wanted to reach out to him, but she couldn't. Everything I've ever loved goes away, Magdalene whispered inside her skull. Everything I love goes away.

Her father closed the door behind him so quietly she didn't even hear the squeaky doorknob turn—how did he always manage to do that? Magdalene swore to herself that she would never find solace in the arms of another. She swore that she'd always stand on her own— and fall on her own sword when the time came. Weakness came from needing other people—her mother, Michael, Christina, Katie—and Magdalene was tired of being weak. She felt her grandmother's blood rushing through her own; she could feel the unyielding cold granite of Rosewood Seton's gravestone against her back. Magdalene lifted her pillow and counted the purple pills: thirteen in all. Maybe not enough to kill her, but a start. She needed to begin severing ties—at least emotionally. Magdalene flipped her journal open to the little calendar she had gotten from the bank and pasted to the inside front cover. All that remained to do was pick the actual date. Solve some mysteries, murder her dog, pick an end date. Magdalene closed her eyes, and far off she could hear water trickling. Without warning, she fell into a warm, dark puddle, surrounded by the hypnotic whirring of dragonflies. Magdalene tried to say the word "no" once or twice, but her mouth filled with water. When she woke, her sheets were soaked. Raven sniffed suspiciously at them.

It rained for the next three days.

A Lab's Ears Are Made of *SILK*

Episode II:

What Pig Said

It didn't take Finn long to become lost. The Wold was new and scary, and Finn had little experience in the Wold. He had no idea how long he'd been walking, but it seemed like forever. When he finally rested, he made sure to keep one eye on his basketball; Finn didn't want anyone stealing it away.

"ACHOO!"

Finn woke in a fit—one second he was playing basketball with the Boy and eating all the cookies he wanted, and the next, he was shivering from the cold. The basketball had rolled away a bit, but Finn was able to retrieve it easily with his paws.

"ACHOO!"

Finn sat up.

"Ga-blesh-you," Finn said.

"Thank ye."

Finn sniffed the air. Even though he couldn't see the sneezer, there was a familiar smell.

"Do I know you?"

"ACHOO!"

"Ga-blesh-you again," Finn said.

"Thank ye again," the voice said.

Sniffle, sniffle.

"Where are you?" Finn asked.

Cough, cough.

Finn decided it might be time to move on.

"Excuse me, mister," Finn said. "Do you know of any place I could go that isn't so cold?"

"Ye were sleeping on the vent," the voice said.

Finn turned around. True enough! He *had* been sleeping on a vent. A steady, cold breeze blasted from the floor. Finn started to lift his butt from the vent—the only part of him still asleep was his butt!

"No, no—don't move. Ye were blocking it nicely."

Finn sat back down.

"Where are you?" Finn asked again.

"Up here, heathen," the voice said. "How many times do we have to go over this?"

Finn looked up, and there, inside of a glass house, just at Finn's eye level, was Pig. The glass house—a large aquarium—had a round food bowl and a water bottle suspended from one side and an upside down shoebox on the far left. On the other side of the aquarium were two gray cardboard toilet paper rolls. Pig was brown and white and black and looked like a chubby log of fur with two little, round, pink ears stuck on one end. He was huddled beneath a blanket of newspapers. Pig appeared to possess a nervous habit: he nibbled on his own whiskers.

"Mr. Pig!" Finn cried.

"Careful," Pig said.

Finn cocked his head.

"Of what?"

"You're breathing on me."

Finn lowered his head and tried to breathe on something else.

"I am sorry, Pig."

"I could catch cold, ye know," Pig sniffed.

"What would you do with it if you caught it?"

"Not *it*," Pig said with a hint of venom in his voice. "A cold."

"A cold," Finn repeated, sniffling himself.

"Sniffles," Pig said. "Sneezing."

"Hmm," Finn said, still not sure, but not wanting to be rude.

"Like hairballs," Pig offered.

"Oh," Finn said, for he knew the danger of hairballs.

Pig coughed a little. He sucked on his whiskers.

"I could die, ye know."

"Die?"

"Yes, die: *morte*. Deleted. Corporally ceasing to exist. Dead."

"Die," Finn said, trying out the new word. It didn't sound so good in his mouth.

"From a cold," Pig said. "Cavies do that. Die from a cold."

"That sure does sound awful, Mr. Pig," Finn said. He still wasn't sure what "die" meant, but Pig certainly seemed upset enough about it.

"Cavy," Pig said.

"Ga-blesh-you again," Finn said.

"I didn't sneeze."

"But you...I—"

"Cavy. *I'm* a cavy," Pig said, chewing on his whiskers. "Of the genus *cavia*. Or the family *caviidae*. To call me a guinea pig is an insult to my race."

"I don't know about any of that, Mr. Pig, sir," Finn said, "but I'm on a Great Journey of sorts, and I was wondering if you could help me."

"And why should I?" Pig said, so upset he flipped off his newspaper blanket and walked into his food bowl. "A Cavy helping a black Labrador retriever? Whoever heard of such nonsense? Besides—what about that time ye barked at me."

"I don't remember, but I am truly sorry if I did. Sometimes I bark just because. Maybe you scared me."

"Oh, so it's my fault?" Pig asked.

Pig noticed he had four whiskers stuck in his mouth, and, as casually as a chubby guinea pig could, he noisily hacked the whiskers out (along with a fair amount of lime-green phlegm) and nibbled on a toilet paper roll. ("To cleanse the palate.")

"Besides: my title is Vicar," Pig said, puffing out his round tummy. "I'm a Vicar to ye."

One of Pig's whiskers flickered in the huffing and puffing and went up his nose.

"ACHOO!"

Finn refrained himself from bleshing Pig.

"Ordained and everything," Pig said. "And for that alone, I deserve your respect. I don't have to do anything else."

Oh my, this isn't going well, Finn thought, and he stood up and yawned, more out of sheer frustration than sleepiness—although, Finn *was* still very tired, despite his nap. He almost always needed an after-nap after a nap.

Pig scurried behind his water bottle and shivered and shoved as many whiskers in his mouth as he could.

"Please, don't hurt me," Pig said, trembling. "Don't."

Finn sat back down.

"Hurt you? I would never—"

Pig stopped shaking and looked embarrassed.

"Heightened sense of fear," Pig said, not looking at Finn.

"I just wanted to ask—"

"Are ye saved?" Pig asked, now staring Finn straight in the eyes.

"Saved?"

Pig tossed his nose in the air, as much to illustrate the importance of his point—being saved!—as to dislodge a stray whisker still stuck between his teeth.

"Saved! Are ye going to go to heaven, boyo, or are ye going to hell?"

"Well, I'm not quite sure *where* I'm going. I've been wandering around for—"

"Ye haven't even left the house, dog," Pig said dismissively.

"I haven't—?"

"Ye don't go to heaven or hell until ye leave the house. Until the Lord calls ye," Pig said. "They'll lie to ye. They'll tell ye, 'Come on, let's go for a ride, dog,' and the next thing ye know: SQUEAK— you're gaspin' for air; you're clawin' the sky. Then ye meet the Lord."

"Who is the Lord?" Finn asked, genuinely curious.

Pig sputtered and spit and turned in a circle. His whiskers were all askew, as if they'd exploded on his face. Finn sniffed at the glass walls in concern. Perhaps all the whisker sucking had made Pig confused about his place in the Wold—more confused than Finn.

"Ye don't who the Lord is?" Pig asked.

"I don't know...I was just...I don't think we've met."

"Do you, um, congregate with cats?" Pig asked in a casual tone.

"Cats? No, Mr. Pig—Mr. Vicar, sir. I chase Alley Cat once in a while."

Pig lowered his voice to a whisper.

"Good, good. Can't get into heaven consorting with cats."

"Consorting—"

"Do ye like girls?" Pig asked. "Ye have to like girls to get into heaven."

"Girls...I wasn't trying to get into heaven...I just—"

"Oh, wait: *bitches*," Pig said. "That's what your kind calls them, right?"

Finn didn't know.

"Never mind...so ye like girls then, dog?"

Finn thought for a moment. Pig had thrown a lot of information at him.

"Well..." Finn began carefully, making sure he used the right words, watching Pig's little face (Finn loved how his nose never stopped twitching!), "I love the Boy."

Pig squeaked.

Pig squealed.

Pig sounded like this: WHEEET WHEEET WHEEET WHEEET!

Finn tried to not look surprised, but the Pig's song was so high-pitched! Finn's ears quivered and quavered.

Pig's circle dance came to a halt in a flurry of dust and chips.

"HACK!"

From Pig's mouth came another tiny pile of green-tinted stuff: bits of newspaper and toilet paper roll, small pieces of what Finn assumed had been Pig's lunch, and there, stuck in the center of the pile: a quivering stalk of translucent white. Pig had swallowed one of his own whiskers!

"Ye love a Boy?" Pig whispered after coming to an unsteady standstill.

"Don't you?" Finn asked in return. "Don't you love the Boy?"

Pig turned his back to Finn.

"You'll *never* get into heaven if ye love a Boy," Pig said. "I'm the Vicar. I know! It's been demonstrated."

Demonstrated.

"It's been demonized," Pig continued.

Demonized.

"The Good Book says, 'He who lays down with the Boy will forthwith have a body defiled.' "

Defiled.

Finn tried to remember all the Blue Books the Boy had read to him. They were all Good Books as far as Finn was concerned.

Pig was still talking: "If ye don't accept the Lord into your heart, dog, ye will not go to heaven."

Finn spoke before he thought: "I wasn't going to heaven."

Pig scampered right up to the glass.

"What d'ye do?" Pig asked, salivating a little on the glass.

"Kill someone?" Pig asked.

"Steal, perhaps?" Pig suggested.

"Did ye—did ye have *relations*?" Pig gasped.

"Relations?" Finn asked, genuinely puzzled

Pig's heavy breathing fogged the surface of the glass.

"If ye did," Pig panted, "ye have to tell me everything."

"I...no...I never...I'm not sure what that word—"

"You're not a Moslem, are ye?"

"No, I'm a—"

"Jew?"

"Ga-blesh-you," Finn said.

"Jesus and a biscuit!" Pig squeaked. "Will ye *please* stop bleshing!"

"I'm sorry, Mr. Vicar, sir. Like I said before, I'm on a Great Journey. I'm looking for some answers. One answer, actually."

Pig showed Finn his butt again.

"All the answers ye need are in the Good Book," Pig said.

"The Good Book? Well, where can I find the——?"

Pig turned around slowly (he had to; Pig was portly) and eyeballed Finn.

"I'm saved," Pig said proudly, puffing his chest out. "For I am the conduit of the Lord."

Finn tried not to giggle. Pig's chest was *so* little.

"The era of subtlety is over!" Pig declared.

"Ask me!" Pig challenged. "I've read the Good Book backward and forward. I know sin, and I know our Lord."

Finn looked down at his paws, embarrassed. The moment was here, finally here. Finn raised his head and brought his nose close to the glass. Pig backed up a wee bit.

"Are my ears made of *SILK*?" Finn asked.

WHEET! WHEET! WHEET!

"That's your question?" Pig's eyes bulged like two tiny, black basketballs. "That's the question ye bring to someone of my stature? I'm *enlightened*, ye know. Oh yes—not every Vicar is enlightened. Mix a pinch of the east into the west. The Good Book and the Path. WHEET! WHEET! WHEET! All this I know, and ye ask me about your *ears*?"

"Yes," Finn said; he was making progress. "I need to know if my ears are really made of *SILK*."

"Sit, please, dog," Pig said. "The draft."

Finn sat down upon the vent. It *was* cold.

"I told ye: if I catch cold, I'll die," Pig said.

"What's 'die' again?" Finn asked.

"No. More. Carrots," Pig sighed, saying each word slowly.

"I don't think I like carrots," Finn said.

"Then ye won't mind takin' my place," Pig said, jumping up (which wasn't very high, as guinea pigs—cavies—as a rule, don't jump).

"That's it!" Pig said, trying to snap his little fingers. "Ye can take my place!"

"Take your place?"

"Yes, yes. I'll tell ye if your ears are made of *SILK*, and ye can take my place."

Finn eyed the glass house.

"I don't think I'd fit," Finn said. "I'm grown."

Pig muttered to himself and kicked his water bottle with his crooked toes.

"Dammit, you're right, dog," Pig said to himself as he fluffed the newspapers together to make a bed. "Goddamn Darwin. Gotta stick with the Good Book, gotta go with the Book."

Finn gestured with black nose (still runny, by the way, from sleeping on the vent) towards the upside down shoebox.

"If you're cold, why don't you sleep in there?" Finn said. "It's gotta be warmer than those old newspapers, Mr. Vicar."

"The Lord will provide," Pig said.

"What?" Finn asked.

"Speak up," Pig said, clearly irritated. "I don't speak 'dog' all that well, dog."

"The Lord will provide what?" Finn asked.

"Shelter. The Wold's a mess. Goin' to pieces. Just look at these headlines," Pig said, gesturing to his newspapers.

"You peed on that one," Finn said. "It's all smeared."

Pig turned around and shuffled the newspapers with his back feet, then turned back.

"A-ha! See!" Pig shouted—then grew quiet. "Oh. The funny pages. Never mind. What the Vicar does is bring all these things together under the…under the…under the protection of the Blanket of the Lord!"

Finn waited what he thought was an appropriate amount of time, then spoke very quietly: "Why are you afraid of dying?"

Pig managed (sort of) another jump.

"Why? Why?" Pig said. "WHEET! WHEET! WHEET! Because when we die—well, when *I* die—when whoever dies—the Lord judges ye according to how you've lived your life. If ye were good and followed the Good Book and stayed clear of the Moslems and the Jews and the cats—especially the cats!—then ye get into heaven. No cages in heaven! No glass! And no colds! Just ye and others like ye—or, rather, me and others like me."

"But why are you afraid?" Finn asked, more confused than before.

"They let blacks in now, I heard," Pig sniffed.

"Blacks?"

"Blacks! Blacks! Jesus on a soda cracker! You're a *black* Lab, for Christ's sake!"

Finn thrust his chest out.

"I have a Little White Tie."

Pig gasped.

"Mixin' the races!" Pig said.

Finn sighed.

"Mr. Vicar, sir, I'm not looking for heaven. I'm looking for an answer."

Finn thought of all the books with the blue covers on the boy's bookshelf.

"It's...it's more of a mystery," Finn said.

"A mystery?" Pig asked, looking interested.

Finally!

"Yes, yes!" Finn said. "The Mystery of the *SILK* Ears!"

Pig waddled away from the glass.

"Back to that," Pig said, distrust in his squeaky voice. "Back to the ears.

"Do ye think *my* ears are made of *SILK*?" Pig suddenly demanded. "Do ye?"

"I wouldn't know, Mr. Vicar. I'm not even sure what *SILK* is," Finn admitted. "Except I know what it looks like in my head. It looks like this."

And Finn thought really hard and used his Smart Bump (all Labs have one) and conjured everything he knew about *SILK* and everything he loved about the Boy:

SILK

"I can't see inside your head, dog," Pig said. "But I can tell ye this: if your kind values ears of this sort, then ye should strive to have those kinds of ears. The price of *SILK* is not cheap! And, if ye are able to attain this state of *SILK*, then ye need to make sure no one else takes it from ye. Ye need to make sure others of your kind don't lay down with those of another kind and pervert the Lord's plan. And no ho-mo-sex-u-al activity of any kind. The Lord really hates that. Make sure ye flaunt this *SILK*. Ye need to be willin' to die for it, and for sure, ye need to make sure others—and there will be plenty of 'em, others without this *SILK*—ye need to make sure they know they will burn for not believing in *your SILK*. Or at least make sure they feel inferior. See, dog: they'll kill ye for your *SILK*. Remember this: who made *SILK*? The Lord made *SILK*."

But Finn had already lifted his bottom from the grate on the floor and retrieved his basketball. Pig made him uncomfortable. It was time to move on. Time to continue his quest. More than anything, Finn wanted to go home, curl up next to the Boy, and let all Pig's nasty words escape in a snore or two.

"Don't ye walk away from me and leave me in the draft," Pig squealed, diving under the newspapers. "WHEET! WHEET! I'll pray for ye! You'll burn too if I don't! WHEET! WHEET!"

Finn was tempted, just a little, to bark and growl and generally throw a gala fit, but Finn knew finding the truth about *SILK* was more important than scaring Pig. Besides: this Lord Pig spoke of sounded like he would know the answer (even if Pig himself was chock full of bile and chewed toilet paper rolls and misplaced whiskers). Pig's Lord had to know what Finn's ears were worth. Finn left the room without looking back.

"The way is narrow, dog," Pig squeaked, "and so our minds have to be too! Don't forget! Narrow is as narrow does!"

And that was what Pig said.

Chapter Seven

The Mother

Christina Fuller had once asked: *ever notice that dentists' kids always have the worst teeth?* As absurd as it sounded to Magdalene at the time (Christina wasn't the most astute observer of students outside her immediate circle; her observations usually had origins in some failed romantic tryst or perceived playground slight), she had to admit that there was a certain, albeit wonky, sense to Christina's blanket statement. Dentists' kids did seem to always be in some state of orthodontic hell. Magdalene believed this theory applied to cops' kids as well; they were always the ones to avoid in school, almost as bad as Stevie Rich or John-John Hagarty. It was like children of police officers were forced into roles that they had no choice in choosing. If a parent was always pounding their offspring with warnings and threats about staying on the right side of the law, it seemed natural that those kids strayed to the other side. It was what Father Dave had called the natural tendency to rebel. Lawyers' kids had it too; how could they have a respect for the law when they were constantly being smothered by it? "The curiosity of the forbidden," Father Dave had said, "will lead many of the flock to the very edge of the cliff. Sometimes the excitement of what awaits them if they were to step off muffles the voice of the shepherd. But the shepherd is always calling for his sheep." Magdalene wondered if it wasn't the scary sound of the shepherd's voice that had sent the sheep to the cliff in the first place.

Her sorta best friend Christina was the daughter of a doctor (Magdalene realized she'd been prefacing the best friend sobriquet with *sorta* lately), and Magdalene knew no one more unhealthy than Christina—at least not their age—except maybe the kid in the wheelchair a couple of grades below them, and the young guy who worked at the record store who had multiple sclerosis. His limp and the prism in his glasses were the only obvious signs to anyone who didn't know, but Magdalene felt sorry for him anyway—and envious: at least he had something to blame his misery on; Magdalene had no idea of the origin of hers. It seemed to her she had always been this way, even before Michael had disappeared or before her father had become a drunk. She remembered being no other way. And maybe this was her rebellion—misery without specific cause. She'd certainly never heard the call of the shepherd, and she was inches away from falling off the cliff.

Jerry Eves worshipped the record store guy. Jerry had said (half-seriously) that he'd rather work in a record store when he grew up than play college football. Magdalene understood how uncool she really was every time she walked into the music shop; rock'n'roll didn't mean much to her—she liked it and sang its refrains softly to herself when she was in the tub, but the performers weren't leaders or thinkers to Magdalene. (Her favorite song was "Moon River," Raven's theme song—definitely *not* a rock'n'roll song. It was wistful, heavy with every goodbye she'd been forced to say. Raven, having been adopted more than once, knew the heft of a goodbye. Whenever she sang the song to him, he pinned his ears back, as if he suspected another goodbye was imminent.) Sure, rock'n'roll bands were artists, but not even Beethoven or Mozart could approach what a *writer* could do in just a couple of paragraphs or even a few words. Writers were detectives of a sort: one wrong word, one misplaced phrase, and the mood would be broken. Magdalene knew that her favorite writer, Franklin W. Dixon, whose name graced the covers of the Hardy Boys books, was actually a consortium of scribblers, but that just proved her point: the clues were there for those who looked. It was all about the story, the characters—extraneous discourses need not apply. All the writers she liked—Harper Lee and Robert Louis Stevenson and Mark Twain, to name a few—held secrets to the universe that Mick Jagger or Pete Townshend could only dream of.

Christina Fuller didn't give a hoot about books. As a point of rebellion, Christina rejected any attempt by Dr. Fuller to ignite interest in any topic that might require cracking a book, and she spoke of her father with practiced disdain. All Christina saw was a fastidious bookworm easily kept in check by Mrs. Fuller's brassy tactics. Magdalene idolized Dr. Fuller. Christina's father always had a smile; his tone was gentle, even when his wife was fussing about an end table she needed to buy or how this or that needed to be cleaned. (Her browbeating exacted a toll: the lines surrounding the doctor's eyes had become more pronounced in recent years; the creases were almost brown.) But he took his time with Christina and Magdalene. After ADA Barrows started drinking, Dr. Fuller's attention became increasingly important to Magdalene. Besides—Magdalene thought

Dr. Fuller liked it when she was around. Christina always seemed bored when Dr. Fuller pulled out a book or explained a procedure or showed them paintings or photographs. Magdalene was enthralled. Christina immersed herself in Reese's Peanut Butter Cups—by the dozen. (Christina also smoked cigarettes and occasionally even pot with some of the less threatening stoners.)

"All they wanna do is cop a feel. What do I care? I get to smoke a joint," Christina had told her once. (Magdalene didn't quite have a frame of reference for 'copping a feel,' but it sounded appropriately creepy.) Christina was the definition of unhealthy. In the summers, when she wore a cut off shirt, her belly stuck out an inch from her belt. "Baby fat," Christina explained. Reese's Peanut Butter Cups, Magdalene thought, how goth. The very nature of their friendship was a mystery to Magdalene. Their fathers had been friends in another lifetime, and occasionally—very occasionally, as in every two years or so—their fathers would take dinner together, but married people tended to isolate themselves and congregate only with other married people in their own occupational circles. Magdalene's father was the Assistant District Attorney—and a widower. Not exactly good company, Magdalene understood—even sober.

The way her father had taken his time with her four nights ago: that was a first. (She hadn't expected the Nancy McAllister suicide revelation either.) Magdalene had long ago designated a spot on her tall shelves for her father, even when he was a drunk. The admiration wasn't mutual. Her father loved Michael best—adored him. Michael was tall and skinny yet muscular, and the insouciant way his hair fell in his eyes made her father laugh. Michael played football; their father coached it. Magdalene suspected she looked too much like her mother, or at least enough to make her dad uncomfortable. (Magdalene saw no resemblance.) Then—*poof!*—Michael was gone, and her father's drinking increased double-time, and ADA Barrows became a ghost—not exactly flitting from room to room—more like crashing from door to sofa. Even now, as the blood flowed back into his face, the warmth back into his palms and fingers, a little flicker behind his eyes, he seemed the kind of person one admired rather than loved—not that Magdalene didn't love her father. But his steely gray temples and his strong features, his old matinee idol good looks—even the way he scrunched his eyes to look at something just a few feet from his face—were characteristics one noticed in old photographs. The tiniest things separated him from mere mortals in

Magdalene's head—and not the obvious things: his taut muscles or sly sense of humor. It was his brain—she could claim no other internal organ. She always wondered where his mind *was*—what problems it was chewing upon—rather than how it worked. Her own mind forever danced from subject to subject (writing, detecting, astronomy, counting); rapid twists in place of stately waltzes—she was, without a doubt, her father's daughter.

"The best way to deal with bullies, Maddie, is to not deal with them at all if possible, or, if that's not an option, confront them head on. I think the former choice is our best course of action. Their emotions always cloud their judgments. If you think like a bully thinks for a half a second, you can stay one step ahead."

The night he had talked to her about the widow Tidwell and 9/11 and Mr. McAllister, her father said many things, but it was his bully philosophy that stuck with Magdalene. She felt, for the first time, that her father had given something of himself to her—he had given her a logical course of action. And, equally true, Magdalene experienced guilt over being so goddamn sneaky—but she was a lawyer's kid after all. Magdalene told herself it came with the territory. Not that she didn't respect the law, but unlike her father, she didn't experience the law as a straight line (loopholes notwithstanding); walking the straightest line would put her no closer to solving the mysteries than her father and the DA's office and the police had been at finding Michael.

She had to think like a bully. To defeat Mr. McAllister—or at least circumvent him long enough to get Katie to a safe place—she would need to think like him. Mr. McAllister had to be scared. Valerie Plum was too dumb, too wrapped up in Paul Stern or some other stupid boy to have noticed the ring of bruises on Katie's arm. Mr. McAllister knew this; there was no other reason for him to prefer Valerie to Magdalene. But God forbid something were to happen to Katie when Mr. McAllister was at work (wherever that was) or at the widow Tidwell's—who was better equipped to handle a crisis? Certainly not ol' Valerie Plum.

The same thought process could be applied to Henry Richard Cabot's death, Magdalene thought. If her bully theory in the matter of the shooting was correct—and she was sure it was on the money—then the only way to save Joseph Bochdan from juvenile hall or prison or wherever the authorities would send a second grade killer, the only way to remove the burden weighing down Mrs. Bochdan, toiling alone at Sol's, husband gone, son in lockdown, would be to think like a bully. Magdalene knew what she had to do: she had to force her way—*bully* her way—into Paradise Lakes, confront Assumption's bully-in-chief Stevie Rich—he was such an idiot that he'd probably brag about picking on Henry—and leave the whole case neatly wrapped for her father after she killed herself. How hard could it be to think like a bully? Not very, Magdalene decided.

Still, she knew she had to glean some information from Mrs. Bochdan. Magdalene couldn't go barging into the Lakes on just a theory. Little kids tell their parents everything; they haven't learned to lie yet, most of them. If Joseph and Henry were being bullied, there was a decent chance Mrs. Bochdan knew about it but didn't quite equate those previous instances of preadolescent violence with the charges at hand. How could she? It took a real detective to even put together a hypothesis like that.

Magdalene figured to think like a bully, she had to act like one, but when her sneakers hit the crumbly asphalt of Assumption's recess area, it was empty. If any younger kids were stuck in summer school, then they were stuck inside. Magdalene wasn't completely sure she could have *really* picked on anyone anyway. Besides, Principal Sister Mary Joseph might recognize her and not be too kind about Magdalene ditching her makeup exams. The convent wall was still festooned with all the colors of the Crayola box in honor of Henry Richard Cabot, but they appeared to be dripping. At the end of the Corridor, a group of older boys in black t-shirts leaned against the bike fence, smoking cigarettes. Magdalene decided to hurry back the way she'd come. Throwing french fries at her was bad enough, but Magdalene had a hunch that if she provoked this particular bunch with her physical presence, she would have her ass gift wrapped and handed back to her. (She was thinking like a bully already!)

And that's exactly what she thought Aunt Tiddy was going to do this morning—engage in the time-honored tradition of ass-handing. After three days of rain, after three days of dusting and waxing the house and playing Monopoly and Scrabble (Aunt Tiddy's favorite) and Risk (her father stopped by to play one game in between the work of the people and the mud of Summer Camp), Magdalene had grown to fully fear Aunt Tiddy. The woman was tireless: one activity or chore led to another. It was difficult to find time for herself; she re-read *The Hardy Boys Detective Handbook* and worked on her novella between assignments. The rains were so heavy, the sycamore tree lost its leaves and the mimosa in spinster Evey Corcoran's yard next door lost its plumage, bathing both yards in soggy pink. Raven was frightened of the thunder. He'd spent most of Saturday night sitting on her bed, shivering. Magdalene had to force him outside to pee and poop, and even then, he took to peeing on the concrete closest to the house. It had been a rough three days. By Sunday, even Raven was showing signs of cabin fever. Tiddy had declared the outside world off-limits to play early on, and Magdalene's father had backed this up. "Plenty of time for exams at the end of the week," her father had said on Monday, winking, as the storm continued. "Do you want me to call Sister Mary Joseph? I'm sure she'll understand." Magdalene assured him (and Tiddy) that the next couple of days held nothing but review classes, and both adults had clapped their hands and proclaimed the weather too inclement to risk going outside.

On Sunday, Magdalene had begun to notice odd medicinal smells emanating from Aunt Tiddy. It seemed to come from her pores; even Tiddy's breath was sour. Magdalene began to worry that Tiddy would rot away during the rain-induced prison sentence. Despite Tiddy's omniscient presence of late, Magdalene admired the way her aunt had risen above the station she claimed her parents had chosen for her (housewife) and the way her aunt had stood up to her father after Mr. McAllister's front porch bully session. Tiddy's refusal to marry had been resolute (Magdalene assumed there *had* to have been suitors; old photographs showed Tiddy to be a very handsome young woman), almost as if she had remained unattached to prove a point. And despite her aunt's attributions of just about anything that tripped from her sharp tongue to William Shakespeare's quill, the old woman had read quite a few of the man's plays. Still, within a single hour during the weather-related incarceration, Magdalene vacillated between wanting to hug the doting, quoting, skinny woman who sprawled on the floor to play Othello for a record ten games in a row ("Shakespeare!" Tiddy had cried) and fantasying about strangling the old woman with her ever-present dishrag. Not that she could ever hurt Aunt Tiddy, but Magdalene was rattled by the latter thoughts nonetheless. She was supposed to assaying the part of the bully, not of the murderer.

Which of course led to the Raven Dilemma. She *was* going to have to murder her dog before she offed herself; there wasn't any other option. The three day rain sentence made this thought more disturbing than ever. Raven took every nap within paw's length of

Magdalene. Sometimes he slept on his back, a position Michael had called Dead Dog. During the night as Magdalene stared at the ceiling, fighting sleep, test driving bully phraseology ("That your lunch? Mine now!" "Who you lookin' at, punk?" You got a problem? No? You want one?"), Raven checked on her whenever he woke up. He rested his heavy head in her lap while she sat on the floor and was forced into bankruptcy by Aunt Tiddy (a Monopoly bully if ever there was one). Magdalene held her resolve against the love flowing between the doomed and the condemned. She fought back tears just thinking of how Raven would respond if he discovered Magdalene dead in her bedroom some morning not too far off. Raven's heart would surely break. It had taken a dog's age for Raven to surrender the anxiety and uncertainty with which he had arrived at the Barrows Bungalow. He trusted Magdalene's love. Magdalene knew his death would have to be swift. She just needed to decide on their day of dying.

This morning, Tuesday, Magdalene had woken to birds singing. Her sheets were scrunched into a bunch at the bottom of the bed. The sun on her face gave it away: the rains had stopped. The air outside smelled earthy; flowers drooped, their petals having been beaten back for three days. Magdalene swung out of bed and swiftly dressed. Tiddy caught her at the bottom of the stairs.

"The games are up, Magdalene," Tiddy said.

Snap fizz whirr.

Magdalene's skin caught fire—had Aunt Tiddy discovered she was missing some medicine? It had been hard to siphon additional pills during the rain internment, but Tiddy usually spent an inordinate amount of time in the bathroom whenever she announced she had to "go to the head," and ADA Barrows was rarely home.

Tiddy placed the Polaroid on top of a stack of other photographs on the dining room table. There were little piles of Polaroids everywhere: end table, top of the stereo, kitchen counter. Tiddy, it seemed, had yet to commence her scrapbook plans.

"We're going to catch up on the laundry today. I've already started. Everything needs to be hung outside to dry. We need to air the house out too, so open those windows. The house smells like feet." Tiddy stared at Magdalene's bare toes.

A basket of wet laundry was thrust into Magdalene's arms. Her sneakers were placed on the back stoop.

"It's muddy," Aunt Tiddy announced, looking down again at Magdalene's feet. Magdalene placed one foot on top of the other.

Magdalene hung the wet laundry in record time, grimacing at the size of Aunt Tiddy's undergarments. *Why were they so big? Aunt Tiddy wasn't a large woman.* Magdalene looked down at her boy hips and sighed audibly. Raven sniffed at a set of tiny paw prints in the mud. Magdalene set the empty laundry basket on the back stoop. Raven followed her and cocked his head when she closed the gate behind her. He had been the Joe Hardy to her Frank thus far, but if she let him continue to plumb the mysteries with her, it would be that much harder to murder him at their conclusion. Besides, Raven could never bully anyone. Unless someone tried to hurt her, Raven would surely greet each potential victim of Magdalene's with a lolling tongue and an eager Labby smile: all hot breath and irresistible ears. He didn't bark or whine when she walked down the driveway to the street, and she didn't turn around. She knew he'd be sitting there, already counting the minutes until her return, like she was sure he still did for Michael.

Counting was a Barrows family curse!

First she headed towards Assumption, half hoping to run into Jerry Eves. Kids were everywhere, free from their foul weather confines, and as she neared the school, Magdalene walked with caution on the opposite side of the street—as much to avoid nuns as to avoid bullies (although, in some instances, most involving Sister Rita, the avalanche of Assumption, the differences between the two tribes were subtle, a habit here, a bad habit there). Magdalene kept her body attuned to an assault by either party as she crossed the street and entered the schoolyard at the eastern end of the Corridor. Signs advertising the weekend carnival hung on wooden stakes driven into the lawn. The rain had ruined a great many of the homemade Henry Richard Cabot tributes on the side of the convent. A few of the poster boards were now nothing more than streaks of color. Some looked like streaks of blood.

(The older kids at the end of the Corridor had blood on their teeth.)

Magdalene retreated and walked around the school to the edge of the Fields and found her tree and fell asleep. When she woke, her skin was toasty and her mouth dry. She'd dreamed of bullies, and they'd all looked familiar—one even wore an apron—but each had black hair styled into a bob. She thought one or two had cowlicks. *Snap fizz whirr*—too late. The air on her face dispelled the last vestiges of her dream, and there it was, on the breeze, hiding just below the smells of cut grass and afternoon cookouts in the Basin: the rancid smell of the Puddle.

Magdalene left the Fields, still a little groggy, and walked northwest towards Paradise Lakes. Could she actually go into the Lakes alone? There were lots of bullies there—bullies, criminals, whores, junkies, and boozehounds. But counting the criminal element in her head settled it—she needed more bully practice than bully observation, she decided, and turned back towards Assumption. Play the part, Magdalene repeated to herself, play the part. Besides: *finding* Stevie Rich wasn't the dilemma; she had to *know* him.

When Magdalene saw the little boy standing on the corner, waiting to cross the street, she quietly quickened her pace to catch up. She didn't recognize him. Good, Magdalene thought. Victim number one.

One, two, three, four, five, six, seven...

"And where do you think you're going?" Magdalene called to boy, but she slowed her walk. What the hell was she going to do when she caught up? Steal his lunch? Pee on his library books?

Again: one, two, three, four, five, six, seven...

The boy turned around. For a brief moment his face seemed to melt, shimmering like a mirage, then resolve itself. *Oh no, not again*, the little boy's face said. *Mommy*, the little boy's eyes screamed. *I'm outta here*, the little boy's brows uttered, as they set themselves on an angle.

Once more, with feeling: one, two, three, four, five, six, seven...

Magdalene was surprised to find her hands bunched into fists; maybe this was going to work out after all! Still, she doubted she could administer a proper bully beating on the little boy. What if she really injured him? What if he told? There goes the lawyer's kid, people would say; no regard for the law, they'd stage whisper. The wrong Barrows kid disappeared.

Fuck: one, two, three, four, fix, six, seven...

Magdalene prepared to rain her fists on the little boy's head; her nails dug into her palms. Rain and run. The kid's feet were not nearly as determined as his eyebrows; he didn't even attempt to run. When Magdalene reached the corner, the boy flinched and smiled.

"Magdalene!"

She was out of breath; how the hell did she expect to play football with the boys when running three quarters of a block winded her?

"Magdalene!"

Magdalene raised her fists over the little boy's sandy brown hair. His eyes followed her hands.

"You're bleeding," he said and whipped out a handkerchief from his back pocket: a perfect gentleman.

"You walked safety with me to the nurse's office a while ago, 'member?" he asked, and Magdalene didn't. She couldn't speak. She wiped her palms with his handkerchief. She'd almost punched a little boy.

"If this were a movie poster," the boy said with genuine seriousness, "it would read, 'Just Because You're the Geek Doesn't Mean You Can't Get the Girl.' "

Magdalene handed the handkerchief back to the boy. He folded it neatly into a square and jammed it into his pocket.

"I upchucked in the hallway, and Sister Jezebel said one of the older kids would walk safety with me down to the nurse. You came, and you didn't make fun of me or stay away from me because I smelled," the boy explained.

"Smelled?" She'd found her voice, and it sounded old, underused, a smoker's voice.

"From the throw-up! You held my hand and told me not to worry about what they said."

"About what who said?"

The boy lowered his voice and looked behind him.

"Stevie Rich and the boy with the sucker."

"Pacifier," Magdalene said. "John-John Hagarty."

"Yep, that's him all right. You told me to look straight ahead and ignore them. They would be in trouble anyway, you said, because it wasn't lunch or recess and they were in the hallways. You said I should have upchucked on them!"

"I...I'm not sure—"

"My mom owns McCullough's," the little boy said. "She said she knows you."

"Danny Kildare?"

"That's me!" Danny cried. "I'm Katie McAllister's friend. We're in Advanced One classes together. She's the luckiest girl in the world to have you as her baby-sitter. My baby-sitter just picks at her zits all night and whines about boys and homework and her parents. She doesn't even play games with me. I thought *everyone* liked Monopoly. Battleship too! My baby-sitter said Monopoly was just for little kids and old people with nothing better to do."

Magdalene winced.

"So you walked me to the nurse," Danny said, "and then I didn't see you again for a long time. Someone said you were in an accident and that you were in a hospital and that you were sick. I thought you were brave."

"Why?" Magdalene asked. She recalled nothing of the walk to the nurse's office. Maybe she really *was* sick; everyone seemed to think she was.

"You weren't scared 'bout walking back," Danny explained. "You had to walk back through the bullies all by yourself."

A little kid whose lips and cheeks were stained with vomit being led by a non-Bod Squader through the hallways—well, those were obvious targets, but targets with a potential stink factor. So why hadn't they jumped her on the way back when she was alone? Had they known that she was Michael's sister? Maybe they'd been caught ditching class and been forced back into their homerooms. She'd been an easy mark; surely the bullies would have picked on her if they had had a chance. Magdalene made a mental note to pick her marks in the future with care; the more she thought like a bully, the closer she would get to Stevie Rich. Bullies knew how to pick their marks. It occurred to Magdalene that Stevie Rich might be in summer school, but Assumption was the last place she wanted to spy on him, let alone confront him. Nuns were natural spoilers.

"Could you walk me to Sol's, Magdalene?" Danny asked.

"I really have to get...okay."

Danny *did* look vulnerable out here on the corner, Magdalene thought. If she planned to save Katie from Mr. McAllister, she'd better be prepared to help out other bully victims when the opportunities arose. Standing alone on a street corner in the County Seat shouldn't be so dangerous an activity.

"Danny, why were you hanging on the corner just now if you were going to Sol's?"

The little boy laughed and put his hand into hers.

"Because I saw you coming, Magdalene, and I wanted to say hi."

"You were walking by yourself?"

"She...my mom...didn't...I was very careful," Danny Kildare said. "I've done it before. Walked home from our inn a bunch of times."

Once they reached Sol's, Magdalene forgot all about playing the bully. Sol's was packed with kids. Mrs. Bochdan was behind the counter, a slanted smile half-painted on her face as she served the kids and got them their candy and rang up their quarters. Magdalene had half-expected Mrs. Bochdan to come at her again with the broom, but the woman didn't appear to recognize her.

Magdalene wondered if maybe she was putting the cart before the horse, as Tiddy was fond of saying. (Magdalene doubted this phrase was attributable to ol' Bill!) Maybe she should just abandon the bully plans and start the next phase of her investigation with Mrs. Bochdan after all. Surely the woman knew if her son and his best friend were being picked on. It occurred briefly to Magdalene that the *best* source for this information (besides Stevie Rich) would be the parents of the dead boy, but Magdalene knew she didn't possess the absolute grace that situation would require. Besides, the Cabots would probably tell on her and ruin everything.

The clock on the wall, surrounded by Ukrainian holy cards and calendars, read 5:45.

Magdalene blinked. It was later than she expected. She was starving.

She asked Danny if he wanted her to walk him home. She wasn't sure where Danny Kildare lived, and Magdalene wanted to make sure she was back when Sol's closed at 7:30, shortly after the lottery was done for the night.

"Okay!" Danny said, as he took her hand again.

The walk to Danny's house took a lifetime. (He lived closer to the Lakes than she'd thought; Magdalene could smell its decay in every step.) Danny stopped to examine (and safely escort) a water bug crossing the street, and twice he paused to interpret girls' chalk marks on the sidewalk.

"She's unhappy," Danny said of the artist of a particularly uneven hopscotch pattern that ended in what appeared to be negative numbers. "Ohh, look. This girl's mad at her mom."

"How can you tell?" Magdalene asked, squinting at the sidewalk.

"I just can."

"And you're in third grade?"

"Yep," Danny said, never taking his eyes off the sidewalk. "Fourth grade in the fall. With Katie McAllister."

"Right."

After a couple of blocks, Danny stopped cold. A white Trans Am sped by and took the corner with a squeal. Its radio spat out words in staccato, bullets from a gangster movie drive-by: "*...you turn a blind* *eye...to a blank wall...and that's our life...*" Magdalene glimpsed the driver—was that Zooey Kildare? The woman's mouth was open: singing, perhaps, or chewing gum. She wore a cowboy hat.

Danny's shoulders slumped. He kicked at a soda tab.

"Was that...was that your mom, Danny?" Magdalene asked. It had been a while since she'd seen Zooey—but the cowboy hat: it couldn't have been anybody else. Zooey Kildare always wore a weather-beaten cowboy hat.

Danny squatted and regarded the soda tab with the eye of a jeweler before popping it into his pocket.

"What do you want to be when you grow up?" Danny asked without looking up.

Magdalene jumped a little. She hadn't been planning on growing up. Her throat constricted, and the words squeezed themselves out.

"I...well...what do you want to be?"

"I told you when you walked me to the nurse," Danny said, a little hurt.

Magdalene forced a smile. "Tell me again."

Danny's face lit up like a Christmas tree on fire.

"The Innkeeper at the End of the World," Danny Kildare said, raising his head. "I play a little piano too."

"To entertain the patrons."

"Right!" Danny said.

"What do you want to be?" he asked again.

Magdalene shrugged. Why not?

"A writer. I'm going to be a writer. And a detective."

"Both!" Danny shouted. "Wow!"

She didn't want to lie to him. When he'd first caught sight of the Trans Am, his eyes had widened like he was expecting—she didn't know—something good. Maybe Danny's mom was supposed to take him to Sol's.

"But I'm not going to grow up," Magdalene said. "Don't tell anyone."

Danny's face was a collection of circles: "Why, Magdalene? Why?"

Magdalene squeezed one eye shut, hunched her shoulders, and hung her head to one side.

"*My time hassss come,*" Magdalene hissed.

Danny shuddered. "I hope I don't get Sister Rita when *I'm* in the eighth grade," Danny said. "I hope she gets retired or something.

"Hey—if this was a movie poster," Danny said, "it would say, 'She's Chasing Ghosts and They're Chasing Her.' "

Danny covered his mouth with both hands as if he'd said something he shouldn't have. Magdalene laughed, and Danny laughed then too and placed his hand in hers again. His hand felt cold and clammy to Magdalene—a dead hand.

At least the subject of growing up was closed. *No good way to explain* that, *now was there, Magdalene Barrows?*

When they reached Danny's front step, he let go of her hand. A long concrete slab led to a porch with an old wooden swing flecked with faded, white paint chips.

"Whatever you're gonna do," Danny said, "be cautious. Look both ways before you cross over."

"Third grade, huh?" Magdalene asked her shoes; her head hung low. Was everything she was about to do scrawled on her face?

"Fourth grade," Danny corrected her with a smile.

"Your mom..." Magdalene said. "She's pretty busy? Yeah, well, sometimes adults are like that. They forget, you know?"

"My mom laughs at me sometimes," Danny said; his smile was gone. "I don't like it, but I don't think she's being mean either. My dad's always in the city or away on business. My mom—well, she picks on me. A little."

"Picks on you?"

"Oh, not like she ever hits me or anything. She just pokes fun at me a little. I'll be singing a song, getting the inn ready, and—"

"McCullough's."

"Yeah, and she'll walk behind me, singing like me and making faces."

Bully behavior.

"Does it make you mad?"

"I don't know," Danny said. "I just feel—silly. My mom's either always laughing it up—even the time the tea kettle caught fire and the curtains too: she just laughed and laughed until my dad walked out and slammed the door—or she's like Chicken Little."

"Chicken Little? 'The sky is falling, the sky is falling!' *That* Chicken Little?"

"Uh-uh. When the world's coming to an end, *I* could be on fire, and she might not notice."

Magdalene nodded her head.

"Then she pretends it didn't happen," Danny said. "I'll ask her about this thing or that thing, about the world ending and the sky falling and stuff, and she just laughs and imitates my voice. I know she's just teasing, but the older boys who work at the inn, they imitate me all the time now too. They're always fighting out behind the inn—the older boys—really fist fighting and all. It's scary."

Danny stared at his sneakers.

"My mom calls 'em her boyfriends."

"But not you."

Danny lifted his head but tried to avoid Magdalene's eyes.

"They make fun of my voice because my mom does. But they're not just teasing."

Danny's voice *was* a tad high-pitched. He spoke as if he were always excited, always on the verge of opening a birthday present.

"And your dad?"

"If my dad was a newspaper headline, it would read, 'Child's Death Ruins Couple's Holiday,'" Danny said. "Except I'm not dead."

"You have a nice speaking voice," Magdalene lied. So much for not lying.

"You want me to sing you a song? I know a bunch."

Magdalene shook her head and pinched Danny Kildare's arm.

"You trying to woo me?" Magdalene asked, smiling.

Danny scrunched his face.

"I don't know woo."

Magdalene was careful not to laugh.

"Danny—my mom lied too."

"She does?" Danny asked, his face a carnival of ovals again.

"Did."

"Did?"

"She died."

Danny nodded his head.

"My Pop-Pop died. That's how come my mom runs the inn. But my dad says the inn's not an inn anymore and hasn't been one in a long time. He says it's just a bar, but I don't believe him. He just can't see it." Danny paused to watch two boys race down the street on their bikes. "My mom's very busy. My dad too, I guess. They're...not together. I go to Sol's by myself all the time."

Magdalene almost hugged him.

"My brother—one time we were at Beach Haven—you've been to the shore?" Magdalene asked.

"Yeah," Danny said, "but it was a different one. A lot of old people."

"Well, my great-uncle, he has a house right on the beach almost," Magdalene said. "Just a few yards away."

"Wow!" Danny said, genuinely impressed. "We have to drive and then walk six blocks and *still* the water was like ten miles away!"

"Sounds like Wildwood," Magdalene said. "So, we're waiting for dinner, my brother and I—"

"Michael."

Magdalene blinked.

"Michael. Yes."

"He's—?" Danny asked; she could see him trying to find the right words.

"Yes. So, we're—"

"You miss him?"

"Of course, but—"

"You wish you were nicer to him and stuff?"

"Nicer to my—?"

"Sometimes when people die," Danny said, "the people that are still alive wish they'd been nicer or lent them money or gave them a better birthday present. Sister Jezebel said that when the end of the world comes, we're gonna have no time at all to do all the things we wish we'd done—not stuff like jump in the Grand Canyon or drive a race car—just people stuff. Being nice."

"I…" Magdalene shook her head to clear the…what? Had she been counting?

"What happened?" Danny asked.

She *had* been counting. She'd been almost up to a hundred by twos.

"I don't remember what we were—"

"Beach Haven," Danny prompted her. "You were telling a story about Beach Haven."

Oh, there we are, Magdalene thought: the lifeguard stand at Beach Haven. Why was she telling the lifeguard stand story?

"My brother—"

"Michael," Danny said.

"Yes…we were sitting on the lifeguard stand. It was late in the afternoon. The beach was pretty much empty. Everyone was getting ready to eat—"

"…or go on the boardwalk," Danny added.

"Well, yeah, 'cept Beach Haven doesn't have a boardwalk," Magdalene said. "But, yeah, people were done with the beach for the day, and they were getting ready for—whatever. Michael climbed up the lifeguard stand. (The lifeguard was gone for the day.) I told him not to. I didn't want to get in any trouble. I didn't think my dad would have liked us even being on the beach then, let alone on the lifeguard stand. But, um, Michael dared me...do you know what a dare is?"

Danny nodded his head.

"I stay away from those games," he said. He pouted his lips and squinted his eyes. "Those are the kind of games Stevie Rich and John-John Hagarty play. Make you do things. A lot of kids are afraid."

"That's what bullies do, Danny."

"Was your brother a bully?"

"What?"

"Michael. Was Michael a bully?"

"I...I don't..."

Danny shrugged.

"Did you get caught?"

"Caught?"

"On the lifeguard stand?"

Magdalene tried to delete the numbers from her head, but she seemed to be in the middle of a multiplication table. She forced words past her teeth, past integer guards.

"Yeah...no...well, not right away. Not caught, per se. We were on the lifeguard stand, and Michael pointed to the horizon. You know: the line at the end of the sky."

Danny nodded his head.

"So Michael points out there and says, 'See that line—that gray line all the way at the end of the ocean? That's England.' And I believed him."

"It wasn't England?"

"No," Magdalene said. "It was just the horizon. I thought you..."

Danny smiled.

"I was just messing about," Danny said, but Magdalene didn't believe him.

"When we ran back to Uncle Jack's for dinner, the house was full: second cousins and great-aunts and uncles and, well, just about everyone on my dad's side of the family. Except my grandmother. She's a politician."

"They don't go to the beach?"

"Too busy."

"Doing what?"

"She...well, she doesn't need anyone. She's too busy doing her own stuff."

Danny laughed.

"Everyone needs somebody."

"Okay, but—"

Danny cut her off.

"That was the innkeeper's job back then, back in history: bringing people together. He'd fix up their rooms and have the cook prepare meals, and then he'd draw beers, and all the guests would sit in the common room around the fire and listen to each other. Bringing people together.

"What happened," Danny asked, "when you went in for dinner?"

"Oh, well, I guess I'd gotten a splinter from sitting on the lifeguard stand. I still had my bathing suit bottoms on, and the lifeguard stand was old and the white paint was all chipped and splintery. I couldn't sit still at dinner. My dad, he was getting a little steamed 'cause of my wriggling around. He thought I was playacting for my younger cousins or joking around or something. He hushes me once, but I can't stop squirming. I don't wanna tell him where we were, you know. He'd be mad. So I'm trying to squirm so he doesn't notice, but he does. Michael's laughing, and so were my older cousins, and my dad stands up and pulls my chair back. He thinks I'm being disrespectful. Some older relatives—older like my dad's age—were there. My Aunt Tiddy too. She's not amused either. My dad asks me to stand up, reaches down, and plucks the splinter from my—"

"Butt."

"Right. Butt."

"Pretty cheeky," Danny said. He bent over and held his stomach, spilling high-pitched giggles.

"Good one," Magdalene said.

Danny straightened himself up.

"Inappropriate..." Danny said.

"Nice word, but I don't know—"

"...for the common room. Nothing too bawdy, in case ladies are present."

"Uh-huh."

"Just bringing people together. An innkeeper."

"Yeah, well—"

"Did you get in trouble?"

"No...trouble?...well, no, not really. My dad knew where we'd been. His eyes kind of lighted on my brother, kind of zeroing in on him. *And then Michael turns and tells my cousins about me believing the horizon was England!* Can you believe it? Everyone laughed—even my older relatives (but not Aunt Tiddy). My father let the lifeguard stand incident go unpunished. He shot one final look at Michael, who was grinning like a madman. I just sat there. Everyone was laughing— even my mom, who told me later what a wonderful story it was. And I just sat there."

"That was *so* mean!" Danny declared. "Did you want to just kill your brother?"

Magdalene snorted.

"Yeah, I did. He was always doing that—catching me out. But I was in...but he was my brother...is my brother. Just...what I'm trying...guess what I mean is this: sometimes people who love you can hurt you. And some people *mean* to hurt you 'cause that's how they are, they're not nice people—like Mr. McAllister—"

Danny gasped.

"Katie McAllister's dad?"

Magdalene shook her head; the numbers were lining up to be counted again.

"No, no," Magdalene lied. "A different McAllister. I just confused the names."

Danny seemed placated.

"What I mean is that sometimes people who love you can be mean, but it doesn't mean they don't love you."

"Sin," Danny Kildare said. "That's what'll get you. Sister Jezebel said that at the end of the world, you die right then and there with all your sins. Hey, Magdalene, what if you haven't made your First Confession yet? You still go to hell?"

"I...I don't know. I would think not."

Danny sucked on his lower lip.

"I think I know you what you mean," Danny said. "Everyone's got a bully inside them. Not the Stevie Rich or John-John kind. A different kind. My dad said that bullies pick on you because they see something weak. He wanted to teach me to box. My mom didn't want me to, so I didn't. (I didn't want to either.) He got so pissed, my dad, he went away on business even longer than normal. But if everyone's got a bully inside them, then they might even bully someone they love, just 'cause they see something weak. My mom said that weaknesses—she said *per-ceived* weaknesses, whatever *that* means—makes people mad, especially people who love you—not just bullies. She said it reminds other people of their own weaknesses. Reminds them of their own sins."

Danny Kildare pulled the soda tab from his pocket and inspected it closely before whisking it away again.

Everyone's got a bully inside, Magdalene considered. Everyone?

Danny Kildare hopped on one foot and spun around in a circle.

"Maybe one time when you're baby-sitting Katie McAllister," Danny said, "I could come over and play with you guys."

After all this, Magdalene didn't want to lie anymore, but she did, promising to check with Katie's dad. Danny—satisfied, elated even— waved bye and ran up to the porch of his house.

"If this were a newspaper headline," Danny Kildare yelled without turning back around, "it would say, 'Blind Kids Defeat Bullies They Haven't Seen in Years.'

"Be careful, Magdalene," he called as the screen door slammed behind him.

She took her time walking back to Sol's. There was a lot to think about. If it was true that bullies knew how to pick their marks, then Magdalene thought she was surely one. Why the heck had what Danny Kildare said brought her down? This was no way for a detective to act: studying her shoes instead of taking in her surroundings. Dr. Fuller had told her that's what writers do: look at the big picture and notice the little things, like the way the wads of dried pink gum, streaked with gray and black, were arranged on Meadowbrook Avenue like a cross, or the way all the starlings in the world seemed to have gathered on the telephone wires to watch her put one tired foot in front of another on her march to Sol's.

She resisted the urge to count the starlings.

There was a line for water ice when she reached Sol's. Magdalene didn't want to be seen, but the few kids that saw her ignored her. She had forgotten: she was a pariah. She could parade around in her skivvies, and most of the kids here wouldn't take notice or even look twice if they did. Resurrection Girl. When she fell asleep on the brick wall across from Sol's, her head in her hands, no one shook her awake or tried to tip her over. When she woke, the world through her bangs looked noticeably darker. The line into Sol's now consisted of all adults, some in suits, others carrying metal thermoses and wearing worn jeans or pants splattered with paint: the lottery line.

Magdalene decided to wait. She'd been gone for hours anyway. She knew Aunt Tiddy had more than likely already called her father. What was another hour now? The sun was already inches lower when Mrs. Bochdan shook the dust from her broom in the little concrete backyard, straightened the garbage cans (now all firmly tied to the small fence), and exited via the front door, pulling on the handle several times to make sure it was locked. In her arms was an overloaded grocery bag.

Magdalene followed her at a safe distance. *The Hardy Boys Detective Handbook* said it was important to keep several yards between herself and her quarry. The *Handbook* recommended using several detectives placed at different intervals to throw off the mark. But Mrs. Bochdan never turned around. She barely looked at the stoplight when she crossed Summerdale Avenue, and Magdalene saw her opportunity. The next cross street was Dungan Road. Mrs. Bochdan ignored the stoplight again, and as Magdalene ran to help her cross the street— she thought the *Handbook* mentioned something about helping old ladies cross the street, or maybe that had been in Michael's *Cub Scout Handbook*, she wasn't sure—a car sped across Dungan, and Mrs. Bochdan jumped back. A carton of eggs fell from her bag. Magdalene slipped in the aftermath, almost knocking Mrs. Bochdan to the ground.

"I'm sorry, I'm sorry," Magdalene said. Mrs. Bochdan let the grocery bag slip from her arms and dropped to her knees, scraping at the eggs with her bare hands.

"I should have never put them on top," Mrs. Bochdan said. Her accent was hard, jagged consonants emerging from her throat, but her tone was resigned and soft.

"Let me help," Magdalene said, and when she looked up to see Mrs. Bochdan's face, the smile, the slanted one Magdalene had notice earlier in the day, slid from the woman's face like egg yolk. Magdalene saw the deep lines etched into her dark skin and the red rivers flooding her eyes.

"I'll replace the eggs, I swear, Mrs. Bochdan. I just didn't want you to cross against—"

Mrs. Bochdan grabbed the front of Magdalene's t-shirt and twisted her hand upward, like gangsters and bullies did in the movies. Magdalene scrambled back on her palms and knees, but Mrs. Bochdan pulled her closer, her mouth open—Magdalene could see her fillings. The woman smelled vaguely of spices and cheese—but the overwhelming odor was one Magdalene associated with the church carnivals: cheap thrills and the cold, cold fingers of fear. It was the smell of oily rides and dirty popcorn and sticky-sweet cotton candy hawked by overweight, sweaty men in too-small t-shirts that hid none of their curly animal hair. Mrs. Bochdan smelled desperate.

"I'm sorry, I'm sorry," Magdalene repeated. "I'm sorry about Joseph and Henry." It just slipped out, and as Magdalene leaned backwards, her backside fully immersed in egg yolk, Mrs. Bochdan's silent, pleading cave mouth descended and buried itself in Magdalene's t-shirt.

Behind their slow ballet, a car slowed. Another car, on the opposite side of the street, honked its horn.

"Hey, kid, leave her alone," a man's voice said.

"Somebody call a cop," said another voice, this one heavier, gruffer. The voice of a bully.

Magdalene pushed her body up and out from under Mrs. Bochdan. The woman collapsed on her side; her head smacked the pavement. Mrs. Bochdan's blouse was smeared with egg yolk. Magdalene heard two pairs of footsteps behind them. A tall hedge was on her right, and Magdalene plunged through it, not looking back. The men would stop to help Mrs. Bochdan, Magdalene thought; they wouldn't bother to give chase to a kid cutting through backyards, but she didn't leave anything to chance and didn't stop until she reached the safety of the berry bushes across from Katie McAllister's house.

Magdalene caught her breath and stared at the blue Chevy in the driveway. She wanted to tell Katie about her failure at becoming a bully. She wanted to tell her about Mrs. Bochdan's breakdown: how Magdalene had sensed the husband, Andriy Bochdan, and his history of violence bubbling just below his wife's creased skin and deep worry lines. Magdalene wanted to tell Katie that Mrs. Bochdan was in need of saving too—that Mrs. Bochdan too knew the weight of secrets. What kind of a world would it be without dares, she wanted to ask Katie. What does a world without bullies look like?

A shadow moved past Mr. McAllister's front windows: Valerie Plum. Magdalene's pulse picked up the tempo. Why had Valerie dimed her out? Magdalene knew Valerie was angry and embarrassed about Paul Stern. Did Valerie figure that everyone should be as miserable as she, or did she just pick up on Magdalene's leper/pariah status? Or had she just been reacting to something in the air, something that told her that Magdalene was different and that different was bad?

Magdalene thought she could probably throw pennies up at Katie's window again, but unless she tied a note to a rock (a method the Hardy Boys would have frowned upon), there was no way to get a message to Katie without Valerie the Wicked being alerted. If Raven was here, Magdalene could fasten a note to his collar perhaps, but that struck Magdalene as possibly too Lassie. How often did Valerie baby-sit anyhow? Seemed like Valerie was here in the morning and afternoon when Mr. McAllister was at work (or wherever), and she baby-sat Katie most nights too, when Mr. McAllister was busy wooing the widow Tidwell. The fat tabby cat knew more about Mr. McAllister's romantic dalliances than Katie did!

Magdalene patted the small wad of bills in her pocket: she had brought the very last of her old baby-sitting money; soon she'd have to brave Michael's room and liberate his stash. At first, she'd been afraid the temptation to use whatever money she had at Sol's for reasons other than the surveillance of Mrs. Bochdan would win out (Magdalene *was* famished), but *writer* and *detective* were callings that required self-discipline—a discipline most kids her age didn't even have a clue about. All Christina Fuller cared about was money, but not in the same way as Magdalene. Christina whined if her father didn't give her enough money to go to the malls in Rhawnhurst or Spring House. And even when he did, Christina would moan about how the high school kids took the train into Philadelphia. Christina said Mondauk Proper and its environs were "pedestrian." She said there wasn't a dollar amount that could keep her in Mondauk County once she graduated from high school. Christina said Philadelphia had character, and all Mondauk County had were characters.

Magdalene decided it was time to stop worrying about not having enough money and to start budgeting for the inevitable. If nothing else, she would have to get Katie on a bus to the girl's Aunt Angela in

New Hope—not a local one, but a Greyhound. Even if Magdalene couldn't reach Angela on the phone, she could secure a map and make sure Katie knew where to go once she got off the bus. A bus ticket, even just one way, was going to eat up most of Michael's stash. (Magdalene thought it a shame that because of financial circumstances and her own impending suicide she couldn't ride with Katie.) Most of what would remain—roughly the amount in her pocket—would have to go to implementing Raven's demise.

With her heart rate back to normal, Magdalene left the safety of the berry bushes and walked south, past Sol's, towards the shops on the Pike. The light was leaking from the sky; Magdalene knew the shops closed at nine p.m. She quickened her pace.

When Magdalene was younger, she'd often ask herself, before any decision that required more than her age and experience had to offer, *what would her father do?* He'd been a man respected in the community. When Magdalene was little—very little—she used to stare at her father's face when they walked to the shops on the Pike. Everyone called out his name. Magdalene swore one of the clearest memories of her mother—and these were fading into old Polaroid territory more and more—was of her mother tearing clippings of her father's name from the newspaper and trapping them beneath magnets on the door of the fridge. *Good news or bad,* her mother had said, *we're proud of who you are.*

Rex's Pharmacy was still open. Its pink neon sign sizzled as it roused itself for another night of sentry duty. The flickering made Magdalene sick to her stomach, reminding her of McCullough's beer signs and the men and women caught inside the bar, frazzled and a little sad.

A bell jingled over the door when Magdalene entered the pharmacy, and she counted her steps. Old Man Rex was in the back of the store, behind the pharmacy counter.

"We're closin' in half a second," Old Man Rex called out. His round head bobbed behind the counter; he appeared to be floating. He wore skinny glasses that clung perilously to the pointed tip of his sharp, shiny nose. Grumpy, lumpy Mrs. Scialfa dusted behind the register and scowled.

"My father sent me," Magdalene said to Mrs. Scialfa. "We have rats."

Mrs. Scialfa sighed, pointed to the back, shaking her head, and resumed her dusting.

Old Man Rex didn't look up from his work.

"What do you need, miss?"

"My father sent—"

"I know who your father is, missy," Old Man Rex said, clearing his throat. "And I know who you are. I'm not selling you anything that you can…well, I'm just not."

He slammed a book cover closed and shoved a pen into the pocket of his smock. The bottom of the pocket was stained blue and black and red.

"My father sent me," Magdalene continued; there was no use deviating from the script. Either Old Man Rex was going to sell it to her or he wasn't. "We have some rats in the basement. He sent me to get rat poison."

"Why doesn't he just call Animal Control?" Old Man Rex asked, but he had already turned from her to open the gray steel cage behind him. "All I got is four pound pails."

Magdalene asked: "Um, how much are they?"

"No, no, here: ten packs, six dollars. You have the trap already?"

"Yes, sir."

"Which one?" Old Man Rex looked over his skinny glasses at her. The skin around his neck looked stringy.

"Oh, I'm sure I don't know, Mr. Rex. My dad sent me."

"You can pay me. Mrs. Scialfa already counted down."

"Yes, sir," Magdalene said, digging into her pockets.

"Your father, he's still not—"

"Sir?"

"Nothing. Six thirty-six with the tax," he said.

"Shouldn't be going after Mrs. Bochdan like that," he added.

Magdalene's skin felt stretched thin. Heat spread over her cheeks and neck almost instantly. Had Old Man Rex been in one of the cars honking at her on Dungan Road?

"Don't mind sayin' so. They always say it's the parents' fault, and it usually is. Never saw my kids in jail, did you? No, but Andriy Bochdan: there's a bag of trouble. Ex-con. Junkie, right? Drinking too, from what I hear. Not what you would call a model father. Mrs. Bochdan's done nothing wrong. She loves her son, sends him to the Catholics for his education, works her fingers to the bone at that little store, cleans rich people's homes. Your father—they should just find Andriy Bochdan and leave the mother and the boy alone. Sixty-four cents is your change."

"Thank you, Mr. Rex," Magdalene said, averting her eyes away from his as she backed away from the counter.

"You know this town can take a lot," he said. "We took a lot during 'Nam. Good part of the county didn't come back, or they weren't whole when they did. The Lakes was a campground then. Folks would come from outta town to sleep in a tent by the Puddle. You could even fish—I mean really get somethin' outta there. You could see clear to the bottom. Now the big fish don't come down this far, and the Puddle is dark, missy, dark and deep."

He looked at Magdalene as if he were in cahoots with her, as if she understood not only what he was saying but why he was saying it. Magdalene squeezed the bags of rat poison, and in the back of her head, she saw Raven lying on his side, his stomach and chest rising and falling like someone had stuck a bicycle pump in there, his tongue hanging out of the side of his frothing mouth.

"Now the Lakes are a slum. We lost a few up there in the Big Apple with the terrorists flyin' our own goddamn planes into them buildings. And now we got ourselves a school shooting too. Little kids. Not some high school ne'er-do-wells. Little ones. Something's gotta be done, but not to the boy—though Lord knows he might need some help gettin' over all this. I know Mrs. Bochdan. There's nothing wrong with that boy. It's his father, plain and simple. This town can take a lot, missy, and we'll go on, but I think it needs to take a rest. Your father and Mr. Matthews and that fool Hugh Greene need to go after the boy's father, find him, see justice served, and let the boy and his mother get on with their lives. This is not a liberal town, missy, but we need to heal. Saddest thing. Filled the Cabot boy's prescriptions. Knew the mother to say hi. Nice people. But they would say the same thing. Your father clearheaded enough these days to see that through?"

Magdalene's body was frozen in the act of turning, but she'd heard enough. Old Man Rex had played his part. She had her murder weapon. She didn't need to hear the pharmacist tell her what she knew to be the truth, then go and blame her father for the whole thing. She had a dog to murder.

+

Tiddy was in the backyard, taking down some sheets from the line in the light of the porch lamp. Magdalene watched her from the kitchen, helping herself to some of Tiddy's fresh squeezed lemonade. When her aunt came in through the back door, Magdalene pretended to wash her glass in the sink. Tiddy ignored her. Magdalene could hear the old woman climb the stairs and stomp down the second floor hallway.

Magdalene stashed the rat poison inside a plastic bag and stuck it behind her father's small computer desk in the dining room. The computer was in the corner of the room. Her father rarely turned it on. Magdalene used it for school projects only on rare occasions when library research was unsatisfactory. Nowadays, the computer was only dust free because Tiddy used a feather duster on it every two days. No one would find the poison if she stuck it behind the snake-tangle of wires. And if Raven found it early...

Tiddy was behind her.

"Fancy turning that thing on," Tiddy said. "I was wondering when you'd get around to it. You kids are supposed to be on the computer all the time. Surfing, right..."

"Right," Magdalene said, her fingers fumbling for the on switch—was there an on switch? She preferred to write long hand or on her mother's old Royal typewriter. Something about the *clack* of the keys tickled her stomach and made her understand that writing was only partially a *craft*—although that's what Sister Rita had called it during Career Day. The stirring in her stomach told her it was so much more, and only those who actually dipped their heads in the well knew what it was like to be wet.

(If Aunt Tiddy didn't look so sinister right now, Magdalene would have congratulated herself on the "heads in the well" image.)

"...or writing your book?" Aunt Tiddy finished.

"I don't write on the...what book?"

Tiddy winked at her. Had Tiddy been nosing around her room?

"You know your mother fooled around with writing," Tiddy said.

" 'Fooled around?' " Magdalene asked, a tad defensively. "I don't think writing is *fooling around*. And neither do you. I thought you loved Shakespeare."

"I *like* ol' Bill just fine, but it's a folly, all the same. 'Lord, what fools these mortals be!' "

Magdalene blinked: "Did you say—?"

Tiddy pretended to wipe her hands on her apron.

"Your mother?" Tiddy said. "Yepper, I did. She wrote a great deal when she first met your father. Always banging away at that old

Royal. Kept a journal too. She'd even pull it out at a restaurant if an idea popped into her head. Guarded that thing like it was made of gold."

Tiddy reached over and pushed Magdalene's chin upward.

"You'll catch flies."

"What did she write?"

"Who knows? Didn't show anybody," Tiddy said. "Not even your father, as far as I know. She even tried to get something published—a novel. Took a bus to the city, the whole bit. Your father encouraged her as much as he could, but by this time, you kids were around, and they had a deal: he worked, she stayed home with you and your brother. So she came home, and the Royal was shelved. The book too, I imagine."

"The lying got worse then, you know," Tiddy added.

Magdalene didn't know whether to hug Aunt Tiddy or vomit on her shoes.

Her mother had been a writer?

"And don't ask. Her novel ain't here. Either are the journals. (I 'spect she kept more than one.) Your father looked for them long and hard after she passed. Maybe she threw them out. Should have seen her face when she was writing though. It was like she wasn't even in the same room anymore. Hell, I'd a-read it! Her lies would have made better movies than half the claptrap on the tube nowadays."

Magdalene felt woozy. It was her fault—her father had *bullied* her mother out of writing because of her and Michael.

"Okay, enough of that, sit," Aunt Tiddy said, pointing to a dining room chair. On the table, in between tottering stacks of Polaroids, was a piece of loose-leaf paper covered in words. Magdalene stared at the old woman's extended finger and followed her instructions. She could see her aunt's namesake in her imperious tone and her easy mantle of command. Magdalene sat down.

"Now, I don't know who you're fooling, or who you *think* you're fooling, but it's not me. I don't know how many of those makeup exams you've actually taken, or if you've woven this summer scheme out of whole cloth—horse hockey, in other words—but we're going to set some things straight right here and now."

Tiddy tapped a finger on the loose-leaf paper.

"I tried this before, but what the hell," Tiddy said. "This is what we're gonna do this summer. No, no. No words just yet, Magdalene.

It's not all chores. Though I did give you a few. They're on the back. You're gonna help me some, and that's that. Nothing too hard. Some cleaning, a little laundry. Give that dog a bath. (Jesus in a bucket, he needs one!) Make your bed. Scrub the tub when you're finished with your bath. See what I mean? The rest of the list is the *fun* stuff. Activities. Plans. We're gonna make the most of your summer, Magdalene, maybe even take a ride to the beach. You and Michael used to love Beach Haven, remember?"

"But—"

"No ifs, ands, or buts. You're moping around the house— sneaking around is more what it feels like. Running away for the day. And God knows what you're doing when you leave. I know it's not drugs or booze, because you're acting as dopey as when you left. But it's as bad as locking yourself in your room. We're gonna take the bus to the city and go to museums or maybe the zoo. Take a day in the park. Go out on the Puddle with a canoe. I think you can still do that."

Magdalene could feel her fingers wriggling in her lap—counting God knows what.

"I spoke to your father about this, and he agreed with me. Enough moping about. It's time to move on. For all of us. So, this paper here lists what days are day trip days, 'less it rains, and which days are for studying, and which days are for house cleaning—not many, like I said. That's my job and that's why I'm here. Every day between now and Labor Day is writ out on that paper. No more shoulda coulda woulda. No more time-wasting."

Aunt Tiddy pushed the loose-leaf paper towards Magdalene. (A stack of Polaroids featuring Raven's nose and open grin and stuffed animals teetered and slid across the table.) There was so little time left; it had been hard enough to get around Tiddy, and now this? Magdalene willed herself not to cry. Mondauk County was enshrouded in mysteries, the truth so much dirt under the fridge. Not one adult in her life seemed to know that anything was awry. Old Man Rex was right: this town had been through too much. Magdalene knew the role she needed to play. She had failed in the past somehow, but like Sister Mary Magdalene de Rosa, Magdalene wouldn't fail this time. If she rescued Katie and Joseph Bochdan and his mother—hell, even killing Raven was a form of rescuing, wasn't it?—then she could go to her death knowing, at the very least, she had risen to meet the times.

And now this? Day trips to the zoo?

Magdalene tore the loose-leaf paper into tiny pieces and left the dining room table. She took the stairs two at a time, stepping over Monien to close her bedroom door. The house was quiet, and when the bedsprings settled under her weight, Magdalene could hear Aunt Tiddy sobbing. She stuck her fingers into her ears and closed her eyes.

When she woke, it was finally dark. Her bed sheets were damp, and a breeze blew the curtains. Her bedroom door was open.

"Raven? Raven?"

Magdalene heard his heavy breathing. She sat up and screwed her fists into her eyes.

"Raven?"

The dog sat in the doorway. The monkey lay on the floor next to him, but Raven was staring at the space between her nightstand and bed.

Magdalene slid out of bed and winced. The floorboards were glacier cold; it was like stepping into a puddle. Magdalene knelt down and ran her hand over the wood. The floor was dry.

Raven glanced in her direction.

"What, Boo?"

Magdalene crawled next to Raven and saw Monien trapped between the bed and the nightstand. This panda gets around, Magdalene thought. Yet another rescue! She reached for Monien— and started counting. When the numbers ceased, Magdalene climbed, shivering, back into bed. Monien and Monkey were in the middle of the floor, leaning against each other. Raven sat before the stuffed tableau as still as Magdalene had ever seen him—as if he was keeping watch. When neither toy made a move or a noise, Raven snuggled his nose between the panda and the monkey and stared at Magdalene. Magdalene stared back until she fell asleep.

+

"Divide, conjugate, bag o' stones;
Next sound you'll hear is the rattling of bones.
Diverge, gin mill, Daddy's dive bar;
Next sound you'll hear is the falling of stars."

Michael wears a halo. It's warm. A writer would call it sultry, Magdalene thinks. Steam rises and surrounds Michael's head. Puddle water drips from his chin and hair and nose onto his hairless chest. He stands before her naked. Magdalene keeps her eyes on his halo.

"You have to respect the dare, Lil."

"I know."

"You have to."

"I know the rules, Michael."

"Well?" Michael asks, shaking his head like a dog—like their dog ("Moon river, wider than a mile...")—spraying water over Magdalene's naked body. He doesn't hide his curiosity; Michael looks at her pale stomach and the puffy nipples on her non-existent breasts; he stares between her legs and at the whiteness of her thighs. He does all this without anything registering on his face: no teasing, no disgust. Michael just looks at his sister, and for Magdalene it's a warmth even the sun can't bring her. Magdalene scolds herself for feeling ashamed in front of her brother. Still, she doesn't want to look between his legs. She knows, soon enough, Michael will get hairier, and the boy-god before her will become a miniature of their father: all cologne smells and scratchy chest hair and deep voice.

"Just this one, Lil," Michael says, pointing to the gnarled mimosa—the Jumping Tree. The other trees on the Puddle's edge are thick with bark that had been turned green by the rising of the water. The mimosa's trunk is still off-white. There are initials and messages carved into its wood: T.T. loves P.A.R. *and* The Stars Rule! *and* J.O. Sucks It! *Its long, slender limbs stretch out and wave over the Puddle flowing swiftly below it. Only the dead sycamore, the Dead Injun Tree, black against the bark of the mimosa and its neighboring trees, offers a more dangerous launch pad, but no one dares jump from its ancient branches. The Jumping Tree and the Dead Injun Tree. Legend enough keeps the Dead Injun Tree from being used; good common sense helps too: its branches are thick enough and wide enough but black with rot and riddled with holes, and although a few of its moribund limbs reach over the Puddle, they do so at such a severe angle that jumpers could easily smack their heads on the healthy branches of the mimosa on the way down or even be misdirected just a tad to the left by the sycamore's other, smaller branches to meet the edge of the equally rotting dock.*

The legend of the Dead Injun Tree, like the legend of Lou's Head, has passed from Cub Scout lips to high school ears and back again. Magdalene knows it well: the boy who would become the last Indian of Mondauk, a skinny Pennypack with the unfortunate name of Ruth, finally finds what he'd been looking for his entire life at the foot of the Dead Injun Tree: a reason to live. Ruth was too skinny to work the family fields for long, too frail to defend the borders of the tribal land, too afraid to hunt. His parents named him Ruth because when he was born, Ruth arrived without a penis—or at least his penis wasn't visible when he exited his mother's womb. Although his father had longed for a son—the couple was older and Ruth would be their first and only child—he tried to make the best of it, allowing the women of the tribe to celebrate Ruth's birth with the appropriate feminine rituals. Until Ruth's penis popped out. How and where it was hidden was the plot point that had kept the story alive in the schoolyards. True or not, there had been a Pennypack Indian boy named Ruth who, it was recorded, had been the last of his tribe. The history of Ruth's penis, Magdalene surmised, was deemed inappropriate and unimportant to the story. The Mondauk Historical Society made no mention of Ruth's penis in its slim history of the Pennypack Tribe (required reading in sixth grade) though surely it was an important point for Ruth—and Jerry Eves. Jerry raised his hand and asked after Ruth's penis every time the class discussed the Pennypack Indians.

According to the legend, Ruth's father, disgraced (yet secretly proud of his only child's budding furtive nature), decreed that his son would keep the name given to him at birth: Ruth. Still, as tradition decreed, Ruth's father gave his son the amulet his father had given him: three tiny purple leaves inside a piece of quartz. Rawhide was strung through the quartz so Ruth could wear it around his neck. His father had told Ruth that the leaves had become trapped inside the rock hundreds if not thousands of years ago, a natural accident. The chief had bestowed the amulet to Ruth's grandfather when he'd been Ruth's age as an award for bravery and loyalty on the battlefield. The amulet was certainly older than that; the Pennypack chief had told Ruth's grandfather that it had been passed from father to son, from chief to warrior, since the days before the white men came. If nothing else, Ruth's father said, the amulet represented the dwindling tribe in a time of great uncertainty. It would be Ruth's job to wear the amulet with honor. But Ruth disappointed his father time and time again (the boy was a terrible archer and a reluctant tracker), and after Ruth ruined a hunting party by making a fuss over a mongrel dog he'd found rolling around in the mud, his father took back the amulet. Pennypack Indians never give a second chance when the first had been blown. Ruth was a failure at twelve years of age.

When the settlers came from the larger towns, looking for more room, Ruth's tribe, a peaceful sort already diminished in number by the scarcity of game in the white men's wake, found themselves pushed to the very edge of the Puddle, and when they refused to cross, the white man who led the settlers, Colonel Maxfield Mondauk, ordered his men to open fire, and the last of the Pennypack Indians were slaughtered along the banks. Except for Ruth. Ruth had been making pictures with the paints he'd whipped up from various plants and oils. He was in the middle of a rather intricate portrait of his dog, whom Ruth had named Muddy Ball. The dog followed Ruth wherever he went, disrupting hunting parties and reconnaissance missions with his incessant barking; Ruth was careful to play far away from the rest of the tribe. Muddy Ball had in fact been barking when the settlers started shooting. He'd paused to scratch at a flea, and Ruth heard the last of the gunshots. He abandoned his paints and sprinted towards the banks with Muddy Ball trailing close behind.

When Ruth reached the Puddle, he discovered the bodies of his tribesmen and women covered in blood and filled with holes. Ruth found his parents among the dead, and he buried them first, at the base of the largest tree this side of the Puddle, a sycamore. Before he buried his father, he removed the amulet from his father's neck and hung it from his own. Then Ruth dug holes and buried the rest of his tribe.

When some of the settlers returned to ravage the bodies for leather or jewelry, they found Ruth leaning against the big sycamore with his dog, next to the graves of his parents. Enraged that Ruth had beaten them to the booty (or, in the least, made their scavenger hunt that much harder—not that they were above digging up the dead for a bit of gold or a glint of silver) and slightly unhinged by Muddy Ball's nonstop barking, they fired their pistols into the air and told the boy to leave, for although they had just, hours earlier, murdered men and women and children, it was easier when the victims were all in a bunch. Ruth was skinny, doe-eyed, with paint on his fingers and face. Ruth refused to leave. Muddy Ball growled and howled. A soldier ordered Ruth to silence his dog. Ruth shook his head and picked up Muddy Ball, shielding him from the muzzles of the enemy with his own body. The men laughed. "Look at the brave brave!" the men cried. Muddy Ball struggled and Ruth lost hold for a second, shifting his body just long enough for the soldiers to see the amulet. They demanded its immediate surrender. Ruth again refused. The white men stopped laughing. They raised their pistols and rifles and shot Ruth until his skinny body was filled with holes like the bodies of his parents and his tribesmen had been. Muddy Ball, too, was filled with holes, but in his last conscious moments, the dog charged the men, barking at the top of his little mutt lungs, leapt, and closed his muddy jaws over one of the soldier's balls. Muddy Ball was skewered with a sword and tossed aside, one of the soldier's testicles still in his mouth. Ruth, meanwhile, was blowing blood bubbles from his mouth. He closed his bony hands over the amulet, and no amount of prying, gunshots, or kicks to the head could loosen his fingers. Ruth curled up into a ball at the foot of the towering sycamore next to the graves of his parents and maintained a grip on the amulet. The men laughed again and set fire to the tree. Muddy Ball, half his insides on the outside, released the soldier's ball, entered the flames, and crawled to his master, barking the entire time.

Magdalene knows that the local fishermen and some old timers believe the Puddle is cursed (so does Jerry Eves), that it was Ruth who'd muddied its waters (giving the fish some cover), killing the giant sycamore and staining the ground with his blood to forever remind the town of its original sin every time someone *tracked the red dirt into their safe, warm homes.*

Whether or not the Legend of Ruth and Muddy Ball is true, the soil along the length of the Puddle is red, and the sycamore is quite dead. No one ever jumps from the Dead Injun Tree.

So that leaves the mimosa—the Jumping Tree. Its pink plumage decorates the dirty water like icing on a birthday cake. The mimosa has plenty of limbs strong enough to hold a person before a jump. The real trick is maintaining balance before surrendering to the air.

It amazes her that somehow she has avoided the dare of leaping from this tree—any tree, for that matter—for this long. Magdalene broods. Perhaps Michael considers this his last chance to pull a dare on his lil sister. In the fall, Michael will be swept away by the currents of high school life at Father Hoskins High, Magdalene left to play catch up, as always. By the time she can join him a year later, Magdalene knows everything will be different, and maybe Michael knows this too. Maybe Michael knows he has only so many dares left to make.

The Puddle is swollen from the previous day's rain. Branches and clumps of dirt and innumerable leaves litter the surface, making the already impenetrable water darker still. But the current is swift. Magdalene watches as the surface litter speeds by. She figures that if she does jump, she has a fifty-fifty chance of impaling herself on one of the larger branches streaming by. The heat of the day has already begun drying the banks; the red dirt is damp, but not muddy.

"I dare you, Lil. I dare you," Michael says, and Magdalene knows as she pushes herself from the ground and wipes her hands on her thighs that she will do anything Michael asks her, dare or not. It's late summer; a tinge of autumn is in the air, its bitter claws dragging everything safe and warm away. Magdalene is struck again with the chill that has haunted her bones all summer long: Michael will soon be gone, rendered unidentifiable by new pals and eager girls; Magdalene will be left with the empty flask of a father.

Michael climbs the Jumping Tree, his hands and feet interchangeable. When he reaches the first decent horizontal branch, he squats and pushes his bottom towards the ground.

"Full moon, I dare *say!" Michael cries, and Magdalene laughs despite knowing that autumn is coming and autumn is greedy and hungry and autumn will take Michael away from her. She laughs despite knowing that their father is this very second hunched over a dirty glass in McCullough's, cleaning his fingernails with a matchbook cover. She laughs and hears her mother's laugh like an unexpected tickle on the down of her neck.*

Their mother told them once that she *had created the Rules of the Dare— codified them—and that the Rules of the Dare were simple:* Honor the Dare, Respect the Rules, Execute the Dare, or Be Banished Forever. *To their mother, dares were harmless little games without danger. There was no sulfur smell in their mother's dares—just silliness and warm, clear laughter. Streak in the backyard for ten seconds. Eat an entire apple pie—without using utensils. Drink all the juice from a jar of olives. Where the rest of the world saw danger and skull and crossbones, their mother saw only more opportunities to release her laughter. If their father, before their mother died, had been all about logic and authority and respect for the law, their mother respected only the shared look between two sets of eyes squinting from laughter.*

Magdalene looks behind her. The last thing she needs is for somebody—God forbid it be one of the Bod Squaders—to see her naked, scaling the Jumping Tree. But they are alone. Don't look down, she whispers to herself, don't you dare look down. There: she had dared herself, and her trembling arms pull her towards her brother. She can hear the bass from the radios in the cars tearing down Dirt Road, blasting oldies. She remembers bumping hips with her mother to Aretha's "Respect" in the kitchen, Michael singing lead into a wooden spoon stained with spaghetti sauce.

She counts backward from fifty. She recites "The Ladybugs' Picnic."

As she nears her brother, he reaches above his head and pulls himself higher. Magdalene listens to the gurgle of the Puddle, choking on its own overflow. She is surprised to see just how swollen it looks from up here; it appears ready to burst, a pulsing vein of runoff scum and discarded pieces of trees.

"Jump," Michael says, as if it is the simplest thing in the world.

"Jump," he repeats. "I dared you. You have to jump."

There is a breeze in the air, and Magdalene, crouching on a scrawny branch, regrets getting naked—starkers, as Magdalene is sure Shakespeare had once put it. Michael stares down at her unabashedly—almost like he doesn't care that she is his sister. It's the dare he lives for and the dare alone. Most of the dares Magdalene has performed at Michael's behest have bordered on the dangerous— and Magdalene felt bullied into every single one of them. Is it possible to bully with love? Michael is everything their father discarded after their mother died. He is sure of himself and ready to seize life as it happens rather than mourn forever what is now dust and bones. Magdalene is continually surprised how quickly they regulated Patricia Archer Rumsey Barrows to a few talismanic objects and Super 8 memories. "They're young; they'll heal quicker," Aunt Tiddy said at the time, but their father was too far into a bottle of gin to fully comprehend.

"Jump, jump, jump!" Michael chants, and he shakes the branches. The smokestack of the abandoned asbestos factory looms on the northern horizon like a spire of an angry church. Beyond the tree line, a car zooms down Dirt Road, radio blasting.

"Sunny, yesterday my life was filled with rain…"

Michael shakes the branches and the tree disturbs the red earth and the red earth tickles the muddy Puddle.

One, two, three,
Four, five, six,
Seven, eight, nine,
Ten, eleven, twelve,
And they all played games at the ladybugs' picnic.
"Jump, jump, jump!"

She is a thousand hundred million miles above everything—from here, Magdalene is sure, she can reach out and touch her mother's long, slender fingers again; she is that close to heaven. Air tickles her crotch and charges into her nostrils—and then she is falling, a pebble into a well, a raindrop screaming towards the concrete. She is immersed—she can't reach the bottom with her toes—and then she is away, the current of the Puddle tense and swift. When her head goes under for the third time, Magdalene closes her eyes and wonders if this is what Sister Mary Magdalene de Rosa felt just before the fire consumed her body and melted her eyeballs.

You have to respect the dare.

+

She wished she'd brought Raven with her. She was beginning to miss him even though she hadn't murdered him yet. Magdalene knew she wouldn't have to miss him for long, but she was beginning to wonder when she would have the *time* to commit suicide. She'd certainly hoarded enough of Aunt Tiddy's medicine to insure a clean break with her body. How did Frank and Joe Hardy find the time to solve so many mysteries and still go to school and participate in extracurricular activities? She hadn't made much progress on her book either; there was too much going on. And too many numbers. The numbers were everywhere.

Magdalene sat on the brick wall across Loretta Avenue from Sol's. She had to try to reach Mrs. Bochdan one more time; Magdalene couldn't shuffle off this mortal coil (as Shakespeare had *really* said, or at least had written) without seeing if her theories could help clear Joseph Bochdan. But with Tiddy breathing down her neck, and her father's increasingly erratic schedule (he was frequently up and out of the house before Magdalene awoke), it was becoming more and more difficult to make plans. This morning, Magdalene had spent an inordinate amount of time in the bathroom, running a shower she had never actually stepped into, trying to stall the inevitable onslaught of Tiddy-related activities and chores. In the end, she simply decided to try the lie again: she had a makeup exam coming up—English—and she had to go to Assumption to meet with Principal Sister Mary Joseph. Magdalene hoped she could gain a few more free afternoons by saying Sister Mary Joseph was tutoring her. Besides, Tiddy would never check. Aunt Tiddy had no parental privileges, and Magdalene's father was soberly swamped in both the Cabot Case and Summer Camp.

The problem was: Tiddy was catching on—or at least Magdalene thought so. She didn't interrogate Magdalene on every detail, but Tiddy's face now carried a weight Magdalene remembered seeing on her father's face before he had started drinking. It was the face Magdalene expected from him when she'd done something wrong, like finger painting on the side of the porch, or that time she and Michael ate an entire cake that Aunt Tiddy had been good enough to bake and drop off. Their mother didn't have a face of reproach. She'd laugh when they misbehaved and caress their cheeks and hold them close to her lightly perfumed neck. It was as if she knew her time was going to be cut short, and she surely wasn't going to waste it chastising her children. Magdalene couldn't remember a single time their mother had seriously scolded her or Michael (even when Michael's room looked like a bomb had hit it). Aunt Tiddy was a different story. Even when Tiddy had lived in her immaculate apartment in Spring House, she had been a frequent visitor to the Barrows Bungalow and had assumed presupposed roles as adjudicator and disciplinarian. Now Magdalene was starting to believe that perhaps Tiddy was a detective as well—and maybe a damn good one. No matter, Magdalene thought. Her father was far too busy to prosecute any judgment Tiddy handed down. Besides, Magdalene hadn't been caught yet.

After spending a day wandering around the town, circling Katie's house, trying to figure the best way to get Katie's attention without alerting Valerie Plum or Mr. McAllister, Magdalene finally decided to skip dinner and wait for Mrs. Bochdan to shut down Sol's for the night. Perhaps if she approached Mrs. Bochdan while the woman was closing her store and just started a conversation, she wouldn't be startled much, and they could avoid a scene like the day before.

"Aren't you the little girl with the black dog?"

Magdalene opened her lids and was surprised to see a pair of brown eyes staring back at her. Up close, Mrs. Bochdan's skin was the color of chai tea with just a splash of milk. There were grooves etched deep into the woman's face; they looked almost unnatural, like movie makeup, as if Mrs. Bochdan had been the victim of a terrible automobile accident—one where the tires had skidded across her otherwise smooth face. Magdalene sat up and swiped at the little pieces of dirt and rock embedded on her cheek. How could she have fallen asleep—again!—on the brick wall?

"Come on, answer me, child," Mrs. Bochdan demanded. When Magdalene returned the stare the woman looked away. Magdalene thought Mrs. Bochdan blushed, but her skin color made it hard to tell. Magdalene wasn't sure if she'd ever seen a more beautiful face this ruined. Mrs. Bochdan didn't seem surprised to see her.

"I assume you wait for me, but I do not pretend to know why," Mrs. Bochdan said. "I assume you will tell me, no?"

Magdalene opened her mouth and shut it quickly. Her tongue was coated with sleep; she could smell her own breath.

That's how we know we're dying, Michael had said. Bad breath. Rotting from the inside. When you're little, your breath is like magnolia blossoms. When your breath turns, Lil, your days are numbered. You can count them.

"Come, child," Mrs. Bochdan said. "You are here to walk me home, no? So, walk then."

Magdalene jumped down from the wall and took one of Mrs. Bochdan's grocery bags.

"No eggs today, child," Mrs. Bochdan said and managed a wan smile. "You are called?"

"I am Magdalene," she said, blushing. Surely Mrs. Bochdan was the most exotic adult she'd ever spoken with. Maybe Mrs. Bochdan would give her one of the colored eggs; Magdalene imagined Mrs. Bochdan's house was overflowing with them.

"So, where is the black dog?" Mrs. Bochdan asked as they walked. Magdalene wondered if any of the same cars from the day before would be cruising by so their drivers could see the two of them walking together carrying groceries.

"He died," Magdalene said, not at all surprised at the words coming out of her mouth, but startled at the tears that sprang from her ducts almost instantly.

"He's dead. He was called Raven."

Mrs. Bochdan lowered her head to look at Magdalene's wet face.

"You must have loved this Raven very much, yes?"

"Yes."

"It is hard to say goodbye, Magdalene."

They walked north in silence, past Magdalene's neighborhood, until they reached Mrs. Bochdan's house, a clapboard single atop a steep driveway. No cars had slowed down during their walk. No Bod Squaders had yelled at Magdalene to make fun of her wardrobe choice (denim overalls). There had been no chalk marks scrawled by little girls on the sidewalk. It was if they were walking through a land where children no longer existed. As they trudged up the driveway, Magdalene saw a little red bike with training wheels leaning against the fence; red and white tassels poured out of the white handlebar grips. Various sports paraphernalia littered the side yard. A clothesline flapped in the breeze, one end tied to a rusty pole.

When Mrs. Bochdan unlocked the front door (she had to push her body against it to force it open), Magdalene's nostrils were filled with the scents of loss. The air was stale and humid, heavy with the smell of wash done needlessly and dinners cooked for no one. The Bochdan house smelled like tears. The living room was dust free, meticulously clean. Family portraits were everywhere: on top of the television in little gold frames and on the walls in big gold frames. The sofa had a plastic see-through cover with gold trim, and on a chair was a large pillow with gold stitching outlining a lion's mane.

"Sit, sit." Mrs. Bochdan took the grocery bag from Magdalene and walked into the kitchen.

"Do you like tea, Magdalene?" Mrs. Bochdan called from the kitchen, giving equal emphasis to each syllable of Magdalene's name.

"Yes, ma'am."

Cups and saucers rang out and a kettle rattled and hissed. Magdalene focused her attention on the large family portrait on the wall behind her. Andriy Bochdan's skin was even darker than his wife's. (She recognized him from pre-mystery visits to Sol's.) He was handsome in an Errol Flynn kind of way (or maybe even in a Basil-Rathbone-as-Sherlock-Holmes way), but a poor man's Errol Flynn: his thin mustache was cut short on one end, and his hair, slicked back, was far too greasy. Robin Hood gone to pot.

Magdalene couldn't determine if the way Andriy Bochdan had thrust his chin forward in the portrait was a sign of fearlessness (like it had been on Michael) or of dumb bravado (like Stevie Rich's). In the picture, Mrs. Bochdan's makeup was sparse: a touch of lipstick, maybe, a dash of eye shadow. She was dressed conservatively. Her dress was buttoned to her neck, and her hair was unadorned and shorter than it was now, with no curls or waves or highlights. Her smile seemed genuine though, and both of her hands encircled the little boy sitting on her lap: Joseph Bochdan, second grade killer.

Joseph's hair was dark like his parents', but his skin was almost fair with a very slight gathering of freckles across his nose and cheekbones, just enough to be caught in the photographer's lens. His smile was huge and confident. Was this the face of a boy who'd murdered his best friend in front of his entire class? There was a bruise on one of Joseph's cheeks. It was small, and if she hadn't been staring at it, Magdalene would have dismissed it as a birthmark or a trick of the light. But there was no mistaking it for something else: it was a bruise. Not the finger-crown of bruises on Katie's left arm (Magdalene chastised herself for not checking Katie all over for additional bruises or bruises that had healed to a dirty yellow), but perhaps the aftermath of a slap or a punch. Andriy Bochdan's hands were folded on his lap, and he wore a large gold ring. Did the bullies take to Joseph Bochdan or had his father? Abuse, dares, bullies: Magdalene was starting not to see the difference; they were all the same because the end result was as well—someone stronger dominated someone weaker either through a flurry of fists or a tirade of talk and torment. What did it matter if it was done in ill will or in the name of fun, or worse: practiced as a form of parenting?

Mrs. Bochdan brought a little gold tray from the kitchen laden with teacups and little bowls for the sugar, honey, and milk.

"Drink, drink."

Mrs. Bochdan sat on the sofa; the plastic covering crackled. Magdalene helped herself to some tea. Mrs. Bochdan drank nothing.

"So tell me, child, why do you follow me? Why do you wait for me?"

"I just...I wanted to...I wanted to..."

The tea was steaming, and Magdalene took a big gulp and waited for the explosion in her mouth to travel down her constricted throat to her stomach.

You see, Mrs. Bochdan, a prime usually stands alone—and I'm a prime— divisible only by one and myself. That's me! But I'm about to perform the ultimate act of division. There'll be nothing left when I'm finished, and I need to have the rest of my house in order before I calculate the final sum. My brother? Well, he was a victim of subtraction, see, and it might have been my fault—I was always better at counting *than* arithmetic, *better at* watching *than* doing.

Anyway, before I am split into nothingness, I need to get to the doing. *Call it what you will: atonement, penance, a pathetic attempt to make up for a failed algebra test. And I've chosen you and your son. You are the lucky recipients of my transparent altruism.*

"I just wanted to help," Magdalene croaked. Her forehead was sweaty; her armpits were damp. She counted the gold stitches on the pillow.

Mrs. Bochdan pointed to the portrait behind Magdalene.

"Who knows the minds of men, huh?" Mrs. Bochdan asked. "Do you have a boyfriend?"

Jerry's face skated through her overheated, numeric brain. *The boy I like—his name is Jerry Eves, but I can't like him too much, because I really have to die soon and just* cannot *dillydally.*

(*Dillydally?* Magdalene thought that was reason enough to kill herself: there was no way she wanted to start co-opting Aunt Tiddy's figures of speech. Of all the thoughts to skate through her mind…Jerry Eves and Aunt Tiddy…of course, there were the numbers. Tiny little numbers.)

"No, I—"

"I see love on your face, child. You cannot hide it from me," Mrs. Bochdan said. "Don't you know mothers know everything?"

Briefly, Magdalene saw Mrs. Bochdan's pure white teeth, the only evidence of the woman inside who had died, tortured and scared, when Joseph pulled the trigger.

"I loved him once or I was supposed to," Mrs. Bochdan said. "Where we came from, love was a luxury and *like* was enough. Do you know *like?* You do not understand, I am sure. But I *liked* him enough, even if his family were ruffians. They took advantage of their own people."

Enough about your husband for now, Magdalene thought. What about Joseph?

Mrs. Bochdan sighed. "But he's gone now. They cannot find him. They will not, I am afraid. He is a true ruffian, and his people will hide him or send him back overseas."

Mrs. Bochdan waved a hand in the air: "It does not matter. He is gone."

Magdalene cleared her throat and swallowed another huge gulp of hot tea.

"Where's Joseph now, Mrs. Bochdan?" Magdalene asked.

"My husband is an addict. He took drugs and he drank vodka. Did I tell you I did not even know what he did for a living the past year and a half? Probably longer, but Mrs. Shumsky told me her husband said my husband hadn't been at work for at least five months. We always had some money, so he was doing *something*. He took drugs with bad people. Other ruffians from back home. I met a few of them. All they talked about was how great it was back home. 'Go back if you like it so much,' is what I thought, but I said nothing. I played my part. I know it well. Yes."

"Joseph...? Are you allowed to see Joseph?"

"And then there was the scum from the Lakes. Not Ukrainian. Frannie is not a Ukrainian name. Mongrels, all of them. They'd eat their own dogs to get ahead. My husband went there to play cards. Cards! Ha! This I know from some of *their* poor wives. Always coming in to buy lottery tickets. 'This is my time,' they tell me. They need to escape, I say to myself. Nothing good comes from the Lakes. They don't even work! We pay for their unemployment checks! Ask your father. He knows."

Magdalene almost spilled the rest of the tea in her lap.

"You know my father?"

"I know who you are, child," Mrs. Bochdan said. "That is enough, eh?"

"I want to help Joseph," Magdalene said, her voice sounding nothing like her own—it had her father's authoritative tone and her mother's frivolous fearlessness.

"So, he's gone. He's not coming back. He knows it is his fault. We're going to lose the store. We cannot afford a good lawyer. We have to take what we can pay for only, and that is not much. My husband took our money with him. I have to clean houses."

Mrs. Bochdan sniffed: "I lost some houses because they thought I was an Arab."

One, two, three...

"There is a lien against the house now—he had stopped paying the mortgage, yes? The only thing he left was the store. He never liked it. Didn't like me working. Didn't like me out there among other people. He was afraid I might get ideas."

Magdalene dabbed her mouth with a small gold paper napkin.

"Was Joseph picked on in school? Or Henry Cabot? Did anyone bully them?"

Mrs. Bochdan dismissed the question with another wave of her hand. Magdalene realized Mrs. Bochdan was staring at the baby pictures on the top of the television set. The woman hadn't looked Magdalene's way for several minutes.

"It wasn't his gun. We never had a gun. I wouldn't allow a gun in this house, not with…and I didn't want one in the store either. I started to think if anyone held up the store, my husband would probably know him! Probably sent him! No, it wasn't my husband's gun to begin with. He showed it to me. Said the fireman's brother owed him—owed us, he said—money, and the gun was a down payment. What could I say? 'I told you no guns in the house'? He was in too deep by then. What kind of men pay off a debt with a pistol? Oh, but all the Ukrainian ruffians my husband 'did business with' loved it! All his friends came over to see it and hold it. Speak English, I told them. You are in America, speak English, but they went outside to smoke their drugs and drink their beers and take turns holding the gun."

"Do you know Stevie Rich?"

Mrs. Bochdan turned her gaze on Magdalene. Her eyes were heavy-hooded and distant. The wrinkles around her eyes looked like knife slashes.

"What did I just say, child?"

"I don't…I'm confused," Magdalene confessed.

"As well you ought to be at your age. You do not want to know everything, but you will when you get older. Then you will know, and you will wish you were young again when you knew nothing."

One, two, three,

Four, five, six…

"Did Stevie Rich pick on Joseph and Henry?" Magdalene asked.

Mrs. Bochdan swept her hand in the air and cleared her throat: "He picked on everyone. That is what the nuns told me. That boy picked on everyone."

Magdalene felt emboldened—Mrs. Bochdan's monologue was morphing into a conversation.

"Then it's true Stevie Rich picked on Joseph and Henry? Is that why you talked to the nuns?"

"Why do you ask me about nuns, child? My husband didn't even go to church. We are Orthodox, of course, but Roman Catholics pray to the same deaf God, yes? What does it matter what you call yourself?"

"But Stevie Rich—back to—"

"I know his father," Mrs. Bochdan said and spit on the floor. "That is enough. The apple never falls far."

"His father...?"

"My husband was never interested in church."

Mrs. Bochdan folded her arms over her chest. Her forehead creased into a flag of a thousand wrinkles, worn and windblown.

Magdalene swallowed the last of the hot tea and grimaced as it scalded her throat.

One, two, three,

Four, five, six,

Seven, eight, nine...

"Did Stevie Rich bully Joseph and Henry?"

Where is Michael?

Daddy, why aren't we looking for him?

Why is nobody looking for him?

"Drained our accounts. All I have is the store."

"I want to help, Mrs. Bochdan. If Stevie Rich..."

Say his name, Daddy. Say his name: Michael. It's Michael.

"...or John-John Hagarty—"

Daddy said his name, dummy. You weren't listening. You were busy counting.

"Where I come from, husbands and wives took care of each other. There was alcohol there too, of course, but not the drugs. Not the sex and the clubs with the women taking off their clothes for dollar bills."

One, two, three,

Four, five, six,

Seven, eight, nine.

Ten, eleven, twelve,

And they all played games at the ladybugs' picnic.

"Say his name, Mrs. Bochdan, say his name," Magdalene said, the tea threatening to evacuate her stomach through her mouth.

What kind of town is it where a kid goes missing and no one looks for him?

What kind of love is it where we can't say his name?

"For what? Still my husband does not pay the bills. Freeloader. Doesn't pay, but I have to work all day on my feet. I have to take all their stares. I have to remember that I don't belong, that I never did. My life is borrowed like a book from the library."

"JOSEPH!" Magdalene screamed; some spit hit Mrs. Bochdan's

cheek and mixed with the woman's tears. "HIS NAME IS JOSEPH! YOUR SON'S NAME IS JOSEPH!"

Mrs. Bochdan's forehead crumpled, and she fell forward onto the coffee table, overturning the gold tray and the little bowls of sugar and honey and milk.

He's a boy and you're a girl, he would say. *Boys think they're invincible. They are reckless with their lives—most of 'em anyway. Then they grow out of it. Football keeps the danger around a little longer. It's a boy's game, Maddie. He's a boy and you're a girl.*

Mrs. Bochdan's forehead was bleeding. The woman remained doubled over, her arms and head on the coffee table. Tea dripped on the gold carpet.

Faster, Michael, faster. Higher, Michael, higher. That's my boy. Okay, again.

"His name is Joseph," Magdalene whispered. She stared one last time at the family portrait behind her, at the gap in Joseph's teeth, the grease in Andriy Bochdan's hair, the way Mrs. Bochdan held her child on her lap, gentle and firm at the same time, as if she were handling an egg. Magdalene's father had told her once that juvenile hall was not the kind of place she ever wanted to see the inside of, that it was a place where wayward kids became mixed up, and where mixed up kids were beaten until they were too far gone to be anything other than bad, plain bad. Magdalene imagined the fear on Joseph's face; she could see him crying for his mother and maybe even for his father and certainly for the best friend he'd shot in the face.

"Joseph." The two syllables stuck on her tongue.

The blood from Mrs. Bochdan's forehead mingled with the spilled tea and milk.

Magdalene gathered herself as best she could—she felt pieces of herself were now scattered in no less than a dozen places.

He shot him in the face.

One little boy shot another little boy square in the face.

Henry's mother had to bury him with the coffin closed.

He no longer had a face.

Magdalene let herself out. Sultry. She didn't bother to close the door behind her. She was counting.

+

When Magdalene returned home, the ignoring was in full effect—sort of. Tiddy placed a large pile of sheets and underwear—all Magdalene's—in Magdalene's arms without so much as looking at her grandniece. Her father was going back to the office after Summer Camp, Aunt Tiddy told her as if to say: *it's just the two of us again and I'm done with you.*

Raven followed her around with Monkey in his mouth. Monien was nowhere in sight, but Magdalene knew the mute panda's absence was as symbolic as its silence. *Monien is missing. Can you find Monien?* Even as she rubbed Raven's head, Magdalene knew she was doing the right thing in murdering her dog.

Standing in front of Michael's closed bedroom door, Magdalene held her breath. She didn't know why she was hesitating. Surely, she wasn't like her father or Mrs. Bochdan. That's what this was all about: not hesitating, answering the bell when it was her call.

Magdalene pushed Michael's door open. It hadn't been shut all the way. Magdalene closed her eyes and listened to the hinges squeak like baby mice.

Jump, jump!

She opened her eyes.

The panda was in the middle of the floor.

And they all played games at the ladybugs' picnic.

His stash was most likely under his mattress, but she decided to look there last. Michael's wine colored shirt—the one he thought made him look like a dude—was draped on his desk chair. His souvenir coin from the Franklin Institute was still nailed to the wall. Swim trunks stuck out from beneath his bed; although he went swimming all the time, Michael rarely wore swim trunks—these still had the tag from the store. His newspaper bag was crumpled in a corner, covered in smeared black fingerprints. Michael had been an industrious delivery boy, raking in a bundle of tips during the Christmas season. There was a photograph of Michael and their mother in a gold frame on his desk. Michael was young in the picture. His hair was bowl cut and parted to the side; his cowlick stuck up like a middle finger. He wore a maroon velour pullover—Michael had loved that shirt—and their mother had an arm around his shoulder; Michael was grinning, his lips tight. There was a blur in the background of the photograph, a blur with a black bob and nervous hands: Magdalene's face was obscured, but her hands flapped as if giving signals or instructions to the photographer. Michael had said that Magdalene was such a ham, she had to be in every photograph. Magdalene knew better: she'd grown bored of the photo shoot— their father had just bought a new camera—and had been amusing herself by tossing a football in the air and catching it, annoying their father to no end.

Magdalene flipped through his school books (Michael didn't read for pleasure like she did; all his adventures were real and paternally sanctioned); she looked through his underwear drawer and found nothing but a very old *Playboy* magazine. Magdalene took one look at the women's blank faces, their obnoxious-sized breasts and scary patches of pubic hair before shoving the magazine back under Michael's tighty-whities. Boys were odd, Magdalene thought. Only boys would find that attractive.

Raven entered Michael's room carrying Monkey in his jaws. He walked around the panda, regarding it warily.

Magdalene shoved her hand between Michael's mattress and bedspring. Her fingers touched the elastic band of another pair of underwear, and she knew before even pulling it out that this particular pair of tighty-whities was wrapped around Michael's bank: fifty-two dollars, most of it in ones, with one twenty—what was left of Michael's birthday money and newspaper tips and odd job money. Their father, even after he had started drinking, used to give them five dollars here and there for doing odd jobs around the house; it had started with just mowing the lawn or swabbing the deck (as Michael called mopping the floor), but had expanded, after their father took up the bottle full time, into pretty much everything else. After their mother had died, Tiddy would come from Spring House once a week to help clean or make a few casseroles, but mostly it was Michael who kept house (except his own room, which he refused to clean as a tribute to their mother). Magdalene shied away from the odd jobs; she kept her own counsel and cleaned her own room, occasionally scrubbing the bathroom sink and tub. It pained her to see dust on their mother's little collection of porcelain angels, but it pained her even more to dust them. To leave them dirty left them untouched; to clean them was to reactivate whatever memories they held and behold their Super 8 fuzziness, and for all of Magdalene's desires to spark certain synapses in order to help solve certain mysteries, she preferred to leave memories of her mother just that: memories—ones she could pull down from the shelf when she wanted to, but nothing close enough for her to polish or dust off.

Magdalene wrapped Michael's stash back in his underwear and shoved the whole wad into her overalls. Raven sniffed at her hands, but she opened them to show her doomed dog how she held nothing of significance—not anymore—and tossed his monkey through the door.

"Good Lord!" Aunt Tiddy cried from the hallway. Aunt Tiddy was balancing another large pile of laundry in her arms. Raven ran after Monkey, his tail swooshing against the walls, as he attempted to navigate past Tiddy's legs.

Magdalene stepped into the hall and closed Michael's door behind her as her aunt lost her claw-like grip on the laundry pile—Raven's tail was ticklish against her bare legs, and Tiddy was wearing one of about a dozen almost identical house dresses—burying the black dog under a pile of white bath towels. Magdalene locked herself in the bathroom and scrubbed her face and hands until every scent of Michael had been sucked down the drain.

+

Snap fizz whirr.
The ignoring was over.
Snap fizz whirr.
"Indoor things too," Tiddy said as she served Magdalene a bowl of Quaker Oats. "In between studying for your exams. I wrote down a list there: checkers, Othello, chess—you do know how to play chess, correct?—cards. Gin rummy. I'll teach you Kings in the Corner."

Magdalene had woken up cranky—now *this* again. She plunged her spoon into the oats and glanced at the silent movie star in the still-developing Polaroids: fuzzy outline, wounded hollow eyes, the cereal spoon in her hand reflecting the brilliance of a star long dead. What had changed between yesterday and today? Last night, Tiddy had barely looked in Magdalene's direction. This morning, the old woman was more underfoot than Raven! Magdalene wondered if Tiddy had noticed the number of pills in her prescription bottles decreasing. Or had it come to her father's attention, through his investigators, that his daughter had been to visit Mrs. Bochdan—and had yet to take a makeup exam? Magdalene hadn't heard her father come home last night, nor had she seen him this morning, but his whiskers were in the sink and a game plan for the Summer Camp team was still on the kitchen table when she'd plunked herself down for breakfast.

"Now, your appointment with Willa Meade," Tiddy said as she unpinned the calendar from the wall, "has been moved up to tomorrow. But you're still going next week too. You're going twice a week for a little while, Tuesdays and Fridays now until you get on your feet."

Magdalene refused to look at the calendar, and Tiddy swiftly removed it from the table and sat back down with a pack of cards.

"Can't spend all summer doing chores, right?" Tiddy asked, shuffling furiously. "Have to have some fun. I was telling your father that maybe if he got a break from Summer Camp, we could *all* take a drive to the shore. Take the Caddy. A little sun, some sand in the shorts. Do him some good. You could teach your father to ride the waves like you and Michael used to. Your mother too. She was crazy about riding waves. Said it kept her stomach flat. Kept her suit full of sand, that's for sure."

Magdalene peeked at the calendar—it was Thursday. Magdalene figured she had maybe another week, tops, before Sister Mary Joseph called her father to ask when she could expect his daughter to complete her exams. As Tiddy shuffled, Magdalene decided she would have to force the situation: four days. Four days to rescue Katie, complete the Cabot Case investigation, and poison Raven. On late Sunday night or early Monday, she would swallow Tiddy's medication. She couldn't bear the thought of even waiting that long, but Magdalene had little wiggle room. To solve a mystery *and* spirit Katie away from Mr. McAllister's clutches in four days seemed almost impossible. Magdalene thought of Sister Mary Magdalene de Rosa throwing her body across the flames to make a bridge for the children. Magdalene knew this was what Sister Rita had been talking about: her time had definitely come. Afterward, when she'd completed her tasks, she'd be able to close her eyes forever and leave this darkened fishbowl of a world.

"Now, with Kings in the Corner," Aunt Tiddy explained, "you start out with—"

There was a bang on the back screen door, and Magdalene jumped up to answer. Jerry Eves stood on the back stoop, one freckled fist hanging in the air. Jerry was wearing his Summer Camp jersey, and his helmet swung at his side from the chin straps. The rest of his uniform—pants, shoulder pads, cleats—was stuffed haphazardly in his open equipment bag. Magdalene smelled dirty socks. Raven pushed his way through her legs to smell for himself.

"Hey," Jerry said, suddenly interested in the space above Magdalene's head.

"Hey back," Magdalene said, looking up too.

"It's okay, you go outside," Aunt Tiddy said. "I'll clean up."

"Ma'am," Jerry said, snapping a salute to Magdalene's aunt, forgetting the helmet that was dangling from his fingers. It smacked against the side of his head.

"Jesus in a bucket," Aunt Tiddy said.

Magdalene pulled Jerry into the backyard, and they sat behind the sycamore tree. The spare tire swung in a lazy circle, and Magdalene could hear some of the neighborhood kids bursting from their back doors, eager to start the day. Summer vacation was still young, and the boredom of near absolute freedom had yet to infect the younger kids. Raven lay next to them (he'd brought Monkey) and rested his head on Magdalene's thigh.

"I thought you had practice this morning," Magdalene said.

"I quit practice early."

"Was my father there?"

"No, he doesn't show up until after dinnertime on Thursdays. It was just the assistants this morning. They won't even notice I'm gone, Tonto."

Magdalene liked the way Jerry's freckles seemed to migrate across his cheeks when he talked and the way his hands appeared to be opening and closing with his mouth, like a nervous little puppet show. But what she liked best was when he called her Tonto. (She imagined Tonto was a girl's name.) It was as if they'd had a long history together (outlaws! heroes!), one filled with not only deeds and dares, but also a romance kept at bay by their chosen professions. Magdalene hoped he didn't call every girl Tonto.

"Did you want to do something?" she asked, and Jerry flinched.

"Something? No, well, yes, you know the End of the Summer Dance at Camp? I was wondering if, well, I was hoping you'd…" Jerry paused to inspect an ant making its way across his left sneaker.

"I won't be here then," Magdalene said. She counted Jerry's freckles.

"Oh, vacation then," Jerry said, his tone pitched between relief and despair. "Yeah, a lot of kids are away when the dance happens. Jersey shore?"

"What?"

"Is that where you're going?" He continued to study the ant.

Magdalene figured it was now or never.

"Jerry, where does Stevie Rich hang out?"

Jerry jerked his chin up, smacking the back of his head on the sycamore.

"Stevie Rich?"

Magdalene gave Jerry her best smile. She hoped she didn't have Quaker Oats in her teeth.

"I need to talk to him a little," she explained. "It's important."

"Talk to him about what?" Jerry sounded jealous.

"Just a couple of things."

Magdalene wanted to look away now but knew she could not.

"He probably hangs out in the Lakes with the rest of the losers," Jerry said. "He lives there. Unless Social Services took him again. They did last year. His dad sells drugs—or takes them. I forget which."

Magdalene maintained eye contact.

"I'm sorry about the dance, Jerry."

"Oh, it's okay. I was just reminding you. No biggie."

"Maybe we could go on our own date," Magdalene said, and although she regretted the words as soon as she uttered them, a warm flow invaded her skin, as if she had peed in a pool."

"A date? We could do that. We could." His blush threatened to obliterate his freckles.

"Have you ever been on a date, Jerry?"

Jerry stuck his mouth guard in his mouth.

"*Mmmpff*," Jerry said.

"Me? Have I gone on a date?" Magdalene asked. "No. I don't even know what to do on a date. I know some of the Bod Squaders go parking. Do you want to go parking? I'm not exactly sure what that entails but—"

Jerry spit out his mouth guard.

"I don't have a car, Magdalene," he said. "I'm in the same grade as you."

"Right."

C'mon, Magdalene—this is no time to get distracted.

"Do you think you could take me to the Lakes, Jerry?" she asked. "I just need to talk to Stevie Rich, just for a little bit."

They pushed themselves from the grass and walked back to the stoop. Jerry kicked at a clump of dirt. Magdalene heard Aunt Tiddy in the kitchen noisily washing the breakfast dishes. Magdalene pulled the back door closed.

COUNTDOWN:

- THURSDAY (today): finalize plans.
- FRIDAY: Willa Meade; reconnaissance on the widow Tidwell; date with Jerry Eves.
- SATURDAY: go to the Lakes for meeting with Stevie Rich.
- SUNDAY: rescue Katie; murder Raven; take pills.
- SUNDAY NIGHT/MONDAY MORNING: die.

Of course, she had to squeeze in finishing her book too, her literary legacy, and leave her dad enough evidence to convict the bullies and free Joseph Bochdan—and write a letter to Michael, in case he came back.

Oh, the heady, heady days of summer, she thought.

"Okay, how about we go on a date Friday night," Magdalene said, "and then you take me to the Lakes on Saturday. Let's say early Saturday."

Jerry's eyes widened. He made no effort to conceal his reaction: he was flummoxed. He dropped his mouth guard.

"A date."

"Like in the movies."

"And you want me to take you to Paradise Lakes on Saturday to talk with Stevie Rich?" Jerry asked. "You know he hangs with a rough crowd, right?—an older crowd, even though he's still in grade school?"

"But he flunked some grades too, don't forget."

"That's true."

"Well, it's settled then," Magdalene said.

Jerry jumped up. Raven sniffed at his forgotten mouth guard.

"We could go to the carnivals," he suggested. "They start Friday night—both of them."

Magdalene shook her head: "Too many people."

"Right," Jerry said, sitting back down on his mouth guard. "Too many people."

Raven managed half a growl and plunged his snout into Jerry's stinky equipment bag.

Magdalene whispered: "I'll meet you at Sol's on Friday night. Around seven, okay? You'll meet me up there?"

Jerry bounced up and snatched his mouth guard a second before Raven could pounce on it. The dog looked sorry that he hadn't claimed it when he had the chance.

"Seven is okay. Magdalene, I—"

"Seven it is," Magdalene said, and it was only after Jerry backed down the driveway that she realized how badly she was sweating.

Aunt Tiddy opened the back door and waved a small plate of brownies in Magdalene's direction.

"You guys want a snack, eh?"

"Jerry…he went home. He needed to know if there was any homework."

Aunt Tiddy lowered the plate and squinted at the figure of Jerry Eves standing at the driveway's end blinking into the morning sun.

"Homework," Tiddy repeated.

"Study group work, I mean," Magdalene said. "For summer school. He has to make up exams too."

"Right, so, Kings in the Corner it is then."

+

"I need a favor, dear," Aunt Tiddy said. Already a large chunk of the afternoon had been wasted; true to her word, Tiddy was intent on forcing every drop of fun from the day. Kings in the Corner. Penny Ante Poker. ("One-Eyed Jacks are wild!") Even Tiddlywinks.

"On Saturday," Tiddy said, and Magdalene heard windows of opportunity slamming shut, "I need you to get out of the house for a little bit. I want to swab it out, top to bottom and back again. Have to run out and get film and some meat too. Why don't you go see Christina?"

Magdalene didn't wait to answer (film and meat?); she scrambled out of her chair and ran upstairs to use the extension in her father's room. Tiddy had a new medication sitting on the nightstand next to the phone, and Magdalene had to restrain herself from playing with the childproof cap. She had known for days that she had to call Christina, if to say nothing more than goodbye. Perhaps their friendship *was* just a shell of its former self. Since Magdalene's first suicide attempt and the leprosy convention in Christina's father's study, their friendship had tapered off to polite nods in the hallway. Magdalene's subsequent second suicide attempt had killed it dead. But it had been dying long before that. The last time Christina had borrowed her homework, in between suicides attempts, it had been returned by a disheveled boy who'd stuck the loose-leaf paper, folded into a square, into Magdalene's book bag—as if she hadn't been standing next to her bag. The boy had backed away from Magdalene when she'd touched his hand. Magdalene had had to rewrite her homework. But still, with events coming to a head, Magdalene could use Christina's help—she only lived a block and a half away from Katie in one of the restored old stone houses. Christina Fuller and Valerie Plum were Bod Squad pals. Maybe Magdalene could ask Christina to drop by, check on Katie. Maybe Christina could help run interference with Valerie (or even Mr. McAllister) when it came time for the rescue.

When Christina's mother answered, Magdalene's stomach grumbled around the oatmeal she had barely eaten that morning; Magdalene felt sure that if she wasn't in her father's bedroom, she would have thrown up instantly. It was bad enough that Aunt Tiddy slept in here—the old woman's spoiled-sweets perfume clung to everything—but the equally sticky fear in Mrs. Fuller's voice struck Magdalene as one more reason to permanently check out: it was like the honey trail between the spoon and the jar; there was always more dripping than first believed. Mrs. Fuller couldn't hide her fear that perhaps suicide and depression were contagious. Even Assistant District Attorney Gregory Barrow's alcoholism was a concern to Mrs. Fuller, if only in the way it could cheapen her family by association. Mrs. Fuller held the Fuller family name, the name she'd taken from the good Dr. Fuller, in high regard. If nothing else, Mrs. Fuller hoped some combination of the name (an old family name in Mondauk County) and her husband's profession would raise the Fullers out of Mondauk Proper (which, to Mrs. Fuller, had become overrun with Methodists barely able to fill weekly collection envelopes) and enable them to move west to Anchor Hop or to a penthouse in the city even.

Magdalene had heard Mrs. Fuller's screed against Mondauk Proper (and Methodists) more than once. Mrs. Fuller often maintained a barely audible monologue when she drove Christina and Magdalene to the shops and back or cooked in the Fullers' spotless kitchen. Mrs. Fuller's phobia of the Barrows family curse infecting her own didn't require detective work. Mrs. Fuller was a fake (all she cared about was money and her social status), and Magdalene knew that fakes wore dread like a headstock.

"Magdalene," Mrs. Fuller said.

Magdalene wondered if Tiddy had spritzed her perfume about the room to make it homier.

One perfume bottle. Two perfume bottles. Three perfume bottles.

"Hi, Mrs. Fuller," Magdalene said, speaking around the clump of Tiddy's perfume tickling the back of her throat.

Four perfume bottles. Five perfume bottles.

"Is Christina home?"

The silence that followed was long enough for Magdalene to hear Tiddy creeping down the hallway. How much of the conversation with Jerry Eves had Tiddy heard? How long had Tiddy been spying on her?

"Christina can't come to the phone right now. She'll have to call you later."

"But—"

"Christina has a busy summer," Mrs. Fuller said in a voice both haughty and shaky, "as I'm sure you do."

But if Tiddy had heard, why had she asked Magdalene to make herself scarce on Saturday? Tiddy had been trying to get her to stay in (or at least stay near the house) since school ended.

"When?" Magdalene asked, and she knew that Mrs. Fuller's expression had changed from one of exasperation (she wore exasperation around the girls as a rule) to annoyance. Magdalene repeated the question, adding the tone of adult urgency she had heard her father use on the phone with the DA or the mayor.

Mrs. Fuller hung up.

In the hallway, Magdalene stepped over Monien. There was no sign of Aunt Tiddy. Raven lay in Magdalene's bedroom doorway, his face resting on his paws. The monkey, damp from a recent chewing, leaned against the door. Magdalene rubbed Raven's ears.

A Lab's ears are made of SILK, Magdalene whispered to herself, *and I'm nothing but a tar baby, Raven. I'm stuck.*

Magdalene kissed the top of Raven's head, watching the dog's eyeballs follow her lips. She tried not to imagine what Raven would look like when he was dead.

"I'm taking Raven for a walk, Aunt Tiddy," Magdalene cried, running down the stairs. Raven almost barreled her over. She snatched the leash from the end table. Tiddy had washed it and coiled it on top of the *Ellery Queen* and *Alfred Hitchcock's Mystery Magazines* under the end table. Raven barked and danced in a circle. Walks were rare since Michael disappeared; Raven usually pooped in the backyard—much to Tiddy's chagrin (though she was in no hurry to walk him herself).

"What about the game?" Tiddy yelled from the front porch, but Magdalene was halfway down the street, and Tiddy's words were lost in the thunder of Raven's paws and Magdalene's bare feet on the asphalt and tar. Magdalene had forgotten her shoes.

+

It would be their last walk together, and Magdalene wanted it to be special, but she found the present to be constantly interrupted by the past. And that was a true struggle, wasn't it—the undertow of memory? It was one thing to reminisce, another to wear a memory down; in between was best. She believed adults lived in the past so often that their memories became worn, like the souvenir coins her father had bought for her and Michael on the Wildwood boardwalk at the Jersey shore when they were little. Michael had driven a tiny nail through his coin into his bedroom wall and displayed his souvenir like an old lady displaying a nice piece of china. Magdalene liked the way the grooves of her coin felt in her palm and on her fingers—so different from quarters and dimes and nickels; she'd kept the coin in her pocket for months, rubbing it so often, she was barely aware of it—until Megan Riley asked her if she had an itch. Magdalene reluctantly retired the coin—not out of embarrassment, but out of fear (ah, there was that word again!), fear that Megan would never let it die. Megan: whose nose for gossip and whose skill for keeping an issue in front of the Bod Squad (and sometimes the entire student body) was unparalleled and malicious. Like the time Zeke Cessna was caught picking his nose during a solitary detention. Two girls—one of them Megan Riley—had peeked in on him through the window in the door. They were spying because he had been deemed "cute" at the start of the school year. By the end of the term, Megan had pontificated so often on nose picking and what Zeke did with the boogie after he had picked it (particularly whether or not Zeke had stuck the offensive material in his mouth, which according to Donna Gaynor, who'd witnessed the excavation, Zeke most definitely did *not* do), Zeke had become a social pariah, almost on the level of the infamous gym-pooper James Orienti. Zeke eventually transferred to Keasbey. Magdalene knew (courtesy of social gadfly Jerry Eves) that Zeke was a regular fixture of late at the Lakes, a companion of Stevie Rich and John-John Hagarty.

Magdalene had grown used to be being a leper, but after Michael disappeared ("Is she the one who…" "Yeah, she didn't even…" "*I* heard…"), the coin made her briefly popular. The school scuttlebutt was that all Michael had left behind was his coin. Megan baited her again and again until the coin became precious to everyone. Magdalene knew she'd be obligated to surrender hers for inspection sooner or later. She was weary, and even Christina told her to show it to everybody already and just get it over with before it grew uglier than it already was. Magdalene heeded the warning (mostly because it was the most Christina had spoken to her since Michael had gone missing), if not the advice, and stopped carrying it in her pocket.

For a couple of months, Magdalene rubbed the coin before she went to bed and when she woke in the morning. If she were stuck on a particularly difficult math problem when she was doing her homework, she'd reach over and caress the coin. She'd count the number of times her fingers and thumb rubbed its surface. When she finally mislaid it, the coin had become as familiar to her as the freckle on the tip of Michael's nose or Aunt Tiddy's hideous perfume or the alcohol on her father's breath. She'd cried through the night when she realized it was gone. There were only two of them in her whole world—and now there was only one, nailed to Michael's bedroom wall, immovable.

Magdalene knew her memory was spotty; holes had deepened where certain events had been stored—holes filled with numbers that never reached a sum. Memories of her mother, for instance, now seemed limited to a handful, and in every one, her mother was smiling like a fool. If her mother had suffered during her cancer, Magdalene couldn't remember. She barely remembered that her mother had had cancer. And despite his current sobriety and the fact that he was back at work, coaching, sleeping on the sofa rather than passing out beneath the sycamore—he was not dead like her mother, in other words, or missing like her brother—her father seemed engraved into the oak bar at McCullough's. Whenever Magdalene thought of her father, her first image wasn't of the man with the graying temples in a neatly pressed suit, ready for court, or of the Summer Camp football coach; it was of the bent coat hanger of a man bowing his head over a cocktail glass and a bowl of dusty peanuts.

She had spent the fall and winter after Michael had disappeared (and she had sufficiently recovered from her first suicide attempt) making posters: *Have You Seen My Brother?* posters. She spent a good portion of her baby-sitting money photocopying Michael's picture. But no matter where she hung them, using the stapler from the dining room computer desk, they were gone the next day. At first, Magdalene thought that someone had seen Michael and had information (she'd provided her phone number on the serrated poster bottom), but no phone call ever came. And there, on the telephone pole on the corner of Orchard and Main, Michael's cowlick was visible on a ragged corner of wet paper beneath a rusty staple. Raven lifted his leg and peed, missing the pole by three inches.

Magdalene wasn't surprised her feet had led her to Katie McAllister's house again. She'd yet to plot Katie's rescue, but she could no longer afford to procrastinate. In order for the plan to work, Mr. McAllister had to be at work or with the widow Tidwell. Valerie Plum was a surmountable obstacle, but if Magdalene timed Mr. McAllister's absence wrong, Magdalene would be left with a dead pooch, and there'd be nothing to prevent further abuse of Katie. Surely, Magdalene would be punished, locked away again in a mental health facility like Friends Hospital or worse—EPPI's public nut house maybe—if Raven were found dead and Magdalene not. Magdalene crushed a red berry under foot and crossed the street, ducking low behind Mr. McAllister's Chevy. When she reached the yard, Magdalene huddled against the back of the house. Raven sniffed along the bottom of the fence. Magdalene hoped Oscar Sceebers was far away, casing the widow Tidwell's driveway. A shadow fluttered behind the curtain of Katie's bedroom window on the second floor. When the time arrived, she could easily toss a few pennies up to the window again. Magdalene made a mental note to make sure she had a few in her pocket on Sunday.

Magdalene and Raven scurried from the McAllister house and headed south. She was in no hurry to return to Kings in the Corner. Magdalene tasted a small twinge of guilt in the back of her mouth, but Aunt Tiddy would have to wait. She loved Tiddy (Tiddy, at least, had thought to look after her and Michael while their father imbibed), but this recent forced togetherness had left Magdalene drained, resentful even. If there wasn't a chore, there was a game or an itinerary. Even Raven seemed ecstatic to be free of the Barrows Bungalow; he was frequently on Tiddy's bad side too. The dog just about bounced down the street, his tongue hanging out of the side of his mouth. Raven took the time to bark at every rabbit and squirrel. He pulled on the leash and tried to pee on half a dozen telephone poles. Though he missed each time and eyed the spillage on the pavement with suspicion, Magdalene rubbed his ears and praised his diligence (if not his aim).

When they reached Assumption, Magdalene was careful to keep her eyes peeled for stray nuns as she entered the northern side of the schoolyard with Raven. Magdalene hoped she was right about having maybe a week before Principal Sister Mary Joseph called her father to report her absence. Magdalene was cautious as she approached the Corridor in the hopes of seeing the bullies hanging near the bike fence before they saw her, but the schoolyard was empty.

The area around the convent wall, however, was bursting: every spare piece of asphalt ten feet out was covered in flower petals. Rain had made the colors on the posters run, and the photographs of Henry Richard Cabot all appeared to be crying. Henry grinned from beneath the tracks of his tears as if he liked the attention. Raven sniffed at a bunch of dried chrysanthemums.

"Well, just bring a bag out then."

Magdalene froze. Raven barked, but the nun yelled over him.

"A trash bag, Sister. A *trash* bag."

There were a few bicycles chained to the fence, and Magdalene ducked between them, pulling Raven with her. She clamped both hands over the dog's snout—a familiar position for both.

Principal Sister Mary Joseph turned the corner of the stone convent, muttering to herself, and stout Sister Edna followed behind, teetering from side to side like a wayward egg. Sister Edna looked as if she'd aged significantly since Magdalene had last seen her, though it was believed that Sister Edna was younger than Sister Mary Joseph. (Sister Mary Joseph was rumored to have witnessed Christ's crucifixion.)

Raven's tongue darted between Magdalene's fingers; his eyes were white saucers. Magdalene whispered in his ear to soothe him ("...a Lab's ears are made of..."), but his tail smacked against the fence pole. Raven was ready to consort with the enemy.

"Just the dead ones. The ones that are dried up," Sister Mary Joseph instructed, and she and Sister Edna knelt in their habits and began stuffing the dead, damp flowers into trash bags.

"Not the posters. Leave them, Sister."

"How about the ones that are water damaged?" Sister Edna asked.

Raven sneezed, and Magdalene let go of his snout to wipe her hand. Sister Mary Joseph put down her trash bag and stood before the makeshift memorial, her hands on her hips, her back to the bike fence. Magdalene had seen her walking the halls just like that: a black and white doll, a wooden stick with a bunch of keys jangling on the end smacking against her thigh. Raven released a half a bark before Magdalene grabbed his snout again.

One Mississippi, two Mississippi, three Mississippi...

Sister Mary Joseph turned away, her hands still on her hips.

Four Mississippi, five Mississippi, six Mississippi...

"Just the ones that really distort his face, Sister," Sister Mary Joseph said. "If you can still see Henry's face clearly, then leave it."

Magdalene watched as pieces of Henry came down from the wall. Some of the posters were hung with tiny nails driven into the cement between the large, gray bricks, and Sister Edna struggled to pull out the nails without tearing the posters.

Magdalene counted the body parts: there was Henry's ear. A couple of teeth. His nose.

"Just tear them down, Sister," Sister Mary Joseph said. "We can come back later and pull the nails out. Here, tie the bag like this...Sister!"

Sister Edna had hiked up her skirt and placed one leg in the trash bag. The bag split with the explosion of a fart. Sister Edna hurriedly lowered her skirt, and rumpled pieces of poster blew across the asphalt. Sister Mary Joseph clasped her hands together tightly as if in strenuous prayer.

Magdalene hung on to Raven's snout. The dog dragged and whined and rolled his wet, brown eyes. Sister Mary Joseph walked towards the bicycles, bending over to pick up crumpled posters and dead flowers along the way. Magdalene held her breath like she'd practiced—like Houdini.

One banana, two banana, three banana, four...

Sister Edna shook her skirt out and waved her hands beneath it.

"Go back inside and get another bag," Sister Mary Joseph said; her breath was short from bending over. "Did your parents just *drop* you off at the convent when you were little, Sister? Don't leave that one here. Take the ripped bag with you and throw it...what are you...?"

"Airing myself out," Sister Edna said as she waddled back to the convent.

Magdalene knew it was time to make a run for it, Raven's barking be damned—but she couldn't move. She was counting.

"Okay, Magdalene," Sister Mary Joseph said, the exasperation that had been in her voice a moment ago now replaced by something softer. "Sister Edna went in to air out...to get a new trash bag. I'll keep my back to you for a second or two, and you and your black dog there can make a break for it. I'll expect you in my office first thing Monday morning for your makeup exams. I won't call your father unless you don't show up. Consider this a pass."

Sister Mary Joseph bent down to pick up Henry's nose. Magdalene and Raven bolted from the behind the bicycles and ran down Shelmire Avenue.

Over Raven's barking, Magdalene heard Sister Mary Joseph call after her: "Monday morning, Magdalene!"

+

Magdalene sat with her back to Rosewood Seton's gravestone. Raven nibbled on a dandelion.

"I tried to find him, I really did. Nobody else even lifted a finger to help me. Nobody. Everyone just accepted that he was gone. No one else hung posters. I called the police detectives twice. Daddy was always in McCullough's. Who the heck knows what Tiddy was doing, but whatever it was, she wasn't helping me. I was the only one."

Raven stopped nibbling, stared at the dandelion, and bit the top off.

"I tried to bring all the pieces of the puzzle together. I made lists of all the evidence; I wrote down all the clues. There weren't many, but I wrote 'em all down—but there was nothing to summarize. Nothing added up. It's no different now, Raven. I'm not convinced that *anything* connects. Sometimes there's no wizard behind the curtain, you know what I mean? There's just so much misunderstanding and confusion out there, and most people just seem to accept it and never try to figure out what any of it means. If I rescue Katie at least, well, then I'll have *acted* instead of just sitting around in the dark. Who knows what Mr. McAllister is *really* up to? Whatever it is, Katie must be in the way. It's a gut feeling, but I think I'm right: Mr. McAllister wants a new wife—the widow Tidwell.

Maybe the widow hates kids. People do, you know. Just like some people hate dogs. Katie's in their way—that's it. I told you about the bruises. Why else would Mr. McAllister do that?"

Raven spit out the soggy dandelion top next to her bare feet. He turned his head and blinked at Magdalene, and then, as if to make sure it wasn't truly edible, licked the dandelion top again. Magdalene glanced down. Her feet were filthy. She had stubbed a toe running from Assumption. A tiny trickle of blood ran between her toes. Raven sniffed Magdalene's feet.

"If Jerry and I can find Stevie Rich and make him confess—he'll probably be so proud, Stevie Rich, he'll brag about it—then Joseph Bochdan can go home to his mom. If Stevie Rich and John-John Hagarty were picking on Henry all the time, then Joseph was more than likely just trying to rescue his friend. Maybe Joseph's aim was off, or maybe Joseph was trying to save Henry from the misery of being bullied the rest of his life. Heck, Joseph saw his mom being bullied by Andriy Bochdan every day! And that's why he shot Henry. Either way, it'll make a difference in the case because then it'll be Stevie Rich who really killed Henry, not Joseph."

Raven closed his eyes but kept one paw on the soggy dandelion top.

"I love you, Boo," Magdalene said, but Raven kept his eyes closed. "I've always loved you even though you loved Michael more. Maybe it was a boy thing. But I love everything about you: the way your fur smells like popcorn, your stinky breath, your loud snoring, all of you."

Magdalene didn't realize she was crying until she lifted her head from his fur, and the salty water slid to her lips.

"It'll be better, Raven. I'll be gone soon, and I don't want you to miss me. It would be great to be like Rosewood Seton here and live out our days as our own, but we can't. The world doesn't work that way. Prime numbers are a myth. So we'll do the next best thing, Boo. We'll disappear."

Magdalene stood up and stretched; her bones were weary. Raven gave the soggy dandelion one last look before following Magdalene out of the graveyard. Out near the southern ridge of the cemetery, the first of the carnival rides idled on a truck on the side of the road. It was the Tilt-a-Whirl, and to Magdalene the obscene angles of its arms and the peculiar positioning of its pods looked like someone falling out of the sky.

278 · Saving Magdalene

When Magdalene and Raven arrived home, Aunt Tiddy was in the backyard, tearing away at the weeds. Magdalene watched the old woman's back from the driveway as her aunt laid the offending stalks neatly in a basket. Magdalene wiped the cemetery soil from her feet on the grass in the driveway. There was just the hint of red in the brown and gray dirt.

"Got you," Aunt Tiddy said.

Magdalene clamped Raven's mouth shut (for the umpteenth time!) and knelt in the grass.

"You're mine now," Aunt Tiddy said.

Magdalene closed her eyes and let the numbers jumble, fracture, then settle. Patterns emerged; equations resolved.

Magdalene opened her eyes.

Everything would go much smoother if Tiddy wasn't always trying to direct the daily goings-on in their little corner of Mondauk Proper.

Fifteen men on the dead man's chest—
Yo-ho-ho, and a bottle of rum!

Magdalene led Raven by his snout to the front porch. She hoped her feet were clean enough for Aunt Tiddy. Raven yelped when she let him go.

Drink and the devil had done for the rest—
Yo-ho-ho, and a bottle of rum!

In the dining room, Magdalene ducked under the computer desk, letting her hands feel for the bag of rat poison, her ears tuned for the sounds of Tiddy. Raven pushed Monkey towards Magdalene with his wet nose. The monkey emitted his loud jungle cry, and Magdalene covered it with both hands. Raven looked at her face expectantly.

"Not now, boy. I'm sorry," Magdalene said. "We'll play later."

At least Monkey had found its voice, she thought. That makes one of us.

Her hands caressed Raven's ears, letting the *SILK* slip through her fingers like the hours of early summer speeding past her. Magdalene knew she needed help if she was going to execute all her plans in the coming days. If Christina couldn't (or wouldn't) help, there might be a chance Magdalene would have to abandon at least a portion of her game plan.

Keeping an eye on Tiddy through the windows above the kitchen sink, Magdalene used a soup spoon to mix a smidgen of rat poison into Raven's food bowl. The dog drooled in anticipation. Magdalene watched Tiddy stand, rub her lower back, then kneel again in the dirt. Magdalene knelt too and placed the bowl in front of her dog. Raven licked Magdalene's face and rolled over so Magdalene could better reach his belly.

Think bad thoughts. Think bad thoughts.

Raven peeing in her bed, his pungent urine soaking through her bed spread and sheets, all the way through her mattress, dripping under her bed. Raven gnawing though a dresser leg or an action figure's head. Raven nibbling on the corner of her journal.

Make-believe.

The real Raven peeked over his belly and blinked at Magdalene. Magdalene tossed his food, now thoroughly mixed with the rat poison, into the sink, running the water to clean away the evidence as best she could, and gave the pooch a dog cookie.

"That you, Magdalene?" Aunt Tiddy called from the backyard. Magdalene ignored her and picked up the receiver, pausing as she dialed Christina's house.

What were the last two digits? Damn. So many numbers in her cerebrum now. Too many patterns. Her brother always said it was best to just hang up when she couldn't remember a phone number, clear her head of everything, and try and dial when she wasn't thinking about it, but Michael hovered over her every stray thought like a guardian angel, peeking from between a rushing current of numbers; she couldn't trust Michael—not even Michael's ghost.

The phone rang on the other end of the universe.

Breathless: "Christina?"

"Hi, no, it's Magdalene, Mrs. Fuller. I was hoping Christina was home."

"Magdalene."

"Yes, ma'am. Is Christina home yet?"

"Christina hasn't come home from swim practice. Her dinner's getting cold, and you're blocking the line."

"I'm sorry. Mrs. Fuller—"

Click.

Probably with some boys, Magdalene thought. The phone throbbed in Magdalene's hand as Tiddy blew into the kitchen. Sweat huddled on the old woman's forehead and upper lip.

"You're gonna have to do the weeding for me next time, Magdalene," Tiddy cackled, looking out of the corners of her eyes at her grandniece. "I'm getting too old for all this kneeling. Getting to be like church out there."

"What?" Magdalene asked. "What?"

She was screaming. Raven hid under the kitchen table.

Fifteen men on the dead man's chest—

Yo-ho-ho, and a bottle of rum!

Tiddy peeled off her gardening gloves and laid them over the edge of the sink.

"Nothing. Nothing at all, Magdalene," Aunt Tiddy said. "Except this: work isn't poison and—"

Magdalene ran up the stairs with her dog, slammed her bedroom door, and counted Raven's whiskers over and over until they both fell asleep.

+

Pretend it's a story.

Christina's mother called three times that evening looking for her daughter. (Tiddy answered the phone each time.) The last call ended poorly. Magdalene heard Tiddy slam the phone back into the receiver and mutter a word that rhymed with witch.

If Magdalene pretended all of this was a story, she could wrap the strands of the narrative around her fingers and pull and jerk them this way and that, controlling every nuance, precipitating every action. She'd been stuck on a single sentence in her own little book; weaving Christina into the real-life mysteries would slow everything down considerably.

When her father arrived home, Magdalene tried to shush Raven (who ignored her, of course, and pushed past her to run down the stairs and greet her father). Magdalene vacated her spot at the top of the stairs and returned to her room, pulling the sheet over her head. When Magdalene heard the liquor cabinet door crack open and the ice clink in a glass, she crawled from her room, down the narrow hall, and stuck her head just past the banister. Her father was pouring a brownish liquid into a short glass packed with ice. Raven sniffed at his shoes, which were caked with mud.

"She doesn't know?"

Her father appeared to be weighing the glass.

"Lord, no. She went to bed early," Aunt Tiddy said. "I think she got sick in the sink."

"Got sick?" her father asked. He moved out of Magdalene's sightline.

"Threw up. Upchucked. Vomited."

"I got it, Tiddy."

"Heaved. Tossed her cookies."

" 'Threw up' was sufficient."

"Isn't it a bit early to file a missing person—?" Tiddy asked.

"Yes and no. Depends how you're looking at it."

"And how are you looking it?"

Magdalene's father cleared his throat.

"There hasn't been a true missing person case in Mondauk Proper since I've in the DA's office, Tiddy. But Dr. Fuller is a friend of ours."

"Yours. And it's 'was,' " Tiddy said.

Dr. Fuller? Something happened to Dr. Fuller?

Raven peeked up the stairs at Magdalene's eyes and forehead.

Magdalene counted the seconds between her father and Tiddy's exchanges.

"You gonna be drinking that, Gregory Barrows?" Tiddy asked. " 'He hath given his empire up to a whore.' "

Magdalene held her breath.

"No, Tiddy," Magdalene's father said, his voice rumbling deep, as if he were pulling the truth out from beneath a very heavy rock "I'm not going to drink it. I'm just going to look at it."

Magdalene exhaled at the same time her aunt did.

"Having a drink at the Hotel Blackburn then?"

The Hotel Blackburn was on the Pike, in a section called the Strip, in the northern part of town. In the first flush of asbestos money, it had been elegant in a rustic way. It looked like a small castle with red turrets. The hotel took up half the block. Now it was a transient hotel; its windows were mostly boarded up except for the odd fan, and health officials had long ago shut down the bar. The Hotel Blackburn was a ghost hotel.

Aunt Tiddy was being ironical.

"Andriy Bochdan. There's a warrant out for his arrest, we haven't found him yet. The mayor wants the case to continue regardless. But I think you're right: as much as this town wants someone punished for Henry Cabot's death, I don't think prosecuting Joseph Bochdan's mother is going to go over well. Did you read the interview with the Cabots in the *Common*? Even Mrs. Banniman is starting to change her mind, and she's the hanging secretary. Andriy Bochdan is the typical wanna-be gangster. He's the one with the sordid friendships and shady business transactions. The poor woman, she sells candy and soda pop to kids."

"The lottery," Tiddy whispered. "She sells a lot of lottery tickets."

"Big kid candy," Gregory Barrows said, and Magdalene pictured her father like she did when she was little, his head huddled inside the pages of a book, his hair falling into his eyes, a pencil behind his ear, his lips pursed in anticipation of an unexpected truth awaiting his eyes and brain on the next page.

"And now the Fuller girl—"

"Shhh," Tiddy said. "The walls have ears."

"Right," her father said, and Magdalene started crawling backward towards her room.

"So, the drink, Gregory?" asked Aunt Tiddy. "Scotch and water?"

"Cheap scotch at that," he said absently. "Would have been a rail drink."

"Cheap scotch," Tiddy repeated.

"A public example. Karl and Hugh want me to charge Mrs. Bochdan, and in the meantime, the boy languishes in juvenile hall, surrounded by our state's finest examples of bad parenting."

"And the cheap scotch, Gregory?"

"If we go after the mother, then Joseph Bochdan becomes a ward of the state. I know a little boy is dead, but I don't see how essentially ending another child's life solves anything. Even the Cabots don't want that. So, I'm just looking at the scotch, Tiddy. That's all."

"You haven't had a drop in two weeks?"

"No, I haven't."

"It wasn't your fault," Aunt Tiddy said. "Boys will be—"

"I know," he said, and Magdalene, back in bed, pulled the sheets over her head.

Pretend it's a story.

This is the story of five little ducks:
Five little ducks went out one day,
Over the hills and far away.
Mother duck said, "Quack, quack, quack."
But only four little ducks made it back.

Assistant District Attorney Gregory Barrows entered his daughter's bedroom, and although she knew the liquor had never hit his lips, Magdalene imagined she smelled the whiskey vapors rising from his warm skin. His tie was askew and his shirt, still tucked in, was wrinkled and sweat-stained. His long fingers touched the journal on her nightstand.

"How's the writing, Maddie?"

"Okay," Magdalene said from beneath the sheets.

"Want me to read the dictionary with you?"

"I don't care," Magdalene said, but her stomach clenched. Why did she feel like Katie's turtle whenever she was around her father?

" 'Titrate: to ascertain the quantity of a given constituent.' "

Magdalene poked her head out.

"Did something happen to Christina?"

Her father looked up from the dictionary. He had deep wrinkles around his eyes. Magdalene didn't remember his wrinkles being that deep before.

"No, not that we know," he said. "Christina didn't come home after swim practice, and, well, you know how Mrs. Fuller is."

Magdalene nodded.

"Nothing for you to worry about. If there was, I would tell you."

Magdalene knew he was lying. *Just leave. Michael isn't here.*

"I want to tell you something," he said. "A story—a true story. It might help you. It might not.

"I used to have to take a bus to school every day," he began, "even in nice weather. I went to Resurrection in Rhawnhurst, so every school day, I would walk to the corner and wait for the bus. I took a bus in high school too. Remember, I grew up in New Hope. All the schools were far away then. I played football, but I was too bookish and skinny to hang with the jocks. They always wanted to copy my homework or cheat from me during an exam. I never let them. When I was a freshman, I got it bad: picked on, teased, the whole nine yards and then some, as Shakespeare said."

Her father paused, waiting for a giggle perhaps, but Magdalene was determined to do nothing more than grimace her way through yet another story of How Things Used to Be. Granted, the telling of these stories, once an everyday occurrence, had ceased when her father began keeping hours at McCullough's. She thought, back then, that she'd give anything to hear those stories again: her father the all-star half back in both high school and college (where he'd squired

Patricia Archer Rumsey to an athletic social), sneaking out of his dorm window to drink beer with his teammates in the woods, his brief stint in the Navy, his law school days which culminated in the courtship of the strange, intoxicating liar who would become her mother. In black and white photographs, her father was just another grinning kid in a military uniform—but a serious-looking kid. His ruddy complexion, high cheekbones, and graying temples were dulled like a plate in a history textbook. His hair was graying even in high school, their mother had told her and Michael; Old Man Barrows, their mother called him when he'd work himself up with worry, a name that never failed to bring a grin to their father's usual stoic countenance. It had been a long courtship, and her father had been very much in love with Miss Rumsey. Magdalene's image of her father had long vacillated between black and white snapshots taken before her birth and the crimson-faced, bent and beaten drunk who'd often slept in his own vomit and blood. She needed to see her father in full, natural color. And now, just when her entire world was coming to a head, the world itself had become fuzzy and black and white—and there seemed to be very little white left.

Four little ducks went out one day,
Over the hills and far away.
Mother duck said, "Quack, quack, quack."
But only three little ducks made it back.

Stoic countenance. Magdalene congratulated herself on properly using not one, but *two* words from her vocabulary book. She had to be careful: her journal would be a book someday (posthumously), but a book for children. There were already a few rather adult ideas in her novella, but children didn't use words like "stoic" or "countenance." Maybe Katie McAllister did, but most kids didn't. Most kids weren't as grown-up as Katie seemed. And some kids never grew up.

Best not to dwell. Best not to dwell.

"In high school, I got jumped in the locker room," her father continued. "A kid named Devlin broke my watch, and Tiddy went down to the school and made that kid's parents buy me a new one. Another time, this boy Tony Buto took a girl I was dating (not your mother) to the movies, so I offered him out. Do the boys in your school still say that? 'Offer you out'? That's what the boys used to say when they wanted to fight someone. Kind of formal for a fight, don't you think?"

Ask Michael—if you can find him. He's a boy.

"By the end of my junior year, I wasn't on the bottom of the heap anymore. Playing football had bulked me up. The seniors were busy getting ready to graduate, so we were the kings of the school. I guess I was acting out my revenge for all the times I'd been picked on and beaten up. There was this kid, Brooks McGee—Irish kid—red hair, freckles, chubby face. Probably not a bad kid—just in the wrong place at the wrong time. I needed to flex my muscles—my brain muscles."

Magdalene turned away from her father and stared out the window at the stars. She wondered if she could see Cassiopeia from her bed. Vain, jealous, petty Cassiopeia. Magdalene thought Cassiopeia's punishment was perhaps the best punishment ever for a bully—and that's the only word to properly describe the wife of Cepheus, the Ethiopian king: bully.

"It started out as just teasing. But here's the funny thing, Maddie: Brooksie wasn't the kind of kid you'd think you could push around. He didn't play any sports, but he was bulky—unformed, but bulky, his muscles buried beneath too many Yoo-hoos maybe, I don't know. But every day, I'd set my sights on him. I'm not even really sure how it began. He was a sophomore, and we spent many hours on that bus together. Too many. I would make fun of his hair, his curly red hair. I would tease him because I knew I could make him blush—make his face match his hair. Brooksie laughed along, this nervous stutter-laugh, but his friends laughed even harder. This one friend of his— John somebody—had a vicious, violent laugh that attacked his body so that he'd swivel around and gape at Brooksie before my latest zinger hit anybody else on the bus. And I did this every day, both to and from school."

In some mythology books, Cassiopeia had promised her daughter, the beautiful Andromeda, to Perseus, then changed her mind—jealous of her own daughter's beauty, perhaps—and convinced one of Poseidon's sons, Agenor, to wage war against Perseus. Perseus was not to be trifled with, however; he had recently slain the Gorgon on a dare and buried her head in a bed of coral. In the midst of battle, Perseus unearthed the Gorgon's head and waved it before his enemies, instantly turning them all to stone. Poseidon was so incensed at Cassiopeia and her husband Cepheus that he placed them both in the heavens. The bullies were now forever targets.

"I even did this at the prom. The juniors and the seniors had their prom together, and I made sure to humiliate Brooksie in front of his date. I thought his head would explode—his face was so red. John somebody and his other pals pointed at him and laughed too— they actually *pointed*. I remember putting my arm around Brooksie's shoulders and saying something stupid, like 'You're alright, Brooksie,' or 'Hey, just kidding, man.' But Brooksie didn't say a word. He shrugged me off and left the prom early."

In another version, Cassiopeia's constant bragging of Andromeda's beauty enraged the sensitive gods. Cassiopeia claimed her daughter was even more beautiful than the Nereids, sea nymphs and Poseidon's courtiers. Poseidon got so worked up, he sent a sea monster to ravage the coastline. Cassiopeia and Cepheus were told to sacrifice Andromeda to appease Poseidon, but Perseus, with the head of the Gorgon (a handy weapon, that head) saved the day. Andromeda was spared. The punishment for Cassiopeia and Cepheus, however, was the same as in the other version.

"But all was not well with me in high school. My mother and I— well, suffice it to say, we didn't get along. I stayed at Tiddy's house more often than my own. Not that my mother wasn't a good woman. But having me was more a statement of purpose than an act of love; she wanted *something* positive to emerge from her marriage to my father. Once I was born, my mother foisted me on Tiddy and set about leaving my father. When she ran for (and won) a seat on the County Council, I saw her political posters more often than I saw her face. Not that I lacked for love. Aunt Tiddy, as we both know, is a fountain of love, but I missed my mother. Maybe not in the same way you miss yours. My mother wasn't taken from me, Maddie—she left of her own accord, but she lived within walking distance. She never failed to me send a present on my birthday or Christmas. Tiddy never said anything to me, but I heard her on the phone telling a friend she suspected her sister of sending a staff member to pick out my birthday present. Tiddy was a hands-on woman, even then. The only reason, I think, that Tiddy doesn't *make* our birthday presents is that she's too damn busy taking care of us."

Her father paused again to allow Magdalene time to giggle or nod in consent, but Magdalene focused on the stars, tracing their fire in her head, counting them. There was Andromeda, and to her left, Pisces. Slightly above Pisces was Ares the ram. And above her daughter, Cassiopeia on her throne.

"I was obsessed at getting even with my mother. Not that I could have consciously articulated what I was thinking. I wasn't sitting in my room, plotting my revenge. And revenge for what? I had a good life. Tiddy loved me unconditionally (as long as I cleaned my room!); my mother was a poster on a utility pole. I was brought out for the photo opportunity when she won her seat. When the reporters left, my mother's aide gave me an envelope with fifty dollars in it. I bought my own football pads with that money. Tiddy didn't seem to have a job—other than taking care of me—but I never wanted for anything, so I guess my mother provided Tiddy with money (or Tiddy had wisely managed what was left of the Wheelwright fortune). But still, something yanked at me; some small part of me was tender. And that part was festering, by leaps and bounds."

Three little ducks went out one day,
Over the hills and far way.
Mother duck said, "Quack, quack, quack."
But only two little ducks made it back.

On her throne: that was where Poseidon had placed Cassiopeia—in the stars, glued to her throne, forever revolving around the Pole Star, so that she spends half the time upside down.

"Like I said, I couldn't put my finger on it. I just knew something wasn't right, and slowly but surely, every night, as I struggled to fall asleep, it was my mother's face I saw behind my lids. Only she wasn't looking at me. She was standing on a dais somewhere, wearing one of those pantsuits that made her look even slimmer, and she was surrounded by men in suits and red, white, and blue posters and people clapping and cheering. My mother's holding my hand, raising my arm occasionally, and just as swiftly dropping my hand. Her palms were clammy, and her rings cut my fingers when she awkwardly sought my hand again. In this daydream or fantasy or whatever you want to call it, I kept trying to see my mother's eyes, until I realized, late one night, that I hadn't actually seen her eyes in years—only on political posters. My mother didn't looked me in the eye when she won her seat; she didn't look at me when she dropped off my birthday present. She would never look me in the eye. Never. So I tried to kill myself."

Jesus Christ in a bucket.

Magdalene clenched her fists beneath her sheets. The provenance of suicide was no longer limited to the enlightened—even her father had tried it! Was trying to commit suicide merely a rite of passage—everyone's little attempt to escape to the stars? Magdalene dug her nails into her palms. Suicide was a punishment and only those who truly deserved it would achieve this lofty goal—and quite possibly find themselves in a place far lower (and hotter) afterward. Determination required discipline; the father she'd had before her mother had died had told her that about a million times. Magdalene knew she had both the determination and the discipline to see her way to the stars. She'd just never imagined the heavens being so crowded or the task being so difficult.

"I never told you that. I was just a kid. It was a half-hearted attempt. I took a fistful of aspirin. Had to go the hospital and have my stomach pumped. Tiddy was beside herself. I don't think she ever told my mother, or at least my mother never brought it up—to me or anyone else. After a week or two out of school, I went back and beat the living hell out of Brooksie McGee. I beat him to a pulp. I beat him until he cried tears of blood, I swear. Then I ripped his shirt and pants off and hung them in a tree.

"I didn't last long when I first went to college—no one to pick on, I guess—and I couldn't afford to go to a college far away. So I joined the Navy. The Navy broke my anger. And my nose. Twice."

Her father cleared his throat; it sounded dry, parched, in dire need of liquid refreshment.

Two little ducks went out one day,
Over the hills and far away.
Mother duck said, "Quack, quack, quack."
But only one little duck made it back.

"That's what a bully is, Maddie: a person so scared of himself, so frightened of the world around him, that he takes it out on someone who can't possibly defend himself. It's a bully's way of gaining, at least in that moment, some kind of control. That's what a bully is all about: control. Peel back a bully's mask, and you'll see a face of fear."

Magdalene hugged the sheets closer to her body despite the heat charging through the open window. Stars blinked from the cloud cover, and Magdalene thought she could smell the start of a thunderstorm. Not many more times to smell a storm, she thought. Magdalene closed her eyes and imagined Cassiopeia hanging upside down. A unique punishment—unlike suicide apparently. Her own father? Perhaps it runs in the family. The family that dies together, stays together—forever.

Magdalene spoke into her pillow: "Where's Mommy's book?"

"Mommy's book?"

"Tiddy said Mommy wrote a book, but you told her she couldn't be a writer because she had to be a mother. You bullied her too."

Her father placed his hand on her arm to roll her over, but Magdalene wouldn't budge.

"She never finished it, Maddie. She never...she never actually finished anything. Just started stories or novels and then put the pieces in a big box and tried to find a publisher for them in New York. They were just pieces, Maddie. I asked her to come home because she was just trying to escape again."

"Escape you?" Magdalene asked into her pillow.

"Maybe. Your mother...she...your mom was sick. Besides the cancer. She had...she had issues. Psychiatric issues. Your mom wanted everything to be more than what it was. So she made stuff up. She lied. She couldn't deal with whatever had happened in her past. And in all the years I knew her, I never figured out what that was. But something had—she tried to tell me a few times, but she'd just weave some crazy story instead. One thing is for sure: she loved us, I have no doubt—all of us: you, me, Michael. But rather than deal with her mental health issues, rather than see a therapist or take medication, she escaped. In her head. She lied."

A tiny piece of Magdalene wanted to turn to her father and tell him the truth about summarizing: she was the daughter of a bully and a liar.

"Maddie, do you want to talk about it?" her father asked, his voice taking on the cadences of the courtroom. "We can talk about anything you like."

Magdalene squeezed her eyes shut and watched the numbers flow by like the Puddle in a rainstorm.

One little duck went out one day,
Over the hills and far away.
Mother duck said, "Quack, quack, quack,"
But none of the five little ducks ever came back.

Her father closed her bedroom door, catching Monkey between the door and the frame. The monkey screamed, and Magdalene made sure to stay perfectly still and wait for her father to say good night or I'm sorry or I know what happened to Michael or anything; she made sure to stay absolutely still, still enough to be dead.

+

There are the Rules of the Dare to consider: Honor the Dare, Respect the Rules, Execute the Dare, or Be Banished Forever. *These are their mother's rules, and now the rules are theirs.*

Of course, there is the rarely invoked Fifth Rule—the Pentagon Rule, they call it, for it destroys the perfection of the four Rules of the Dare. Rarely invoked because the Fifth Rule is inherent in the others. It's a given. Thinking outside the box—a phrase their father has used on many occasions (mostly involving homework), a phrase that seems to be catching on with their teachers at Assumption—has no place in the Established Rules of the Traditional Dare. Honor the Dare, Respect the Rules, Execute the Dare, or Be Banished Forever. *It is simple.*

And she is about to tread upon the Fifth Rule; Magdalene is about to destroy the four perfect corners of the Rules of the Dare.

Magdalene knows this act could break the spell of the day; just spending the afternoon with her brother is enough of an incentive to not *break the Rules of the Dare—jumping in the mucky-muck of the Puddle is enough of a spell breaker on its own. The smell of burnt hamburger drifts over from Paradise Lakes. People who live in trailer parks, Christina said, either cooked out or ate straight from the can—unless they went to McDonald's. Magdalene found this revelation startling, as Christina's breath at the time was heavy with the grease of a Big Mac or a Whopper, and her fingers were leaving french fry stains on her schoolbooks. But not even the scent from the Lakes can ruin a day with Michael. Nothing could except the Fifth Rule.*

Don't Cheat the Dare.

There: she whispers it to herself: Don't Cheat the Dare. *A dare could go on and on until Michael has his fill. He* is *a boy after all.* Don't Cheat the Dare.

It occurs to her, during this internal debate of the Rules, that she'd better make up her mind soon. Her mouth is filling up with Puddle muck, and she knows she can't keep dog-paddling much longer.

Magdalene lifts her head, gulps a heaping helping of air (and a bunch of what Michael calls swamp flies)—then lets it out. Her pale, little body sinks until at first just her toes, then her shins and knees and palms grip the grit and pebbles on the floor of the Puddle.

Magdalene has timed this exercise many times, but until now, she never knew why. She always wrote it off as a just a dream—a recurring dream, but a dream nonetheless—not a practice exercise. In the dream, she is holding her breath, and she invariably wakes gasping, her hands at her throat. At first, the dream was beyond frightening; she'd actually peed the bed twice. (Being in charge of the wash, no one ever found her out.) But as the years went on and the dream returned unabated—and unchanged—Magdalene grew used to its shape. She knows exactly when in her dream to emerge one last time and fill her lungs with oxygen. She knows how to hold her breath and count.

She thinks briefly of Sister Mary Magdalene de Rosa saving the children, the wind knocked out of the martyr nun as the children use her as a bridge to safety, the smoke choking her, invading her throat, baking her insides. Surely Sister Mary Magdalene had held her breath for as long as she could; the Church condemns suicide. If the good Sister had been able to save herself after the children were safe, Magdalene knew she would have. And for a while, Magdalene did think the dream was preparing her for her Moment, her time to rise above the muck, but lately, that Moment has become murky—like the Puddle right now. Seems silly: all those dreams just for this, but she is *drowning. Any second now, the Puddle will fill her already exhausted lungs. Michael is back in the Jumping Tree; she heard his laughter the last time she gasped for air. Good a time as any to break the Fifth Rule. Besides: Michael might take his good ol' time rescuing her, but he will never let her die.*

The funny thing is this: she is in the bathroom in the old school building, crouching over the cold porcelain, peeing, listening to the squeals of the second graders and waiting for the first signs of smoke, when Michael pulls her from the Puddle. His breath reeks of cigarette smoke.

"Were you smoking?" is what Magdalene wants to ask, but she throws up on the muddy red banks. Michael drops her in a salad of bottle caps, candy wrappers, and beetle skins. The Puddle water is like a twist of noodles, snaking up her throat.

"Don't tell Dad," Michael says, and Magdalene throws up on his feet just as the sky starts to drizzle on their heads.

"Oh, man," Michael says. "You just chucked on my toes!"

"You were smoking?" Magdalene asks between hacking coughs.

"Earlier today. This morning. With some of the guys. It's not like a habit or anything."

Michael wades into the Puddle to clean his feet. Magdalene catches a whiff of vomit and forces another deluge back down to her stomach.

"Wear my sweatshirt," Michael says, draping the hood over her head, and she sits there in the darkness of the hood as Michael climbs the Dead Injun Tree.

Magdalene blinks.

Michael is climbing the Dead Injun Tree.

"Why are you doing this?" Magdalene asks.

"Smoking cigarettes?"

"No. Climbing the Dead Injun Tree. It rained last night. It's raining now. The Puddle's swollen. The Dead Injun Tree's not safe."

Michael flexes a muscle.

"I'm pushing myself, Lil. Like Dad always says: the only way you know you're alive is if you push. *So I push."*

"Dad stopped pushing," Magdalene says.

"Well, I didn't. Like my head to a gun! As long as I only push myself a little further each time, I'll be okay. Nothing too radical. Like my last jump: way out, smacked my back against the surface of the Puddle, and, voila!*: nothing changed. Except me. Then I rescued you. My heart's a-racing and my skin is kinda creep-crawly. I feel alive. Besides, someone has to do this stuff. Geeks and gawds."*

Magdalene spits something green.

"And I got to save my sister. How many brothers can say that, Lil, huh? Not many."

Magdalene pulls the hood from her head. Michael is higher in the Dead Injun Tree than their last leap together from the Jumping Tree. He inches himself along a narrow branch. It creaks under his weight. His foot slips a bit and he waves at Magdalene in the air.

Magdalene jumps to her feet.

"You okay?" she hollers up at him, noticing the way the rain appears to embrace his body for a heartbeat, cascading down his sun-ripened skin like water on a car that's just been waxed. His skin shines like a face fresh from a cry. Here, along the banks of the Puddle, within a stone's throw of Paradise Lakes, in the shadow of the asbestos factory smokestack and the visible church spires of Mondauk Proper, her brother is a god. Here, now, he is Perseus, his body an armor the color of iced tea, his eyes two lighthouse beacons. His ears are made of SILK.

"Rain is slippery," her brother says." Rain is goddamn slippery."

Magdalene woke screaming. Raven's mute panda was perched on her pillow. She stared into Monien's reflective corneas. Raven snored from the end of the bed, and Magdalene heard Aunt Tiddy moan in her sleep, a dying foghorn in the hall. And, somewhere in the back-back of her head, behind the numbers and the dream that seemed to come a little more into focus each night, the Puddle lapped to its polluted shore, making a trail of gritty green foam amid the beer caps and cigarette butts decorating the dusky red dirt, taking with it the Established Rules of the Traditional Dare, leaving only a girl sitting in the mud with her brother's hood over her head as the rain poured from the sky.

Chapter Eight

The Widow

It occurred to Magdalene on her way to the medical office building, as she watched a bunch of younger kids slip and slide down a piece of wet plastic set up on a front lawn, that *everything* was slippery—especially the truth. If the truth were easy to find, there wouldn't be libraries, or at least they would be smaller. Novels would be more like manuals and textbooks. Although the world had become a very black and white place, it still required guesswork and detecting; shadows were the favorite lurking places of banana peels. And just lately, the black and white were beginning to run together. It was Friday, which meant Magdalene only had three days left; Sunday night was curtain call. This wasn't the time for her thinking to become muddied; the black and the white needed to stay as stark and as separated as possible—if only to stop the random thoughts that had nothing to do with her myriad missions from infiltrating her throbbing skull. She'd fill the colors in as she found them. It was enough to keep up appearances around Tiddy and to have to suffer through this—yet another session with Dr. Willa Meade. Still, Magdalene knew she could use Willa; Willa surely had information pertinent to Katie's case. She just had to stay focused and use her time wisely.

Extraneous thinking, Magdalene was sure, had prevented the town—particularly her father—from continuing the search for Michael. It was something Magdalene could never quite get her head around. If everyone loved Michael so damn much, why had everyone stopped looking for him? To be sure, her father's ass had been superglued to a barstool, a circus monkey eating bar nuts, slurping away at shots of whiskey, gin, vodka, fuck-all, but what about Aunt Tiddy? Hell, what about Mayor Greene? Or Chief Hagen? Even Dr. Fuller had seemed to accept that Michael was gone. Any words spoken about Michael were in the past tense, as if it was generally accepted that Michael was no longer here. Magdalene clung to each and every syllable like her father had to his damn whiskey. (And what the hell was with all the cursing? She'd never cursed this much before.) There'd been no funeral—at least not one that Magdalene could recall. There'd been some tears (but Magdalene suspected they were mostly her own) and an unusual amount of head shaking from adults, as if they were attempting to clear their brains of something unpleasant (or extraneous), as if head shaking was the accepted greeting of the grieving.

But what Magdalene knew that every other human being in Mondauk Proper didn't (Raven was privy to this information on whatever level he could compute it) was that if Michael had died, his death would have been significantly more spectacular than a missing person case. Disappearing wasn't Michael's style. He was a show-off, a whiz, a minor god descended from the heavens, destined to carry the ol' pigskin the extra mile so mere mortals (and that included Magdalene) could stand in openmouthed wonder at the miracle of skin and blood and bone sprinting into the end zone. Wasn't that what Michael said the day they had gone Puddle Jumping? Michael said he pushed himself because not everyone did—not everyone pushed themselves. He didn't want to just get by. Michael told her once that the world was divided into writers and readers. But someone, Michael said, needed to be the subject, the protagonist (although Michael hadn't used that word). If it was Magdalene's job to jot it all down, and everyone else's job to read it (or not— Magdalene believed most folks would rather suck their own toes than read a book), then it was clearly Michael's job to be written about. Michael wouldn't have just *died*; he would have gone out with a significant bang, something worthy of a couple of chapters at least, and mournful family members and coaches and Bod Squaders would have flung themselves from the banks of the Puddle in genuine remorse and guilt—guilt because it wasn't them, guilt because they were all, to a person, secretly relieved at having been spared, even at the expense of losing such an example of living, if only because they no longer had to be reminded of what they could not do and what Michael could.

In rescuing Katie from Mr. McAllister's negligence and abuse and saving Mrs. Bochdan and Joseph from the ignorance (and maybe even the prejudice) of Mondauk County officials (including, it hurt to think, Assistant District Attorney Gregory Barrows), Magdalene was removing herself from the sidelines, placing herself center stage. A good detective knew when and how to enter a room, book the accused, free the victim. A good detective knew when to *act*. Magdalene had done her research. And a good writer knew that moving the plot forward was all that mattered. Long passages of internal debate just delayed the obvious (or the not-so-obvious if the book strove for something beyond the ordinary). If Magdalene had been in charge of Michael's investigation from the very beginning, he would be here now. (Well, maybe not in Willa's office because there'd have been no reason, none at all, for Magdalene to have tried to die—twice.) It was just that when it had happened—Michael's disappearance—Magdalene's world had been very, very gray. Nothing as easy as black and white. Nary a hint of contrast. And zero color. Quite fuzzy, thank you. A bit on the blurry side. But love will do that to you.

Ahh, there it was—a piece of the mystery best left unsolved. (And Magdalene, using all the wisdom gleaned from the Hardy Boys, Sherlock Holmes, and even ol' Bill himself, knew there was rarely, if ever, a mystery not worth solving.) If searching for the truth concerning Michael's disappearance had led her to interrogate herself—and hadn't Principal Sister Mary Joseph, who taught advanced English, told her class (Magdalene among them) just that: all great literature involves the search for self—then the truth was this: Magdalene always figured she'd marry her brother.

In Willa's office, Magdalene strained to keep her blushing face from burning down her hair; she didn't want Willa to become aroused in any way. Willa was mostly useless, a turd, as Michael once said of people who liked to hear themselves talk—and, oh boy, did Willa like to talk! When Magdalene walked into her office this morning, Willa had greeted her with, "DINGLE FART!" Magdalene, mystified enough by the reference to a bodily emission as to the legendary dingleberry (which Michael had described to her as the last little piece of poo that clung to your butt and smeared itself all over the place if left unattended, a phenomenon that had never effected Magdalene, and one, she'd told Michael on several occasions, she had little interest in discussing), had plopped down on the bean bag chair she'd previously avoided as if it were molten lava—the chair was meant, like the crayons and the coloring books and the construction paper, for the little kids who were either forced to see Willa by parents who couldn't communicate, or else chased to Willa's den of art deconstruction because of copious amounts of "bad touch"—and promptly lost herself in her mysteries and a waterfall of prime numbers while Willa rearranged her chair to face her patient and emitted a stream of questions and leading statements and occasional exclamations involving a dazzling array of defecation references.

Magdalene was the only logical choice—blood be damned. Christina was too...Christina. All the other girls who swooned in Michael's wake wore their mothers' eye shadow like the Lone Ranger's mask and couldn't think their way out of a Sears catalog without a matching color guide. If Michael were to marry anyone, common sense (that slippery sister of logic) dictated it should be Magdalene. Yes, yes, Magdalene knew that brothers and sisters weren't allowed to marry; and yes, she knew their offspring, were they to sire any, would be of a decidedly left-of-center bent. But Magdalene, knowing little of lusting and even less of love, couldn't picture making babies with Michael; even thoughts of kissing Michael made her shiver. For Magdalene, it was all in the *sleeping*. The origin of love was all in the smells of the parental bed. That Magdalene could recall her mother's sleep scent was actually more distressing than Magdalene would have ever let on, but the smell itself Magdalene remembered as the most comforting smell of all. It wasn't the best smelling smell or even the most inviting, but it was home. Her parents' bed had smelled of sweets gone bad and fermented apples. In science class, Sister Edna had told the students that Homo sapiens (words that inspired quite a few titters from the boys and a low-level fake fart from the obsequious Jerry Eves) shed x number of layers of skin a year—dead cells accumulating into dust. "When your mothers are dusting the house, they are cleaning away little pieces of the family history," Sister Edna had intoned as if it were some cautionary tale, but Magdalene could never quite figure out the moral—and whenever Magdalene found herself in the parental bed, she luxuriated in the dead cells, hoping some of hers would join the fray, twisting history both far and near into tomorrow's laundry. And it was during those times, before they got too old for "that sort of thing" (another Shakespearian pronouncement from the indefatigable Aunt Tiddy), when Magdalene and Michael would share the same bed—sleepovers, they'd called them, even though they were just in each other's rooms—tickling and giggling and whispering and spooking each other with a penlight, that Magdalene had become convinced that she should marry her brother.

It was simple: Michael smelled like she did when he was asleep. Okay, maybe not *exactly* like she did; his sleep scent was slightly muskier, as if he'd been out behind the house, digging in the dandelions for hours on end, but otherwise, it was pretty much the same. Magdalene had smelled her own sheets; she was quite familiar with her own scent. Magdalene knew one didn't need to be a detective to sense one of her own.

Magdalene had never made her intentions known, however, until an unfortunate moment in the fourth grade—unfortunate because the ensuing unveiling of her desire to commit what amounted to, at least in the eyes of her captive audience, a dire mortal sin, reached the ears of the terrified and quite humble Sister Edna, she of the hairy arms and jittery disposition, back when the fourth grade homeroom was the stout nun's educational domain. Magdalene had been daydreaming during religion class. Sister Edna had been prattling on about the sacrament of marriage and related commandments. Magdalene tried to tune her out and finish the short story she'd been writing for her mother; besides: nuns couldn't marry. What would Sister Edna know about marriage? The wedding bands the nuns wore symbolized their marriage to Jesus. Jerry Eves had said that even Jesus wouldn't be able to raise Sister Edna's beaver from the dead. Jerry Eves had said that Sister Edna's beaver was dead as a doornail.

"How many of you would like to get married?" Sister Edna asked. The thick fingers that sprouted from her hairy arms gripped her pointer as if she would rise swiftly to the pockmarked ceiling tiles or possibly find herself magnetically attached to the blackboard was she to let go.

The classroom was hot, the students lethargic.

Megan Riley jumped from her chair and raised her hand. Sister Edna shuddered.

"I want to have babies," Megan said.

"Lots of them," she added, sinking back into her chair.

Megan's fellow nascent Bod Squaders exchanged glances; there was little doubt, their glances said, in Megan's aptitude for having lots of babies.

"Good, good. Anyone else?" Sister Edna asked, her eyes trying to avoid Megan's, as if there had to be something wrong with the pixie-haired schoolgirl knowing this early that she wanted to lie down with a man.

Donna Gaynor raised her hand. Sister Edna stared down at her scuffed nun shoes. Magdalene knew that if Megan got around, Donna Gaynor had been there first—even in fourth grade. Sister Edna seemed to possess the same information.

"Yes, Donna, yes?" Sister Edna asked. "You want to get married someday?"

"I know who Megan wants to marry," Donna Gaynor said. "And Megan's sister."

"Shut up," Megan said, blushing to the tips of her freckles.

"Now, now," Sister Edna said, gripping her pointer tight enough to make her hairy knuckles white. "Remember: you're only in the fourth grade."

"Megan's sister showed her hoo-ha to John-John—"

"SHUT UP!"

This roused Magdalene slightly; Megan Riley's sister, Maggie, had a rather torrid reputation for someone only in the seventh grade. Maggie wore heavy eye shadow and smoked cigarettes with boys beneath the Assumption rectory fire escape or on the dock at the Puddle; it was rumored she sometimes drank beer with a few of the older boys in the Lakes. Whether or not Maggie had shown her hoo-ha to John-John Hagarty—an unworthy recipient, Magdalene thought; in Health class, John-John had mislabeled the venereal diseases and confused a cold sore with a clitoris—Megan obviously had a lot to live up to and to defend.

Sister Edna's face was ashen.

"It's true," screeched Donna Gaynor. Her breath smelled like week-old potato chips. Donna's family was one step away (ascending or descending, Magdalene wasn't sure) from the Lakes. Even her clothes evidenced a rather sharp odor, like a cheese sandwich left in a locker too long. The effluvium of her hair was reminiscent of gym sneakers left in the rain. Magdalene prayed often for a seat change.

"Everyone's seen Maggie's hoo-ha!" yelled Jerry Eves, and while that may have been true, Magdalene felt quite confident that Jerry had not. He could barely speak to Magdalene without stuttering or tripping himself up in the wiles of a compound sentence unless he had an audience.

"Everyone's taken a shot at that beaver," Jerry Eves added.

Sister Edna snapped a piece of chalk in half.

Magdalene went back to working on her short story. She had known as early as the second grade that she was going to be a writer. Nothing else interested her in the same soul-shattering way—except maybe being a detective, and Magdalene had already begun to see the two occupations in a similar light. Sure, she liked studying the stars and *loved* playing football, but as occupations, the former seemed foolish (all the stars were dead anyway, according to her Earth Science textbook; no sense in studying the dead if no one had killed them) and the latter was forbidden due, solely, to her gender, despite her ability to throw perfect spirals.

"Maybe *you* showed *your* hoo-ha to Jimmy Lonergan," Donna Gaynor said to Megan Riley, "since you wanna marry him and all."

Megan stood up again, her face submerged in a sea of crimson.

"I DO NOT WANT TO MARRY JIM LONERGAN!" Megan screamed.

Magdalene wondered if Jimmy had crawled beneath his desk yet (she didn't want to turn around like everyone else); he was not a boy who liked to be called on in class.

"I know who *you* want to marry," Megan sputtered to Donna Gaynor, but sputter was all she could do. Magdalene, like Megan, knew that Donna Gaynor was destined for School Slut status; Donna's sisters, both pregnant by their sophomore years in high school, had forged the way. Megan would never be able to come up with a potential suitor for Donna Gaynor, not even as a retort. Magdalene sighed. She had begged her father to home school her or to send her to one of those special schools where she could jump grades and graduate high school by the time she was twelve. Not that Magdalene considered herself a genius, but she would sacrifice her throwing arm to escape hoo-has, Donna Gaynor, and the trembling Sister Edna.

Megan turned to face her tittering chums. (Megan had so many freckles in so many interesting patterns—as if the Milky Way had exploded—Magdalene couldn't meet Megan's eyes; she couldn't find them!) Christina, for one, could barely contain herself. She was bent over her desk; one would be inclined to believe she was upchucking on her saddle shoes, Magdalene thought, if it weren't for the staccato giggles spraying from her heavily lipsticked mouth.

"I know who *Christina* wants to marry," Megan announced, and Sister Edna's lips were moving silently. The laughter increased tenfold; it was more of a howl, really, and Magdalene drifted back to her short story. *There was this bluebird, you see, and—*

"Christina wants to marry Michael Barrows," Megan hissed. Christina paused long enough in her laughter to glare at Megan, as if marking her for near-future schoolyard revenge, then continued guffawing into her shoes.

"No," Magdalene said, although—as had happened many times before—she had no idea she was actually speaking aloud; sometimes thoughts just squeaked out, "Michael's going to marry me."

In retrospect (here and now in Willa's office, Willa's voice some distant train whistle in another town), Magdalene realized the subject and direct object should have been switched, for marriage to Michael had been *Magdalene's* desire. Now that she was but a summer and a failed suicide away from Hoskins High, "desire" seemed too dramatic, tragic even, sad; Michael was missing, and, besides, Magdalene had long ago surrendered any hopes of merging their scents. By placing the impetus of desire on Michael rather than herself, Magdalene had been concerned, back in the fourth grade, that she'd created an uncomfortable situation for her brother; but if that was the case, Michael had never mentioned it. He was the only one.

As Magdalene struggled to immerse herself back into her short story, the fourth grade classroom had erupted into a shit-storm—one that Sister Edna, squeezing an eraser, its chalk dust blossoming like a little nuclear mushroom, had zero control over. Christina shot Magdalene a look: disgust or contempt or jealously; Magdalene wasn't sure and didn't much care: Christina would never be able to define any of those words, let alone use them in a sentence. Magdalene felt above the fray.

After class, Sister Edna, words stumbling past her lips, her breath hot and curdled, explained that it was a mortal sin for a brother and sister to marry, and Magdalene shook her head as if she'd already forgotten what Sister Edna was referring to. (Magdalene would have Sister Edna as her homeroom teacher again in the seventh grade; although the nun certainly seemed to find it easier to control seventh graders, her fear was always palpable, and Sister Edna never again broached the subject of sibling marriage.) But if there was any point where Magdalene could see the oh-so obvious advantage of keeping certain thoughts hidden, of carefully maintaining secrets, it was then. Any good detective could have taught her the danger of tipping her hand. Writers knew this instinctively. Her father had once said of Hemingway that he only needed to write of the tip of the iceberg, and although Magdalene wasn't quite sure this was true in every case, she longed to re-submerge the bulk of her character.

So Magdalene had let Sister Edna blather; besides, in the fourth grade, she harbored no secret greater than being in love with Michael, and despite her unfortunate exculpatory shout-out during class (the echoes of which she was sure would pursue her from the mouths of classmates in perpetuity), she felt no reason to debate her secret's merits with a clearly shattered nun. Magdalene knew love. She loved her brother above all men—maybe even more than she loved her father, and she worshipped her father. If she was guilty of anything, it was of worshipping too much. Her list of idols was long, and as she'd grown older, the list had grown too: the writer (or writers) of the Hardy Boys' mysteries, Mark Twain, the Lost Generation of the '20s (thanks to her mother), Harper Lee (of course!), Robert Louis Stevenson (*yo, ho, ho, and a bottle of rum*), Professor Tolkien (*O Elbereth! Gilthoniel!*)—so many others. Even if she didn't understand much of Faulkner or Woolf, the beauty in the way each syllable crashed upon the next, the way their words undulated on her thick tongue like dazzling dragonflies hovering over the shit-swamp of the Puddle made her shudder with excitement. They resounded in her chest when she remembered the words falling from her father's lips on those nights so long ago when he'd read her to sleep. (Heroes fall hard.) She also loved football; she picked a new favorite team each year based purely on how she felt about the team's name or uniform. She loved stargazing too and the myths behind them. So she knew love; and with Michael, Magdalene knew being in love too. And from fourth grade onward, she knew the value of secrets.

And now, here, in Dr. Willa Meade's office, shades drawn, bean bag chair hugging her sides, amid Willa's opulent hand gestures and the clanging of the plastic hippie beads dangling over her therapist's almost nonexistent bosom, Magdalene realized, that yet again, secrets were best left for writing. Willa was trying to get Magdalene to turn over her journal. Magdalene was glad she had left it at home. Willa wanted to mine Magdalene's journal for secrets.

Teachers were worse: they wanted writers to be *explained*. Magdalene's teachers prattled on and on about the *tools* of writing, dismissing the *magic* of putting pen to paper (or the spell the clacking of typewriter keys could weave). Magdalene hated Career Day: she couldn't choose "detective" for fear of being laughed out of class, but choosing "writer" meant she had to listen to endless banter. It was as if her English teachers were angry that they were merely teachers and not smiling benignly from the back of a book cover jacket. Magdalene suspected her English teachers lacked the discipline to write. Oh, they may have had the discipline required to get their college degrees and commence teaching careers, but writing required a gnawing need—the same gnawing need the detective feels as she sniffs out the elusive in the demonstrative, the specific in the common, the unique from the among the sedentary. Magdalene had this need. And if nothing else, she knew she had the vocabulary.

In seventh grade, Mr. Butler had chastised her for being too prolific with her extra-credit compositions. (She'd written five of them.)

"It appears that Miss Barrows," Mr. Butler had said (in front of the entire class), "has been infected with a case of verbal diarrhea."

"Logorrhea," Magdalene muttered to herself while the class tittered—exactly the word, it turned out, the *Mondauk Common* had used in a review of Mr. Butler's first (and only) novel, *Teaching Latin, Feeling Greek*.

"You didn't read the review?" Sister Mary Joseph asked her after Mr. Butler, the little black curls atop his perfectly round head just about the only visible part of his body not beet red, had sent her to see the principal on charges of "gross insubordination."

"No, Sister," Magdalene answered. She'd barely been able to get through ten pages of Mr. Butler's book. She returned it to the library on the very last day so Mrs. Stanley wouldn't call the Library Police; it was the only book Magdalene ever started without finishing.

"And why all the compositions?" Sister Mary Joseph asked.

Magdalene shrugged.

"But why so many? Mr. Butler only required one for extra credit."

Magdalene squirmed in her chair.

"I like to write," Magdalene said. "I like to make up stories."

"Were you trying to show off?"

Magdalene shook her head.

"I just needed to write them all down—the stories—before I forgot them."

"No one *needs* to write, my child," Sister Mary Joseph said. "It's a myth. Writing is simply something that one *does*. There is no magic; the art *is* the craft. Some writers spend hours, days even, contemplating a single comma."

Magdalene thought Sister Mary Joseph was up to her hoo-ha in dingleberries.

"I knew where all the commas went," Magdalene said. "I just wanted to tell the stories."

She watched Sister Mary Joseph flip through a stack of stories.

" 'The Whiskey Bar at Midnight.' 'The Secret of the Snipes.' 'The Case of the Dead Injun Tree.' " Sister Mary Joseph crinkled her nose.

Magdalene looked down at her saddle shoes. Here comes the soft-pedaled *I-know-your-mother-passed-away* speech.

"They're…they're mysteries," Magdalene admitted.

"And you're the detective?" Sister Mary Joseph asked. "In the stories—you're the detective?"

"Yes, Sister."

"What in heaven are you looking for?"

The problem with writing, Magdalene felt (this was not a theory she had shared with Sister Mary Joseph), was this: everyone wanted to explain writers when writers were the ones charged with doing the explaining. (Everyone suspected the protagonists to be her—even if the protagonist was a bluebird.) Maybe it was just her eighth grade brain (correction: soon-to-be-freshman brain—another correction: soon-to-be-shut-off brain), but no one seemed to question Bruce Springsteen's (who stared over his shoulder from Michael's ceiling on a raggedy poster Michael had won at the Catholic carnival) or former Phillies third baseman Mike Schmidt's or Alfred Hitchcock's motives or methods. They'd made music or played baseball or shot movies because they *needed* to; the urge to express themselves overtook every other aspect of their lives, obliterating other concerns until they perfected the very self-discipline others could never fully understand. Sure, her dad had books on Hitchcock's method, and her mother, who had been overly fond of Mike Schmidt (Michael teased her all the time, calling Schmidt Mommy's boyfriend), often spoke longingly of the arc of the retired Phillie's swing, the ease of his stance—but all the books in the world (as her father had promised the family) could never prepare them for when Raymond Burr turns to stare at Jimmy Stewart in *Rear Window*. And Magdalene's mother, who'd seen Mike Schmidt once during a school trip from the vantage point of third baseline seats, had told her and Michael that baseball was a game of moments and watching Mike Schmidt seize his was the closest she'd come to believing in God. (Magdalene had nodded eagerly along with her brother—any hint of their mother's past was worth hearing as many times as she wanted to tell it.)

And there were those who carved careers out of explaining art and beauty. Hell, every damn week, some guy whose face appeared as a pixilated black and white grin (the kind of grin John-John Hagarty sometimes flashed at Magdalene in the hallways of Assumption; the kind of smile that hid his teeth and gums, which Magdalene was sure were black and green with the remains of all the lunches he'd stolen from the younger kids) reviewed movies, grading them with one to four stars. Although Magdalene had no problem with rating movies (she knew what Mr. Pixilated considered a four star flick and what he was likely to condemn to a single sputtering star, so she could gauge her own interest against his), sometimes this near-faceless writer (Magdalene shuddered; Willa offered Magdalene her sweater) gave away salient plot points. And that was a sin her teachers, especially in seventh and eighth grade, were guilty of committing. Granted, reading (or acting out) Shakespeare lines was no walk in the posies— some extrapolating was helpful—but to tell the advanced reading group what the green light at the end of *The Great Gatsby* represented (which escaped Magdalene at the moment, so overstuffed was her brain) and *then* to demean F. Scott by qualifying his great accomplishment (no small part of which, Magdalene thought, was that he had been able to squeeze a masterpiece into a skinny book only slightly longer than the Hardy Boys' *What Happened at Midnight*) as merely a successful effort in craft—no way could Fitz have *needed* to put his pen to paper for the tragedy of Jay Gatsby, no sir—well, the whole lot of them were out of their heads. Writers *were* detectives; ideas and phrases sprung forth untethered from their minds, and they spent the rest of their lives chasing them down, following the clues, deciphering their meanings, honing the nuances.

Sister Mary Joseph wasn't a writer (as far as Magdalene knew), but she *was* a teacher and an administrator. How could Sister judge the process Magdalene or any writer used to make something up? It was on par with Sister Edna teaching marriage! Willa was the same way. (Magdalene knew she had to quiet this interior monologue; after all, her father, or his insurance, was paying for these fifty minutes.) Willa, as far as Magdalene knew, hadn't lost her brother. (And if Magdalene was wrong, then Willa Meade was worse than Magdalene originally thought, for surely the therapist should spill her own beans.) Willa didn't know about bullies and the havoc they wrecked upon the world (at least not like Magdalene knew); Willa knew about bullies secondhand: perhaps a patient or two had been terrorized. Willa was a peeping tom (Magdalene blushed, remembering her trash can episode outside Mrs. Tidwell's), no different than Sister Mary Joseph and the Assumption faculty trying to debunk the magic of writing from the safety of a classroom. But Magdalene was sure Willa, because of her profession, knew of abuse, and abuse was an extreme form of bullying.

And bullying, Magdalene now understood, was *everywhere*.

Magdalene had sat in the waiting room before her appointment, perusing old news magazines (she'd read every *Highlights* at least twice), and all the well-thumbed, slick pages of the news weeklies seemed to have the same photographs: the twin towers ablaze, a plane crashing into the south tower, little dots in even littler colored dress shirts and work uniforms and casual clothes from the Gap, leaping from the torches that had been buildings just moments before. And ash. In every picture, an ash blanket covered faces and hard hats and police caps and fire helmets. Ash outlined the tracks of tears etched into a screaming woman's skin. Ash clouds obscured the destination of the leaping colored dots.

Magdalene had clenched her stomach. Even now, not even a year later, it seemed too close to be consigned to a history book. How adults went back on airplanes, how life went back to normal was beyond Magdalene's comprehension. It was no different, she felt, than everyone accepting that Michael was gone. Where were the search parties? Where were her missing posters? Why wasn't Michael's face on the back of a milk carton?

It all came down to bullies. The terrorists were bullies. They didn't even have the guts to come fight. Just crash and die. And who were their enemies? Just little colored dots in Gap shirts; little falling dots with moms and dads and kids and husbands and wives and dogs. There were no enemies here—none that Magdalene knew of anyway—but the adults in McCullough's, when she had to get dinner money from her soused father, had other opinions, which they expressed in loud tones of outrage.

They want what we got.
We need their oil.
They want our cable TV.
We've been involved with things we shouldn't have been involved with.
We have to defend Israel.
The White House had done business with these guys before 9/11.
Fucking Jews—it's all their fault.
Patriot Act, my ass.
This is a Christian nation.
Just bring our boys home, that's what I say.
Towel heads.
Sand niggers.
Blast the fucking lot of them.

Iraq was in the crosshairs now, but even Sister Rita had managed to spit out that this was but "a shhhhaggy dog taillll." Bullies begat bullies, Father Dave had told the class.

In the waiting room, surrounded by photographic evidence of the terrorist bullies' handiwork, Magdalene knew she couldn't put off asking Willa about abuse any longer. If all went according to plan, she wouldn't get a second chance. And if the plan failed, Katie would be doomed to the fate of Mrs. Bochdan. The face of a pretender had fallen upon Mrs. Bochdan. Katie had lied to Magdalene about her bruises; full-blown denial (a Willa word!) wouldn't be far away. Soon Katie could join Mrs. Bochdan for tea service amid gold-framed lies of familial bliss—if Mr. McAllister didn't kill Katie first to make room for Mrs. Tidwell.

Willa pushed a box of Crayolas across the low table separating them. Willa had moved to the floor; she was sitting Indian-style, her legs under the table, already hard at work coloring a picture of a rabbit surrounded by baby bunnies. A small gold clock sat on the edge of the table, its face staring at Willa.

"I'm not a baby."

"I know," Willa said without looking up from the rabbit.

"I'm not a little kid."

"I know that too."

"I read better than anyone else," Magdalene said. "I read at a college level."

"Still read the Hardy Boys?"

Magdalene ignored the question. So what if she still read the Hardy Boys? Adult mystery books were all about sex; Magdalene didn't want anything to do with sex. She tried to refocus her mind back to the tasks at hand; bantering with Willa was as helpful as bantering with Aunt Tiddy.

There: there was Raven catching the little orange and blue striped basketball in his mouth and parading around the house, showing it off; a victory parade Michael had called it; no one could take the little basketball for further play.

There: there were Katie and Magdalene lying in Katie's backyard, just as night fell (Katie giggling nervously: "I hope it doesn't crush me!"), Magdalene pointing out various constellations and gods and goddesses, and Katie repeating each name carefully, sounding out the syllables.

There: there was Raven trying to lick Magdalene's face; she was home from the hospital (after the first attempt, or "incident," as she'd heard Aunt Tiddy say), and she was crying and Michael still wasn't home; there were no mentions of him in the paper, no missing posters, no search posses, no smoking guns.

Festooned along the wall on Magdalene's right were dozens and dozens of crayon and magic marker drawings on construction paper. Magdalene focused on one she'd seen before: a little blue dot falling from a window. Everything was out of scale: the window was too large, the dot too small, the flames that rose up to meet the dot (or perhaps, shrunk away from its swift, descending lines of navy blue) too hungry, too eager. Magdalene could barely make out the title scrawled in the corner in shaky cursive.

"That's 9/11," Magdalene said, the words creeping past her lips, slow and measured.

Willa twirled her fingers around her beads. Her hair was cropped short today and styled spiky, dyed an annoying orange-red. Magdalene thought she looked like a cross between a Bod Squad fashionista and a circus clown—or at least one in hippie beads and open-toed sandals.

"Yes, it is," Willa said, her eyes cruising the breadth of the wall. Magdalene shifted her focus away from the out-of-scale drawing and took in the entire wall too. Every piece of construction paper was on fire; one jumping blue dot became a dozen, maybe two dozen; flames crept out of windows, clouds, women's hair, men's suit coats; an airplane with an evil looking pilot, his grin pitched between a devil's and a skull's, appeared in at least six drawings. Over and over: little colored dots fell from absurdly over-scaled buildings of actively melting steel and dripping glass.

"Does looking at them make you sad?" Willa asked.

"I don't know," Magdalene replied. She wanted to strangle Willa in her love beads; the condescending tone of her voice made Magdalene want to tear Willa from the floor and turn the therapist and her sandals and her love beads and her bromides into so many dots sailing from the office window.

(*Condescending*—had she used the word correctly? The word felt appropriately overbearing, a perfect adjective for Willa's tone, as if the therapist were not sitting on the floor, pretending to be "just one of the kids," as she did, Magdalene knew, with so many of her younger patients, but rather ensconced in some high judge's chair, Magdalene's father arguing one side, Mr. McAllister the other. "Yes," she imagined Willa saying, "it is *my* recommendation that this child is in *deep* need of an enema; she has swallowed too much of the Puddle!" Magdalene smiled to herself, remembering a line from *West Side Story*: "*I'm depraved on account I'm deprived!*")

"You don't know what makes you sad, or you don't know if these pictures…" Willa asked, sweeping her hands through the air, a large sparkling ring on one finger, her nails painted a deep, deep red; how un-hippie like, Magdalene thought, "…make you sad?"

Magdalene shook her head. She'd heard the phrase "the apple doesn't fall far from the tree," but until the past couple of days they had just been a string of words, something Shakespeare had probably said—but here she was: thinking bully thoughts! Meek, hippie-wanna-be Willa was no different than any of Stevie Rich or John-John Hagarty's playthings. Magdalene wanted to smash her.

She refocused on the drawing of the falling blue dot, taking in the gash in the disproportionately sized buildings. She twisted her head to one side.

"It looks like a bloody wrist," Magdalene said, instantly covering her mouth. She had to learn to stop speaking her mind out loud. Before long, she'd be counting so everyone could hear.

"Have you ever cut your wrist?" Willa asked.

Dammit! Magdalene needed to move the conversation away from herself. If she didn't grill Willa about bullies and abuse, it probably wouldn't make *much* of a difference, but Magdalene had grown increasingly aggravated that she saw herself in bully terms and increasingly apprehensive about securing transportation for Katie to her Aunt Angela's. Was there anything Magdalene needed to do for Katie once she rescued her? Would Katie be better off if Magdalene took her to the orphanage on Lindenwold Estates? She'd heard of abuse victims—battered wives on daytime talk shows—needing years of therapy to stop cringing at the sound of a door slamming and requiring tons of medications to be able to look at themselves in the mirror.

"Do you want to draw me a picture?" Willa asked.

Magdalene suppressed her rising desire to bully Willa and snatched a red crayon from the table and slashed it across a piece of construction paper.

"They're along her wrist—like thumbprints, like someone grabbed her—but not," Magdalene said, "just anyone."

Willa nodded her head, encouraging Magdalene to continue.

"And there are other bruises, I'm sure—and there's a scar on her face."

"And what is her name, Magdalene?" Willa asked. "You said 'she.' Does 'she' have a name?"

Magdalene shut her eyes for a second. This wasn't all that different than the research she'd done for the paper Sister Edna had assigned her seventh grade class on the saints.

"Katie," Magdalene answered.

"Hi, Katie," Willa said.

Magdalene looked behind her.

"What?

"I was just saying hi to Katie."

"Oh."

"Tell me more about Katie. What does Katie look like?"

"That's not important," Magdalene said; the experiment was starting to irritate her.

"Okay," Willa said. "What would Katie like to talk about?"

"Her father—"

"Her father?"

"Her father leaves her alone all the time," Magdalene said, "and yet he *never* leaves her *alone*, if you know what I mean."

"I'm not sure I do. Why don't you explain it to me?" Willa asked.

"There are bruises on her arms...like a man's hand."

"Her father's?"

Magdalene ignored her. "I never looked, but I bet there are more. She uses Minnie like a metaphor."

"Minnie?"

"The turtle!" Magdalene said; exasperation seeped through her skin.

"Minnie is a turtle?"

Willa ran the beads of her necklace through her wrinkled fingers, as if they'd been discussing nothing more urgent than what tea to have with breakfast.

Magdalene shot Willa what she hoped was a withering look, but she doubted it. Magdalene's bones sagged in her skin. This was going poorly.

"Minnie's always trying to escape. She changes the color of her shell like a chameleon does, although she doesn't really; that's just what Katie thinks."

"Do you want to draw me a picture of Katie?"

Magdalene stared at Willa; Willa let her love beads cascade through her fingers. Magdalene had never seen so many wrinkles on the fingers and hands of someone who wasn't quite old enough to have them marking the eyes or brow. Forget love beads—these had to be worry beads.

"So Minnie is a metaphor for...?" Willa asked.

Magdalene dismissed the question with a shoulder shrug.

"You know the shooting at Assumption?"

"Assumption of Our Lady?" Willa asked. "Of course, but—"

"Well, Joseph Bochdan and Henry Richard Cabot were best friends."

"I had read that, yes, in the papers, but—"

"And bullies picked on them all the time. I can't *prove* it yet, but I will—tomorrow. I mean, I'll have my proof tomorrow. Stevie Rich and probably John-John too."

"And this Stevie Rich: he shot Henry?"

"Are you even listening to me?" Magdalene yelled. Her voice rattled the construction papers hanging on the wall; if she looked down at her arms, she knew her skin would be bubbling.

"I'm listening," Willa said. "I'm right here."

"What do you know about bullies?" Magdalene asked. "This is not about me. This is for someone else I know."

"Can I speak to that someone else?

"What?"

"Can that someone else speak to me? Or can I please speak with Katie?"

"You want to help Katie?"

"Of course, Magdalene," Willa said. "This is what I'm here for."

Magdalene's eyes soaked themselves; a large, wet stone shifted inside her chest. She knew the Aunt Angela Plan was a plan of sheer desperation—what if Katie's Aunt Angela was down the shore or visiting a friend? Magdalene could do no more than just stick Katie on a bus; she couldn't go with her. Once Magdalene accomplished everything else—gathering evidence against Stevie Rich, poisoning Raven, finishing her book—she *had* to take her own life; if just a tiny part of any of her plans went wrong, she'd find herself immersed in a swollen river of trouble. Besides, the biggest and most important mystery of all—Michael—was beyond her reach; she could feel her fingers slipping and something tangible sink away. She'd rather be dead than live without Michael.

Words crowded against each other in Magdalene's skull; it was almost comforting to count the syllables. She thought she might vomit—not because she was sick, but because she would have an ally. Even hippy-dippy Willa Meade was better than going this alone—assuming Willa didn't sink the plans in a puddle of adult rhetoric. Ha! *Rhetoric!* Magdalene gently squeezed herself; she loved her goddamn vocabulary.

Rhetoric.

Three syllables.

Rhet•o•ric.

"Yes! We have to act quickly though. Katie lives on Orchard Street. Now, I'm not sure of Mr. McAllister's schedule, and I'm banned from babysitting because Mrs. McAllister committed suicide a couple of years ago and I tried twice. Valerie Plum's got my job. But I know Mr. McAllister is dating the widow Tidwell. Katie's left with Valerie almost all day, so we just need to lie low and watch for when he leaves or create some sort of distraction to make *sure* he leaves. I have a plan for this too; I'll have to use some of Michael's money..."

"Your brother's money."

"...but if I don't have to put Katie on that Greyhound to her aunt's, then—"

"Greyhound?"

Words, unlike numbers, were pretty concrete. (Numbers were flexible.) Words could have various meanings and nuances, but those were stalactites from the original rock. And even the rock had roots—Latin, usually. (One of the few items on the Agenda of Possible Futures that made Magdalene wince when she thought of missing it was the chance to study Latin, to actually peek at the roots outside of their dictionary museums). Magdalene had built her vocabulary like she had practiced holding her breath—one word, one second at a time. Words could entangle—water could sweep everything away. Words could confuse and carry the faint whiff of lies and sins; words could sting and hurt and pop the skin; words could burrow—water could fill you up. The same water that gave life could take it away if it exploded past your throat, filling your lungs. But practice: vocabulary words, counting, holding one's breath—these were ways to harness everything that slippery hands and soft hearts could not.

She had to choose her words carefully.

"Greyhound," Magdalene pronounced slowly. "You know: the bus line."

"Katie is real?"

"Of course she's goddamn real!" Magdalene shouted. Inside her chest, her fingers slid from the wet rock.

Willa looked relieved, but quickly donned a mask of stern concern Magdalene recognized from Aunt Tiddy's broody countenance.

"What are you doing with Michael's money?"

"I don't know what you're talking about," Magdalene said. The rock, the roots, the syllables, the numbers—everything was now covered in slippery moss.

"You mentioned Michael's money."

"I didn't," Magdalene said. "I was just making stuff up."

"You were talking about bullies—and then the boys from your school. Then you said something about sending Katie on a bus—"

"Katie's a turtle."

"I thought you said Minnie was the turtle."

"The turtle's name is Katie. I lied the first time. Minnie was her code name."

Magdalene tried to compose her face into something resembling *sheepish*.

"I wanted to rescue the turtle. I don't think Mr. McAllister takes very good care of the turtle. I mean, the turtle isn't his, per se, but it lives in his backyard, and Mr. McAllister's always going off about the shit in his backyard."

"But didn't you baby-sit Mr. McAllister's little girl? What was her name?"

Magdalene knew in a town this size, Willa could easily check, but hell, by the time the lies caught up to her, Magdalene would be well on her way to being dead—all Willa needed was a name.

"Christina."

"Popular name."

Magdalene blushed. Had she mentioned Christina Fuller to Willa before?

"Guess so. They say Michael is the most popular boy's name. Joseph's up there too."

"I'm sure you've heard of the missing girl."

The missing girl?

"Her name's Christina too," Willa said. "I thought you might be in the same grade as her."

"There are a couple of Christinas in my grade."

"I can't remember what they said her last name was."

"But she's missing?"

"Yes, according to the radio this morning," Willa said. "Never came home from swim practice."

Magdalene's skin erupted again, only this time what bubbled beneath the surface were eggs—not beautiful Ukrainian eggs, but thin-shelled eggs, baby blue robin's eggs, one stiff breeze away from tumbling into hell—and now the incubating mess would spread into Magdalene's veins and find its way to her heart.

Magdalene opened her mouth but closed her ears; she didn't want to hear herself ask the question.

"Are they looking for her?"

"Yes," Willa said. "It's a bit early, but the county already has a team of officers and citizens scouring the town. The missing girl's mother apparently has some influence with the county. By tomorrow it will be a full blown manhunt."

Magdalene's gripped herself; if she could just crush every egg now, maybe she could go home, swallow Tiddy's medication, and start the unraveling of the coil ahead of schedule.

"I'm sorry, I thought you knew. This must remind you of Michael, no?" Willa's wrinkled knuckles rubbed against her love beads. A little light peeked through the drawn curtains and blinked off of her oversized ring.

"Do you blame yourself, Magdalene?"

Fuck Willa. Not even Christina could steal Magdalene's thunder now. As much as it pained her to be cavalier (every thought was like an aching muscle sputtering under extreme duress) Magdalene knew they would find Christina—if she was actually missing and not holed-up in a lengthy make-out session with any number of eager boys. There was too much to do; let Christina be a distraction for everyone else. Fuck Christina too.

No matter where she turned, the dark secrets of Mondauk—or at least the secrets of those inhabitants closest to her fluttering heart—were unveiled and dragged into the light: her father the bully, Nancy McAllister the suicide, and Mondauk County's apparently unwavering and perhaps premature search for Christina Fuller. There was no way she wanted to live in a world where Christina was tracked down and

Michael was consigned to heaven without so much as a memorial service or professional posters—a town where Mrs. Bochdan (crazy as she might be) was to be held liable for the actions of her son Joseph, who clearly (most likely, anyway) was trying to save Henry from the bullies with a weapon deadlier than fists.

Magdalene walked to the windows and snapped the shades. She let her eyes gather in the drawings. The light fell on the wall she'd been facing, but lit the adjacent wall as well—it too was festooned with exploding airplanes, falling colored dots, and larger-than-life flames consuming shaky towers of dripping steel and shimmering windows.

"Do you blame yourself, Magdalene?"

Magdalene walked out of the room and closed the double doors behind her. Her mind was already concocting a whopper of a lie she could tell the widow Tidwell when she gave her the movie tickets. The movie ticket idea had come to her in the middle of the whirlpool of thoughts and numbers in Willa's office. (She realized after she'd left that she'd been counting the number of drawings hanging on the wall with her toes while Willa prattled on—Jesus, she was getting good; it wasn't that different from holding her breath, and she was damn good at holding her breath.) Magdalene smiled. Michael would have enjoyed this part of the plan. This was a dare—a self-dare, really—and the Rules of the Dare had long ago been decimated, flotsam and jetsam caught in the swift currents of Magdalene's endgame.

+

Magdalene dreaded her date with Jerry Eves this evening. She dreaded it in the way she had dreaded her confirmation party and its crush of jolly adults and distant relatives—not dreaded it like she did the possibility of makeup exams (a dread not squashed by her soon-to-be untimely death). Magdalene's knowledge of dates were limited to the possibly-missing Christina's tales of mashes with various boys' lips and teeth and underwear—none of which Magdalene truly believed. What boy would stain his own underwear just because soft-around-the-middle Christina had lifted her shirt to show off her enormous bra, all clamps and desert-tan pansies fluffed with baby powder? Magdalene had only worn a bra twice and both times she had ditched it halfway through the family functions. Those were the only two bras she'd ever owned. After her mother died, her father never bought her another one or enforced any sort of undergarment code. She'd seen Michael using her tan church bra to toss rocks at the side of Frankie Bean's garage; the other one was as lost to her as Michael was now. Gone is gone, Aunt Tiddy (channeling ol' Bill no doubt) had said more than once.

Obfuscate.

Three syllables.

Ob•fus•cate.

(ŏb fŭs' kāt)

Just thinking of Christina made Magdalene's stomach feel like she'd swallowed angry balls of cement. If Christina had succeeded where Magdalene had failed—*twice!*—well, that was enough to break an already bent friendship. On the other hand, if someone had kidnapped Christina—whisked her away for unknown pleasures or sold her off to gypsies or buried her beneath layers of plywood and wormy dirt—then there was yet *another* mystery slipping through Magdalene's fingers. Either way, it stung; Christina had surely not put in the man hours necessary to refine a self-inflicted tragedy (which in Magdalene's case would follow a series of quick altruistic triumphs), let alone suffered enough to wander into the half-light of suicide— which was how Father Dave had described the act in one of his boisterous sermons: a broken, blinking, intoxicating Christmas light. Christina's father was Dr. Fuller, for fuck's sake. Dr. Fuller had never spent entire days hunched over a dusky bar. Dr. Fuller had never drunkenly run in the rain to pull the hood off the wrong survivor.

Altruistic.

Four syllables.

Al•tru•is•tic.

(ăl' trŏŏ ĭs' tĭk)

Def.: Regardful of others; having regard to the well-being or best interests of others (opposed to egoistic).

Pulled the hood off the wrong survivor?

Magdalene shook her head. The bus stop was empty, thank God, and Magdalene patted the wad of bills in her pocket. If she believed what she'd seen in old movies, dates took place at soda fountains (which Magdalene had never seen in Mondauk Proper; Tiddy had said that Rex's Pharmacy was once such an establishment)—or in movie theaters. In the old films, it seemed as if the boy picked the location of the date. She didn't know where Jerry would take her.

But thinking about the movies had given her an idea. Her father had placed Mrs. Tidwell and Mr. McAllister's relationship in the spotlight of tragic romance—a romance brought together only because their spouses had died in spectacular ways: Nancy McAllister via suicide (spectacular or not, the poor woman had obviously been successful in a way that Magdalene had not quite managed) and Bobby Tidwell at the World Trade Center. Romance was in the air—that much Magdalene had seen for herself. Hence the movie tickets.

She had to admit, it seemed absurd to just present Mrs. Tidwell with two tickets to the movies, but enough pint-sized salespeople had knocked upon Magdalene's door hawking candy bars or magazine subscriptions, even offering seed samples or a free week of newspaper delivery. What if Magdalene just knocked upon Mrs. Tidwell's door and presented her with two tickets for a Sunday evening show? It was a long shot for sure. Maybe Mr. McAllister and the widow Tidwell didn't like movies. Maybe they didn't have a date planned for Sunday. If Magdalene was sure Mr. McAllister was out Sunday night, then she'd only have to deal with Valerie Plum during Katie's rescue. The chance was worth the sixteen dollars. Besides, Mrs. Tidwell looked like the kind of person who'd enjoy going to the movies; she looked like someone who didn't leave the house very often.

As much as Magdalene adored the stars, she had little patience for horoscopes and the other ephemera (e•phem•er•a—four syllables—ĭ fĕm' ər ə—def.: anything short-lived or transitory) that were often lumped in with astronomy. Still, she couldn't help but feel that the stars were anything but aligned when she reached the Ambler Theater. Magdalene studied the movie posters. Everything was rated R except a sub-par Disney romp that Magdalene had skipped the first time it had been released. It was one of the later, cringe-worthy efforts—not a classic like *The Jungle Book* or *Robin Hood*. (She and Michael had worn out those tapes!) Magdalene bought two tickets to the Disney flick out of guilt—she'd been holding up the line, trying on different facial expressions and attitudes (she never had a problem getting into an R rated movie) before abandoning it all and surrendering sixteen of Michael's dollars for an inane animated feature no two people over the age of four would want to see. The smell of popcorn had weakened her—that was it. Magdalene loved popcorn.

In its previous incarnation, the Ambler Theater had been the

Christian Cinema. Magdalene couldn't remember which Protestant denomination had run the place then, but it had always looked derelict—like a pornography theater, Tiddy had said. Now it was considered an art house: foreign and independent films plus repertoire movies (and occasional blockbuster dreck). The theater had been restored to its former glory thanks to a grant from the County Council. The yellow bricks had been cleaned and polished. The big AMBLER sign had been repaired and rose vertically above the marquee; you could see it all the way from Wings Field. Tiddy said the new sign was garish, but Tiddy didn't like anything new. (Tiddy had said she'd gone on a date to the Ambler back when it was still a magnificent example of Mondauk prosperity, before the factory closed and the theater fell to the Christians. Wouldn't that be odd if Jerry and Magdalene had their date in the same building where Tiddy may have shared popcorn with a potential suitor?)

The bus was late (she was spending money left and right now, it seemed), and she almost missed it anyway—she'd been counting the stars that were now competing with the sun for the sky. The husky exhaust brought her back, and from her seat, she sought the skies for Draco.

Cadmus had killed him—Cadmus had slain Draco, the terrible dragon—after failing to find his sister Europa. Cadmus had been sent to search by his father, who believed Zeus had kidnapped Europa. Unable to discover where Zeus had hidden his sister, Cadmus wandered the world to avoid his father's wrath over his son's failure. Desperate, Cadmus begged Apollo to assist him in finding somewhere to call home. In what would become the city of Thebes, Cadmus sent his men into a cave to find fresh water to offer as libation to Zeus. When his men failed to return, Cadmus entered the cave and there discovered Draco the dragon. A fierce battle was pitched, and Cadmus, who'd been so unsuccessful in his quest to find Europa, overcame and killed Draco. At Athena's suggestion, he buried the great dragon's teeth in the ground, from which sprang a battalion of warriors who battled amongst themselves until only five remained, and these five, led by Cadmus, founded Thebes. Another version has Draco being placed in the heavens after being slain by Hercules, but Magdalene understood the true glory of Draco's death was in Cadmus' victory in the face of defeat. Having lost Europa, Cadmus banished himself—but not before accomplishing a task worthy of being celebrated in the stars.

As the bus climbed into the Heights, Magdalene wondered if leaving the tickets in Mrs. Tidwell's mailbox was such a good idea. What if her mail came early, and Mrs. Tidwell didn't check it again until Saturday morning or early afternoon? Did that leave the widow Tidwell enough time to call Mr. McAllister and make a date?

And there she was on the next corner in a worn, tan sweater and thick, dirty-gray corduroys, despite the early summer heat: the widow Tidwell! She was hunched over and there was a little stoop in her walk. Magdalene thought she recognized the stoop; Mrs. Bochdan walked the same way. It was the stoop of defeat. Mrs. Tidwell's fingers were red and raw, clinging to two plastic supermarket bags, their handles stretched way past the recommended stretching point. Magdalene yanked the bus cord and dug into her pockets for the movie tickets. She pushed the doors open with her tiny frame before the bus came to a complete stop, tumbling from the steps and just about colliding with the widow. Mrs. Tidwell flinched and squinted, straining over her bags. There we no broken eggs this time. Magdalene wondered if this tremulous activity (trem•u•lous—three syllables—trĕm' yə ləs—def.: characterized by trembling as from fear, nervousness, weakness)—the straining of the plastic handles, the hunching over tonight's dinner and tomorrow's lunch, the flinching at a young girl with sockets where her eyes used to reside—was the end result of living beyond one's time. Magdalene found her mouth more than willing to take over for her recently Willa-fried brain. She let her toes do the counting

"Mrs. Tidwell, my name is...well, I'm Michael Barrows' sister and...let me help you with those bags."

Magdalene's mouth tasted like metal, and her underarms were damp. She slid one of the plastic bags from Mrs. Tidwell's hand, the plastic handles greasy with palm sweat, and slipped the movie tickets into the stunned lady's free hand.

"I go to Assumption. Or I did. I'm thirteen. I just finished eighth grade. I still have to take some exams, but it's been a busy summer."

Mrs. Tidwell's face was one big worry line: her little mouth was open, and Magdalene could see what was once pretty—even still pretty—about the middle-aged woman standing before her on the pavement. Her mousy brown hair was full of split ends, and even her eyebrows were in need of trimming; they exploded like Raven's whiskers. (Magdalene's stomach clenched itself—she imagined she was doubled over rather than planted on her own two feet—when

behind the numbers and definitions and plans and dares she glimpsed
Raven asleep at the foot of her bed, his curiously unrestrained muzzle
hair jutting like antennas tuned to a channel dedicated to cookies,
football, and Michael.) Mrs. Tidwell looked a little like the girls who
lived in Paradise Lakes Trailer Park, a few of whom attended
Assumption or Resurrection up in Rhawnhurst (if their parents could
afford the adjusted tuition). These girls: their skin was gray and
scratched; instead of pimples, there were pits. Their pallor matched
their parents', as did their nicotine-stained fingers. But the Lakes girls
were portraits of flesh in descension (de•scen•sion—three syllables—
dǐ sěn' shən—def.: *now rare*: descent). Whoever Mrs. Tidwell had been
was buried beneath the weight of the twin towers, this much
Magdalene was sure of. (She willed herself not to think of the swiftly
falling colored dots raining down from the melting giants of steel and
glass; she forced herself not to imagine the late Bobby Tidwell
trapped inside a red no fire engine paint could replicate.) Mrs.
Tidwell's decline was not completely of her own doing.

"I like helping people, and I have here…there, in your
hand…two tickets to the Ambler to see…well, you can exchange
them. They're for Sunday night's picture—Sunday night."

Mrs. Tidwell backed away from Magdalene and stared into her
palm. The woman's mouth worked itself over and then clamped shut,
as if trying to decide which words to choose and then abruptly
abandoning all choices.

"So, only take 'em if you're gonna use 'em," Magdalene said,
trying to force a laugh.

"Don't grow on trees," she concluded, cursing Tiddy and all her
goddamn little clichés. If Shakespeare had ever said that, someone
should have shot him in the face.

Someone should have shot him in the face.

The widow Tidwell looked up from the movie tickets.

"No, we'll use them." Her voice was creaky, underused. "What
did you say your name was?"

How pale her own face must look, Magdalene thought, and how
shiny, framed by her sweaty, black bob.

She answered without thinking: "Magdalene."

*No—take it back—Mary, Maureen, Madeleine—hell, even the dreaded
Maddie.*

"Magdalene," Mrs. Tidwell repeated, like she was trying to speak
a foreign language, not seeming to equate the name with the recently

deposed baby-sitter. Perhaps Mrs. Tidwell was a trifle slow in the uptake. That could explain a whole heck of a lot.

"Magdalene," the widow repeated.

Mrs. Tidwell looked down at the tickets again and laughed. Higher pitched than her voice, it trickled from the woman's mouth like drool. Disconcerting—but it was a laugh nonetheless. Magdalene couldn't help the grin she knew had invaded her own lips; she buried the fact that this ticket giveaway was far from an altruistic act and tried to seize the moment as it drifted in the still air, arid and tangible—a connection made between two broken parts—not at all like the tea service with Mrs. Bochdan or the shouting match between Mr. McAllister and Magdalene's father. Magdalene realized she was standing on her toes and eased herself down.

"Are you a friend of Stevie's?" Mrs. Tidwell asked, still laughing, and the last of Magdalene's smile sunk into her gums.

Magdalene held her breath.

Count: *one, two, three, four, five, six, seven...*

Mrs. Tidwell paid no attention to Magdalene's lack of breath.

"He's my nephew," the widow Tidwell explained. "Stevie Rich. My husband's nephew, really. Do you know him?"

Big grin.

Easy.

...eight, nine, ten, eleven, twelve, thirteen...

She was under Michael's blanket; she was seven years old—no six—maybe eight—and they were camping in his room, propping up his old velour blanket with various pieces of football equipment. Outside, the rain splattered and painted the windows. Downstairs, their mother was bent over a stove working on a mystery soup; she had *shooed* her children from the kitchen: "You can't possibly see what's in the soup."

Michael was outside the blanket tent, Magdalene inside. He was being very quiet; she couldn't even hear him breathe. In fact, she could only hear her own muffled, anxious breaths. Was that a lightning flash? A series of thuds landed on her head, timed with the thunder. She pulled her extremities in tight. The thudding ceased. Magdalene peeked out from beneath the blanket.

Big easy grin.

"Avalanche," Michael said by way of explanation.

Magdalene retreated back into her cave tent. The blanket smelled like her brother did, only older and somewhat spicier. It was slightly rancid, but Magdalene couldn't help but suck in huge gulps of future, stinky Michael smell.

"Ready?" Michael asked.

Magdalene nodded, her head under the blanket.

"Lil? You ready?"

"I nodded yes."

"No cheating."

"Just do it."

"Okay, in case of emergency—"

"I know, I know." She was bored. Already this morning, Magdalene had been pushed from a lifeboat, had been forced to jump from a cliff, and had reenacted Sister Mary Magdalene de Rosa's body bridge.

"By the wrists."

Magdalene snorted. *This is a test of the emergency broadcast system...*

"As long as you can, okay?"

Magdalene ignored her brother. *If this had been an actual avalanche...*

Everything outside of the cave tent grew quiet—Indian quiet, as Michael called it.

...you would have been instructed to...

The blanket pushed against her face. Magdalene dropped to a horizontal position and stopped breathing.

One, two, three, four, five...

The Hardy Boys Detective Handbook says: "Surveillance comes from the French word *surveiller* meaning 'to watch.' "

...thirteen, fourteen, fifteen, sixteen, seventeen...

Nebula.

Three syllables.

Neb•u•la.

(neb' yə lə)

Def.: a cloudlike, luminous mass composed of gaseous matter or stars far beyond the solar system.

...twenty-eight, twenty-nine, thirty, thirty-one...

The Hardy Boys Detective Handbook says: "Of the millions of persons fingerprinted to date, no two have ever been found to have even one fingerprint identical."

...forty-six, forty-seven, forty-eight...

Vega, one of the three brilliant stars of the Summer Triangle, belongs to the constellation Lyra, named after the musical instrument Apollo had given to Orpheus. Orpheus played so beautifully, even savage beasts stopped being savage—and his lyre was placed in the heavens after his death.

    ...seventy-nine...

Raven.

    ...eighty...

"Get in the pool, Boo."

"He won't get it in."

"Raven!"

"Yellin' ain't gonna help, Lil."

    ...ninety-four...

"It's *his* pool!"

    ...ninety-six...

"Lil, he has to *want* to get in his pool."

"He follows you everywhere. You get in the pool."

"I don't want to get in the pool."

"Michael, please? Get in the pool."

    ...one hundred and sixteen...

"Why do you care so much if Raven gets in the pool?"

"I bought the pool with my allowance. He always looks so hot, panting like crazy. You said it yourself: 'the dog days of summer are upon us.' "

    ...one hundred and twenty-seven...

"Michael, get in!"

"I have practice."

"Not for hours!"

    ...one hundred and forty-three...

"What will you do for me, Lil? What will you do for me? I feel a dare coming on."

    ...ONE HUNDRED AND FIFTY-SEVEN...

Underwater, everything looked like it did in a funhouse mirror: distorted, obscene, stretched. Underwater, her hair waved and shimmied, finally free of the strictness of the practical bob. Underwater, Magdalene's hair flowed like her mother's.

    ...ONE HUNDRED AND...

The weight shifted. Michael had her by the wrists and pulled her out from beneath the blankets. Michael had saved her. The taste in the back of her throat was a mixture of metal and the bologna she'd had for lunch.

"Where's Raven?" she gasped.

"Sleeping on the floor. Lil—"

Michael's hands were still grasping her pale, skinny wrists. Her nails were digging into his skin.

"He won't get in the pool, Michael."

"I don't think I know—"

Magdalene turned her head, and her hands clawed at the air. As her peripheral vision returned, Magdalene thought she was awash in a sea of dandelions, swept under a blanket of whisker wishes.

Magdalene listened to her own voice: "...I don't think I know him."

Mrs. Tidwell sighed. "I don't know him that well myself." The widow's sundress, under her gray sweater, was a yellow pattern of sunflowers.

"They're for you and Mr. McAllister."

The movie tickets Magdalene floated to the warm pavement.

"Oh, I see what this is," Mrs. Tidwell said. "Is this some born again thing?"

Magdalene counted the seconds before they landed.

"You don't understand," Mrs. Tidwell said. The widow's face was nose to nose with Magdalene's.

Magdalene stared at the tickets at her feet. Mrs. Tidwell's breath smelled like the inside of an attic trunk, like gravelly, corroded coins. It was stale, this air—not at all like Michael's ripe, blanket smell. This was grave stink. She wanted to return to the (relative) safety of the blanket; Magdalene could hold her breath all day long. But she could squeeze her eyes shut, pinch her nose, cover her ears—it wouldn't make any difference. The volume of Mrs. Tidwell's shattered, underused voice would never dissipate, never decline, never descend into its previous worried whisper.

"YOU DON'T FUCKING UNDERSTAND!" Mrs. Tidwell screamed. "NO ONE DOES!"

One, two, three,

Four, five, six,

Seven, eight, nine,

Ten, eleven, twelve,

And they all played games at the ladybugs' picnic.

Such a kid thing—the safety blanket—the security blanket. If Magdalene had her brother's old blanket—his stinky, Michael-stained blanket—she'd hold it over her head right now and jump. She'd parachute to some place where maybe she wouldn't be the only person aware that walking wounded was the equivalent of dead-in-the-water. Every single soul in Magdalene's Mondauk—the widow Tidwell, Mrs. Bochdan, Katie McAllister, even needy, eager-to-please Jerry Eves, straining against the leash of puppy love—limped, hypnotized by some kind of love that no longer existed. No one was whole. Least of all their father.

Their?

Someone had stolen Michael's security blanket; someone had eased Michael from the story. Someone had erased his colored dot.

"I LOVED BOBBY. I CAN'T *POSSIBLY* LOVE LIKE THAT AGAIN. WHAT THE FUCK IS *WRONG* WITH YOU PEOPLE? LEAVE US ALONE!"

Mrs. Tidwell's colander-strained voice echoed as if the streets were empty, as if forcing itself raw would somehow make itself understood. It was the voice of a banshee slouching from Pennypack Woods. Magdalene tried to turn her head—nothing but numbers. No one would hear them; no one would even look in their direction. Mondauk Proper had grown deaf to the wails of the banshee.

"FUCK!" Magdalene screamed to her sneakers. A slight breeze had blown the movie tickets to a scrub of yellowed grass.

Mrs. Tidwell's voice had drifted away too. "Jack McAllister is a good man."

"FUCKITY FUCK." Magdalene's voice muscled past her constricted throat, and by the time her breath had returned (*twenty-seven, twenty-eight, twenty-nine*), Mrs. Tidwell had taken back the bag and shuffled past her. Magdalene didn't turn around; she couldn't imagine looking at Mrs. Tidwell's stooped shoulders. Just hearing the plastic shopping bags rubbing together was painful. The sound was so familiar. She covered her ears and listed all the prime numbers less than 100.

Michael had rescued her: he'd pulled her by her wrists. There was to be no suffocation for Magdalene; no dirty bridge over a fire. Michael had saved her, rescuing her from thick blankets of brother-scent and interminable counting.

Magdalene knew what that sound was. The numbers wouldn't help.

The *swish* of Mrs. Tidwell's plastic bags against her dirty-gray corduroys sounded like the Puddle lapping up stray cigarette butts and used condoms from the endemic shoreline.

The numbers wouldn't help her at all.

Chapter Nine

The Date

It was Carnival Day! Magdalene had almost forgotten in the wake of her failed encounter with the explosive widow. (She had tried to ignore the fliers stapled to the telephone poles where her missing posters used to be.) Friday was the kickoff of ten days of competing carnivals. Calvary United Methodist Church's carnival was smaller than the Catholic event and had fewer games, but their haunted houses were legendary: spongy floors, college kids with vampire teeth, rubber spiders hanging from the ceiling, waiting to bounce against foreheads in the dark. Assumption's carnival always had the better rides, and Sunday was Feast Day. Father Dave would give a speech after the noon Mass, and members of the Faith Board would parade through the Corridor and past the convent with a statue of John the Baptist. This year, the Baptist's birthday fell on Monday. But it close enough to give the carnival at least the veneer of a religious event. Tiddy said it was an excuse to make money, but that each parish was responsible for its own financial well-being, and wasn't that a hoot and a holler? There was an actual feast in August to celebrate the Virgin Mary's Assumption, but most of the parishioners were busy with vacations, and for the last few years, the Assumption was commemorated with a spaghetti dinner in the school cafeteria after Mass. Magdalene didn't know if the Methodists feasted the birth of John the Baptist. Tiddy had said Calvary held their carnival on the same week to siphon Catholic dollars, but that anything that blew wind up the bloomers of the Faith Board was okay by her. Both carnivals lasted ten days, an extraordinary length; by the final weekend, most of the kids had ridden every ride, tramped through every haunted house, and played every game of chance at least three times. On the last weekend, their parents' wallets and pocketbooks would have long been shut, and even the hot dog vendors would be slumped in their seats catching catnaps.

Walking to Mondauk Common, Magdalene could smell popcorn and hear the screams of the early arrivals. She and Michael used to look forward to carnival season; they'd go to both, and Michael would ride every ride. Magdalene preferred the haunted houses or wasting her money trying to toss a softball into a tilted basket. Her absolute favorite carnival game was the one her brother and Christina and the rest of the Bod Squad ignored: guessing the number of gumballs in the large fishbowl. When their mother was ten years old, she had guessed correctly; the prize had been a brand new apple-red bicycle that she was banned from riding the next day when it was discovered she'd caught a bad case of chicken pox that would lay her up for two months. Magdalene had won the gumball game twice (annoying Mrs. Fuller who administered the games of chance), but the prizes were significantly less exciting than an apple-red bicycle. The first year she'd won a goldfish in a bowl; the fish died during the night, and the ceremonial flushing was disturbing. The next year, the prize was a children's picture Bible. But Magdalene was proud of her counting.

Like her father with his little red AA book, Magdalene thought she could probably now stand up among others of her kind (if there were any) and say with a lump of Puddle mud in her throat, "My name is Magdalene Harper Barrows and I'm a counter." Despite her sieve-like memory regarding semi-recent events (Michael), she could remember, if she concentrated, a time when she didn't count. But that was long ago.

It made sense then, as she made her way north to County Hall and the Common, that she'd count the cracks in the pavement, categorize the different colored wads of gum stuck to the pavement, keep track of the number of times the girl with the pigtails on Edgewood Street skipped rope. If nothing else, it kept part of her mind focused; the other part, the part that wasn't counting, ruminated on Mrs. Tidwell's revelation: Stevie Rich, Assumption's king bully and Magdalene's chief suspect in the Cabot Case, was Mrs. Tidwell's nephew.

It made sense too that Magdalene was able to hold her breath for lengthy durations: holding one's breath was all about counting—there was simply nothing else to think about when one couldn't breathe. Time was like summer or a good movie—it didn't so much stand still as skip rope. Or bounce on a pogo. Or dribble in one place. Or *drip drip drip* like the leaky faucet in the Sister-Mary-Magdalene-de-Rosa-sanctified girls' room. Or pulse like the Puddle slurping along the shoreline.

Float float float.

To make it through to the other side of Michael's games in one piece—the challenges, the wars, the dares—she'd swallowed hard and counted. Sister Anita had told the class, as they were making Father's Day cards in the fourth grade, that TRUE LOVE was unselfish; it took the good with the bad: the Dad who told you not to play with the lawnmower was the same father who pulled you from the undertow at the last second. Sister Anita had told the class they couldn't choose *when* to love—not if it was REAL LOVE. But how to survive REAL LOVE, how not to lose oneself in an undertow of love—the nuns never taught those lessons. The nuns were too busy subjugating themselves to God, principal, school. (Subjugate—three syllables—sub•ju•gate—sŭb' jə gāt'—def.: to make submissive or subservient.) No one had taught her how to survive Michael.

So Magdalene countered by counting. It was her only method of grounding REAL LOVE. In counting, every number was accountable to itself only, its own uniqueness less a measure of separateness than a subtle distinction among similars—a snowflake in a curtain of snowflakes or a fingerprint on a smudged window. She'd counted when Michael tackled her in the backyard, or when Michael chased her with raw hamburger, or when she was submerged, on rainy days, beneath his blankets and pillows, smothered within his sleep smell. She could never have screamed or cried—God forbid! Michael would have branded her a traitor if their father had grounded him (unlikely as that punishment—or any—was); her brother would mark her a coward if she turned down an opportunity to be buried in a pile of his dirty laundry or to be stuck in the mouth of a street hockey net, a severely worn goalie's mask her only protection. So Magdalene counted.

Only when she emerged on the grassy Common (fourteen steps from the edge of the square to the dirt walking circle which was surrounded by twenty sickly elms; County Hall was inside the circle, fifty two steps from the inner rim) did she stop counting. (It had been a long walk from the Heights to the Common in the north.) Usually, inanimate objects held the most counting potential, if only because they couldn't move; she could go back and re-count if necessary. But people were the real counting quarry—even if syllables were more reliable. People could be sorted by weight or hair color or nationality. Hell, she could sort them by Christian denomination if she wanted to: guilty-looking but smiling Catholics (Magdalene assumed the true nature of the sacrament of confession had something to do with insouciance—*insouciance*: now *there* was a decent gathering of syllables!—lie, cheat, steal, kill, then ask for absolution and say a few Hail Marys) and austere, dirty Methodists—not dirty as in sinful or pornographic, but dirty as in poor. A large portion of the Methodist population lived in Paradise Lakes in tin trailers that had, like their inhabitants, long ago lost their mobility. How the economic split between denominations had come about, Magdalene didn't know. During the golden days of Mondauk Proper's prosperity (spurred by the opening of the asbestos factory), the economic and social tier had been reversed: the Catholics, mostly Irish and Italian, had composed the bulk of the workforce; the ruling class had consisted of various Protestant congregations. Miss Rosewood Seton, grand dame of the old Methodist cemetery, had certainly come from money—or so Magdalene imagined. Some of the chiseled letters on her gravestone had been beaten smooth by years of rain and snow and wind, but the stone was still shiny and the largest in the cemetery. By contrast, the pavements of the Common Square and County Hall were dull, the elms malnourished, the circle path worn, tramped down by thousands of pairs of feet, the accompanying bodies consumed by their heads' endless counting. Mondauk Proper's Catholic Faith Board was involved in its own secret counting (secrets being the town's homegrown currency): which of these *other* people are sinners? Which are Methodists? Oh, there's a black person—a Baptist! That woman's fat. His shorts are too tight. He once stole a box of condoms from Rex's Pharmacy—a sinner!

Towards the center of the Common was an almost-obscene, seaweed green fountain. It was dominated by a sculpture of a large-mouthed fish, frozen in the act of jumping out of the Puddle, its mouth inches away from the chipped tail of a diving, wanton mermaid. The mermaid was barely dressed (massive cleavage, a hint of buttocks), and both the Catholics and the Methodists had taken turns attempting to address the offending pieces. And so the fountain remained empty—it had been empty for years. Magdalene sat on its smooth ledge. For a Friday—for any day—Mondauk Common was empty. A lot of folks must have left their jobs early to run to the carnivals. Magdalene had sensed footsteps scurrying away in her approach, and now their tinny echoes were the only things remotely human left to count. It was like a '50s sci-fi flick, the kind she and Michael had watched on rainy Saturday afternoons, their mother burning a bowl of popcorn for them to share (Michael had an almost perverse desire to stick kernels in Magdalene's ears), their father maybe still at his office, or out back hacking at the damp weeds—the bar still a cancer victim away. Magdalene hollered her own name and waited for its return. Only the yawning, stained-green fountain carried her echo, and it was weak, the fizzle of a long-dead signal.

There was a scraping sound behind her—a sneak attack!—but when she turned, there was only a lump of shadow. Magdalene thought of Raven sitting at the top of the stairs where he could just about see out of the little octagonal window on the front door (during fall and winter) or parked with his nose against the screen door (in spring and summer). Raven: barking at the kids chasing balls and riding bicycles, or howling at the tailless tabby who took pains this past spring to antagonize her dog by cleaning itself inches from the door.

Magdalene walked to the inner edge of the circle and penetrated the shadow of Raven. He wasn't there; her dog was nowhere near Mondauk Common. Her dog was home, awaiting execution by rat poison.

Two, three, four ounces.

Magdalene tiptoed away from the fountain and made her way behind the shrubbery and the news boxes that threw bulky, canine-shaped shadows at her feet. She knew she should be getting home, preparing for her date with Jerry Eves or helping Tiddy with the chores one last time. Or murdering her dog. Or finishing her book. (What the hell was the old lady up to on Saturday that she wanted Magdalene out of the house?—*ahh*, better to not look too closely— " 'pleasure and action make the hours seem short,' " Tiddy was fond of saying, quoting the Bard.) But Magdalene was drawn towards her father's office; she wanted to see him, feel his presence, smell his aftershave—quite the opposite of what she'd been feeling recently. During the past year, unless sent on a specific errand—one that perhaps required her father's signature on a report card or a truant slip—Magdalene had skirted her father and avoided walking anywhere near McCullough's. Once, when going to the bar couldn't be avoided, she'd passed fire-breathing Mrs. Stanley, town librarian, consummate curmudgeon, and teetotaler for Jesus, as Magdalene neared McCullough's worn, green door. The woman's sour mug had been contorted into what Magdalene assumed was a mask of empathy. Magdalene had ignored her but wondered if she could somehow facilitate the murder of Mrs. Stanley amid the library stacks—maybe somewhere between the tattered Agatha Christie paperback mysteries and the Jesus-Loves-You books. Magdalene had felt then she neither deserved nor required looks of sympathy or empathy—especially from Mrs. Stanley, her reptilian eyes trapped beneath volumes of flesh. After all, inside the bar was a man Magdalene barely knew; inside McCullough's was a man who'd loved her brother above all people and the law above all things. The nifty balance of heart and brain, already made tipsy from the loss of his wife, had come undone when Michael had vanished. She'd stood in the doorway of the bar, a vestige of the afternoon sun on her back, and he'd slouched towards her, blinking, his empty spaces filled to capacity with liquor.

Near the west side of County Hall, the doors to the offices stood open, as they sometimes did in the spring and summer, and a secretary's radio blared out corporate messages to the empty corridors. Magdalene poked her head into the hallway. A newsbreak was about to start as they always did on the quarters and the halves, the jocular DJ announced. His voice then took a solemn turn: "*...and coming up, we'll have more information on the missing child from Mondauk Proper...*"

The third door on the left was her father's; it was the only closed door in the hallway. The radio blathered from the next office. When Magdalene pulled the door open, Mrs. Banniman, her father's absurdly tall and round secretary—*ahem*: administrative assistant— flinched, startled, her chins wagging, as if...why, as if she'd seen a ghost.

He was drunk again. Magdalene just *knew* it.

"Why, young Miss Barrows. Come to see the Assistant District Attorney, have you?"

Mrs. Banniman's face was flushed, as if she'd been caught doing something she shouldn't have been—and caught by her boss' moody, unstable daughter no less. No telling what that girl was capable of, no telling at all, Mrs. Banniman's scrunchy face said.

"Hi, Mrs. Banniman. Is my father in?" Magdalene asked.

Mrs. Banniman reached under her desk. She placed a bottle of clear nail polish on a white notepad.

"In a meeting, he is."

Mrs. Banniman spoke like the old biddy from the village surrounding the haunted castle in those black and white Universal horror movies. Tiddy had told Magdalene she thought Mrs. Banniman's English accent was put-on, something to impress the painted coots that ruled Assumption's Faith Board, something to distract attention from her chins.

"Big doings," Mrs. Banniman said. "Lots of shouting."

So he wasn't drunk. Magdalene shook her head. Hard to know what to know anymore.

"*...police are stymied, Jim. There appear to be very few clues and even fewer leads. The child's father, a prominent local doctor, has posted his own reward. Now, the police say they haven't ruled out...*"

Mrs. Banniman huffed her way around her desk and pushed the door closed with two puffy fingers.

"Mrs. Taylor doesn't seem to be aware, lassie, *that sound travels.*"

The secretary raised her voice on the last three words and, pulling at her pearl choker (Magdalene imagined the circle of impressions it left on her plump, middle-aged neck), hobbled to a filing cabinet to fondle the manila folders.

"Now, now. Duplicate, triplicate. Hard to track. Hard to track. Have to keep it together, eh, lass?"

Magdalene slid past the bulk of the secretary and peeked into her father's office. Papers were stacked in random fashion upon his desk. In fact, *stacked* was the wrong verb; *tossed* was a better choice. Folders were open, closed, bent. There was one on the floor. Two coffee cups crowded the edge of the desk as if about to jump to the relative safety of the floor—itself home to stacks of large books with red covers and gold embossing.

"Come now, come now."

Mrs. Banniman led Magdalene back into the outer office. The woman's thumb was as thick as a bagel. The upper sleeves of her blouse squeezed her arms pink so they resembled the intestine-like wares hanging in Bard's Meats. If, as Father Dave lectured in multiple homilies, the human body was the temple of God and should be kept as such, Magdalene thought Mrs. Banniman's also housed the Son *and* the Holy Ghost. Magdalene had once witnessed Mrs. Banniman devouring an entire box of doughnuts at an Assumption Christmas bazaar.

"Ye can wait in the chair here and keep me company, or I can take a message," Mrs. Banniman said, her annoyance no longer hidden. "Can't be scampering about now."

Ye? Had Mrs. Banniman actually said *ye?*

The secretary held open the door for Magdalene, the decision made.

"*...the rescue team gathered near Paradise Lakes. Chief Hagen would not comment on the search other than to say that the community and the authorities are committed to...*"

Magdalene slammed the door shut behind her and followed the radio report down the hall.

"*...thank you, Carl. Thank you, Steve. We'll have more news for you on the half...now back to the* rock *that doesn't* roll *you over on 93.3...*"

Mrs. Banniman opened the office door.

"Being difficult, eh, lassie? I'll be informing your father."

She didn't sound displeased.

Magdalene ignored her and headed for the stairwell. She climbed the wooden steps, counting each one aloud, until she was far enough away that she couldn't hear Mrs. Taylor's transistor radio. The fourth floor was a ghost town. Light from a small round window at her end of the hall illuminated spots the cleaning crew had missed. The hardwood floor creaked as if she was walking across the deck of an ancient pirate ship. She made her way on tiptoes to the double doors at the far end of the hall; shadow figures shuttled behind the frosted glass. The air was stale; the hallway was insanely hot. Magdalene imagined herself trapped in one of the twin towers and instantly admonished herself—one didn't playact with tragedy; there was enough to go around. The colored dots falling from the towers hadn't started out their day as dots—they'd begun their day as Mrs. Banniman or Mrs. Taylor or Chief of Police Cutter Hagen or even Mayor Greene or Assistant District Attorney Gregory Barrows. The hallways of the towers hadn't been ghost towns either—they'd been tunnels of fumes and flames, filled with faces of fear. The windows that had remained were no longer illuminated. They provided an option: jump and maybe the curtains will act as a parachute. Jump and the hell that has swallowed everything behind you will be over. Jump and fly rather than stay and burn. On 9/11, there was no Sister Mary Magdalene de Rosa to smother the flames.

Float float float.

She'd been counting again—the doors, the splits in the wooden floor, the fingerprint swirls hidden in the frosted glass. Her mind felt thick, as if she'd been holding her breath under Michael's stinky blankets, waiting for her brother to either rescue or abandon her; the blanket over her head had always been both parachute and morgue sheet. But despite her very real concerns, Michael had never let her down; he'd always brought her to safety. He'd pull her from certain death; he'd grasp her wrists and she'd clutch his, just like he'd taught her. Together they'd run from the ghost house and escape their increasingly inebriated father figure and the mother whose ghost had slowly slid from the immediate part of their memories.

Magdalene leaned on the doorknobs. The hallway buckled and the walls moved in towards her shaking body. She dragged her nails across the pale inside of her left arm, drawing a little blood. She dipped her pinky in the crimson and brought it to her lips. Voices rose from behind the smoky glass.

Uno, does, tres, quatro.

COUNTDOWN:

- FRIDAY (today): date with Jerry Eves.
- SATURDAY: go to the Lakes for meeting with Stevie Rich.
- SUNDAY: rescue Katie; murder Raven; leave evidence for Mrs. Bochdan (and ADA Barrows); take pills.
- SUNDAY NIGHT/MONDAY MORNING: die.

And finish her book: nothing like a posthumous release to spike the sales, she thought.

Stevie Rich was the key in the Cabot Case. She'd have to lay out any evidence she found for her father in lieu of a suicide note. The fact that Stevie Rich was Mrs. Tidwell's nephew only heightened her resolve. It was all connected. Mr. McAllister wasn't the sharpest card in the deck—Magdalene had heard Aunt Tiddy say the same thing many times (with and without attributing it to ol' Bill)—but he knew the best way to start a new family was to get rid of all the vestiges of his previous one. (Here we go again: vestige—two syllables—věs' tĭj—def.: a mark, trace, or visible evidence of something which is no longer present or in existence.) Maybe Katie would be forced to live with Mrs. Tidwell's relatives in the Lakes while the happy couple split their time between the Heights and the McAllister house. Maybe Mr. McAllister and the widow Tidwell would simply split town altogether. Maybe Katie would go "missing" too. And maybe that was where Stevie Rich came in.

It was all starting to make sense.

The voices on the other side of the frosted glass were loud, ferocious—even Magdalene's father's

"And where does prosecuting Mrs. Bochdan leave us, Hugh? Goddamn it, our backs are up against the wall on this thing."

"My point exactly. The State Police can't find Andriy. The ATF can't find him. The governor even called me. I didn't know the SOB even knew my name."

"That's what I'm saying here. Are we going after the mother because she's the only one left?"

Magdalene placed her ear against the glass. What had *The Hardy Boys Detective Handbook* said about eavesdropping? She could smell the mayor's cologne. Whenever he visited the Barrows Bungalow—which hadn't been often since Michael disappeared—the older man insisted on picking up Magdalene and her brother, long after they'd passed the picking up age. His cologne always smelled like it was trying to hide something dirty. Magdalene knew her father regarded Hugh Greene with a jaundiced eye. (Magdalene grimaced; she may have overshot a vocabulary word. Her father often regarded many things with *bloodshot* eyes. She made a mental note to look up "jaundiced" later, but she doubted there would be time, what with having her first date tonight, not to mention a kidnapping and a canine murder all crowding her social calendar.) But Karl Matthews was a man her father respected, even if they did cross the river at different points—to quote Tiddy, not Shakespeare. Tiddy had said it was almost natural to distrust Mr. Matthews—he *was* a Republican after all. But Tiddy had also said Karl Matthews was a Republican by birth and wallet only. DA Matthews had fought to hold Assistant District Attorney Gregory Barrow's position during the latter's indisposition—a mark of true friendship.

"There is an election to think of, Gregory."

"To hell with the election."

"Easy for you to say," the mayor began. "You've spent the better part of two years inside of a taproom."

"Okay, okay," Karl said. "Separate corners, gentleman. No need to take this outside of the arena of discussion." The DA's voice was as steady and even as Magdalene's father's (if not as sonorous); the mayor was a blustery windstorm in comparison.

Tense silence followed. Tense at least for Magdalene. Karl Matthews was a recovering alcoholic too (she couldn't stop thinking of what his teeth must have looked like sitting there on the bar!), and he wasn't going to allow the mayor to run her father down. But Karl wasn't exactly on her father's side either. Mayor Greene sounded like a whiny county government bully who would rather just start wailing on Magdalene's father than even try thoughtful discourse.

One of the doors swung open, trapping Magdalene in the corner. She didn't know whether to bolt for the stairs or remain where she was. The frosted glass offered little cover. Better to count her breaths. Calm, cool, collected. What she wouldn't have given for Michael's smelly, old blanket now!

"I'm sorry, Gregory, I didn't—"

"Pay it no mind, Hugh."

"Heat of the battle and all."

"The question here is this," Gregory Barrows said, "are we prosecuting Mrs. Bochdan only because we can't find her husband? Now, I know we have nothing besides her word that she didn't give the child the gun, but she has no priors, she's an upstanding citizen with a popular business, whereas her husband's rap sheet could be rolled out like a carpet. The guy is bad news."

"We have to think about the Cabots here as well."

"I am thinking about the Cabots, Karl, and they are *not* vindictive people. They are good church-going people. They have repeatedly spoken to the press about the need for healing. What more convincing do we need?"

"There's still the matter of the boy," the DA said. "Pre-Columbine, we had a little more wiggle room, but not anymore. Pennsylvania law requires that a minor accused of murder be tried as an adult, unless the accused succeeds in having the trial transferred to juvenile court. Section 6355, Title 42. This office has a responsibility—"

"Karl, we are fulfilling our responsibility. We try Joseph as a minor and recommend that he be remanded to a state facility—"

"A mental...facility..." the mayor said.

"Yes, Hugh. A mental facility," Magdalene's father explained. "It's the best option we have."

"He'd be out when?" the mayor asked. "Eighteen? No."

"The judge would have the final word, of course," Karl Matthews said, "but during sentencing, our office could—"

"The people want justice, Karl."

"But we know he didn't have malicious intent," the ADA said.

"Wait—we know that how?" Karl Matthews asked.

"Joseph was standing there showing the gun to Henry when it went off. Some of the children said the nun ran in after it discharged, some say before. But all say the same thing: he was showing the gun off. They weren't fighting."

The mayor cleared his throat. "I recommend that Joseph Bochdan be tried as an adult and be remanded to the State Correctional Institute at Waganer.

"Justice," he added in the silence after his pronouncement.

"I won't do it," Magdalene's father said.

"This isn't multiple choice."

"But this *is* a tragedy, Hugh," Gregory Barrows said. "Why are we playing the blame game here? Something went horribly wrong in one of our classrooms, with two of our kids. An unfortunate, tragic, deadly incident where one little boy shot and killed his best friend—wait—with a gun we *know*—yes, mayor, we *know*—was used in a robbery-homicide in Rhawnhurst over a year ago—the main suspect of which is Andriy Bochdan. I'm not saying Joseph didn't know what the gun was capable of doing. That's best left to the clinical psychologists. I'm saying this child grew up in a home where one parent is a career criminal with more time in than out, and the other works around the clock to pay the mortgage and send her child to Catholic school. Trying Joseph as an adult has to be off the table."

"What are you suggesting?" Karl Matthews asked.

"Yes, yes," Mayor Greene said, sounding less sure of himself. "Suggestions, suggestions."

"What I've been saying. Knocking Joseph's charge down to involuntary manslaughter, prosecuting him as a minor, and recommending supervised counseling in a controlled environment."

"The press are going to eat us alive," the DA said, but he didn't sound unconvinced.

"Just until we find out everything there is to know. How did Joseph get the weapon or who gave it to him, for starters."

"We have to be quick and thorough then in tracking down Andriy Bochdan," Karl Matthews said. "A little boy shot another little boy in the face, for God's sake."

"In the face," the mayor repeated, "for God's sake."

The room went silent again except for Mayor Greene's husky breathing. Magdalene counted his wheezes. The mayor was more than a tad overweight. Magdalene doubted he could even tie his own shoelaces.

Her father's voice pierced the wheezing. "I would dare say that God had very little to do with this, Hugh."

"Parental responsibility, then," Karl Matthews said, "in the matter of the mother. The grand jury might—"

"We both know that's a dead end," the ADA said. "It's Andriy we want. It would hold up for the father. We'd just be feeding Mrs. Bochdan to the wolves."

"The press is slavering for action," Karl said, "and the archdiocese *demands*—"

They all exploded at once. Mayor Greene stuttered his way through a proclamation that his authority was "more authoritative" than the cardinal's. Karl dismissively called the mayor's rhetoric a "stump speech," ignorant of "consequences." The Catholic Church has political influence in the state beyond the mayor's, the DA argued. Magdalene's father's voice rose above the rest. She imagined the lines that would be traversing his forehead and the way the front swoop of gray from his carefully-combed hair would be falling across his eyes like a little boy's.

"Mondauk is not going to stand by and watch Mrs. Bochdan be persecuted for—"

"And you know that for sure?" the mayor asked. "*You* know what the people want?"

"The people want justice, Hugh, yes" Gregory Barrows said. "They want someone punished for this crime, yes, but the people, *our people*, know this tragedy—the death of one child at the hands of another cannot be wrapped into a nice, neat package. We arrest the father, and we'll more than likely find out what we need to know. Just being aware that there was a manhunt taking place would placate the populace. So don't just leak it to the *Common* and the *Inquirer*. Plaster his face across the nightly news. Mondauk County knows Andriy Bochdan. They know the family, they know Sol's. They know that Mrs. Bochdan keeps the store afloat by cleaning their houses—the ones that still let her. The Cabots want peace; they want reconciliation. And—no, let me finish please—yes, they want answers. We all do. The county does. But the answers are not going to be found in prosecuting the boy's mother. If our justice system is to dole out what you call appropriate punishment, then we may very well be crossing into cruel and unusual territory in this instance. If we incarcerate the mother, we essentially ensure Joseph a fairly bleak future. He'd become institutionalized, a virtual orphan. It's tantamount to taking his life. These are little boys we're talking about. Again, we know the gun was registered to someone now behind bars in Waganer—someone we know did business with Andriy Bochdan, or at least we know his associates did. We don't know for certain how Andriy came into possession of the gun or how it ended up in Joseph's hands. But we have two accounts that say Henry Cabot *knew* Joseph had the gun, *knew* he'd brought it to school that day. There might be more to why Joseph—"

Magdalene covered her mouth with her hands.

Criminy. She was counting aloud.

"What is it?" The mayor was impatient.

Magdalene eased herself from behind the closed door, then froze. Her father's head appeared in the movie-projector-dust that guarded the otherwise empty hall. Magdalene ticked the counting up a notch and held her breath. This wasn't going to end well. She hoped she wouldn't pee.

The dust was a blanket; it refracted both the unnatural neon flickering of the old tubes suspended from the humming ceiling with their dead-bug-carcass-polka-dots, and the persistent sun attempting to crash the wake from the window at the other end of the hall. Magdalene wished the blanket over her head and closed her eyes tight—if she couldn't see her father, maybe he couldn't see her. Wasn't that a game her mother had played with her and Michael? Peek-a-boo? *Float float float.*

Just before the door slammed shut, District Attorney Karl Matthews asked: "And now what about the missing Fuller girl?"

+

The wind about her ears as she ran home was the breath of a lion: it yawned and growled and screamed and purred. A constant barrage, it hurt her ears. Still, she'd rescued herself—or was at least trying to. Behind the lion's breath, there were other noises as well: Aunt Tiddy's Shakespearean bromides, the condescending practicality of Willa Meade, the *flap-flap-flap* of a thousand singed birds rising to escape the hell of what had been the World Trade Center.

Magdalene didn't dare look down; she knew her feet were hundreds if not thousands of feet off the ground. Funny—the drawings of the World Trade Center in Willa's office rarely showed the pavements, the streets, the rubble. Things unspeakable lurked at the bottom of the drawings like the creature Michael had said lived at the bottom of Loch Linden. On 9/11, there'd been a continuous raining down of things (*things?*) hitting bottom. Hundreds of Sister Mary Magdalene de Rosas swallowed fire and dust and bone and not a single blanket diminished the flames. At the bottom, Fireman Bobby Tidwell, onetime member of the Mondauk County Volunteer Fire Department, rookie New York City firefighter, escapee of Paradise Lakes, and the special love of a mousy woman in a natty sweater, swallowed a big lungful of black smoke from a thousand moments shattered, and as the last of the birds took to the air, fell to his knees and thought not of his wife, but of his nephew: *what would happen to his nephew now?*

The blanket flapped a little in the wind, and Magdalene kicked her feet, anxious to avoid the sticky pavement. She needed to keep moving. *"Whhhhat wwwwwilll you doooo whhhhen yourrrr time comessss?"* Sister Rita wailed, and Magdalene knew she didn't need another dare, there was much to do, and she narrowly avoided falling on Raven, who'd been napping on the blanket and the sheets she'd kicked to the floor.

Jesus—how long had she been asleep? She hated falling asleep in the afternoon.

The room was a scorching ninety degrees or more. Magdalene's t-shirt clung to her back and chest and underarms. Her legs were sore from running all the way from County Hall. She's been using Monien the panda as a pillow, and she tossed it to the floor. It fell noiselessly. Raven stared at it and pushed it with his nose.

Magdalene retrieved the panda and squeezed its stomach.

Nothing.

Raven watched Magdalene thoughtfully, expectantly, from the floor. He didn't seem too eager either to play with the panda or to leave it unguarded.

Magdalene pulled the panda's ears.

"C'mon, Monien, speak," Magdalene whispered.

She poked the panda's rear with her fingers and pulled away stray panda fluff with her chewed, ragged nails.

Raven yawned but kept his eyes on the panda.

Magdalene clutched Monien to her chest in a bear hug.

Still nothing.

Tiddy's knuckles rapped on the door.

"Magdalene, dear? You alright in there?"

Raven licked Magdalene's leg and padded to the door. His tongue felt cool although she imagined he must be suffering in his heavy black coat. Magdalene placed Monien the mute panda on her nightstand. The panda was a Goner, Magdalene thought—just one in a long line of Goners. They were all that were left behind—Joseph Bochdan, the Cabots, Katie McAllister, the widow Tidwell, Raven—Goners. Everything from here on out for the Goners of Mondauk, the whole cast, was forgone—out of their hands. They were amputees, all of them, forever scratching phantom itches. And half of nothing is less than nothing. Goners.

Magdalene sniffed her sheets but didn't recognize her own smell—good, I'm disappearing, she thought—and started smoothing them to make her bed. The last thing she needed was Tiddy getting her wrinkled fingers between the mattress and the bedspring and finding the pill stash.

Tiddy was in the hallway and her arms were heavy with laundry. Magdalene grimaced—how much laundry was there for three people? Her aunt smiled, and Magdalene turned her head. During the past couple of days, Tiddy had swung back and forth from a blunt, deliberate, cold shoulder to being almost omnipresent (at least as far as housework went.)

Omnipresent.

Four syllables.

Om•ni•pres•ent.

(ŏm' nə prĕz' ənt)

Def.: present everywhere at the same time.

Magdalene shook her head. Afternoon naps usually threw a blanket over her thinking, and not the good kind of blanket, not something soft and warm and familiar, but the blanket kept in the trunk of a car in case of emergencies: harsh, rough, a blanket Raven would forgo.

Tiddy was in the bathroom now, her voice sonorous, her echoes endless. "I know you think I'm a batty old woman who should leave well enough alone…"

Magdalene reached under her mattress to grab Michael's money and the tissues wrapped around Tiddy's blue pills. These she stuffed into her pockets. At the last second, she snatched from her nightstand a handful of dogwood leaves that she'd saved from Katie's backyard. For luck, she told herself, although petals from the progeny of the tree used to crucify Jesus couldn't possibly be very lucky—it was a Judas Tree according to the Legend of the Dogwood. Tiddy barreled her way into the room, interrupting Magdalene's musings, Raven right behind her, his huge tongue dancing in his eager grin. Magdalene's fingers caressed the worn cover of her journal: she hated the thought of leaving Finn unfinished when she shrugged off ol' Bill's curly-cue.

Tiddy gestured to Magdalene, and together they shook out her blanket and sheets, and the breeze lifted her brother's wallet-sized school picture from the dresser. Magdalene covered it with her foot as Tiddy went to grab the blanket from her hands. Magdalene tugged back, and Tiddy smiled. Together they smoothed the sheets and finished her bed. Magdalene used her toes to pick up Michael's picture and shoved it into her pocket.

Tiddy had never stopped talking.

"...but I watched you play catch with your brother. Michael. See, I said his name: *Michael*. I know you loved the game as much as he did—as much as Michael did."

Magdalene looked around her room. The bookshelves were overloaded. Her walls were plastered with pennants of teams she didn't follow anymore and posters of bands she'd never listened to. She had tried, over the years, to obliterate the girly yellows and pinks her parents had foisted upon her before her birth. Who ever heard of a writer or a detective—those plumbers of truth—toiling under soft pink and yellow wallpaper?

She looked at the clock. It was less than two hours until her date with Jerry Eves. Magdalene wondered if she should shower first, then dismissed the idea as frivolous and girly.

"Well?"

Magdalene let her fingers sneak into her pocket and touch Michael's picture. She never thought she'd be out on a date with anyone but Michael, and seeing how Michael was her brother, Magdalene always assumed dating was not in her future. A writer-detective-nun!

It's not a date, silly, it's a mission. You need Jerry's help—in case you need to make a quick getaway tomorrow. No telling what will happen in the Lakes.

No telling was right. Drug addicts, alcoholics, prostitutes, parolees from Waganer, bullies: they all lived in Paradise Lakes. Magdalene imagined them surrounding the few good people stuck there like bugs crowding a porch light.

"Well, what?" Magdalene mumbled back.

"Play catch with me," Aunt Tiddy said. "Now. Let's go outside."

One, two, three, four, five, six, seven...

"You think I'm too old to throw a football, that it? I got a few surprises left in me, Magdalene Harper Barrows."

As if on cue, Raven scampered down the hallway—as much as a six-year-old, slightly overweight, definitely under-exercised, black Labrador retriever could scamper—and returned to plop his monkey, in mid-jungle cry, at Magdalene's bare feet. How many times had Magdalene woken to Monkey's death cries? In the deep recesses of a dream, Monkey's cries spoke for all the Goners of Mondauk, not just Monien the panda; Raven's monkey knew the pain of watching and being unable to act.

"*Whhhhat wwwwillll* you d*oooo whhhh*en your*rrr* time come*ssss?*"

Magdalene tried to count Tiddy's wrinkles. There was no way she'd be mentally alert for her date if she let herself continue to fret and fuss. Jerry was essential to dissipating the darkness of Mondauk. Magdalene knew she was a Goner; she imagined her lot in life slashed into her forehead like the mark of Cain, the blood dripping into her eyes. But she could reverse the trend for others; she could actually act this time, not just sit there…

This time?

…like a lump on a log, as Shakespeare would say.

"Well, toss the ol' pigskin around, Magdalene?"

This time?

"Can't play catch with yourself," her aunt said. "Come on. Let's beat the rain."

Air rushed past her cheeks, and inside her fuzzy, fuzzy brain, she pulled the blanket and sheets over her head to make a parachute. And the Goners—who maybe, with Magdalene's beneficence, could get gone from this ghost town, all of them, Katie, Joseph, even sleepwalking Mrs. Bochdan with her gold tea tray and sad family portraits—cuddled up tight and waited for Magdalene to stop holding her breath, to stop counting, for her time had surely come.

+

From next door, Evey Corcoran's kitchen radio played the soft hits of summer in between fast food and muffler commercials and urgent minute-long newsbreaks.

"There's nothing like athletics to stimulate the brain," Aunt Tiddy said, "besides maybe reading, and you got to have some pretty time on your hands to do a whole lot of that. The true athlete is an artist of sorts, wouldn't you say? For the rest of us, it's just one plus one plus one. Throw the ball, catch the ball. Follow the dots."

The old woman threw a perfect spiral, and Magdalene, too under the blanket to follow the pass, connected with the football using only her forehead. Aunt Tiddy didn't even blink.

"Now, you take your father. Or rather, your father's job. He has to work with the facts given to him. His office represents the people; his office speaks for Mondauk, but, first and foremost—*uhh*, got it— he speaks for the law. Connecting the dots. If the final picture is blurry or what appears is altogether *different* than what was previously thought—look at that spin!—then it's not the DA's case to win. That's where religion got it wrong. Too many dots, not enough *real* connecting. People don't want any more mysteries in their lives. If you need some church, well, you should just go. Don't need to do much. Just bow your head, pray some. See if anything comes to you. But they have their silly rules, the Catholics, and the priest can refuse you Communion if he feels like it—which I'm sure Jesus, who consorted with hookers and IRS men, is fully behind."

Magdalene's fingers were tingling. They were starting to notice the funny shaped ball cupped in her palm, remembering not only the smack of a good catch, but the way to grip the ball like it was an egg. Pure muscle memory.

" 'Judge not, lest ye be judged,' " Magdalene said.

"Matthew 7:1," Tiddy replied with a wink. "Know they enemy."

Raven ran into Magdalene's legs, turned around, and departed in a Warner Brothers cartoon *puff* for Tiddy's side of the yard, barely paying attention to the trajectory of the ball.

"The Methodists ask too much. Austerity is for the birds. The whole Kingdomtide thing is all about assistance to the poor, which is all fine and good—but most of *them* are poor! Now their sign has Korean writing on it, which don't mean Calvary United Methodist is gettin' any richer. And the Catholic Church is too busy trying to control to really lead. Governing. Collecting. *Tisk-tisking*. Each parish is responsible for its own financial solvency. That's going to be tough in places like Mondauk. Tougher as the county grows; tougher because it forces the Catholic schools to accept more non-Roman Catholics—those that can afford it anyway. As the county grows— *uh*, almost!—the congregation's actually going to shrink. The well-off are going to put their kids in the Prep in Cornwall Heights or send them out of state like they're going to college to escape what they figure are the lower classes. Vicious circle. Damn it, dog, don't slobber on it!"

Raven tried to grab the football—Magdalene had missed the pass when she realized she could smell her own sweat; she'd have to take a shower now before her date—and it slipped out of his eager mouth, skidding across the grass. The harder Raven tried, the slimier the ball became.

"Connect the dots. Seems to me the bishops don't do that; they live in a bubble—but the parishes do. They connect the dots. The priests in Mondauk know that you'll come when you need it—which is better than going because you think you have to. Just because you don't go to church every Sunday don't make you a sinner. Connect the dots. Too many rules—too many bishops in gold hats with their hands out, sticking their noses and God knows what else in—and the people'll stop coming. Come here, dog!"

The blanket served many purposes: it could force you inside to count and smell your brother's smell; it could—maybe—be used as a parachute to safety. And not only that. It could also connect everything together. But the blanket was gone.

The ball slipped out of Magdalene's hands, and Raven lunged, his jaws snapping an inch away from Magdalene's fingers.

"That's what's gotta happen with your friend. The police have got to ask themselves if she ran or was taken or something else."

Tiddy's voice trailed off, and Magdalene drifted away from counting—sixteen passes; two fumbles; four recoveries by Raven—to stare at Tiddy as the football whizzed past Magdalene's ears.

"I'm sure you heard by now, and I don't believe in hiding too much. I never had kids of my own, but I had you and Michael. God*damn* it, dog. Is he trying to drown the ball? You can't think of the worst, but you can't pretend it's something it's not either. Town's got enough going on with Henry Cabot's shooting. Can't say I've seen much of Christina around lately. Were you girls on the outs?"

The football landed in the little plastic baby pool, full from the rain, that Magdalene had bought for Raven a couple of summers ago. Every morning for weeks back then, Magdalene checked that there wasn't a drought warning, which there hadn't been for quite a while, and ran the hose over to the pool and filled it. Not that Raven ever put as much as a paw in the water. If Michael tossed Raven's basketball in, Raven would circle the purple plastic pool and bark. He might dip his nose in the water if he was thirsty, the gray of his snout glistening like silver as he squinted into the summer sun, but he'd never lie down in the pool and cool off.

Just then, the announcer on Evey Corcoran's radio mentioned that all the recent rain—and more was expected—would make the search for the missing Fuller girl more difficult.

The football floated to the center of the pool.

Magdalene shrugged. "Different summers, I guess. I have makeup exams."

Magdalene's face reddened—not so much at the lie as for why she had to go to summer school.

"Makeup exams, right," Tiddy said. "And how's that going?"

"Fine," Magdalene said. She tried to lift one of Raven's paws into the pool. The dog yelped, backed away, and released a little gas.

"Well, it's been forty-eight hours now," Tiddy said. "Found her diary, that's all."

Magdalene turned and faced the pool. *Diary?* Christina, queen of goth and lip gloss and spin the bottle, kept a diary?

"Not sure if there was anything there. They're looking for…well…maybe a mention of an older feller. Maybe she was keeping a rendezvous. She was always a little fast, that one. No offense meant to the doctor. And her mother's not exactly Mother Theresa, is she? A little too good for Mondauk. Fired Mrs. Bochdan. Didn't want to bring shame to the family is what I heard."

Magdalene could see Tiddy's reflection in the water, her sleeves rolled up, her hands on her hips, dark circles around her hillbilly house dress. Her aunt's skinny chest undulated in the water.

Raven turned to investigate the noises that continued to emit from his rear.

What if Christina had killed herself? Magdalene couldn't see it. To commit suicide required a force of will and ingenuity one would never associate with Christina Fuller—an ingenuity that Magdalene seemed to lack, granted. Hell, Christina seemed adept at only makeup and boys—and the latter was a toss-up; there was a remote possibility that Christina was just easy—or a liar.

Raven ripped another one and backed away from the pool.

"He's so scared of that pool," Aunt Tiddy said, "he's 'bout ready to poop." Magdalene ran her fingers across her aunt's reflection. The shadows from the sycamore tree painted Tiddy's forehead. The water wavered but the old woman's image remained.

"Can't erase me that easy," Tiddy said, touching Magdalene's shoulder.

Somewhere near the porch, Raven farted and howled.

"Whatcha been feeding that dog, girl?" The image wobbled as her aunt laughed. "That dog's got the devil in his rear today, and it's lookin' like judgment day."

Magdalene rested her eyes. Could it be that easy to die? Henry Richard Cabot. Nancy McAllister (another suicide). Poor Bobby Tidwell. Her mother. Now Christina. Seemed to Magdalene that the actual Goners were the ones left behind. That she didn't feel an ounce of sorrow at the thought of her best friend dying had no effect on her. Christina had accomplished—okay, *may* have accomplished— what Magdalene had been meticulously planning for days on end. The only thought that kept her from dunking her head right now— besides the indignity of being rescued by an old woman from a baby pool—was that Magdalene had a purpose: her time had come—right?

Mr. McAllister, perhaps under the influence of beverages he'd previously sworn off, satisfying the anger that had swelled like his belly, had perhaps taken his grief out on his daughter, who looked nothing like her father, but rather was a miniature of her mother. Maybe Mr. McAllister had just switched punching bags from wife to daughter after the poor woman had checked out. Men like Mr. McAllister—bullies—fed off the fear of others. If other people weren't afraid, then being a bully would be boring. To be a bully was to *need* to feel above someone. Katie was too easy a target, but still, a target she'd become. But Mrs. Tidwell: a mouse in old sweaters, her husband buried beneath the rubble of the ultimate bully attack— she'd be a good mark. He was softening her up; Mr. McAllister had a plan and was sticking to it. Magdalene had to admire that.

Think like the bully.

There was no way, however, that a man like that would cotton to being a caretaker to the late Bobby Tidwell's nephew, arch-bully Stevie Rich. That would be too much. Better to shuffle the brat off with Katie. They could scratch together in the Lakes, living in a rusted tin can with basic cable but no hot water. Hell, kids were going missing left and right in Mondauk County. What's one more, especially a little girl? No one looks for them anyway. Yeah, the Fuller kid, the doctor's brat, was making all the headlines, but so had the ADA's little snot of a son, and no one's looking for his skinny ass anymore. No one's hanging missing fliers or dragging the Puddle. Maybe just get young Stevie Rich to take matters in hand with his soon-to-be step-cousin. Stevie had been instrumental in Henry's shooting. Who doubted that?

A blanket held it all together. A blanket of conspiracy. (Although at times, it seemed more like an afghan—there were so many holes!) A blanket that kept quiet the down-dirty sins of a community too entrenched in the warfare between the Catholics and the Methodists or the battle over the fate of the old asbestos factory to worry about the disappearance of a grade-schooler—now two grade-schoolers. (Although one disappearance was getting more press than the other.) But the shooting couldn't be ignored. As the *Mondauk Common* had put it: it was child-on-child violence, and the only thing worse was adult-on-child violence—something that was going on right under the town's heavy-lidded eyes. While citizens fought the good fight over cemetery zoning and which denomination laid claim to the Common on which holiday for such-and-such demonstration of faith (prayer services for public officials; Passion plays; Nativity plays; pro-life rallies—curious since neither church seemed all that concerned, at least as far as Michael's vanishing act had gone, with saving an actual living, breathing citizen), children were disappearing.

It was like a movie marquee: *Something is Happening to the Children of Mondauk!*

Did the town not know how to handle bullies? Or were they just blissfully unaware of the terrifying education offered their children even in Catholic school? To look at Stevie Rich meant to look closely at Paradise Lakes, and no one seemed to want to do that. The laymen and women of the Catholic Faith Board had the local government in a chokehold. (Tiddy had said the Church owned more land in Mondauk County than Carter had pills.) The Methodists had newer recruits—South Koreans mostly—but most were at or damn near the poverty line. Tiddy had told Magdalene she didn't think the Faith Board wanted to see that change. Was the apple cart so precariously on edge—Magdalene could see the apples falling: *one, two, three, four*—that no wanted to ask the hard questions: why had Joseph Bochdan brought a revolver to school? Why had Joseph Bochdan shot his best friend? Sure, Andriy Bochdan sounded like Puddle scum, but he hadn't sent his son into Assumption to carry out a contract like a crime kingpin would in a television show. But a bully like Mr. McAllister would.

Someone had to stand up for the Henrys, the Josephs, and the Katies, even if only one time. If there was a bad, there had to be a good—both denominations taught that. Everyone, Magdalene thought, regardless of their past, was worthy of redemption—even her. Tiddy had said as much about ADA Barrows (attributing it to ol' Bill): there are two sides to every coin. It was the tarnished, rubbed-down side of Gregory Barrows who argued against those in the administration who would have Mrs. Bochdan and her little boy hang without knowing the truth. Magdalene sliced her hand through the dirty pool water, cutting her reflection in two. By the time the weekend was over, her father would know the truth.

Tiddy called her name—maybe she'd been calling it—and when Magdalene looked up from Raven's pool, the football, dripping with drops of drool that danced in the summer air, spiraled towards her. She reached her hands out and tucked the ball into her stomach, hunching over, her whole body involved in its capture.

Tiddy cackled from the shade of the house.

"You should try out next year."

"For football?"

"Didn't drop a one," Tiddy said, "not when your head was in it, anyway. Hell, probably not too late to get in Summer Camp."

"Football?"

"Freshmen can try out for junior varsity. Michael was going to."

"Daddy would never let me."

"You let me worry about your father," Aunt Tiddy said.

Raven gently nosed the wet football Magdalene had laid at her feet. Magdalene rubbed him behind his ears. The dog lunged, finally ensnared the ball, and carried it away to the back stoop with a triumphant prance.

"You going to get out tomorrow so I can air the place out?"

Magdalene counted Raven's paw prints.

"Yes, ma'am."

"Good, I have to—what in God's name, dog?"

Raven sneaked a peek at Magdalene and, after several dramatic hacks, vomited on the football. The dog moaned and turned away.

"What the Sam Hill did he eat? Get some paper towels. Turn on the hose. Oh, hell, better get some regular towels. He's at it again."

Magdalene held Raven's ears. They were made of *SILK*. This was her fault, she knew. If Raven died right now—forget inconvenience, forget her plans—there was no way she could live her remaining two days while Raven was in the ground. His graying muzzle tilted towards her face, and his stinky tongue licked away her tears.

Tiddy had followed her own instructions and was busy kneeling over the back stoop, picking up the larger chunks with a paper towel.

"If I told you once, dog, I told you a thousand times: don't eat my flowers."

And true to Tiddy's admonishments, colored petals populated the sticky piles. Raven looked longingly through Magdalene's encircling arms at the remains of Tiddy's African violets.

When the rain came, Tiddy left Magdalene on the stoop with Raven. The dog refused to leave her lap. His warm stomach rested on her bare thighs. Magdalene could feel all of his 95 pounds. The rain made the black fur on his muzzle and around his eyes seem like little frozen ripples of ebony. His large, brown eyes constantly sought out hers; he wasn't going to leave her. What vomit Tiddy hadn't picked up washed away under the summer rain.

Tiddy sat at the kitchen table, her back towards the screen door.

"Your father's going to have his hands full Monday, dear."

The newspaper rattled in Tiddy's hands as she summarized the lead story aloud calmly, as if her niece and her niece's dog weren't sitting out on the steps in the rain.

"The mother testified today before the grand jury. Not her gun, her lawyer told the *Common*. Didn't even know her husband kept a gun in the house. The *Common* didn't sound convinced."

Raven heard Jerry before Magdalene caught sight of his lanky frame or his tan freckles or the cowlick that made him seem taller than six foot two.

"Gonna have his hands full," Tiddy repeated, now standing at the back door. Raven barked and slipped down the steps to greet Jerry Eves. "I'll fetch a towel, dear."

Raven danced in a circle as Jerry ambled up the driveway, looking every inch like his alter ego Stick Man. Raven jumped and offered his paws to Jerry. Raven liked boys a little bit more than he liked girls. Magdalene kept trying to remind herself of this slight.

Snap fizz whirr.

"Caught you, ya Irish potato!" Tiddy cackled from behind her Polaroid.

Jerry Eves smiled and Magdalene counted.

+

Magdalene hadn't known how to dress for a date and found herself, for reasons she blamed on the silly magazines her mother had read, picking out her prettiest pair of underwear.

Magdalene kept this to herself as she walked at a snail's pace with Jerry Eves. At first, his nervous Jolly Green Giant strides kept her at a half jog, and her few conversational responses were spoken in a runner's pant. Eventually he had slowed himself down without mentioning it, and now his long, slender fingers swung at his side, occasionally brushing her light blue skirt.

"Going somewhere fancy, are you?" Tiddy had asked when Magdalene scrambled down the stairs in the skirt and a long-sleeved white blouse. *Snap fizz whirr.* Magdalene looked down at her clothes—she'd spent so much time mulling over her underwear, she hadn't given much thought to the rest of her attire, except to choose a skirt (and don her bracelets over her scars). Magdalene had thought corduroys or jeans perhaps too casual for a date—only to realize, when she faced Jerry, sitting with his stuttering hands between his knees in the living room, a black Lab at his feet, a Coke bottle on a coaster on the edge of the coffee table, that he was wearing blue jeans.

"Is that what you're wearing?" Aunt Tiddy had asked, and Magdalene resisted the urge to run back up the stairs and don a sweat suit.

"You look pretty, Magdalene," Jerry said once they were a few blocks away from the house. "I think so, anyway."

On the outside, Jerry had been all "yes, ma'am, no ma'am, not sure which one yet, ma'am, have to finish high school first, ma'am," to Aunt Tiddy, but inside he was a rebel; it had nothing to do (as far as Magdalene was concerned) with Stick Man or cutting up in class. A quiet rebel. Jerry was waiting for his first real adventure too; he just didn't seem as aware of it as Magdalene.

"Do you want to get a Coke or a burger?" Jerry asked.

Magdalene shook her head. His cowlick reminded her of Michael. This was going to take some doing. This was going to take some kissing. At *least* kissing.

"I, um, I looked at the movie schedule," he said. "We could go to the Ambler."

Magdalene took his fingers into hers. She didn't know about tonight's shows, but she could have easily recited all the movie times for Sunday night's. Magdalene closed her eyes, and Mrs. Tidwell's frightened, skinny, blotchy face was before hers, hunched beneath her raggedy, tan sweater; Magdalene could smell something rotten on Mrs. Tidwell's breath.

Jerry Eves squeezed back.

"I know you don't want to go to the carnivals—too many people," Jerry said. "After thinking about it some, I don't really want to go either, although the first night's always pretty cool."

Jerry's hand was as sweaty as hers.

"I really don't want to see Father Dave," Jerry said explained. "I still owe him a couple of detentions."

Magdalene's chest hurt. She didn't want to go the carnivals either. The Bod Squad would be out in full force, kibitzing on Christina's disappearance. She knew she'd look for Michael on every ride.

"It's terrible about Christina," Jerry said.

Magdalene said nothing. She wondered if she was thinking out loud.

"They found duct tape and stuff in her room," he said, "like someone came and took her away."

Magdalene stared at the sky. The rain had stopped, but it was only temporary. They'd been walking south. The clouds in the distance looked thick and dirty.

"I'm gonna be a veterinarian," Jerry Eves said, and Magdalene inched her body closer to his as they walked. He smelled like grown-up men did when they dressed for Church on Sunday. (Not that ADA Barrows had taken his children to Church very often, but she'd been forced out of bed on the bigger holidays.) Jerry's cologne had been liberally applied. Magdalene was slightly disappointed; she thought Jerry Eves had his own cut-grass, boy smell.

"I think Raven's going to be okay," Jerry Eves said. Magdalene willed herself forward.

"My mom had a dog when she was little," he continued. "A shepherd-lab mix, she said. Yellow with pointy ears that half stood up and half flopped over. Two of 'em. Ears, that is."

Jerry turned to look at her, and Magdalene made sure to flash her teeth. Jerry's eyes jumped back to the sidewalk. Magdalene held her grin and ran her free hand over her little fangs. (Tiddy called them the Curse of the Wheelwrights.) She was going to have to be more careful. Jerry wasn't going to want to kiss her if she leered at him like a bride of Dracula.

"So one day, the dog—Loodle-Loo—catches this baby rabbit in the backyard. Kills it dead. He wasn't eating it or anything. Maybe he was playing too hard with it. Maybe he thought it was a toy. Anyway, he kills this bunny, and my mother, she goes bat-shit."

Jerry's free hand went up to his mouth, and Magdalene squeezed his other hand to let him know it was okay. Magdalene had been expecting some of Stick Man's humor—what a surprise! In the back of her head, she replayed Christina's tall tales of boys conquered.

"My mom's hopping mad. She yells at Loodle, really screams at him. Swats him. Dogs: now I don't know if they retain for long periods of time, most of them. If you don't punish them right away, they're gonna be confused as to why you're yelling in a second. You know, they used to say you should push their nose in it if they, um, if they—"

"Poop?" offered Magdalene. "In the house?"

"Right. Poop."

"Take a shite?" Magdalene suggested.

"Um, yeah..."

"Make a doodie?"

Jerry had stopped walking. Magdalene tugged him along. Better to keep her mouth shut. Stick Man humor didn't sound as funny coming out of her mouth.

"Go 'head. Finish the story. I'm sorry."

"No, it's okay. My mom, she really laid into Loodle, you know, and for the rest of his life, Loodle avoided the little rabbit holes back by the shed. He'd just sit on the back porch sometimes, looking at the shed, howling and crying."

Jerry's feet were so big, every time he breached a puddle, Magdalene felt the water on her ankles. What was it Christina had said about the size of a boy's feet in relation to his penis size? Penises were funny, funnier than pooping. She remembered that Christina had said the trick was to act as if the penis was a separate being, as if it didn't belong to the boy breathing heavy next to her.

Jerry walked with his eyes down.

"You don't have a dog now?" Magdalene asked, although she thought she knew the answer.

"Too many of us," Jerry said. Magdalene knew this too. Jerry had three brothers. Mick, Brian, and Patrick. Mick was the oldest. Jerry was next. Mick was the one with the GTO.

The whole town seemed to emerge in the wake of the rain. A car passed them on the street, and Jerry waved. Magdalene shirked back, but Jerry didn't seem embarrassed at all. Sol's was closed, so Jerry asked her if she wanted to walk to Rex's for a soda. Magdalene declined and diverted their path northwest.

"With Christina, it could be a serial killer," Jerry said. "Like in the movies. *'Clarice'...*"

"Do you know why they're called 'serial' killers rather than just killers?" Magdalene asked.

Jerry scratched his head. " 'Cause they like Cheerios?"

"A serial killer's murders are a series of similar actions. It means more than one victim. It even means more than two."

Of course, Jerry was referring to her brother. Although Michael had disappeared almost a year ago, serial killers, Magdalene knew from a television program, didn't always strike one right after the other like in the movies. Sometimes they waited and planned. And that was the only good news about Christina being gone: if she'd been taken by a psychopath, then maybe the authorities would have to reopen Michael's file. All the attention was focused on Christina now. It was unavoidable. Even the radios in the passing cars broadcasted reports about the search. They were beating the reeds along the Puddle. They were fanning out in the Fields behind Assumption. They were looking for hitchhikers on the road into Spring House.

They had done none of this for Michael.

There had been no search parties that she'd heard of. No rescue missions.

Just her father, out of breath and drunk on the shore of the Puddle.

Why was a doctor's daughter worthy of a search party, but not the Assistant District Attorney's son?

Just her father, out of breath and drunk on the shore of the Puddle?

Christina's disappearance was a thorn, a real annoyance, doubling Magdalene's discomfort. (Hadn't Christina been her best friend? Sorta?) Christina was the kind of girl who, when she grew up, would voluntarily go see someone like Willa Meade to whine about her shitty husband or her shitty job or her shitty car. Christina wasn't the kind of girl who vanished with a flourish in the third act.

"One time," Jerry Eves said, "my mom had to stay after school. I think she was in high school. And her mom was at work. Her dad was dead from cancer. And Loodle was still new, just a puppy. The pooch had been holding it in all day, and when my mom came home from school—she was the first one home that day—Loodle got so excited, he exploded and pooped all over the living room. Like a bazooka, my mother said. She said it was everywhere."

Magdalene remembered how to smile.

"That's a good story."

"Yeah," Jerry said, "it is."

They were on Orchard Street across from Katie's house. The sky was darkening above their heads. Magdalene wondered if the monster was home, or if he'd already made his way to see the widow Tidwell. If Mrs. Tidwell told Mr. McAllister about the movie tickets incident...

"Come sit in the berry bushes with me," Magdalene said. "There's room."

Jerry knelt down next to her, and Magdalene heard his heart *thump-thump-thumping*, and when he went to kiss her, it was over before her brain registered the smoothness of his lips, the nervous, metallic taste of his mouth, or the way his hands shook when he squeezed her shoulders.

Above their heads, Magdalene knew Cygnus the Swan flew from the center of the Northern Cross. Cygnus the Swan—Zeus in disguise, a masquerade in the name of duplicity, something dark and ugly and sinister in the body of something beautiful. Two pieces, joined together.

Very little to count.

Jerry finished kissing her.

"You're beautiful," Jerry Eves said, and Magdalene waited for her wings to crumble into so much dust and red dirt.

+

The Hardy Boys Detective Handbook was quite specific on the art of two-man surveillance. Crouching in the berry bushes, kissing Jerry Eves, Magdalene knew, was surely not one of the approved methods. Not that the kissing itself was terrible. She'd only ever kissed relatives: her father's dry, matter-of-fact kisses; Aunt Tiddy's slightly sloppy kisses; her brother's reluctant smack on the cheek. Only her mother's kiss remained a mystery. Of all the clues she could recall of her mother, Magdalene couldn't remember kissing her.

The *Handbook*, so wise on so many matters, failed to properly address interrogation techniques or coercion, and how the two could be used together. Jerry would spill the most face-reddening facts if pressed, but she needed a ride more than she needed information. One thing was for sure: the more she kissed Jerry Eves, the easier it became to lay out Saturday's plan.

"It'll be in the morning. He works all day at Pep Boys on Saturday, right?"

"Mick? Yeah."

Magdalene felt the tip of his tongue in her mouth. She recoiled and then pretended to cough lightly. A red berry exploded between her fingers before she realized she'd been clawing at the ground.

"Your brother might not even notice it's gone."

"Right," Jerry said. "He loves that car."

His arm brushed past her breasts once, then again. An exploratory mission.

Over Jerry's shoulder, she saw Valerie Plum's shadow pass by the front windows of the McAllister house, which meant Mr. McAllister was out. Better to stay here until he comes home, she thought. Who knows what shaky Mrs. Tidwell will have said to him?

"We'll just ride up to the Lakes and back."

Jerry's hands were on the move again, but nothing untoward. Still, Magdalene was glad she'd worn her church bra; it was only the second time she'd worn it. It was tan and thick and belonged, Magdalene thought, to some older time when women's breasts were in danger of not just appearing wanton but of falling off altogether. Jerry could draw Stick Man adventures on her church bra, and her breasts would never feel it beneath their armor.

"If he's working at the garage Saturday," Magdalene said, "there'll be a million cars in the lot. We'll be an hour. He'll never notice."

Jerry pulled away from her neck, and Magdalene submerged an urge to count his freckles again. They twinkled like the stars above their heads.

"You want me to steal Mick's Goat—I just graduated eighth grade too, remember—take you out to the Lakes, look for Stevie Rich—*Stevie Rich*—and talk to him about—what are we talking to him about? Doesn't matter. I'm not jacking Mick's car. It's a '68 GTO, Magdalene. Mick's whole life revolves around that car."

Magdalene held her breath (*two, four, six, eight; who do we appreciate?*) and let her hand rest (briefly) in the crotch of Jerry's blue jeans. Whatever was in there—and Magdalene knew; she just didn't want to think about it too much—was stiff and aiming towards his belly.

"What time tomorrow, Tonto?" Jerry asked. He was out of breath.

+

Magdalene never thought she'd be glad to see Mr. McAllister, but Jerry's breathing had become more hitched and he'd undone his button-fly—nothing more, but that was enough.

Mr. McAllister didn't look happy. Not that Magdalene could see his face—Jerry kept kissing her, and the berry bushes didn't make the greatest surveillance spot. It was the way Mr. McAllister walked, the way his work boots (*work* boots?) stomped the pavement. He didn't finger-flick his cigarette into the street; he threw it into the driveway where it exploded in a shower of sparks. Mr. McAllister yanked open the screen door and let it slam behind him.

He knew.

Valerie Plum flew out of the house, dared a look behind her, and scooted down the street.

This was not good.

She pushed her tongue further into Jerry Eves' mouth to give herself time to think. She counted his teeth—peanut butter; he'd eaten peanut butter sometime today—and kept one eye on the front windows of Katie's house. Nothing could happen to Katie tonight. She had to make sure of that. She'd get Katie out in forty-eight hours. Nothing could happen tonight.

Magdalene pulled on Jerry's belt loops.

"Come on."

+

She wasn't surprised the blue Chevy was unlocked; Mr. McAllister worked on it constantly; he could easily forget. But she was surprised at how clean it was. The smell was the only thing: it smelled strongly of gasoline.

Jerry sat in the back seat of Mr. McAllister's car, his knees knocking.

"Ten tomorrow morning, okay?" she asked. She'd rolled down the back window on her side just a little so she could hear if Katie started screaming. All the windows were open at the McAllister house. Mr. McAllister was too cheap to turn on the air conditioner, Magdalene thought, even though tonight was looking to be as humid as the day.

"Ten. Right. Yes."

Jerry Eves was bordering on the monosyllabic. This was Christina territory. Although she liked kissing his jittery lips and counting his freckles (she'd given in; she couldn't help it: there were *millions!*), she hadn't thought she'd have to go this far.

"Ten," Jerry repeated. He was bungling with her bra clasps. Somehow his hands had crept under her blouse.

Concentrate. If Katie started screaming, she had to be ready to just rush in. The plan would go to hell, but if Mr. McAllister was angry…

Jerry Eves was unbuttoning her blouse, her fancy white blouse, the one she had saved her baby-sitting money for so she could wear it to Christina's birthday party/make-out session last year, the same party where sweet Jimmy Lonergan and that fireplug Kevin Meany had spilled their "Happy Punch" (which smelled a bit like Hawaiian Punch and tasted like gasoline) in Magdalene's lap, narrowly missing her new white shirt.

Magdalene bit her lip and started counting the number of fingerprint smudges on the Chevy's windows.

Best not to think too hard on Jerry Eves.

Besides, he'd just undone the third button of her blouse.

There are two halves of every person, the person her father had told her we tried like hell to be—the angel we shed as soon we as learned the power to cry—and the person we quite often are. In the course of a daily life, it takes *another* person—the outsider, although the role could only be taken by someone we already love—to buttress our quiescent divinity, so that we may see the Halloween mask for what it is and not be fooled by our own foolish reflection.

Quiescent.

Three syllables.

Qui•es•cent.

(kwï ěs' ənt)

Def.: being at rest, quiet, or still; inactive or motionless.

Fingerprints were better identifiers than mirrors. *The Hardy Boys Detective Handbook* noted eight basic fingerprint patterns: the plain arch, the radial loop, the ulnar loop, the tented arch, the plain whorl, the central pocket loop whorl (tickets please!), the double loop whorl (whoops!—lost her cookies on that ride!), and the accidental whorl. From these eight patterns, a detective could discern the identity of a perpetrator. A villain's uniqueness would be his undoing. Who made me? God made me. If she accomplished her mission, if she laid her body upon the flames and departed the world having saved another, anyone, *someone*, at least her whorls would not have been in vain.

In other developments, her nipples felt like they were going to explode. It was (to quote Aunt Tiddy) suddenly as cold as a witch's tit in the car; her teeth chattered like her old Royal.

Jerry fumbled with her ancient bra clasp.

The outsider coming in…

The outsider, Magdalene knew, the friend who reminds us that we're wearing a cheap, plastic Halloween mask from Rex's, is quite frequently the person laughing next to you in the mirror—for the outsider knows, for good or ill, it's better to shore yourself up when you can't see the bottom than to merely accept what's on the surface.

M4: now there's a cluster you could easily miss without a telescope like Katie's. To the west of Antares, the smudge was discovered in 1746 and has more than 100,000 stars all mashed into one cluster, each jockeying for position, as if they were huddling for warmth. M4 has roughly a 75-light-year diameter. It looked like an ulnar loop that had been squished from either side.

You could spend an entire evening trying to count your way through M4. You could spend years, lifetimes, trying to find out if stars were like snowflakes—no two alike. Was it the distance between the stars—a 75-light-year diameter was a respectable amount of space, cluster or not—that caused them to fall and expire like snowflakes on a warm tongue?

Magdalene shifted her body so Jerry would have easier access to her back.

Often, more than one person completes us, Magdalene thought, though we are too blind to see even one, just as we are blind to our own two halves. Walk away from the sun, to a darker side of your orbit, and in the midst of your blindness, a glare, a refraction, a reflection reveals your best smile or your laugh lines or the way the cords on your neck stand out when you sing or the way your black bob haircut bounces when a real belly laugh emerges.

And what a mystery it was to find our other halves! You need more than a telescope or a detective handbook. It was Magdalene's experience that most adults were less obsessed with finding themselves than trying to pinpoint where certain *other* people belonged and where those *other* people ought to look for themselves. This, of course, was an excuse for a mass market, new agey kind of self reflection which was no kind of self reflection at all. (Hence Mrs.

Stanley's carefully tended bin of paperback self-help books—a bin on wheels, no less, as if there might be a need to *whisk* them away should someone of Magdalene Barrow's comportment crack their spines or mark their pages with a bent corner. Popular titles that designated which planets—Venus or Mars, say, or the ever popular Uranus, planet of choice for Jerry Eves and compatriots—represented which gender.) Magdalene didn't have to hang out at McCullough's drinking a pint with the second most powerful attorney in Mondauk County to hear the Crayola Role Call: kike, nigger, papist, dago, mick, injun, limey, spic, wop, faggot, dyke, retard, fat pig, bitch, bastard, chink, jap, sand nigger. The last was especially popular now. Assumption had taken it one step further: the soggy cafeteria fries were no longer considered European in origin; instead they were now designated Freedom Fries, although the grease-laden strips of potatoes seemed anything but free, but maybe that was the point. There seemed to be very little to really bring people together. Groups like the Faith Board were more like gangs huddled together for protection, attempting to impose their will and beliefs on the rest of the populace, than democratic social clubs. Post 9/11, the prevailing mood was of suspicion—and not just of Al-Qaeda or Saddam Hussein: anywhere but here, it's okay as long as they don't touch me, back where they belong.

Jerry Eves had succeeded in separating the two halves of the ancient bra clasp. Magdalene half-expected to see a dust-up with moths fleeing the scene. She felt the rough scrape of the bra as it slid from her chest.

Jerry was breathing *awfully* heavy. Almost an inhale or an exhale every half-second. Although his head was currently buried near her shoulder blades (and creeping ever so awkwardly south), Magdalene thought Jerry would be better served breathing into a lunch bag. She'd seen that once on a detective show, and more than once at Assumption; Megan Riley was forever escaping pop quizzes or turns at the blackboard by breathing so hard and so fast—kind of like Jerry now—that she would end up in the nurse's office, staring into one of the brown lunch bags the good sisters of Saint Joseph kept for just such occasions.

Here's something *The Hardy Boys Detective Handbook* doesn't mention; here's a factoid not noted in her old copy of Menzel's *Field Guide to the Stars and Planets*: when faced with Irrational Opposition—a bully, for instance—the person you think you are splinters just a little bit more, even while clinging to that old self-image.

That's where they all come together, Magdalene knew: writing, detecting, stargazing. Picking up sticks. Connecting the dots. Carefully removing a splinter.

Jerry was feeding like a baby. His fingers were on her thighs.

Michael.

Surveillance was the art of watching people without them knowing. Astronomy was the study of the stars after they've died. Writing was a way of capturing the living and the dead, with the living often in disguise and the fictional standing in for the dead.

Jerry's warm palm rested on the inside of her leg. Bowing her head, Magdalene eased his hand up. Jerry was nice. She wasn't using him for Mick's GTO; she was making him a character in her story.

The problem with surveillance, the dilemma with stargazing, the conundrum of writing was this: while not exactly passive, these were not defining moments of action.

Whhhh*at* wwwwi*llll you d*oooo whhhh*en you*rrrr *time come*sss*s?*

And when the person you love is a bully, when a bully is *exactly* whom you love, the splinters split—they halve, they quarter. You become incapable of action—startled in the headlights, lungs full of smoke, chest filling with water.

Jerry fumbled under her skirt—a funny phrase for a football star—until his fingers, his long, slender, freckled fingers found a place that up until a few moments before she hadn't been entirely aware she had.

Jerry's fingers were inside her.

Two halves.

Of the same whole.

Michael.

This last jump is even more wild than the previous one. When Michael hits the surface of the Puddle, it sounds like a gunshot—not an unfamiliar sound so close to the Lakes.

The rain makes its own noise as the drops grow into falling stars. She doesn't notice Michael standing in front of her until she looks up. He is a lithe, bronze statue. His penis stands straight up like it does sometimes during their blanket games. Magdalene knows the blanket games only continue at their age because the games provide opportunity for their bodies to be close. They never speak about it; it's never discussed in even the most schoolyard of terms. They both know.

And they both know something else: it's like double-sided tape. They're caught either way.

She doesn't want to touch Michael's penis.

She can't stop thinking about its smoothness.

Michael could force her to touch it, Magdalene is aware. He's forced her to do *just about everything she's ever been in trouble for: lighting dog poop on fire, cutting school, sipping from the discarded, not-quite-empty Budweiser cans after a family picnic (back when they were members of a family rather than increasingly strangled tentacles), mumbly-peg, peeing together behind the tree in the yard.*

Magdalene also knows Michael knows that she likes looking at it: when it accidentally slips out of his underwear or when he emerges from the shower while she's brushing her teeth. It's scary, this thing, *and ultimately ugly: wrinkled when tiny, crimson and stretched to the breaking point when it stands up. Magdalene is aware of the power Michael holds over her. And it has little to do with his penis. He is everything she wants to be. She writes about it; he actually does it. She can only gaze at the stars; Michael is luminous, a half-turned spiral pass caught in the speckled halogens of a night game, his feet dancing on invisible clouds that lowered just to raise him up. If Magdalene searches for clues and facts, connections between the dots, concrete evidence, then Michael is an immutable, concrete conclusion: everything their father wanted in a son: brains, brawn, a sense of adventure, an air of danger.*

Magdalene knows what sex is.

Sister Theresa scrawled on the blackboard in fifth grade: DO NOT TRY BEFORE YOU BUY *(her singular piece of advice and her solitary warning), eliciting giggles and wide-eyed stares from the girls and snickers and high-fives from the boys. Christina Fuller actually turned her painted mouth downward and stage-whispered, "Too late," to Donna Gaynor. Magdalene remembers Donna Gaynor turning to look Magdalene straight in the face as if to say:* need Cliffs Notes? *And truth be told, it was a while before she fully understood what sex was. Mrs. Stanley guarded the sex books in the library like a rabid dog. Magdalene's mother never got around to "the talk." "Not in front of the children." Magdalene's first period still has yet to arrive. She could have asked Michael back then, but even years ago she knew that would be akin to lighting a firecracker in a closet. So she learned what she could in the schoolyard without actively asking, but the information was often wrong and frequently made her even more confused.*

Once Magdalene overheard two boys—one was skinny, ol' freckled face Jerry Eves, that beanpole, that class clown!—discuss FUCKING *in the Assumption Corridor during fifth grade recess. Jerry told a dirty joke involving a Polack, a Mick, a Wop, and lots of* FUCKING. *The other boy was mystified, terrified even; it seemed as if he didn't want to let on that he didn't know the word* FUCK *beyond its myriad uses as an adjective. (Even in fifth grade, Magdalene read beyond her peers; she'd been forced to stop bringing her Hardy Boys books to school the same way she'd been forced to ditch her Green Lantern lunchbox in favor of brown bags—perhaps forced was the wrong word, but Magdalene was aware that the power to coerce was not exclusive to her brother, and she worked hard at discovering the weaknesses inside herself that allowed her to give in and give up, hoping to drag them beneath the light of the stars for a good ass-kicking.) The other boy tucked in his chin and released a poor imitation of a knowing laugh. "Yeah, yeah," the other boy said. Jerry seemed less convinced of the boy's wisdom. True to his good nature, Jerry tried to let it go. But more kids had wandered over. Magdalene pushed herself further back against the bike fence. A few of the less self-conscious members of his audience clamored for further explanation. Jerry lowered his voice. "Fucking's when a guy puts his thing into a girl and they both pee. If they pee together, they make a baby."*

Magdalene spent the better part of what remained of her fifth grade year making sure her brother flushed. Michael didn't always remember to flush, and often it looked as if he'd been dancing while he was peeing. Sometimes even the toilet paper roll would be damp. Magdalene was careful to clean up after Michael used the toilet; the last thing their father needed as their mother wasted slowly away to a skeleton smile on the bottom of a bald head was another baby.

Magdalene's sexual education has advanced considerably since then (and the toilet baby nightmares have long ago ceased). She understands why the Church places so much emphasis on sex. Sex is a genuine mystery. She is as drawn to the forbidden as Frank and Joe Hardy are to a haunted tower. But for Magdalene, curiosity doesn't equal complicity, which means little when it comes to a dare.

See, the Rules of the Dare go like this: Honor the Dare, Respect the Rules, Execute the Dare, or Be Banished Forever—*and of course, the just-broken Fifth Rule, the Pentagon Rule:* Don't Cheat the Dare. *But there is a codicil to the Rules of the Dare, enacted by the caller usually when the dare has been cheated: best the first, cheated dare with another of greater value (either in execution or audacity, it doesn't matter), and the second dare takes precedent.*

You can't cheat the second dare. There are no provisions for that. Cheating the second dare calls for a punishment worse than banishment—whatever that could be.

This dare has been coming for a while: the dare involving the penis. With Michael entering Hoskins High next year, their constant companionship will end; their silly games they know they are too damn old for will become obsolete. (They are too damn old, according to Aunt Tiddy, for their favorite activities, especially untying Tiddy's apron strings, or, even better, distracting the old busybody while one of them ties the apron strings to something else—anything else: a chair, the handle of the stove or fridge, once even an arrangement of dogwood flowers in a glass vase. Too damn old to be taking it that damn far.) What high school kids pretend to be stranded on a raft in the middle of a bed overflowing with blankets?

The Puddle was the precursor. He's gotten her to jump. Michael had been waiting years for that moment, she knows, and she'd cheated the dare. Now he stands before her, rain bouncing off his penis. It throbs in the rain. She's never seen it hard this close before. Oh, she's felt it against her back and once against her bottom during a particularly rough game, but that was normal brother nuisance shit, or so Christina Fuller said. (Odd, since Christina didn't have a brother.) Magdalene once even peeked into Michael's pajama bottoms when he was asleep. The flap was partially open, and the little head was poking out. Magdalene quietly, softly, widened the opening and stared at it for—well, it seemed like hours. Magdalene wondered how to make it grow big, but Michael rolled over, and the moment passed.

Lately, he's taken to undressing and changing in front of her without turning around. Magdalene knows her brother is, in his own not-so-subtle way, encouraging her to do the same, but Magdalene is embarrassed by the changes taking place in her body: although her nipples have grown big (big?—Magdalene thinks they look like saucers, big ugly flying saucers), her breasts remain submerged. Pubic hair has sprouted almost overnight. One minute: nothing; the next: jungle sod. (Tiddy calls it her lily pad, which makes Magdalene want to go toss frogs like Stevie Rich and John-John Hagarty do at the Puddle.) But Michael never forces her to undress; he is as casual about her nakedness as he is about his.

The hood of Michael's sweatshirt hides her eyes from his. Up close, his penis is huge. If he dares her—and what is a dare but a refined form of bullying—the jig is up. She wants to touch it. She wants to cup it smoothness in her palm. She wants to run a finger down its shaft and cup the egg-shaped balls. She loves him. She wants to marry him. She even wants to kiss him. Married people touch each other down there all the time. Jerry Eves' pee theory aside, it's how babies are made. Being in love with your brother—well, that's a sin. All the good sisters of Saint Joseph and all the priests and just about everyone she knows could tell her that much. Even Christina, who follows Michael's muscles with a salivating look and heavily made-up eyes, knows it's a sin. "If he was my brother!" Christina has said. "Shit! I'd be in jail or hell by now!"

The rain pelts the ground, and Magdalene's feet, pulled close to her body, are sinking in red mud. Better off sitting in mud than pulling dock splinters from her bottom, she thinks. She extracts a cigarette filter from between her toes. One thing's for sure, they'll definitely be alone in the rainstorm. Not that their peers frequent the Puddle much anymore. The dock at Finch's Landing has become a hangout for the burnouts, a home away from home after dark for the denizens of

Paradise Lakes (when it's not pouring). Here the trailer park kids smoke their cigarettes and drink their beer and take their drugs and practice fucking, if the half-buried condoms and the ones clinging to the huge reeds alongside the Puddle are any indication.

Michael takes one step forward.

"Lil," he croaks.

Any second now.

Count them.

One little piggy, two little piggies, three little piggies.

One for the road, two drink minimum, three's usually my limit, four to the floor, five and I'm flagged, six and I'm outta here, seven and I'm gone, gotta big case tomorrow. Got more cases than Carter's got pills: murder one, robbery two. Got more cases than kids. Count 'em: one, two. Girls, they count as one, right? Hahahahahaha. All join in: Pete, Zooey, you in the corner, one, two, three, down the hatch. Here she is now: number two. Come to lead me home, gents, two blocks, four blocks. How many feet, darling? How many yards? You see my boy, Stan? Kid's got the golden arm. Ain't shit to do with his coach. Been coaching my boy for years now, Zooey. Little one's gonna take me home now. One bed. One parent. Two kids. How does that add up, Stan? You tell me, how does that add up?

Hold your breath and count to ten. Spin around and do it again.

"Lil," Michael says, and his voice is hoarse. His lips are peeled back. His teeth are chattering.

"One, two, three, four, five, six, seven; all good children go to heaven."

Red rocket! Red rocket!

Two, four, six, eight! Who do we appreciate?!

This is what Michael says.

Three words.

Three syllables.

A thousand stuttered little breaths later:

"I

dare

you."

She stares at him. She stares at his penis. He can't see her eyes. That is good. Never let 'em see your eyes. Shakespeare? Humphrey Bogart? Franklin W. Dixon? From Dirt Road comes the sound of tires skidding over loose stones, and from a car radio, a heavy metal band rattles on in anger. ("Hand's are shakin', got your finger on the trigger / Jesus ain't complainin', gonna figure it out.") *A hundred scenarios, a thousand thoughts.*

She reminds herself to breathe. No escaping now. Gotta breathe. She was damn close to a hundred and twenty seconds—half a breath away, as a matter of fact.

Michael's words hang in the thick air of Pennypack Woods. The whirr of dragonflies can't pierce Michael's words. All the songs of all the frogs can't smother Michael's dare. Not now.

She could try to best the second dare. She could try. The codicil allows for a last-second turnabout. The Rule of the Bests.

One, two, fuck you. Three, four, you little whore.

The Dead Injun Tree is so black, it looks fake, like someone has painted it for a play. The tree belongs on a Robert Louis Stevenson cover, a sea-worn vessel in the distance flying the Jolly Roger with impudence and insolence. It is a tree as old as treachery.

Magdalene thinks if she pulls the hood from her head, reveals her pale, softer (but not much), more dour version of her brother's face, that he will see: if he dares her (which he's done, but there is always the ancient kindergarten rite of Take-Backs for Michael to consider; it isn't too late; no, it sure isn't; one, two, three, four, can I have a little more?), she will have to dare him back; if he dares her (which he's done, of course, but when you count, and she is a counter, an enumerator, there exists a continuum—you learn this—and though it may seem that you're climbing, ascending—counting backwards is silly unless you're blasting-off in a rocket ship—you're really just floating; there is no end to the river; there is no end to the river; one more time for the folks back home—folk, singular, drunk: there is no end to the river), she'll dare him back and then berate herself LOUDLY inside her head once she is home in bed, and Michael is in his making his sheets all smelly, for NOT just r-e-a-c-h-i-n-g out and...

"The Dead Injun Tree again—higher," Magdalene says, and she sees her brother's face droop (nothing else does) as he realizes she's pulled out the Rule of Bests. Magdalene's dare, for sure, bests his second dare if only because she can't hurt herself touching his penis; the threat of physical injury always bests emotional damage. He can't even try the Double Dare now. The time to use the Double Dare (which, admittedly, is extremely *kindergarten, so much so, that it is rarely used) has surely passed.*

"Climbed it once, right?" Michael says. "Tempted fate. What's once more?"

Michael turns to look at the blackened bark and absently runs his hand along his penis. The heavy metal music stops abruptly, and all the frogs open their mouths to sing a croaking blues loud enough to make branches leave their trees. The Puddle smells like water that's been left standing in a dirty pot overnight, and the frogs are vocal grease spots. Magdalene's toes and bottom (and lily pad) are buried in the wet, dirty shore. Michael laughs, and on Dirt Road someone cranks Skynyrd, and Magdalene is quite sure in a bar several miles to the east, amber liquids are cracking ice with their warmth, beer caps are being popped off, and their father is sucking on a Camel (when he inhales, it sounds like tiny pieces of paper being ripped), forcing smoke to jet past his soon-to-be-yellowed teeth and his white-coated tongue to enter the lungs that used to raise a baritone over their mother's alto when the two voices would entangle just enough to raise the hairs on the back of Magdalene's neck.

"'Where have you gone, Joe DiMaggio?'" *her parents sang,* "'a nation turns its lonely eyes to you...'"

Michael stands at the foot of the Dead Injun Tree and kicks the trunk several times with the side of his heel.

"Testing the tires," *he says.*

Magdalene wants to crack a joke about Mr. McAllister always being in his driveway, doing little more than kicking and cursing at the Chevy he was legally restrained from driving, but sitting naked in a thunderstorm doesn't make her feel very funny. Michael laughs as if she made the joke anyway.

Two halves.

Of the same whole.

Magdalene had been counting the lightning bugs, and although she'd surpassed one hundred and forty, she'd become convinced it was just the same half-dozen or so, lazing around the outside of the Chevy. Jerry's breathing was locomotive-like now, and there was little sense in stopping the train. Jerry Eves was a nice boy. He treated her like a pal in school—a pal that made him blush. Even now, his bumbling in the back of Mr. McAllister's car was sincere: equal parts excitement and awe. When he succeeded in removing Magdalene's pretty, white blouse, he pulled his head back to stare, wide-eyed, then whispered in a husky, morning voice, "Magdalene, Magdalene," before lowering his head back onto her chest.

Michael climbs the Dead Injun Tree. He is careful, testing the give of the branch before committing his full weight. Magdalene follows his ascension and counts. When a branch Michael stands on goes SNAP, Magdalene's face registers concern, but she congratulates herself for her dual concentration. She's not only counted all the cigarette butts frescoed on the shore, but she's also separated them into two categories: white filters and brown filters.

Jerry Eves had a hard-on.

What if Mr. McAllister had somehow convinced Stevie Rich to torment and antagonize Joseph Bochdan and Henry Richard Cabot in order to send a message to Andriy Bochdan? Mr. McAllister could have wooed the widow Tidwell in order to have access to her nephew. Perhaps Mr. McAllister was doing business with Andriy Bochdan. What did McAllister do for a living anyway? Perhaps Andriy Bochdan and his Ukrainian associates had somehow contributed to Nancy McAllister's suicide. Maybe Mr. Bochdan was holding a secret over Mr. McAllister's head. Maybe Andriy Bochdan had had an affair with Nancy McAllister, and the affair had led to her suicide. (Something sticky brushed Magdalene's hand for half a heartbeat.) That would have explained Mr. McAllister's drinking— he'd discovered the affair and had done nothing out of fear. His wife had needed rescuing, and he'd done absolutely nothing. And what better way for Mr. McAllister to enact revenge on Andriy Bochdan than by having Bochdan's son bullied by Assumption's Head Bully, thus setting into motion a confrontation that even wily Mr. McAllister couldn't have expected (so distracted was he by his second set of plans involving making his own daughter disappear so he could elope with the widow Tidwell). Or had he? Had the only unexpected part been who'd pulled the trigger? (And that's what Jerry's penis felt like when he placed her hand on it—a gun; Jerry may have been putty in her hands, metaphorically speaking, but at least one very distinct part stood up for itself.) Magdalene didn't believe Stevie Rich was smart enough to understand the subtleties of intimidation. To Stevie, bullying was bullying: he could so he did. Even Magdalene's father had said as much about his brief foray into bullying. Had Stevie been recruited by Mr. McAllister to do more than bullying, but told to back off if or when the situation took care of itself? Had Stevie developed a taste for it—a taste for something beyond the everyday drudgery of stealing lunches and copping feels, tripping first graders and forcing heads down toilets? (Magdalene's hand moved Jerry's penis up and down, up and down. His breathing had become erratic, and his eyes were shut tight. Magdalene closed her eyes eventually too. It was easier to count the strokes if her eyes were closed.) On the mean streets of Mondauk Proper, Stevie Rich had already become an urban legend, a spook tale. He killed animals with his bare hands. He and John-John Hagarty peed together in Pennypack too and held each other's wieners when they did. If Stevie Rich killed pets for kicks, and Stevie could be bought and sold by the likes of Mr. McAllister or Andriy Bochdan (who's to say the Ukrainian gangster didn't have a prior relationship with Stevie?), what would stop Stevie from taking the next step towards total immersion in his extracurricular activities: killing other kids?

Her hand went up and down, up and down.

"Magdalene…"

"Yes…?"

Float float float.

How many kids had gone missing from Mondauk County in the past few years? Had the police even checked for similarities between the cases? Had the *Mondauk Common* published any exposés?

What if bullies were killing the children of Mondauk?

What if the bullies had killed Christina?

What if they'd killed Michael?

Michael calls her name again. He is balanced on a short, broken branch that appears to have been struck by lightning; its missing portion is violently gone. Michael stands bronzed and naked, his body toned and shaped by football and stickball and wrestling on the front lawn. His presence seems to aggravate the storm-darkened sky; the gods thunder as the rain-soaked deity climbs his way to heaven. The lightning illuminates the contrast between the zombie husk of the Dead Injun Tree and the bronze angel storming the skies, as if to remind them both of how even the mightiest can fall.

Magdalene hears her mother's mellifluous tones, which delivered even the direst of proclamations with a smile full of healthy, milk-stained teeth: "Always wear a slicker in the rain and don't hide under a tree if there's lightning, for lightning will always find you."

SNAP.

Magdalene looks up, and Michael isn't where he was. Neither is the truncated branch. She searches the sky for his tan frame and watches the afternoon take its last breath and die. A beetle climbs the Dead Injun Tree. Two beetles. A ladybug. Three ladybugs. A fourth. The rain drenches her upturned face, pelting it with drops as big as footballs, and the warm fingers of the swollen Puddle tickle her buried toes as it begins to take the shore. Michael calls, "Lil," then says something that sounds like, "It's a goddamn whirlpool." The thunder boxes her ears. She realizes he's been standing on the edge of the dock a few feet away from her. He survived the Dead Injun Tree. He survived the dare.

Michael yells: "Cannonball!"

Magdalene waits for the splash.

Jerry offered Magdalene his handkerchief so she could wipe her hands, and outside the Chevy, the McAllisters' porch light suddenly came on.

+

It was sweet that Jerry Eves carried a handkerchief; Magdalene thought only the old men who played chess in the Common still carried handkerchiefs (and Danny Kildare), but today, the Common had been a ghost town, and tonight, in Mr. McAllister's blue Chevy, Jerry Eves was carefully cleaning her hand with his handkerchief.

Had Jerry Eves peed on her hand?

The McAllister screen door opened.

Magdalene pressed her fingers together. No, they were sticky—pee wasn't sticky. Jerry placed her arms back into her bra and worked patiently to clasp the hook.

Mr. McAllister stepped out to his front stoop and lit a cigarette.

"Holy shit," Jerry whispered, as he scrunched down and buttoned his blue jeans. He pulled Magdalene down next to him. "What do we do?"

Magdalene interrupted her count of his freckles.

"Pray," she giggled. "Count."

Splinter.

SNAP.

Float float float.

Jerry's freckles went slack, and Magdalene regretted the joke. She was still somewhat surprised to find herself in the back seat of Mr. McAllister's Chevy in Mr. McAllister's driveway watching Mr. McAllister suck on a butt roughly a yard away. And Jerry's liquids notwithstanding, Magdalene was completely stunned to find herself (partially) dry and dressed in a pretty blouse and a light blue skirt, rather than wet and muddy beneath Michael's smelly, old hooded sweatshirt, the one she'd slept with for a month after he'd disappeared, the one, she was sure, Aunt Tiddy had secreted away. Tiddy wasn't one for hanging on to the past. The past for Tiddy was the provenance of movies and books. Even Shakespeare was only as good as the timelessness of his advice and admonishments. Magdalene wondered what Aunt Tiddy would think of her grandniece now. Magdalene wasn't even sure what she had just done.

"Okay, Tonto, how do we get out of this one?" Jerry asked.

Mr. McAllister released a noisy fart. Katie—they were here to keep an eye on Katie. She tried to clear her head of numbers and rhymes. What would Frank and Joe Hardy do? Magdalene knew for sure they wouldn't be trapped in the backseat of a Chevy having just finished a heavy petting session. Mr. McAllister seemed awfully content (content enough to rip one on his front stoop), but there was no way they could escape without being seen. Mr. McAllister would as surely kill her as blink. Magdalene wished he would just finish his smoke and go inside.

"He just lit another one," Jerry whispered.

Jerry's eyes were wide, and he covered her body with his. His heart raced like she imagined Mick's '68 GTO would.

Magdalene buried her nose in his hair. Oh, to count all of his dirty-blonde hairs!

"We need a plan," Jerry said. "A good one."

"What would Stick Man do?" she whispered, at least half-serious.

Jerry kissed her forehead. His lips were warm.

"Good question."

In the dark, Jerry's eyes sparkled, but his chin was set and determined. The air in the Chevy crackled like a potentially spectacular movie moment.

"Stay low until you hear me go inside," he said, "or until you hear him chasin' me. Then skedaddle. I got me a terrible thirst."

He kissed her lips and didn't open his. It lasted exactly fourteen heartbeats. Seven of hers. Seven of his. Fourteen.

"All this kissing's drying me out, Tonto," Jerry said, as he climbed over the front seat and pushed the squeaky passenger door open. He folded his handkerchief before replacing it in his pocket and winked at her.

"What the *fuck* is this?" Mr. McAllister asked.

Jerry knocked on the trunk as he walked around the back of the car. Magdalene jumped up and hit her head on the roof.

"That's what I'm asking, mister," Jerry said. "*What* the fuck?"

Magdalene lifted her head so she could see through the rear window. Mr. McAllister made as if he was going to rush off the stoop, but stopped suddenly and merely shifted his weight instead. He appeared stunned that a lanky kid had just emerged from the back of his Chevy. Mr. McAllister's mouth hung open. Magdalene ducked.

"No, no, I don't like the way she drives," Jerry said. "Not gonna take her, I don't think. Hey, she got Fuelie heads? A Hurst on the floor? I didn't think so. What else ya got?"

Magdalene lifted her head again and wiped at the rear window with her palm. Jerry and Mr. McAllister were staring at each other, then Jerry pushed past Mr. McAllister—actually *rushed* past him and fumbled with the screen door. She had to hand it to ol' Jerry Eves: he fumbled quite a bit, but he got the job done.

"Lemme take a peek at your kitchen," Jerry said. "Maybe I'll buy the stove. Maybe. Man's gotta have appliances. That's what my daddy always said. Say, got any soda pop?"

Jerry yanked the door open—hitting Mr. McAllister's arm with the door in the process.

"No? You comin' in?" Jerry asked, holding the door open. "You don't live in a barn, do ya? Want me to air the place out?" Jerry swept the air with his hand. "That last fart's still hangin' 'round. You better check your skivvies for skid marks!"

Jerry popped into the house, and the screen door closed with a crack.

Mr. McAllister stood on the stoop for *one Mississippi, two Mississippi, three Mississippi*, his mouth agape (not looking all that different than he normally did, Magdalene thought), his latest cigarette burning forgotten in the driveway, before ripping the screen door open and following Jerry inside.

Magdalene climbed out of the Chevy and eased the door shut. She heard Mr. McAllister's back door open. She hoped Katie was safe in bed. The back house light bounced on, and there was Jerry Eves, Assumption's wide receiver, creator of Stick Man, record store idolizer, school joker—and now what? her boyfriend, paramour, soul mate?—jumping the metal fence with one hand, his gangly frame receding into the darkness.

Magdalene realized she stood within the circle of the front porch light and quickly retreated across the street to the berry bushes. Damn—if Mr. McAllister took chase after Jerry, this would be the ideal time to get Katie out of the house, but that would be the end of it: no GTO ride to the Lakes, no solving the Cabot Case. Part of her—hell, a *chunk*—wanted to hop fences with Jerry Eves; that was summer, wasn't it? Before the dares had taken over and before the penis had become part of every game with her brother, her summers had consisted of hopping fences, skipping stones at the Puddle, playing Freedom way past dark, staying up late to watch old movies. She couldn't blame Michael for the changes in their summer activities; she *was* in love with him, right? And in some part of her number-addled brain, some splinter, some unexplored whorl, under the darkest part of the blanket, beneath the brilliant death of yet another star, Magdalene knew she was no longer the sum of her parts; she was just *that*: parts. In Willa Meade's office, if she had looked closely, if she had had a magnifying glass, instead of a falling dot, she would have seen a thousand million billion little, tiny, infinitesimal dots barely held together and seconds away from coming apart.

+

Magdalene was beyond punishment now. Tiddy was back to ignoring her again; the old woman didn't even pick up her camera. It was what Magdalene had hoped for though. Her aunt said nothing as Magdalene climbed the stairs. Magdalene had tried to display a fair amount of guilt upon her exhausted face. At least Tiddy tried. Her aunt may have been a pushy busybody, but she tried. Magdalene bet that if anyone had beaten the bushes and scoured the environs for Michael, it had been Tiddy. The woman knew how to dole out the silent treatment, as well as how best to lash out with a forked tongue, but she was loyal, and as Magdalene worked feverishly to finish her novella (she would need to write the letter to her father tomorrow, after Jerry drove her to Paradise Lakes; not a suicide note, which seemed pointless, like a third-rate sequel to a half-decent movie, but rather a detailed report of the results of her investigation—and she wanted to leave a note for Michael too, just in case), she heard the conversation that must have begun outside and had now spilled into the living room. Her father was home. Raven barreled down the stairs to bark his greetings.

"I don't care if she hears. I'm tired of secrets. I'm tired of pretending about school. I don't understand what the course of action is here."

Her father's voice was tired and cranky: "Goddamn it, Tiddy. No is no."

"We're doing her more harm than good, by God!"

"Harm? The harm—"

Tiddy's voice escalated: "You're not here all day. I am. Something needs to be done and done now."

"With Christina Fuller, it's just…" Her father's voice lost its bearing.

"It's terrible, but—"

"It is, Tiddy."

Magdalene imagined ice rattling in a hundred empty glasses, a thousand cigarette smoke rings scorching the good sense of a single parent of one. She stopped writing. Assistant District Attorney Gregory Barrows sounded almost heroic, struggling over his words.

"It is, Tiddy," her father repeated, and his *voice* was back: stentorian, authoritative, theatrically paced. "And, as much as we can, we have to shield Magdalene from it."

"Well, she *was* fast, that Christina Fuller."

"That has nothing to do with the horrors she might be going through right now," Magdalene's father said. "She's somebody's daughter."

End of subject. Magdalene thought that if Franklin W. Dixon (or whoever wrote under that name) ever decided to update *The Hardy Boys Detective Handbook*, he should include a detailed section on forensics and persuasive speaking and their myriad uses: grilling suspects, questioning witnesses, shutting down nosy relatives. Her father had a way of making the general very specific, bringing the eyeglass to the dot.

"The Fullers are a wreck. He's a good man, Dr. Fuller."

Tiddy couldn't resist: "Sure, seen him around a lot after—"

"Enough."

There was no anger in her father's voice, just bone-weariness. Had her father hopped fences in his youth? Had he ever pulled a daring escape like Jerry Eves had tonight?

"*Criminy!*" Aunt Tiddy said. "New subject, old argument then: it's time: let your daughter join the team."

"No, Tiddy. The answer is no. It's hard enough to coach with everything that's going on, but I owe the county, I owe the mayor, I owe everyone. I fell on my face. I refused their help, and they waited. My son played football, Tiddy. Magdalene is…she…Magdalene is artistic. Once we get through this case—"

"…and then through the Fuller girl mess and then through: what?" Tiddy asked. "What excuse is next, Gregory? Your daughter is a Goner, you don't pick up the pace. Life's not going to wait around and give you a second to breathe just 'cause you want it to. And you can pray all you want if you still do that sort of thing. Your bosses weren't the only ones waiting for you to come down from that barstool. Look around you, Gregory, look 'round. It's not like when I was young—or even when you were. Oh, yeah, there were drugs and communists and Nixon, but today it's different, and after 9/11, *everything* is different—or at least it seems different. More precious.

The world doesn't stop to let you off, and the shit doesn't stop flowing just because *you* decide to stop squatting."

Raven lumbered up to her pillow and deposited Monien next to her head. Her dog's hot breath was in her ear. Magdalene squeezed the panda.

Silence.

"Goner," she told her dog.

Raven ignored the panda as if this information were nothing new. He pushed the lump next to her pillow.

"Oh, Monkey too. Not now, Raven." Magdalene could just hear Monkey's jungle shrieks bringing an end to Tiddy's speech.

"Tiberius Willamena Wheelwright," her father said. "What in the hell are you talking about?"

"She'll be a Goner," Aunt Tiddy said. "I don't need Shakespeare to tell me that."

The monkey erupted.

Magdalene heard Tiddy stomping up the stairs and shoved the screaming monkey under her pillow, but Raven kept pushing his nose, then his whole big, black noggin under the pillow after it. Magdalene's forehead connected with Raven's brow. She snatched the monkey, faked a throw, and stuffed it down into her sheets. Raven sniffed over by the bureau, tracking the elusive simian. Tiddy's skinny shadow graced her doorway. Magdalene shut her eyes and faked a couple of snores. When she dared a peek, the shadow was gone.

When she heard her father prepare the sofa for bed (and Raven had found Monkey in the sheets and was munching contentedly on its fur), Magdalene tore a page from her journal and began a letter to Mrs. Bochdan. For all her self-ascribed writing talents (okay, some of the nuns had complimented her book reports and such, and Willa Meade had practically had a bowel movement when Magdalene showed her one page of *A Lab's Ears are Made of* SILK), the letter was a mess. After tomorrow's expedition to the Lakes, there would be almost no time to complete her book and all the letters she had to write. But she had to let the woman know the truth about the shooting. More than half the letter to Mrs. Bochdan would be conjecture, a summarizing of all that Magdalene thought to be true.

As soon as someone is gone, the summarizing begins.

Magdalene thought Mrs. Bochdan would be very familiar with summarizing.

Outside of the Barrows Bungalow, summarizing was what passed for careful consideration and meaningful meditation for most folks. The events of 9/11 were played out in fitful clutches of flag waving and sworn fealty to leaders who seemed hell-bent on starting another war in Iraq. Because the Bochdans' skin was browner than most in Mondauk Proper, there'd been talk of boycotting Sol's in the aftermath of the terrorist attacks—talk of boycotting and whispers of much more—until it was discovered the Bochdans were Ukrainian. They weren't Arabs. The whispers migrated elsewhere—blindly criticizing those who spoke out against the impending war in Iraq and embracing the baritone voices who declared that it was *our* time to kick some ass—until new local targets could be established. (Magdalene was convinced that the fervor with which the Catholic Faith Board attacked the Methodists' mounting of a competing carnival on the Feast of the Baptist was partially due to misplaced rage as local targets diminished.) Magdalene's Social Studies class had studied these events with due diligence. Magdalene found it difficult to see beyond the summarizing. Even the government's reckoning of the terrorists' rationale seemed wonky. In her textbooks, she'd read about the U.S. support of these very terrorists in their battle against the Evil Empire in Afghanistan. Either we backed the wrong horse way back when, Magdalene thought, or there was more to this story than the summarizing presented by a caught-in-the-headlights president spouting platitudes like a bad guy in a Nancy Drew book.

The president also claimed to talk to Jesus, and Magdalene knew this for certain: no matter where your particular bent lay on the divisive issue of God, fighting the fundamentalists of one religion with another brand of fundamentalism was not only plain ol' silly but also smacked of the Crusades. Our God is better than your God.

Poppycock, as Aunt Tiddy would say. Bullshit. Horse hockey. The good sisters of the Order of Saint Joseph didn't delve much beyond the summarizing (why discuss the issues? wave a flag instead!), but class debate was encouraged in the eighth grade in an effort to prepare the students for high school and beyond. Many of the finer points of much of the discussion eluded their intellectual grasp; many talking points were no more than reiterations of arguments heard at the dinner table: WMD (real and imagined); government contracts and high officials' connections to said contracts; possible theaters of war in the near future.

"My daddy says if we don't get 'em now, it'll be like grandpop and them didn't do nothin' fightin' back the dinks in the '50s."

"Please avoid using a double negative, Jimmy."

"Yes, Sister."

"My daddy says we need to lock up all the Arabs that are here now before they go aiding and abetting."

"Wouldn't that be unconstitutional, Bebe?"

"Not if they're Arabs, Sister. They're not Christian."

And so on.

Mrs. Bochdan's civil liberties and those of her son had been in danger long before Joseph pulled the trigger and made his best friend's face disappear. In the end, however, the citizens of Mondauk Proper proved resilient to the machinations of the White House Cowboy. It was either that, or Spring House was too far a drive to buy lottery tickets (an opinion expressed by Mr. McAllister). Between suicide attempts, Magdalene had heard this opinion and many others, including an endless list of countries that deserved American boots on the ground. Still, Magdalene preferred to think the good people of Mondauk County were just that: good people—scared, perhaps, but not easily rattled. Economic divisions were as prevalent as before the terrorist attacks, and religion continued to be a problem (at least between the Roman Catholics and the Methodists), with the Faith Board keeping their thick fingers in every issue from the carnivals to the removal of the asbestos factory's waste, but neighbors still brought in each other's trash cans from the curb, and Sol's continued to sell lottery tickets, gallons of milk, bubble gum, and baseball cards. If Magdalene had understood her father this afternoon, it was the will of the people (and the Cabots) to not prosecute Mrs. Bochdan or even Joseph for the murder of Henry Richard Cabot, but rather to find an alternate method of resolution within the pliable confines of the law.

Magdalene wrote the letter as if Mrs. Bochdan had complicit knowledge concerning the mood of the town. The woman knew her husband was a bad apple. Mr. McAllister and Andriy Bochdan; Mr. McAllister and the widow Tidwell; Mrs. Tidwell and her late husband's nephew. Magdalene wrote it all out, the connections between the principals: her cursive penmanship swirling and twisting with whorls and loops and arches, all lines leading to buck-toothed bully Stevie Rich and John-John Hagarty, Stevie's pacifier-sucking sidekick. Magdalene made sure to indicate that not every single clue had been collected, but that if her fishing trip to the Lakes tomorrow proved at all successful, the burden of proof would be that much lighter.

She hoped the letter would inspire Mrs. Bochdan to act. If Magdalene's information was right (and she and Jerry escaped the Lakes intact with the information), her father's office would be contacting Mrs. Bochdan the very next day (or at least as soon as they checked it out). Magdalene was aware that the process could be delayed by her own funeral, and there was always the possibility of her father resuming his place at McCullough's after she died, but she doubted it. Her father had visited the absolute bottom and found it crowded (at least Magdalene told herself this; there was no way to be sure): nobody there read the dictionary, nobody there loved words and studied them and honored them, not a single soul at McCullough's seemed to know they were on the bottom floor and it was time to get up, olly olly oxen free.

In the end, Magdalene hoped Mrs. Bochdan's love for her son would pull her away from depressing living room shrines and endless hours of minding Sol's or cleaning other people's toilets. Joseph was an only child. Wherever he was being held, no matter how much he missed his mother, no matter how dense his confusion and unexplored grief over the shooting was, Magdalene thought Joseph would be able to cope until his mother pulled together his defense. She was sure he was scared and wounded, but he was probably used to being alone. Magdalene had only less than a year in which to inhabit that particular stasis herself, and she knew well its confines and comforts.

Except Magdalene wasn't an only child.

She couldn't write Mrs. Bochdan about that.

Michael had been the firstborn and thus imbued with certain privileges, that if not actually denied to the second child, then not offered either. Their father may have never bought her a football, but she never wanted for anything. (She was sure the kids who lived in the Lakes wanted for a lot of things.) If an inordinate amount of time had been spent ferrying Michael from field to field, from game to practice, their father had never ignored his daughter. He bought her a new telescope one year and a whole box of used books from a garage sale another.

Before their mother had died, Michael had been her favorite too. And Magdalene had been the dutiful princess: adored, worshipped from afar, and cherished, but never in the line of ascendancy. It was annoying, but she'd grown used to it. After their mother's death, Magdalene (who had neither her mother's easy smile nor her sunny disposition, only her secretive nature) had faded into the wallpaper and law briefs and whiskey labels.

Michael had been allowed to stay up later than she had been, even when they were younger, to watch *Perry Mason* and *Ellery Queen* reruns or music video shows. Beneath their tent of blankets, Michael would detail the cases and the clues, and every single time, Magdalene would pick out the murderer before Michael told her. At the breakfast table the next morning, Michael would always try to tell their father of Magdalene's mental detective work, but it was difficult getting through to ADA Barrows, and when they were older, their father, who normally never sat down for breakfast until he was clean-shaven and showered, could be found sitting with his head in his hands, an untouched cup of coffee steaming into his slack, rough-hewn face.

"Lil did it again, Pops," Michael said. "She figured out who the killer was."

"Uh-huh," their father said, busy reading his own palms close up.

"I'm gonna make one a hell of a detective," Magdalene said, just to see if her father was paying attention. "A damn good one," she added.

Michael giggled. "It's elemental," her brother said.

"What time is practice?" their father asked.

"No practice today, Pops," Michael said. "Day off, remember?"

Their father removed his hands from his face, and Magdalene wished he'd put them back. His matinee idol jaw was swimming in a slight layer of flab, his eyes were trapped behind haphazardly strung red razor wire, and the less said about his breath, the better. Raven avoided him altogether.

Her father reached for...*what had it been? sugar? surely he hadn't meant to*...and missed; his big, soft hand, its fingers stained yellow, connected with Magdalene's jaw. She and Michael sat still for a beat, then two, before their father lifted his head and stared at Michael with eyes of fire. There was sweat upon his brow.

"I'm sorry, Michael, I really am," their father said. "I'm really sorry."

Magdalene looked down at her letter and was surprised to find the paper was filled with her tiny script. She had no idea what she had written, but she was sure it said enough. Her father's gentle snores climbed the stairs. It was a wonder he could sleep.

The world wasn't coming apart: it was coming together, all the pieces crashing into place—all except one. Tiddy had once said of Assistant District Attorney Gregory Barrows, football coach and father (now) of one: "Sometimes brave men fall the hardest." Her aunt hadn't attributed the words to a dead playwright or an infatuated butcher or acted as if the nugget she'd spat out was common knowledge among the learned, as she sometimes did. Magdalene had been between suicide attempts, and Tiddy, still living in her apartment in Spring House, was hurling towards ubiquity; it was as if Tiddy had just discovered the telephone. Michael had been gone a couple of months maybe; it was goddamn hard to remember, seeing how it was as if he had never existed. The missing person fliers Magdalene had stapled to every single telephone pole from Lindenwold Estate to the Fields were gone, replaced by carnival advertisements—Catholic *and* Methodist. Almost every day after school, she'd walk out of her way to check on her father and make sure he was still holding up the bar, still filling Zooey McCullough's till. One crisp afternoon, with the smell of burning leaves in her nostrils, she'd found him in McCullough's parking lot, still dressed for the office except he was missing his shoes. He was on his hands and knees; vomit and blood ran down the front of his powder blue J. C. Penny dress shirt and matching tie. The large stain on the front of his pants indicated he had pissed himself. Magdalene stood near the lip of the parking lot and watched her father crawl towards a still-smoldering cigarette and bring it to his cracked lips with a shaky hand. Gravel and dirt were pressed into his cheek. She'd never seen him this bad before. Oh, he'd peed on the front lawn and had had a few fender benders, even tossed his socks in the sink one night and set them on fire, but after another head-in-hands morning, he'd trudge to the office. But not tomorrow morning, Magdalene had thought then, and she'd been right. Whatever had happened in the parking lot of McCullough's had been the end of one chapter and the beginning of another.

It was that night on the telephone when Tiddy had said, "Sometimes brave men fall the hardest."

But that wasn't *all* that Tiddy had said, was it?

Magdalene turned in bed and extracted the screaming monkey from between her pillows. Raven's eager breath invaded her face and relieved her of Monkey duties. He rested his head upon the ragged toy and resumed his snoring.

Tiddy had had more to say that night on the phone. What she'd said had reminded Magdalene of Sister Mary Magdalene de Rosa, the patron saint of fiery lavatories.

"Sometimes brave men fall the hardest," Aunt Tiddy had said, "because they don't know that they're brave."

But what, Magdalene had wanted to ask, *about little girls?*

Sugar and spice and everything nice, right? But if the ingredients didn't add up? What if that was all she had become: ingredients, parts, pieces, splinters?

She had heard someone say that in the aftermath of 9/11, we were all widows and widowers, and Magdalene understood that that statement made more sense than all of Shakespeare put together. The whole country was missing parts of itself. And there was nothing the country could do but go through the mourning process. War, flag waving, stupid country songs: none of those could bring back the dead. They were forever falling, brightly colored dots imbuing every thought and every action, bruising the far-flung pieces of those that remained, so thereafter the survivors could only identify themselves by recognizing the stains.

Where do the brave stand when the sky is falling?

Magdalene switched off her reading lamp and held tight to her dog.

A Lab's Ears Are Made of *SILK*

Episode III

What Turtle Said

The glass door was one of those sliding kinds, and it looked comfy inside. And it was open. The Great Journey had been an arduous one thus far, and Finn's issues regarding *SILK* were more perplexing than ever. The Vicar Pig had been little help. Pig's Lord sounded scary and kind of piggish—not at all the loving God Finn remembered from the Boy's *New Catholic Picture Bible*.

Finn tiptoed into the house (as much as a black Labrador retriever could tiptoe) and found a nice spot of sun on the rug. He soon fell asleep, but inside his noggin, in every single dream (and he had a bunch right in a row), his ears were on fire, and when he woke, he shook his head violently to hear them flap and make sure they were still there. He didn't sleep very much after that. Finn stayed on the rug, in the sunspot, just staring at his old basketball.

Can't lose my ears now, Finn thought. They were all he had left in the Wold—besides the orange and blue striped basketball.

"I say, I do say, you there!"

Finn jumped to his paws. The fur on his neck and back stood straight up in their alert positions. His mind felt as fuzzy as his belly. He'd walked forever before finding this house (which smelled familiar), resting only when necessary. The basketball had gotten slippery from all the drool, and the road had seemed to go on forever. Plus Finn was still shaken from his encounter with the Vicar. He'd left Pig's place, hoping to find another old acquaintance, Mr. Turtle, but he'd forgotten where he'd seen Mr. Turtle last.

And now this: someone calling Finn by his proper name—the name the Boy had given him!

"*Ahem*! I say, Mr. Huckleberry Finn, dog!"

Finn hoped it wasn't Daddy Big Un. His Second House was now in the same place his First House was: nowhere. It was sad, but Finn believed this much to be true: once he knew how much his *SILK* was worth, *everyone* would want him in their homes because he would be so valuable. Then, and only then, could he even *think* about maybe, possibly, going back to the Boy and the Big Uns. Of course, by then, the Big Uns would be clamoring for him!

"Finn," the voice said. "Down here."

Now Finn's nose may have been as old as the rest of his body, but as far as sniffers went, Finn thought it top notch, and while Finn didn't completely follow or comprehend the television programs the Big Uns preferred, he thought he would have made a good police dog—as long as there were naps. Finn lowered his big noggin, and his sniffer struck another aquarium—this one smaller than Pig's—on a shelf below eye level.

"Who's there?" Finn asked.

"Down here, Finn."

Finn positioned his body so he could lower his sniffer into the little aquarium. He instantly regretted the maneuver. If Pig's place had smelled, well, slightly piggy, this aquarium smelled like—Finn didn't know what. The only reference he could conjure was the Big Un vacation to Beach Haven, which happened just about every year, but one year, galloping on the beach, entertaining the Boy and Daddy Big Un by catching their Frisbee, Finn had paused to investigate a load of seaweed. Finn had been hungry—Finn was pretty much *always* hungry (he was hungry now, but never mind that)—and after a tentative sniff or two, he had sucked the seaweed into his mouth in one gulp. His first thought had been: salad meets bubble gum. Later, when he had thrown up for the tenth and final time that night, with his stomach ginger, and the Boy whispering *SILK* into his ear, Finn swore off bubble gum and salad.

The little aquarium smelled just like bubble gum salad.

Finn pulled his head out and knocked it on the shelf above.

"Sound the alarm!" the voice cried. "Call the militia! Call the minutemen!"

The top of Finn's noggin HURT. His Smart Bump t-h-r-o-b-b-e-d. His Little White Tie raced the devil. For a second (a pretty long time in canine reckoning), he wished the Boy were here to rub his Smart Bump and brush away his tears.

"Did they hurt you, son?" the voice asked. "Are ya hit?"

Finn shook his noggin. He was afraid if he opened his mouth, the voice would hear him cry.

"Are you the scout? The advance man?" the voice queried. "I didn't even know you were one of us!"

Finn wanted to tell the voice that he was no longer one of *anything*—that he was just *one* alone—but he said nothing.

"Or," the voice whispered, "are you *undercover?*"

The *t-h-r-o-b-b-i-n-g* began to subside. Finn cleared his throat.

"I'm not allowed under cover anymore," Finn said.

"Whatcha do, Finn? Go AWOL? Friendly fire? Frag a sergeant?"

"I ate some shoes," Finn replied.

It hurt just to think about eating the shoes. Finn hoped he never saw another stray pair of shoes his whole miserable life.

"By accident," Finn added.

"Thought they were shoe bombs, eh?" the voice chuckled. "Or were they just your size?"

Finn could hold it back no longer. The bump on his Smart Bump had opened the floodgates, and now tiny pieces of Little White Tie dripped from his eyes. Finn was sure that if he could see his Little White Tie, it would be faded away to nothing.

"I ate the shoes," Finn explained, his words rushing together in a series of quick, short barks, "because I wanted to play basketball and I missed the Boy and he'd been gone a good long time, sir, and I don't remember everything in quite the right order because I don't, and maybe I don't because I just bumped my Smart Bump and the Big Uns, they were mad and—"

"The Big Uns?"

The voice was creaky, crusty, pitched somewhere between a southern drawl and a crusty New England accent.

Finn lowered his head carefully to see the source of the voice. Inside the aquarium, between a bowl filled with lettuce and another, larger bowl filled with water and poop, a bright green rock with oddly shaped panels shifted ever so slightly.

"Yes, the Big Uns," Finn responded, for he was nothing if not polite.

"Sir," Finn began, his leaky eyes forgotten momentarily, "are you a rock?"

"You could say that, Finn," the rock said proudly. "The rock this great country was built on!"

Finn kept his eyes on the rock. He swore the rock was moving back and forth!

"How do you know my name, Mr. Rock?" Finn asked.

The rock rocked a bit more, then waddled closer to the side of the aquarium and went POP!

A small, arrow-shaped head stuck out of the big green rock!

"It is I, Finn," the arrow-shaped head said. "It is I!"

"Mr. Turtle!" Finn shouted.

"Shhhh, soldier," Turtle said. "Lights out and all that."

The Little White Tie on Finn's chest burned with what Finn could only identify as HOPE. Mr. Turtle was exactly the sage Finn's situation needed! The Boy had told Finn, on more than one occasion, that some turtles lived to be a hundred years old. Finn couldn't count to one hundred, but the Boy seemed impressed by the number, so Finn was too. And the past being the past and all, Finn hoped Mr. Turtle understood that Finn hadn't meant to bother Mr. Turtle that morning two summers ago, but the tennis ball Finn had been chasing had taken an odd bounce, and Finn's noggin had followed its bounce into the side of the little aquarium. "Oooh, be careful of the Colonel, Finn," the Boy had said, lifting a green rock into the air. "You'll scare him!"

"Mr. Turtle, sir!" Finn whispered now.

"Colonel," Turtle corrected.

"It's me, Mr. Turtle," Finn said. "You were right the first time. It's Huckleberry Finn."

Mr. Turtle's head disappeared in a *whoosh*, then POPPED out again.

"Sorry," Turtle said, "had something on the burner. Now, where were we?"

"Well, you called me Colonel, sir, and I'd said—"

Turtle sputtered and spun in a circle—twice.

Finn sat back on his haunches. Mr. Turtle wasn't very fast. Two complete spins took about a half an hour (give or take ten or twenty minutes; Finn was terrible at time, as was mentioned earlier).

"You, Finn, were not decorated on the Fields of Backyard. I'm the only Colonel here."

"I'm sorry, Mr. Turtle, sir, I didn't mean—"

Turtle *humpfed* and sputtered and *humpfed* some more.

Boy, Finn thought, do I know how to put my paw in it!

"I do say, Finn, you know how to give a fellow a start," Turtle said in his strange southern-New-England accent once he'd calmed down.

Turtle stuck an odd-looking toe in the air.

"Back in a flash," Turtle said and *whoosh*: his little head was sucked back into his shell.

Finn scratched an itch.

Finn nibbled on a crumb lodged in the rug.

Finn fell asleep.

"Finn!" Turtle shouted, and Finn snapped to attention. Little wisps of smoke eked out from the neck of Turtle's shell.

"Sir," Finn said, "I think you're on fire."

Turtle waved his little hand and *pooh-poohed* the thought.

"Just a roast," Turtle said. "Left it in too long, son."

"You can cook in there?" Finn asked. (Finn's tongue involuntarily hung out of his mouth; Finn enjoyed a good piece of roast.)

There followed more sputtering on the part of Turtle.

"Of course, soldier. Full amenities. I'll own the damn thing in two years."

"Own...?"

Turtle ignored Finn.

"What brings you to these here parts?" Turtle asked, indicating his surroundings slowly (s-l-o-w-l-y) with his arrow-shaped head.

Finn cleared his throat. Asking was always the hardest part.

"Well...mister sir...I—"

"Colonel," Turtle suggested.

Finn was confused, but smiled politely.

"Thank you," Finn said.

"You're quite welcome, son," Turtle replied. "My shell is always open to you."

Finn wanted to ask how that was possible, but didn't.

"I had a question..."

"Ask away, my boy."

"...but now I have two questions."

The mood in the aquarium changed instantly.

"Oh, you think you'll get away with this?" Turtle asked. "They'll hunt you down for this, son. Hunt. You. Down. One does not *question* orders. One does not *question* the Supreme Commander. Ever."

Finn dropped his noggin to the floor. The Wold made him dizzy.

"Who is the Supreme Commander?" Finn asked, although he was too weary to really care. He'd never heard of a Supreme Commander before, and the identity wasn't one of his two questions. "Do you mean the Lord?"

Turtle's tiny tongue sprung from his pointy mouth then retreated.

"The Lord!?" Turtle screamed.

Finn's eyes were getting heavy.

"Yes, sir. Pig said—"

"PIG!" Turtle roared. "The traitor!"

"Pig said that if I read the Good Book, then I could go to heaven—not that I wanted to go. He just sort of told me all on his own."

"Pig," Turtle muttered.

"Cavy," Finn said.

"Ga-blesh-you, son," Turtle said.

Finn hasn't sneezed, but he thanked Turtle anyway.

"Mr. Turtle, sir…my questions?"

"Yes, yes," Turtle said. "You came for wisdom, and here I am dispensing tactical advice to a junior officer. You may approach the Colonel."

Finn looked around to see if the Colonel was talking to someone else. Mr. Turtle had closed his eyes—what sheer little lids he had!—and appeared to be murmuring in his sleep.

"Ask ask ask," Turtle murmured. "Ask."

"The first question is this," Finn said. "What happens when we die?"

Turtle spat and strutted (in a turtle-like fashion). Finn lowered his head to the floor again. He seemed to have a way of setting off his superiors.

"You listen, son, and you listen good," Turtle said. "To die in battle is glorious. To die in service to your country is the biggest sacrifice a citizen can make. To die in the Lord's name—"

"You said 'the Lord,'" Finn interrupted.

"Not *Pig's* Lord," Turtle snapped. "'The Blanket of the Lord!' *Pah*! God helps those who help themselves only. There is *not* room for everybody. That Pig's Blanket Theory doesn't hold water. You can't cling to the Blanket Theory. No one will save you, son, if you don't save yourself. Goddamn pinko Vicar."

"Actually Pig is white and brown and—"

"To die in battle is glorious—"

Finn interrupted: "You said that part already."

"Of course, of course." Turtle cleared his throat; he'd become quite phlegmy. "What happens when you die? That is the question."

"It's simple," Turtle said. "If you do the will of the state, why, you go to heaven, son."

That was pretty close to what Pig had told him, but Finn thought better of mentioning it.

"Heaven," Finn repeated.

"Do you kill baby turtles?" Turtle asked.

"I don't kill anything, sir," Finn said.

"Good, son, good. Killing turtles is *not* an activity that will get you into heaven. The Lord Our God says so."

"The Lord is *God?*" Finn asked.

Turtle stamped his little feet.

"God blesses our country. God gave us the land. God gave us the right to clear the land of all the what-have-yous squatting around in feathers and costumes. God, Finn, God."

"God," Finn repeated. "No killing baby turtles."

"Now you're talking, soldier!" Turtle shouted in a voice that sounded like it should have been accompanied by a slap on the back. "We kill only the enemy."

Talking with Turtle made Finn's noggin ache.

"Who is the enemy?"

"The enemy," Turtle responded, "is anybody who threatens our way of life. Attack and parry."

"Oh," Finn said, but other than Alley Cat, Finn didn't have any enemies, and Alley Cat wasn't a *real* enemy. One afternoon, during the previous summer, Finn had spied Alley Cat lounging in the sun within striking distance, but the sun was toasty, and Finn, trying to keep one eye peeled (in case Alley Cat tried anything sneaky), lounged the day away as well.

"What if I don't have any enemies?" Finn asked.

"Terrorists!" Turtle screamed. "What about terrorists?"

"Oh," Finn said again. There was no sense in pretending he knew what a terrorist was.

"And *suspected* terrorists. Got to wipe them out too," Turtle said. "And animals of the same genus as the terrorists. We can't be too careful. Unless they have something we want. Then we befriend them and attack them later. Or is it the other way around? I don't think it matters. Terrorism gives us the license to do whatever we want in order to protect the state. God will protect us, legally speaking."

Finn thought God must have as many faces as Turtle had accents.

"Violence is all the terrorists understand," Turtle explained, "and so violence is what we give them.

"In God's name, of course," Turtle hastily added.

Finn wasn't sure he wanted to meet this God any more than he wanted to meet Pig's Lord.

"I hope that answers your question, son," Turtle said. "Now, if you'll excuse me, I have a roast to baste, a war to plan, and a Vicar to kill."

Finn navigated his snout into the little aquarium. Finn hated being pushy, but he'd come such a long way. Turtle's head disappeared in a *poof!*

"*Hello,*" a mechanical voice said from inside Turtle's shell, "*the Colonel is not currently available to take your call. If you'd like to leave a message, please do so after the long beep.*"

"BEEEEEEEEEEEEEEEEEEEEEEEEEEEEEEEEEEEEEEEEE EEEEEEEEEEEP!"

Finn wedged his nose underneath Turtle and was about to flip the shell when it occurred to him that Turtle might not to be able to right himself again. Finn extracted his noggin and sat back down. He was not a very happy Labrador retriever. No one wanted to answer his questions.

Turtle peeked out of his shell and blinked twice.

"Did you know God spelled backwards is dog, son?" Turtle asked.

Finn sighed. "No, sir," he answered.

"You could be a god. War raises even the lowest among us. War raises us above the struggle of the common man."

"You can come out again," Finn said. "I'm not going to hurt you. I am sorry if I scared you."

POP!

"Scared, son? Hell, no. I've been in worse campaigns. I remember back in—"

"Excuse me, sir, but could I ask you my other question?"

Turtle smiled—or tried to; turtles don't really smile as much as grin.

"Answered your first query with precision, did I?" Turtle chortled. "Of course, my dear, dear Finn, ask away."

"Are my ears made of *SILK*?" Finn asked, tilting his head so Turtle could get a better view of his ears.

"Do *you* think they are?" Turtle responded. "Made of *SILK*?"

If Finn could have turned red, he would have. In truth, Finn was very intelligent (even if he did place more emphasis on sports than book-learning), but not very Woldly, despite having lived in two homes since he was taken from his Goner of a mother.

"I don't know what *SILK* is exactly, sir," Finn admitted.

"Exactly!" Turtle cried.

"Exactly?" Finn asked.

"Exactly!" Turtle said. "That's exactly what we're fighting for! Freedom! Exactly that. At least *our* freedom."

Finn's noggin throbbed.

"Can I trust you, soldier?" Turtle asked. "You're not with *him*, are you?"

"Who's *him*?"

Finn wondered what he was getting himself into.

"The Vicar Pig," Turtle said.

"No, we were just talking."

"Did you give Pig an envelope? An offering?"

Finn surely didn't and said so.

"Good, good. Fine, fine. Calm, cool, collected," Turtle said. "Here's the toughie, son. Did Pig touch you?"

Finn shook his head.

"Good touch *or* bad touch, soldier."

"No touch, sir," Finn said.

"Fine, fine. Good, good," Turtle said. "The Supreme Commander won't like me telling you this, but if something should happen to me (and let's just hope something doesn't), but if something should, if something did, then I want *you* to carry on with the directive.

"And if the Vicar Pig did touch you," Turtle added under his breath, "I want you to keep it a secret. Don't ask, don't tell."

Turtle's head *whooshed* back into his shell. Finn could hear clanking and clanging and unzipping and the sound of a motor idling, then shutting off.

"Keep your eyes peeled, soldier," Turtle said from inside the shell. "Cover me if necessary."

With a *creeeeeeak*, a tiny panel on the side of Turtle's shell opened, and a pale, skinny sliver of liver wearing Turtle's head stepped out. Finn drooled; he enjoyed a nice piece of liver when he could get it.

"I know. Don't say it. I've heard it a million times from the non-coms," the sliver of liver said. " 'How do you keep that body, Colonel?' Let's just say, a little bit of God and a whole lot of chemical assistance."

Finn's mouth hung open. The sliver of liver: it was Turtle!

"Go ahead, don't be afraid now, son. Take a look-see," Turtle offered, pointing to the open panel on his abandoned shell. "Snap to it, soldier!"

With a heaping helping of trepidation, Finn lowered his head into the little aquarium and peeked inside Turtle's shell—and what he saw, well, it's safe to say Finn had never seen a carapace like it before. (And while it's also true that Finn had *never* seen the inside of a carapace, the lack of experience took nothing away from his initial wonder and honest appraisal.)

"COOL!" Finn shouted. His bark echoed briefly inside the shell before being dulled by the thick carpets in what Turtle told him was the Sitting Room.

"Soundproofed," Turtle said. "Now, if you'll turn your head to the left, you'll see the Baby Grand and the Picasso above it. And over by the fireplace—just for show, mind you, son; no fires in the ol' plastron—that's an original there. Helmut gave it to me himself. The dining room table? Sixteenth century. Got the price tag to prove it. Elizabeth I ate her jams sitting right at this table. Never mind those magazines. Someone left 'em here. There—in the breakfront: Ming. The bar? The wood is from a nineteenth century pirate ship. Shores of Tripoli and all that. Bar's fully stocked, of course. Oh that? Something Versace and the boys whipped up for those rare nights out. Three-day pass, you understand. Wink, wink, nod, nod. Now the pool table has to be re-felted, but..."

Now of course, Finn saw none of these objects d'art, but that did little to affect how impressed he was. He wasn't quite sure, however, how long he could keep holding his head in such an uncomfortable position. He could only look inside Turtle's shell with one eye, and the only way he could get his noggin that low inside the aquarium was to lean against the glass. The pressure on his belly was making him gaseous. Any second now...

"...always cleaning. There's no end to it. Had to hire a fire-newt, some lieutenant's nephew. The more stuff you have, the more you want to protect—"

"*PFFFFFT!*" went Finn's heinie.

"INCOMING!" Turtle yelled and dove into his shell. Finn retracted his noggin and sat back, slightly embarrassed. He hadn't eaten since he had begun his Great Journey, but his gas still managed to somehow smell like week-old bologna. And despite knowing that it was quite silly, the smell made Finn hungry.

"Come in, soldier. Are you there? Over," Turtle said from inside his shell, making a crackling noise with his pointed mouth: *screeeeeek.*

"Distress signal! Distress signal! Over," Turtle said. "*Screeeeeek.*"

One of Turtle's stubby arms crept out and felt along the ground.

"How many wounded, son?"

Finn inspected his extremities.

"None, sir," Finn reported. "All intact here."

Turtle's head reappeared.

"That was close," Turtle said; he wore a tiny helmet on his arrow-shaped head. "This war is never ending."

"I didn't know we were having a war," Finn said. "Why won't it end?"

"Bad for business," Turtle said. "If we ended it, how would the military industrial complex and the weapons contractors make money? It's goddamn unpatriotic. These people have to eat. Buck up, soldier. We're in it for the long haul."

Finn loathed to bring the subject up after such a display of heinie activity, but...

"My questions, sir," Finn said in as quiet a voice as a Labrador retriever could muster.

"Are you dense, soldier?" Turtle asked. "I just demonstrated. I just deconstructed. I just declassified."

Finn thought his noggin was going to explode like his heinie had.

"Let me spell it out for you, son," Turtle said. "Get a number two pencil and have your den mother take notes. I'll dumb it down. I'll give you the Cliffs Notes version. The Classics Illustrated edition."

Finn shrugged.

"Three words for you, son. Three words. Ready?"

Finn nodded. He had to *PFFFFFT* again, but he held it in out of respect for Turtle.

"Protect. Your. Neck," Turtle said.

"Neck," Finn repeated, not wanting to mention that Turtle didn't appear to have done such a great job: when he'd been outside of his shell, the sliver of liver didn't seem to have a neck!

"The Other Party—the Simpers and the Wimpers—they talk about civil *rights* and the Bill of *Rights* and equal *rights*, but they're all Lefties!" Turtle declaimed. "They forget what makes us superior. They forget what makes us the mightiest and the proudest and the freest: *we have stuff!* Stuff makes us unique. Oh, sure, other countries have *some* stuff. But we have LOTS of stuff. Hell, we have stuff we don't even need, but if we have it, then nobody else can, and that makes us top dog—no offense meant."

Finn hadn't taken any.

"It's like this, soldier: paw prints, tracks in the snow, droppings," Turtle declared. "If you see a pile of little round poops and some scampering, hesitant tracks, you know the Vicar and his ilk were about. If you see a deep groove in the ground, then, why, that's a turtle! Fingerprints, soldier. They aren't just for clues anymore. They are what make us unique. That's our *stuff*, son. We're tied to our stuff; our stuff defines how free we are. Hence, freedom!"

"But aren't there Labrador retrievers and turtles and pigs and alley cats and goldfish in other countries?" Finn asked. "Wouldn't the fingerprints of a turtle from another country look similar to yours?" Finn was unaware of other countries, let alone Other Parties, but the Turtle's dissertation seemed to be in pieces—like a cookie after Finn executed the first chomp—rather than something whole and embraceable like Finn's basketball; Finn struggled to keep pace. But Finn believed himself to be an expert on fingerprints, having been read almost all of the Blue Books by the Boy. In the Blue Books, two other Boys, Hardy brothers, undertook quests like Finn's and solved difficult mysteries. Fingerprints were often involved; droppings were not.

"No! Haven't you been listening, Finn? Ours are superior because they're ours!" Turtle screamed. "We have stuff! The outside Wold? Bullies! The Other Party? Wimps!"

But Finn's mind had turned to his basketball. Where was his basketball? He swore he'd left it next to the sunspot on the rug, but the sunspot had moved to the wall, and Finn didn't see the basketball.

"Protect what's yours," Turtle continued. "That's it in a nutshell. Think our way, and you're one of us. Everything comes down to politics, son, and all politics are local. Your precious *SILK*? My precious shell? I'll tell you: the *SILK* is yours and the shell is mine. And that's it: freedom, soldier, freedom. Love it or leave it!"

"You just left your shell a few minutes ago," Finn said, but he was distracted. Where *was* his basketball?

"Ownership is freedom; consumerism is worship," Turtle said, distracted himself and making little sense.

Finn sniffed at the rug near the sliding glass door. The basketball had been *right* here…

"It doesn't matter," Turtle said. "With God at our backs—"

"I think someone stole my basketball," Finn said, slumping to the rug. First the Boy, then the basketball. Finn cried softly to himself.

"The Bullies!" Turtle yelled. "The Bullies stole your basketball!"

"The Bullies?" Finn asked.

"Look," Turtle said, pointing (as best he could) with his tiny stub of a hand. "The door to the Other Country is wide open!"

"The Other Country…?"

"Pa-ti-o," Turtle whispered. "Then the Fields of Backyard."

Finn sighed. He missed his bed and his Boy and the Boy's Blue Books.

"The time for subtlety is over!" Turtle stated. "Here—stick a paw right there on the edge of my shell. Flip me like a tiddlywink."

Finn did as instructed. Turtle went *FLIP!*

"Good job, soldier," Turtle said.

It was Turtle's voice Finn heard, but where was Turtle? Finn spun around.

"I can't see you, Colonel," Finn said. "Did you die, sir?"

"I am on your back," Turtle said. "Safety in numbers, son. Together we'll ride towards our destiny. Together we'll rescue the basketball from the Bullies and decimate their ranks once and for all. I'll be directing the campaign, of course, so I'll need a ham radio, a deck of cards, a couple of number two pencils…"

Finn turned and looked at his reflection in the aquarium. Turtle was indeed on his back. Although Turtle wasn't wearing a Colonel's hat or a helmet of any kind, Finn watched Turtle in the reflection adjust one nonetheless. The Colonel dug his feet into Finn's back like he was spurring a horse (which was annoying), but thoughts of the basketball kept Finn focused on the task at hand.

"Now is the time," Turtle said, "for heroes and for ghosts, for might for right, four score and seven years ago…"

Finn heard it first: *THWACK!*

"My basketball!" Finn cried, and indeed, once Turtle piped down, Finn was sure the Colonel could hear it too.

THWACK! THWACK! THWACK! THWACK!

Someone was dribbling Finn's basketball.

"Charge!" Turtle yelled.

"Basketball!" Finn barked. He leapt through the open sliding glass door and landed on the stone patio. To the right was a gate, to the left was a dead earthworm and beyond the patio: the Fields of Backyard. Finn galloped to the left.

"Tippecanoe and Tyler too!" Turtle cried.

And then: nothing. The backyard was empty. No *THWACKING*. No basketball.

"It's a setup," Turtle said; his beak was chattering. "It's an ambush. It's a doomsday scenario. Pull out your *New Catholic Picture Bibles*, men!"

One short whistle. One long. Another short.

"They're using code to call more troops," Turtle said. "We're outnumbered, out-manned, out-whistled—"

"Shhh," Finn said.

One short whistle. One long. Another short.

And there, perched atop the tall wooden fence surrounding the backyard, was a tiny, muscular steel and black tabby with emeralds for eyes and a tail that appeared to have its own agenda.

"Alley Cat," Finn said, nodding his head in greeting.

Turtle tried to burrow into Finn's fur.

"Huckleberry Finn, I presume," Alley Cat replied. "We meet again."

"Why don't come down from there," Finn suggested. He was anxious to recover his basketball.

"You know why," Alley Cat said. "If I come down, then you have a better chance of catching me."

"You're fast," Finn said. "Aren't you?"

"Don't throw me in that there briar patch, Brer Fox," Alley Cat said, imitating Finn's bark: rough on the outside, maple syrup on the inside.

"So, once again, we're at an impasse, you and I," Alley Cat said.

WHEEET WHEEET WHEEET WHEEET!

"That sounded like Pig," Finn whispered to Turtle, but Turtle had retreated into his shell and did not seem to be currently accepting any calls.

"A protester," Alley Cat said with a laugh, jerking his head towards the WHEETS.

"I want my basketball back," Finn said. "Did you take it?"

"And if I did?" Alley Cat hissed.

"The basketball's mine, Alley Cat, and I've had it forever. I came to the Big Uns' house with it. I could have even had it on the farm."

"Coulda," Alley Cat said.

"Shoulda," Alley Cat continued.

"And Woulda," Alley Cat concluded.

The fur on Finn's neck and back stood at attention. He bared his teeth and growled low in his throat.

"Is that a growth on your back?" Alley Cat asked.

"A growth?" Finn replied, trying to peek behind him. Was this a cat trick?

"Oh, you mean—"

"Keep it down, soldier," the Turtle's shell whispered.

"But I thought the time for subtlety was over," Finn whispered back.

"A tactical retreat is *not* subtle," Turtle's shell said. "We need reinforcements."

Finn blinked.

"What about the earthworm?" Turtle's shell suggested.

"He's already dead," Finn said.

"We could attack *him*," Turtle's shell said.

There was a loud rustling noise on the other side of the wooden fence.

"Oh my," Turtle's shell said.

"Sit!" Turtle's shell commanded, and Finn, who'd attended a number of obedience classes, descended into a sitting position. Turtle's shell slid slowly down his back.

"Obligations," Turtle said. The very tip of his beak protruded from his shell. "We're out of supplies."

Three more felines had lined up on top of the wooden fence on either side of Alley Cat. They were much larger than Alley Cat, but they seemed to treat Alley Cat with deference.

"Shoulda," Alley Cat said, pointing to his left. A fat tabby nodded his head in Finn's direction.

"Left the water on," Turtle muttered to himself, crawling back towards the open sliding glass door.

"Coulda and Woulda," Alley Cat concluded, gesturing towards his right. Coulda was an older Siamese wearing a black eye patch. Woulda—well, it was hard to see just what kind of feline Woulda was. Woulda was a huge ball of gray fur with a tail where his nose should be! A monster cat!

"Ass backwards," Alley Cat said, rolling his eyes.

Coulda nudged the gray monster. Woulda apologized and turned around in great haste, lowering a Lone Ranger mask over his face. Thankfully (to Finn), he had a rather normal face after all.

"I'm looking for my basketball," Finn said. "Have you seen it? Any of you?"

All four cats stood in unison and began strutting along the top of the wooden fence. They flicked the back of their necks with their claws like they were flipping up collars on leather jackets. All four cats began wiggling their toes, as if they were snapping their fingers, but their faux snapping made no sounds that Finn could hear.

"No opposable thumbs," Alley Cat said by way of explanation and shrugged.

"Are you a gang?" Finn asked.

"A bevy," Woulda said, and Coulda knocked him off the fence with a well-aimed swoop of his tail.

"Despite the fantastical notions and exertions of my *compadres*," Alley Cat said, "we prefer to call ourselves the Realists."

"The Realists," Finn said to himself. The word fit comfortably in his mouth—despite having originated from a cat.

"Jesus God," Turtle's shell said. "The Realists."

It was taking Turtle a long time to reach the sliding glass door.

Woulda climbed back to the top of the wooden fence and attempted to adjust the collar on his imaginary leather jacket. Woulda's head looked like it was surrounded by two black wings stolen from two different blackbirds.

"If you're going to join us, Huckleberry Finn," Alley Cat said, "then you'll need to become a Realist too. Or, if you prefer the Groucho method, we'll grant you membership without you actually joining. Realists, of course, know of the safety in numbers, but accept that each of us dies alone. The price of freedom."

Finn scratched himself. He hadn't been planning on joining any gangs, nor had he expected to be asked. But still—safety in numbers. Finn had to admit he didn't have a compass inside him to navigate the scary Wold outside the Big Uns' front door. All Finn had were his Little White Tie, which was pounding out a furious jungle beat, and his whiskers, which were twitching like mad.

"Are with us," Alley Cat asked, "or are you against us?"

Shoulda the fat tabby crept the length of the fence, all the way around, until he was behind Finn. Finn kept his eyes on Alley Cat. Coulda the Siamese followed Shoulda's path.

"What's it gonna be, Finn?" Alley Cat asked. "Are you ready to open your eyes, or do you prefer to trip around in darkness the rest of your life?"

Turtle popped his head out.

"Don't listen to him, soldier," Turtle hissed. "They're Realists! They see things *as they actually are*! They do things because they *like* them. They think heaven doesn't exist. They mix ketchup and mustard. They believe that if it looks green, then it probably is. They want to hold the government accountable for its actions. They believe that it matters more how you live your life than which deity you bow down to."

Shoulda and Coulda leapt from the fence and stood on either side of Turtle.

"They think Elvis was a good guy," Turtle said, "even when he was fat!"

Coulda raised his arms straight up in the air and ducked his head. Shoulda stepped backward a few paces and squinted his emerald eyes.

"They think the Constitution is stronger than any one person!" Turtle yelled to Finn.

Shoulda took a running start, and his left hind leg connected with Turtle, who was too far into his diatribe to retreat inside his shell in time.

"They eat French food!" Turtle said, as his head and stubby legs flapped in the air, easily clearing Coulda's raised-arm-goalposts. Shoulda took a victory lap. Coulda spiked an imaginary ball. Woulda jumped up and down, waving an imaginary pennant, before taking a header off the fence, and landing, snout first, in a pile of leaves.

"They believe love is all you need! They want to give peace a chance!" Turtle yelled as his shell sailed over the wooden fence. "They never buy lottery tickets! They will soil your *SILK*!"

And that was what Turtle said.

Chapter Ten

The Grandmother

The hand surely wasn't her own. It flapped, waved, belly flopped, and did a silly dance from the '50s, like something she'd seen on a jittery, old black and white program. Surely the hand undulating in the wind outside the car window was *not* her own.

Jerry Eves said little as the blue GTO tore up red dirt and disturbed gray pieces of slate on Dirt Road. Magdalene had lied and told him they could walk. Hell, she and Michael walked to the dock all the time. But Paradise Lakes was further north, a couple of miles maybe, and, besides, they might need a getaway car.

"A getaway car?"

"Don't worry about it," Magdalene said as she watched her hand shimmy and shake in the wind. "It's just in case."

"If something happens to my brother's car…"

"You can drop me off at the entrance as long as you promise to wait for me."

Jerry looked at her for a long time (which was slightly disturbing since they were flying up Dirt Road), then shook his head.

"Right, Tonto, right."

But her offer was sincere. This was her mission. She had "bullied" Jerry into stealing Mick's '68 GTO. She wasn't completely sure she was still a virgin. There hadn't been penetration by any appendages other than a finger or two, but she definitely felt different—not slutty and scummy, but no longer shiny and new either. Just different. She had used her womanly wiles (a slight smile almost blew past her teeth, but Magdalene concentrated on her hand, dancing in the *whoosh* outside of the passenger window) and beguiled Jerry into "borrowing" his big brother's car.

They'd left the Pep Boys parking lot (where they'd liberated Mick's Goat) and circled behind Assumption, past the Fields, empty on a breezy Saturday morning. The radio had said it would be humid in the afternoon, but the breeze carried scents of the ocean in its tail, as if promising an altogether different forecast.

Their getaway car skidded on a curve (Jerry wasn't a bad driver for a thirteen-year-old, but turns were taken at top speed), and

Magdalene pulled in her hand briefly to avoid the trees reaching for the car like crabby holdouts from *The Wizard of Oz*. As the GTO trundled over a crumbling stone bridge, Jerry pointed down to a clearing in Pennypack Woods.

"Little City," Jerry said, and Magdalene realized she might have to reward Jerry after all was said and done this afternoon. There was so little of her left to go around.

For all its torrid reputation, Little City didn't look so hot in the late morning. Carved out of an abandoned picnic area and surrounded by trees, the Mondauk make-out capitol was accessible, Magdalene could see, only by an even smaller dirt road that ran up a hill to join the one they were traveling on. Little City looked like a more extreme version of Finch's Landing: bottles—beer bottles most likely—trash, and even clothes were strewn everywhere. Condoms too, probably, although she couldn't see any. Magdalene hoped Jerry didn't have a condom in his wallet. She knew some of the high school kids carried them. Stevie Rich claimed to have used an entire box in one weekend, but Magdalene didn't know of any girls who dated the pimply behemoth. Maybe he'd raped them.

"Why is it called Little City?" she asked, knowing the answer already. This was a game.

Although the Joker surely lurked inside, the boyish cockiness in Jerry's voice (the cockiness most boys' voices had) had been replaced with confidence: the confidence of her father's courthouse voice or of Aunt Tiddy's quoting Shakespeare or of Michael's as he climbed the Dead Injun Tree.

Michael climbing the Dead Injun Tree?

" 'Cause at night, when you drive over the bridge," Jerry explained, "all the parking lights on the cars make it look like a little city."

"Have you…?"

Jerry laughed. "No, no, no. But Mick's taken me on beer blasts before in the Basin—though they usually happen in the Fields—and a couple of times we drank beer on the dock at Finch's Landing. One time, Mick and the boys were going to drive to the Lakes and fight some guys, but it didn't happen. I forget why."

Magdalene offered a wan smile to the side of his face. She was tired. Her eyelids pulled down on her forehead, and her eyes themselves were tight. She'd finished the final chapter of her book last night after beginning the notes to Mrs. Bochdan and her father—

and even though it was a book for children (and for Raven, who'd watched her leave this morning with a resigned look and a couple of exaggerated Labrador sighs), she'd wanted it to be perfect. If all her other plans failed, she'd at least have left the book behind. It had taken her most of the night. She'd slept intermittently, and it had been a sleep interrupted by nightmares of a literary bent.

In one, a nun was accusing her of plagiarism. The nun shook *A Lab's Ears Are Made of* SILK in front of Magdalene's face. "It's *The Wizard of Oz* all over again." As the nun spoke, her wimple became a pointy hat, and the nun's face morphed into Margaret Hamilton's, the Wicked Witch of the West, the lady from those old coffee commercials.

"But I wrote a new version," Magdalene said to Margaret Hamilton, but the nun was now the single-toothed, swollen-headed, purple Aunt Taminella from the ancient Muppet production of *The Frog Prince.*

"A better version?" asked the evil Muppet around a mouth of drool. "Trying to keep the story alive or just couldn't think of anything original?"

Magdalene tried to raise her arms to protect herself from all the spittle—then the witch Muppet was gone and Sister Rita was there, her face melting like peanut butter and jelly in the heat.

"Judas*ssss*! B*rrrr*utu*ssss*!" Sister Rita hissed. "Ba*rrrr*ely a *wwww*oman!"

"But I'm only thirteen," Magdalene protested. "I haven't even had my period yet!" And they encircled her, all of them: Sister Rita, Margaret Hamilton, Aunt Taminella.

"I never plagiarized!" Magdalene cried.

"Bowdlerized!" the creatures screamed. "Copycat! Derivative! Unoriginal!"

"You're not your brother," they shrieked. "It should have been you! It should have been you!"

"I *was* trying to keep the story alive," Magdalene admitted. Her voice had become a hush.

The circle was suffocating. The monsters pointed and howled at Magdalene until the circle broke, and a little nun with burnt clothes stepped into the center. Her wimple barely shaded the burns of her face.

"Like you kept Michael alive?" the diminutive nun asked, and the circle of creatures was gone. In their place were ancient sycamores, dripping mimosas, sad dogwoods. Magdalene could hear the sound of lapping water somewhere behind her, and there was a dirty, red condom at her bare feet.

Magdalene blushed, and something in her chest loosened. Everything was in there, waiting to come out. How she had made missing posters and stapled them to every telephone pole and bulletin board in town. How everyone had stopped looking for Michael. How she had never stopped. Of course she was trying to keep Michael's memory alive! Who the hell was this charred little nun to question her love for her brother?

"The bully?" the burnt nun asked.

"My brother!" Magdalene screamed.

"You kept Michael alive?"

Magdalene's teeth were about to pop from her jaw.

"YES, I FUCKING KEPT HIM ALIVE! NO ONE EVEN SAYS HIS *NAME*! THEY ALL STOPPED LOOKING! I *NEVER* STOPPED LOOKING!"

"That's not what I was asking," the burnt nun said, and she began to lift her face from the shadow of the wimple, and Magdalene wanted to avert her eyes, look away, but she could not, dared not.

"I was asking if you saved him," the burnt nun said. "I was asking if you saved Michael."

Magdalene tried to count—anything, everything.

"There's nothing left to count, Magdalene," the burnt nun said. "*Summe. Summa.* The final sum is one. The cheese stands alone."

In Mick's GTO, Jerry was still talking.

"I think it was because Mick and the boys were too drunk to find where the fight was supposed to take place. Somewhere near Finch's Landing, outside the Lakes, but still on their turf. I remember that, but off Dirt Road in case the cops came."

Magdalene pulled her hand in from its dance. Her fingers were covered in little red slices, like miniature versions of what she had tried to do to her wrists not so long ago. Magdalene pulled her bracelets in place over her scars.

"You don't have to hide them from me," Jerry said. "I don't care. I mean, I care, but I don't care that you tried what you tried. What you went through—if something happened to Mick or Brian or Pat, Christ, I'd go a little nuts too."

Magdalene offered a slight lift of the skin around her jaw; it was all she could manage. She thrust her hand out of the window again.

"I didn't mean 'nuts' like you were certifiable."

Magdalene shook her head. A large bug flew into her hand and died there.

"You gotta be crazy to like me, right?" Jerry asked. "A little, at least?"

When she'd woken up that morning, her bed was wet with sweat and the alarm clock had been blaring some inane approximation of nothing but a good time. The sun was already up; the house was quiet. At first Magdalene thought she'd overslept, but she wasn't due to meet Jerry in the Pep Boys parking lot for another hour. Still, she had to hurry. Raven nuzzled her leg with his nose and leapt from the bed. No wonder she was all sweaty! Raven had snuck into her bed! She must have been moaning in her sleep. The bedroom door was ajar, so there was a good chance Tiddy had checked on her if she'd heard Magdalene moaning. Magdalene made sure her book and letters were tucked away and accepted good morning licks from Raven; the dog's breath smelled like pepperoni.

The hallway was clear. She stared at herself in the bathroom mirror and splashed water on her face. She was still wearing the underwear she'd had on the night before, the underwear she'd let Jerry ease his long, freckled fingers into. Magdalene shucked them off and stuffed them into the bottom of the hamper, then thought better of it, and buried them at the bottom of the trash can. She hadn't looked for any stains or other telltale signs of illicit activities, but she didn't want to get Jerry in trouble after she killed herself Sunday night. Raven watched her from the bathroom doorway, smiling his eager Labby smile, patiently waiting for Magdalene to let him outside.

She thought for sure the rest of it would have come to her by now: the Puddle, the Dead Injun Tree, the Rules of the Dare, but she hadn't dreamed of Michael last night, just of witches, and as Magdalene opened the screen door to let Raven relieve himself in the backyard, she realized that she might never reach the end of the dream. The dream came in pieces and not always when she was sleeping. It had come when she was heavy petting with Jerry Eves in Mr. McAllister's Chevy. But her time was *tick-tocking* away, and only this morning, watching her doomed dog pee on Aunt Tiddy's African violets, did she realize she'd been watching the dream, taking notes, reading clues—*counting*—and waiting, like a damsel in distress, like a housewife glued to her daytime stories, like Jerry jumping out of his freckles to touch her skin.

It took Magdalene a few more minutes to realize Tiddy had already left. She checked outside. The Cadillac was gone, just an oil stain in the driveway. It was odd for the house to be so empty. ADA Barrows had probably broken camp at dawn. Damn, Magdalene thought, an empty house would be perfect for tomorrow evening, but fat chance Tiddy would make herself scarce on Sunday night. (Coach Barrows would be at Summer Camp.) Monday morning played a big part in the weekly cleaning; Tiddy wrote her lists on Sunday night. But Magdalene had to admit: just the thought of Tiddy driving that big ol' Cadillac was enough to give her the willies. About the only places the old woman ever drove were to the mall in Rhawnhurst or Bard's Meats in Spring House; she walked everywhere else: Sol's, the library, the shops on the Pike. And she rarely drove back to her stuffy apartment in Spring House, with its worn area rugs and frequently dusted, but never disturbed, breakfront china display. Tiddy drove in a stop-start fashion that precluded the presence of other vehicles; she ignored meridians and treated street signs as sudden, surprising commands. The roads of Mondauk County were being haunted by the Baby Blue Cadillac of Doom.

"You need me to clip Raven's nails?" Jerry Eves asked her, and Magdalene yanked her hand into the car again. Little tufts of red and brown from Dirt Road mixed with tiny sharp stones to attack the GTO.

"Hope this stuff doesn't scratch Mick's car." Jerry said, but Magdalene was thinking about her great-grandfather's pocket watch.

Magdalene's mother loved to laugh, and the backward clock in the kitchen, the one where the numbers circled the face counterclockwise so that three was where nine should be and vice versa, was just one of the little things Patricia Archer Rumsey Barrows collected that could make her face explode into a fireworks display of dimples and white teeth. The funniest part of the clock was that time was irrelevant to their mother; she ran in the extremes, either embarrassingly late or hours early for appointments, parties, and movies. Magdalene recalled seeing her mother sitting on the curb outside Assumption reading a book when Magdalene was in the second grade, waiting to walk her children home. Magdalene's heart had pushed against its cage until she looked at the clock: it wasn't even eleven in the a.m. Their mother never understood time.

Patricia Barrows hadn't known how little time she had left either. Perhaps if she had, Magdalene had thought more than once, she would have rescheduled the doctor appointments she'd missed because she'd shown up either hours late or sometimes even a full day ahead. The clocks in the Barrows Bungalow were in complete agreement with Magdalene's mother: the funny clock in the kitchen was a full hour and a half off. The alarm clock in her parents' bedroom was set seventeen minutes ahead (seventeen minutes her father could never get used to). The little gold clock on the end table in the living room was roughly two hours and twenty-one minutes behind. The VCR flashed 12:00 twenty-four hours a day. Their mother could glance at one of the clocks and know the exact time— or so she claimed. (They all claimed this ability for her.) Rather than set the clocks, the Barrows family lived their lives around the broken minutes and shattered hours. The only reliable timepiece in close proximity was Tiddy's father's pocket watch.

After Magdalene's mother passed away, the Assistant District Attorney made an executive decision and eliminated all the clocks— except the backward clock in the kitchen. It was as if he didn't want to discover which of the clocks had been right, which of the clocks had indicated how little time had remained for Patricia Barrows.

Tiddy had little time for silly clocks or clocks with the wrong time. Her father, Jonathan Wheelwright, had been a watchmaker, and Tiddy found time far too precious to leave to the random markers of the Barrows Bungalow. If Tiddy were underfoot, Magdalene and Michael were on time for every appointment. Tiddy carried her father's pocket watch everywhere. The watch was silver and plain, as if anything more ornate would take way from the mechanism's basic function: the trapping of time. But Tiddy, like the rest of the Barrows family, fell victim to her own interpretation of time. The old woman would pull the pocket watch out of her apron or house dress, then *tsk-tsk* and shake her head before stuffing it away.

"It's losing time," Aunt Tiddy would say.

Rather than have the watch repaired (she considered the local watchmakers too young and clumsy), Tiddy lamented the passing of the time she felt the watch indicated she had missed.

"We're all losing time," was all Tiddy would say on the subject.

The Goat turned a corner and its wheels spun out just enough for the car to give birth to a wave of dirt and pebbles.

"Shit balls," Jerry Eves said.

They were losing time. It was only morning, and they were already losing time.

Magdalene stuck her head out of the window, and as the dust cloud dissipated and Jerry switched gears, Magdalene saw the GTO's tire tracks etched in the dirt, waiting to be erased by a breeze or an animal or another car speeding its way to Finch's Landing or Paradise Lakes or beyond. "The Case of the Shabby Shoes" (the third chapter of *The Hardy Boys Detective Handbook*) had a guide on how to make plaster casts. The tracks the GTO left on Dirt Road would make handy casts if they were driving anywhere else but on Dirt Road. Here, red and gray dust would devour their tracks and cover their trail; here, on Dirt Road, the smell of the Puddle strong in their nostrils, memories were momentary, and everything was ephemeral.

Jerry fiddled with the radio. ("Remember what station it was on, okay?" Jerry asked her, "Mick'll know for sure if we don't." Magdalene nodded her head without looking at the radio dial). And there she was, in all her new found celebrity: *Christina Fuller...Missing...If You Have Any Information, Please Call or E-Mail...Parents Holding Press Conference Later Today...Reward...Please, Please, Please.*

Magdalene wanted to throw up.

"I know you shut down my theory before on the basis of math, but maybe it was a serial *bully*. Someone who thinks of people as human " Jerry Eves said after losing the Christina Fuller Radio Report and discovering "Start Me Up."

Magdalene straightened her spine and grabbed Jerry's right arm. The car swerved before Jerry gained control.

"What the heck?"

She hadn't meant to do that, but it was startling to hear a couple of her stray thoughts coalesce in someone else's mouth. It was true: she'd previously blown off Jerry's Hannibal the Cannibal hypothesis, but who defined Irrational Opposition better than the Zodiac Killer, the Night Stalker, or the Son of Sam, bullies all.

"You said—"

"Serial bully. Christina. You can't rule out that a serial something-or-other might have gotten to her. Seems like there's a lot of strange stuff going on this town."

Magdalene stared at his profile.

"Jerry, do you know what the standard profile of a serial killer is?" she asked.

"I know the story of Count Chocula and Franken Berry."

Magdalene punched his arm.

"Back off bully," Jerry said, grinning. His freckles rose and fell like little stars.

Bully, Magdalene thought. Hard to shake that sobriquet.

"*You make a grown man cryyyy,*" Mick Jagger sang.

"No more cereal jokes, I promise."

"They were jokes, huh?"

Jerry sighed and launched into a monotone: "A serial killer is someone who kills over and over. A serial killer doesn't kill for revenge or for love or anything like that. He kills because he likes it. Most serial killers are white males and were abused when they were kids, and they killed animals—pets and whatnot—before moving on to their first human victims. Whether they were born this way or made this way doesn't matter: they're still bullies."

Magdalene nodded her head. Jerry was on fire today: stealing a car, driving a stick, criminal behavior analysis. If she wasn't planning on dying, she'd marry him!

"How'd I do, Teach?"

"Where'd you learn all this stuff?" Magdalene asked.

Jerry smiled. "Would you believe me if I said the public library?"

"The people he kills—assuming it's a he—aren't even people to him," Magdalene said. "They're just...momentary. Human bayonet dummies, like you said. He needs them, but they're disposable. Only the act is important."

Just like bullying, she thought. Jerry was right.

"You go to the library too?"

Magdalene didn't answer.

"I heard through the grapevine that Christina had sex with Joseph Connelly," Jerry said.

"I don't believe it," Magdalene lied. "Did you ask him?"

"Joe? Heck, no."

"He's your best friend."

"I mean, I like him and all," Jerry said. "I just—"

"If you asked him, then he'd ask you," Magdalene surmised.

"Something like that."

Jerry kept his eyes focused on Dirt Road. Dead bugs were piling up on the windshield.

"So lie."

"He'd want names," Jerry said.

"Oh."

"I'd have to tell him a name. Then that girl would...you know."

"She'd get bullied and be branded a whore."

"Well, maybe," Jerry said, "but I'd be acting like a bully if I made something up."

"You haven't...before..."

"No. Just what we...no."

"Well, she's gone," Magdalene said, returning to the missing. "Christina's gone. And the whole fucking town is looking for her."

"Whole *fucking* town? Young lady!"

Magdalene ignored him: "Christina the Astonishing. Wonder if she'll be at the carnival. *Either* carnival."

"Nobody disappears into thin air, Tonto."

The GTO followed the road around a bend to the left, and visible just ahead, through a thicket of trees, was a flock of television antennas. Magdalene jerked around in her seat; they had passed the dock without her realizing it, and her stomach gnawed at itself; numbers flew through her head. She hadn't dreamed of Michael last night, and now she'd passed the dock and the Dead Injun Tree without so much as blinking.

The GTO took one more slight turn, this time to the right, completing a giant S, and the front gate of Paradise Lakes (such as it was; the gate appeared to have been removed long ago, leaving two rusted poles) loomed ahead amid an explosion of waist-high weeds.

"Momentary lives," Magdalene whispered, and Jerry nodded his head, tightening his grip on the steering wheel. Something exploded to the left of the GTO, and Magdalene jumped in her seat.

"*You make a dead man come*," Mick Jagger sang.

"Schlitz," Jerry Eves said. "Someone dropped a can of Schlitz. I ran over a can of shitty beer."

+

If astronomy was the ancient art of detecting, the first serious connecting of the dots (and Magdalene considered it so), rooted in a primal need for order and origin, then Paradise Lakes Trailer Park was a prime example of absolute chaos: this was the bottom, where, failing to fit or cling or adhere, failing to accept their own inherent yearning for the stars, the ephemera, the unclaimed flotsam and jetsam, gathered in clumps of convenience, ignorant (or so Magdalene guessed) of how they had gotten here and (Magdalene assumed) uninterested in how to escape. The trailer park was the endgame for shooting stars whose limp trajectory began not with a big bang but with a misfire: the pull of a beer tab, the hiss of a Doral extinguished in a stained toilet bowl, the insouciant shrug when a Trojan broke.

Magdalene hoped that if Jerry did have a condom in his wallet, that it was of recent vintage. (Christina Fuller had told her an old condom could develop tiny pinprick-sized holes.) She might have to let him use it. But what the hell—no one would know. She'd be nothing but a whisper on the lips of the Mondauk wags by Monday morning.

They drove through the front gate in silence. Other than their time together in the backseat of Mr. McAllister's car, Magdalene had never seen Jerry Eves with nothing to say. She almost said something just to break the spell.

Almost.

The road, more pebbles and red dirt, littered with candy wrappers and garbage and glittery astronomical facsimiles fashioned entirely from broken beer bottles, narrowed as they entered Paradise Lakes and never entirely widened enough for two cars to pass one another comfortably. Despite this, cars were parked on both sides of the road at random points, so that Jerry steered the GTO in a shaky figure eight pattern.

They passed a tiny side road, but Jerry shook his head and continued to pilot the car down the main road until they reached a fork. Jerry bore to the left. His fingers gripped the wheel so tightly, Magdalene wouldn't have been surprised if his knuckles popped off.

The first kid—dirty blonde hair, Nike t-shirt two sizes too big—darted between a Rabbit and a red pickup truck. Jerry slammed on the brakes, covering the GTO in a cloud of red dust. From just outside the cloud, they watched the tyke flip them the bird before disappearing behind the overgrown weeds surrounding a wide, graffiti-covered pump. Before the dust settled, two more kids ran in front of the GTO. One of them threw a fistful of—*something*—that splashed on Jerry's window. Jerry didn't flinch, but Magdalene noticed that the color seemed to vacate his freckles.

The first few kids had been like warning shots. Soon the cars parked—or abandoned—along the road (now dotted with trailers on the right and left) were festooned with the youth of the Lakes. Magdalene stared out of the dirty car windows. Here were the true ghosts of Mondauk County. Yes, Mrs. Bochdan, the widow Tidwell, even scary, old Mr. McAllister were ghosts—Magdalene's father too, at least for a few years there and soon to be again. Not dead, but barely breathing, the ghosts of Magdalene's Mondauk were the very definition of living dead, every breath, every thought and movement predicated upon missing an essential part of themselves, whether it be spouse or child. The ghosts of Magdalene's Mondauk Proper were wraiths, poor, flimsy copies of their former selves; they hadn't intended to become ghosts. But here in Paradise Lakes, being a ghost was part and parcel of living. Here, Magdalene thought, she and Jerry stood out, for they had not yet given themselves over to the world of the dead.

Well, maybe Jerry hadn't.

Magdalene examined her face in the rearview mirror. How far had she to fall before she reached the standard of living (purely in terms of existence regardless of economic factoring) evident in the eyes of the Lakes' finest? Magdalene looked for her face in the frame of limp, black hair. When had her eyes become saucers? She looked like a pencil drawing of a scared, little boy in a children's book.

"I have to pull over," Jerry said, for the road had narrowed considerably. The kids leaning against the beat-up, parked cars (or sitting on them, some standing on them even, others sitting inside, all of them smoking) were older—older than the kids dodging the GTO a few yards back. Jerry pulled to a spot on the right side of the road alongside an ancient Gremlin hatchback facing the opposite direction, and the ghosts surrounded the Goat.

And what beautiful ghosts! The boys' arms were skinny, but muscular in their cutoff concert t-shirts—t-shirts surely belonging to their parents (or parental guardians); Magdalene doubted any of these kids had witnessed concerts by Peter Frampton or Heart or Def Leppard. (She silently thanked Michael for enrolling her, frequently against her will, in the school of rock, for though it meant little, very little, in the real world, it gave her a point of reference, some place where a possible dialogue with the ghosts could be established.) The girls were the true paragons of otherworldliness though: their bodies vacillate between mathematical boniness and wanton fleshiness, with stomachs sloping from half-shirts over button flies. The ones blessed with breasts showed them off; their nipples pushed against the thin fabric of their shirts. Makeup was *de rigueur* and applied like camouflage paint, all heavy eye shadow and dark eyeliner. Stained yellow teeth snapped gum between waves of blood red lipstick.

Magdalene couldn't take her eyes off of them. She counted their nipples.

"Now what?" Jerry had reached over Magdalene to push down her lock and now sat staring straight ahead.

Magdalene had seen a few of the Lakes kids before at Assumption (most of the Paradise Lakes population were Methodists), but the navy blue uniforms rendered cliques as disparate as the Bod Squaders and the ghost girls into (as Donna Gaynor had put it) one giant ball of Jesus Sluts. (Donna's family had moved from the Lakes when she was little, granting her a cachet of coolness the other Catholic girls alluded to only in their less than judicious use of language and carefully practiced makeup strokes.) Thus, even the kids who trudged to Assumption from the Lakes didn't look all that different from everyone else during the school year. And with Christina and Megan and the rest of the Bod Squad dressing, at times, as if *they* were from the Lakes, it made little difference—except the Lakes kids were poor and Methodist and *belonged* only when the ruling cliques desired illicit thrills only the ghost children could provide (most involving getting high).

The difference in person was plainly obvious. The Bod Squad dressed up as the Lakes girls, copying their fashion styles and garish makeup, like it was Halloween. Here, the costume was uniform and worn with pride. But it was their eyes—eyes not all that different from the ones that had peered out at Magdalene from the rearview mirror—that truly set them a race apart. Their eyes stared out of concave trenches (made more obscure by their extreme makeup, but quite a few of the boys sported black eyes of their own), glassy-eyed but self-aware. If the kids' casualness evidenced a practiced (and maybe, Magdalene thought, a learned) laziness, their eyes betrayed them, for even as they appeared quite stoned or drunk or some wicked combination of both, a not-so-latent wariness kept them from wallowing in complete somnolence.

The silent movie star stood in the middle of the group; she seemed to be in thrall to an orbit all her own. She looked like someone Magdalene swore she'd seen a million times before, but it wasn't until the girl slouched against the car, her raccoon eyes looking into hers, that Magdalene remembered: the girl in the turquoise shorts she'd seen in the Basin! With the exception of those Magdalene labeled Goners without hesitation, the other kids lounging in, around, and on the Gremlin carried their jungle senses on their sleeves beneath a gauze of pharmaceuticals and Schlitz. But this girl's heavy eyelids were part of her character; although she may have been under the influence of one or all of the available party substances, her *awareness* of her state was obvious. Magdalene thought the girl looked like she'd been stolen from Tiddy's blurry Polaroids of her grandniece or torn from an old movie poster, all eye gestures and projected vanity: *I know I'm fucked up, but you have to look at me.* The silent movie star. The girl's clothes were a mismatched ensemble of designer sneakers, what Magdalene was sure were hand-me-down cutoff jeans, and an extremely tight, faded purple t-shirt commemorating a long ago musical event. Her eyes were encircled with black lines so deep, yet so faded, they looked like old tattoos. And there was what looked to Magdalene like a real tattoo just under the girl's left eye: a teardrop, too full and fat to be a freckle.

The silent movie star never broke eye contact.

Magdalene glanced down at herself to make sure she wasn't naked.

"Why are you counting?" Jerry asked.

"I wasn't."

"There's thirteen of them," Jerry said, "which is roughly twelve too many, if you ask me."

The crowd of stoned vampires squirmed around the abandoned, yellow wreck. ("A goddamn Gremlin," Jerry muttered to himself.) A few of the larger kids huddled against its passenger side door.

"If they touch Mick's car..."

The silent movie star was gone, swallowed by the mob.

Without turning his head, Jerry's right hand drifted below his knees, and returned with what looked to Magdalene like a mini-baseball bat swathed in black electrician's tape. He stuck it behind his back.

"Better safe than sorry," Jerry said, the words easing out of the side of his mouth, a detective in an old film noir. Magdalene realized how gray the Lakes were: even the yellow of the Gremlin, the faded purple of the silent movie star's too-tight t-shirt, and the stunning crimson of the bloodshot eyes of the bevy of boys gesturing towards the GTO were facsimiles, like flashbulb traces behind closed eyelids.

"Here goes nothing, Tonto," Jerry said, and for a brief second Magdalene thought he was going to lunge out of the GTO and beat the answers out of the ghosts. "Don't get out of the car."

Instead, Jerry leaned his sunny face out of the window.

"Hey, what's goin' on?" Jerry asked. "We're looking for Stevie Rich."

"Who's lookin' for him?" asked a kid in a glittery Styx t-shirt, tossing his cigarette to the ground. "Is there a beef?"

Silly boys, Magdalene thought, always playing at something, never knowing the difference between a true calling and copycatting. She'd heard innumerable times that girls mature faster than boys, and although her nubby breasts refuted this theory, at least biologically, she couldn't help thinking that perhaps the truth was this: boys tended to act in the opposite manner of whatever a situation called for by simply (unknowingly) parodying appropriate behavior; the harder boys tried to maintain a respectful silence during Mass, the more violently their shoulders shook. Girls (especially the Bod Squad) knew they were playacting, dressing up or dressing down; it was a dangerous game, but a game to the Bod Squaders nonetheless. These ghost boys weren't playing a game despite the gangster dialogue. Jerry was precariously balanced on the fine line between assaying a role and committing to one. Magdalene could sense that the boys leaning on the Gremlin were anxious to cross that line.

To Magdalene's relief, Jerry retreated into his classroom shtick: he wiggled his ears.

"Nope, no beef, guys," Jerry said. "Hey, where's the beef, right?"

The huddled Lakes boys looked confused.

"You gettin' wise?" another kid asked, comically punching a fist into his open palm. Magdalene should have gotten out of the car and asked the silent movie star, but she knew it was too late for that. Jerry had eased the car back into drive.

"No, man, no," Jerry said. "We're looking for Stevie Rich. We go to school with him, and we're just seeing what he was doing today. Told us he lived here in the Lakes somewhere."

"What, you're gonna play basketball with him?" snickered the palm puncher, and Magdalene hoped that if the ghost kids did lead them to Stevie Rich, that they (she) could confront him without an audience of bored, violent boys. Jerry had already escaped Mr. McAllister; Magdalene didn't want him to have to fight his way of the Lakes.

"Nah, just hang out, whatever, no big deal," Jerry said. "Maybe take a spin in the Goat."

"Ain't that Mick's car?" an older kid asked. He was stretched across the trunk of the Gremlin, his head resting on the curve where the rear window met the roof. His eyes were obscured by greasy bangs, but Magdalene felt that both the grease and the carelessness were less than casual. This kid wasn't a kid anymore; he looked to be in his early 20s but trying hard to cling to his miscreant youth. He had a pencil-thin moustache.

Jerry's ears reddened. "Yeah, yeah," he said, squeezing a laugh between the *yeahs*. "He's willing it to me. Figured we'd cruise around today, get used to how she runs."

"I could be up for that," the older kid said, and there was the silent movie star: dangling a hand above the older kid's waist, a cigarette—one of those long, skinny, all white cigarettes; even the filter was white—balanced between her skinny fingers. Magdalene caught a glimpse of the teardrop tattoo for a heartbeat, and then the shifting boys swallowed the silent movie star again.

Jerry half-turned to Magdalene as if to ask how the hell would they get out of cruising around with the ghost kids of Paradise Lakes, but the mangy circle suddenly dissipated, and the topic seemed dropped. The older kid began nodding his head to an invisible kick drum.

In the distance, a police siren announced the discovery a new crime. It would soon be afternoon. Dandelion wishes crowded the air where the crowd had parted, and an extremely large, feral boy shambled towards the car. (*Two, four, six, eight, who do we appreciate?*— concentrate!) He wore a dusty black trench coat despite the early summer heat. Jerry popped the door, shoving the blackjack into the back of his jeans.

The feral boy came to a halt and fell into a slouch. Even his face went slack as he sucked on a cigarette (all of the ghost kids smoked), and the ember was like Sirius, the jewel of the dog's collar. *Canis Major*? Or was he *Beta Canis Majoris*, simply the announcer?

And they all played games at the ladybugs' picnic.

Or maybe he was Sirius B, the Pup. The white dwarf. So dense, one book said, a tablespoon of its own matter would weigh twice as much as the earth. Once powerful and majestic, now so much sputter and window streaks. *One, two, three, four. Yellow dwarf, red giant, white dwarf*, then—*black dwarf*. Sputter and die.

The feral boy's slouch was a mashed potato mirage: one minute thick and full, the next drowning in gravy. Magdalene was familiar with this kind of drowning. The feral boy's Budweiser breath battled the sour wind of the Lakes. Maybe the trailer park's stench came from the town's runoff pipes or from corroded septic tanks. Or maybe it was just the accumulation of *years* of once-feral boys and washed-out girls exuding the contents of their bloodstreams into the frothy muck of the Puddle.

The feral boy's bloated face squinted at Jerry, and his left arm took a slow motion route to his mouth, so his yellow fingers could loosen the dangling cigarette from his chapped lips. Some of the white pus clinging to his lips came away with the cigarette.

"I know you, man," the feral boy said.

Jerry's right hand felt blindly behind his back for the blackjack.

"You never know, man, right? Can you ever really know someone?" Jerry grinned. "You guys gotta beer for me?"

The feral boy spit in the general direction of the GTO.

"Out, man. Could get you some bud, but it'd cost ya."

Jerry turned his head and winked at Magdalene.

"Too early for that, man," Jerry said. "I'll be nodding off in my toast and jam." An easy laugh tumbled from his mouth and died— *one, two, three, four: yellow dwarf, red giant, white dwarf, black dwarf.*

And they all played games at the ladybugs' picnic.

"Never too early for weed," the feral boy said. "Ya pussy or what?"

Jerry ignored the boy's mumbled taunt. Magdalene twitched in her seat. They were losing time. She'd watched the stoners in the playground near Sol's before; navigating the monkey bars took them half an hour.

The feral boy's bloated skin shifted so his crooked, yellow teeth were revealed and words tripped past the pus on his lips. "...he'll have some or his stepdad will. Frannie's always holdin'. Cost ya though. You got that kind of dough on you now?" He gestured to the ghost boys lurking behind him who seemed to close in.

"Hell no!" Jerry laughed. "I'm as a broke as a priest's dick."

Whatever spark had temporarily lit the feral boy's face expired (*yellow, red, white, black*) and the ghost boys shrank back. He turned his eyes to the red dirt and tossed his cigarette; his lips puckered as if he'd just popped a lemon drop.

"Keep goin' that way." With huge effort, the feral boy pointed north, then dug around in his back pockets. "In the same lot as his grandmother's trailer, that big ol' silver thing."

The feral boy brought out a pacifier and popped it into his infected mouth.

"John-John?" Jerry asked. Magdalene placed her hand on Jerry's shoulder blade as he backed into the driver's seat and gently shut the door. "You look like shit, man."

"Yeah?" John-John Hagarty asked, then blinked and stared back up the road. "It's really Frannie Tidwell's grandmother, so I guess it's Stevie's great-grandmother." He spit again. "I don't fuckin' know, man. He'll hook you up, though, Frannie will. I won't buy my crystal from nobody but Frannie."

Jerry choked (Magdalene thought it was supposed to be a laugh) and said, "Yeah, I know what you mean. Thanks, man," as he eased the car into gear and pulled away from the ghost kids returning to the Gremlin. A few feet up, the road widened, and Jerry jerked the car to the left, then yanked it into reverse and turned around.

"Jerry!" Magdalene yelled.

"Stevie Rich's father is Frannie Five Fingers Tidwell? No way, Magdalene. No way. Did you see John-John? If it weren't for Mick being my brother...we're history; we're outta here."

The tires spun in the dirt.

John-John Hagarty was still standing where they had left him, staring up the road as Jerry navigated the parked cars at an alarming speed. Jerry's teeth were visible. He stared straight ahead as the GTO skidded to swerve past the Gremlin.

"Watch out!" Magdalene screamed.

The GTO passed within an inch or two of John-John. The feral, pudgy boy never blinked. He just sucked on his pacifier, his eyes still squinting north, as if seeking out the crystal meth currently in the possession of Frannie Tidwell.

The silent movie star, her eyes twinkling from the bottom of two long abandoned wells, was stretched on the trunk of the Gremlin next to the older boy with the pencil-thin moustache, who appeared to have his hand down her cutoff jeans. The girl's eyes were laconic despite their brilliance, blinking in slow motion; they were like two sponges, and Magdalene was soaked into their stare, which was neither scornful nor haughty nor hateful nor needy. These were the eyes of someone watching, Magdalene thought, always watching, but never daring to truly participate—other than to take a swig or a snort. The parade had passed the silent movie star by, and still she watched for it, unmoved by its pageantry or cheekiness. Her eyes were open, but everything the girl saw was already old. Her past—like Magdalene's—had become fugue-like and unavoidable. But the silent movie star had chosen to ignore it by staring straight into it. Either the summarizing was too chilling or the girl had long ago ceased to be moved by the accumulation of events that had led to copious amounts of pharmaceuticals and beer and her being felt-up on the trunk of an abandoned Gremlin.

Magdalene lifted her hand in a wave; Jerry grabbed her fingers and deposited them in her lap. Never daring to participate, Magdalene thought, except that once—Magdalene had heard the words (or words just like them) a million times in the playground: "Want a taste?"—and Magdalene imagined the silent movie star's eyes hypnotized by the older boy's or the playground pusher's or the horny stoner's. (Magdalene had never quite figured the appropriate application for "horny" before parking with Jerry Eves, and knowing now what boys were capable of, even a good boy like Jerry, and how sticky everything, literally *everything*, had become, she was struck by how inappropriate a word it was—hard, callous.) The silent movie star's fingers were yellowed by nicotine; her nails were improbably long and painted alabaster, perhaps manicured at the Korean nail salon where all the female employees wore surgical masks and where Tiddy had said all the white trash went for such services. Who had this girl been before putting on her costume (if the Bod Squaders only knew!), before taking her first swig of Hawaiian Punch and gin, or her first pull on a smoldering joint, or naïvely accepting her first fistful of little M&M colored pills? Who had she wanted to be before the first time had become a lifetime, and the lifetime had thus far been squeezed between an elementary school education and a future turning tricks in the city? (The girl couldn't be much older than Magdalene.) As Jerry gunned for the front gate of the Lakes, Magdalene squirmed around in her seat to watch the silent movie star exhale her cigarette smoke, one hand in the lap of the older boy, their heads leaning on the roof of the car.

The parade had passed her by.

"Jesus Christ," Jerry said, "did you see John-John's face? It's like he was burnt out. I didn't even recognize him." He steered the car east, back towards Bethlehem Pike.

Magdalene contemplated jumping out of the car, but the thought passed. Jerry gunned the engine. The grand scheme, the plan: blown to bits, shot to hell, squashed like a bug on the Goat's filthy windshield.

And they all played games at the ladybugs' picnic.

The telephone poles and outlet stores on the Pike went by in a blur, but if Magdalene concentrated, she could see carnival fliers on almost every utility pole. The 35th Feast of the Baptist Carnival was what the Catholic fliers proclaimed. Rides! Games! Face Painting! Funnel Cake! The Calvary Methodist fliers were more austere, of course; most weren't even on colored paper. The Catholics liked their holidays. In Mondauk, the summer was marked by three religious holidays (observed, Aunt Tiddy had said, to milk the populace during the dry season between Easter and Christmas): the Feast of the Baptist, the Feast of the Magdala (in July), and the spaghetti dinner held to commemorate the Feast of the Assumption in the dog days of August. The Feast of the Baptist Carnival was the best of the three. School had just ended; even parents were excited at the prospects of summer. The Feast of the Magdala, celebrating Magdalene's namesake saint was an almost secular affair—especially bizarre considering Mondauk Proper had its own martyr in Sister Mary Magdalene de Rosa.

But then Saint Mary Magdalene had always gotten the shaft, Magdalene thought, despite being the first to see the risen Jesus (according to the Gospel of John). But almost anytime the saint's name came up, it was usually in connection with prostitution, a rumor begun by Pope Gregory I in 591, who'd merged Mary Magdalene with Mary of Bethany and the sinful woman in Luke who anointed Jesus' feet with her tears. (Pope Gregory seemed especially fixated on the line in Luke where she is described as having been possessed by seven demons before they were exorcised by Jesus.) Sister Fatima had said that the Church reversed themselves officially in the late '60s, freeing the saint from her reputation as the Holy Harlot, but Magdalene felt the damage had been done. She'd endured more jests and jibes than she'd care to count for simply sharing the saint's name. In France, where according to legend Mary had fled after leaving Jerusalem, Mary Magdalene was revered; here she was a hippie hooker. In Spain, boys on stilts danced with her picture. In Florence, they ran a race on her feast day. In England, she was the patron saint of lepers. Here, Sister Rita, possible leper, referred to the saint as the Fallen Woman, which always reminded Magdalene of the old chestnut about the college student who wrote in an essay, "The girl tumbled down the stairs and lay prostitute at the bottom," and the professor who responded in the margin, "My dear sir, you must learn to distinguish between a fallen woman and one who has merely slipped."

They prayed to Mary Magdalene's relics in an abbey in Burgundy; they built a basilica in St. Maximin in Provence in her honor. Her body, thought by most Catholics to be a vessel of sin before her redemption, was venerated in Europe. Tradition held that after fleeing the Holy Land, Mary Magdalene died in a cave on a hill in Marseille, and angels carried her body to her resting place in a grotto founded by St. Maximin. Her relics as well as her body were thought to have been moved to Vézelay, where they attracted thousands of pilgrims, but in 1279 her purported remains were found hidden beneath a church in Mary Magdalene's holy cave, La Sainte-Baume. Pope Clement VIII had her remains placed in a sarcophagus, but the saint's head was placed in a separate reliquary. (Lou's head!) Although the church at La Sainte-Baume was built and rebuilt during the ensuing centuries, Mary Magdalene's head was still there, the destination of countless pilgrimages.

In the Orthodox Catholic Church, among the Czechs and the Greeks and the Ukrainians, a popular legend connected Mary Magdalene with the beginnings of the Easter egg tradition. (Magdalene found this story particularly fetching.) After Jesus' crucifixion and resurrection, Mary Magdalene used her position as "apostle to the apostles" (*apostola apostolorum* according to Hippolytus) to wrangle an invitation to a banquet given by Emperor Tiberius Caesar—Aunt Tiddy's namesake! Mary Magdalene presented Tiberius with a white egg and proclaimed "Christ is risen!" Tiberius was said to have laughed (which was Tiddy's reaction when Magdalene and Michael expressed their desire to have their picture taken with the Easter Bunny at Sears). Emperor Tiberius responded that Christ rising from the dead was no more possible than the white egg she held in her hand turning red—which it did before he finished speaking, and Mary Magdalene was invited to preach the Gospels to the entire royal household.

In Mondauk Proper, the Feast of the Magdala was celebrated with an annual dog parade.

It was one of Mondauk Proper's biggest and most popular events (right up there with the church carnivals, Independence Day fireworks, and the lighting of the Christmas tree in the Common). It was fun when she and Michael had been little (before they'd adopted Raven), even if the day did begin with Mass, but as they grew older, the parade became superfluous. Nothing ever happened. The dogs (and their owners) marched north on Butler Avenue for about five blocks, ending up at the shops in the parking lot shared by Pep Boys and Sears (who sponsored the dog parade and, by extension, the Feast of the Magdala). Employees in blue vests swarmed the parking lot, attending the hot dog and water ice stands. Priests shook hands with assistant managers who all seemed to have mustard stains on their clip-on ties. Dog poop was everywhere, and blue-vested teens, lowest on the corporate totem pole, ran to and fro, scooping shit. There was even a yappy dog wearing one of the blue vests.

The feast before Michael disappeared, Magdalene had walked Raven down to the parking lot. Raven was always nervous around other dogs. Magdalene thought they could at least join the parade for the last block and then split a hot dog in the Sears lot. Michael wouldn't go; he said he'd outgrown parades (with the exception of the Hoskins High Homecoming Parade, a county tradition for the football teams). Raven insisted on carrying Monien the panda in his jaws the entire walk there, and when they reached Butler, Raven growled and cried around the panda, and Magdalene and Raven watched the parade from the safety of the record store's doorway across the street. She remembered seeing a group of boys hanging around outside Pep Boys and wondering if Jerry Eves was among them. She purchased a balloon from a vendor and tied it to Raven's collar, and it remained suspended above her dog as they walked home, his only souvenir of his only dog parade. The parade had passed Raven by as well.

"It's not worth it, not worth it at all," Jerry said. The GTO flew towards home. Magdalene counted telephone poles.

If it was over now, it was strangely hollow. The world would swirl on and all the tragedies and comedies and histories would become just that: history. The same way time had already turned Mondauk, in the aftermath of Michael's abduction (or murder), into a ghost town, it would sweep away Magdalene and Henry Richard Cabot and Raven and Katie McAllister. *Yellow, red, white, black.* Ghosts all around and not one to ring the bell, not one left to scream *wake up and breathe*! Michael had told her once that the most sinister part of the year was Deep Autumn, when the clocks were turned back in October, and suddenly it was dark by dinnertime. Of course, by then, their father had just about glued himself into the well-worn stools at McCullough's, or at least made reservations for the next couple of years, so dinner, that staple of the family unit, was an anomaly, and Oodles of Noodles were the special of the day almost every day. Deep Autumn was the most sinister part of the year, Michael had said, because it reminded you that the weather heralded by spring and celebrated by summer was being mourned; you could see it in the trees, Michael said, you could feel it in the wind.

"Anything can happen in Deep Autumn, Lil," Michael had said. "That full moon shit is shit. Just a precursor to Deep Autumn. The fishermen'll tell ya."

"You don't know any fishermen."

"Read about them."

"In *Highlights*?" she suggested.

"Or maybe Mick told me about them."

"The source of all knowledge."

"The thing is Lil," Michael explained, "once a year *they* come out of Pennypack Woods and take a kid. That's the secret of Mondauk. Paying our dues. Hell, the town's practically surrounded by Pennypack, except in the Heights. Across the Puddle there, that's part of Pennypack too."

Magdalene snorted: "The only 'things' living in Pennypack are hobos."

"I'm telling you. Mick's got a cousin, and his cousin's best friend—*poof*, gone, right after Deep Autumn."

They were walking home from Sol's, sharing a Rocket Pop, and the sun had vacated the sky twenty minutes before.

"Michael, if this is another lifeguard stand story—"

"Think about Halloween, Lil. You see witches and goblins and about a thousand Draculas, but you never see any angels, right? Halloween's an old ritual to appease whatever lives in Pennypack."

"That would explain the older kids dressing up as bums every year with cork on their faces. Mr. Butler would call that a *homage*."

"One kid. Every year."

"And if I drink soda and Pop Rocks, my stomach'll explode. I thought *they* were appeased by Halloween."

"One kid," Michael said. "The town knows, but no one makes a big deal about it. It just happens quietly. *Poof!* We'll see; we're of age. They only take kids between the ages of ten and twelve."

" 'They?' "

"Whatever's in the woods, Lil."

"You don't even know what *they* are?"

"I don't have to. I just gotta make sure I'm not walking alone when it's Deep Autumn."

"Just that one night? When the clocks turn back?"

Michael scratched his chin, and then rubbed his fingertips on Magdalene's arm.

"I'm not real sure about that part. Mick said it was our rite of passage. Every couple of years, the older kids tell the incoming freshmen. I forget when they come for you though—the things from the woods, not the older kids. Could be earlier than Halloween."

Michael continued: "Some of the upper classmen say it's some sort of creature, but Mick told Jerry it was a couple of wild kids from the Lakes. Like fifty years ago or something, their parents' trailer burnt down. Joe Connelly said it was 'cause they were burning candles for Satan, but Mick said they were cooking meth. The county never found their bones—the kids' bones—two brothers. (Joe said there were four, but he has three brothers and so does Jerry, so I think he was confused.) And now the brothers live in Pennypack, on the banks of the Puddle."

He cleared his throat; his breath smelled like charcoal. Magdalene suspected he'd been smoking.

"So, they come out—the two brothers—every Deep Autumn and steal a kid because no one ever looked for *them*, and they were little and scared and had to find food for themselves. They run around naked, Jerry said."

Magdalene wished she'd worn a sweater; she had goose bumps on her bare arms.

"Horse hockey," Magdalene said. "Deep Autumn stinks, Michael, because it means school's started and the nice weather's over. And you see no angels 'cause we're expected to be angels all year long, so it's more fun to dress up as something scary and ugly and messy. Even little girls grow out of fairy princess costumes."

Michael looked her up and down: "Except you, tomboy bookworm. Except you."

Magdalene ignored his looks and counted lightning bugs. "Lifeguard stand," she said. "That's all I'm going to say."

"Lou's Head!" Michael said, laughing. "Don't go losin' Lou's Head!"

She had to duck her chin and close her eyes, for she would have done anything he'd wanted during the breadth of his laugh, and she had become quite sure Michael knew it.

422 · *Saving Magdalene*

Magdalene spit out of the window of Mick's GTO and felt it smack back against her cheek. It wasn't Deep Autumn, but it sure as hell felt like it. Her temples throbbed with memories of Michael.

Two, three, five, seven, and done! Got no factor 'cept myself and one!

"Is that Aunt Tiddy?" Jerry asked.

"What?"

"This blue Caddy we're about to pass."

"Hell," Magdalene said, ducking down in her seat. She watched Jerry wave confidently as if this were an everyday occurrence: an eighth grader passing Aunt Tiddy on Bethlehem Pike.

"She was heading towards Spring House? She has to be going...Tiddy doesn't drive anywhere really except—"

"Bard's. I know, Tonto. There and the occasional fire sale, right? Well, she's gotta hit the road to Spring House occasionally. Her boyfriend ain't choppin' meat in Mondauk Proper."

"*Boyfriend?*"

"Mothers' talk," Jerry shrugged. The darkness of the previous hour had dissipated from his freckled brow, and he seemed to be enjoying himself tooling around in Mick's GTO.

"We gotta get this back to the lot. If Mick notices it's gone, he'll call the cops. He's usually too busy on Saturdays to stick his head out of the bays, but it's getting on—I bet it's after noon even. Someone's gonna see the Goat on the road and see that it ain't Mick behind the wheel."

Magdalene realized she was biting her lip and stopped. What will you do when your time comes, indeed? She could still get Katie to Aunt Angela's house. She could do that much. The thought of dying with these big messes unresolved made her stomach hurt. Her body parts beat out of time. Best to think of something else.

"Jerry, tell me about Deep Autumn."

Jerry cleared his throat and did his best imitation of Mr. Peitzman.

"Deep Autumn is a fisherman's term for the time when the clocks are turned back."

"No, no, tell me what you know about the wild Lakes brothers or whomever coming out of the woods and snatching kids."

Jerry smiled and said: "Snipe hunting."

"Snipes?"

"You know: snipe hunting. Boy Scouts do it all the time to Cub Scouts. Seniors do it to freshman. They take 'em out to the woods or down to Finch's Landing, arming 'em with a sack or a paper bag. They tell the Cubbies to lie down in the grass and whisper, 'Snipe, snipe, snipe!' Then the older kids come running at them in the dark with their flashlights bouncing. Funny as hell. They usually do it right around Deep Autumn. Mick's done it to a hundred freshmen at least, and they're not even little."

"Doesn't sound funny at all. Scaring little kids."

Jerry tried to look chagrined but kept a smile on the tips of his lips.

"It's just a rite of passage, Tonto."

"Bullying," Magdalene said.

"Magdalene—"

"Stop the car."

"But—"

"STOP THE FUCKING CAR, JERRY!"

The GTO pulled to the side of the road. A cloud of dust swallowed the car. Magdalene thought that if she could be swallowed by this cloud with Jerry Eve at her side, then none of this would have to happen.

The dust settled and they sat on the shoulder of Bethlehem Pike. They were only a couple of miles from their safe, middle class homes. Magdalene could see the asbestos factory smokestack and the tips of the antennas from Paradise Lakes behind them. Utility poles lined either side of the road. With the exception of one old carnival flier, every pole was bare.

Magdalene pushed at the car door with her feet, hopped out, and ran towards the closest telephone pole. Jerry hesitated long enough for a car to pass around the GTO—Magdalene had seen the rolling curtain of dust heralding its approach; she turned her face to the dead corn field on her left in case it was Aunt Tiddy trawling in the Baby Blue Cadillac of Doom—long enough for Magdalene to doubt whether Jerry would follow her; where would her plans be (what was left of them) if he just took off and returned the GTO to the Pep Boys parking lot?

The car passed, an obscenely green Volkswagen, like a cartoon car in the dust—heading towards Philadelphia maybe, hurtling past the ghost town of Mondauk Proper to a film premiere or a nice dinner at an expensive restaurant with an unpronounceable name. Jerry jogged towards her. Magdalene raised her fists, punched the telephone pole, then sprinted for the next one.

The utility pole closest to the car didn't appear to have any staples at all, and the next one had a single dangling, rusty specimen. Magdalene punched it flush. The third pole was bare.

"See, not even *evidence* of a poster, Jerry. Not one poster."

Her knuckles were bleeding, and Jerry wrapped her hand in his handkerchief. Magdalene wondered how many handkerchiefs he had. She spoke into his face, an inch or two away. She didn't think about her breath; she didn't think about kissing him. (Maybe a little, but *one two buckle my shoe; one fish two fish dead fish blue fish.*) And she told him everything—everything she thought he could handle. Telling Jerry about the planned poisoning of her pooch and her own curtain call— that would be too much. To tell Jerry how much she had loved her brother, how much she loved him still—she couldn't do that. The true love would spill through, and Jerry would see he had little to no chance against Michael. She couldn't tell Jerry, no matter how hard the words forced themselves into her mouth, staining her teeth, that she knew somehow, some way, in her very *blood*, she was responsible for Michael's vanishing. Michael had slipped her grasp. She didn't want to die, but she had to; she couldn't stay on living and hear the sounds of boys practicing in the Fields knowing her time really had come and gone, and she had failed. Michael, never labeled a Goner, was, in fact, gone, and not a SINGLE FUCKING POLE had even a remnant of a missing poster. Just one rusty memorial staple.

And the little one said, "roll over, roll over..."

Back in Mick's GTO, Magdalene leaned against Jerry. As the car headed west, back the way they'd come, then skidded south down Dirt Road, Magdalene thought how nice it would be to stay here, snuggled against this confused, freckled, skinny boy who had listened and with very few questions—very few—had turned the car around and headed back towards Paradise Lakes.

The Goat ate the road and Magdalene thought of Raven, gobbling a cookie, eager to retrieve a ball or lick her ear or have his big belly rubbed. Every car they passed was Aunt Tiddy's Baby Blue Cadillac of Doom, fresh from picking up sausage links at Bard's, a secret boyfriend lodged in the back of her scrawny head. They'd passed a combination bar and lunch counter, and Magdalene could see her father's bar stool in McCullough's, could smell the spilt beer and old peanuts and hear Hank Williams sing his songs of doom from the jukebox, and Frank Sinatra too, detailing the life of a sophisticate far from Mondauk County. But in her head, the bar stool was empty, and Magdalene realized she couldn't place her father anywhere else. Would she always miss who he was? Would she always watch his silhouette from behind his office door or hear him from the top of the stairs or listen to his lawyerly tones as he read the dictionary from the other side of her blanketed back? In person, he was part shadow; Magdalene assumed it was because that was all that was left. But there she was in the GTO's passenger mirror: purple bags under her eyes, lips cracked, hair limp. *Who's the shadow now, girly-girl, Maddie Monkey?* There's more than one silent movie star in this town.

The radio spurted and cackled. Ruth Brown was singing, "*You're the world...*" bending the lyric, "*to me, you know...,*" snapping it in half, "*you've been mine so long...*"

Michael had heard music this way. Michael heard the nuance in Seattle feedback, the heartbreak in up-tempo Motown, the joy in the Delta blues. He worshipped record labels like Stax/Volt and Sun, and loved bands with names like Hüsker Dü, Echo and the Bunnymen, and the Afghan Whigs. Of all the pieces, of all the clues of Michael, music was the most ignored. If she thought more like Michael, felt more like he had felt, she'd be able to find him wherever he was. Was he buried alive in a shallow grave, kicking at the splintery wood as the *thud thud thud* of the *clump clump clump* grew weaker? Was he chained in someone's basement, waiting to be basted? Was he gasping in the trunk of a car, thinking of her, humming "Hey Jude" to steady his thoughts as he attempted to undo a complicated knot?

The antennas of the Lakes wiggled and blinked in the sun.

"What if he doesn't say anything?"

"What?" Magdalene struggled from beneath her blanket of thought.

"What if he doesn't say anything, Magdalene? What if Stevie's as stoned as John-John was? He could just get pissed and wanna fight."

"I'm sorry, Jerry. You don't have to go with me. Just drop me off."

"Don't be silly. I don't care if he wants to fight. I don't know if he's done what you think he's done, but he deserves an ass kicking anyways." Jerry grinned and pointed to his mouth. "*Pow!* Right in the kisser!"

Magdalene pressed her body closer to his. *God, he was warm.* When she placed her fingers on his jeans, he squirmed like a worm. She wished boys weren't this easy (despite what Christina had said, she'd never have guessed it before this weekend), but when she'd told him everything—almost everything—he hadn't hesitated: he opened the car door for her after inspecting her knuckles one final time and turned the car around. If she'd planned on living longer than a day and a half, she supposed she'd have to learn to cohabitate with hard-ons. They just seemed a silly extension, a dangling dare, a biological weakness of boys.

Jerry told her that if they found themselves in a pinch or somehow separated (the Hardy Boys *always* made this mistake, but Jerry shook his head as if to indicate that this was just a contingency plan), she should kick Stevie Rich in the balls and run. He'd take care of the rest.

"*The police have started combing the area along Pennypack Creek, known locally as the Puddle. Although they have not ruled out foul play, Chief Hagen says the Fuller family and the investigators remain optimistic. Contrary to earlier reports, the police* have *questioned a few youths that were seen loitering near the Puddle the day of Christina Fuller's disappearance.*"

Jerry clicked off the radio.

"And you think—"

"Christina? I don't know."

Jerry spit out of the window, a careful, practiced spit that caught the wind and left nary a drop on either the GTO or the spitter.

"You know Stevie's not going to just admit he terrorized Henry and Joseph," Jerry said. "You know that, right?"

"He's a bully."

"No shit and all that, but Henry's dead. If Stevie *was* involved, he ain't gonna say nothing, Tonto, nothing."

"No, he'll talk *because* he's a bully. If we can get him alone and confront him—nothing physical—if we confront him, he'll brag about it even if he's scared."

"Magdalene—"

"If forced, he'll brag. He's a bully. I know. I come from a long line of bullies."

+

It wasn't the drugs and the beer, Magdalene thought, it was a fading hope and maybe a little jealousy that she saw in the silent movie star's face as they drove towards the Gremlin. The girl was stoned, but she watched, maybe even counted. Maybe she counted the number of cars that left Paradise Lakes and never came back. Oh, she could get a car. Any of these boys would drive the silent movie star anywhere for the promise of a few sticky minutes in the backseat near the dock or in Little City, but she'd always come back. The drugs could never erase the nagging, back-of-the-skull, tag-you're-it, simple truth that every Lakes girl swallowed young: there's no escaping the trailer park. One of the stoners pawing at her faded purple t-shirt would someday father her child, conceiving him in a barely functioning hatchback or out behind so-and-so's trailer when the beer ran out and every other girl was smearing her mascara with ashtray-mouthed boys sporting peach fuzz moustaches that tasted like hotdogs and mesquite. Hope, Magdalene knew, didn't die suddenly; it petered out (*yellow, red, white, black*) and strangled most everything else with it.

The ghost kids still sprawled around the Gremlin didn't seem surprised to see the GTO navigating the parked or abandoned cars along Dirt Road. One boy in a mesh half-shirt even waved—it was a little girl's wave—and Jerry gave a heads-up nod (the choice of greeting, Magdalene knew, among semi-familiar boys). Magdalene turned in her seat and watched the silent movie star detach herself from the Gremlin and the boys to stand in the red dust cloud of the Goat's wake. As Jerry steered north towards the patch of yellow grass (the bits of green poking through looked positively fake, like Easter grass), Magdalene watched the silent movie star walk up the road after them—her pace slow, deliberate, a horror movie monster's pace. Magdalene counted her lumbering steps. In the red dust, the silent movie star appeared to be floating in a careless, loping fashion, towards the twin silver trailers set back from the road amid the dead, yellow grass.

Jerry pulled the GTO up to the trailer on the left. It was the larger of the two, and appeared to be the least lived-in—no bicycles or car parts or buckets or children's toys, just a once-white laundry line, now gray and fraying, running from one rusted pole to another. Jerry turned the car around ("At least we'll be facing the right direction if we gotta make a run for it.") and reached for the blackjack. Magdalene shook her head, and Jerry caressed her cheek instead. His voice was muted, strangled, deep: "Last night...I never...I really, *really* like you."

Magdalene struggled to find the appropriate response, the right words—any words. But if she opened her mouth, she knew numbers would come tumbling out. She managed a small nod and ignored the puddles in her eyes. In the shadow inside Mick's GTO, Jerry's freckles twinkled like the constellations of the summer sky. Here: one, two, three freckles over was Cygnus the Swan. Oh, and there was Capricornus the Sea-Goat, the next constellation east of Sagittarius. And there, between Antares and Vega, lay Ophiuchus the Serpent Bearer: the forgotten constellation of the zodiac.

"I think I love you," Jerry said, and the screen door of the silver trailer creaked open.

"Jimmy, that you?" an old voice cackled, and it sounded to Magdalene like static electricity, like the sound of pulling two socks apart or yanking a sheet off your sister's bed to see if she's sleeping naked—but she hadn't been, or if she had been, she didn't remember: she'd been busy counting; she'd been practicing holding her breath. The beauty of numeric memory was really like the beauty of flight: Magdalene could count and count and count (like the little vampire on *Sesame Street*), she could move between the perfectly ordered numbers, recognize precedents, witness premonitions, but she never had to touch the dirty ground. "Jimmy, that you?" The screen door slammed shut, and inside her mouth, Jerry's tongue touched hers.

Ophiuchus the Serpent Bearer was a doctor, and his healing skills were so great that Hades, ruler of the Underworld, was forced to appeal to Zeus—Hades was running out of fresh customers. Zeus killed Ophiuchus with a thunderbolt and as an honorarium placed him in the sky holding the snake Serpens—for snakes molt and are reborn and such was Ophiuchus' skill.

Twelve constellations of the zodiac. Ophiuchus made thirteen. Serpens was divided into two parts: the head pointed west, the tail east. Fourteen freckles on the right side of Jerry's cheek, on the area closest to his nose—all she could see—and behind them, in the rearview mirror, were two silver trailers.

Counting was wonderful.

The trailer on the right side of the lot was smaller and surrounded by junk—tire rims, milk crates, garden tools (although Magdalene could see that the small patches of grass that weren't yellow hadn't been mowed even once this summer), and lots and lots of bottles: soda bottles, wine bottles, beer bottles, all lined up or balanced upon each other like at the carnivals.

Magdalene blinked, and she and Jerry were out of the car, walking towards the trailer on the left. (How had the embrace ended? Had she pledged her love back to Jerry? God, she owed him that much, didn't she?) The trailer on the right, although surrounded by the effects of the living (and the sloppy), appeared almost unlivable. A heavy sulfur smell emanated from its direction. As they approached the trailer on the left, what Magdalene could see of the one on the right proved true of its twin: it was silver only by happenstance. The sun weakly fought the cloud cover and glanced off the trailers (both were turned on an angle so walking towards the center of the two would have been like walking into a large V—except that the two trailers were as far apart as they could be on their large (for this area) plot of land—maybe a hundred feet). The light bouncing from the trailers' siding made the dormant vehicles appear silver. But as they reached the screen door of the trailer on the left, Magdalene saw that it was tombstone gray, and even that color was patchy—literally. There were little patches of what appeared to be tar and paper all over the trailer's side. The screen door had been just about eaten away by rust, and the rust itself was flaking away in large pieces.

Jerry exchanged a glance with Magdalene (she was going to owe him big; Little City, here we come!) and banged on the screen door. His knuckles came away covered in freckles of rust.

"Jimmy? That you?"

The old woman wore a pink taffeta dress; its wrinkles crisscrossed the fabric like the tracks of a dying animal, matching the lines on her face. And her face appeared to be in danger of sinking into itself, of being sucked towards the pucker of her lipstick-smeared kisser. The woman stood absolutely still as they mounted the cracked wooden steps. The trailer smelled like a mixture of lanolin, cough syrup, and cigarettes smoked at close quarters. It appeared to be immaculate at first glance, perfectly preserved even, but Magdalene couldn't help but notice the lone cup and saucer drying in the drainer and the large cracks in the plastic covering the tiny sofa. The plastic was filthy; it looked like someone had smeared a light brown layer of Crayon or peanut butter over it. A large tan lampshade, its brown tassels swaying just a little as they entered the trailer, was enshrouded in a giant spider's web. Magdalene could feel her sneakers sticking to the floor.

The woman turned her back to them, her fingers creeping out from her palms, her palms jutting from twig-like wrists.

"Jimmy? Eh? That you, Jimmy? Gonna be late. Late, late, late. Now, somewhere there's the collection envelope."

The old woman snatched at a Calvary United Methodist calendar from 1984 that hung on the wall near the Formica kitchen table. The table's legs were covered in rust halfway to the tabletop. The calendar swung on a thumbtack.

Jerry's mouth hung open. The woman placed a pink bonnet on her head. Her hair was pulled back tight, like harvested straw, and it crunched when the hat landed on her head.

"Ma'am? Sorry to bother you," Magdalene said; her voice felt foreign, funny, fuzzy. "My friend and I are looking for Stevie Rich. Some of the kids outside told us he lived here."

The woman turned and peered myopically at their faces and then at their shoes.

"Jimmy?" she asked weakly.

"No, ma'am. I'm Magdalene and this here's Jerry."

"Jimmy?" the old woman asked brightly.

"No, ma'am: Jerry."

"Jimmy?"

The old woman was retreating now, becoming smaller, fading into the trailer. She eased the hat from her head and placed it carefully on top of a stack of newspapers that teetered on a wooden chair with a straw seat.

"We're looking for Stevie Rich, ma'am. Do you know him?"

"He wasn't a good boy," the old woman said, easing herself into a chair at the kitchen table. "But he said he was comin' back. He said he would be back. Jus' had to wait a spell. Francis, he don't know nothin'. *His* father didn't either, God rest his wicked, wicked soul, but then, his father came from the seeds of pumpkin whiskey and lust. The Bible, it says…"

Magdalene moved a stack of catalogs, some of them dating from the '80s, from the kitchen chair opposite the old woman's and sat down. The trailer was stifling; despite the early summer heat, the windows were shut. The old woman lifted her gums into a smile and patted Magdalene's hand.

"Sit, sit. Sit for a spell. Would you like some sugar water, my dear, some tea?" the woman asked, halfway out of her chair. There was a rattle behind the trailer, and Magdalene watched the light go out of the woman's eyes.

"Was that the phone, dear? Did I miss the phone call?"

Magdalene looked around the trailer. The phone's tangled, stringy cord peeked out from behind a frayed, gold sofa pillow.

"I don't think so," Magdalene said in a careful tone. "It was probably just a squirrel out back."

The old woman eased her bony frame back into the chair, then squinted towards the doorway, as if seeing Jerry for the first time.

"Jimmy?"

"Jerry," Jerry croaked. His shoulders were hunched as if he was afraid he would bang his head on the ceiling. "Ma'am," Jerry added, glancing over at Magdalene.

"Eh?" the old woman asked, shooing her hand towards Jerry. "I always wear the pink dress on Saturdays and Sundays. Jimmy told me he liked this dress best."

"Jimmy's your son, ma'am?" Magdalene asked.

The woman cackled, then stared at the filthy window. Magdalene thought it was like someone was switching a light on and off in the woman's head.

"Sit, sit," the woman said, gesturing to Jerry. Her eyes glanced shyly Jerry's way, then hid behind their lids. Her eyebrows were pencil thin, fading away to almost nothing halfway from their thickest points to their thinnest. Jerry took a seat at the cracked Formica table.

"Ma'am—" Magdalene began again, but the woman *pooh-poohed* the air.

"Grammy is what Francis always called me, his sister too before she became too good for Paradise Lakes. Had to study in the city, she did. Can you imagine? Leavin' your own people? Said her brother needed 'professional help.' Tryin' to claim he touched her this way and that. Brotherly love, I said. 'Course their father wasn't around none by then, but I raised 'em." Grammy snorted. "Couldn't raise her none. She said she was done bein' raised and that was that. Wouldn't go to Calvary." Grammy squinted at the window again. "Francis, he don't take me to Calvary United anymore anyhow neither. And what with Bobby…" Tears splashed into the crevices on the old woman's face. Magdalene offered her a paper napkin that lay across a stack of envelopes and paper.

" 'Course that's what I get for choosin' Tommy," Grammy said. "They was both so handsome in their own way." Grammy straightened her frame, made as if to rise, then settled back down. She rearranged the brown, rotting bananas in the bowl near the window. Magdalene saw a plate of something moldy and green-hued just behind the bowl of bananas. "Could have had my choice. I was that pretty. My mother always said it. My paps, he said I was plain, that Ginny was the pretty one, that she had the smarts." Grammy snatched Magdalene's fingers in a bunch. "Sent her off to college, he did! Said I could find an office job, maybe take a typin' course. Said I should get hitched! Thank the Lord he passed before I went and met the Tidwells. Pappy wouldn't have liked them trailer trashies one bit. At least they were Methodists, Mother said. Don't bow to no king in Rome. 'Gotta bow enough in *this* world,' Pappy always said. Mighta been the only darn thing he was ever right about."

Then she was up. "I know how you like your tea, Chloe," Grammy laughed. "Don't have to tell Grammy, no, no, no."

Grammy touched Jerry's shoulder gently; Jerry recoiled, but Magdalene's stare held him fast to his chair.

"What's this tall glass of water want, you think? You need a beer, huh? A cold one? Francis keeps some cans in here."

The old woman struggled with the refrigerator handle; Jerry leaned over and pulled it open for her. Grammy smiled—at least Magdalene *thought* it was smile—pitched halfway between salacious and embarrassed.

"Why, thank you! Guess the old bird don't have the fight in her she once had, eh?" Grammy bent over, her head in the fridge. Magdalene could see runners in the old woman's ankle hose.

"Ah, here's one for the man of the house," Grammy said, tossing a can of Schlitz towards Jerry, who caught it deftly, pulling it back towards his body like it was a football.

Grammy laughed. Magdalene looked away. The old woman had no teeth.

"That's the way to catch 'em, boyo," Grammy said. "Won't fizz up on you."

Grammy laid a saucer out in front of Magdalene, then a sugar bowl and a quart carton of milk that had expired last month.

Magdalene caught Jerry's eye as he raised the beer to his lips. Jerry lowered the can and placed it in front of him, a wistful look in his soft, brown eyes. Magdalene would have to make sure Jerry had another romantic encounter tonight—if they ever finished their quest. Jerry pointed to his watch; Magdalene shrugged: it was out of her hands, at least for the time being.

"Now I know you heard this, Chloe. Must have heard it jus'

about one hundred times. *Ahh*, but you were always a good girl, weren't you? Told me you were afraid of ghosts, remember that? No, no, don't be embarrassed. This tall drink of water, he don't look like he leaks, eh? Told me you didn't want to be a ghost. Told me you wanted to be an actress." Grammy leaned her face into Magdalene's. Magdalene held her breath. "Still actin'?"

"Well, ma'am, I—"

"Call me Grammy, dear. You hurtin' my feelin's. After all the time we gone and spent together."

"Grammy. My name is…" Magdalene cleared her throat. "My name is Magdalene Barrows and this is—well, this is my friend—and we're looking for Stevie Rich. We're looking for your…" Magdalene searched Jerry's face, but he was sneaking a peek at his beer. "I think, I'm guessing, I think he's your great-grandson: Stevie Rich. We need to talk to him."

Grammy placed a chipped green tea cup that looked handmade in front of Magdalene, a silver spoon propped inside of it. Magdalene peered down; the cup was empty.

"Sip it now," Grammy said, easing herself back into her chair, using Jerry's shoulder for balance. "Don't burn your tongue. Remember when you burned your tongue? 'Grammy', you said, 'I can't live with no ghosts, and ghosts is all I got.' Hmm, hmm, hmm. 'I see no angels,' you said. *Tsk*. All you kids: so many of you come to Grammy when your folks hit the sauce or worse. Time was when Paradise Lakes was—well, it weren't *paradise* but it was somethin', somethin' better than what we'd expected. We'd come so far, you know. German and Dutch, touch of the Irish. Paradise Lakes *seemed* like paradise to us at first, 'Course my Tommy couldn't wait to get out. Said that as soon as we moved here. Said: 'Gonna get us out soon enough.' But, you know dear, the curtain had gone down on that man long before we moved to the Lakes. Guess he always knew second best. Ain't no comin' back from second best, baby doll. Nosiree. If you don't know what you're worth, you're always bringin' up the rear." Grammy stared at Magdalene. "How's the tea, Chloe?"

"Still hot."

"Chamomile. Your favorite. Oh, Grammy remembers, she does. Watched you all the time. Here, let Grammy blow on it," Grammy said, reaching for the teacup. Magdalene picked up the tea and blew across the lip.

"Wonder when Jimmy's callin'. Hmm. Used to be the same time, every week. Kind of all over anymore, his callin'. Can't remember. 'Course he's an old man now too, I guess. Not in my head though: in my head Jimmy's still fightin' his bangs. They always fell in his eyes, that boy. Heh, heh, yesiree, Bob." Grammy's head jiggled side to side. "What will you do when your times comes? Not what Tommy done in the strawberry patch. That bully-boy, no, no, no."

"Magdalene, we should probably…" Jerry started.

She had been trying to count—anything she could: Grammy's wrinkles, the crumbs on the table—but her concentration was shot. The numbers were ill defined, vague. Grammy thought Magdalene was family. Grammy was a clue.

"Grammy, tell me again: who's Jimmy?" Magdalene asked. "Who's Tommy?"

"…go." Jerry nodded with his eyes towards his wristwatch. Magdalene ignored him; the GTO would be back in plenty of time. They could always park it behind the shops, even help Mick look for it.

"Well now, Chloe dear, you done heard this story a million and a half times. Shucks. Nothin' wrong with wantin' to hear it again." Grammy reached for the sugar bowl.

"No, ma'am."

Grammy winked as she pried the sticky lid off.

"Nothin' wrong with that at all, what with your momma…well," Grammy said, gesturing her head towards Jerry, "maybe it's best we don't say in front of the boy lest we give him the vapors. Heh, heh." Grammy pulled two plates of yellowed teeth from the sugar bowl and shook them off.

"Likes to keep 'em sweet, sweetie," Grammy said.

"Jesus Christ," Jerry said.

Grammy popped the teeth into her mouth and shifted the plates around. It was like she was changing right before their eyes, Magdalene thought. Grammy's cheeks puffed and her jaw titled, and when the teeth settled with an audible sugar-crunch, the old woman straightened her back and brushed away stray sugar crystals from the table.

"He was the better lookin' of the two, Jimmy. Tommy was older; he was goin' places. Now, in the South then—that's where we lived, although not so far south that we were of a secedin' nature—when a boy took a fancy, he courted you, came a-courtin'. You took walks when you was allowed. You might go to dances. Chaperones were the order of the day, Chloe dear. 'Member when I used to sit you when your momma was indisposed? Used to watch those old black and whites. You loved you Ingrid Bergman, I 'member. Me? Tyrone Power! Well, it was like that: Jimmy was a swashbuckler. Always a-quippin'. Always with an eye for the ladies. The first time he kissed me, I broke out in a rash of tears!"

Grammy squinted at the clock above the kitchen counter behind Magdalene. Magdalene turned to look too; Jerry shook his head.

"Can you believe it?" Grammy asked. "Can you?"

The clock had a white face with large black numbers—a perfect clock for an old lady, except the arms were missing.

"Was wearin' this very dress, I was. Well, no, this part's a lie, but you don't know that, so I was wearin' this very dress. Pink taffeta. Daddy weren't rich. Ha—no! Down by the water, I was, gatherin' wild strawberries, and Jimmy, he says if I went and fell in, why, he'd jump in and rescue me. Then I'd *have* to kiss him. I thought Jimmy was so funny. Not at all like Tommy, so serious with his studies all the time. He wanted to go away to college so bad, Tommy did, but his daddy could never afford it. Now I knew Jimmy had been with girls. Hell, everyone in town knew! He had a weakness, and a pencil moustache, like he jus' got back from safari. I liked to listen to his stories, even though he was disturbin' my gatherin' jus' at the moment. I played along; I pretended to faint by the water's edge. Jimmy never let my back touch the reeds. He swooped me up, his fingers rough from workin' in his daddy's fields—college didn't have much of a callin' for Mr. Jimmy. His fingers were on the back of my neck, all sweaty, and then he kissed me. Well, I jus' about pitched a fit! I was promised to his brother. I was promised to *Tommy*! Serious, stern Tommy."

Jerry sipped at his Schlitz and picked at the cracks in the tabletop.

"I was so ashamed. Kissin' Jimmy Tidwell! You can imagine, Chloe dear. The shame of it. Well, I told ol' Jimmy I wouldn't be sayin' nothin' to his brother, and you know what Jimmy does? He jus' laughs. Says maybe Tommy better get to the kissin' sooner than later. Jimmy says maybe Tommy better teach me some manners too. I went to strike him, but he jus' turned and walked off, and my hand was swishin' air like a fly swatter in a swamp." Grammy nodded. "Was jus' goin' to clock him. Ran out of time."

Grammy's chin plummeted to her chest, and her body started to slip from the chair. Her decline was swift. Magdalene watched in silence as Jerry propped the old woman back up.

"Need a beer, do ya?" Grammy cackled; she was back. "Boys like their beer, don't they?"

Magdalene shook her head. "He doesn't need any more beer, Grammy."

Jerry glowered at his sidekick.

"You seen Chloe 'round, dear? Been worried sick about that one. Old Miss Lars, she says Chloe's been hangin' 'round with my grandson."

"Stevie Rich," Magdalene ventured. She was getting confused.

"Hell, no," Grammy said, "Stevie's my *great*-grandson. Francis' boy. (More Bobby's boy though.) I only had one child myself, and he's gone now too. Jus' like his father. Left his wife and all. Had to get out, he said. Smotherin' him, he said. His name was Jimmy, jus' like his father."

"You didn't marry Tommy?" Magdalene asked.

Grammy's chin crashed into her scrawny chest again.

"Hm-huh," Grammy said when she came to. "Married Tommy. Took his name. Named my Jimmy after his brother, he did. To keep his mother happy after Jimmy had that accident in the pond. How's your tea, Chloe?"

"Chloe's back," Jerry whispered to Magdalene. Magdalene kicked him under the table. She resisted the urge to turn and stare at the armless clock—something was missing, and not just the arms. She sighed. At *some* point, they had to return the GTO. She had hoped Grammy would lead them to Stevie Rich. If time had stopped in Grammy's trailer, it was ticking away outside of it.

Grammy patted Magdalene's arm, and Magdalene could see the multitude of threads sticking out this way and that from the cuff of the pink dress. The sleeve was stained with brown splotches and yellow smears, and the dress itself was ragged from being taken out and hung back up so many times. Magdalene pulled her mind away from the clock.

"So I went ahead with the engagement to Tommy. He was gonna work in the bank. A promisin' career. In the meantime, my mother still knew people at Pappy's factory, so Tommy could work there 'til the bank was ready for him. Took some extra math courses and whatnot, my Tommy did."

"You were talking about Jimmy, ma'am," Magdalene said. "About his accident in the pond."

"Hell, that weren't no accident," Grammy said. "You 'member that boy went down in the Puddle this summer past? Now *that* was an accident. You go down three times, they say, but only come up twice."

That was it, Magdalene realized: the counting! The numbers were gone from her head! Well, she was sure they were still there, like the numbers on Grammy's clock, but they were silent. In all the places *not* to hold her breath—just now something egg-salad-sour smacked into her nostrils—Magdalene was fully aware of every breath and of *not* counting them. She must be close. She remembered reading about writers getting into the zone when they were on fire. Magdalene was sure the same applied to detective work. A good sleuth should be able to block everything out until nothing's left but the quarry.

Jerry was staring at her. Magdalene squeezed his hand—she didn't know why, but she'd seen women do that to worried men in dozens of black and white movies.

"I guess we were, oh, maybe a month away from the weddin', and them darn strawberries were everywhere! I jus' had to pick some. So there I am down by the water again, betrothed now, not jus' promised, and who wanders up but ol' Jimmy, lookin' dapper, a little veneer of sweat paintin' his forehead, his hair slicked back, no hat even! 'Course no one wears a hat no more 'less it's a ball cap, but back then," Grammy said, "*phew*, men wore *hats*. No sillier than the bonnets women wore to the church, I guess. But Jimmy, he didn't play by the rules. He said he was a proletarian and was bein' kept down. Forced to work. Always meant to look that word up. Proletarian."

Grammy looked at Jerry as if seeing him for the first time.

"You're a tall glass of water, Irish! Can we fetch you a beer?"

"He just finished one," Magdalene said, and Jerry crunched the can with one hand to prove it.

"So?" Grammy said.

"He doesn't need another—"

"What does it mean, big fella?" Grammy asked. "Proletarian. What's it mean? Always meant to look it up. Never did. After what happened, didn't want to."

Jerry's eyes were saucers.

" 'Belonging to the lowest or poorest class of people,' " Magdalene recited, " 'contributing nothing but offspring and labor to the state.' "

Jerry looked relieved. "I wasn't so great at vocabulary," he whispered out of the side of his mouth.

"That he did!" Grammy said. "On the last day of his...on the last day I ever saw him, Jimmy did jus' that, so I guess he was right."

"Jimmy was right?"

"Oh, Chloe, you know this old story. Don't tease Grammy now." Grammy looked down and seemed to realize she was wearing a dress. "Get now. Gotta get ready. He could be here any time."

"Tell it one more time, Grammy," Magdalene said. "Tell it one more time, please."

Jerry sighed and peered into his crushed can of Schlitz.

The old woman's head swept up and her eyes twinkled. Thank God Aunt Tiddy wasn't as gone as Grammy, Magdalene thought. Tiddy was a pain in the rear, to be sure, but Magdalene couldn't imagine being forced to live in the shadow world of Grammy Tidwell.

"I could have saved him," Grammy said.

Tidwell. Magdalene's every sense heightened (which was regrettable, considering the egg salad and medicine smells). The trailer next to Grammy's had to be where Stevie Rich lived.

Two trailers. One. Two.

"I could have," Grammy continued, "yelled out, saved him somehow."

"Jimmy?" Jerry asked.

Grammy patted Jerry's leg.

"You been listenin', Lord bless ya. Methodist, are ya? Never seen you down Calvary United."

"We go over in Spring House," Jerry lied.

"Do ya?" Grammy scrunched up her face and pinched Jerry's leg. "Get to church, boy. I know you young people don't cotton much to church, but you need it more than me. I'm one step away. Lord keeps me awake jus' to wait on Jimmy when he arrives. It's like a dream, but my knees ache."

Magdalene's focus was gone as quickly as it had come. The dream of the Puddle. The dream of the Dares. The rest of the dream *should* have come by now, Magdalene thought. What was the point of all the fragments if she never reached the final reel? Magdalene understood Grammy a little: her dreams were so real, Magdalene felt she could just reach out and...

"I said, Chloe dear, you still with us? You look a trifle pale."

Grammy produced a crumpled tissue from one of her pink sleeves and pushed it across the table to Magdalene.

One pink sleeve had three buttons.

The left one had only two.

Jerry reached for Magdalene's hand. His was *covered* in freckles. There must have been a hundred freckles on one side of his hand alone! Oh why, oh why did she have to wake her numerical somnolence? Magdalene forced herself to stare into Grammy's face.

One wrinkle. Two wrinkles. Three wrinkles. Four...

"He was in shirtsleeves too, Jimmy was," Grammy said, shaking her head. "Well, it *was* summer, but that don't give him no excuse. I'm a-pickin' strawberries and sorta hummin' to myself. Not that I was ignorin' Jimmy, mind you, but I didn't think it proper for him to be accompanyin' me uninvited while I harvested them wild berries along the shoreline. He's yackin' about this, yackin' about that, all the while gettin' closer, mighty close. Then, clear out of the blue sky, he says to me, 'I want to kiss you. I been thinkin' 'bout it all summer long.' Can you imagine the sheer nerve of that man?"

Grammy blew out a long breath, and Magdalene smelled liverwurst and onions; the old woman must have just finished her lunch before getting dressed in pink taffeta.

"Well, I must admit to you, I thought him handsome. Tommy, now he wasn't nothin' you'd shoo away, but Jimmy was like one of them Roman statues. The pencil moustache—we all made fun of that thing—but it fit him. He was this side of rugged, like you knew he wouldn't be in the fields too long, but since their daddy could only afford college learnin' for one, he'd have to make his own way, but you jus' *knew* he'd find it, that scallywag. Heard he gave it to Brinkley Dotter's daughter, but she always fancied Jimmy. Weren't that much of a surprise. But she was the only one rumored that I believed. I wasn't quite sure what *it* was he gave her, and, if I'm spillin' the truth here, Chloe dear, I was both scared *and* curious. I wanted a baby inside of me once I married, but I wasn't so sure I wanted a *man* inside of me to get one, if you know what I mean. Oh, forgive me, Lord. But, still, I'd thought about Jimmy, fresh off them fields, an hour from his bath, and him gyratin' on top of me all sweaty-like. Lord knows I thought about it."

After a respectful silence, Magdalene asked, "Do you know where we can find your great-grandson Stevie? We need to talk with him."

"Some men," Grammy said, "take what they think is theirs

whether it is or not. Take your tall glass of water here. He'll take it, Chloe. He'll snatch it from you if you let him. Some men take what they think is theirs whether it is or not. It's in what they *covet* that makes the difference between a criminal and not."

Magdalene felt like she was back in Mrs. Bochdan's living room, staring at the gold tea service.

There were 102 wrinkles on Grammy's face.

"Stevie Rich, ma'am?"

"I was jus' stretchin' for a big, fat strawberry, feelin' full of myself. Gonna marry one brother in not but a few weeks, and the other brother, hauntin' my daydreams and my berry pickin' now too."

Grammy reached across the table, and her crooked fingers hooked into the front of Jerry's shirt.

"I stretched for that strawberry. It was so fat, lookin' so juicy, and that was it: Jimmy was all over me like he had eight arms and a thousand fingers. Tore my dress, suckled on me like I was a pig. He took what he wanted, what I'd never given no other man before. The sweat on his forehead was on my face, and his back arched, and it was like he was doin' push-ups on top of me. I couldn't breathe none hardly. His breath, even his sweat, smelled of pumpkin whiskey. It hurt so bad. Like I was getting' pierced in my lily pad."

Grammy released Jerry's shirt, and Magdalene was surprised to feel the warmth on her cheeks crawling towards her eyes. Is that what Jerry wanted to do? Pin her down and pierce her thirteen-year-old lily pad with his push-ups? Jerry didn't know where to focus his eyes; he seemed to be studying a scuff on the side of his sneakers.

"I didn't see Tommy come up. What with all Jimmy's breathin'—you know, that breathy-breath—and me yellin' stop (at least I *think* I was yellin' stop, some things bein' hard to recall) and Jimmy sayin' my name over and over, like it was a prayer. Like he was countin'. Jus' sayin' my name. Didn't see my Tommy. Didn't hear him comin' through the brush. Didn't see him standin' over us. Didn't know he was there until it weren't sweat comin' off Jimmy's forehead no more, it was blood, and it was in my eyes, and I know for sure that I was screamin' then. Jimmy was rugged, but Tommy had the rage of angels on his side. Jus' kept hittin' Jimmy with that big branch. When Jimmy rolled off me, Tommy hit him in the face with it. Couldn't even see Jimmy's nose no more. It was like Jimmy didn't have no face left. Uh-huh. There was blood on my strawberries."

The trailer was silent except for the hum of the refrigerator. Outside, Magdalene heard a car pass down Dirt Road or one of its bastard auxiliaries. A bird sang, then stopped, its song dying in the baking heat of the trailer. Magdalene ran a hand under her armpits; she was soaked.

"That's when he said it. Under all the blood, Jimmy says to me, 'I'll be back for you.' 'I love you,' Jimmy says to me. I don't know if Tommy heard. He was in a fit, I can tell you, Tommy was. He's lookin' at me, starin' at my stomach peekin' through the tear in my dress. And I wanted to hit Tommy with a big stick or a rock or somethin'. Not Jimmy, *Tommy*. Jimmy's jus' lyin' there, breathin' funny, bleedin' hard. Tommy turns away from me. He says, 'Get yerself dressed.' Coulda smacked his skull silly with a stone, but I didn't. Shoulda coulda woulda. But the moment had passed, and there I was: already fallin' through the underbrush and then the trees. And I kept a-runnin' until I'd swore I'd never run no more. I buried my dress and told Mother it fell apart when I washed it. Then it was suppertime, and there at the door was Tommy. My mother was happy to see him: good future and all. Mother was happy for me, I guess. Tommy walks in, fresh shirt on, hat in his hand. 'Got any of them strawberries you was pickin'?' Tommy asks me. 'You picked some berries today, dear?' my mother asks me. And I went and got 'em. I'd left the basket and what berries hadn't bounced out, the whole mess of it, on the back stoop, and I collected 'em and washed the blood off 'em and served 'em and ate 'em next to my fiancé."

Grammy dabbed her eyes.

"He called me by my Christian name, Jimmy did, right before I ran. That much I remember. Everyone called me Maddie, Tommy too, and how I hated that. But Jimmy called me by my Christian name, lyin' there after Tommy did what he done, and that was worse. I like Grammy now. It means somethin' to some of you kids, like Chloe here, but it can mean nothin' too, and nothin' is jus' enough of alright for me 'bout more than half the time." Grammy rescued another tissue from her sleeve.

Magdalene counted the tears on Grammy's face.

" 'Course I was so sick afterward. Couldn't sleep, eat, nothin'. Gettin' sick every mornin'. Waitin' for news. But that was it. Jimmy had left town after a job, the note said. His mother—Lord, she was upset. But that was Jimmy, everyone said. Plenty of sharps in his head, but not a solid stone to whet them against. His mother—poor thing—she wanted to postpone the weddin' for a bit. 'Can't get married without your best man,' she told my Tommy, but I 'spect that Tommy had only asked Jimmy 'cause their mother had wanted him to. Different branches from the same tree, 'cept Jimmy's branch was floatin' somewhere down the river. That's what I thought. Thought that for years until I was gonna move. Yep, yep. Them kids 'round here, they forced me to wonder 'bout movin' back south with my cousin, Ellie. Ellie don't have two sticks to rub together, but she calls 'bout twice a year and always sends the nicest cards, sometimes for no reason, or no reason I can remember. That little wretch, that Chloe, and my great-grandson and that boob of a boy he's always with, they *stole* from me. Stole! Chloe wasn't but a child. I sat her for years. *Years!* Told her to stay away from my great-grandson, but they always played together when they was little, so it's natural. But the rest of 'em—some I even sat for—do nothin'. Take drugs or take drink. Steal things. Fisticuffs. No good, the lot of 'em. Lost Stevie long before I even knew it. One minute he's watchin' cartoons on my floor, the next the police are bringin' him back from this place or that. Won't look me in the eye no more. Comes over for money when his father don't have none. I tell him all I got is what the state gives me. I always stash it—well, *somewhere*—cookie jar, maybe. Sugar bowl."

"That's for the teeth," Jerry whispered to himself. Magdalene kicked him under the table again, but lighter this time. Maybe cracking wise was to Jerry what counting was to Magdalene. Jerry was rarely mean about it. He was a good boy, that Jerry Eves. So many freckles. So many.

"Jus' about to move. Started packin' a little. When you're my age, when you're—dear, tell me your name again?—you do things a little at a time, buildin' towards it, you know. It's not 'cause you're slow or 'cause you're old, although I was and I am. It's 'cause *everythin's* a clue. Everythin' takes you back, piece by piece. It all takes me back. Everythin's eventual, and eventually the river takes us all. And from time to time, the river gives some back. Jus' a little. Jus' enough. That's when Jimmy started callin' on the phone. I knew it was him. He had what my pappy would have called *dulcet* tones. His accent had smoothed itself out—hell, we hadn't been that *far* south—and he knew so many things I had only told my favorite girls, like Chloe here—there you are dear." Grammy squinted at the mound of envelopes and newspapers on the table. "Thought you went away.

Grammy missed you!" She patted Jerry's leg.

"We talk every week. He told me things 'bout the places he'd been, and I told him 'bout what I done and how Tommy ran off not soon after my little Jimmy was born. I told Jimmy 'bout them all stealin' from me here, and where I hid my money after I cashed my check, and about how Bobby would come over and drive me to the bank each week. Wanted me to keep my money there, Bobby said. I told him about Ginny and her car accident. My sister: she couldn't even speak after a bit. I think she tried callin' once or twice too, but I could never seem to understand her. Her jaw was broke in that crash. Always mad after me, Ginny was. Thought the Tidwell brothers were country trash, she did. So, I never left the Lakes. Stayed put. Didn't move back down South to Ellie's. What if Jimmy couldn't find me down there? Ellie don't like usin' the phone. Probably wouldn't like me usin' it none either. I stayed put, right here in the Lakes, where Tommy had done brought me and little Jimmy, Jr. That's what Tommy said to name him. Said it was in honor of his brother. He was drunk when he said it. Smelled like his brother: all pumpkin whiskey and sweat, but meaner, littler. Tommy was a little man. All his muscles were in his brain. His brother had both, he did. Maybe not as book smart, but Jimmy was no runt. And Tommy kept gettin' smaller and smaller. Ellie asked me once, back then, if there were problems in the marriage bed, and I laughed! Oh, how I laughed. Tommy never slept in a bed with me 'less he was drunk and then *I* would leave the bed to 'scape all his snorin' and such.

"So I had my Jimmy, Jr., and then Tommy didn't pass some test or such, didn't end up goin' to college. Moved us up to the Lakes. There was 'posed to be work in Philadelphia, but we couldn't afford nothin' in the big city 'cept some wee little one bedroom place. Here, by the water, we could get a fresh start. That's what Tommy said, but he never started nothin' but drinkin'—and usually first thing in the mornin'. Had to sell off a good part of the lot here," Grammy gestured behind her, "to pay off our debts—his debts. I was raisin' a son. Jimmy, Jr. looked nothin' like Tommy. He was gonna have brains *and* bones, you could tell. So Tommy left. Jus' up and gone. Boy can't get along without his father. The Puddle got polluted, and the blacks moved in and the Ukies and some other Russian types. Jimmy, Jr., he got caught up in no good, he did. Tore my heart in two when they took my Jimmy, Jr. Then I had no Jimmys at all. They took him away for that convenience store thing which he did *not* do.

Jimmy, Jr. didn't use his smarts like he shoulda. Too proud to take a trade. Didn't want to be no apprentice, he said. Wanted to make his own way. Sounded like Tommy, but reminded me of Jimmy! Jimmy woulda done it too—well, I guess he did, the way he talks without an accent now on the phone. Refined himself real good, he says to me. By the time Jimmy, Jr. went to prison, he had three kids, two of 'em by that woman—Deirdre, some French name—all hairspray and chewin' gum, that one. I think Bobby was by some other girl, but I'll be darned if I recall. Doesn't matter: I got 'em all: Francis and Bobby and their sister. Oh, their sister. She was too good for the Lakes, but not too good to pass judgment on her brother Francis. But she loved Bobby. Everybody loved Bobby. He had this no-good tramp of a girlfriend, knocked him for a loop though. When he got out of the Lakes, he did it right, married a nice girl—a trifle mousy, maybe, but better than what's 'round here—moved to the Heights, became a fireman. Used a cousin's address in the Big Apple to get the job. Said he wanted to be of use. Always thinkin', Bobby was. I know he was thinkin' that day in September. I know he was thinkin' 'bout Stevie."

Magdalene stopped counting the grease stains on the peeling wallpaper behind Grammy. The light outside was shifting, and the patterns were changing too fast for Magdalene to count.

"Stevie Rich," Magdalene said.

"Bobby took an interest. The mousy wife, she wrote checks to charities and what-have-you. Volunteered. 'You have a quarter more than the bucket, why go and give what you got away,' I asked Bobby, but after that *tramp* shook him silly, well, the mousy wife must have seemed a godsend, so maybe it was her idea, all the charity stuff. After that business with the gun, Bobby took an interest in Stevie. Takin' Stevie to the city, feedin' him dinner in the Heights, tryin' to get him to play sports or swim or somethin' instead of jus' hangin' on the corner with that big flunky and the little thief, Chloe. Burnouts, all of 'em. *Tsk.*"

"Stevie Rich," Magdalene repeated, trying to steer the conversation.

"Now Stevie's Francis' boy, but Bobby knew better. He had *direction* then, Stevie did. Bobby took an interest. Francis, well, Francis has got problems. Needs to take medicine to help him get by. Gets checks from the government too. Told me he started his own business and not to mind the smell 'cause it's imported what he's workin' on. I don't know how he affords to live the way he does, but he's no dummy either. That's what his sister didn't understand. So, he took some money from her once. It's a brother thing. He could, so he did. That don't make him a bully. She says he needs professional help. Heck, ain't that what the medicine's for? Costs enough. Always borrowin' ten here, twenty there from me for his medicine. Hard to live without a mother and a father. 'Course, he could see Deirdre anytime, plyin' her wares behind the Blue Bell Diner, but I don't tell him that's his mother. Would do no good. His sister never understood that. Wanted to know. So, she leaves—not leaves like Bobby movin' to the Heights, but leaves. That's it. Get a card at Christmas—or maybe I'm makin' that up. Forget when Christmas is sometimes, 'less Francis asks for present money."

"The business with the gun," Magdalene pressed.

"That weren't nothin'. He wasn't gonna use it. Not my Stevie. Bobby takes him under his wing. Francis got pretty sore, but it was good for Stevie, and Francis needs to take care of himself, get his health back. The cost of his medicine goes up every year, did you know that?" Grammy asked, shaking her head.

"Stevie had a gun?" Magdalene asked. Jerry held her hand under the table.

"A cap pistol," Grammy sighed. "Not the best way to start off the school year."

Magdalene willed herself to not look at Jerry. *Not the best way to start off the school year.* It was hard enough trying to focus on Grammy. The grease stains danced enticingly in the light behind Grammy's head.

"I was losin' hope when that happened, I'll tell you. Not another one, I thought. Stevie's mother? Connie Rich? Who knows? Takes advantage of Francis, breaks his heart, has Stevie, drops him off. Came by maybe twice. *I* never saw her. Stevie's got her name. I'm sure she thought she'd get a windfall from Bobby's money when the government or whoever coughed up that check for what happened on 9/11, but there weren't a whole lot tricklin' down. His mousy wife, Beth, maybe she needs it, maybe she don't, but she was Bobby's wife and she loved Bobby, not like that tramp. So, let her have it, I say. Francis," Grammy giggled, "he don't agree."

"Grammy?" Magdalene asked.

"Yes, dear?"

"What did Stevie do with the cap gun? In school?" Magdalene had heard plenty of tales concerning Stevie Rich and John-John

Hagarty, but none involving a cap gun—or any gun—in Assumption of Our Lady.

"He calls once a week, Jimmy does. Says he's comin' soon to take me away from here. Says it's my turn to get outta the Lakes. He's gonna take me back to another body of water, he tells me. Says he's got a hunger for strawberries. Tells me to be ready, so I am. I'm always ready, waitin'. I don't wanna disappoint him again. There's a fine line between takin' what's yours and stealin', and maybe Jimmy did a bit of both that day, but maybe I was waitin' to be stole. Maybe. Well, I gotta get myself freshened up. Thought this strappin' young man was my sweet Jimmy. Sweatin' enough to be him, he is." Grammy laughed to herself.

Magdalene had held her anger in as long as she could. She pushed at the table with both hands. The teacup crashed to the floor; Jerry's chair fell backward as he tried to catch the cup. The edge of the table caught Grammy on her right arm. Magdalene could see a little blood seeping through to join the stains already decorating the pink sleeve.

"Oh, God, oh God, I'm sorry, Grammy, I never meant—" Magdalene cried, and inside her head, behind her furrowed brow and damp black hair and drowning eyes, the numbers multiplied themselves: there would never be enough time to count them all. There would never be enough time to find the root, the starting point. And that was it, wasn't it? Not counting *forward*. Magdalene needed to count backward. She'd wasted so much time already. To start now would take years maybe. Freckles. Breaths. The grease spots on the wall in Grammy's trailer. Losing time? Magdalene had lost it.

Grammy *shooed* the air, pulling another tissue from her sleeve to dab at her arm. The tissue already had blood on it. The old woman's expression never changed. Her face was like a saint's face on a holy card, Magdalene thought, the kind they gave out at funerals. Grammy stared at a point several feet above Magdalene's head.

"He called me by my Christian name, Jimmy did. Tommy was bashin' his skull in, down by the river. Tommy was beatin' his brother with a big branch, and blood and brains and pieces of skull— so white—flew in the air, and Jimmy, he looked at me, and said my name. I heard him. I heard him say, 'Magdalene.' Jus' once. I heard him. He says it now. He says it on the phone."

Jerry picked himself off the floor and righted the chair. Magdalene gasped for air, but there wasn't any—there wasn't a bit of fresh air left in Grammy's trailer; all the air here had died years ago, Magdalene thought, *decades* ago. Ash was all that remained.

Magdalene? Grammy's name is Magdalene?

Outside, the cloud cover fought with the summer sun. The world must be spinning fast, Magdalene thought. She held on to the seat of her chair. Her legs were weak, like she'd been dog paddling for hours.

Count, count, count.

One, two, three, four, can I have a little more?

Magdalene ignored Grammy blotting blood with her wisp of a tissue. She ignored Jerry pulling at her. She ignored the phone that sounded like tiny, annoying echoes from the bell tower at Assumption. Magdalene ignored the black makeup dripping down Grammy's face from where her eyebrows would have been.

Grammy picked up a rotting, brown banana from the bowl.

"Jimmy," Grammy said into the banana, "that you?"

Magdalene held her breath. The phone was still ringing. Count the rings! Count the grease spots. Don't let them move on you. Count, goddamn it! Count!

The sun won a minor skirmish and sent light down through the window where it passed Grammy cooing into a banana, her eyebrows melting to her chin, and lit the moving wall where hundreds of cockroaches scrambled and squirmed and danced before dissolving into extremely mobile grease spots as the clouds took the next battle. The sun retreated, skipping over a chicken carcass rotting on a plate just behind the bananas, and then gave up the ghost altogether, surrendering the trailer to shadow.

The phone rang and rang and rang.

Twenty rings now.

Twenty-one, *tra-la-la*.

Ooooh, twenty-two.

"Oh, Chloe, the phone, get the phone!"

Jerry was pulling Magdalene through the trailer door.

"Ta, ta, Chloe," Grammy said. "Ta, ta."

Inside Grammy's trailer, the phone continued to ring: was it twenty-four rings already? Oh dear. Oh my. Twenty-five. No one here gets out alive. Twenty-six. Pick up sticks. Twenty-seven. All good girls go to heaven...

Jerry pinched her cheek, and Magdalene held her fist a moment to follow Jerry's pointing finger. There in the trailer not a hundred feet from Grammy's, the one surrounded by the debris of the living and the touchstones of the living dead, a sour face scowled from a tiny ship's window.

The face had a phone to its ear.

Magdalene held her cheek, counting her breaths. Now or never. Do or die. (Well, it was kinda going to be both now, she thought, wasn't it?)

As Magdalene straightened her hair and smoothed her shirt, she felt it: somewhere, out in the world, Magdalene's future self (if she had a future) was wearing sharp business suits and taking meetings in tall glass buildings, winding down in the evening, sipping Merlot, in a penthouse overlooking a park, glancing wistfully at an old photograph leaning next to a Royal typewriter. That's what escapees did, right? Enjoyed the good life while they could, while the past lapped at the shore behind them, ever ready to take them back if they so desired? But they were never the *same* waves, were they? Never the same water. The past changed quicker than the present or the future. Just me, Magdalene thought, I'm the same. The same scared little sister, clinging to the ancient Rules of the Dare. Clinging because once the Rules were broken—oh, and she'd broken them that day at the Puddle—once they were broken, that trust—go ahead, Magdalene, say it: four letters, one syllable, thirteen definitions in *The American College Dictionary* alone—that LOVE, it could come back, driftwood, polished maybe, or crusty and riddled with holes, but it was never the same. Never the same.

Magdalene curled her hand and punched Jerry in the cheek—lightly. Got to keep him on his toes. They were going to call on Frannie Five Fingers Tidwell. Time to grab time by the ass and drag it down—down by the river, if need be, down near Jimmy Tidwell's watery resting place, and God knows who else was down there. Time to vanquish the clouds and let in a little light.

Jerry rubbed his face, and Magdalene kissed him on the lips. His breath was sour, but so was hers. It was like Michael had said: they were no longer children; they were already starting to die.

Chapter Eleven

The Bully

All Magdalene's father had ever wanted, besides presumably a healthy family and a prosperous career, was a house in the mountains, a cabin. He didn't put on airs about it or act desperate; it was just something he dreamed of for the future. "Folly," her father said of his own wishes. "A pipe dream." Magdalene remembered her mother encouraging his fantasies at the breakfast table even as her father backed away from the idea—it was *fantasy* after all, not the hard reality of the courtroom—with a barely perceptible tilt of his strong jaw (scraped clean before the day began), his eyes alternately drilling into his morning toast and seeking some crumb, some wink, some truth in Mother's blue eyes. The way he seemed to have never been young fascinated Magdalene; even in old photographs, the unassailable bearing and manifest destiny on his brow were impossible to ignore—and inexplicable in the neon light of last call, which just proved Michael's theory: sometimes, for whatever reason, you have to put your head to the gun. In Gregory Barrows' case, the gun was family-owned and nearly the death of him. Magdalene was sure he'd never expected *family* to be the fantasy.

Who can arrest a shooting star?

Frannie Tidwell was the kind of celebrity Magdalene had heard tales about before she knew his full Christian name. He was one of the first neighborhood boogiemen, one of the first evil, mythological figures of the playground. *Don't take nothin' from Frannie Five Fingers*, the older kids said. *Did ya hear Frannie Five Fingers passed out on the Ferris wheel?* It was startling to Magdalene to hear fourth and fifth graders, even third graders, invoke his name. He was a drug dealer, child molester, welfare bum, trailer trash, pimp. A real B and E expert, the boys said; a combustible Robin Hood type, said the girls. As actual sightings dwindled (or lies about sightings—*hey, one time, Frannie Five Fingers drank a beer with my cousin behind the Gas and Go outside Spring House*), his reputation flourished, increasing the power of familial invocation in terms of schoolyard braggadocio (*my sister made out with him once*) as well as plain ol' self defense (*fuck with him, you fuck with Frannie*). Increasingly, it had become less about what Frannie Five

Fingers Tidwell had actually *done* (hold up a gas station, rape someone's sister, swallow a live field mouse), then what he *stood* for: the mad grab for whatever was just out of reach—but nothing *too* far. Frannie Five Fingers had grown into a local legend among the susceptible students of Assumption and the worshipful high school loner set. Magdalene's investigation had led her to think of Frannie Tidwell not as the poster boy for the bad, but simply every lazy boy's ideal: the whole world at your fingertips, but not actually in your hand.

Who can arrest a shooting star?

Frannie's relationship with Stevie Rich had, until recently, been murky to Magdalene. But there was little denying either of their stains on Mondauk Proper. Magdalene recalled her father and Chief Hagen talking on the porch in hushed tones:

"How 'bout Tidwell? I like Frannie for this."

"Chief, no one's seen hide nor hair of that reprobate in a dog's age."

"Dogs have a way of findin' their way home."

"Virtual shut-in," her father had said. "He's got his hand in some drug business, guns too, that's for sure, but his influence doesn't extend beyond Paradise Lakes. Even the meth lab boys up Bristol way shrugged him off quick. Francis has been known to more than dip into his own snuff."

Magdalene could see, standing in his trailer, that clearly the world had swirled past Frannie Tidwell. He'd spied on them through the tiny ship's window when they left Grammy's, but when Jerry knocked on his door, there was no answer, and they had to let themselves in—and hold their noses. It smelled to Magdalene as if all the eggs that had been burnt in Grammy's kitchen had found their final resting place in Frannie's trailer; a heavy, choking, chemical smell hung in the air too. He must have gotten off the phone quickly then, Magdalene thought—Frannie was entangled on the sofa with a much younger, slightly chunky, naked girl. It was like he was putting on a show. Frannie was at least partially clothed. (Thank God, Magdalene thought.) He wore threadbare boxer shorts that clung tenuously to an elastic band (his tiny penis sprouted through a hole in the front) and a stained tank top t-shirt, the kind the boys called a wife-beater. The girl was straddling his lap, and her generous buttocks rubbed against the small coffee table that had been shoved within an inch or two of the sofa, making the few objects on the chipped wood surface (including, Magdalene couldn't help but notice, a tiny *Treasure-Island*-like chest) shuttle and rock. A big, expensive-looking television was balanced on gray cinder blocks opposite the sofa. There was barely enough room for Magdalene and Jerry to stand. Jerry was hunched over as he had been in Grammy's trailer, as if his head would hit the roof. (It wouldn't.) Magdalene had never been in a trailer before Grammy's. Grammy's was roomy at least; this trailer seemed bereft of air.

For the first time, Magdalene understood the origin of *wife-beater*. Frannie looked capable of beating any number of people, although it had nothing to do with size. He wasn't very big, but he appeared to be very angry, furious, barely contained. (It was almost as if, like a rabbit in a small cage, Frannie had grown no bigger than his environment allowed.) Frannie was sucking on the girl's neck—Magdalene didn't dare look at what his rapidly moving hand was doing, and she tried her best to erase any glimpse of the tiny root the naked (and obviously intoxicated) girl was tugging on with joyless aplomb—and when he finally acknowledged his guests, Magdalene saw that her host had succeeded in branding his barely-legal companion. A large, wobbly F pulsed in purple and red on the girl's neck.

Ahh, a shooting star indeed.

What becomes a legend most, Magdalene asked herself: keeping a low profile. Not one of the stoners or bullies or punks or Bob Squad princesses living outside of Paradise Lakes would elevate Frannie Tidwell if they saw him in his element.

Oh, good, he was taking off his wife-beater.

Of course he was Stevie Rich's father. Stevie had gotten his father's jutting chin and sloping forehead, and like Stevie, Frannie Tidwell was in the habit of talking chin first. Magdalene could see Frannie's whiskers grew in patches, as if his development into an adult had arrested itself. Stevie's big, angry mug was dusted with peach fuzz, but it wasn't a stretch to see Stevie's face on the sniffling runt heavy petting on the tattered sofa with a girl maybe only slightly older than his son. It was the eyes: no matter what Stevie's fists did or his mouth said, his eyes were always darting, watching for the deference, the reverence, the fear, and the slight. Frannie feigned indifference, but his eyes were in constant motion.

"Social Services?" Frannie Tidwell asked from behind the chunky girl.

"Um, no." Jerry's face was twisted, his lips ascending towards his nose. Was it the smell, Magdalene wondered, or just the tragic trajectory of a schoolyard snipe? Frannie was a twitching mess. His right cheek bounced intermittently, forcing one eyelid to a slit. *Yellow dwarf, red giant, white dwarf, black.*

The naked girl stayed put on his lap, her forehead on Frannie's shoulder. Frannie rolled himself a joint with his free hand. His deftness surprised Magdalene. Frannie's other hand explored the vastness of the naked girl's bottom.

"Speak up, Eves," Frannie Tidwell said.

Jerry's mouth hung open.

"I know who you are," Frannie said, caught midway between laughing and inhaling his little cigarette. "All you Irish runts look alike. Irish runts, Irish cunts. What? You wanna take a run at me, right? Heh heh heh. I'm just FUCKING with you, man. Oh, get off me, will ya?"

Frannie rammed his hand into the girl's doughy middle, and she rolled away, flapping into another room—presumably the bathroom. Unlike Grammy's trailer, there was no wall demarcating one area from another. Frannie loudly sniffed his hand.

"Wanna smell?" Frannie asked, offering his hand to Jerry, who made to slap it away. Magdalene grabbed Jerry's fingers and held them behind her back. "Good pussy for a fat chick. Still clean. No fish. Fish-free! Heh heh heh."

"I wish you wouldn't—" Jerry started, but Magdalene squeezed his fingers.

Frannie's right cheek started bouncing again. He flicked some ash from his lips and placed his bare feet (so dirty, they were almost black) on the coffee table amid the collection of ancient watermarks of various sizes. Frannie's belly looked like the distended stomach of a starving African Magdalene had seen in a photograph.

"Is, uh, is Stevie home?" Jerry asked.

Frannie's toenails were neatly clipped and clean. For a man who looked like he hadn't worn shoes and socks since his elementary school days, his toenails were immaculate. Magdalene couldn't stop staring at his feet. What becomes a legend most? The details. The Bad Boy of Mondauk, sire of the Assumption's bully chieftain, was fastidious about his toenails.

"Oh, he must be in the east wing," Frannie Tidwell said. "Let me get the butler. Oh, Jeeves! Heh heh heh."

Frannie's eyes traversed Magdalene's face. Magdalene resisted the urge to hide behind her hands. Was he looking to see if he knew her? Did he want *her* on his lap next? Or was he seeing Michael's face buried in hers, like the way she could see Stevie's in his? It's no wonder Stevie Rich was the way he was, she thought. Stevie Rich could never escape his father's face.

The formerly naked girl, now wearing mismatched earrings and a Def Leppard t-shirt two sizes too small—but still no underwear—returned to the living room. She leaned over Frannie and squeezed her hand into the little opening in his boxers.

"Ya'll want the same thing, right?" Frannie coughed, as he popped the latch on the little treasure chest. "You and Social Services. Stevie, Stevie, Stevie. Go bother his bitch mother." He wheezed, and the semi-naked girl plopped beside him on the couch. Her knees were bruised, as were the insides of her arms. Her breasts strained against the t-shirt; her nipples were enormous.

"Here," Frannie said. He handed the semi-naked girl a clear little baggie with a clump of white powder huddled near the bottom. "Split it with Chloe."

Magdalene jumped back and would have hit the television if she hadn't been holding Jerry's hand. Grammy had thought she was Chloe for more than half of their visit. Did Frannie mean for the semi-naked girl with the huge nipples and hungry veins to split the contents of the *Treasure Island* baggie with Magdalene?

"Tell her I want to see *both* of you later," Frannie Tidwell said, smacking the girl's oversized backside as she heaved herself from the sofa, stomach first. As she waddled towards the trailer door, Magdalene noticed she was pigeon-toed.

"Good girl," Frannie said after the trailer door slammed shut, "if ya know what I mean, jelly bean." Frannie winked at Jerry. "But I can see you got yourself a fine filly right here."

Jerry stiffened and released her hand. His breath was hot on her neck. She patted his leg. Magdalene knew Jerry would hold it back. Jerry was loyal to her; he wouldn't do anything to aggravate the situation. They had been together one, sticky time (*one times one is still one even though it looks like two*), and he was hers. The responsibility was enormous—for both of them. Would Jerry wander the rest of his days like Cain after he knocked off his brother when Magdalene slippy-slid into the next world, seconds behind Raven? If nothing else, Magdalene thought, Jerry needed to know that what happened or was going to happen in Paradise Lakes today was for a reason.

"Tell you what, Eves, tell you what," Frannie Five Fingers said, "give you a dime of sinsemilla for this one right here, right now, no questions. You can come back and collect her. Give you the bag up front."

She could hear echoes of her father's courtroom voice before the first syllable tripped past her dry tongue. She could feel her mother's laughter, pushing the words up and out: bravery in the face of—oh, what was it?

"Actually, we came to talk to Stevie about Henry Cabot," Magdalene said. A roll of perspiration somersaulted down her cheek. "You know. The boy who was shot at Assumption. Shot by another little boy. We came to ask Stevie about it. We're here to ask Stevie about the shooting."

Cancer—that was it! *Cancer* had eaten away at their mother. God—*their*! Once fragmented, it was nearly impossible not to itch. A detective, a good one, was always able to see the whole story, see past the summarizing. Magdalene had suspected that Fenton Hardy, Frank and Joe's father, was halfway to a permanent stool at McCullough's, so prim and prissy and proper, so calm, cool, and collected, such a bastion of the community. He was constantly involving Frank and Joe in cases apparently too complicated for himself, but not for goody-goody Daddy-pleaser Frank and rebel-without-a-clue Joe. What would happen to Fenton Hardy if one of his sons disappeared after splitting up with his brother inside some lighthouse or Injun Joe's cave? Would he crack up, Humpty Dumpty style? Would he count the lines inside his palm to see how much longer he had to stay put on the stool? Would he forget about the other brother? This much was true, Magdalene knew for sure: *someone* was responsible for whisking Michael away (and probably Christina too), someone (or some ones) had kidnapped him or enslaved him or sold him, but everyone else, the whole goddamn town of Mondauk Proper, had sealed his tomb by giving up the search. To give up on yourself is one thing (hell, to quote a song her mother had loved: "*You got to know when to hold 'em, know when to fold 'em...*"), but to give up on another, well, it was Long John Silver's black spot then, wasn't it? And there he was: Stevie Rich's plump stomach and jutting chin and clipped speech and scared eyes, smothered inside the grizzled, twitchy pedophile Frannie Tidwell—it was like seeing the origin of a superhero in reverse. A good detective brings the fragments together;

a good writer shows only the tip of the iceberg 'cause she already knows what the rest looks like. Fuck summarizing. *"You never count your money when you're sittin' at the table; there'll be time enough for countin' when the dealin's done."*

Cancer—her mother had died of cancer.

A writer, not a counter.

A detective, not a metronome.

But it was hard: Frannie Tidwell had three pimples on the left side of his face; to the right of the treasure chest were four straight lines carved into the coffee table; Jerry had three fingers on her back; the sofa pattern, a repeating approximation of a dying, turd-brown weed, had a total of sixteen visible leaves; Magdalene hypothesized that Frannie Tidwell's oversized rear covered another eight.

Frannie coughed out a plume of smoke and waved it away with his hand.

"Bobby wanted him to go that Papist school. I didn't want jack-shit to do with it," Frannie intoned with a grimace that Magdalene thought looked more like the face she imagined she made when she had to go number two and couldn't.

"I'm on disability."

The bemused look vacated his face, and his eyes took a tour of the inside of his skull before pinpointing on Magdalene.

"Saint Bobby. Right. Heh heh heh. I knew when Bobby could snort through a weekend's worth of blow in about two hours. So, his girlfriend gets dusted and steals his wheels with her dealer. Drives his car off the road down an embankment. When the police find the car, her head's barely attached, but she's still got her dealer's cock in her mouth. Heh heh heh."

The sound of laughter exited Frannie's mouth, but his chapped lips barely moved.

"Bet you suck a mean dick, honey-child," Frannie Tidwell said—and it was hard, so hard to be out-bullied, for in that moment, regardless of consequence, Magdalene could see white-bellied Frannie flopping on the trailer's threadbare rug, amid its hair balls and tiny pebbles, the little wooden treasure chest shoved so far into his throat that if she were to open its lid, she would be able to scoop out his yellow and black teeth.

"Oh, Bobby goes on the straight and narrow. 'I want outta the life,' he says to me, like we're in some fuckin' movie, huh? Oh man, Bobby could party back in the day. Got him some *poontang,* he did.

Heh heh heh. At least he didn't get all Jesus-freaky. Just wanted to clean up. I told him: hell, we ain't forty yet, why we gotta act like it, huh? But fuckin' tellin' me my kid's gotta go the Papist school. Like the Methodist school ain't good enough."

Jerry's voice was steady and strong in her ears, no shakes, no shivers. She could have fallen in love with him right then and there, maybe loved him more than Michael, but, no, no: *one two three four five six seven, all good children go to heaven.*

"There aren't any Methodist schools around here," Jerry said.

Frannie blew a tunnel of sweet smelling smoke into Jerry face. Jerry didn't blink. He dug his fingers into Magdalene's back; her shirt was soaked through. Standing inside Frannie Tidwell's trailer was like being between two pieces of cheese inside a toaster oven.

"No shit, Sherlock," Frannie said. "But we ain't Papists. We don't bow to Rome. Hell, we're *all* Methodists, the Tidwells. Way back, we were Methodists, and we're Methodists now. 'Bout the only thing the Papists is good for is them little Catholic schoolgirl uniforms. You got one of them, missy?"

Magdalene held his stare until he shrugged and looked away.

"They owe me," Frannie said. "I'm owed, is all I'm sayin'."

He was a Goner, Magdalene thought, a classic case: a Goner clinging to the summarizing before it was necessary (if it ever was). Magdalene heard it in his voice. The summarizing brought together bare facts (fragments, even) and forced a conclusion, like some lame detective television show. For all the bluff (and it wasn't *all* bluff; Frannie Tidwell's legend, like every legend, had some basis in truth: Magdalene was glad it was still afternoon; she didn't ever want to encounter Frannie Five Fingers after dark where she would only know he was on top of her from his dead mouse breath), Frannie had come to certain conclusions, and Magdalene knew, after multiple eavesdropping sessions from the top of the Barrows Bungalow stairs, that adults, once they had pasted together whatever fragments were handy, married themselves to their conclusions. There was very little flexibility.

"Don't even get me started on the settlement money," Frannie wheezed, "the 9/11 settlement money."

His wheeze sounded like a whale dying. Outside the trailer, there was the faintest echo of a second wheeze.

"I even gave the old bat the bigger trailer 'cause I thought we was movin' on up, ya know, to the east side." Frannie winked at Jerry.

"Hey, if the Negroes can do it, why can't good white folk, huh? Heh heh heh."

Outside, someone laughed: a sonorous, resonant laugh.

Stevie Rich?

"And now I got the kid most nights on the sofa, stinkin' the cushions up. Always knee-deep in shit, fuckin' kid. Hell, I don't really know where he crashes the other nights. Not Grammy's. Says she's got roaches. I don't know. Don't go over there much." Frannie turned his head and spit on the floor. "I was owed. I was due, if ya know what I mean, jelly bean."

If it was Stevie Rich, outside, laughing it up, this was not the time or place to confront him. Magdalene needed to speak with Stevie away from Frannie. The last thing she wanted was to deal with both of them at the same time. Frannie was already pretty wound up. As much as she wanted to grab Jerry and run, maybe Frannie knew something. And not just about Henry and Joseph. Maybe he knew something about the snipes. Maybe he knew something about Michael.

The screen door slammed and the pigeon-toed girl entered the trailer, no longer semi-naked; the tiny Def Leppard t-shirt was still squeezed over her cushiony frame, but she wore a pair of slinky, flesh-colored underwear. A shadow behind her coughed a smoker's cough. The shadow was too skinny to be Stevie Rich's, too self-contained. This shadow had hollow eyes.

"Damn, you're dumb, Sue," Frannie said to the no longer semi-naked girl. "I told you: *later*. Well, fuck it. Come right the fuck in, why don't ya?"

The shadow behind Sue unfolded itself, accordion-like, and the silent movie star with the teardrop tattoo under her left eye squeezed past her pigeon-toed friend and dropped a rolled up, brown lunch bag next to the little treasure chest.

"This here's Chloe," Frannie Tidwell said, squeezing the girl's right breast through her purple t-shirt. Chloe shrugged him off. Chloe's eyes were like two tractor beams, and Magdalene jumped back (bumping into the television, almost taking Jerry down with her) when she realized if she stared long enough, she could see the bottom; she could see to the bottom of Chloe's eyes, and there was nothing there to see there.

Frannie watched their staring contest in open-mouthed silence, his pumpkin-sized head drifting like an old osculating fan on its last legs. Magdalene blocked him out as best she could; even when he turned his rodent eyes on her, Magdalene stayed locked on Chloe. Looking at Chloe was like looking in a mirror (except for the teardrop tattoo): a mouth without laughter, skin without sun, eyes without any real hope. And despite all that, despite everything already ruined in Chloe, the bottom wasn't *that* unappealing—it didn't look safe and warm, but it looked *familiar*.

"What the fuck?" Frannie Tidwell finally asked, and the moment was over. Chloe smiled and sat next to Frannie. The pigeon-toed girl plopped down on his other side. Magdalene could see pubic hairs poking out of the sides of her underwear.

Chloe produced a cookie from the bag.

"Fuckin' leave the old bag her cookies, would ya?" Frannie Tidwell grumbled.

The pigeon-toed girl picked at a sore on her lip.

"She thought you were me," Chloe said, her eyes focused on the cookie. She nibbled at the edges, stared at it, nibbled a little more.

"Who?" Frannie asked. He sucked on the joint, but it was no longer lit.

"Grammy," Magdalene answered. "Grammy thought I was Chloe."

Frannie's face lit up. "Yeah, what were you doin' in Grammy's trailer?"

"Not having cookies, that's for sure," Chloe said. Her voice was raspy.

Frannie seemed satisfied with the answer and pushed at the brown bag with a chunky finger; his fingernails, unlike his toenails, were almost black with dirt.

Sue, the pigeon-toed girl, glared at Chloe.

Chloe looked up.

"You gonna eat that or what?" Sue asked.

"I'm eatin' it."

"Fuckin' eat it, then."

Frannie pulled a lighter and a bent spoon from the little treasure chest and lined them up next to a chipped compact disc.

"Eatin' it out is what it looks like," Frannie cackled to himself.

"You burnin' now, Frannie?" Sue asked. "You cookin'?"

Chloe turned her cookie over and examined the bottom. She picked a chip out with one fingernail and flicked it towards Magdalene, letting their eyes touch again briefly.

"Always wanting what someone else has, Sue," Chloe said.

"Shut up," Frannie said to no one in particular. He concentrated on the objects laid out before him with an exactness Magdalene didn't think was possible in the lumpy Frannie Tidwell. Only his hands shook.

"Here," Chloe said, tossing the brown lunch bag over Frannie to Sue. "I ate all the chocolate—"

Frannie's knuckles pulled away from Chloe's nose, and Chloe sat still for a few seconds—*one, two, buckle my shoe*—and a red flower bloomed under her nose, spreading, stretching, then dropping, dripping down over her full lips. She locked eyes with Magdalene again, and Magdalene watched whatever lay at the bottom of Chloe's eyes spill out in shimmering, emaciated drops.

Frannie pushed a box of tissues towards Chloe. Jerry reached into his pocket (that kid and his handkerchief!), but Magdalene stopped his hand with her own. Frannie Tidwell had stopped fiddling with the drug paraphernalia and was focused on Jerry's hands. Jerry let his arm drop to his side.

Sue peeked into the brown bag, and Frannie knocked it away.

"You want some too?" Frannie asked. "You need a cookie like you need a hole in your head." Frannie grabbed the meaty part of Sue's thigh. "Gonna all be flappin' cellulite soon enough, girlie. Who's gonna want your fat snatch then, huh? *Roomy!*"

Jerry poked Magdalene in the back. "Maybe we better go."

"Nonsense, we got issues, you and me," Frannie said. "We got discussion points. We got minutes to take, don't we, Eves? Ya'll came to see me, remember?" He inserted a finger into a nostril and then wiped it on the sofa cushion between his legs.

"No, really," Jerry began, "we have my brother's—"

"Mick's Goat?" Frannie asked, laughing *heh heh heh* to himself. "That stuck-up fuck lent his precious car out to a bunch of wet-behind-the-ear private dicks like yourselves? Regular Starsky and *Butch*, huh? Heh heh heh."

Sue huddled in the corner of the sofa, crying loudly.

"Here," Frannie said, tossing Sue a little baggie of what looked like oregano. "Knock yourself out." Sue pushed herself to her feet with some effort and gestured to Chloe with her eyes.

"You get your ass back here later," Frannie said. "I'll be done with these two soon enough, huh? You get your ass back in the saddle, hear?"

Sue pushed open the screen door.

"And don't let it slam," Frannie said as the door slammed back on its frame.

Chloe stood up and cleared her throat. A pile of bloody tissues littered the coffee table.

"Take them with you," Frannie commanded. He didn't look up from his little movements. His hands, partially hidden by the open lid of the treasure chest, were in constant motion. "The tissues. Don't leave your bloody shit here. Got enough blood with piggy flushing her fucking monster pads down the shitter."

Chloe scooped up her tissues. Frannie handed the girl what looked to Magdalene like a couple of cold capsules. Chloe stood next to Frannie and caressed his neck with her fingers. He handed her a few more capsules.

"And that's it. Don't come askin' me for more tonight, tomorrow, fuckin' Monday. That's it. 'Less you got the dough, that's it."

Chloe went to squeeze past him to retrieve the cookie bag, but Frannie blocked her with his legs. "Gimme a tug, babe, huh?" Chloe reached down into Frannie's boxers. "You come back later with Sue, huh? I'll see if I can't hook you up with more, okay? Alright?" Chloe's face was blank; nothing came through, nothing was getting out. Magdalene could see a pink tint fight to escape Chloe's alabaster skin.

Frannie grabbed Chloe by the neck. "Don't do it all tonight. I ain't takin' you down the free clinic if you do. You got it?"

Chloe brushed past him and kicked the door open.

"And don't let it…"

Look at me, Magdalene willed. *Look at me Chloe. Don't take what he gave you. Don't cross the threshold. Do you see the bottom of my eyes, Chloe? Does the darkness look familiar? Do you see the numbers? Do you see how they reflect and waver and jumble themselves up like they were floating in the muck of the Puddle? Do you see how I have to count them? Do you want to escape this? Do you see the bottom of my eyes, Chloe? Do you? Do you?*

"…slam."

Chloe stepped into the afternoon heat and shut the door gently.

Frannie reached between his legs, beneath the sofa cushion and placed a gun on the cluttered coffee table. The gun was so big, it was almost absurd; it was easily the cleanest thing in the house, cleaner even than his toenails.

"So—just so we're honest with each other, huh?" Frannie said. "Let's talk about what you were doin' in Grammy's trailer. Let's us chew it over and see how we're gonna handle this."

Frannie patted the gun like a puppy, picked it up, spun the barrel, placed it to his head, then pointed it at Jerry's face.

"Let's jaw it over a bit," Frannie Tidwell said. "Sit."

+

"It was my brother who died. *My* brother! The terrorists or the Jews or whoever the fuck flew into the World Trade Center there, they killed *my* brother. And what I'd get, huh? Nothin'. I'm the one who told him how to get the job without havin' to move. Gave him Billy's address, fixed it with Billy. I'm the one who worked on his car so he could drive there. I did that. Bitch. Fuckin' mousy bitch. Says he stayed here 'cause of Stevie. As if! As if they could have afforded to live in New York. Not 'cause of me or Grammy, but Stevie. Wanted Stevie to go to that Catholic school with ya'll. Huh? Tidwells ain't no Cath-O-Lics. We're Methodists. I even let Grammy have the bigger trailer 'cause I thought I was outta here soon. But no. Huh?"

The sofa smelled like feet or really old cheese. Magdalene sat next to Jerry, and when their knees touched, Magdalene was surprised to feel Jerry's leg twitching. Her own legs were perfectly still, but wet with sweat, which was understandable being between a psycho and Stick Man.

"Let's shoot the shit," Frannie Tidwell said, aiming the gun at Jerry's kind, freckled face again. With his free hand, Frannie reached between his legs a second time—and came up empty. He knelt on the floor and shoved his left arm up to his elbow between the cushions, his right hand wobbly but still pointing the pistol at Jerry. Frannie grunted and dislodged a smaller, but no less clean, gun.

"No, I don't get no raghead settlement money. I'm his own brother, for God's sake. Big Bobby Tidwell. Moves up the Heights with that whore. Shit, now *she's* tryin' to look after Stevie's welfare, she says. Gonna call Social Services if I don't let her, she says. Fuck, I knew McAllister when he was a drunk. I knew McAllister when you had to *drag* him outta McCullough's. Then his wife, that little bird of a thing, she kicks away the stool. Eats the proverbial bullet. Yeah, Eves, just like you soon, baby. Ya know, I could let 'em have Stevie—hell, that's what they want, fuckin' love birds. McAllister's gettin' his meat secondhand now. Sloppy seconds. Gonna make that whore kill herself too, I'm guessin'. If I let 'em have Stevie, then I want a taste of that 9/11 money, the insurance money, whatever. I got it comin' to me. McAllister thinks bangin' my brother's widow entitles him to *my* money? Motherfuckin' bully."

Magdalene had to will herself to concentrate: all she wanted to do was count. But it wasn't anything specific: not syllables or wallpaper patterns or freckles or perfect numbers. Now it was *just* numbers, and there didn't seem to be an end to them. She peeled her tongue down from the roof of her mouth.

Frannie nodded to himself as he lined up little gold bullets next to the treasure chest.

"McAllister's a bully?" she asked.

"What? No! He's a pussy," Frannie said, "jumpin' on another man's family. Didn't do such a great job with the first one, huh? I told Stevie. I told him a thousand fuckin' times: don't end up a fuck like McAllister. Make your own way. When Bobby wanted him to go to that Papist school, I told Stevie: you take what you can if ya gotta go. Don't go puttin' on airs like the niggers over in Perkasie Park. You go and kick some ass and take some names. Kid's gonna be in there a few years longer than everyone else anyhow."

Frannie Tidwell laughed into his arm and wiped his nose at the same time. The snot stuck to the little hairs on his fish-belly white arm. He stood up and climbed over Magdalene, squeezing her thigh as he passed. He had a chemical stench beneath his body odor. His laughter ended in a wheeze, and he steadied himself against the television as he caught his breath.

Jerry shifted his weight, but Magdalene placed her hand on his bouncing leg. Frannie still held the larger pistol sideways towards them even as his body shuddered and shook with bone-rattling coughs. Jerry's eyes, wide like train tunnels and just as dark, gestured towards the coffee table.

The gold bullets were arranged on the table, lined up all nice and neat.

What did Jerry want her to do? Throw a bullet at Frannie?

Frannie shoved the big gun into his waistband and counted his ammunition: "Eenie meenie minie mo; catch a nigger by the toe. My mother said to pick...this...one!" Frannie made a show of picking up a single bullet to load into the little gun, which he then did out of their sight lines.

"And what about Henry Cabot?" Magdalene asked.

Frannie lowered the pistol so it was level with Magdalene's face. Magdalene stared back at Frannie. She wasn't afraid to die. Frannie slammed the little gun down on the coffee table and paced in the tiny space in front of the television, stopping to suck on a tinfoil pipe.

"I heard about that shit—fuck, Stevie goes to that school. I told you that. Fuckin' Ukie wanted to collect his shares. Goddamn Ukies. Worse than niggers somehow. Least we brought the niggers here. Who asked these half-Russian bastards, huh? Thinks the world owes 'em somethin'. They don't realize they got to wait in line like every other workin' class stiff. He's got that store, right, but it goes right up his nose, so his old lady's gotta scrub other people's floors. That's what I hear. Takes the guns. I told him I ain't got nothin' for him. I told him, fuckin' wait your turn like everyone else. The shit's comin' down, and the big guy's gonna make sure everyone's got a taste. I told him: you don't know from guns, but he's happy as a nigger in shit. Big man, ya know."

Frannie sucked on his homemade pipe. For a second, Magdalene swore his fingers were on fire. Little blue flames escaped from the tips. Then they were out, and Frannie sucked on the ends of his fingers.

He pointed the gun at Jerry.

"Take up that pistol there, Eves," Frannie said. "Good boy."

Jerry picked up the little gun.

"Alright, alright. You know how to do this, Eves? Your big brother show you how? He's into all that shit, huh? Just raise it up."

Jerry winked at Magdalene, but she kept her eyes on Frannie Five Fingers.

"So, Mr. Bochdan got the gun from—" Magdalene wasn't even sure she was speaking English. Her tongue tripped over her teeth.

"Shut the fuck up," Frannie Tidwell said. "Grab his cock. Go on, do it. Put your hand on his cock 'cause it's gonna get so fuckin' hard when he does this. Russian Roulette. Adrenaline and shit. Heh heh heh. They don't tell you this the first time, but you get so fuckin' hard, you could hump a Buick."

Frannie paused and examined his fingers. They *were* burnt. Frannie peeled away a sliver of skin and flicked it towards Magdalene. Magdalene kept her hands in her lap. Frannie placed the pipe on top of the television. Jerry turned the little gun over in his hands.

"Hell, this town ain't got but a million secrets. Oh, yeah, sweet pea, oh yeah." Frannie reached over and ran his dirty, burnt fingers down the side of her neck. He pointed the gun at her head. "You and me, sweet pea, you and me, we gonna dance before this day is through. Right after Baby Huey here gives himself a buzz cut. He'll come before his body hits the floor. Now, do it."

Magdalene reached for Jerry's pants, but he pushed her hand away and raised the gun to his sandy hair. "I'm ready, Frannie. I'm ready to play."

Frannie's eyes went dark and focused on a point on the trailer wall above their heads; his gun hand shivered. Jerry nodded at Magdalene then at Frannie's gun, but Magdalene shook him off, just as Frannie leaned back and felt his pockets.

"Did you fuckin' take it, bitch?"

"It's on top of the TV," Magdalene said.

Jerry leaned forward and pointed the gun at Frannie just as Frannie turned to the television. Magdalene shook her head no again. The numbers were piling up now, almost to her eyes; she could barely see past the digits falling like snowflakes—but instead of each one being unique, they were all multiples of three, the numbers, and they didn't melt when they hit the soft, spongy ground of Magdalene's brain matter; instead, they took root, falling on top of each other, entangling, piling up, blinding her with their perfect fit that no amount of confusion could dissuade.

The bullet went through the wall behind Jerry's head. Smoke curled from the end of Frannie's pistol. Jerry sat back down and placed the little gun to his temple. Frannie stared at Jerry, as if willing him to make the next move, then shook his head, took a drag from the tinfoil pipe, and blew a wobbly smoke ring. (Watching him light the pipe with one hand while trying to aim the gun with the other would have been comical, worthy of Abbott and Costello, if the noises outside didn't indicate that Frannie's girls had witnessed the bullet exiting the trailer.)

"Bochdan and his Ukie wanna-be mobsters. So, I sold 'em some blow. Cut him in on deals. This one time, he wants to be paid in guns. So I paid him in guns. So what? I told him: don't keep 'em in your house, huh? Cops find 'em, they're hot, you know. Plus, he's got a fuckin' little kid." Frannie took another hit from the pipe. "Musta kept one around, huh? Fuckin' Ukie."

The trailer door creaked. "You come through that door," Frannie yelled, "I'm gonna shoot you, ya hear me? Don't care who you are."

"Frannie," said a voice that sounded like Sue's.

"Fat bitch keep your goddamn nose outta this!" But the door had been returned to the frame, and the voices outside were reduced to whispers, like the sounds numbers made when they fell from the heavens, evil-manna, not meant to nourish, but to choke and obscure.

"You ready, Eves?" Frannie asked. Jerry nodded his head.

"Then go, already," Frannie Tidwell said. "Spin the barrel. Put it to your head. One bullet, baby. Could be yours."

"Not everyone has a secret," Magdalene said.

Frannie lowered his gun for a half-second, then raised it again. His hands shook and his lips had turned chalky white.

"Everyone, bitch, everyone's got one."

"Mr. McAllister?"

"You bet McAllister's got a secret. Oh, he goes around pretendin' he's God's right hand man now—joinin' Big Brothers, making Stevie go to them meetings. Man's all about meetings. Twelve steps? Gonna take more than twelve steps to erase a life full of stumblin' 'round drunk as a skunk, ain't it? Huh? Wants to take Stevie campin'. Yeah, right. Wants to hump him in a sleepin' bag. Gonna take him campin', right? Fuckin' kid sleeps outside most of the spring and summer anyway. And all 'cause McAllister's bangin' my brother's widow, spendin' my raghead 9/11 money. You have to make up for your sins, don't you little girl? Even us poor-ass Methodists know that. McAllister needs to take care of his own.

"You," Frannie said, pointing the gun at his own head and then back at Jerry, "up, up. Keep it to your skull, Eves."

"What's his secret then?" Magdalene asked, peering through the numbers, punching through a couple, sticking her head through the holes in the eights and the zeros.

"Heh heh heh. McAllister? They say when he found his wife hangin', she'd poured out all his booze and left the bottles lined up on the counter. No note, nothin'. Left him with the kid. Not that he seems to care 'bout anything 'cept my 9/11 money now. All over Stevie 'cause 'that's what Bobby would have wanted.' " Frannie's voice went up an octave, and he pursed his lips and spoke through his teeth. " 'He'll have a chance in Catholic school. Won't cost you a cent.' Like I don't know it's my money. Yeah, where are all the fuckin' jobs, right? I ain't got no job. County won't fix my leg, won't pay for nothin'. It's my fault? It's my fuckin' fault?"

Frannie stumbled and the gun went off. When Magdalene opened her eyes, the little treasure chest on the coffee table was in splinters, and the air was thick with white powder. She breathed through her mouth.

"McAllister's tryin' to fill my brother's boots," Frannie screamed in a spray of white spit. "Ain't gonna fuckin' happen. Christ, you people. I fuckin' eat people like you for fuckin' *breakfast*. PUT THAT FUCKIN' GUN TO YOUR HEAD, EVES, OR I WILL BLOW THIS BITCH'S FUCKIN' HEAD CLEAN THE FUCK OFF!"

Jerry returned the gun to his temple. Frannie's breathing sounded like a dog's—Raven!—and he smiled at Jerry, all blackened teeth (there weren't many), bopping his head to some internal tune.

"Don't worry, now, don't worry. This how they all go. You'll be in good company. Coulda been a workin' stiff like Mick, but you like a taste now and again, don't ya, Eves? Come up to see Frannie now? Need a taste? Need a hit before you eat this piece of chicken here, huh? Spin the barrel. Pull the trigger, man. You pull it twice and you still breathin', I'll give ya a bag."

Magdalene looked at the ceiling; the white powder circled the air at the behest of Frannie's rancid breath. She could feel the numbers still clinging to her waist and legs and feet as she climbed through. She slipped past the last round number and narrowly avoided a tumescent fraction.

"Do it now, Eves, or I'll shoot the bitch in the face."

Magdalene looked down: Jerry's pants were wet.

Click.

Frannie whooped and leapt up. "See, see, now ya get a taste before the next round. Spin the barrel first though. Gotta spin now."

Magdalene stood up and pulled her t-shirt over her head.

"Magdalene, no," Jerry said. "I'll pull it again, Frannie, I'll pull the trigger again."

"Little chicken wants to play? Little chicken thinks she ain't gonna get her turn, huh? Heh heh heh. Want me to fuck you so Eves here can watch, right? Think I won't when your boyfriend's brains are stainin' my sofa? Yeah, he can watch—his eyes can watch when they're slidin' from his face to the floor. Sit the fuck down, little chicken. Put your shirt on. I'll eat you when I'm good and ready." Frannie slapped the side of his head with his gun. "Christ, you people. Always tryin' to step on our heads to get above. You need us to feel good about your lives. Bully Henry, right? Probably bullied

Stevie, fuckin' Catholic pricks. Our whole fuckin' lives, you bullied us. OUR WHOLE FUCKIN' LIVES." Frannie wiped white gunk from his lips.

"You can't even keep your own intact, can you? You lower that gun, Eves, I will put a bullet in your girlfriend's twat. Ya'll come here for weed or speed or dust, but ya can't keep track of your own. I'll make you disappear. I'll erase YOU. I'll make you never exist, just like that little piece of ass on the radio every ten seconds. Gonna find her in the trash somewhere 'cause they are LOOKIN'! You think the county'd be out lookin' if it was one of them out there," Frannie said, gesturing towards the door, which Magdalene noticed was open a crack.

"McAllister needs to take care of his OWN! Now ya'll got my dander up, so you're either gonna flick a clip one more time there, Eves, or I'm gonna shoot your girlfriend in the pussy, and *then* fuck her. Told you: this is what happens to all you rich kids. Come to the Lakes for a taste, leave at the bottom of a dumpster, huh?"

Frannie hadn't noticed that the door was opening. Magdalene stood up again.

"SIT THE FUCK BACK DOWN, LITTLE CHICKEN!"

Frannie snatched her hair and pulled her head over the coffee table towards his chest.

"PULL THE TRIGGER, EVES. PULL IT OR WE'LL SEE HOW BIG YOUR GIRLFRIEND'S BRAINS *REALLY* ARE!"

Jerry cocked the gun.

The door swung open.

"The door, Frannie," Magdalene yelled, punching at his bare chest. Frannie raised the gun and shot at the door. The pigeon-toed girl tripped into the trailer and started screaming. Frannie shot a second time, and Jerry dove to the floor, crawling towards Magdalene. Magdalene, still on her feet, pulled Jerry to his, pushing him towards the back end of the trailer. Maybe there'd be a window. Maybe they could find a phone and call the police, someone, anyone.

Chloe ran into the trailer, stepping on the pigeon-toed girl. "Sue Ann? Sue Ann?" Frannie turned the gun on Magdalene. His eyes were all red latticework and twitches.

Click.
Click.
Click.

"Go! Run!" Chloe yelled, just as Frannie brought the butt of his gun down on the bridge of her nose. Blood sprayed from Chloe's face and hit Magdalene's arm.

" 'Un, Mag-a-lene, 'un!" Chloe said, as she clawed at Frannie's face with her nails, and Magdalene and Jerry ran, sprinting between the sofa and the coffee table, stepping over the pigeon-toed girl.

Frannie yelled after them. His voice rose above Sue's screaming. His voice carried outside the trailer as Jerry took her deep into the brush between Grammy's trailer and Frannie's, away from Mick's Goat. (The same kids who'd earlier decorated the stranded Gremlin were now sprawled on the GTO.) They could still hear Frannie's voice, chummy, conversational, convivial, his tongue clicking like an obstinate crow straining on a headless scarecrow:

"YOU FIND YOUR BROTHER, NOW, LITTLE CHICKEN. YOU FIND HIM, HUH?"

Chapter Twelve

The Head and the Cadillac

"Back here."

"Is he following us?"

"I don't think so. I don't think he could run very far."

Frannie Tidwell's voice, broken into chunks of sobs and admonishments, had only carried as far as the edge of the woods behind the trailers, thank God; Magdalene didn't want his voice rattling inside her head, now oddly free of numbers. Her skull felt empty, but not dumb, just: EMPTY. All her plans for the weekend were most likely shattered. She could recite them if necessary (but wouldn't; Jerry had had enough scares for one day). She could list all the facts of the Cabot Case. She could rattle off evidence proving the abuse of Katie McAllister. For sure, she could pinpoint every telephone pole where she'd hung handmade missing posters last year. She could try and catalog Raven's whiskers and stray eyebrows, even draw a map of their locations. But inside her was an airy space. The numbers were stored away. If she were to hold her breath at this very moment (which she couldn't imagine doing; her chest burned from running so far into the woods, every snapping branch an angry mob of dusted children an inch of air away from her sweaty, black bob), she would actually have to think: *count*. Had she fallen so far that even the numbers, her precious, important numbers, had abandoned her?

Or was she getting better?

Willa would be so proud.

Fuck Willa.

No, no: quiet.

She sat down at the foot of a tree, her back scratched by the rough bark. Jerry lay in the dead leaves next to her, remainders from last year's Deep Autumn, and she watched his chest rise and then fall as if from a great height. Heat from her own skin rose to her nose, and she remembered: Jerry had wet his pants. She had dragged handsome, freckled, funny Jerry Eves into her endgame, and he had soiled his pants trying to be a hero.

Seriously: if she wasn't going to die in roughly twenty-four hours, she could see herself carving their initials inside of a heart in the damp bark of the Jumping Tree. Seriously.

Right: boys just wanted to hump. All they were interested in (according to Christina, now a slave to the snipes or fish food at the bottom of the Puddle) was rounding the bases.

The Jumping Tree?

The Puddle?

Christina said boys thought with their, well, *you know, Magdalene: their cocks, their dicks, winkies, wee-wees, wee willy webbers, the doink* and *the balls.* For a doctor's daughter, Christina had a bizarre grip (no pun intended) on the male anatomy. Jerry wouldn't have come this far just to repeat last night's backseat love performance, would he? Magdalene watched Jerry roll on his stomach, trying to dry his jeans off in the dead leaves.

"Don't worry," Magdalene said. "We can walk back to my house after we return the car. Throw 'em in the dryer."

"No biggie," Jerry said into a pile of crunchy leaves. "Think that ape spilled some beer on me."

"Schlitz!"

"The King of Shits!"

"Budweiser!"

"The Beer To Have If You're Having More Than Six!"

"Kiss me," Magdalene said, and he did. He crawled over to her, keeping his stomach to the ground, and kissed her ankle where it peeked through between the top of her socks and her jeans.

And instead of listing all the beers she knew (and she knew quite a few; her father had let the empties pile in the sink or in the recyclable can) or continuing the classic beer continuum to infinity ("Ninety-Nine Bottles of Beer on the Wall" was for wimps), she thought of how Jerry had helped her zip and button up the night before in McAllister's car. He had taken his time. It mattered to Jerry. She mattered. It was like the way her father took the time to read the dictionary...

That was *before.* That wasn't now.

Yes, it was.

Do-over.

Summer repeat.

It was now.

Jerry's fingers caressed her ankle.

"Well, what did you think? About Frannie?"

"Do you smell that?"

Jerry curled into a ball. "It's just that Frannie spilled beer on—"

"Not you," Magdalene said. She tilted her head in the air. "Shhh. Smell."

Banana peels, two week-old bread, hamburger gone rancid, filthy diapers, sweat-stained handkerchiefs, smeared napkins, chicken bones, turkey bones: garbage. She could see Jerry had a whiff.

"You're not thinking—"

"Frannie said: 'Come to the Lakes for a taste, leave at the bottom of a dumpster.'"

"Heh heh heh."

"It's not funny, Jerry."

"I was just imitating Frannie."

Magdalene studied the top of Jerry's head. His hair stood out in every possible direction.

"You're my sidekick now," Magdalene said. "Frank and Joe Hardy."

"Whatever you say, Tonto, but I'm not going anywhere near a garbage dump..."

Magdalene leaned down and kissed his lips—was this evil? Was she bullying Jerry with her kissing and heavy petting? His breath tasted like hers: like water from the playground fountain—tired, expired, mineral.

"...unless you're going."

Jerry stood up and took her hand. "I peed myself back there," he said, trying to avoid her eyes and failing.

"It's okay," she said. She wanted to kiss him again; the taste of fear and batteries in his mouth was comforting: she wasn't in this alone. But she needed his attention; Jerry couldn't be thinking about kissing or parking or unzipping. She didn't think he truly understood where they were going and what they might find. Or who.

"Did you?" he asked. "Did you, um, did you pee yourself?"

Magdalene had, in fact, not peed herself. As she looked down at her hand, interwoven with Jerry's, the pair almost imperceptibly twitching, she knew, without turning her head, that her other hand was completely still—zero tremors.

"Maybe a little. With a girl, it's different. It's hard to tell sometimes."

"Oh," Jerry Eves said, and hand in hand, she led Jerry deeper into the woods towards the source of the smell of rotten apples and leftover egg salad and cooking grease and cheese gone green and the bodies of kids stowed away by blind rodents and desperate carrion crows.

+

He hadn't heard them come up through the woods, holding hands, their free arms thrown across their noses and mouths. He hadn't heard them because in the middle of the dump—a ring of maybe a dozen once-green dumpsters circled by bags and mounds of garbage and bricks and bottles, the dumpsters surrounding an even bigger pile of ripped bags and rotting food—Stevie Rich was balanced on his large stomach over a rusty dumpster. His head, indeed almost the entire upper half of his body, was submerged inside in the dumpster; his lower torso, legs, and feet, were dangling a good foot or so from the ground.

Jerry tried to pull Magdalene back towards the underbrush, but Magdalene never lessened her pace. For reasons she wouldn't have been able to explain (in order to talk, she'd have had to open her mouth and she knew she'd vomit on her sneakers), she *did* feel brave (*naked* and brave—not the naked of the backseat of Mr. McAllister's car, but naked as in number-free), full of herself actually. Only she *couldn't* be this brave; only firemen and policemen were this brave. Her bravery was temporary: adrenalin, perhaps; knowing she was near the end of, well, of *everything*: her time had come.

Having failed at holding her back, Jerry's second instinct—and Magdalene guessed this had to do with having just soiled his pants and been made to play Russian Roulette with Frannie Tidwell—was to lift his free hand, aim the little gun, the very one Frannie had forced him to place against his freckled temple, and fire a round into the air.

Stevie Rich fell backward into a puddle of liquid garbage the color of the Puddle. Magdalene's writer's eye clicked into focus. Stevie Rich's head wasn't big per se. His body was underdeveloped— even at six-foot whatever. Undernourished perhaps, despite the belly sloping over his Lynyrd Skynyrd belt buckle. Stevie Rich hadn't grown into his head yet. But Magdalene couldn't tear her eyes from his shorts. They were at least two sizes too small and looked extremely uncomfortable.

"Start fucking talking," Jerry Eves said.

"Whoa, whoa, I had nothin' to do with stealing them tires. That was the Bristol boys, not me, man."

"Stop whining," Jerry said, "and start talking."

"About what?"

Jerry risked a glance at Magdalene who still held his other hand in her warm grip.

"About what?" Jerry asked her out of the side of his mouth. "Specifically."

Magdalene let go of his hand slowly, almost a finger at a time. This is how you let go of someone. This is how you let someone go. One finger at a time.

"Eves?" Stevie Rich asked.

It occurred to Magdalene that she had rarely (if ever) seen Stevie Rich without John-John Hagarty, and although they'd encountered John-John earlier in the day, Stevie seemed unaware of their presence in Paradise Lakes.

"Your time has come," Magdalene said to Stevie Rich.

Flat. Stifled. Maybe it was the nun's habit that brought the phrase its eerie authority.

"My time has what? Look, stop fuckin' around, alright?" Stevie Rich said. "I wasn't doin' nothin'. It is Eves, right?"

"Um, yeah," Jerry said. "It's me. Jerry."

"Yeah?"

"Hi," Jerry said.

"What the fuck, Eves? Who's the bitch?"

Jerry fired another warning shot in the air. *Jesus—Frannie had cheated; there had been more than one bullet in the little gun!* Stevie Rich jumped, took three giant steps backward, turned, and slipped on a banana peel.

A banana peel.

At least Magdalene hoped it was a banana peel. Anything else wouldn't sound right if she decided to live and write the whole tale down.

If she...

...decided to live.

One, two...

FUCK YOU!

"Okay, okay," she whispered to herself. "Here we go.

474 · *Saving Magdalene*

"Stevie, I want to ask you about Henry Cabot," Magdalene said. "And Joseph Bochdan. And I want you to tell me the truth."

Magdalene looked at Jerry, but Jerry was concentrating on the gun, squinting down the barrel with one eye.

"Or Jerry will shoot you."

How many bullets were left anyway, Magdalene wondered. Damn. No counting, no counting.

"Right, he won't—"

"Call her a name again," Jerry Eves said, "and you can pay the wager from hell."

"That was good," Magdalene whispered. Jerry would make a swell detective. Maybe he could help Magdalene with her book. He was usually better with stick men than words. Maybe he could illustrate it.

He was good with kissing.

Where's your head Magdalene Barrows? You're finally here. This is it.
COUNTDOWN:

- Rescue Katie.
- Murder Raven.
- Leave evidence for Mrs. Bochdan (and ADA Barrows).
- Take pills.
- Die.

In another world, Raven waited alone for her at home (if Aunt Tiddy was still out). Maybe chewing on Monkey. Most likely trying to make the panda sing.

This is how you let go of someone, Raven. This is how you let someone go. One song at a time. One song.

"Look, I was just dumpster divin'. No harm, right?"

"You're a bully," Magdalene said.

"You're the ones with the gun," Stevie Rich said.

"In school. You're a bully at school."

Stevie pushed himself up and brushed at the dirt on his shorts with exaggerated swipes. Magdalene thought the stains looked as if they dated from an era before the banana peel slip.

"Yeah, you say. The nuns say. The fuckin' teachers say."

"Are you?" Magdalene asked.

"Am I what?"

"A bully. Are you a bully?"

Stevie Rich laughed, and Magdalene forced her head not to turn around and follow the echoes. He laughed like an adult. Stevie Rich's laugh had grown exponentially with his head.

"Oh, yeah, I'm the big bad wolf. I'm the fuckin' pit in the olive, right? Fuck you. And fuck him." Stevie gestured behind him, beside him, in the air. "This is my whole fuckin' world, right here. Don't need to go much further than that. That trailer back there, the bigger one? That's my Grammy's. Ninety-one if she's a day. My...Frannie...lives in the other one. Sometimes I stay there. Sometimes I crash wherever." Stevie wiped his nose with the same hand he had used to brush at his shorts. A shiny, gray stain glistened from his upper lip. "Wherever I want, matter of fact."

"Right, but—"

"Bully, right? You try and go to a school where no one wants you. Fuckin' uncle's widow keeps payin' the tuition. Buyin' the ties and shoes and shit. And then McAllister. Jesus, what a fuckin' Jesus-wimp, right? Must be. Pussy-whipped is what Frannie says. Like it's my fault I live in a goddamn trailer park. I know what people say: trailer trash, poor white trash, all kinds of things. Not nice things, not Cath-O-Lic things, but I hear 'em. Think they're gonna gimme a job when I'm eighteen? The fuckin' county, think they're gonna gimme a break on them taxes or help a guy who needs it? I may be a kid, but I know what I'm gonna do. I wanna pump gas and fix cars and shit like that. You think the town's gonna help me out there? You know who Frannie is. You know what he does for a livin'. What are people gonna think 'bout his son?"

Magdalene hadn't expected a speech from Stevie Rich—especially not after one from his great-grandmother and another from his father. But what was most unexpected was Stevie Rich's voice. It was nasally and whiny; it hadn't turned. She'd forgotten how old he really was—maybe even her age. He'd been left back so many times, it was a wonder he didn't have his own office at Assumption. But his voice hadn't turned like so many of the boys in her grade or the boys that used to pal around with Michael.

Michael.

"What's in the dumpster, Stevie Rich?" Magdalene asked.

"Trash..." Stevie said, glancing at Jerry, who still squinted the down the barrel of the little silver gun, "...bitch."

"Where's Christina?"

"Who?"

"Christina," Magdalene repeated—not that she felt like saving Christina. The friendship had seemed to sever on Magdalene's suicidal insistence—fair enough, she guessed, but damned judgmental. Still, how could she save Joseph Bochdan and Katie McAllister and *not* save Christina?

Stevie slipped on another piece of fruit, and Magdalene wondered if she would have to save Stevie Rich before the day was out.

"I don't know a Christina," Stevie said, pushing himself up again. He didn't bother brushing his shorts off this time. One of Stevie Rich's balls peeked out from a hole in his shorts.

"Christina Fuller. Dr. Fuller's daughter."

"Right. Big tits. Dick tease."

"She's gone missing," Magdalene said.

Why hadn't she canvassed the Lakes after Michael had disappeared? Had she even hung missing fliers anywhere near the trailer park? How about near the dock, Magdalene? Ever hang any on the Jumping Tree? Ever hang any on the Dead Injun Tree?

"Shut up," Magdalene said.

"I didn't say anything," Jerry Eves and Stevie Rich said at the same time.

"Not it!" cried Jerry.

"Not it!" responded Stevie Rich, out of habit.

"Firsties," Jerry said, lowering the gun a little. "I called firsties, dickweed."

Stevie, at warp speed: "I'm rubber, you're glue; whatever you say bounces off of me and sticks to you."

Jerry looked impressed.

"Christina," Magdalene said through gritted teeth. "Christina. My brother. The snipes. WHAT ABOUT THE SNIPES?"

Magdalene snatched the gun from Jerry's hand. A bullet discharged and *clanged* off a not-so-green dumpster.

"THE SNIPES, STEVIE RICH," Magdalene said. "WHO ARE THE SNIPES?"

Stevie Rich fell backwards with a squishy sound.

"Henry Cabot," she whispered.

"Look, I don't know what you're talkin' about, okay? Yeah, I was there, okay? Happy? I saw the whole fuckin' thing, but just because I live in the Lakes don't mean I had anything to do with that kid gettin' shot."

Stevie Rich looked up, and Magdalene would have sworn on a stack of Bibles—Catholic Bibles, Methodist Bibles, did it really matter?; *my* Jesus is so much stronger than *your* Jesus—that preparing to surface on Stevie Rich's surprisingly crystal blue eyes (but they weren't clear blue, were they?; one eye sported a shiner, and both were bloodshot; the blue, upon closer inspection, *floated* in his eyeballs, detached from their own beauty, darting to and fro like his father's) were a pair of fat teardrops.

Stevie Rich was scared. (Magdalene could smell his breath, eggs and cigarettes, over the garbage—or maybe that was the garbage.)

"The one kid, the Ukie kid, he whips the gun out of his book bag when the sister leaves the room—catchin' a smoke; I could smell it on her habit. Fuckin' kid could dance. You ever see him do the Ukie dance? Like they're sittin' down, but kickin' out their legs. Kinda gay, but kinda cool too."

Magdalene spit to the side. The smell was growing. It was the smell of excess, other peoples' excesses: *mommy, I can't finish the peas— mommy, wipe please!—mommy, will you ever leave us?*—Q-tips with earwax, rancid fruit, stinky sweat socks, a soiled football uniform.

"Stop with the 'cool' and the 'gay' and the sweat socks," she said.

"Sweat socks?" asked Jerry.

"Just finish," Magdalene said to Stevie Rich. Stevie was still on his butt in a pile of garbage.

"Bochdan brings the gun out. Big fuckin' gun. Shiny, you know? I been pickin' on him and his little buddy, the kid with the big head."

"Henry Richard Cabot."

"Yeah, that's him." Stevie Rich nodded his head three times and shook it twice. "His head was so big. Like a pumpkin. Couldn't figure out how he even walked, you know? Just a melon of a head. Big noggin."

"We get it," Magdalene said. "Come on."

"Kid did have a big head, Tonto," Jerry said.

Magdalene ignored him. Frannie Tidwell had been real enough to scare the pee literally right out of Jerry Eves, but not this: a girl with a gun and a dope in the garbage.

"*Ton-to*," said Stevie Rich in a mocking, sing-songy voice. "You ridin' the Lone Ranger, Tonto?"

"You got a pretty big head there too, Stevie," Jerry Eves said, focusing down an imaginary barrel. "Easy fucking target. No mess, either. Nothing in there."

"Knock it off," Magdalene whispered. She aimed the gun at Stevie Rich's admittedly large skull.

"Continue."

"I, uh, I think Bochdan wanted to, um…"

"Yeah?"

"I think Bochdan wanted to impress me. With the gun."

"Why?"

"All the girls thought he was so fuckin' cute. Me? I figured if there was any good gonna come from me goin' to remedial readin' class again, it would be pickin' up on the hot little girls. There are a few, you know? Right, Eves?"

Jerry turned his head away and spit.

"Did you beat him up?" asked Magdalene.

"That day? *Hell*, no! He was the one holdin' the—"

"No, before that."

"I may have roughed him up, just rough housin'. What's the big deal? He liked it."

"Did Joseph think it was just 'rough housing'?"

"Look, I didn't kick the kid's ass, alright? I just messed with him is all. No big deal."

"Henry too?"

"Henry what?"

Magdalene wouldn't have been surprised if her forehead blew off its hinges and her brains splashed all over Stevie Rich's sloping stomach.

"Next subject. How'd he get the gun? Joseph. How'd he get it?"

"How the fuck? His old man. Bochdan told Henry he saw Andriy wavin' it at his mother, braggin' he clipped some nig—some black guy in Rhawnhurst owed him money. Kid said his old man was screamin' at his mother to torch Sol's or sell it or somethin' so he could get his."

"And you know this how?"

"I have my sources. Right, Eves?"

Jerry didn't answer. He just kicked a soup can.

"Look, word gets around. Ain't but two or three guys bother with me 'less they wanna kiss my ass, and a lot do. Not you, Eves—but you always stop and say 'hi' or at least yell it across the hall or the lot."

"Yeah, I do." Jerry peeked at Magdalene. She reached up to her eyes to make sure they were still there and not dangling from the sockets. The gun was heavy in her hand; she held it high to avoid Jerry's glance.

"Why'd you do that?" asked Stevie Rich, and Magdalene thought she could see, beneath the wariness and early beer fat, the kid Stevie Rich *wanted* to be. It wasn't the Catholicism so much (most of that had been impressed upon him; Magdalene would have bet Stevie Rich didn't give a good goddamn about organized religion) as it was being different: trailer trash in a school of relatively well-off suburbanites, who, until 9/11, had little to unite them except for religious and neighborly empathy for personal tragedies—suicides, robbery, child abuse—crimes of the home. After the terror attacks, there was an immediate sense in Mondauk of wanting to pull the person next to you closer. Then it dissipated, evaporated. Adults argued over the president and war in the middle east and gas prices, and everything went back to normal—except wariness had become the norm, wariness of adherents to political parties other than one's own, wariness to rival religious congregations (there not being any Moslems in Mondauk, or at least none that Magdalene knew of, the Christians took to tearing each other apart, scorning the small Jewish community altogether), wariness to any signs of differences. Pre 9/11, Stevie Rich, inundated as he most likely was with the Frannie Five Fingers Doctrine of Tolerance, at least only had to battle himself and a general prejudice against people who lived in trailer parks; now, Stevie Rich was a combatant. Magdalene had heard it again and again: *why's he going to* our *school?* Differences were worth fighting for now, whereas, Magdalene liked to believe, before the terrorist attacks, everyone had at least *tolerated* everyone else. Mrs. Bochdan had darker skin than most of Mondauk's white population. How many times had Magdalene heard that crack about Mrs. Bochdan falling into her brightly colored Easter eggs? She didn't remember hearing jokes like that before the terrorist strikes. Before the 9/11 tragedy, Mondauk Proper rallied around the football team (even public school families sold booster stickers for the Assumption teams) and the handicapped kid who ran in the sack race at the Catholic carnival; the blood drive always had the longest lines, residents of the Heights and the Lakes, elbow to elbow. Post 9/11, her brother could still be missing without so much as a whisper—or rather, that was all Mondauk Proper had become: a town of whispers.

Magdalene wished Stevie Rich knew how to whisper. Everything he said came out as a boastful roar.

"Why'd you do that, huh? Say 'hi' to me and stuff?" asked Stevie.

"Why not?" answered Jerry Eves.

"Jerry." Magdalene rubbed the side of her head.

"Oh, sorry," Jerry said, raising his hand, aiming the imaginary gun at Stevie Rich.

"*Pow*," whispered Jerry Eves.

Whispers.

It was like when you got off one of those rides—the Octopus or the Screamer—at the Catholic carnival for the Feast of the Baptist. Magdalene's father had told her and Michael, over and over, that those rides weren't safe, and Michael had gotten tossed right out of the Octopus one night, landing on his rump in the middle of the convent lawn with a bump and a laugh. But premature ejection aside, the shaky legs, unsteady gait, and general silliness of having survived the ride imbued everything else with an insouciant glow that surged through the brain and swaggered in one's walk.

"Bochdan told Henry he'd fix it so his old man never bothered his mom again. He'd show his old man, is what he told Henry, the way I heard it. Henry, that boy was kinda uncomfortable with kids 'sides Bochdan, if you know what I mean."

"Uncomfortable?" Magdalene asked.

"Yeah. Word was that Bochdan showed Henry the gun at recess. Guess it gave Henry something to brag about, right? John-John, right away, he says Bochdan stole his father's gun 'cause of what Frannie was rantin' about that week: 'fuckin' Ukies, pay 'em in guns they don't know how to use, worse than nig—blacks; who let 'em in this country?' Shit like that. If you meet the bastard, you'll hear the speech—and a few others. So John-John gets the skinny. Henry's avoidin' him, but John-John plays it off, you know, gives the kid a lollipop, and sure enough, John-John comes back and says the gun's for real. 'Course we don't for *sure*, but John-John double-swears it up and down. Got a thing for guns, John-John does. Likes to shoot at rats out here. Shot a cat once. Sat down next to it to watch it die. Some bullshit about its spirit risin'. Put it on Lisa Singer's doorstep 'cause she wouldn't suck his...'cause she wouldn't kiss him."

"Then what happened?" Her temples throbbed; her vision was blurry. Stevie Rich pushed himself from the ground with a grunt. "After Joseph pulled the gun out, when Sister Agnes Ynez left the room—what happened next?"

"Some of the girls were screamin', some of 'em were laughin', but a couple of 'em, a couple of 'em actually went up and *touched* the barrel of the gun. Like it was his cock. Sorry, man, sorry. You know what I mean. And they didn't just go up and, like, touch it—they grabbed at the honker, you know? Not to take it away, and Bochdan didn't flinch. He had these bangs, like a Beatles-cut, and he just turned his head this way and that, watchin' all the girls. And Jenna Horseman—Jenna Horsehead—she reaches over and *pets* his hair. That was what done it. Watchin' him bask in it. Watchin' him just shake his perfect little haircut. Just blew my cool. John-John, he was all crouchin' down already. Fuckin' pussy. Sorry, sorry. I just lost it. Fuckin' Ukie. I knew who his dad was. Ukie gangster, right? Beggin' Frannie to give him and his boys a job to do. Like case a bank or run a scam. Woulda done anything for Frannie, his fuckin' dad."

Magdalene tried to count the number of times Stevie Rich said 'fuck,' the number of cigarette butts, the number of banana peels. But she could count nothing. She knew how the story ended now.

"I charged at him, just full blown, you know? Sister comes runnin' back in 'bout the same time, all smellin' of smoke, you know? Fuckin' nuns, right? The bigheaded kid—God, his head was big, wasn't it, Eves? God. Big fuckin' head. Like his hair didn't cover his head. Am I right? Okay, okay. I'm finishin'. This is what you wanted to know, right? The bigheaded kid—Henry—is standin' kinda to the side of Bochdan, but kinda facin' him, grinnin'. Grinnin' like a retard. No—I know he wasn't. Anyway, he turns his head towards me as I'm comin'—Henry does—and he's grinnin', like I said. He's missin' his two front teeth, and I 'member thinkin'—ain't no use getting' mad about it now, okay?—I 'member thinkin' that when I was done with the Ukie kid, I was gonna take the rest of Henry's teeth."

Stevie Rich wiped at his eyes with his dirty hands.

" 'Member that story—the one about the nun and the fire in the girls' bathroom?" Stevie Rich asked Magdalene, looking directly in her eyes for the first time.

"Yeah?"

"Well, Sister What's-Her-Name, she sees the gun. I know she did, 'cause I tried to slow down when I realized she was on my tail. Thought she was after *me*. She wasn't."

Stevie took three steps forward until he was within arm's length of Magdalene.

"Go on, Stevie."

"I'm done talkin'. Go get a paper. Extra, extra, read all about it." His eyes danced around in their sockets.

"Go on. Finish." Magdalene moved the gun closer to Stevie's face. She knew if she slipped even a little, Stevie Rich would be all

482 · *Saving Magdalene*

over her, and she and Jerry would join whomever at the bottom of the once-green garbage dumpsters.

Stevie Rich gently moved the gun away from his face.

"I don't like guns no more."

Magdalene blinked once. Twice.

"Fuck it. Okay. Fuck. Bochdan—he sees me, he don't see the nun, I don't think. I don't know what Henry saw. Like I said, I slowed down. I slowed down enough for Sister to run right past me. I slowed down, but I didn't stop."

Magdalene took a step back.

"I'm too big to just stop. I was chargin'. Bochdan had his hand out so the girls could squeeze the gun, but the girls had moved away. Then Bochdan lifted the gun. I swear to fuckin' God, I thought he was gonna shoot my fuckin' head off. Then fuckin' Sister— unbelievable—fuckin' Sister *dives outta the way*! Dove right into the desks. Hit the deck. Bochdan fires the gun. I run right past him, and I couldn't believe it: he missed me. Fuckin' Ukie missed me. I turn around, and for a split second before he fell, the Henry kid is just standin' there, but where his face and his mouth with the missin' teeth were supposed to be, there was nothin'. I mean *nothin'*. Just his big, round head, and that blonde fuckin' hair and not much more. No nose. No fuckin' eyes. No nothin'."

Magdalene lowered the gun; Stevie wiped snot from his nose.

"I kept on runnin'. Just ran right the fuck home. Figured the cops would come 'round soon enough 'cause of Frannie, and sure enough, they came, sirens wailin', the whole bit. Frannie's flushin' shit down the john. Grammy's thinkin' her date's here. John-John—he don't come out of hidin' 'til the whole thing blows over. Goes to some cousin's in Rhawnhurst. I gave myself up. I mean, who else could have done this, right? Had to be a Tidwell. I can't read so good, so it had to be me, right? I didn't tell 'em shit though. Nothin'. Fuckin' Sister jumps outta the way, and the cops come and hassle me. All 'cause I roughed him and Bochdan up a couple of times. But I didn't touch 'em that day. Even the fuckin' girls said the same thing, which surprised the shit outta me. I figured they'd lie, but I'm not sure they even saw me. Too busy lookin' at Bochdan's big, shiny gun, then too scared when Sister Spanish comes runnin' from the door. Police had to let me go, and they did, but not 'fore they clocked me once or twice."

Stevie Rich pointed to a scar on the side of his forehead, but Magdalene barely glanced at it before she started walking back towards the woods. She hoped Jerry would follow her, but if he didn't, she'd understand. She turned her back to the boys. She'd walk home if she had to.

Stevie Rich came running up beside her, his footfalls echoing at the edge of the woods.

"Shitty things happen everywhere, Magdalene. What? That's your name, right?"

Jerry placed his body between Magdalene and Stevie Rich. Magdalene gently tapped Jerry's stomach.

"It's okay," she said, but it wasn't—not that Stevie Rich posed much of a threat anymore. Magdalene was convinced she could have handed him the gun and he'd spend the rest of the afternoon shooting garbage or rats or pigeons. Stevie Rich was a spent force.

"Shitty things happen everywhere. But 'cause we're Methodists and 'cause we're poor or whatever and 'cause we like to party, 'cause we get high sometimes, it's our fault. It's our fuckin' fault. Sister jumps outta the way, but it's me they pick up. Bochdan brings the gun to school. Where'd he get the gun? Two guesses, right? Fuckin' Ukie wanna-be. But they haul me in, toss Frannie's trailer."

Stevie Rich bunched his hands into fists, and Jerry did the same.

"Worse fuckin' thing I ever seen. And I seen a lot out here. Guys' pipes blowin' up in their faces. Bad crackups when they drag on the Pike. Fella Frannie knew blew his own leg off, but he was too stoned to know it, so he sat himself down, stowed the leg in his catch sack, and had a drink until Hagen's boys found him the next day. I seen him though. We went up. Drank his booze, peeked at his leg. Thought about hidin' it, you know, but we didn't. I dunno why."

Stevie Rich turned his back on them and started back towards the dump.

"I 'member thinkin' how much Sister smelled like smoke when I ran out past her, but it was the gun—it was gun smoke. The room was filled with it. And the chalkboard..."

Magdalene wanted to count. She didn't want to hear anymore. Her head was thumping, drumming. If only Jerry wasn't here, she'd lift the little gun to her own head and...

"...it was covered with it—him."

Stevie Rich turned around.

"He didn't have no face left, Magdalene. He wasn't anybody. Just pieces. Just a bunch of pieces."

Magdalene could barely hear Stevie for the drums in her head—no, not drums: but birds taking flight and dragonflies buzzing and the Puddle lapping at the dock and the gunshot splashes of rain on the Puddle.

"You know my brother? Michael?"

"I don't know," Stevie Rich said. His eyes became little slits.

"Michael Barrows?"

"Yeah, the kid who—"

"That's enough, Stevie," Jerry said.

"Yeah, I knew him. Sorta."

"You have a fight with him?" Magdalene asked.

"Me? No, Barrows was a tough little fuck."

"That it?"

"Pretty much. Always said 'hi' like the Lone Ranger here. Don't think he liked me much though, but he never let on."

"What makes you think that?"

Stevie Rich coughed into his fist. " 'Cause I like to fight."

"So does Michael."

"It was different. He had football and all that. Me, I had to defend myself."

"Against second graders?"

"Look, you're the ones with the gun, bullyin' *me* around, so go on and say whatever you want."

Without warning, all the numbers flew back into her head and jumbled themselves up like a new jigsaw puzzle.

"I'm sorry," Magdalene said, and she meant it.

"For what?" Stevie didn't appear interested in the answer.

"You know you should go the police," Magdalene said.

Stevie Rich snorted. "Like hell."

"Joseph fired the gun because—"

"He fired 'cause he was scared," Stevie Rich said in a little baby's voice.

"Of you, Stevie Rich. He was scared of you."

"As he should be," he said, but there was little conviction in his voice. He slumped forward, and his eyes betrayed how elusive sleep could be—Magdalene knew the posture well.

"He was scared because you beat him up before. And Henry too."

"Right, and that's why I ain't talkin' to the police."

"Joseph's going to jail, and they're gonna try to convict his mom too. Negligence, something like that. Never mind how I know. No more Sol's. No more pops for John-John."

"Kid's into heavier stuff than lollipops and pacifiers these days," Stevie Rich said.

"No more Joseph. You think the Lakes are bad. Growing up in jail's gotta be worse. Nothing to think about except the hole in his best friend's face."

"They'd charge me with—I dunno—something."

"You think that once all those little kids calm down, they're not gonna remember you *chargin'*, as you said, across the classroom?"

"They'll say it's my fault. Not everything has a happy ending, right?"

"It's everybody's fault, Stevie Rich. But we're the only ones who can fix it. I know what I know now, what you just told us, but I think it would go better for you if you talked to the police on your own." Magdalene cleared her throat; even the slightest movement triggered waves of pain in her head.

"You*rrrr* time ha*sss* come," Magdalene hissed in her best Sister Rita voice. Steve Rich grinned back, then covered his mouth.

Magdalene laid the little gun on the ground.

"What are you doing?" Jerry asked, reaching down.

Magdalene stopped him. "No."

"I don't want nothin' to do with no guns anymore," Stevie Rich said.

Magdalene shrugged. "We have to go. We stole his brother's car, and we have to give it back."

"Why'd ya steal it if you're just gonna give it back? Go joyridin' at least."

"We stole it," Magdalene said, "to come and see you."

Stevie Rich thought about this for a second or two, then reached down for the little gun.

"Maybe I'll shoot some bottles out, you know? Maybe pop a few rats."

"Suit yourself," Magdalene said. "I don't know how many bullets are left. But it might be better if you stuck with the bottles. Noisier. More fun."

"Right," Stevie Rich said, but he was already walking away, his head down, inspecting the gun. "Happy endings suck."

"Let's go," Jerry whispered, "before he realizes it's one of his dad's guns."

"It won't matter if he does," Magdalene said. As they entered the woods, the sounds of beer bottles or soda bottles breaking into a thousand little pieces, left to twinkle and wink back at the stars, followed them until their echoes were swallowed up by the whirr of the cicadas.

+

This is how you let go of someone. This is how you let someone go: one moment at a time. One moment at a time.

She had to let go of Jerry—and soon.

She'd solved the Cabot Case—sorta.

It wasn't clear-cut. Stevie Rich wasn't a monster, at least not yet. But he had taken after Joseph Bochdan that day in the classroom, but so had Sister Agnes Ynez. Either way, Joseph had panicked. Either one would have been enough, but seeing Stevie Rich barreling towards him and Henry: that would give ADA Barrows motive. Stevie Rich wasn't a good kid, but he wasn't without hope. Too busy fighting Frannie Five Fingers' phantom wars. Too busy drinking, drugging, and leading a crew that included John-John Hagarty—and too young to care. Magdalene wondered how Stevie Rich had acted when Bobby Tidwell had taken him places and gave him the Big Brother treatment.

She doubted Stevie Rich would turn himself in and talk to the Chief Hagen, but she would write it all down nonetheless. In the end, maybe justice would be served, maybe not. Stevie was responsible for his actions, but who was responsible for showing him right from wrong if his mother was gone and his father sold drugs and guns and fondled teenage girls? Joseph Bochdan at least had his mother. Who did Stevie Rich have—especially now that Bobby Tidwell was dead, and Frannie seemed in no hurry to have Mrs. Tidwell in Stevie's life (unless it was for her 9/11 money)?

(Mrs. Tidwell certainly did not appear to be living in the lap of luxury, so how much of Frannie's 9/11 rant was true was another mystery altogether.)

At least Magdalene could rescue Katie tomorrow night. Get her away from Mr. McAllister. But what had Frannie been going on about? Mr. McAllister helping out Mrs. Tidwell, wanting to take up with Stevie Rich where Bobby Tidwell had left off—isn't that what Frannie had said?

No: the bruises. The way Katie wouldn't look her in the eye.

She had to let go of Jerry. And soon.

But she owed Jerry. He'd driven her to Paradise Lakes, stayed by her side the entire time, never backed down an inch—even when the guns came out. So what if he'd peed his pants and she hadn't? His time had come, and he had taken time into his large, soft, freckled hands.

If they got out of Paradise Lakes intact, Magdalene would let him take her to Little City. How long had their first assignation lasted? Regardless, it would be nice to kiss Jerry Eves again before she drew the shades and turned out the lights. Kissing Jerry was nice. Whatever else he wanted to do, he could do. As long as he kissed her—and kissed her quick.

"Alright, Tonto," Jerry said, squeezing her hand. "Moment of truth."

The sun was on the other side of the sky. It had been a long afternoon, and now the clouds that had played hide and seek with the sun were out in full force. Soon it would rain like it did...

...like it did when?

"What did you say?" Jerry craned his neck over the brush they were crouched behind.

"Nothing."

"There she is. The Goat. No kids around," Jerry said. "Mick's gonna kill me."

"It's my fault. I could talk to him."

Jerry let go of her hand and placed his warm palms over her cheeks.

"I don't want you to worry a lick about Mick."

"Thank you, Jerry."

He kissed her forehead. She felt suddenly ashamed of how much she had perspired.

"We had to. We had to. Everything is someone's fault."

Jerry chuckled. "To Stevie Rich, *everything* is someone else's fault."

"Yeah, yeah," Magdalene said, excited again. Her head was still like the sky above them, crowded and growing darker by the second, but to know that Jerry understood even a little—maybe he would be okay when she died. Maybe he would look back fondly on this moment, this slice of something beautiful, something that could never be summarized, never be broken and scattered like the stars: Jerry and Magdalene—J. E. loves M. B.—with garbage dumpsters and Stevie Rich behind them and Frannie Tidwell's trailer ahead. Jerry's warm lips on her sweaty forehead felt like the greatest thing that had ever happened to her.

"Someone's *else's* fault," she repeated. Her eyes were shut tight.

"Not everything," Jerry said in between forehead kisses, "can be your fault."

+

The GTO was still there just as Jerry said, and as Magdalene and Jerry sprinted towards the car, Magdalene's peripheral vision caught Grammy standing at her screen door, still in her pink taffeta dress.

"Jerry—"

"Just ease the door shut when you get in. We don't know if they did anything to it. We'll slam 'em shut once we get clear of the front gate, okay?"

Grammy opened her screen door.

"Jimmy, that you?"

"No, Grammy, it's—"

Jerry had his door open. "For Christ's sake, Magdalene, get in the car!" he hissed.

Grammy lifted one slipper in the air, an inch or two from the ground, and shook it like she was shaking out a bad case of pins and needles.

"Grammy, go back in, okay?

"Chloe?"

"Yes, it's me, Grammy, now go back in," Magdalene whispered. "Please."

There was a rattling coming from Frannie Tidwell's trailer. Magdalene saw something flit by the trailer's little ship's window.

"Jesus Christ, Magdalene," Jerry pleaded.

"You stick your hand in my cookie jar, Chloe?" Grammy asked, lowering her foot.

"No, Grammy, I wasn't even hungry."

Grammy's foot missed the trailer step, and the old woman tumbled onto the grass face-first.

There was a tinkling sound—like glass breaking—from inside of Frannie's trailer.

"Jesus God," Jerry said, running towards Grammy. Magdalene reached her first and knelt next to her.

"Is she breathing?" Jerry asked. His own breath came in short, clipped bursts.

Magdalene gently rolled Grammy on her side.

"Grammy, Grammy? Can you hear me?" Magdalene asked.

The old woman's face was stretched like a Silly Putty comic, her makeup was smeared, the chicken skin of her neck rested to one side.

"I think Chloe took my cookie jar money," Grammy mumbled.

"Can you stand up?" Magdalene asked. "Grab hold of me when I stand up. Jerry can ease you up from the back. You think you can do that for me, Grammy?"

"Why would Chloe go into my cookie jar?" Grammy asked. "I took care of those kids. I raised 'em up."

"What the fuck you do to my Grammy?"

Stevie Rich stood in the clearing, his father's little gun in his outstretched hand.

"Stevie, she fell," Jerry said. "She tripped out of the trailer."

Another glass shattered inside Frannie Tidwell's trailer. Magdalene willed herself to ignore it.

"Looks like you tryin' to roll my Grammy," Stevie Rich said. "You tryin' to roll my Grammy, Eves?"

"No, I *told* you—"

Magdalene ran straight at Stevie and closed her fingers around the muzzle. It was warm to the touch. With her other hand, she snatched Stevie Rich's chin—greasy and pimply—and held his head still.

"No, no. Look at *me*."

"Jimmy, that you?" Grammy squinted from the ground towards her great-grandson.

"Grammy fell. She tripped from her trailer. She thought Jerry might be someone else. She was—no, look at *me*, Stevie, goddamn it—waiting for someone—you know who. She fell, that's it."

"Magdalene," Jerry said. "I, uh, think our time has come, if you know what I mean."

Frannie Tidwell's trailer seemed to rock on its supports.

"He's lookin' for a gun," Stevie Rich said, looking down at the one in his hand. "Gonna be hell to pay."

Magdalene stepped on Stevie's bare feet.

"Help us get Grammy up and back into her trailer. She's old. I don't know if she broke something or not, but you're gonna need to call—yes, Stevie, yes—you're gonna need to call an ambulance. Not the police. They might come too. But you'll need to call an ambulance to make sure Grammy didn't break anything."

"Jimmy, you're late," cackled Grammy between coughing, little laughs. "Been a-waitin'."

Stevie Rich let his eyes rest on Magdalene's.

"I wouldn't hurt your Grammy, not for anything in the world, okay? Let's just get her up. You know we can't stay here." Magdalene nodded towards Frannie's trailer.

Stevie Rich blinked once or twice, pushed Magdalene aside, and raised the little silver gun.

"Just let 'em go," Stevie Rich said.

Frannie Tidwell stood at his open trailer door in a tattered bathrobe and not much else, a revolver in his hand, a cigarette dangling from his lips.

"You talkin' to me, boy?" Frannie Tidwell asked, the cigarette dancing in his mouth.

"Grammy fell outta the trailer," Stevie Rich said. He had the little gun aimed at his father. "She's waitin' for someone, and she thought..." Stevie paused.

"Cat got your tongue, boy?" Frannie bellowed.

"She thought my friends here were who she was waitin' for," Stevie Rich said.

"Jimmy, that you?" Grammy asked.

"Well, get her off the fuckin' ground, will ya?" Frannie yelled.

"You know who she was waitin' for, right, Frannie?" Stevie Rich said. "You know."

Frannie's eyes shifted from circles of surprise to narrow slits. Magdalene took a step back towards Jerry and Grammy.

"That my gun?" Frannie asked. "That my fuckin' gun?"

"Found it," Stevie Rich said. "And if it is, don't matter. Grammy fell. We gotta call an ambulance."

"Yeah, you gonna pay for that ambulance ride, boy, huh? You gonna pay the medical bills?"

Magdalene eased next to Jerry and tried to prop Grammy up.

"Chloe?"

"No, Grammy, it's Magdalene. Just like you. Magdalene."

"Redeemed we are, dear," Grammy said, patting Magdalene's hand with her own little sheath of skin and bones. "Redeemed in the eyes of our Lord."

"Let her down," Stevie Rich said. His eyes glanced over at Magdalene and Jerry and Grammy. The little gun was still aimed at his father. Frannie had lowered his pistol and stared at the tableau in front of him.

"I'll fuckin' be..." Frannie Tidwell muttered under his breath. The cigarette dripped from his mouth, hitting his bare feet with a shower of sparks.

"Goddamn shit," Stevie Rich said, shaking his own feet in sympathy.

"Let her down?" Jerry whispered to Magdalene. Magdalene shrugged. There were so many numbers now, as many as there were raindrops. She found it hard to think. The rain was falling hard.

"Case she broke something," Stevie Rich said. "Just let her down. My uncle was a fireman. He told me, unless you gotta 'cause of fire, you leave 'em be 'til the paramedics get here. Frannie, you go in and call..."

"And who's gonna pay for it?"

"...before I have to go and shoot you."

Frannie Tidwell turned and went back into his trailer, slamming the door behind him.

"No, Magdalene, let her down easy. She'll be okay in the grass. Get goin'. Now, go. I'll take care of it. He's on a tear, I can tell. Gonna be a long night. The cops are gonna come out no matter what 'cause it's the Lakes. Just hope Frannie can hold it together when they get here. He hates cops."

Magdalene and Jerry eased Grammy down onto the grass.

"You come back and see Grammy. I'll whip up some eggs."

"Okay, Grammy, okay," Magdalene said, feeling bad for lying, but feeling okay that Stevie Rich was in charge.

Magdalene and Jerry backed towards the GTO and eased into the bucket seats.

"We can call an ambulance once we're outside of the Lakes," Magdalene yelled.

"Yeah, that might be best," Stevie Rich said, never taking his eyes off of Frannie's trailer door.

"Get rid of the gun," Jerry said, "before the police get here."

Frannie kicked open his screen door and fired a round in the general direction of the GTO. The bullet clanged off a rusty folding chair.

"Don't worry," Stevie Rich said and fired the little gun (that *had* to be the last bullet, Magdalene thought) above Frannie's head. (Frannie scampered back inside.) "I'll be long gone when they get here. I don't like cops much either."

"Just don't do anything foolish."

"Get," Stevie Rich said, never turning his head. "Thank you for Grammy. Won't forget it."

"Don't go losin' Lou's Head," said as she closed the car door.

"Jimmy, that you?"

"No, it's Stevie, Grammy. Gonna have an ambulance here soon, okay. They're gonna check you out, alright?"

The GTO's wheels spun, and Jerry's easy grin was now skull-like, his lips peeled back. A cloud of red dust swallowed the car despite the rain. Magdalene tried to roll her window back up, but it was too late. They were swallowed, swallowed whole.

"*...don't you go losin' Lou's Head, Lil.*"

"*And God said to Jonah: 'Arise, go to Nineveh, that great city, and cry out against it, for their wickedness has come up before me.'* "

The basement chapel at Assumption was a smaller version of the main church upstairs. It was a particularly solemn place, as if monks and cardinals were buried beneath its slates of scuffed grays, bruised reds, mournful violets. Like the main church, the pews were divided so that, if seen from above, the aisles made a big cross—or in the case of the basement chapel, a little cross.

Sometimes nuns and lay teachers brought a class there for special spiritual instruction—or to scare them, Magdalene thought. (Sister Rita loved using chapel attendance as a scare tactic.) In the main church, even on Sundays, squished into pews with family and neighbors, the urge to act out remained unabated—at least for many of the boys. Christina and her Bod Squad buddies stood in the back of the church on Sundays, Marlboro-breath at the ready for Communion, then a quick duck outside for one last smoke beneath the rectory stairs. In the basement chapel, no one acted out. No one chewed gum or wrote notes on the corners of hymnals or planned rendezvous for the evening hours. No one acted out, period.

Perhaps it was the size of the chapel. A single classroom of children was a tight fit, and the shuffle of saddle shoes and the smell of the chalk dust that had settled on their clothes were strong. If someone had bad breath, the whole class knew instantly. Sister Rita quite frequently had bad breath. It was rancid, like bologna left sitting out next to a dead cat and a pile of steaming dog turds—it was that bad. Sometimes there were little traces of blood in the spaces between her odd, misshapen, yellow teeth. It was close quarters in the chapel.

One of Sister Rita's favorite scary stories to hiss at her charges as they settled into the chapel pews was the story of Jonah and the whale. Father Dave used Jonah's woes often too. But Magdalene had been under Michael's blanket; she knew the story of Jonah well. Hailing some fisherman, the reluctant prophet Jonah took to the sea after refusing to raise the Lord's ire against Nineveh, but the waters became embroiled and the sailors frightened. Jonah instructed the men to toss him into the sea, since he reckoned the storm to be God's response to his cowardice. Along came the whale, and Jonah was swallowed whole.

The chapel was the domain of Father Demetrius. Its maintenance, according to the nuns, was the elderly priest's single ecclesiastical duty. The job seemed to consist (if Magdalene skipped over general cleaning duties) of lighting and dousing the various chapel candles. Father Demetrius was at least eighty years old, maybe older, and he shuffled from wick to wick, his eyes focused straight ahead on the wick in question, limping an inch at a time, sometimes right past the priest celebrating the Mass. If his goal was to light the candles to help illuminate the general gloom of the chapel, then he failed miserably. Sister Edna had said the chapel was one of the first things built when Mondauk was settled, and if Magdalene could judge age by gloominess, then the chapel could have been held over from the time of the cave men—even the frames of the decrepit Stations of the Cross, festooned along the pockmarked stone walls, were broken and misshapen by age or weather or something far more sinister. The corners of a few of the frames appeared to have melted, dripping with prehistoric sweat. Often by the time the last of the children were arranged mutely in single file for the march from the chapel back to the classroom (or, *please, please, please,* the black asphalt of the recess area for a gulp of air not emanating from either Sister Rita's perpetually bleeding gums or their gloom and doom ancestors), they were in complete darkness. The underground chapel, according to Sister Edna—who's idea of God was not the martyr-eating deity of Sister Rita nor the gentle, bespectacled paternal figure of Father Dave's homilies, but rather a God who inspired an awed fear—was the last remnant of the original church, destroyed by marauding Methodists. There were no windows. Little outside light penetrated, and the chapel was home to more than its share of candle stands, maybe a hundred. Regardless of historical context or particular fears, Father Demetrius often succeeded in dousing the last candle, placing his little silver cup, which jutted from the end of a short silver stick, over the last flame about halfway through the service, tossing the proceedings into total darkness.

Poof.

" 'And then he said to them: Pick me up and throw me into the sea that it may quiet down for—' "

"Donna Gayno*rrrr*, are you *chhhhewwww*ing gum?"

"*Ow*! Sister, stop pinching! I'm not Donna—it's me: Jimmy Lonergan!"

"W*hhhh*y a*rrrr*e you *wwwwea*rrrr*ing a ssssskirrrrt*, young man?

"Sister, that's my tie. It's my dad's, so it's a little long."

Donna Gaynor would never have chewed gum in the chapel—and Donna Gaynor was rarely without gum. Magdalene had become convinced the acne and the blackheads that had spread across the bridge of Donna's nose was the result of being forced, almost every day, to stick the remains of her gum there. But it had been a long afternoon; concluding the school day with a sermon in the basement chapel had made everyone edgy, including Sister Rita and Father Dave.

" '…and Jonah was in the belly of the fish three days and three nights'…Sister, is there a problem?"

Sister Rita, in addition to being disfigured in several ways, also seemed to be hard of hearing.

"Ou*rrrr* Fathe*rrrr*, *whhhh*o a*rrrr*t in hea*vvvv*en—"

"Sister," Father Dave said, "we haven't reached that part yet."

"I don't think it'*ssss* app*rrrr*op*rrrr*iate fo*rrrr* the *chhhhillll*d*rrrr*en to fa*rrrr*t eithe*rrrr*," Sister Rita replied.

Father Demetrius lit a candle in the back of the chapel, throwing Sister Rita's shadow against the tiny stone altar. Because of the size of the room and the tightness of the tiny pews, Sister Rita usually leaned against the wall, and where she chose to lean today—between the utter heartbreak of the Fourth Station (Jesus Meets His Mother) and the mini-miracle of the Sixth (Veronica Wipes Jesus' Face)—was both auspicious and suspicious, for the Fifth Station (Simon Carries the Cross), where Sister Rita leaned the damaged remains of her possibly leprous body, was missing.

Father Demetrius spent the remainder of the service lighting every available candle, sometimes even dragging in additional candle stands so that the children had to wind their way down the aisle for Communion like an obstacle course—but in a half-darkness: Father Demetrius immediately began putting out the flames as soon as he lit the last one in an effort to catch up on his day. And every time Sister Rita attended to some perceived student waywardness, Father Demetrius shuffled to the ancient wall where the Fifth Station had hung for time immemorial and stared mutely at the blank space.

Poof.

They could never get the nuns to talk. But older siblings and younger parents remembered a time when Father Demetrius was the pastor of Assumption—on his way to bigger and better capes and hats. Like so many stories where the whispered truth was so far removed from the actual truth (and probably less spectacular), there was no consensus, except: whatever had happened had taken the priest's sanity (and his career trajectory) with it.

Even Magdalene's father had spoken of Father Demetrius (before the pastor's fall) in tones of quiet respect. He had often quoted his sermons and sought his advice. "A man of faith, a true man of faith, Maddie, doesn't need to worry himself over the minutiae of a single parish. Father Demetrius is a man of vision, a leader. He sees the Catholic Church in roles normally the province of the Methodists, at least around these parts." Her father saw in Father Demetrius a fortunate lack of magic—a man grounded by his faith, rather than lost in its mysteries or weighed down by the inevitability of doubt.

And a leader he had looked to become. Father Demetrius had been invited, it was announced in a breathless Church bulletin, to speak in Philadelphia on some pertinent Church issue; the Holy Roman Church wanted the opinions and teachings of Mondauk's own Father Demetrius, not the musings of a big city priest or some seminarian professor of theology. They wanted Father Demetrius—*their* Father Demetrius: the slightest trace of a Greek accent still buried beneath his worthy tongue, his subtle jibes at the Irish Father Tuffy for his beer quaffing, his self-deprecating humor regarding his Orthodox Catholic upbringing—"Spent more time painting eggs than I did mending fences," Father Demetrius had said from the pulpit more than once. In other words: *do* rather than simply *worship*. Action rather than magic. To Father Demetrius and his learned Disciples (Magdalene's father and Dr. Fuller among them), the

Church was a tool to do good. No magic needed. Magicians need not apply.

Until the car accident.

The version Magdalene knew was this: it wasn't Father Demetrius' car (although he had one and drove himself, a fact mentioned again and again in stories about Father Demetrius, as if he were already an archbishop or cardinal with a chauffeur at the ready), and the identity of the driver of the other car, who's head had either been cracked open after passing through the windshield or had been severed completely at the neck by jagged glass, was unknown. Fuzzy. The police were already there and maybe an ambulance or two when Father Demetrius happened upon the scene of the accident on the state turnpike. (There never seemed to be any mention of the other vehicle involved.) The vehicular companion of the headless (or nearly headless) man had noticed Father Demetrius, sitting in his car, his head nodding along to a book on tape. The priest had been on his way back from a symposium in Philadelphia. Another detail that emerged in the years of telling: to some, it was a tape of Richard Burton or Burl Ives reading from the Old Testament, usually *Leviticus*, to others it was classic literature, to some a trashy piece of popular pulp, or, God forbid, Joyce Carol Oates—Catholics in Mondauk deemed her particularly dangerous. One persistent rumor was that Father Demetrius had been engaged in a session of vehicular, aural stimulation via a tape of lascivious letters detailing illicit encounters with busloads of public school cheerleaders. Regardless, the passenger of the mortally wounded man hailed Father Demetrius by knocking on his window or throwing rocks at his car (depending upon the version and/or the teller).

There was little Father Demetrius could do for the injured man other than spiritual succor. (Here Magdalene inserted her own spin to the story, as she imagined, from the events that followed, Father Demetrius to be a proud man—like her father. Magdalene imagined people who valued their intellect above all else to be at least slightly prideful, if for no other reason than to perhaps make up for the fact that their brains were inside and everyone else's beauty and muscles were on the outside—not that Magdalene considered *all* smart people unfortunate in appearance, but a quick glance in the mirror usually shored up that opinion right quick.) Father Demetrius jogged past the other cars to administer the final rites.

Here's where it got sticky. Here's where the story of Father

Demetrius and Lou's Head tripped over itself into Alice's Looking Glass or Dorothy's Oz. (The tale was well-known to Magdalene; she'd heard it from adults sipping beer or wine coolers during summer backyard parties and from classmates huddled in whispering circles in the back of the library during Study Hall.) Father Demetrius knelt down next to the man and began, with the seeing-without-looking efficiency of someone who had done this a thousand times, to anoint the driver's forehead with oil.

Only the driver was not in possession of his head.

The driver's head had rolled to the shoulder and had been surrounded by police and fire workers and those oddly pink-red road flares.

Father Demetrius waved a quick sign of the cross over the body and allowed himself to be ushered to the head.

Now, here's where good Father Demetrius lost *his* head. And like the driver of the car (in the version adopted by Magdalene), he was never to be in possession of it again.

Father Demetrius' Disciples had had their own opinions. (They called themselves this—Disciples—except for her father; how many times had he said to her and Michael, his rich voice, thick with the gravel of the courtroom and a young man's predilection for smoking: "Never a disciple nor a lender be," always laughing at something that neither of his children understood, she and Michael dismissing the statement and the fatherly guffaws that followed as that strange, dry, adult humor they rarely found funny?) Father Demetrius' Disciples had lamented aloud, "If only he hadn't stopped," or, "If only he had left the city earlier," or sometimes even, "If only the man had been able to hold onto his head."

Not: why hadn't Father Demetrius *jumped* from his car to administer Last Rites or prayers for the wounded? All of the versions had his vehicle among the first couple of cars in the police backup. Surely, if he had been that close, Father Demetrius had witnessed the accident scene.

Not: why had Father Demetrius, after attempting to execute the responsibilities of his office, his vocation, been found babbling next to a tiny excuse for a brook? (Most likely the brook itself was not babbling due to its diminutive description; more likely it was trickling—another unexplainable portion of the story that *every* version had: he was found next to a little, nearly dried up brook.) The priest had been found naked except for a scapular and generously applied sunscreen; the latter, according to police reports, he had taken from a startled observer's car. Father Demetrius had walked up to the sun-conscious man's Fiat, absolved him of his sins, reached into the backseat, and liberated the sunscreen.

Back to the *really* sticky part:

Father Demetrius knelt next to the head and tried to extract the necessary items for the Catholic passage of death from his handy Last Rites travel kit, but his fingers betrayed him, and the little bottle of oil almost rolled into the head's open mouth. (The driver had apparently been surprised when his head ejected from his body like a dandelion flower popped by a five-year-old.)

A police officer retrieved the vial and handed it back.

"Here ya go, Father. You want we should kneel?" the police officer asked.

Father Demetrius nodded—words were failing him. With the exception of certain passages from the last sacrament (and even those, it was reported, were not in the preferred order), Father Demetrius stopped speaking in complete sentences. The jumbled religious phrases were the last words he ever spoke—if you discount the babbling by the brook, but sometimes, the "last words he ever spoke" part was omitted from the telling. They were certainly the last words he spoke before he sang (most likely for the final time as well.) Magdalene found it hard to piece together the truth, impossible really. The important things in the story of Lou's Head, for Magdalene and Michael, was the lesson learned: don't go losin' Lou's Head.

So Father Demetrius began the sacrament of the Last Rites, bungling the order, mumbling words, skipping others, almost leaning on the policeman who had retrieved the oil.

Eventually, Father Demetrius' mouth would stop making noise altogether—at least for a little while.

But the head didn't.

The head, it seemed, still had a lot on its mind.

"Chicken soup," said the head.

And that's about where the story has Father Demetrius' mumbling depreciate into hyperventilation. His right hand kept moving, however; Father Demetrius' hand flew over the head in a rapid sequence of the sign of the cross—over and over and over. Father Demetrius maintained his perpetual blessing—as if this head needed more than the usual recommendations to enter heaven, as if this man's body had long struggled with the man's head, one part keeping the laws of God, the rest desiring to root in a more earthy cellar.

"Like he was making shadow puppets," the policeman, who was all but holding up Father Demetrius, reported in the *Mondauk Common*.

The priest was on his knees, his hand flying through the air, his body slumped against the cop's.

"Ruthie," said the head, which then spit.

According to the policeman (Magdalene thought of him as Frank; she didn't remember his real name, but Frank seemed appropriate), it was around then that Father Demetrius skipped ahead past the penitential part of the rite. Maybe Father Demetrius had said it to himself, or maybe he'd realized, despite any powers vested in him by the Holy Roman Catholic Church, that absolving a head of *anything* might prove difficult to explain should he ever be questioned about his highway activities and the duties performed there at a later date.

Or maybe he just didn't like kneeling before the talking head.

"Ham, Ruthie," suggested the head, perhaps looking forward to a roadside lunch. "Ham with mustard."

Officer Frank reported to the *Mondauk Common* that Father Demetrius had started humming to himself right about THERE. Not quite humming—murmuring, talk-singing, roadside a cappella.

"I think it was Neil Diamond," Officer Frank told the reporter. "But I can't really say. It's all in the report. I don't follow music much. Not since Ol' Blue Eyes passed away, God rest his soul. But it was a Hello Song, if you know what I mean, not a Goodbye Song.

"But then he stopped humming a bit. Seemed to find his feet, you know, his sea legs. Can't say I blame him. I know these sacramental things can't be rushed, but if you're not used to seeing heads or toes or sometimes the insides of—well, never mind—if you're not used to seeing stuff like that, it can blow your top, I know. Can really get inside a guy's head—no offense to the victim, of course. No offense. Anyway, Father seemed to get ahead of himself. He kinda got all entangled in the words."

Magdalene knew all about dead people getting inside one's head.

Aunt Tiddy had dragged Magdalene to easily twenty funerals during the years since cancer had taken Patricia Barrows. Michael had been dragged too—until the snipes snatched him. Before Tiddy moved in, Magdalene often slept over Tiddy's little apartment on the weekend. The weekends were sacrosanct to her father. Two dollar drink specials and Saturday football practice; Coach Barrows never missed a practice, even if he showed up unshaven, reeking of McCullough's, a Camel dangling from his chapped lips, a curious, damp stain on his trousers. Sometimes Michael stayed over too, but he was often excused for football practice and Summer Camp. Magdalene suspected that her banishment was Michael's doing. At least on weekends, with football practice dominating Saturdays and the games being played on Sundays, Michael could take an active role in their father's extracurricular occupations. But that wasn't the worst part of the weekend—although it was pretty bad; Magdalene pretended it wasn't, a trick she had learned from her mother (and wasn't it funny, how in this cloud of red dust inside the vicious boundaries of Paradise Lakes, her mother came into view, clearer than ever, not just perfume traces left on an old sweater, but actual flesh and blood—there, there's the little scar on her cheek that she refused to explain, that she'd tell her children was from another life altogether)—no, the worst part of the weekend wasn't not playing football (or even not watching it), it was witnessing Aunt Tiddy's morning scan of the obituary page—and seeing dead bodies.

Maybe it was Tiddy's way of embracing her transition into senior citizenry, but to Magdalene, Aunt Tiddy had always been old. Whatever the reason, Tiddy would circle the most promising prospects in the *Mondauk Common* with a red felt pen.

"I knew him!" Aunt Tiddy would cry. "He used to cut your father's hair when he was a little boy.

"My God," Aunt Tiddy would exclaim, her hand fluttering at her chest. "I had no idea she was even still alive! And now she's dead. She worked at the fish market. Poor Mary," Aunt Tiddy said, adjusting her reading glasses. "Matilda," she corrected herself. "Poor old Matilda."

Tiddy would then yank the calendar from the wall (always the right year, not like in Magdalene's house, where a calendar was apt to mark the second anniversary of a 1998 holiday before being replaced, as if trying to compete with the vacillating accuracy of the various clocks' effort to lock down a specific period of time), marking the date of the services.

"Wash out that navy blue dress," Tiddy would instruct. "No, better give it here. You're better at flailing *in* the mud than removing it."

Magdalene accompanied Aunt Tiddy to almost every funeral—even if Tiddy wasn't quite sure if she knew the deceased or not. One memorable time, after waiting in line for what seemed like an hour, her aunt's smart, black change-purse at the ready with tissues ("If Lawrence knew how long we had to wait to see his dead body, he'd have had a bird," Tiddy hissed in Magdalene's ear, her breath medicinal even then), Tiddy snatched her hand out from Magdalene's, whom she'd been leaning on for support.

"Sonofabitch," Aunt Tiddy said, whipping around from the coffin and plunging back towards the doors of the church, directly through the line of mourners. "It wasn't him," Tiddy said over her shoulder to Magdalene, who dodged indignant mourners and angry stares. "That means—I can't believe it! *My* Lawrence Burrell is still alive!" When Tiddy reached the vestibule, she turned and sprinted back up towards the *other* Mr. Burrell. "I don't know *who* the hell *that* is!"

Magdalene tried not to look at the dead bodies. Although she rarely knew the deceased, the few times she had known the wax replicas, with their posed praying hands, they looked nothing like they had when they'd still been breathing. She didn't remember her mother's viewing (other than being afraid her father would drunkenly bump into the coffin), but Magdalene was sure the absence of Patricia Archer Rumsey's impressive breasts, long removed, would have sent her off the proverbial deep end. She'd have lost her head for sure. When Tiddy approached a coffin, Magdalene would close her eyes and keep them closed until Tiddy was done *tsk-tsking* and was yanking her grandniece to the exit—it wasn't all that different from holding her breath.

By virtue of having attended an almost innumerable number of funerals (innumerable at least right now, in the red dirt cloud, ensconced in Mick's GTO, hunched in the passenger bucket seat, watching Jerry navigate his way through the cloud to—where?—safety?), Magdalene knew the choice of funeral Biblical passages quite well. If the deceased was unknown to the officiating priest, he could always fall back on a few favorites.

Some were troubling, like: "Whoever eats my flesh and drinks my blood has eternal life, and I will raise him up at the last day, for my flesh is real food and my blood is real drink."

Others were just plain confusing: "I am the way and the truth and the life. No one comes to the Father except through me," to which,

Magdalene concluded, several hundred generations of Jews could only reply with an irritated shrug. Who was to know when God would pull out the rug again? Assistant District Attorney Gregory Barrows referred to this as a possible *proviso*.

Magdalene preferred John 15:4 above all others: "Remain in me, and I will remain in you."

Short, simple, and to the point.

Of course, becoming lost yourself could increase the possibility of losing everyone else around you.

But Father Demetrius, faced with nothing more (and nothing less) than a driver who had lost nothing more (and nothing less traumatic) than his noggin, could not conjure up even the simplest of these passages.

The head wouldn't shut up.

"Soup, Ruthie," said the head. "I'd like some chicken noodle soup."

"And so we know," Father Demetrius started again, "and rely on the love God has—"

"No crackers. I'm so thirsty," said the head. "God, I'm so thirsty. No crackers."

"...the love God has for us and the love...God is love...whoever loves in love—"

"I pledge allegiance to the flag," stated the head, "of the United States of America—"

"...whomever lives in love lives in God and God lives in him forever, for I am—"

" *'Goo goo goo joob,'* " the head added. " *'I am the eggman.'* "

Father Demetrius switched tactics: "Whoever so believeth in me and die shall live for—"

" 'Four score—' " began the head.

" '...and seven years ago...' " finished Father Demetrius.

Officer Frank noted that Father Demetrius did manage to mumble what sounded like the Prayer of the Dead. Magdalene knew it by heart due to Aunt Tiddy's funeral haunting: "We come to you, O lord, the soul of this your servant..."

"Father?" Frank the cop nudged him; the priest was still leaning against Frank for support.

Father Demetrius looked down at the head, then placed his face as low to the ground as he could, holding on to Officer Frank with one hand.

"What is your...?" asked Father Demetrius.

The head appeared flustered, then elated.

"Lou!"

"...of this your servant Lou...redeemer of...as in your love...and the number of the blessed..."

"He just sorta petered out," Officer Frank reported. "Started humming again. Real loud."

" '*Hmm-hm*-hmm / *hmm-hm*-m-*hm*, *hm*-m-*hm*,' " hummed Father Demetrius.

" '*Hmm-hm*-hmm / *hmm-hm*-m-*hm*, *hm*-m-*hm*,' " Lou's head began.

"It was like they were humming independent of each other—the victim and Father. They...they just kept humming. Until they got to that part, you know, what do they call it? Right before the chorus. Then they started singing out loud. Real loud."

" '*...touching hands...* ' " whispered Father Demetrius.

" '*...reaching out...* ' " whispered the head.

" '*...touching me...* ' " sang the priest in almost full choir voice.

" '*...TOUCHING YOU!*' " concluded Lou's head, at a volume described as being at the top of his lungs, if he had still been connected to them.

Several stories had circled around Mondauk, some sordid (Father Demetrius had had an affair with the man who'd lost his head), others less so (Father Demetrius had broken down when he saw the head roll its eyes up), and some just plain silly (Father Demetrius had snatched Lou's head from the shoulder of the highway and made for the woods with the police in hot pursuit). But what happened next, according to Officer Frank (and a couple of "eyewitnesses" quoted in the *Common*) was this: Father Demetrius smiled at Lou's head, and Lou's head smiled back, and they charged into the chorus together.

"With gusto," Officer Frank said. "That head could really sing Neil Diamond."

" '*SWEET CAROLINE—BA BA BUMP—GOOD TIMES NEVER SEEMED SO GOOD—I BEEN INCLINED—BA BA BUMP—TO BELIEVE THEY NEVER WOULD!*' "

Yellow star.

Red star.

White star.

Black.

Father Demetrius was still singing when they found him slathered in suntan lotion, but he was far beyond words. Some of the more rabid Disciples said he had been speaking in tongues, but Magdalene liked to think he was just making noise to block the sound of God's wrath. He had shattered the pieces of his life he'd given over to God. Maybe he thought God had failed him when he needed God most. Maybe the administrative and political duties he enjoyed were his true calling. Magdalene recognized the prayers, mumblings, and Neil Diamond lyrics for what they were: pieces.

Lou's head told Father Demetrius: "I'm sorry."

"And I forgive *myself*," Lou's head concluded triumphantly.

According to Officer Frank, the head then took the second verse and bridge of "Sweet Caroline" solo, before realizing it was dead. Officer Frank said it was the saddest, most terrifying look he had ever seen on a human being ("…or a piece of one.") "One minute, the head was singing Neil, doin' okay. I heard worse. The next, *boom*, he notices that he's just a head. Never finished the song."

"Funny thing," Officer Frank told the reporter, "but it was more of a Hello Song than a Goodbye Song, like I said."

With Assumption's main church nearing the end of a community-funded facelift (Dr. Fuller chaired this particular board), much of the decor—the long candle snuffers, the incense lantern that swung on a chain of gold, the red confessional cushions, the cracked and fading Stations of the Cross—were relocated to the underground chapel. It had rarely been used until Pastor Father Demetrius allowed young Father Dave—a cheerleader for Jesus if there ever was one—to conduct singing masses in the chapel, masses where the entire liturgy, even Father Dave's parts, were accompanied by a trio of hippies: a terribly skinny couple with acoustic guitars and one young woman, endowed with tremendous boobs, rattling a tambourine: the Bonnie Happy Three. The singing masses were popular with the younger congregates. Magdalene suspected this was because of their brevity; Father Demetrius' occasional lapses into monotony and his tuneless execution of key lines were successful only in elongating a Mass already stretched to the breaking point by Father Demetrius' impossible-to-follow homilies (which were peppered by little knowing laughs from the Disciples, an act Father Demetrius encouraged and allowed to fetter away before he would even think of continuing). (God forbid someone miss a word while locking eyes with a fellow Disciple and exchanging a wee chuckle!) But Father Dave's singing masses were so popular that the stairs leading down to the chapel became a fire hazard, chock full of worshippers eager to sing or escape the droning of Father Demetrius and the tittering of his clique upstairs, and eventually Father Demetrius rearranged the schedule in the main church so Father Dave and the Bonnie Happy Three (upcoming secular trio appearances at the Drafting Room in Spring House were advertised in the Church Bulletin—tips appreciated!) could assault the heavens with the jangle of an Apostolic Creed sung at the speed of a sneeze. Besides: the chapel was far too gloomy for Father Dave—and Father Dave was too ambitious to remain in the basement long.

Following Father Demetrius' slide into mute shuffling and candle snuffing, singing masses became de rigueur (and the Bonnie Happy Three ubiquitous). The basement chapel was left to student suffering and Father Demetrius and his deleterious candle duty.

Even Aunt Tiddy never seemed to doubt the story of Lou's head, which, true or not, was a part of the local fabric.

"He was so far up his own backside that he couldn't *deal* with a talking head," Aunt Tiddy had said. "He probably couldn't deal with a silent head either, come to think of it. (Heads don't come with wallets you know.) Father Demetrius was used to people kissing his holy ass. Asses he was used to. Talking head? That's a whole 'nother roll and butter, as Shakespeare said. The only thing Father Demetrius liked better than fund-raising and books was beating the Methodists out at carnival time. Always made sure we had the best carnival.

"And now we got the Bonnie Happy Feet," Aunt Tiddy said. "Win some, lose some. I don't know *who* said that. Poor Father Demetrius. Can't save someone else's soul if you don't know how to save your own.

"Hell, in my time, there've been priests who forgot to absolve a man before he died or failed to baptize a baby before it went back from whence it came. But there was no one to help Father Demetrius. Ol' Bill, he said the proud fall the messiest, but here he was wrong (and that man is rarely wrong, lemme tell you): Father Demetrius didn't fall. He ran," Aunt Tiddy concluded. "Ran like the dickens."

Of the great writer's oeuvre, Magdalene had only read *A Christmas Carol*, so she decided not to ask Aunt Tiddy how Charles Dickens applied to Father Demetrius. Magdalene had learned the hard way that some things were better left—

"And before you ask, it's just an expression. Run like the devil. Only nicer."

Magdalene failed to see the more pleasant side of Father Demetrius' situation.

"Like 'Shakespeare said that'? " Magdalene countered.

"No!" Tiddy snapped. "Ol' Bill's a real fount of wisdom. Won't shut up half the time."

Magdalene shrugged.

Not soon after Father Demetrius was installed in the basement chapel, Father Dave (now officially Pastor Dave, but no one called him that) shrugged as well.

"But it's *missing*," Mrs. Fuller said, elongating the last word so Father Dave could take his time and soak it in.

"So it is, Bernadette," Father Dave replied, somehow managing to look her in the eye with a kindly tilt of his head and stare above her hairsprayed helmet as if calmly observing angels in action at the same time.

They were on the steps of the Church, Magdalene tagging along because she'd slept over Christina Fuller's house. Michael had gone missing not long before, and Magdalene had already failed her first suicide attempt. It was their final sleepover. Dr. Fuller hadn't accompanied them to Mass; he was at a symposium somewhere. (Magdalene wondered if he was happy to be separated from the spastic harlequin in designer clothes he had married.) Dr. Fuller never treated Magdalene any different, always asking after her, as if she had just gotten over a cold or the flu and had not just tried to swallow a sword. Mrs. Fuller narrowed her eyes in Magdalene's presence as if searching for forensic evidence, as if Mrs. Fuller didn't want Christina to catch what Magdalene had. Magdalene was careful in Mrs. Fuller's presence.

On the Church steps, Magdalene watched Father Dave count the angels avoiding the ozone levels around Mrs. Fuller's coiffed coil.

"Well?" asked Mrs. Fuller. "Are you going to speak to Father Demetrius?"

She stressed every syllable of the former pastor's name. Father Dave sighed and Magdalene watched him mentally bid farewell to the angels.

"We have convened an inquiry to—"

"Don't play with me, Father," Mrs. Fuller warned, but Father Dave, the sun glinting from his little, red beard—little because, as Dr. Fuller had explained, every man has a different beard pattern, and apparently Father Dave's beard only grew into two thin strips that met at his chin, like straps for an invisible hat—seemed to tune his ears away from the shrill audio of Mrs. Fuller.

"I am *talking* to you, Father," Mrs. Fuller said, stamping her foot. "The Board raises the money for your—decorations."

Father Dave cast an eye in her direction and then caught Magdalene attempting a smile.

"These were old, Mrs. Fuller, older than me. Even older than—" Father Dave stopped himself. He liked an audience. Christina was indifferent, distracted, as she usually was around adults. Magdalene followed the exchange carefully.

"Decorations," muttered Father Dave. "Can't wait to see your house at Halloween."

Father Dave cocked his head to one side and sniffed the air, oblivious of Mrs. Fuller's full-on righteous indignation.

"The Faith Board has *certain*—" Mrs. Fuller began, the syllables rising from her lowest register to her highest.

"Shhh," Father Dave instructed, turning away from Magdalene, Christina, and a now terrifically fuming and quite put out Mrs. Fuller. Father Dave made a quick sign of the cross in their direction and winked. Magdalene crossed herself, watching Christina take the easy way out, jostling her hand in one place, her bracelets clanking in the cool breeze that drifted across the Church steps. Mrs. Fuller stood with her hand on her hip. Father Dave walked on his toes to the stone railing, his nose stuck in the air.

Magdalene could smell it now too. Was that cigarette smoke?

Father Dave leapt over the side of the Church steps and reached into the berry bushes, lifting Jimmy Lonergan and Jerry Eves by their collars. Jimmy Lonergan had a Marlboro dangling from his lips.

"Well, I never!" Mrs. Fuller exclaimed.

"Yes, you have, Bernadette," Father Dave said without looking up. "Have a nice Sunday."

Magdalene thought she caught the priest winking at her again.

Jerry swore he hadn't been smoking, just hanging out, but Father Dave had collared them both. Because the infraction hadn't occurred during official school time, just on church grounds, Father Dave couldn't initiate the recommended punishment as noted in the school's Parental Handbook. Instead, he assigned Jimmy and Jerry rectory duty. He gave them chores that the chubby, tiptoeing maid and the old booze hound Charley Murphy took all week to accomplish. (Everyone knew that Charley could be found most nights—and days when not polishing chalices—firmly planted at McCullough's, making eyes at the young woman who owned the bar.)

"He wants to tire us out," Jimmy Lonergan said later in school.

" 'This is what smoking will do to you,' " Jerry Eves said, imitating Father Dave's sardonic tone. "Damn," Jerry said, chewing on a pencil. "I really didn't do anything—this time!"

Jerry smiled at Magdalene. He knew she was eavesdropping. Jerry punched Jimmy in the arm then stuck the pencil up his own nose.

"Gettin' the lead out," Jerry said, looking again to see if Magdalene was paying attention.

She wasn't—well, okay, she was, but: *Jerry Eves*? She had plans, embryonic plans—plans that didn't, couldn't, involve lanky funny bone Jerry Eves.

She thought she could hear his voice, even now, in the cloud of red dirt surrounding the blue GTO—or was it white chalk dust from banging out the erasers?

Clues. Everything was a clue.

But there were no clues in the Case of the Missing Fifth Station.

They didn't need any.

Jerry Eves found the missing portrait of Simon helping Jesus with the cross on His way to Golgotha.

Again, eavesdropping—which always made Magdalene giggle (inside)—*eaves*dropping on Jerry *Eves*!—and with Jerry aware (again) that she was listening, he told Jimmy Lonergan and Joseph Connelly (no Bod Squaders around, thank God) what had happened.

Father Dave knew Jerry hadn't been smoking; Father Dave had known Jerry's father and had witnessed the cancer take his father's lungs and then the rest of his body. So Jerry was assigned laundry detail. Jimmy had to polish the wooden staircase, mop out the bathroom, help with the dishes, and empty the trash into the dumpster. Jerry, not happy with the thought of handling holy skivvies, was dawdling after Father Dave left the rectory, hoping to kill some time and maybe get away with doing only a load or two of laundry—he hadn't been the one smoking after all.

Boredom sent him knocking on Father Demetrius' door. Jerry figured since he'd started a wash cycle, he was free to explore the rest of the rectory. Father Demetrius took his time shuffling to the door, Jerry said, as if the priest was coming from a long way off. When he reached the door, Jerry could hear him breathing. The chubby maid passed Jerry as he knocked again.

"He don't come out, that one. He'll leave his laundry out if he wants it done. A quiet bully, that one," the chubby maid said between gum snaps. "Gets what he wants 'cause everyone's afraid of him. Supposed to be brilliant," she concluded, eyeing Jerry's tall, skinny frame up and down. "You brilliant?"

Magdalene thought Jerry made the last part up, but she didn't care. The chubby maid's role ended there. (Jimmy tried to sweet-talk the horny help on the next floor and apparently had little luck— Jimmy punched Jerry in the arm when Jerry started to relay Jimmy's version of the failed romantic rendezvous, and Magdalene could tell from Jimmy's red face that part of it was true.)

Jerry couldn't let it go, however, even as the maid sashayed down the stairs, and he began tapping the rhythm of Neil Diamond's "Sweet Caroline" on Father Demetrius' door.

When the door swung open, Jerry's nose prepared himself for a shut-in, musky smell, but the room smelled like flowers, he said: "…like the wildflowers on the edge of the Fields."

"You sniffin' flowers now, Eves?" Joseph Connelly asked.

"Only to clear my nasal passages of your mother's—"

Jerry shrugged—he knew Magdalene was listening—and continued.

Father Demetrius stood with his back to Jerry in the center of the room. When Jerry asked if he had any laundry, Father Demetrius shuffled and pointed to a little adjacent room.

"When I passed him, *he* smelled—like he hadn't bathed in weeks or something. He reeked, but I felt sad for him. He looked sad. Like he wanted to die. So I go into this little room—there's not even a door; it was more like a big closet—and there it was, leaning against the wall, but in pieces—the frame I mean—but not in pieces. It's hard to explain."

The painting of Simon and Jesus was indeed in Father Demetrius' tiny sitting room, still in its frame, but the rows of bronze palm fronds that had decorated the frame (all the Stations in the underground chapel had the same design) had been broken off and were in pieces—many, many pieces—then glued back on. In some cases, tape had been used. Simon and Jesus appeared to be exploding, the haphazardly applied rusty fronds either exclamations of gratitude from Jesus amid a world of hate, or shrapnel from the bursting of Simon's heart at the treatment of this peaceful stranger. Jerry knelt down to get a closer look, and Father Demetrius was behind him, breathing heavily through his nose, placing a firm hand on Jerry's shoulder. He wanted Jerry to leave, but Jerry ignored him, and snapped off one of the fronds. Father Demetrius extended a claw to retrieve it, and Jerry broke off another one.

"See, they go this way," Jerry explained, fishing around with a free hand for the tube of glue he had seen before he'd knelt down; he didn't want to take his eyes off the priest who had once supposedly sang a duet with a severed head.

"See," Jerry said, gluing the fronds he had broken off back on in an approximation of their original position.

Father Demetrius again clasped Jerry's shoulder, but it was different this time—and Jerry went to work: snapping, gluing, mending, breaking again, until the frame at least held some semblance of its former, dilapidated glory. Father Demetrius made him tea that tasted like leaves. Jerry drank it anyway—he was admiring his handiwork. If Jimmy Lonergan was finished his chores (and romantic endeavors) and was waiting for him downstairs, then so be it. Jerry hadn't been the one smoking.

"Screw you, Eves," Jimmy Lonergan said. He attempted to give Jerry a noogie.

"Let him finish," Magdalene said. "Let him finish the story."

Jimmy blushed. Jerry cleared his throat and continued:

"How'd it break?" Jerry asked the priest.

Father Demetrius ignored him and showed Jerry his back.

"The frame," Jerry continued, "how'd it get that way?"

Father Demetrius turned back around and clasped Jerry's face with both hands, lifting him from the floor. Their faces were inches apart. Father Demetrius' smell was unbearable—but it wasn't the smell of dirt, Jerry said. It was the smell you get after burning rubber. The room smelled of wildflowers, and the shuffling, bent priest smelled of burnt rubber.

"How'd it break?" Jerry asked a third time, too curious not to ask, too afraid to pull away.

Father Demetrius released Jerry's face and shrugged.

"That's it?" Jimmy Lonergan asked. "He shrugged? That's the big mystery? That's what you kept me waiting for? You know, Father Dave made me—"

"He shrugged," Jerry said, shrugging. "He didn't know how it broke, and he tried to fix it, but since he probably never had to fix anything before in his life (being a bit of a bookworm) and he didn't know how it broke, he could never fix it. So he just glued and unglued, glued and unglued. Sad."

Father Demetrius' decline brought about the end of the Disciples. The lay Faith Board gained in power. Theology came in a distant second to creating an unofficial political machine, Magdalene's father had said many times. Dr. Fuller resigned from the Board, but Mrs. Fuller became chairwoman and then (simultaneously) editor of the Church Bulletin. Father Dave, keenly aware of which way the fund raising-flag blew, kept his insolence to a minimum, undermining the authority of the Board only when it was unavoidable—such as squashing the *What Method?* handout Mrs. Fuller had intended to distribute at the Methodist carnival using Catholics disguised in overalls or rock'n'roll t-shirts. "She actually suggested going to the Thrift Shoppe and buying old AC/DC shirts," Magdalene's father had said.

"What the hell is a 'Skynyrd?' " Aunt Tiddy had asked.

Father Demetrius began sleeping in the basement chapel after meeting Lou's Head and being released from the hospital. Magdalene had overheard Mrs. Fuller complaining to Dr. Fuller.

"*Someone* has to put a foot down," Mrs. Fuller said, standing over Dr. Fuller's reading chair. He was attempting to lose himself in a book after dinner.

"Did you speak with Father Dave?" Dr. Fuller asked, pretending not to be distracted.

"Father Dave!" Mrs. Fuller exclaimed, her hands shooting into the air.

"Father Dave," she repeated to herself quietly.

So Father Demetrius slept in the chapel, on a hardwood pew. As the chapel reeked of burnt candles, there was no worry of Father Demetrius' increasingly deleterious personal hygiene "stinking up the joint," as Jerry Eves put it.

And it just got worse; Father Demetrius rarely, if ever, left the chapel anymore. Perhaps with the frame of the Fifth Station intact, Father Demetrius had run out of extracurricular activities to occupy his non-candle-snuffing time. But Magdalene suspected it was something else: Father Demetrius couldn't face what he'd seen—in the Fifth Station or on the turnpike. Jerry Eves had described the painting as particularly unnerving up close: Jesus didn't look serene— His teeth were yellow and broken, His skin cracked, His eyes already dead. But it was Simon who was the scariest, Jerry had said. "Simon's eyes were about ready to *pop* out of his skull, and his mouth was open in that way that you just knew he was trying not to vomit on his sandals." Simon's hands were outstretched, reaching for the cross— itself a formidable log with a jagged, crooked crossbeam. Simon's hands were tentative and soft-looking; Jesus' hands were covered in blood and dirt. The sacrifice of *both* men was evident in the painting, and Jerry said he'd avoided looking at Simon's eyes during the reconstruction of the frame.

"It was *that* scary," Jerry Eves told Jimmy Lonergan and Joseph Connelly (and Magdalene Barrows). "Jesus looked goddamn awful, like a slasher movie victim, but Simon—he looked like he was in the middle of falling, like he couldn't believe the bottom was coming."

Jimmy Lonergan's attention wandered; he was trying to look up Magdalene's uniform. Joseph Connelly was adjusting the center of his trousers.

Magdalene let Jerry catch her eyes, and she nodded. *Like he couldn't believe the bottom was coming*—this from the author of Stick Man!

And maybe that's what it was: Father Demetrius couldn't stand to look at a frightened-to-the-core Simon helping a tortured Jesus take the next step towards execution. Maybe when Father Demetrius looked at Simon's terrified visage, it took the priest back to his time with Lou (or Lou's head). Maybe Father Demetrius caught a glimpse, in Simon's expression, of Lou's horror when the head realized it was no longer part of Lou. Maybe Father Demetrius, knowing that awareness would come to Lou's head sooner or later, had been filled with inextinguishable grief during their duet, precipitating the good priest's descent into sun lotion theft and perpetual candle-snuffing.

Humpty Dumpty was a cad, Magdalene thought. He sat on a goddamn wall—an eggman! " *'Goo goo goo joob,'* " as Lou's head had sung.

Father Demetrius was of the exact opposite character of Sister Mary Magdalene de Rosa. Father Demetrius had taken a vow—an oath to God—to save souls. Heads, apparently and most unfortunately, were too much for Father Demetrius. He had leaned too far over the wall. It was easier to work on the puzzle of the shattered picture frame than to probe the mystery of Lou's head's separation from Lou's body.

So Father Demetrius descended into the chapel one morning, not soon after Jerry had reassembled the frame of the Fifth Station of the Cross, and never returned.

Mrs. Fuller and the Board's bullying couldn't budge him. Father Dave left him alone. Father Demetrius slept in the chapel and spent the better part of each day lighting and snuffing candles—busy work, Magdalene thought, to tamp down the sound of Lou's head harmonizing on the chorus of "Sweet Caroline."

Her father was sitting, as usual, on the back steps when she came home from school, the day she'd eavesdropped on Jerry Eves. The liquor on his breath was startling—like he had swallowed a large container of ammonia. With her second suicide attempt still in the early planning stages, Magdalene knew her father's pose well—not that she ever assumed the same position, but inside, she felt about the same as he looked: beaten down, bullied, in pieces.

Her father glanced up and seemed to recognize Magdalene. (Magdalene didn't know which was worse: her father's drunken hugs and slurry *I loooooove yoooooo, yoooooo knows* or those times when he seemed to look right through her, as if she was invisible, but since the former happened rarely and the latter just about every day, she had become almost—*almost*—immune to being invisible.) He patted the step next to him, and Magdalene sat down. He lit the wrong end of a cigarette. Magdalene reached up to take it from his lips, but her father snatched it back.

"Poor Father Demetrius," her father said.

Magdalene stared at her father's red-tinged eyes and unshaven cheeks—did something *else* happen with Father Demetrius? The priest's Humpty fall had been a couple of years ago. Had the news just now penetrated the thick, rising whiskey tide?

"Poor, poor Father Demetrius," her father repeated.

"Did...did something else happen?" Magdalene asked, trying to speak and not breathe in the alcohol fumes at the same time.

Of course, the numbers helped then. The numbers always helped then. Not like now. (She heard Jerry speak to her, but the Goat's engine drowned him out.) Once the numbers had risen like the Puddle after a strong rain. Now...

"They took you by the hand, Father Demetrius and Father Dave, one on either side, and took you down to the..."

Magdalene went inside, slamming the screen door behind her.

"...for the memorial service."

+

The numbers were gone.

She was sitting in Mick Eves' blue 1968 GTO, which, having just executed a reverse spin, was now hurtling from the safety of the recently rain-enclosed Pike (it had been warm in there, hadn't it? had it?) towards the front gate of Paradise Lakes.

Jerry Eves leaned forward in the driver's seat, squinting through the window, turning the windshield wipers on and off, on and off. The red dust was everywhere.

But in Magdalene's head: the numbers were gone. Her temples throbbed above the roar of the engine—then stopped.

It was as if the first reel of the Short, Happy Life of Magdalene Harper Barrows began not with a baby's wail or a mother's shout of relief and pain, but with heavy metal guitars: the sound of a plastic pick scraped across nickel wound strings pulled taut, and someone, someone in pain, screaming, drowning in the feedback. Oh, and the drums—oh, oh: the bass! Thunder was too quaint a word. (Angels bowling, right?) CRACK BANG FLASH. "Count the seconds between the thunder clap and the lightning," Michael had taught her one night, forcing her to stand on the back steps, her nightgown whipping around her cold, cold ankles. CRACK BANG FLASH. "Getting closer," Michael had said. "That's how you know: count, Lil, count." CRACK BANG FLASH. There was no mystery to this music; this was the sound of a mystery exploding, its entrails and clues and bones visible to all. And she could see everything, *click click click*, but just clips, snapshots blinking awake, *snap fizz whirr*, then *yellow star, red star, white star, black*, on to the next: her mother laughing; the backs of men hunched over a bar; a man leaping from a great height with a curtain for a superhero cape; a little boy with a gun, another instantly without a face; her brother's tanned arm, curved and slightly muscled, its little golden hairs standing on end, and her fingertips caressing it for a second before he swiped blindly as if at a bug; hulking shadows coming towards her, and the gap toothed grin of the bully emerging from the dark to crash into her face; Aunt Tiddy squinting at a spot of red dirt; a little girl—Katie!—handing Magdalene a bunch of flowers, and the petals all had bruises like fingerprints; a hospital room; a tube being forced down her throat; a priest leaning over in the street, as if retching; and always, again and again: her brother running, sprinting at top speed, a lithe, bronze blur tearing down Finch's Landing, gripping the air, grabbing his legs, cannonballing into the murky water. Her eyes tilt, and there they are, flashing by, the edges of the film reel burnt and charred, two trees: the Jumping Tree and its dead brother, the Dead Injun Tree. The picture wasn't complete without both. Michael climbed the Dead Injun Tree once, then again...

She couldn't go losin' Lou's Head.

She was alone. She stood alone in the middle of—she didn't know what—it could be almost anything she wanted: a field, a road, a train platform, but she chose none of the above. The guitars were gone; so too the drums and bass. It had never been her music; it was her brother's. It was hers by default for the Barrows Bungalow had thin walls. But there was no sound now—nothing. She thought she could probably hear the splash of the Puddle if she chose, but she did not. The air was cool on her legs. She was dressed for some formal occasion, a white dress with scrunchy material along the hem. She pulled the skirt down over her legs and sat down...

...on the road. It *was* a road now. She was waiting. But this couldn't be it—this *nothing*. She had a pocketful of clues. (Along with Tiddy's pills, dead dogwood petals, and Michael's school picture and money.) She knew the plot, the characters—nothing too outside of the plot was going to happen. She had plans, a list. Being alone was all fine and good, and that's how she planned to leave—alone (as if, she shook her head, everyone didn't die alone pretty much—how silly to think otherwise!)—but she might need a ride home from wherever she was right now. Maybe she could convince Jerry to boost Mick's car (again). Okay, one person—she needed one person. Convincing Jerry, manipulating him: that wasn't bullying, was it? She smoothed the wrinkles in her dress. And bullying—well, *everyone* knows the true root of evil is bullying. Look at Cain. Marked forever. A bully. And it doesn't take a huge effort to reach the Cain inside, now does it? Magdalene shook her head no. The air was so clear, so fresh, it sparkled, a push of heat on her face, a cool sideswipe kissing her cheek. The air was busy with dandelion wishes, like shooting, sneezing stars. Was this what heaven was like? Was *this* heaven?

No—it couldn't be. Raven wasn't here. There couldn't be a heaven without Raven—his hot, stinky breath, his popcorn scented fur, the murder-squawk of his monkey, the silent solemnity of Monien the panda. She could just about touch the little white spot on his black, black chest...

Of course, Raven *couldn't* be in heaven. Not *wouldn't*, despite what the uppity nuns said—couldn't.

Raven couldn't be in heaven.

She hadn't killed him yet.

Something foul struck her face—a bad smell on the breeze. A clue?

Sometimes things just happen.

Sometimes *things* just happen.

Who'd said that? Not Shakespeare.

It was coming—she felt its presence approaching. If this was heaven…God? Shit! She looked down and her nice white dress was gone; she was wearing Michael's pullover hoodie and nothing else; she was soaked. Her fingers were wrinkles; her hair was flattened against her skull.

It was coming and sometimes: Sometimes. Things. Just. Happen. *Things.* And this *coming*—this was like their mother's lies. (*Their.*) They always knew when to expect the lies, but never knew quite what to expect or how to react. Their father tried to explain it away, some sort of reaction against *her* father's expectations, some flaw in her back-story, and *blah blah blah.* Their mother was a liar, and a good one, if you judged the lies purely on their storytelling merit, but bad, if you took into consideration that everyone knew when she was lying—everyone in the Barrows Bungalow anyway. Not Old Man Rex. Certainly not mean and nasty Mrs. Stanley, the town librarian— Magdalene's mother could return books practically whenever she wanted; whatever story she returned with the book was payment enough for excitement-starved Mrs. Stanley. The nuns too, Patricia Archer Rumsey Barrows fooled 'em all. Karl Matthews? Yep! Mayor Greene? More than once! As a writer, Magdalene was proud of her mother's ability to fabricate entire trilogies out of an ear of corn— except she never stopped. Her mother was no more capable of telling the truth for any goodly length of time than their father, in the years after her passing, was able to carry on any conversation or engage in any activity that did not include a nearly-empty glass in one hand and an unfiltered Camel in the other. And they could all see it—Michael, their father, even Aunt Tiddy—it was plain as the scars on Magdalene's wrist, as Shakespeare would say.

"Patricia, did you take the car in for inspection this morning?" Gregory Barrows would ask. Magdalene and her brother would wait breathlessly for her response, and they'd hang on every word of her answer.

"I did, but there, in the middle of the street—I *was* on my way and in quite a hurry—was this little baby chick. Yellow little baby chick. So I stopped and picked him up. It was a he—had a little gray feather on the top of his *very* yellow head. And I drove him out into farm country."

You see? The devil's in the details: the gray feather.

"Met the *funniest* older gentleman out there. It was his chick, he said, been looking for it all day, said it was *his* chick—can you believe it? He made me some possum soup, and we jawboned most of the morning and afternoon away, I'm afraid."

Yep, there it was: the whopper. "It was *his* chick."

(It was still coming—rolling, even. Not slow, but making good time. Although Magdalene knew the skies were blank, when she looked up, the storm clouds she'd pictured in her head jostled with anticipation.)

Magdalene thought her mother simple, in that good, wholesome way—like, say, baby chicks or black Labrador retrievers were simple—like homemade applesauce or those long florescent colored Popsicles in the summer. Not much to figure out—simple that way. What you had in your hands, what was in front of your eyes, was what you got. Suffice it to say (and Magdalene liked to remind herself of this after her mother, laughing with her wide, toothy smile, lied her way to the cemetery), they were *nothing* alike, she and her mother.

And that's what attracted their future father to Patricia Archer Rumsey, Magdalene was sure. Magdalene surely didn't miss the irony (especially after she'd learned what the word meant): her father, a lawyer, one of the good guys, falling for the world's most insistent and imaginative and terrible liar (if truth be told). But with Patricia Archer Rumsey, what you saw was what you got, and after years of detecting (isn't that what lawyers do: hunt down the vagaries of the written law?), Gregory Barrows wanted someone who required no looking glass or fingerprint kit or law degree. Gregory Barrows wanted what he saw.

Sure, sometimes the whoppers got Patricia Barrows in hot water, but she always managed to step out of it, dry as a bone and needy as a tick for the next story. There was the time the rear part of the backyard fence was missing—that whole run of whitewashed wood: gone. Mother said a traveling salesman selling dog brushes was responsible. (The detail: "God, did he ever stink of Brylcreem! It was like he'd bathed in it!") When Patricia tried to explain to the salesman that they didn't have a dog ("I even showed him the yard—no dog poop there, I said to him…"), the man emptied the contents of his car, which was filled to the brim not with dog brushes but with actors. *Actors.* Actors who took one gasping look at the backyard fence and asked Patricia Barrows if she could see it in her heart to spare a portion of the fence for their play. They were performing *Tom Sawyer* and were in desperate need ("…*desperate* need, Gregory…") of a white picket fence.

Couldn't say they didn't see it coming.

Whopper.

(Whatever it was, it was getting closer. The air was tight, close—everything good had seeped out. She could smell the Puddle close by, its banks festooned with cigarette butts and crushed beer cans and fast food wrappers and used condoms. Beetleskins. It was coming? It was nearly here. She tried to cover her knees, but they were damp with red mud.)

Whatever actually had happened to the back part of the fence, they never did find out. It was just gone. Magdalene and Michael had run outside to investigate. There was a line of folded dead grass where the fence had been, a straight line. No footprints. The actors had been quick, neat, and quite handy. Father had a new fence erected on the weekend. He didn't seem happy about it, but he wasn't angry either. Magdalene caught him later that night, smoking out where the missing fence had been, looking, just as she and Michael had earlier, for *anything*, looking for clues.

It hadn't occurred to their father—or any of them—that Patricia Archer Rumsey Barrows was a Goner.

"Guinness called," their mother said one day when Magdalene and her brother came breezing through the back door. Their mother was reading a book at the kitchen table.

"The beer?" Michael asked.

"No, silly," their mother said, tapping him on the head with an invisible magic wand. "*The Guinness Book of World Records.*"

"What did you do?" Magdalene asked, wary and careful.

"Oh my God, Lil—remember the fattest guy in the whole world? He was in Guinness!" Michael ran upstairs to find his well-thumbed copy.

" 'Sea of Love' " said Magdalene's mother. "Phil Phillips and the Twilights."

"I don't get it," Magdalene said.

"I've been whistling that song now for ten years. Since right before I met your father. Guinness called. World record, they said."

Magdalene knew asking questions would force their mother to dig deeper into her story. When they were younger, she and Michael would do it just to see where their mother would take them. Now Magdalene usually nodded her head and went about her business. Michael always wanted to see how far their mother would go. "I can't help it," Michael said. "They're good stories." But Magdalene couldn't help herself either this time—to Magdalene, "Sea of Love" was the First Song, the first song she remembered hearing. Their First Lullaby. Their mother had whistled it constantly when they were little.

" *'Come with me, my love / To the sea, the sea of love / I want to tell you / Oh, how much I love you.'* "

The song was like the tide; it came and went in the Barrows Bungalow. Their mother's version was like the last song of sailor boys doomed to the sea. Magdalene's father didn't care for the song. He called it a Goodbye Song.

"How did they—?"

Michael ran into the kitchen with a small stack of books in his arms. His thumb was stuck inside one of them, and he flipped it open.

" 'The longest recorded solo singing marathon is one of 105 hours by Eamonn McGirr at the Bower Club, Stalybridge, Manchester, England, on August 5-10, 1974,' " Michael read.

"Are those my old books? Gosh, they're from, what, 1977?" their mother asked Magdalene, as if Magdalene understood that *anything* from 1977 had to be suspect. "I hadn't even met your father yet."

" 'The world record for voluntarily staying underwater is 13 minutes 42.5 seconds by Robert Foster, then aged 32, an electronics technician of Richmond, CA,' " Michael read, " 'who stayed under 10 feet of water in the swimming pool of the Bermuda Palms at San Rafael, CA, on March 15, 1959. He hyperventilated with oxygen for 30 minutes before his descent.' "

Michael laid the book on his lap.

"Mumsy, what does that mean? 'Hyperventilated with oxygen.' "

"Means he cheated, dear," their mother lied.

"The record's yours for the taking, Lil."

"How did Guinness know to call you?" Magdalene began again.

" 'The longest recorded period for which a person has voluntarily gone without sleep is 288 hours (12 days) by Roger Guy English, 23, in a waterbed showroom in San Diego, CA,' " Michael read.

Magdalene thought that if Michael didn't shut his yap for five seconds, she'd help him break the record for the longest period of time unconscious after a knuckle sandwich from his little sister.

" *Do you remember when we met / That was the day I knew you were my pet...*'" their mother sang. Her voice was more pleasant than good, and she tended to warble when she had to carry a note. Their mother was a better whistler than singer.

"Whoa!" Michael said, his face buried inside *The Book of Lists.*

"General Chang Chung-Ch'ang. 'The Chinese warlord was dubbed "72-Cannon Chang" because his *manhood*,' " Michael read, " 'supposedly equaled 72 stacked silver dollars in length and diameter!' "

"Not exactly a record like *singing*, is it," their mother sniffed.

"They have Napoleon's penis in a jar!" Michael said, his eyes glued to the book.

"Don't say penis, dear," their mother instructed absently.

"How 'bout vagina?" Michael asked. "Hey Mumsy, can I say vagina?"

"Yes dear. In context."

"Says here," Michael read, " '15% of married women prefer rear entrance or doggie fashion.' "

"Absurd," their mother said.

"Did they call you first or did you call them?" Magdalene asked.

"Who called?" their mother asked.

Michael continued reading, " 'Advantages: allows manual stimulation of clitoris. Good for pregnant women, males with small penises, women with large vaginas.' "

"Makes perfect sense," their mother said. "Plus, the man has a place to put his ashtray."

"Really?" Michael asked.

"No dear," their mother said. "I was kidding."

Michael and Magdalene exchanged a quick glance.

Kidding.

"Although I knew a man," their mother began, "who had a tattoo of a squirrel running up one leg, and down the other was a tattoo of the same squirrel with two nuts in his mouth."

A whopper, a tine one.

Michael read the disadvantages: " 'does not allow easy entry or face-to-face intimacy. Penis tends to fall out.' "

"This is true. Unfortunately," their mother said. "Don't say penis."

"Saint Augustine: 'abstained from sex because sperm comes from the same organ that produces urine,' " Michael read.

"*Very* unfortunate," their mother said.

" 'Pope Alexander was an enthusiastic orgiast!' "

" 'Fraid so," their mother said.

"Did you really know that?" Magdalene asked.

"Of course, dear," their mother replied. "He was a Catholic."

"Lewis Carroll: 'Hobby was photographing naked prepubescent girls.' English publisher Leonard Smithers: 'Hobby was deflowering little girls.' "

"What's deflowering mean?" Michael asked.

"Not what you think," their mother said.

" 'Oscar Wilde said of Smithers: he loves first editions.' "

"Bullies," their mother said. "Picking on little girls and boys, abusing them. The true mark of a bully."

"How did they find you?" Magdalene asked.

"Who, dear?" their mother asked.

"Guinness."

Their mother shrugged. It was a simple enough gesture, but one their mother made both insouciant and contrite. When their mother spun a lie, she could never be made to give it up. Despite, or maybe because of, her great love for their father, their mother wanted to be somewhere else. Where, Magdalene didn't know. It wasn't like their mother hated her life as a Barrows, but it was obvious to her brood that the horizon and what lay beyond held her heart in chained sway. But it was more than that, Magdalene thought: their mother wanted to be *someone* else. Anyone else. They didn't really know Patricia Archer Rumsey Barrows, this stranger they all adored. She drove Magdalene and Michael closer than either parent would probably have liked if they'd known. Her eventual exit led their father to look for her at the bottom of a bottle, and when Michael went missing, Gregory Barrows just about drowned in there.

"Says here: 'Empress Maria Theresa's doctor recommended' to her that 'Your Most Sacred Majesty's vulva be titillated for a considerable time before coitus.' "

"Don't say vulva, dear."

"Why not?" Michael asked.

"Sounds too…"

Their mother smiled, showing all of her blinding white teeth.

"…abstract," she finished.

"Abstract," Michael repeated.

"When I was little, a girl who lived down the block got a piece of hot dog stuck in her ginny."

"Ginny," Michael repeated softly, his head tilted just a little.

"Had to have it surgically removed," their mother said.

Michael stood up. "Her ginny?" he asked.

"No dear," their mother answered. "The meat by-product."

"Meat by-product," Michael repeated in the same awed voice.

Magdalene thought her own ginny was going to explode.

"Mom, mom," Magdalene said, clapping her hands together, but her mother was far away again, perhaps imagining the fate of the white picket fence or accepting her award from Guinness.

(Magdalene stuck her head out of the Goat's window. It was chasing her now, moving so fast, it made a whistling sound. She shivered in the rain; it was raining buckets again.)

Of course, it was cancer. Magdalene believed her father never forgave himself for not seeing what was in front of his face—which was what he had liked about Patricia Archer Rumsey in the first place. It was cancer, and Mother hid the results, and Father was too busy ignoring Mother's sudden desire to buy his dream house in the mountains; Father was far too occupied climbing what Aunt Tiddy called the Mondauk Stepladder of Success. He managed to ignore the coughing fits ("Have a cold, love?" he asked over a pile of legal briefs on the dining room table), the thinness ("Really? You ate already? Okay, I'm late for practice," Father said, the screen door bouncing on its frame behind him), the excavations around her eyes. Her eyes were sinking. Magdalene wouldn't look at her mother's body when she was laid out; she was afraid her mother's eyes would be sunk all the way into her skull. Instead, she did what she did at every viewing: she practiced holding her breath and counted.

(Was this a test? This—whatever *this* was—this sequence? Oh, it was barreling on in now, just rollin' on up, motoring.)

(Whistling?)

(No, no—humming.)

(Loud humming.)

("'*Hmm-hm*-hmm / *hmm-hm*-m-*hm, hm*-m-*hm*.'")

(Again.)

(" '*Hmm-hm-*hmm / *hmm-hm-*m-*hm, hm-*m-*hm.*' ")

(She knew it was Lou—or his head—before it actually reached her feet, but she couldn't help herself. She sang at the top of her lungs, tears huddling in the corners of her raw eyes, her hands scooping up Lou's Head from the banks of the Puddle.)

(" *'SWEET CAROLINE—BA BA BUMP—GOOD TIMES NEVER SEEMED SO GOOD—I BEEN INCLINED—BA BA BUMP—TO BELIEVE THEY NEVER WOULD!'* ")

"Sometimes, Maddie, things just happen," her father was saying, and even though she had to fight the crust that had built up around the tears that refused to exit, she opened her eyes, and it was nighttime, and she was sitting on the back steps with her father. His head was in his hands, and Magdalene wanted to reach out and hold him, cradle his head, tell him she was sorry, but the NUMBERS, the goddamn NUMBERS. She had tried holding her breath until she almost passed out—that's how the NUMBERS started, right, under Michael's stinky blankets?—but the NUMBERS, they accumulated on their own now, and her father might as well have been six feet under or at the bottom of Davy Jones' locker.

"Sometimes, Maddie, sometimes things just happen," her father said. He smelled—nay, *reeked*—of booze. "When the times comes, you'll, you'll be able to piece it together. And I'll be there," her father said. He *actually* said that, as if the smell of McCullough's wasn't rising from his soaked body in the evening heat. "You don't have to, I mean, make a statement or anything. I talked to Cutter. It's okay."

The NUMBERS were huge, massive, monolithic even. If she could just *o-p-e-n* her mouth—there, easy enough. Roll past the tongue. Good, good. Leap over the teeth. Great, okay—*al-most there...*

"I'll find him, Daddy," Magdalene said, and her father vomited down the side of the steps. But she'd meant it, and when she lost the trail, she tried to die. There being no honor in failure and all that. But she got back up on that horse—Magdalene thought Shakespeare had never come up with a better catch phrase. The horse ran with her and the hunt was on, but the trail had grown cold. Her time had come and gone. Her time had come, and her father, the drunk, soaked, weeping man holding his own head, the smell of vomit all but overwhelming, was gone. The second suicide hadn't taken and Mondauk moved on and Aunt Tiddy moved in, and the creeping sickness, the hidden marks of Cain and all their various meaning and divinations, had shown their hand. She had one final chance, one more swing of the pendulum.

I'll find him, Daddy...

"Magdalene!" Jerry Eves yelled. "Jesus Christ!" There, stumbling, nearly tripping over herself in the middle of Dirt Road: the silent movie star.

"Chloe!" Magdalene screamed, and the last of the red dust cloud passed over the GTO. She was still in Paradise Lakes, still with Jerry. The rain had stopped momentarily. There was shouting behind them and what sounded like a gunshot. Stevie Rich and Frannie Five Fingers? The sky wasn't clearing up. Magdalene could smell the ocean—or maybe it was the Puddle.

Jerry slammed the GTO to a halt, Magdalene jumped out, and suddenly it was raining great big gum drops. Chloe turned around and arched backward, fumbling with a pack of smokes. Her face was cut, and blood ran down from her forehead.

"What did he do to you, Chloe?" Magdalene asked, approaching Chloe at a brisk run.

Chloe held out her hands in front of her body.

"No, no. Bad touch. Stop. Right. There," Chloe said. "Whoa—who's the big guy?"

Magdalene spun around, but it was just Jerry, his hair flat against his forehead, red dust dripping down his face.

"I think Frannie beat—"

Chloe open her mouth and laughed—a broken, chipped, utterly spent laugh.

"Frannie?" asked Chloe. "*Frannie?* No, he didn't do this," she said, trying to light a damp, bent cigarette with a pink lighter bearing a sticker with the words "Hot Stuff" written in flames.

"Fell. Black beauts. *Fucked* me *up!* 'Posed to meet Rick," she said, emphasizing the "k." She giggled into her fist. " 'Posed to meet at the Gremlin. I do think I'm late. I'm late, I'm late! For a very important date!" She undulated her hand like someone showing off prizes on a game show. "Oh my fur and whiskers!"

"Jesus Christ. With her hair all flat like that, she looks just like you," Jerry whispered.

Chloe dug into her pockets—she had dropped the lighter and given up on the cigarette—and brought out a tissue, unraveled it, and held up a little black pill in the rain.

"Want one? Help you get through. I swear on 'em. When the shit gets too heavy," Chloe said, shaking her head and popping the pill, "I just call on my pharmacist." She swallowed the pill and opened her mouth wide. "See—all gone!"

Another gunshot and there: a distant wail...

"Christ, Magdalene. It's the police."

"We didn't do anything," Magdalene said, holding Chloe up by her shoulders.

"Mick's car..."

"Chloe," Magdalene said, "come with us."

"What?"

"Jerry..."

Chloe watched their exchange in silence, her tongue licking her full lips over and over.

Jerry shrugged. The sirens grew louder.

"Come with us, Chloe," Magdalene said.

Chloe squinted her eyes and laughed. Her teardrop tattoo danced and crinkled.

"Oh and I suppose I could stay with you, right? Sleep in your bed? Careful, sweetie, *care-ful*—I may not be as clean as I look. Objects in the rear may be itchier than they appear."

Jerry pulled at Magdalene's sleeve.

"Methinks boyfriend-boyfriend's shot his load a tad early," Chloe remarked, looking down at Jerry's stained jeans.

The heavens opened up again.

"Magdalene—"

Chloe imitated Jerry's voice: "*Mag-da-lene.*"

"You can't like it here," Magdalene said.

"My mother...my mother, she was a stewardess," Chloe said. "You know—on an airplane. Trailer trash like her: a stewardess."

"Chloe—"

From behind them, a roar: "MOTHERFUCKERS!"

"Okay, now we go," Jerry said, pulling Magdalene by the arm towards the GTO. "That was Frannie, Magdalene. He's out of the trailer."

"Please make sure your trays are stored in the upright position," Chloe said, using inappropriate arm gestures.

Magdalene pulled free of Jerry.

"Chloe, please come with us."

Chloe's face fell.

"That's all I remember. The 'upright position' line."

"Magdalene," Jerry said. "The sirens?"

"About what?"

"Huh?"

"That's all you remember about—"

" 'Stow your trays in the upright position.' I don't even know what an upright position looks like."

Jerry's arms encircled Magdalene. He picked her up and placed her in the car. Magdalene's stomach clenched. She couldn't leave Chloe behind. The girl needed help. Magdalene rolled her window down. The rain had stopped.

"Call me, Chloe. Or stop by. I'm at Candy and Hendricks."

Now she was just being silly, and she knew it. She would be dead in roughly twenty-four hours. Let's send poor, doomed Chloe on a wild (dead) goose chase. Magdalene shut her mouth.

The rain stopped abruptly.

"Just…just be careful, Chloe," Magdalene said.

"The cops are coming up Dirt Road," Jerry said.

Magdalene saw their red dust clouds, swarming, buzzing, wailing from the direction of the front gate.

"I knew your brother, Mag-da-lene," Chloe said. "Can't believe you just sat there. Why didn't you—?"

Jerry had the car in motion, and Chloe raised her middle finger in salute before being swallowed by the red dust. As Jerry navigated a 180 degree turn, Magdalene tried to see Chloe—standing absolutely still, middle finger in the air, the first of two police cars swerving to avoid her—anywhere but in Paradise Lakes, in the sky perhaps, working a flight from Duluth to Boston or serving drinks and sandwiches on a plane that had taken off in St. Louis, destination: Europe! Asia! Canada! But every time she blinked, every time Magdalene rubbed her eyes to keep the fading dot in the purple t-shirt, now bent over a squad car, almost obscured by the dust, square in her sights, Magdalene realized it was all immovable—the trailers, the little black pills, the red dirt, even the police cars. Chloe had been summarized and had accepted it wordlessly—her defiant finger gesture notwithstanding. The only difference between Chloe and her, Magdalene thought, was that Chloe didn't know she was trapped. Change the particulars, and nothing else really changed.

A Goner recognizes another Goner and waves goodbye.

+

Another gunshot—the bang short and sharp, the echo oddly vertical. The squad car that had been tearing after Mick's GTO squealed and skidded, and Magdalene caught a glimpse of Stevie Rich ducking into the underbrush as they headed towards the northern exit.

"Why didn't I do what?" Magdalene asked. "What did Chloe mean?"

"Magdalene, you saved Grammy," Jerry said. "Isn't that enough saving for one day."

Jerry's driving was erratic. Magdalene fumbled for the seat belt, holding her hand against the dash.

She changed her tactics: " 'McAllister has to take care of his own.' "

"Yeah?"

"That's what Frannie Tidwell said. What do you think he meant?"

"I dunno," Jerry said. "He just sounded pissed 'cause he thought that some of his brother's money should have been his. Because Mr. McAllister's dating Mrs. Tidwell and being nice to Stevie Rich, Frannie thinks McAllister's after his money."

There were trails of dirt painted across Jerry's face like war paint.

A sign ahead read, "You Are Now Leaving Paradise Lakes! Won't You Bring Your Family Back and Stay Awhile?"

"At least the rain stopped."

"How could you have been in the same trailer as me?" Magdalene asked.

Jerry ignored her. "Jesus, you know what time it is? Mick's gonna—I'm a Goner, that's all I'm gonna say. He's gonna kill me."

"Subtext," Magdalene said to herself. "Subtext."

Stupid boy—how could so many detectives, so many writers be men?

"He is gonna *fucking* kill me," Jerry whispered. "He loves this car. Worked a paper route for years to buy it."

Magdalene glanced at Jerry: his jeans were damp with rain and pee, his face dirty and red, his hair plastered to his head. His hands, scuffed and bleeding, gripped the steering wheel. His arms were jumpy. It was as if Jerry had stepped down from one of the Stations of the Cross, and she was an angry, vile mob of one, lobbing spit and insults and rocks at his menagerie of freckles.

"I'm sorry, Jerry."

"For?"

"For everything." And there they were: big globes of salt and water and God knows what else—only she *did* know, didn't she? Cigarette butts, empty cans of beer, fast food wrappers, busted Trojans. "I just...I thought that...I...I had a plan, and this was the first part, and now I have to rescue—"

Jerry laughed; Magdalene froze. They had just been held at gunpoint, chased by the police—

"Rescue—listen to yourself. Chloe's going to do what Chloe wants to do."

"But—"

"But nothing. You went for info from Stevie Rich. Then you rescued Grammy. *We* rescued her."

Magdalene crossed her arms.

"She wouldn't have come outside if we weren't there."

Jerry curled his lips into his mouth and let them go with a *pop*.

"True. Maybe. Either way. You weren't gonna let Stevie Rich scare us away with a gun. I'll leave out the fact that you gave him the gun, but—"

"We stole the gun, Jerry."

"You say tomato..."

"What did she mean—Chloe—when she—"

"You saved Grammy. That's it."

"I don't—"

Jerry pulled the car over to the shoulder. The road had petered out to a long, thin stretch of pebbles and debris. Magdalene didn't recognize the landscape. The air was still heavy with the stink of the Puddle. Magdalene realized with a jump (Jerry patted her leg), that it didn't smell all that different from Michael's blankets—or had she known that all along?

And still no numbers. It was hard to even recite her To-Do-Before-I-Die list.

Jerry left the motor running.

"You know my Uncle Paddy, right?" Jerry asked.

Magdalene shook her head no.

Jerry reached out with both hands, all bleeding knuckles and red dirt, and held Magdalene's head still.

"Listen to me," he whispered. "Please."

"Uncle Paddy Irish Potato."

"Yeah, my Uncle Paddy Irish Potato."

"From the Church carnival," Magdalene said. She kept shaking her head.

"That's him," Jerry said. His voice flowed by, even, straight, narrow, as if all the trees in Pennypack would topple and crush them both if he missed even one syllable,.

"He does the potato toss game," she said.

" 'Cept he can't use real potatoes. Well, he wouldn't anyway, but, yeah, that's him, that's Uncle Paddy. Pat. Patrick, that's his name."

"I didn't know he was your real uncle. Everyone calls him Uncle Paddy."

"My dad's brother. His only brother."

Magdalene tried to look through the windshield, but she couldn't move her head. What she could glimpse peripherally was covered in dead bugs, hundreds of them.

Okay: one, two…nope, nothing.

Jerry held onto her head.

"Every Thursday night, every single Thursday, Uncle Paddy came over for dinner. My mom made corned beef and potatoes, and my dad and Uncle Paddy would sit on the back stoop and have a smoke and a glass of whiskey. Real Irish shit.

"Sometimes, Uncle Paddy would be there and my dad wouldn't. He worked at the quarry all hours, my dad. Not much granite left, my dad said, but it was his job to make sure they got it all out, and more importantly, to make sure all his guys got out okay. That's why he stayed so late, well after dark sometimes. Wanted to make sure everyone got lifted out in the buckets with all their fingers and toes."

Jerry smiled. "Guess my dad saved people too."

Magdalene's head was heavy and Jerry held it.

"So, one Thursday night, me and my brothers, we're doing whatever outside, and my mom calls us in. Dad's place is set, but he's not there, but like I said, that wasn't too unusual. But there's not a setting for Uncle Paddy. And we're all yelling, laughing, 'Paddy, Paddy, Paddy!' Bangin' our forks. Uncle Paddy, he liked to play games and pranks, so he could have been hiding. He didn't usually do that sort of stuff around my mom (she's so serious), but still, you never know. One time, he put all these frogs in this vat of mash…"

Magdalene wondered what life would be like with *three* siblings. If they lost one, there'd be three left to huddle together and whisper the missing's name. Now she whispered alone.

Four minus one is three, three minus—gone.

"...so Aunt Betsy freaked out, all these drunk frogs hopping and pooping in her bed. Uncle Paddy had a way with...well, anyway."

Jerry cleared his throat and looked away. Magdalene took a photograph with her mind, for her files. Her detective agency would be filled with them, sorted and alphabetized by secretaries while Magdalene, ensconced in her office, pounded out her latest opus on a Royal typewriter. *Snap fizz whirr!* Jerry as a little freckled kid among a bevy of little freckled boys and pooping amphibians. *Snap fizz whirr!* Jerry as he would be. Jerry the adult. *Snap fizz whirr!* Jerry the husband. Jerry saving his future wife and children from the Stevie Riches and Frannie Tidwells and Mr. McAllisters of the world.

"So we're all yellin' for Paddy, and my mom is telling us to keep it down, and then, without stopping what she was doing, settin' out dinner and such, she says, plain as day, 'Paddy's dead.'"

"Your Uncle Paddy died?"

"Wait...so the little ones are crying. Brian worst of all. Pat's huggin' himself, as if just being named after Uncle Paddy would make the angels rush down and snatch him from the dinner table. Mick's just sitting there sniffling. Me too. Maybe I was crying. I dunno."

Being in love with your brother brings with it certain responsibilities; Magdalene knew them well. They weren't all that different from the Rules of the Dare. Love Your Brother (which she did simply because he was her big brother and significantly cooler than she could ever hope to be), Respect the Fact That He Is Your Brother (which she took to mean that at some distant point in time, she would have to shed the "in" part of "in love"), and Love Him as Much as Is Allowed (which was more than she bargained for perhaps, in hindsight, but in so many ways, not nearly enough). It was confusing. But when you were in love with your own brother, well, there wasn't quite a rule that covered his behavior. Especially if he knew.

And he knew.

"So Mick stands up—he's the oldest. I'm thinkin' he's gonna say something. Mick's not the type to lead us in prayer or anything like that. But Pat's already punching Brian—who knows why?—and Mick figures our mom must be all broken up, so he stands up. To take charge. We figure Dad's at the hospital or wherever. We figure Dad's with Uncle Paddy. But Mick sees the boots."

Magdalene's mother used to tease her all the time: "There's

kissing cousins, Magdalene dear, but no kissing brothers." And Magdalene would blush and giggle. It was true: Magdalene *adored* her brother. Michael was everything she wasn't: sure of himself, outgoing, popular, and a better athlete (although, as they grew older, Magdalene wondered if that last was true).

Then her mother lied and ADA Barrows buried her and she disappeared from the Barrows Bungalow like the back part of the white picket fence. Only Magdalene's father didn't have any stories that didn't come from a whiskey label. There were no gypsy actors dressed like Tom and Huck and Becky and Jim. No baby chicks parading down the street. Their father adopted Raven so there were *three* displaced instead of two. And she'd thought their father had fallen in love in again. A young woman had brought him home a couple of times. By then, her father was settling into a regular barstool and other patrons moved over when he walked into McCullough's; Magdalene had seen it with her own eyes. The dim lights blinking like stars off half-empty bottles lined up on shelves behind the bar, their colored liquid like quicksand, sucking her father down, blinding him to a simple fact: all stars die. *Yellow star, red star, white star, black.* It had taken a while for Magdalene to realize (blinded as she was by the afterglow of her mother's dead star) that the woman tucking her soused father into bed was Zooey McCullough, the new proprietor of McCullough's taproom. (What kind of a name was Zooey, Aunt Tiddy had sniffed, what kind of spelling?) Zooey's father had died suddenly (although how a man in his nineties died *suddenly*, Magdalene wasn't sure), and he had left her his bars. Zooey closed the one in Rhawnhurst and ran McCullough's in Mondauk Proper by herself. Magdalene heard the stage whispered summarizing at Sol's: the wags said Zooey's husband had left her and that she was a tramp and her business was in trouble and the Faith Board wanted the bar shut down. Zooey McCullough had a worse reputation than James Orienti, the infamous gym-pooper.

Magdalene wasn't sure what to think about Zooey the leper. Zooey had brought Gregory Barrows home and poured him into bed a few times. She always stopped by Magdalene's room before she left and always asked the same thing: "How ya doin', kid?" Zooey never waited for an answer. Except one time.

But Zooey brought Magdalene's father home too often, in Magdalene's opinion. She wasn't ready for her father to have a girlfriend. Michael didn't care; neither of them spoke of their mother much, except in hushed tones beneath his blanket:

"Remember how she smelled, Lil?"

"Like a flower, like lilies."

Or:

"Do you remember when we came home, and she had, like, hundreds of cakes, all in them boxes, piled up on the dining room table?"

"The Indians. She told Daddy Indians gave them to her…"

"…because they were running out of room at the reservation!"

"She *had* to help them."

" 'Member what Daddy said?"

" 'Awful lot of wigwam!' "

Zooey had been helping their father up the stairs when Magdalene heard ADA Barrows say to the recently divorced taproom proprietor: "You know, I love you."

"Why are *you* always bringing my daddy home?" Magdalene demanded when Zooey had deposited the Assistant District Attorney between the sheets. Raven licked at Magdalene's heels. Raven didn't like voices being raised. The louder the voices or the angrier the tones, the more he licked. Michael could sleep through anything.

Zooey paused in the hallway and lit a cigarette.

"How ya doin', kid?"

"Daddy doesn't—"

"Your daddy is three sheets to the wind right now, girlie-girl."

She walked past Magdalene and sat on the top step. Zooey wore a cowboy hat and a loose-fitting shirt with a tie front, open at the throat. Zooey's hair was long and jet black; her hands were wrinkled and worn, though Magdalene thought she was no older than thirty.

"Your mother—"

Zooey glanced at Magdalene's face. Hardly anyone mentioned Magdalene's mother anymore, as if her mother had done something wrong and had not been eaten alive by a disease no one could cure.

"Yeah…okay," Zooey said, blowing a tunnel of gray smoke down the stairwell.

Magdalene willed courage to fill her up, and she released it like a popped helium balloon. "Are you in love with my daddy?" Magdalene yelled. Raven jumped up and tried to lick Magdalene's nose. She pushed her dog down.

Zooey laughed. "No, kid, no," she said. "Your dad's a gentleman. He just…you miss your mom?"

Magdalene sat down next to Zooey on the stairs. Raven crept behind them and chewed softly on his panda, the stuffed animal's song muffled and echoed in Raven's mouth. It didn't sound like a lullaby anymore. Gone were the gentle cascading notes. It was funeral music now: all low baritones and conciliatory details and prayers for deliverance. Nothing could muffle the song of the dead: the low, steady hum of a silenced yawp.

Magdalene felt sick to her stomach.

"C'mon, kid. Lemme put you to bed."

"I don't even know you."

"You do now. My Danny knows you. He says you walked safety with him a few times. Danny Kildare."

Danny: now there was a Goner if ever there was one. Danny flinched if someone broke the lead in a pencil. Danny was terrified of nuns. Danny was an easy bully target. She thought he was in Katie's grade.

Zooey tilted her head a little but still wore an easy smile.

Magdalene pointed Zooey towards her bedroom. Raven bounded ahead of them, carrying the panda.

"You're Danny's mom? I thought—" Magdalene was glad her room was dark; she didn't want Zooey to see her blush.

Zooey laughed again (it was an easy laugh too) and pulled the blankets back, gesturing for Magdalene to get in. "I'm sure you heard *lots* of stuff, kid, but I'm not all bad. A woman running her own bar gets a rep in a small town."

Zooey tucked her in bed. Magdalene struggled between feeling uncomfortable with a stranger sitting on her bed, rubbing her arm, and oddly comforted by Zooey's quicksilver laugh, her sparkling eyes and wide mouth.

"Your dad…he's a good man. It's just that…well, he's in love. No, no, kid, not with me. You see: some people love what's right in front of them. Drinking's always chasing, and the drinkers, they always catch it. At least until they wake up the next morning. Then it catches them."

Magdalene could hear Michael moving about in his room. She thought it was safer to be with this familiar stranger than under Michael's blanket.

"The rest of us," Zooey the bartender said, "well, the rest of us, we just love what we can't have, right?"

Zooey regarded her cigarette and its long, cylindrical ash.

"Get some sleep," Zooey said, kissing Magdalene's forehead.

Zooey closed the door behind her, and Magdalene heard the sizzle of the cigarette drowning in the toilet.

Michael was in her room within seconds of the front door closing.

"Was that Zooey?"

Magdalene didn't roll over. "Yes."

"What she want?"

"What the rest of us want."

Michael was next to her in bed.

"I dare you," Michael said.

"Are you listening?" Jerry Eves asked.

Magdalene opened her eyes.

"Mick saw the boots," she said.

Jerry smiled. He was still holding her head.

"So he thought—"

"…your dad had come home already."

"Right, 'cause that's what my dad did, shuck his boots off and leave 'em by the basement door."

"But he wasn't home."

"No. No, he wasn't home. He was in the hospital. You know that he—"

"…yeah, I know."

"Lung cancer."

"My mom—"

"I know," Jerry Eves said, and she couldn't explain it, she wasn't even sure she'd ever be able to write it down, capture it with only a pencil or her Royal, but it was there, this *fluttering*, as if all her veins were trying to push past her skin to see for themselves the source of the powerful *thump thump thump* of her heart.

"My dad smoked. Smoked a lot. Not too much at home 'cause my mom hated it, but at work." Jerry cleared his throat. "Picked it up from Uncle Paddy when they were kids. Uncle Paddy used to beat on my dad something fierce when they were little. They used to laugh about it, but not my mom. They were from the same town in Ireland: my mom's family and the Eves. My mom knew the Eves brothers. Said Paddy used to just *wail* on my dad, really go at him, and my dad kept coming back, never wanting a fight, not even when he started getting big from working, before they all came here. My dad, he was working when he was my age. That's just what they did. My mom said my dad was all wires and muscles. But still, Paddy beat the pulp outta him. And my dad kept on hanging 'round Paddy. My mom said that and his smoking were my dad's only bad qualities. She said they were one in the same. See, my dad wanted to be around Paddy no matter what. Looked up to him."

"Like you do with Mick."

"Yeah, but Mick never beats me up for no good reason."

"Oh."

"So my dad started smoking when he was a kid 'cause Paddy did. When he and Paddy moved here with my grandparents, my mom and her sister came along too. Everyone knew they were going to get married and they did. But my mom, she could never get my dad to stop smoking."

Jerry swallowed.

"It was pretty fast. He never came home even. Couple of weeks."

"And Paddy...he was...?"

"Paddy was alive. But not to my mom. To my mom, she buried her brother-in-law before she buried her husband. But my dad, he didn't understand all this. He was pretty sick. Me and Mick, we were at the hospital one time, and Daddy says to Mom how he wished she could make the peace with Paddy, and Mom tells him, right in front of us, that Paddy had passed on. My dad was too far gone to understand what she'd said."

"Did Paddy ever visit him?"

"My mom wouldn't let him. Me and Mick went to see Paddy after Dad died, and told him what Dad had said about making the peace."

"What did Uncle Paddy say?"

"Not much. He gave us each a pack of smokes and sent us off."

They sat there for a few minutes, Jerry holding her head, Magdalene letting him. Jerry squeezed his eyes shut, his freckles engaged in an internal struggle not to cry, then smiled.

"Did you love your brother?" he asked.

Magdalene tried to shake her head free of Jerry's warm, dirty hands, but she couldn't.

"Did you love Michael?"

"I mean, just like a sister."

"Sometimes things just happen."

"Okay," Magdalene said.

"Sometimes things just *happen*."

"Okay," Magdalene repeated.

"*Sometimes* things just happen."

He kissed her on the lips—and there it was again: *fluttering*. She pushed herself away from Jerry, but slowly. She didn't want to upset him. *Fluttering* was not good. She was a Goner. She bore the Mark of Cain. She—

"What was Chloe going to ask me?" Magdalene whispered. "She said, 'Why didn't you—' What did she mean?"

Jerry let go of her head. "Sometimes bad things just happen."

Both of them sunk back in their seats.

"I love you, Magdalene," Jerry said.

Magdalene tried, searched, failed. Maybe because the numbers were gone, all the good words were gone now too. Maybe dying starts from the inside.

"I'm writing a book," she said. "Or, I mean, I *wrote* it."

Jerry's face vacillated between genuine interest and a little boy's hurt. She hadn't said "I love you" back.

"What's it about?"

"A dog named Finn."

"A-huh."

"It's a children's book—sort of. At least it started out that way.

"It's a secret," she added.

"A secret book? Why is it a secret?"

"I dunno. It just is."

"Secrets are bad," Jerry said.

"Would you illustrate my book?" Magdalene asked, blushing.

Jerry smiled, the freckles on his cheeks reaching for the stars.

"I just draw Stick Man cartoons."

"I want you to do it anyway."

She tried as hard as she could to make it sound like 'I love you, Jerry Eves.' She tried again: "I want you to do it anyway."

Jerry kissed her cheek as he put the Goat in gear.

"Sure thing. It's an honor."

"With Stick Men?"

"No, I'll buy some books and learn some other techniques."

"No, with Stick Men."

Jerry let the car idle for a few seconds.

"I meant what I said," Jerry asserted. "I never said that to someone I liked before."

"Me too."

"You too?"

"I never asked anyone to illustrate anything I wrote before."

Jerry laughed. "Okay, Tonto, okay. Let's get the Goat back before Mick has the entire state out looking for it."

Magdalene, Magdalene, Magdalene, she thought to herself, do you want to do this?

Yes.

"Take me to Little City," Magdalene said. "Please," she added.

Jerry shook his head.

"We need to get you home and the Goat back," Jerry said. "I'm hopin' there'll be plenty of kissing in the future."

Magdalene slouched back in her seat.

Boys.

"Don't be sore, Tonto," Jerry said. "Besides, I'd like to put on a fresh pair of jeans, if you know what I mean."

Was she going to cry again? Everything Jerry had done for her today...

"Tell you what. We're close. Let's drive to Spring House. I'll buy you an egg cream at the Bald Eagle. Place smells so bad, no one's gonna smell me and my jeans. Pretty good egg creams though. What do you say? It won't take long."

Magdalene nodded her head, and the GTO was soon moving west towards Spring House.

Jerry fiddled with the radio. "You like the Stones? I like the Stones."

"I'm not sure," Magdalene replied. The air felt good on her face.

"You're not sure if you like the Stones?"

A song ended and an urgent sounding man announced his own name.

"You want me to change the station?" Jerry asked as they crossed the bridge.

"No, it's okay, it's—"

"*This morning's press conference in Mondauk Common,*" the urgent man reported, "*was a bombshell to the community, Shelly, and to the Roman Catholic Church. Speaking without her husband, Bernadette Fuller, mother of missing Mondauk-area elementary school student Christina Fuller, accused Assumption of Our Lady pastor Father Dave Browne of being privy to the whereabouts of her twelve- year-old daughter, missing now for forty-eight hours. Mrs. Fuller serves on the Church's lay Faith Board and...*"

"THAT'S NOT TRUE," Magdalene screamed. "THAT'S NOT GODDAMN TRUE!"

"Turn the car around," Magdalene said. "We have to go back."

"Magdalene—"

"Jerry, turn the car around."

"*...the priest voluntarily answered questions from detectives for two hours this morning. He was released without incident. Back to you, Shelly.*"

"You know how Mrs. Fuller tries to bully Father Dave around, how she tries to bully *everyone* around. We have to tell the police."

"Magdalene, I'm not sure—"

"We can tell Stevie Rich to go the police and spill his guts, but not us? Not you? Not Jerry Eves?"

"I'll do it, of course I'll do it, but Magdalene...Magdalene, you can't save everyone, you can't—"

"OH YEAH?" Magdalene screamed. "I'LL JUMP OUT OF THE CAR, JERRY, I SWEAR!"

"Magdalene, I said I would...we don't need to go back to the Lakes. We can go to the station in town—"

"TURN IT AROUND NOW!"

"Magdalene—"

"FUCK THE FUCKING EGG CREAMS, JERRY!"

As the GTO crested a hill on Bethlehem Pike, the road ahead was blocked with police cars, sirens silent, but with lights swirling.

"Jesus. Mick'll—"

"TURN! AROUND! NOW!"

A car was on its side in the middle of the road, smoke huffing from the engine.

"Magdalene—"

"I DON'T CARE. WE CAN'T LET MRS. FULLER DO THIS—"

"Magdalene...isn't that Aunt Tiddy's Cadillac?"

The car on its side was indeed a baby blue Cadillac, and swarming around it were men and women in uniform. The trunk was open, and a trail of items led away from the car.

The Baby Blue Cadillac of Doom.

A policeman directed the GTO to the shoulder. Magdalene jumped from the car before Jerry rolled to a stop. The policeman reached for Magdalene, but she ducked and ran towards the Cadillac.

"Get back...will someone get her outta here?"

One shoe, from a pair of sensible shoes, lay in the middle of the road. A few feet away were a pair of blinding white shoulder pads. And there was a football helmet. And a cleat.

A police car hummed on the opposite shoulder, its engine smoking, the front of the car all smashed to hell.

Two men were hunched near the hood of the Cadillac. They reached through the windshield and lifted out a small white package. Other men in EMT uniforms rushed past, knocking Magdalene backward into Jerry. She couldn't take her eyes off the shoulder pads.

"Go back," she said to Jerry. "Go home."

"We don't split up. We're not the Hardy Boys...aren't those...?" Jerry asked.

One of the men squatted down a few feet from the Cadillac and peeled open the white package.

"...is it...?" his partner asked.

"...no, no, it was so small..." the squatting man replied.

"...thought it was a baby's blanket..."

"...she's still out cold..." a third man said.

There were too many voices to count.

"...what is it...?"

"...just meat...some pork chops..."

"...the ambulance is here...toss the meat..."

A voice behind Magdalene asked, "Is that your GTO?" and Jerry answered yes. The police officer crooked his finger and said, "Come with me."

"...pork chops..."

"...Frankie, what the fuck happened...?"

"...just toss them for Christ's sake..."

"...but where...?"

"...gonna have to cut the roof to get her out..."

"...is she breathing...?"

"...radio had said all units to the Lakes..."

"...shots fired in the Lakes, yeah, I heard..."

"...someone call Chief Hagen...?"

"...have that head looked at, Joe..."

"...we were cruising the Strip...

"...missed the turn before Olde Bridge, checking a plate..."

"...but the skid marks...the Caddy was going so slow...

"...it must have drifted into our lane before the rise..."

"...almost head on..."

"...it's fresh...the meat..."

Jerry asked the officer leading him back to the GTO, "Is she...?"

The cop just said, "License and registration, please."

"...will you stop with the pork chops...?"

"...fire department's on their way with the Jaws of Life..."

"...but the registration says *Michael* Eves..."

"...aren't the chops evidence...?"

"...and you're not Mick...I know Mick from..."

"...Cutter's on the radio, Sarge..."

"Turn around, please," the officer said to Jerry. "Assume the position."

There—there: on the left shoulder pad: a drop of blood.

"Tiddy?" Magdalene whispered to herself as the saw screeched into the metal of her aunt's Baby Blue Cadillac of Doom, and the sky, filled to the brim with prayers and curses and wishes and the metallic shriek of the saw, began to cry.

The sky was crying and Tiddy was...

The sky was crying.

The scream of the saw, the shouts of the men in navy blue, their radios squelching, the clink of the handcuffs squeezing the slender, freckled wrists of Jerry Eves, and still, she could hear it, leaking from some trap door in her skull, overtaking even the shriek of metal on metal: the sound of rain splashing on the Puddle.

Michael!

A Lab's Ears Are Made of *SILK*

Episode IV

What Alley Cat Said

Finn was a Goner.

Alley Cat leapt from the top of the fence to the long, twisted bough of the dogwood tree. Coulda (the Siamese) and Shoulda (the fat tabby) closed ranks and stood behind Finn, so close he could smell tuna fish on their breath. Woulda, the big ball of gray, extracted himself from the pile of leaves, marched across the backyard, and planted himself (backward) a few feet from Finn's twitching whiskers.

Finn willed the fur on his back to stand at attention, but the anger wasn't there. Oh, the fear was—but not enough fear to fight. (Being a Goner wasn't so bad.) What Pig said and what Turtle said had confused him at first—but, truthfully, what they had said (or squeaked or grunted) helped begin to clarify Finn's thinking, but Finn wasn't yet aware of these clarifications. He saw the finger-snapping feline Realists as a death squad and felt quite ready to embrace them if necessary: surrender.

"Can I please have my basketball back?" Finn asked, his voice barely above the buzz of a bee.

"Shoulda," Alley Cat commanded. "The basketball."

Shoulda waddled past Finn and climbed the fence. A few seconds later the basketball flew over the fence and hit Woulda on top of his head.

"You're just giving it back to me?" Finn asked.

"It's yours, isn't it?" Alley Cat answered. Woulda wandered in a woozy daze and came to rest, face down, inches away from a pile of dog excrement.

"Who are you?" Finn asked.

"You know who I am," Alley Cat said.

"I think I do," Finn said. "I thought I did."

"Stop conjugating, Huckleberry," Alley Cat said. "Say what you mean."

"Are you the Lord?" Finn asked. "Or...or God?"

Alley Cat laughed. Shoulda and Coulda giggled too. Woulda snored next to the pile of dog excrement. A tired fly, who'd been buzzing the poop, took a brief respite on Woulda's nose.

"Who are you?" Finn asked again, deeply embarrassed. As we mentioned earlier, Finn wasn't very Woldly, but he wasn't aware of not being Woldly. Until his recent adventures, Finn thought life revolved around loving and being loved. Religion, politics, Leonard Bernstein musicals—these things occupied little space in the places between his whiskers and his Smart Bump.

"Count Bjørn de Vagabond," Alley Cat said, introducing himself and bowing deeply—but not so deep that he fell out of the dogwood tree. Shoulda and Coulda bowed too. Woulda snorted in his sleep, scaring the fly. He rolled over and continued to snore.

"What does the D stand for?" Finn asked.

"The D?" Alley Cat replied.

Finn nodded. "The D."

"As in, 'D Vagabond,'" Finn continued.

Shoulda and Coulda guffawed until Alley Cat whistled sharply.

"The D, Huckleberry?" Alley Cat said. "*D*angerous."

I already knew that, Finn thought.

"*D*elightful. *D*electable. *D*ecidedly *not D*astardly—though all the lady cats might disagree. '*Singin' the blues while the lady cats cry.*'"

" '*And all the colored girls go doo doo doo, do-do-doo-doo,*'" Coulda sang. Shoulda nodded gravely. Woulda curled up into a ball and snored into his armpit.

"What else, what else? *D*ependable. *D*emonized—at least by your kind, aye Huckleberry?"

Finn nodded, but it was more of a nicety than an affirmation. Woulda had just rolled into the dog poop. None of the other Realists paid attention.

"*D*epraved," Alley Cat continued. "But only on a *D*are—not an adjective, but it counts."

Coulda and Shoulda snickered.

"And when it rains: *D*amp," Alley Cat said. "*D*evilish—again, a sobriquet granted by the *felines feminine*. I could go on forever."

Woulda snapped awake and sniffed at his chest; his gray fur was caked with poo. He stretched out his little tongue-comb, but Shoulda reached him first and conked Woulda on the head. Coulda ran over to join the violence, slipped in the poo, and skidded into the wooden gate.

"Of course, only one D word matters in the end, dear Huckleberry. You know what that word is, don't you?" Alley Cat asked.

Finn tried to concentrate on D words, but his vocabulary was limited. He wasn't sure if "dog cookies" was one word or two.

"Bologna?" asked Shoulda, rubbing his considerable tummy. "That a D word?"

Coulda smacked Shoulda's nose with Woulda's tail.

"I'll tell you," Alley Cat said, leaping to a lower branch. "*Dead*. That's the last D word you'll ever need to know."

"*Dead*," Finn repeated. He didn't like the way the word tasted in his mouth. Just thinking of dog cookies had made him think of the Boy and the Boy's bed and the stuffed animals and the Blue Books— and, yes: dog cookies. But: *Dead*...

Shoulda pointed to a spot on Coulda's dusty, golden chest, then flicked Coulda under his chin with his paw. Coulda fell backward and smacked his head on the gate.

"Isn't that one of your three questions?" Alley Cat asked. "I believe the Vicar Pig led you down that dark alley."

"Yes!" Finn barked. "I only had one question when I started my Great Journey, but now I have *three* questions.

"What happens when I die?

"What is freedom?

"And are my ears made of *SILK*?"

"What happens when you die?" Alley Cat sighed. "Some things are better left to the learned. Most would do better, at times, to remain ignorant. But this is not to be."

Coulda wandered back from the gate, rubbing his noggin; Coulda appeared to be cultivating his own Smart Bump. Shoulda was in stitches; anything that involved violence struck him as very, very funny. Shoulda laughed so hard, he farted. Coulda forgot all about his injury and farted back. Woulda turned quietly on his side to try to clean the dog poop from his stomach surreptitiously, but he caught a whiff of his fellow Realists and farted himself in sympathy.

"Boys!" Alley Cat said sharply, and the Realists fell into formation. Coulda's head had little bloody scrapes from his encounters with the gate. Woulda covered his poo-plastered tummy with his paws. Shoulda, his face twisted with effort and strain, tried in vain to hold it in, but...

RRRRIP!

The Realists fell about themselves and into the poo. Alley Cat waited until they had recovered and assumed formation before returning to the subject at paw.

"Yes," Finn said. "The Vicar told me I had to read the Good Book in order to go to heaven. He said I couldn't be..."

Finn couldn't remember.

"Oh, we can help you here, can't we, boys?" Alley Cat asked.

"Jewish?" Coulda said.

"Moslem?" Woulda said.

"Black or brown or any unacceptable color?" Shoulda said, eyeballing Finn. "No offense, Huckleberry."

"None taken," said Finn, the very black Labrador.

"Right," Alley Cat said. "It's not just following the rules of the Vicar Pig's Good Book, is it then? No, it's following the *Vicar's* rules."

"For..." Coulda began.

"...he is..." Shoulda said.

"...the conduit..." Woulda said, surprising himself and his comrades by pronouncing "conduit" correctly. Shoulda and Coulda pounded him on his back.

"...of God," Alley Cat concluded.

Finn scratched at a flea and shook his ears.

"The Vicar Pig believes in the Lord, and Colonel Turtle believes in God," Finn said.

"Same difference," Alley Cat explained. "They want you to live *their* way. Imagine the kind of life that has time to protest gay marriage. What does their Good Book say, Coulda?"

Coulda produced a red covered Gideon from a hidden pocket with a flourish. " 'Judge not, that ye be not judged,' " Coulda read.

"Matthew 7:1," Coulda added. The Siamese fell back into formation and tossed the Gideon behind him where it grazed a squirrel trying to sneak by the conclave.

"See, Pig wants you to live according to his book," Alley Cat said. "If you're gay, you're damned. If you believe in another deity, you're damned. Hell of a D Word: *Damned.* Don't misunderstand me: the way *is* narrow, but its narrowness has *NOTHING* to do with bishops and popes and following the letter of the Good Books (and there are many). It's all about how you live your life. Nothing more. Nothing less."

"But Pig said we were all protected under the blanket of the Lord," Finn said.

"Would you jump out of a window with only a blanket?" Alley Cat asked.

"No, but—"

"No buts," Alley Cat said, and Shoulda, Coulda, and Woulda collapsed in a pile of snickers and chortles, covering up their rear ends. "In a situation of unbearable fear, you might reach for the blanket. But the blanket doesn't do anything in and of itself. Other than keep you in the dark. Which is what most (but not all) purveyors of the Good Book want: a congregation in the dark."

"Have you read the Good Book?" Finn asked.

Alley Cat scaled the trunk of the dogwood to reach the next branch.

"Sure have. Know thy enemy," Alley Cat said. "There is a reasonable amount of wisdom in Pig's Good Book, to be fair. Even the parts of the Good Book Pig's ancestors tossed out (no *Dissenting* theologies—*wink, wink*) have passages that will make your Little White Tie thunder and swoon."

Finn ducked his noggin to try and see his Little White Tie. Shoulda waddled up, pointed to Finn's chest, and when Finn looked down, Shoulda smacked Finn under his chin.

"Fellas!" Alley Cat said before Finn could even start to growl.

"I still don't understand," Finn admitted, keeping a stern eye on the rest of the Realists.

What happened next burned beneath Finn's Smart Bump for years after, for the sky didn't *grow* dark—it was more like someone turned the lights out. Shoulda banged on a piece of tin: THUNDER. Coulda stood in front of Finn (a few feet away, just in case) and blinked his eyes, open and shut, open and shut: LIGHTNING. Woulda ran behind Finn and spit into the air: RAIN.

There appeared in the middle of the backyard a pile of bones, and on top of the pile, spun Alley Cat. No, not *spinning* as much as *dancing*. As Alley Cat danced (and Coulda blinked, Shoulda thundered, and Woulda spat), a bunch of bones shook loose from the pile and scattered across the backyard. Then the most amazing spectacle Finn had ever seen happened: the scattered bones scurried towards one another and joined up with a terrible CLICKING. Once they were satisfied with their appearance (some of the more astute bones helped the littler bones build themselves), they danced in a circle around the pile: cat skeletons, clacking and creaking, shimmying their bone bodies, raising their bony paws to the dark sky, bowing their skulls to the suddenly cold earth beneath their bony feet.

Shoulda, Coulda, and Woulda cheered and mewed encouragements. Alley Cat raised his paws towards the heavens, and in the last crackle of Coulda's lightning, fell into pieces and melted into the pile of bones. The backyard went silent except for the rattle of bones as the remains of Alley Cat settled into the center of the pile.

Finn shut his eyes. Alley Cat has just died—right in front of him. Finn regretted all the times he'd chased Alley Cat and barked at the Count. Finn's eyes were soaked, and the tears traveled the length of his snout to hang off the end of his already-runny nose.

Shuffle shuffle shuffle.

Finn shut his eyes even tighter. Death had come for Alley Cat. Surely, it wouldn't pass up an opportunity to add Finn to its pile of bones.

Then something soft tickled his nose. Finn's Little White Tie pounded (*ba-BOOM, ba-BOOM, ba-BOOM*) until Finn's chest was its own thunderstorm.

"Blow," Coulda said.

Finn dared a peek: Coulda was holding Shoulda's tail and using it to wipe tears off the Lab's snout. (Shoulda giggled, for Finn's whiskers tickled.) The lights had been turned back on. The sun painted the part of the backyard it couldn't reach in shadows. The pile of bones was gone. Alley Cat was back in the dogwood tree, cleaning himself. Woulda used the fallen dogwood leaves to wipe the remaining poo from his tummy.

"And that," Alley Cat said as Finn blew his nose into Shoulda's tail, "was the Dance of the Dead Cats."

Chapter Thirteen

The Rescue

"*Ain't no sunshine when she's gone....*"

The song lied. The sun lit the backyard.

"*...it's not warm when she's away...*"

A neighbor's radio broke the buzz of the cicadas. The bass was tinny—a transistor slung over a fence pole probably—anything to keep company while mowing the lawn or pulling the weeds or burying a dead pet.

"*...ain't no sunshine when she's gone...*"

It was her fault, and she knew it. Magdalene never considered it any other way. The police had been responding to calls from the Lakes, shots fired, EMTs on their way, and they had responded in force. It was the Lakes, for Christ's sake: white trash, trailer tramps. Better step on it.

"*...anytime she goes away...*"

What to do about Jerry Eves? If Jerry had shown a little light into her cave, she had devoured it.

Surely, Mick wouldn't press charges. Her father could help, couldn't he?

Her dreams were vacant if she dreamed last night. Michael hadn't come. She'd barely slept—the night sounds repeated themselves endlessly. How long had it been since she'd *really* had a good night's sleep? Michael seemed to be further away from her now—just little camera flashes in the corner of her eye when she least expected it. Maybe she would never know the end of the dream—her and Michael and the Puddle and the Jumping Tree and the Dead Injun Tree.

Monien the panda sat in the kitchen doorway, and when she stooped down to reach for it, Raven bounded in from the dining room and snatched the panda from her hand.

The panda didn't make sound.

It used to sing a song. The song her mother had whistled.

It was ten thirty on Sunday morning.

Raven dropped the panda at her bare feet. The bear was covered in drool. Her toes were damp.

"Not now," Magdalene said, kicking the panda—Raven charged after it—instantly regretting the kick.

"No, Raven, I didn't mean—"

There was little use in explaining. Raven was doomed anyway. He was a Goner. They all were.

Aunt Tiddy...

Magdalene's father hadn't come home from Holy Redeemer Hospital; he'd stayed there with Tiddy. He'd paid little attention to who took his daughter home; he just wanted her home in bed.

"And walk Raven. At least let him out in the yard to pee."

Her father hadn't said much else. At least not to her.

It *was* her fault, after all.

When she'd woken this morning, she checked the living room, but her father hadn't slept there. No coffee cup. The bathroom was dry.

"*...wonder this time where's she's gone...*"

So Cutter Hagen had driven her home (nervously focusing on the police radio rather than the ADA's moody daughter), and she'd waited all night for a phone call or for her father to come charging through the door, relief on his face, punishment on his mind. He was the Assistant District Attorney; surely he'd heard about her and Jerry stealing Mick's car. So Magdalene waited, her head hung low.

She *was* a dentist's kid, after all. The bad seed.

But he'd never called. He hadn't come home.

And it was her fault.

Again.

Again?

"*...wonder is she's gone to stay...*"

Her sleep had been erratic, and she'd woken to Raven's stinky breath in her face and a sinking feeling in the bottom of her tummy.

In less than twenty-four hours, she'd be dead. There was no margin for error this time. She'd counted out the medication; it had taken forever—the numbers were so gone. To insure a smooth transition, she'd crept into Aunt Tiddy's bedroom (really her father's old bedroom, but now the room smelled like Tiddy) and secured a few extra pills. Better safe than sorry.

Magdalene looked around the house. She'd swept the porch and cleaned up her breakfast dishes. She hadn't been able to eat a bite, but she'd wanted to try. No sense attempting to rescue Katie on an empty stomach. She'd brought the Sunday paper in from the porch.

The headline on the top fold contained the word GUN in big letters. More on the Cabot Case. Had her father's bosses taken the ADA's advice, or was Mrs. Bochdan handcuffed with Jerry Eves? Had the authorities traced the source of the gun?

She tried to read the article, but the newsprint smeared and ran.

Magdalene didn't turn the paper over.

There had been enough time for the Baby Blue Cadillac of Doom to make the Sunday *Mondauk Common*.

The massive manhunt for Christina the Astonishing would be detailed there too below the fold. Magdalene knew she couldn't read that either.

Raven sat facing the back door, Monkey in his mouth. Sometimes Monien the panda was even too sad for Raven. Magdalene let her dog into the yard, and he sat on the stoop, waiting for her, drooling around his monkey.

"...*I know I know I know I know I know I know*..."

She tried to count the pills again, then wrapped them back in the napkin and shoved them into her pocket—never know: might need 'em on the run. She planned to die at home, in her bed, but she had to be prepared in case rescuing Katie proved to be more dangerous than she'd first thought. If Mr. McAllister didn't have a date with the widow Tidwell tonight—well, the jig would be up, and Magdalene would have failed again.

In her other pocket was Michael's money and what was left of her baby-sitting cache, along with the wrinkled dogwood blossoms from Katie's backyard—for luck (although what kind of luck Jesus would bring a thirteen-year-old girl intent on destroying herself, Magdalene didn't know). But if God really loved her like the nuns and the priests said He did, then He would see: He couldn't let what had happened to Stevie Rich happen to Katie McAllister. Even if Katie survived her father, how easy would it be for Katie to slide into the life lived by Stevie?

"...*ain't no sunshine when she's gone*..."

She'd finished the letter to Mrs. Bochdan, copied it for her father, stashed his beneath her pillow, and folded Mrs. Bochdan's carefully in an envelope. After the rush for the Sunday papers, Sol's would be closed for the rest of the day. Magdalene could slip it through the mail slot. Her letter meant little if Stevie Rich didn't talk to the police. She hoped he'd been picked up at the Lakes for firing the gun. He could be in a holding cell right now with Jerry Eves.

Jerry!

It was all her fault. All of it. In attempting to undo, she'd entangled. In attempting to help, she'd hurt.

That's the way the cookie crumbles, as Shakespeare would say. That's the way the Easter egg bounces.

She knew she should leave a note. A suicide note. That was the protocol. The letter to her father contained just facts concerning the Cabot Case. Nothing gut wrenching or dramatic. Nothing like: *I've gone out the window.* She hadn't even mentioned her death. There was also the problem of where she would leave such a note (if she did write one). If her father came back from the hospital early, he might see it before she did the deed, assuming, of course, that he wasn't preoccupied. (And why wouldn't he be? It was nonsense for Magdalene to think otherwise. Aunt Tiddy was the only family her father had—besides Magdalene. And that would soon change.)

As a writer, she wanted to leave the most poetic, heart-wrenching suicide note she could think up. She'd gone through several drafts in her head, but none made it to paper. She could go the opposite route too: a couple of words, a few lines maybe, nothing too obtuse, but nothing too elaborate either.

Perhaps:

"See you later."

Or:

"I took the medicine."

Or:

"I'm sorry."

She did none of those. What she did do was write a short note to Michael—in case he came home and she was gone.

Magdalene left Raven on the back steps. In the dining room, she shuffled Tiddy's stacks of Polaroids and slid Michael's school photograph in the middle. She was out of breath when she returned to the yard.

Raven dropped the football at her feet and wagged his tail. The ball was slimy. Long strands of Raven spittle stretched from the ball to her fingers. Raven looked like a puppy now: his eyes wide, bright and aware, his tail moving a million miles a minute, his mouth open in that easy grin of his—just like her mother's.

Magdalene tossed the football—a perfect spiral. Raven pounded on it when it hit the ground and wrestled with its slippery surface. There it was between his legs—now behind him—pounce!

She had to leave the house before her father came home. She'd waited for him throughout the night, but his not coming home made everything easier. If she waited for him now, she might never be able to leave—though there was a chance he might not notice her if she was home.

Raven brought the football back, and Magdalene tossed it high; the ball was slick and the spiral wobbled and Raven lunged for it and missed. The football landed in the baby pool. Raven sat near the edge and watched it float towards the middle.

"...*I know I know I know I know I know I know I know...*"

It wasn't a radio. Was lonely spinster Evey Corcoran playing the song over and over?

Raven cried softly by the edge of the pool. His pose was noble, his *SILK* ears pinned back expectantly; only the tip of his long tail still wagged.

The song finished a few seconds later. How many seconds? Magdalene couldn't count now if her life depended upon it—and it didn't. Not her life.

Not her *life?*

Silence, then a needle bumped and scratched. The record went *hsssssssssss*, like Sister Rita telling the spook story of Sister Mary Magdalene de Rosa and the lavatory fire; it went *hsssssssssss* like thunderstorm raindrops splashing into the Puddle.

An organ? A calliope? Whatever it was, it caught the breeze for only a wink before the record started again.

"*Ain't no sunshine when she's gone...*"

The calliope sounds were gone.

Magdalene retrieved the football from the baby pool, and when she threw it, little beads of water painted the morning air, stars blinking themselves out of existence.

The song ended again. There it was! The calliope! The bells! The smell of popcorn and cotton candy!

Raven dropped the football to sniff the air. His tongue hung out of his mouth.

"...*only darkness every day...*"

Whoever was playing the old 45 was doing so to block the sounds of...

The carnivals!

The Assumption of Our Lady Carnival!

The Calvary United Methodist Carnival!

The kickoff for both ten day events had been Friday night, and today was the celebration of the Feast of the Baptist at Assumption.

Magdalene pumped her arm, but the football slipped from her fingers and thudded to the ground a few feet from her bare toes.

If the carnivals were gearing up, she was losing time.

Raven snatched the football and followed her into the house. He pushed the ball towards her with his nose. Magdalene ignored her dog. There was no time. The kitchen clock said noon. Time was hard to know in the Barrows Bungalow.

Raven barked and placed a paw over the ball, grinning up at Magdalene.

Did anyone ever play with their aging pooch anymore? Tiddy surely didn't. Her father wasn't home enough to even establish a relationship with the dog. And Magdalene? She never had time for Raven. Not anymore.

The ball slipped out from under his paw and skidded across the kitchen floor. He was all over it, trying to keep it in his mouth; drool dripped from its surface. His eyebrows needed trimming. His nails too. Raven dropped the ball at her feet again, waited a few seconds, then gave up, sulking into the dining room.

Magdalene brought his food bowl to the counter and filled it halfway with his crunchy dog food. Normally, Raven would run into the kitchen when he heard the rustle of the bag, but he seemed to be otherwise occupied. Magdalene tiptoed into the dining room and reached behind the computer desk for the rat poison.

Raven was lying next to the desk, quietly crying, chewing on the panda. Monien had seen better days. One eye was missing. Its fur was matted. The white parts were dark, and tufts were missing from the black parts.

"He's not coming back, Raven," Magdalene said.

The dog tilted his head. God, the entire lower part of his jaw was gray, she noticed. The fur around his neck hung loosely. Magdalene rubbed his ears. *SILK*. His ears were still made of *SILK*.

"Michael…"

Raven's ears perked up.

Surely, Raven couldn't remember Michael's *name*?

She knelt down in front of the dog and rubbed her face against his ears.

"…he's…I don't think he's…no one else is even looking for him…and when I'm gone…I don't think he's coming back."

Raven licked the tears from her face. He smelled like popcorn.

Magdalene walked into the kitchen and applied the rat poison to Raven's food. Raven sat appreciatively nearby, licking his chops. But when Magdalene presented him with the bowl, Raven sniffed at it twice then trotted into the living room.

She had to get out of the house before Raven started eating. She couldn't watch Raven die.

But she could come home and find him dead?

Her father would be home before her. That was the plan, right? Slink home in the dead of night and die?

Maybe she should die elsewhere.

Shoulda coulda woulda.

Maybe she should just walk down to the Puddle (once Katie was safely on the bus to her Aunt Angela's) and lie on the dock at Finch's Landing and smell the garbage and listen to the far-off sounds of the carnivals winding down and die.

Raven was by the front door. He had dragged his leash out from the low shelf on the end table. Magazines and newspapers were scattered on the floor.

Magdalene patted down her pockets.

"No, Raven. You have to stay."

Magdalene nudged the dog out of her way and eased the front door open. Raven stuck his snout between her legs; the leash still dangled from his jaws.

"No, you're gonna bite right through it if…no…Raven, I have to go."

Raven pulled his head back and jumped on her, yelping, his breath rough and raw and inviting—like Michael's stinky blankets.

"NO!" she screamed. "GET! GO EAT. GET INSIDE. I CAN'T PLAY WITH YOU. NO WALK. GET INSIDE NOW! I DON'T WANT TO PLAY WITH YOU! GO EAT YOUR STUPID FUCKING FOOD AND LEAVE ME ALONE! GO!"

Raven hung his head and crawled on his tummy.

Magdalene backed out to the porch and closed the screen door.

She couldn't see anything. It was like it was pouring just where she was standing.

"Go, Raven," she whispered. "I can't love you anymore."

Raven whimpered and pressed his nose against the screen.

"…and you can't love me anymore. Go eat. I'm sorry. I am so, so sorry."

"*...this house just ain't no home, anytime she goes away...*"

Was she going blind? Raven was a fuzzy, popcorn-smelling, blurry ball, pawing at the screen door, crying a high, keening wail, and as Magdalene ran from the porch, Raven's song followed her and filled her head. It was a hymn. A hymn for Mondauk. A hymn for the Barrows. There were no words. There was no melody. It was just: sound. A sound that didn't belong to anything or anyone. A sound that everyone recognized, but couldn't—wouldn't—dare interpret. Magdalene knew eventually everyone heard the sound, whether they wanted to or not. And either the sound fit, the final, missing puzzle piece, or went ignored. It didn't matter: the wail of the missing was the only song worth knowing by heart.

+

Sol's was already closed, and Magdalene slipped the letter through the mail slot. Mrs. Bochdan was so far gone, Magdalene thought, she might not know what the letter meant, but Magdalene had made sure to mention in her father's version that she'd written one to Mrs. Bochdan, so it wouldn't be ignored. The letter might not help at all if Stevie Rich didn't talk to the police. It was obvious that either the witnessing nun was keeping a vow of silence or really didn't comprehend what had happened. Joseph Bochdan surely shouldn't have stolen the stolen gun, and most definitely he shouldn't have brought it to school. Although Joseph's motives were unclear concerning just *why* he'd brought it, the reasons behind its eventual use were crystal clear to Magdalene: he was about to be attacked—Henry too—*again!*—and he panicked and fired and removed his best friend's face.

Magdalene stopped walking and listened to the competing sounds of the carnivals. The carnivals were held so close together that the more ingenious of Magdalene's schoolmates would pay for one then find a break in the cheap, temporary red wooden fencing and move on to the next carnival. Their proximity was more one of convenience than of competition, the Methodists said, an opinion with which the Catholic Faith Board vehemently disagreed.

Assumption held its carnival in its parking lot and recess area and the northern-most part of the Fields, with the various games of chance and food stands erected on the east lawn—far enough away from the football field to insure the minimum of unwanted trampling. Calvary United Methodist held its much smaller carnival in the large parking lot in front of the shops on the Pike. Their church's parking lot was too small, and the church itself was smack dab in the middle of a residential neighborhood. The shops' lot provided just enough room—the Methodist carnival didn't have games of chance, just a couple of rides, a bouncing tent (the Moonwalk), some face painting, a puppet show, and tons of greasy food.

The Catholic carnival had everything—even a strongman contest to see who could ring the bell. Magdalene always attended both events—and paid for both. She had always found it exciting to have two carnivals at the start of summer on the same day. The residents disagreed.

Before Father Demetrius descended into the basement chapel, he waged an ongoing debate—some would say war—with Pastor Earl Mockingbird of Calvary United Methodist. Father Demetrius would take pot shots from the Sunday pulpit, playing on the pastor's unfortunate name—one time even going so far as to call him Pastor Copycat. The Catholic carnival celebrating the Feast of the Baptist, according to the Church Bulletin, accounted for a large part of the summer fundraising. Aunt Tiddy said Father Demetrius would hump Lucifer himself and make him a sandwich afterward if it increased the coffers.

Father Dave took a different approach to the controversy when he assumed parishional power, requesting a meeting with Pastor Mockingbird, even taking him to dinner. Father Dave wanted the Methodists to hold their carnival on another weekend—even the weekend after Assumption's ended if possible. But Pastor Mockingbird was immovable; the overflow from the much larger Catholic event was what put the Methodist carnival over the top financially.

In the end, Father Dave raised his hands and let it go. Unable to change Pastor Mockingbird's mind, Father Dave went the opposite route, offering to host, on the grass on the east side of the Church, a competition between the two denominations: a sack race, a pie eating contest, even a Biblical trivia contest. The Faith Board went bonkers, naturally, led by the incredibly offended Mrs. Fuller. How dare Father Dave join forces with the Methodists? How dare he back down from a decades-old battle to have the Methodists move the date of their carnival—or at least move it away from the Catholic one. The Methodists attracted a good many of the residents of Paradise Lakes, and their pre-carnival carousing lent a seedy, after-hours nightclub atmosphere to Calvary's event—or so insisted Mrs. Fuller.

Magdalene had to admit: she found the war of words and ideas between the Catholics and Methodists endlessly entertaining, if for no other reason than she loved watching her teachers, especially the nuns, entangle themselves explaining a recent dust-up between the faiths. There were never any disparaging words—just hints, tantalizing bits. If a fellow student's parents had filled him or her in (or if the kid had overheard after-dinner wagging or phone-gabbing whispers), Magdalene could always tell: that student's head would nod knowingly, the lips would purse, and the student would try to catch the instructor's eye—especially if the student wasn't doing well, grade-wise, or if that student was Jerry Eves, class clown. Magdalene doubted Jerry ever had inside information about a single event the nuns tried not to talk about. His mother was too busy keeping house for four boys to gather and disseminate gossip.

But Magdalene loved it. Not the obvious prejudice dog-paddling the surface—it was hard enough to fight that urge within herself: the urge to label things and people, especially Methodists, and especially the Methodists who lived in Paradise Lakes, if only because they seemed so foreign and lived so close—but figuring out what the nuns were clamoring about. The Good Sisters of the Order of Saint Joseph never stooped to actually pointing a finger at the Methodists or even name checking the denomination, so every screed against "…those so-called Christians who believe otherwise…" (as Sister Jezebel once put it) was a mystery to be solved. Of course, it was invariably disappointing. The Methodists had refused, once again, to move the date of their carnival. The Methodists were asking the borough for a permit to expand their cemetery. The Methodists (thanks to Father Dave) were coming to Christmas Eve Mass, and some of the less reticent (and snooty) Catholics were attending Vespers.

Magdalene approached Assumption from its east side. In the Corridor, booths of every size and shape were lined up against the bike fence on the left and the convent wall on the right. The pictures of Henry Richard Cabot and the notes and posters had been removed. A booth with shelves of doomed goldfish in plastic bowls took up a large part of the convent wall. When a giggling group of kids rushed through the entrance, waving their arms in the air to show proof of prior payment (a stamp on the back of their hands), Magdalene ran after them and lifted her hand the same way (funds were limited). Mrs. Stanley, the fussy librarian, didn't even look up from her counting. She just licked a fingertip and flipped through a stack of bills.

For all the religious fervor accompanying the events, Assumption's carnival was just gaudy enough to make Magdalene forget it had *any* connection to religion. Packs of young girls giggled in halter tops, all chewing gum and jangly bracelets, their developing breasts barely contained. Nascent Bod Squaders. Boys roamed in packs too, collars upturned, candy cigarettes dangling from their mouths, bodies dowsed in Daddy's cologne. Magdalene recognized few faces and even those were distorted. Freedom, even closely supervised freedom on the grounds of the Church and school, stretched the familiar to the funhouse grotesque. Pimples were volcanoes. Long noses: glaciers. Buckteeth: ravenous, rabid rabbit choppers. The beautiful were rendered ugly, the ugly extreme.

And the extreme, it seemed to Magdalene, worked the carnival booths. Oh, for sure, various faculty members manned a few booths (if they weren't on patrol for eighth graders necking behind the food tent or sixth graders sharing a discarded Marlboro). There was Sister Jezebel hawking three throws for a dollar: toss the bean bag through all three rings, the Father, Son, and Holy Ghost, each ring successively smaller, and win a "Don't X Christ Out of Christmas" t-shirt or a Baby Jesus action figure, complete with gold, frankincense, and myrrh (all nicely labeled), an oversized farm animal at His feet (a goat? a sheep?—possibly a supine opossum or a spare camel left by the wise men), and, clutched in His little plastic hand, a disturbing crucifix, upon which a very brown, distorted Jesus appeared to be moaning at His younger self. Assorted outfits for the Baby Jesus action figure could be bought (or won) separately, although His swaddling undergarments were painted on. (No peeking at the Holy Penis.) Sister Rita supervised the pie-eating contest, the instructions—commands!—whistling out of her mouth, spittle flying, bits of blueberry pie stuck to her chin. Magdalene avoided eye contact then doubled back; there was little telling *which* eye Sister Rita was using to look out of. But faculty only worked the booths directly set up and run by the Church. The carnival as a whole had been rented, and manning the booths were the extreme of the extremes.

(Michael used to call it the Sad Circus Syndrome: so sad, it was hard to look at, so bizarre, how could anyone look away?)

Some hadn't shaved—or most likely bathed—in some time. Hair

stood on end. Cheap cologne masked a boozy smell Magdalene was familiar with. One man's head was significantly smaller than the rest of his body—like a pea atop a watermelon. Two women ran a ring toss game, their bodies shaped like bowling pins, their bottoms improbably huge, their pants possibly sewn together from old stage curtains. Another man picked his nose and wiped it on his shirt, in and of itself disgusting, but made more so because, strictly speaking, in a cartilage sense, he didn't have a nose: just two holes in the middle of his face and a lump of flesh, like an anthill slum, affixed right above them. Another man had no legs; he walked on his hands and snatched money and miniature basketballs and cheap prizes with his mouth, from where stalactite teeth caught the blinking lights and many mirrored rides, reflecting back only sullen, yellow decay.

Magdalene stared wistfully at the Pennsylvania Dutch Funnel Cake truck, but decided better of it. The money in her pocket had a specific purpose. She wouldn't have snuck in otherwise.

"Want a bite of mine?"

Danny Kildare!

"The Innkeeper at the End of the World! You keep popping up, don't you?" Magdalene asked, tearing herself a piece of Danny's funnel cake. It was still hot, and Magdalene bounced the dough around in her mouth before swallowing it.

"If this funnel cake had a book jacket blurb," Danny Kildare said, "it would say, 'A steamy read that's nonetheless hard to swallow.' "

"Been here long?" Magdalene asked around the funnel cake.

"Been here all day!" Danny Kildare said proudly, and his face bore the evidence: Magdalene could probably have told Danny just what he'd eaten since he'd arrived. "Been on the Tilt-a-Whirl three times!" he said, holding up three fingers as additional evidence.

"Your mom here?" Magdalene asked, declining an additional piece of funnel cake. The first piece had given her instant heartburn; her stomach and throat were on fire.

Danny shook his head.

"My mom's at the inn."

"McCullough's."

Danny nodded; his mouth was full again.

"Your dad?"

Danny shrugged.

"Your mom know you're here?"

Another shrug.

"I asked her if I could come. She didn't say no. She gave me a twenty dollar bill, and I had some change left in my Jesus bank."

"Jesus."

"Yep."

"Your mom still working a lot?"

"Uh-huh," Danny Kildare answered around a mouthful of Pennsylvania Dutch Funnel Cake. "It was my Pop-Pop's inn, 'member? Before that, it was my great-grandpop's. People stayed there if they were traveling through town, and my great-grandpop would take care of 'em. Brought people together for more than just drinking and fighting and cussing."

Magdalene nodded her head.

"And you're the Innkeeper..."

"...at the End of the World."

Danny didn't seem all that happy at the self-proclaimed sobriquet at the moment.

"You know they canceled the sack races and stuff," Danny said.

"But I saw Sister Rita with the pie-eating contest."

Danny shrugged. "Maybe she likes pies. The whole Jesus Challenge with the Methodists was canceled."

Danny crooked his finger, and Magdalene lowered her head to hear his whispers.

"Father Dave was arrested."

Magdalene fought to hide her surprise.

"Do you know for sure? The radio said—"

Danny shrugged.

"I like Father Dave. I like his red beard. I want a red beard when I grow up."

"You have to have—" Magdalene stopped. Why couldn't Danny have a red beard if he wanted one?

"Brian Eves said both the Methodists and the Faith Board liked that the Jesus Challenge was canceled."

"Have you seen Jerry Eves around?"

Magdalene didn't have to look down to know Danny had shrugged. She didn't know how he was faring as the Innkeeper at the End of the World, but he was in the running for King of the Shruggers. But just hearing the name of Jerry's brother had made her wince.

"Did you ask Mr. McAllister if I could stay with you and Katie when you baby-sit her?"

A squeal of feedback. Someone tapped a microphone.

"Yeah, I don't know, Danny. Mr. McAllister's a tough nut to crack."

"Hmm," Danny said. "If Mr. McAllister was a newspaper headline, it would be, 'Iraqi Head Seeks Arms.' "

A woman dressed head to toe in steel gray, from her bonnet to her sensible shoes, marched towards the duo.

"Mrs. Nicholas!" Magdalene cried, pulling Danny closer to her.

"Who's that?" Danny said. Magdalene felt his body shudder next to hers. Danny's head turned this way and that. "A bully?"

"No…well, yes," Magdalene whispered. "Groundskeeper Nicholas.

"A Methodist," she added.

"Oh," Danny Kildare said. "Look—dogs!"

Danny ran towards a booth in the western corner of the recess lot, as Mrs. Nicholas stomped past Magdalene without so much as a glance. Magdalene decided to follow Danny; she had nothing but time to kill, she thought, cracking herself up. Gallows humor, her father called it. Laughing all the way to the noose.

Danny was waving her over, jumping up and down, his oversized white t-shirt flapping like a flag in the wind. Magdalene weaved her way through the crowd. Danny must have run between their legs to reach the far end already.

An older boy with a pencil-thin moustache blocked her way for a heartbeat then stepped aside. He was accompanied by a feral boy who hid his double chin and yellow teeth in the half-light of the carnival. Three more boys in half-shirts with cigarettes tucked behind their ears trailed a few feet back.

The feral boy winked as he passed.

"Shit."

Magdalene ducked behind the cotton candy booth.

The kids from the Lakes—John-John Hagarty and the pencil-mustached kid who'd been copping a feel from Chloe! She recognized the others as the ones lounging stoned around the Gremlin. What were they doing at the Catholic carnival?

Magdalene watched them approach a game of chance—the one with the oversized water pistol strapped to a board.

That's right, Magdalene thought: the Methodists don't allow games of chance at their carnival. The Lakes boys were most likely Methodists. (Although John-John attended Assumption with Stevie.)

A girl with a large bruise on her face and what looked like a teardrop tattoo under her left eye joined the Lakes boys at the booth, and an exchange was made between palms—hers and the older, mustached boy's. The girl took a long drag on a cigarette, flicked it away, and turned, catching Magdalene's eyes for a brief second before striding away in the crowd.

"Chloe!" Magdalene cried, breaking cover, but the girl (if it was Chloe) was gone, vanished between the Porta Potties and the milk can toss game.

Magdalene walked to the northern side of the convent. The Calvary United Methodist carnival blinked in the east. There were fewer squeals of delight from the rival carnival, too few sounds of kids having fun. Most of the Methodist kids from the Lakes had come to Assumption's carnival.

Magdalene made her way back towards whatever had gotten Danny all worked up. The crowd was tight. The air was thick with body odor. Many of the carnival goers wore tank tops. Quite a few smoked cigarettes. A large number had tattoos—some of the women even.

A large, clammy hand attached to an arm thick with curly black hair grabbed her wrist.

Pastor Earl Mockingbird pulled her between two booths, one of which had an impossibly swollen Scooby-Doo strung above it, the flashing lights from the rides trapped in its marble eyes. Magdalene smelled bologna on Pastor Mockingbird's breath. Mustard too.

"My child. Magdalene," Pastor Mockingbird said, only "Magdalene" came out sounding like "Mag-da-win."

Magdalene tried to pull her arm free. For a doughy minister, the pastor had an iron grip.

"It's okay, Mag-da-win," Pastor Mockingbird said.

"Let me go!" Was Pastor Mockingbird one of the snipes?

"But I have a message from Father Dave—"

Magdalene punched the pastor in the stomach with her free hand. Her fist sunk into his fat then rebounded, thudding back against her chest. It seemed as if all the air left her body. She reached for the pastor's eyes—

He didn't blink.

She touched his glasses.

No reaction.

The pastor was…

Sister Jezebel, Katie McAllister's third grade teacher, stood behind him, making boo-boo faces.

Both lenses in the Methodist pastor's glasses were thick with prisms. She'd never realized.

"…blind?"

"Thank you, Sister," Pastor Mockingbird said. A plastic cup of warm water was brought to Magdalene's lips. Sister Jezebel was kneeling, looking up at her.

"Knocked the wind out of herself when she bumped into me," Pastor Mockingbird said. "The good Sister Jezebel recognized you or I would have missed you altogether."

Sister Jezebel stood up and smoothed her habit.

"I have to get back. If Sister Mary Joseph finds that I've left my booth…Miss Barrows can help you to the stage, Pastor…"

The nun fluttered back to her flock.

"Mostly," Pastor Mockingbird said to Magdalene, only it sounded like "mos-wee." He smiled as if she'd never punched him. (Had she?) "Mostly blind. Legally blind."

She couldn't find her voice momentarily so she nodded.

"Can you walk?" he asked.

She could. The pastor latched onto her elbow. The carnival swirled around them, the crowd chock full of staring Methodists.

"What are you doing here?" she sputtered. He kept his face uncomfortably close. She wondered what her breath smelled like to Pastor Mockingbird.

"Father Dave asked me to come, seeing how he is currently incapacitated," Pastor Mockingbird said, only "currently" sounded like "cur-went-wee."

"Incapacitated?"

"He'll be back in the rectory shortly," Pastor Mockingbird said.

Wectowee.

Shortwee.

Pastor Mockingbird shook his head, smiling.

"Thank God," Pastor Mockingbird said. "Now Mondauk Proper can rest in peace."

West in peace.

"Father Dave knows how close you and the Fuller girl were— are—and he wanted me to check in on you if I had a chance after the carnival, but here you are.

"He wanted me to tell you…well, I hope it doesn't come across untoward, but he wants you to know that nobody has to be alone. That's exactly what he said: 'Nobody has to be alone.' He was worried about you with this whole Fuller girl business, what with your brother—"

Magdalene slid her arm out from Pastor Mockingbird's grip. Her toes were tingling; her face was hot and flushed and sweaty.

"What did you—?"

Pastor Mockingbird appeared not to notice her question or her body temperature.

"In a jiff, Vince," Pastor Mockingbird spoke over her head, only it sounded like "Wince." "I'm on, my child. Go see Father Dave when he returns to the rectory."

Weturns to the wectowee.

Magdalene sputtered again: "Where are you going?" The pastor turned and regarded Magdalene with a gentle smile. (Pastor Mockingbird seemed to always be smiling.)

"I'm the guest speaker. Father Dave used his one phone call to call me."

Father Vincent took Pastor Mockingbird by the arm.

"Please, Pastor. The Board is waiting."

"Ahh, your Board. Yes, yes. Good night, dear," Pastor Mockingbird said to Magdalene, waddling away, a perturbed Father Vincent, his bald head as red as his face, leading him by the arm.

If she could remember how, she'd count. Right now. Just wallow in it.

Danny Kildare was jumping up and down in the far western corner of the recess lot, yelling Magdalene's name. There was still plenty of light left in the day—it wouldn't even get dark until a little before nine. She glanced in the direction of the makeshift stage, erected on the wheelchair incline behind the bike fence. She could just make out Father Vincent's severe pate, at least a head above everyone else's, navigating, with the slightest hint of impatience, Pastor Mockingbird's path to the stage. Sister Edna crept to the microphone, stopped short, and turned, whispering loud enough for the mic to pick up her cringing voice: "But *how* should I touch it?"

Danny Kildare ran straight into Magdalene's legs.

"Ohmygodyouhavetocomesee!"

Sister Edna again: "But tap it *how?*"

Now it was Danny's turn to get plowed into. It happened so fast, Magdalene was sure Danny was dead. He was flat on his back, the creature on top of him. A second creature bounded into Magdalene's legs, and she dropped and curled into a ball.

Whhhh*at* wwww*i*llll *you d*oooo whhhh*en you*rrrr *time come*sss?

"Snipe!"

Magdalene curled her fingers into a fist and swung blindly.

Something licked her ear.

"Magdalene!"

Danny!

"Why'd ya hit me?"

Danny?

Magdalene opened her eyes.

A chocolate Labrador retriever with a gray muzzle licked her nose.

"Huh, Magdalene?" Danny asked, kneeling next to her, rubbing his arm. "That smarts."

"Two for flinching," Magdalene said absently, although she'd only hit Danny once.

The chocolate Lab wore an ID tag.

"Emma Lou.

"And this," Danny said, wrestling with an older yellow Lab, "this is Murphee. Murph I call her."

Someone whistled, and Murphee and Emma Lou (slurping Magdalene's face one last time) took off for the booth in the farthest corner of the recess lot. There an overweight woman with wires for hair and fat little carrots for fingers stood behind a long table laden with literature (each pile secured by a stone), trying to light a very long cigarette. A tarp hung on either side of the table from rickety metal poles, and Polaroids of dogs—all Labrador retrievers and all smiling—were hung with scotch tape.

"Pat O'Brien," the woman said, sticking her chubby carrots out towards Magdalene, pumping her hand vigorously. "Brookline Labrador Rescue."

"I'm Magdalene." Her name felt funny in her mouth, as if it no longer belonged to her, as if she'd lost the right to use it.

Emma Lou licked Magdalene's hand. Inside the Brookline booth, Danny rubbed Murphee's belly.

"Do I *blow* on it?" Sister Edna stage-whispered into the microphone. "Like this?" The loudspeaker broadcasted what sounded like a herd of buffalo passing gas.

"Jesus, Mary, and Joseph!" Sister Mary Joseph said, loud enough for the mic to pick up her exasperation.

"I didn't see you here last year," Magdalene said to Pat.

"Was over at Calvary's carnival last year," Pat said, shooting smoke between her words. "This year, I'm here." Pat shrugged. "We don't have any religious affiliation."

The shrugging was contagious.

"You're spitting all over it," Sister Mary Joseph said. "Will you...*let go*...no, I'm not mad, but I will be if you don't...Sister, sit the hell down!"

"Lot more fireworks here though," Pat said, gesturing towards the little stage.

"Methodists don't have nuns," Magdalene said (trying hard not to shrug). "Not anymore." Emma Lou walked behind Magdalene and stuck her head between Magdalene's legs.

"Don't I know it," Pat O'Brien said. "Different world."

"Wince?" Pastor Mockingbird breathed into the microphone. "Wince? Wince, is this on?" *Tap tap tap.* "Wince?"

"I don't understand what the pastor's doing here," Magdalene said.

"Saying the opening prayer for the carnival," Pat answered. "There he is," Pat said, her voice turning child-like. An off-white lab with pointed ears ran towards Pat barking. "You do good business? You do good business?"

"Wince?" said the loudspeaker. "Wince?"

"You're already *on*, Pastor" Father Vincent said, and Magdalene imagined the rising red tide on Father Vincent's shiny bald head.

"Father Wince, everyone!" Pastor Mockingbird announced to an explosive crowd.

"Father Wince!" the crowd roared.

"Didn't realize Father Vince was so popular," Magdalene said.

"Father Wince!" Pastor Mockingbird said again, and the crowd went bonkers.

Pat O'Brien spat to her left and regarded the end of her cigarette. "Pulling on a mallard's leg and calling him a swan." Pat had a slight Southern accent; her words, even the little ones, sounded important; they weren't rushed, and each one was properly pronounced. "Might have more to do with the pastor's palate than Father Vincent's popularity."

The off-white dog stood up on his hind legs (an effort; the dog was well fed) and cried softly while he licked Magdalene' face. He looked like a white version of Raven (except for the pointy ears).

"Kirby knows," Pat O'Brien said, rubbing the dog's neck, "doesn't he?"

"Kirby?"

"Vacuum cleaner. Eats everything. Half Lab, half German shepherd."

"One hundred percent slobber!" Danny Kildare announced, and indeed, he was covered in it. Murphee alternated between cleaning Danny's face of all traces of carnival fare—cotton candy stains and water taffy smudges and a dab of mustard from right under his nose—and rolling onto her back for tummy rubs.

" 'Uproariously Funny,' " Danny Kildare said, " 'I Couldn't Put It Down.' "

"Kirby knows is all I'm sayin'," Pat O'Brien said.

Adults and their pronouncements. Magdalene wanted to give Long John Silver's black spot to each and every one of them—even the ones she liked. And she liked Pat O'Brien.

Tunnel of smoke.

"He knows you're sad. Kirb's a regular mind reader. You know that Christmas carol: *'He knows when you've been bad or good...*? Well, Kirb knows when you're sad."

Kirby turned around and sat on Magdalene's feet. Underneath the table, Emma Lou, the chocolate Lab, snored loudly.

"I'd like to thank Father Dave for asking me to speak to you," Pastor Mockingbird said. "Together, we bear witness to Christ's victory over Lucifer. And together we celebrate the mysteries of our faith."

Wictorwee.

Woocifer.

Mysterwees.

Emma Lou's snoring wasn't loud enough, Magdalene thought.

"So next year, you'll go back over to the Methodists?" she asked Pat.

Pat shrugged. "Guess so. Does it matter? Anyway, we don't have enough staff for two booths. I'm it out this way."

Pastor Mockingbird said something that sounded like "wee-weg-on." The carnival crowd exploded.

"Does he know why they're cheering?" Magdalene asked.

"I don't think he cares. He's just about blind, ain't he? So he talks funny."

Shrug.

"I don't think the Catholics like him being here," Magdalene said.

Pat O'Brien laughed.

"That's right. I heard about your *Faith* Board."

"They'll turn on him—the crowd."

"You don't know your congregation very well, do you?" Pat asked, lighting another 100. "There's not much difference between the two, you know. It's not like they're different religions."

"But—"

"Way I heard it, Father Dave and Pastor Mockingbird have been talkin' about speaking at each other's carnival kickoff ceremonies for quite some time, seeing as how they couldn't agree to choose different weeks. But Father Dave was indisposed, so Pastor Mockingbird took the torch and ran with it. And why not? This town could use a little healing."

Kirby farted and titled his head back to smile at Magdalene. Danny, lounging between Emma Lou and Murphee, his head on the chocolate Lab's belly and his stocking feet (he had abandoned his shoes) on the yellow Lab's side, giggled and released one himself. Emma Lou lifted her nose into the air. Murphee sniffed at Danny's socks.

"But—"

"Shhh," Pat O'Brien said. She cocked her head towards the small transistor radio suspended from the edge of her table. "Damn. Missed it."

"Wictorwee!" Pastor Mockingbird declared, his fat hands raised in the air.

"Wictorwee!" the crowd repeated, syllable for syllable. Magdalene imagined Sister Mary Joseph covering her face with her hands.

"Wictorwee over evil!" Pastor Mockingbird said. "Wictorwee over twerp-e-tood."

The crowd didn't quite know what to do with that one. Some repeated the phrase back. Others just muttered amongst themselves.

"Um, uh," Pastor Mockingbird stuttered. "Wince!" he shouted, attempting to bring the crowd back to his side. (It worked; the crowd went ballistic.) Magdalene watched Father Vince's bald head bob up and down as he acknowledged his name and the crowd's recognition.

"He's usually a way better speaker," Pat O'Brien said. "But

there's a lot riding on this: the Methodist pastor speaking to a largely Catholic crowd when their own pastor is behind bars."

Kirby farted again. The dog stood up, turned in a circle, discovered nothing worthy of inspection, and sat down again on Magdalene's feet. Danny Kildare, snuggled between Murphee and Emma Lou, released another one as well. Murphee groaned low in her throat. Emma Lou resumed her snoring.

Magdalene wondered if Raven would be upset if he smelled other dogs on her.

Let it go.

"Are you a Methodist?" Magdalene asked, backing up a little bit. She hoped the question didn't offend the dog lady.

Pat O'Brien's laugh was raspy.

"Hell, no. Your two camps can have at it. I'm a Baptist and lapsed at that. Sweetheart, it's only *people* who want everything separate and in easy categories. You think God gives a rat's ass if you're a holy roller or a Papist? You think God gives a good goddamn if you marry a Jew? I don't think so. I don't think God cares about all that shit and Shinola."

"But—"

"There you go! Between your 'buts' and their butts," Pat O'Brien said, cocking her thumb at Danny Kildare and his new furry friends, "there's more than enough hot air to go around."

" 'Every Doggy,' " Danny Kildare intoned, " 'Has a Dark Side.' "

Magdalene scratched the top of Kirby's head and studied his pointy ears as they turned back and forth trying to catch all the aural activity. Pastor Mockingbird had launched into the actual sermon, seemingly convinced that the Catholics were on his side, and he was a damn better speaker than Magdalene would have guessed. With the exception of Father Dave's homilies (which usually revolved around stories of his sprawling Irish family and their mother's faith in the face of all sorts of odds one expected to run into with twelve children), most of the Catholic priests' homilies were boring and pedantic. Magdalene had no more interest in how Saint Paul's letter to the Ephesians affected her life than she did on how it actually affected the Ephesians. (Not very much, she gathered; where were the Ephesians today?) But Pastor Mockingbird appeared to be on a roll—his tone was conciliatory, and the subtext, as far as Magdalene could discern, wasn't the need to build bridges as much as recognize them. She even found herself ignoring his funny manner of speaking.

(Funny in that sad circus way, because this was how Pastor Mockingbird made a living: preaching.) The crowd, however, was dispersing. They failed to hear how his speech had started to upright the words laid flat by his tongue. Soon his voice, drifting through the loudspeakers, melded with the rock'n'roll blaring from the flashier rides and the squeals of little kids jumping in the Moonwalk.

"It's only *people* who want the differences. Gives 'em something to do," Pat O'Brien said, smoke pouring out between her words. "People gotta break things into pieces. Tiny little pieces sometimes."

Pat O'Brien placed her hand dramatically over her chest, her other hand fluttering in front of her face like a fan, the cigarette stuck between her cubby lips.

"You know: 'This here's *my* God and yours is over yonder, and *yours*, well, I can barely say...' "

Magdalene couldn't help but laugh.

"You see what I mean, sweetheart. The Catholics, they want you to fear God, fear damnation. It's a vindictive brand of faith."

Magdalene nodded her head. Kirby stretched out and laid his head upon Magdalene's sneaker.

"So the Church either tries to scare the congregation—although that's mostly in your Catholic schools—or ignores the whole Lucifer thing altogether. You know: Baby Jesus, the Easter Bunny."

Great: a seminar, Magdalene thought. She had to focus on the COUNTDOWN, goddammit. Coming to the carnival was supposed to have been an exercise in recharging, a time killing expedition. Now time was standing still.

"The Methodists, on the other hand, they're needy for some sort of contact with God. They don't want much to do with the saints and all that. It's the Methodists who are severe—not God. It's like the whole thing with the crosses. The Catholics have Jesus on the cross, the Crucifix, died for our sins, redeemed us through His suffering. The Methodists? No Jesus up there. For the Methodists, it's *all* about the Resurrection and life after death. God ain't as scary for them; life is scary enough."

Danny Kildare was asleep between Murphee and Emma Lou. Kirby watched Magdalene, his chin on her sneaker, his eyes cast skyward, ever ready to lick her should she grow upset again.

"They don't sound all that different to me," Magdalene said, not wanting to be rude. "I mean, they both believe in Jesus and the Resurrection."

"More or less. You got it."

"So—that's it? They just choose different ways to keep everyone in line?"

"Yep. The horror show Crucifix versus the plain ol' cross everyone's got to bear every day."

"That's—"

"Silly?" Pat O'Brien teased. "Hear, hear!"

"Why are you telling me all this?" Magdalene asked.

" 'Cause nothing's what it seems," Pat O'Brien said. " 'Cause we're all unique but not all that different."

Magdalene turned and looked at the wave of bodies behind her. They were mostly white, but some were black. A few were dressed to the nines, but most were in cut-off jeans and tank tops and t-shirts. It was getting harder to tell the differences between the congregations.

"And the Baptists?" Magdalene asked.

"We're no different," Pat O'Brien laughed. "Well, I guess we sing more than *both* of y'all. Mostly black folk in my church, and they got them a mean choir. Only reason I go sometimes: to hear 'em sing. I sing with 'em too—not official, but when I go, I sit in the back and I sing. I like singing. My dogs like my singing too."

"Are these all your dogs?" Magdalene asked.

"Just the one on your shoe, darling," Pat said. "Just the one cracking nuts."

Kirby did indeed seem to have severe gas.

"I don't like the singing Mass," Magdalene said.

"Sweetheart, singing's the soul's way of freeing itself," Pat explained. "We get so bogged down in *stuff* that doesn't mean *anything*, like your Catholic-Methodist feud here. When *we* sing, we're freeing our souls. We bring everything together, all the little pieces that we broke the week before, all the hate and the joy, all our anger and our frustrations—and, oh yeah, the love, darling, the love. Then we open our mouths and sing."

Pat O'Brien lit another long cigarette.

"That's why I like dogs better then people. Sure, dogs bark when they're excited or scared or curious or mad or hungry, but they get it out. Dogs are *always* singing. That's why dogs can be adopted. They have it easier than people. See, dogs learn to love again. They don't care about what you mighta done before or who you mighta been. You're good to them, they're good to you, and they will *learn* to love again. You know why?"

Magdalene shook her head. She wanted Raven here *now*. She longed to see his big sloppy grin and his huge tongue lolling out past his strong teeth. She imagined him running amuck with Murphee and Emma Lou and Kirby—or just napping with them.

"I'll tell you why," Pat O'Brien said. " 'Cause dogs learn to forgive themselves. See, darling, dogs think *everything's* their fault. They were given up for adoption because of something they did. That's what dogs think, hand to God. Dogs learn to forgive themselves, and 'cause of that, they learn to love again."

Pat O'Brien stuck the cigarette between her lips and raised her chubby hands to testify.

"Simple, darling."

"I want both of these guys," Danny Kildare said, now awake, his droopy eyes taking in his canine surroundings.

"Take some of the literature there home to your folks, Danny," Pat O'Brien said. "Those two, Emma Lou and Murphee, they were Goners. Hand to God, they were. Usually we rescue surrendered dogs from people who suddenly have kids or a new job or they meet the love of their life, and the dog—the *old* love of their life— seems…"

"Superfluous," Magdalene suggested.

"Well, I don't know about all that, but these ain't bad folks. Just folks whose lives changed. Why the dog can't change with them, I don't know, but I'm not judging. I just work at the Rescue and go to events like this and facilitate adoptions.

"But these two clowns," Pat O'Brien continued, hooking a thumb towards Emma Lou and Murphee, "they came from bad situations, both of 'em. We think we got it rough: lousy boyfriends, bad job, or you: exams and nuns and bullies and everything that goes with school. Think about how bad these guys had it. Hell, Labrador retrievers, if they ain't trained for specifics, like fire rescue or hunting or comfort work, all they *do* is love. That's it."

Pat O'Brien blew an impressive smoke ring. Magdalene stuck her finger in the middle of it and watched it dissipate.

"That's what we do. We just rescue 'em so they can love again. And they always do. They end up rescuing you! And both you kids look like you could use some rescuing. Right, guys?"

Kirby yawned, sat up, and scratched at an ear.

"One time," Danny Kildare said, "one of my mom's boyfriends said he was gonna buy me a dog."

Magdalene winced.

"And?" Pat O'Brien asked.

"He didn't." Danny shrugged. "Then I wanted to get a turtle—you know Magdalene, like Katie has—but my dad said he didn't want anything smelly in the house."

Danny lowered his head back on Emma Lou.

"Like he's ever home to smell 'em!"

Murphee got up and licked Danny's face.

"See?" Pat O'Brien asked.

"Hey, Magdalene," Danny Kildare said, "tell her about Raven!"

Magdalene shot him a dirty look.

"You got one of these, do ya?" Pat O'Brien asked.

Danny shot one back.

"Didn't know it was a secret," Danny said. "Jeez. It's not like it's the end of the world."

Magdalene could see why her mother had been addicted to lies. They were easy.

"He died," Magdalene said. "He was a black Lab from...from another rescue, I think."

"Raven's dead? Oh, Lordy," Pat O'Brien said. "No, no, darling, Raven came from us, from Brookline. Your dad came and adopted him. Think I don't know who your dad is? Raven's dead. Boy, oh boy. What a good pooch. A tad morose, if you know what I mean, but he liked a good belly rub and a cookie."

Danny pouted.

"I never even got to see him. Katie told me he was cool. Liked to play football. She said…"

"How did he…"

"…he had this monkey and this panda, but the panda didn't sing anymore, and Katie said…"

"…go, darling?"

Magdalene cleared her throat.

"Rat poison," Magdalene said.

Not quite the whopper she intended after all.

"Lordy, Lord," Pat O'Brien said, shaking her head. "Poor guy."

Danny raised his hand as if waiting for a teacher to call on him.

"Oooh, in school...in school, Katie McAllister told me Raven was old—like fifty years old. That's old!"

"He was eight," Magdalene said. "He was fifty-six, I think."

"And Katie said that he doesn't know he's that old. He thinks he's a puppy, and he wants to play and run around and fetch stuff all day."

"*Didn't. Thought. Wanted*," Magdalene corrected. If she could count right now, she'd never stop.

" 'Panda Mating Fails; Veterinarian Takes Over,' " Danny Kildare said.

Never never stop.

"Actual headline?" Pat O'Brien asked.

"And you know what, dog lady, you know what?" Danny asked.

Pat O'Brien lit another cigarette from the end of the previous one.

"No, what?"

"Raven *loves* football. He'll chase that football all day long if he has half a chance!"

"*Loved*, dear," Pat O'Brien said.

"And Katie said that Raven *always* smells like *popcorn*! Popcorn!"

Pat O'Brien laughed.

Danny Kildare scrunched his face up so his lower lip just about met his nose.

"Katie also said you never take him to the dog parade."

Magdalene: "He...he would bark...he was scared of—"

"Hey, dog lady?" Danny Kildare began affectionately. "Can—"

"Pat."

"Hey, Pat?" he started again without skipping a beat as Tiddy would say. "Can Emma and Murph go to the dog parade?"

"Actually, Danny, we're going to have a booth there. If Murphee and Emma Lou haven't found homes yet, then I'll make sure to bring 'em. How 'bout that? Kirby too."

"If they find homes, then I won't be able to see them ever again!"

"Danny—remember what I said to your friend here about dogs learning to love again and learning to forget?"

"Nope."

"Maybe you were asleep. Well, dogs *never* forget the good times. N-e-v-e-r. Never."

"So..."

"So, maybe one night when it's thunderstorming and such and they're scared, they'll think back about when Danny used one of 'em as a pillow and one of 'em as a footstool. You'll come back to them in their dreams—and they in yours. Happens all the time."

"Cool," Danny Kildare said.

"Not all the time," Magdalene said.

Pat O'Brien exhaled.

"Yep, Danny" Pat concluded, ignoring Magdalene. "Cool."

"Wish they had the sack races today," Danny said—crisis resolved, he'd already leapt to the next subject. Magdalene closed her eyes and tried to think of *any* numerical sequence: prime numbers, multiples of three, nursery rhymes.

She opened her eyes, and she was staring at one of Aunt Tiddy's Polaroids: a blurry, slightly off-centered Assumption carnival; a round feminine blur with fire in her mouth reaching towards a shiny, shimmering, silver box and—

"...*the accident took place a half mile from where Dirt Road dead ends into Bethlehem Pike...police removed the woman's Cadillac from the scene early this morning, but they kept the Pike closed off while they waited for the Mondauk Volunteer Fire Department to hose the road down...gasoline from the...*"

"Poor woman," Pat O'Brien said. "Didn't give a name. Wonder if she's from these parts."

"Did she slip in the gasoline?" Danny Kildare asked. Kirby ambled over to lick his ear.

"No, the police were responding to a call and smashed into her car. She's—"

"She's what?" Danny asked.

"Shhh," Pat O'Brien said, "they're going back to the Fuller girl."

Magdalene was underwater. The pollution was thick here: soda cans and beer cans and condoms and THERE WAS MICHAEL. Thank God she'd dove in! Thank God she didn't think of all the times he'd abused her love, made her the butt of his jokes, the victim of his dares, the tackle dummy! Thank God she'd—

"...*the police had searched the area twice before, and an undisclosed source said they were close to asking the state to drag...*"

Pat O'Brien shook her head.

"I mean, who could have guessed *that*? Oh God, poor Father Dave," Pat said.

"...*police say the young girl, Christina Fuller, age twelve, could...*"

"I'd say it was an ambush."

Magdalene emerged: "The snipes?"

But Pat O'Brien was looking over her head, smiling. Danny Kildare jumped up and smoothed out his shirt.

"Magdalene, dear. We just heard." Sister Mary Joseph said.

"Sister," Danny said, taking a deep bow.

"Mr. Kildare," the principal said. Murphee rubbed her body against the nun's habit, leaving a trail of yellow-white hairs across the skirt.

Behind the nun were two Faith Board veterans. Broad and malodorous, Mrs. Stanley held both of her palms together as if she was going to start praying right then and there; her hands were inky from stamping kids on their way into the carnival, or perhaps from lingering over late library returns and running her fingers over the date stamp. Mrs. Banniman, the ADA's towering secretary, stood there too, looking like she wanted to straighten up the Brookline Lab Rescue booth.

"Lassie—" Mrs. Banniman began.

"No, his name is Kirby and this is—" Danny tried to explain.

"Your father is with your aunt now, lassie, and he'll see her through, do what's proper," Mrs. Banniman said.

"As he should!" Mrs. Stanley scoffed. "That man owes Tiberius Wheelwright everything."

"Now, now, dearie," Mrs. Banniman said to Mrs. Stanley. "I've worked for Mr. Barrows going on these many years, and I think I know a thing or two about—"

"And how many of those years was he sipping the devil's whiskey in that whore's tap room?" Mrs. Stanley asked.

Magdalene wondered if her father had overdue library books.

"Now, dearie, our Mr. Barrows has been through quite enough without your sour puss. You don't even *like* Tiberius Wheelwright. And as for what she thinks of you, well…"

"I am a pillar of the community!"

"You are a sour pussy," Mrs. Banniman concluded.

"Ladies!" Sister Mary Joseph said.

"If there's anything we can do for you during this difficult…" the principal said to Magdalene, but Magdalene's attention was elsewhere. She'd seen the bully. He was on the move.

He wasn't subtle. He didn't move in and out of the shadows. Bullies don't do that. He was heading her way, his head down, his fists in a bunch: Stevie Rich!

"…time, please don't hesitate to come by the convent or…"

Magdalene shifted her weight so maybe the unholy trio would block her body from view.

"Magdalene!" Danny Kildare yelled, and Magdalene tried to look for him out of the corner of her eye.

Emma Lou was standing on her hind legs, dancing with Danny. Kirby edged next to Magdalene. She reached down and rubbed his ears—betrayal, right? Raven was probably throwing up, lying in a corner, thinking her name over and over, Monkey and the damn silent panda hopelessly out of reach. Magdalene felt the fur on Kirby's neck stand up.

"Magdalene, Magdalene!" Danny cried.

"...reschedule your makeup exams, of course. Maybe we could..."

Kirby growled, but not at the oblivious principal, the totalitarian librarian, or the ADA's bossy secretary.

Stevie Rich had heard Danny. The bully gestured with his hands over his head and started a beeline towards the Brookline Lab Rescue booth.

"...her own person..."

"...stubborn, if you ask me..."

"...no one, did, dearie...fussbudget..."

"...ladies!..."

To the right of the surging crowd—and it *was* surging, like the Puddle in a thunderstorm—one head floated above the rest, his face so red, his freckles stood out like stars.

Don't go losin' Lou Head's now.

Jerry Eves!

"Come to think of it," Sister Mary Joseph began again, her tone shifting slightly, "I'm surprised you're here instead of with your father at the hospital."

Jerry, look to your right, Magdalene willed, look to your right!

Stevie Rich pushed through two kids sharing a huge wad of baby blue cotton candy, just plowed right through them.

"I—"

"Why don't you come with me? We'll call your father and take you—"

Kirby bared his teeth. Pat O'Brien attached his leash and pulled him back.

"I'm sorry, Sister," Pat said.

"It's not 'cause of them," Magdalene said absently.

She stood on her tiptoes, and Jerry saw her. He pointed towards Stevie and then made a beckoning gesture.

Stevie Rich stepped on a balloon.

"Heavens!" Mrs. Banniman yelped.

"Heaven's got little to do with this," Mrs. Stanley said, wiping sweat from her brow. A blue streak of ink ran from one side of her forehead to the other.

Stevie Rich upturned a trash can.

Jerry bounced up and down—he was running defense, trying to head off an aggressive offense.

Stevie Rich grabbed a kid's pretzel, took a huge bite out of it, and tossed it behind him.

"Dearie, here, look, you've got ink all over," Mrs. Banniman said, lifting a handkerchief to Mrs. Stanley's head.

"And you've got the world by the...what?" Mrs. Stanley lifted a hand to her forehead. "See! It's these kids, they..."

Stevie Rich ripped his own t-shirt in half revealing his barrel chest and encroaching stomach.

Sister Mary Joseph stared at Magdalene. Her eyes were kind and her mouth held the barest hint of a smile. She reached out and stroked Magdalene's arm twice.

"Maybe we've been—maybe *I've* been too hard on you," the principal said. "After everything that's happened—well, it's God's plan, not ours, and—"

"Oh, it's in my eyes!" Mrs. Stanley the librarian cried. "It stings!"

Magdalene kept her own eyes on the bully heading her way.

"No, it's not, dearie," said Mrs. Banniman. "It's just the sweat from your forehead."

Mrs. Stanley snatched the back of Sister Mary Joseph's wimple. "No good can come of all this," the librarian said, rubbing her large face vigorously with the wimple. "Methodists and Catholics and—"

"Baptists," Pat O'Brien chimed in. "Oh my." She had filled a little bag of dog adoption information for Danny and was taking down the Polaroids of Murphee and Emma Lou and Kirby for him.

Stevie Rich grabbed a gold fish bowl, swallowed the fish, and drank the dirty water.

Mrs. Stanley stopped wiping and looked up, ready for battle. Sister Mary Joseph was leaning almost backward, glaring at the librarian and the administrative assistant. (Mrs. Stanley, frosted hair freshly-coiffed, easily hit the six-foot mark without shoes; Mrs. Banniman might have been taller, if not as broad.)

"Sister, oh my, apologies, apologies," Mrs. Stanley said, backing down. "It's just...the Methodists...they get my dander up."

NOW!

Magdalene turned and ran past Danny Kildare and Pat O'Brien and Kirby and Murphee and Emma Lou, knocking over Pat's folding chair, sending several Polaroids, their tape weak from the heat, fluttering like snowflakes, shooting stars, dandelion wishes.

"I'm sorry about your brother!" Pat O'Brien shouted to her back.

Magdalene shut her ears, but it didn't help. Even several blocks away, she couldn't shake the sound of barking dogs.

+

Focus was everything.

What will you do when your time comes? Run like the dickens or fight like hell?

By now, her father might be home. He might have poked his head into her room, but he wouldn't have looked for a note, not just yet. He might even have noticed a dying dog in the kitchen. If she made it home (which seemed less and less likely), she could die in bed. If she didn't, he'd find the note eventually, and as it wasn't actually a suicide note at all, but one filled with instructions and clues, the Cabot Case being well beyond her scope now, it would give him something to go on. That was all she had to leave her father, this blanket of clues—especially after what had happened to Aunt Tiddy.

Hold on to this, the note said, *hold on to this, rescue this scared little boy and his crazy mother, focus on this and keep your nose out of the tumblers.*

It was no different for her. She too was jumping out of a burning building with a bed sheet. Only her jumping wasn't out of pure necessity, nothing like the poor souls trapped in the twin towers, the flames of Hades behind them, God's clear, open sky below them. Nothing they had done had made them deserve their fate. Magdalene knew she wasn't as innocent. Not by a long shank, to quote Bill the Bard.

Old Man Rex hadn't blinked when she'd bought the Swiss Army Knife. Maybe he figured since she was the Assistant District Attorney's daughter, being bad was just a natural occurrence—like a cop's kid. Maybe Old Man Rex figured she had just as much chance at being a lawyer as being a criminal, and far be it from him to circumvent the process of either nature or nurture.

Or maybe he just didn't care anymore.

She ran as fast as she could without attracting attention.

Magdalene thought that was the real problem with not just Mondauk County, but the whole world: nobody cared for very long. (The exception being groups like the Faith Board; their brand of caring knew no salve.) After 9/11, neighbors hung flags and sang old songs of freedom and war and secretly applauded when those neighbors with darker skins or mysterious religions were detained, questioned, released, harassed. The separation of church and state, that old First Amendment chestnut, was slowly being erased. Gay marriage was *so* gay. It was a religious war, with the Ruling Party's religion and God (which, admittedly, was her God too, but she hated to admit any affinity with the Ruling Party) proclaimed as righteous and holy. Magdalene had watched the nuns and lay teachers stutter to explain the suspension of civil liberties for naturalized citizens with a Moslem background and the ban of embryonic stem cell research.

The world went back to not caring, like the Ruling Party knew it would, and although the flags, now soiled and forgotten, still hung from front porches and car antennas, making it seem like a united front, it wasn't. The world double-locked its doors, slammed the windows shut, banned any foolish or seditious talk against the Ruling Party, and regarded each other out of the corners of their eyes.

Not that situations like Katie McAllister's or Joseph Bochdan's (or even Stevie Rich's) hadn't existed before September 11, but now they were openly ignored. What else would explain the complete abandonment of the search for Michael? What everyone else had failed to realize was this: *their time had come!* And they had failed.

She would kill Mr. McAllister if necessary. Having Frannie Tidwell's gun would have been better than some ol' Swiss Army Knife that Old Man Rex had to blow dust from before he could read the price, but beggars, to quote her poor Aunt Tiddy, could never be choosers. Hopefully, Mr. McAllister was planning to take up the widow Tidwell on her dinner offer. Or take her to the movies after all. And if he didn't, if he was home…

No shoulda coulda woulda.

She would kill him if necessary.

+

Magdalene shifted her weight to her other leg. She was crouched behind the red berry bushes across the street from the McAllister house. The night was minutes away from swallowing the day, and Mr.

McAllister had yet to step foot out of his house. How late was Mrs. Tidwell planning on serving dinner? Magdalene had been hiding in the bushes for what seemed like hours.

From the next street over, Magdalene heard the sounds of a late game of touch football: scuffling feet, boys exhaling with force, a muted shout, and somewhere behind them, the *phewww* and *pop* of a Wiffle ball bat sweeping the air and making contact. Magdalene was sure the younger kids giggling down the street were playing Freeze Tag or Freedom.

She rubbed her legs. They were sore. She'd run just about the length of Mondauk Proper and back. If Stevie Rich had been following her, then she'd lost him for sure. Had the police pinned what had happened to Aunt Tiddy on Stevie Rich? He looked pretty darn angry, charging towards her at the carnival. Okay—so maybe he hadn't been *charging*, but it had sure seemed like it.

Maybe Jerry had reached Stevie in time. She pushed the invisible gun from her head. Stevie Rich wouldn't be that stupid. Just thinking of Jerry Eves made her rib cage ache, but it was better than thinking of Aunt Tiddy. Or Raven.

"Touchdown!" a boy cried, and Magdalene hung her head. It would always be a boy's game. There would be no room for Magdalene Harper Barrows. Even Assistant District Attorney Gregory Barrows concurred, your honor. When she thought of slices in time that rose above the rest, they almost all involved football—practicing with Michael in the backyard, watching Raven tackle the slobbered ball. Even making out with Jerry Eves had had a football flavor to it. And that's the closest she would be allowed to come: brought up to love a boy's game of which she could never officially be a part.

Magdalene opened the Swiss Army Knife and pressed the blade against her palm. She could charge into the house, stab Mr. McAllister before he realized what had happened (surprise was her only ally against a man his size), and snatch Katie from her room.

Or perhaps it would be easier to simply finish everything right here in the berry bushes. Not as regal as hanging from a dogwood tree like the Quayle boy over in Anchor Hop, the baseball player who'd swung in his own backyard—now there was a statement (if one could get past the summarizing). Hiding inside the berry bushes and finishing herself off with a dusty Swiss Army Knife didn't have the same *panache*.

Magdalene shook her head: only a condemned person would actually consider the artistic integrity of suicide. Only…

Baby-sitting usurper Valerie Plum flounced down the street, singing an off-key version of "If Ever I Would Leave You" from the musical *Camelot*. Magdalene crouched as far back into the berry bushes as she could—but it wasn't necessary. The music seeping from Valerie's headphones was loud enough for Magdalene to hear the *real* words. (Valerie, of course, was singing the *wrong* words.)

" *'If ever I would leave you, it wouldn't be in summer,' for in summer I think of you, Paul!'* Valerie Plum sang.

Obviously, wayward boyfriend Paul Stern was back.

Valerie didn't take her headphones off, nor did she knock—she just let herself right into the McAllister house, slamming the door behind her.

Okay, Magdalene thought, now here's where counting would come in real handy. Magdalene fingered the pills in her pockets. She closed the Swiss Army Knife and shoved it into her back pocket.

Goodbye, Raven.

A light flickered from the top floor of the McAllister house.

Goodbye, Jerry.

The light went out.

Goodbye, Daddy.

"…call if you need anything…"

Corduroy suit jacket, too small. Dress shirt, no tie. Cologne so strong, Magdalene could smell it from inside the berry bushes. Dress a pig up, he's still a pig, she thought.

Click, lock.

Mr. McAllister pulled on the door handle, then, satisfied, *leapt* down the steps and headed up Orchard Street.

Jingle, jangle, went the keys in his pocket.

Magdalene held her breath—she had no idea how long—and with her head ducked down like a cop's in the movies, she sprinted towards a car parked on the street. She peered over the trunk and through the back window. She could make out Mr. McAllister heading towards the bus stop—whistling. The son of a bitch was actually *whistling*.

Magdalene waited until she could no longer see his shadow, then she crept her way around the parked car, keeping cover until she reached Mr. McAllister's Chevy in his driveway. She waited a second or two—should she just sneak in and try to get Katie out without

Valerie knowing? She checked behind her—nobody—and she ran for the front windows and raised her head (slowly) so she could peer in: Valerie Plum had her feet up on the coffee table and was talking on the phone (of course), eating peanut butter out of the jar with a spoon. The television was blaring: a news crew was down the by the Puddle, and lots of people spoke in hesitant but excited voices into the camera. There was Chief Hagen, the veins on his nose fluorescent on television, and—

"There you are," Mr. McAllister said, and Magdalene dropped to her stomach. She hoped the weak light from the television set wouldn't reveal her kissing the grass.

Where was he?

"I got you now," Mr. McAllister said.

Magdalene curled up like Ruth, the last of the Pennypack Indians, guarding the amulet of his ancestors, Muddy Ball at his side, but she hadn't thought of bringing Raven. She'd been too busy planning to kill him.

"I'm gonna make sure you don't get away again," Mr. McAllister said, and Magdalene pulled out her Swiss Army Knife. With her eyes squeezed shut, she flicked it open and stretched out her arm. She crawled backwards and tried to squeeze her body into the lip of the front basement window.

"Damn."

Mr. McAllister walked up the drive, jostled his keys until he found the right one, and opened the door. His cologne was stultifying.

Magdalene climbed up from the basement window lip, keeping a firm grip on the Swiss Army Knife. Back to the berry bushes? Run in and stab him now? Magdalene ducked down as a car turned on Orchard Street, its headlights momentarily splashing across her hiding place.

Inside the house, Katie screamed.

Whhhh*at* wwww*illll you do*ooo whhhh*en your*rrr *time come*ssss?

Magdalene placed both hands on the handle on the Swiss Army Knife and made for the front door.

Katie screamed again—this time longer. It was a squeal. It was a squeak. The monster had thrown a pot of boiling water on her. The monster had stuck her hand into the garbage disposal.

Mr. McAllister stood in the doorway, his back to Magdalene.

"Gotta get a lid for that thing."

The porch light flickered. He handed something off to someone inside. "Cover it up with something for now and keep it on, okay?"

Magdalene stood in Mr. McAllister's driveway, both hands thrust forward, sweat outlining her skin, a can opener projecting from her Swiss Army Knife.

"You hearin' me?" he barked as the door closed again.

Magdalene dove behind the passenger side of McAllister's Chevy. *It wasn't her time after all.*

Mr. McAllister stopped at the end of the driveway and muttered to himself as he walked to the car and popped the trunk.

"I know just the thing…"

Magdalene lay flat on her back; both hands were still out in front of her as she tried to find the blade.

Screwdriver, corkscrew, scissors.

"Just enough," Mr. McAllister said under his breath as he slammed the trunk shut. "Tonight…"

Mr. McAllister's heavy footsteps (and heavier cologne) receded. When Magdalene had composed herself (and inventoried the entire contents of her Swiss Army Knife), she lifted her head. Mr. McAllister was gone, swept away in a wave of shadows. She crawled with caution and crouched down by the back of the car. What the hell was in Mr. McAllister's trunk? Magdalene pushed her palm against the lock. It popped open without effort.

Oscar Sceebers, the fat tabby, sauntered up the driveway. Magdalene shut her eyes, hoping Oscar wouldn't see her, but the cat purred and rubbed against her legs.

A car skidded to a halt at the next house up from Katie's. Oscar sprinted under the Chevy.

"This it?" a voice asked: deep, almost an adult's tone, but not quite.

"Um, no, next one I think." The second voice (obviously a boy's) was tremulous, excited, concerned.

The Chevy's trunk was filled with junk: tools, trash bags, hubcaps, and what looked like one side of an unbuilt cage. Something long and cylindrical was wrapped in trash bags and stashed at the far back of the trunk.

"Are you sure this is even the right street?" the older boy asked.

"Yeah, yeah. Hey, is that him by the bus stop?" the younger boy asked.

"Get out of the goddamn car," the older boy ordered.

The rattle of a fence being hopped, then sneakers running on grass, then pavement. The car gunned it, then skidded in front of Katie's house.

Magdalene jumped into the trunk and pulled the lid closed. She kept a tight grip on the metal latch.

"Anything?" the older boy asked. Was that Chloe's boyfriend, the one who'd been lounging on the back of the Gremlin?

"No, fuckin' nothin'," a third voice said, nasally, whiny. "Where's—?"

"I sent lover boy on foot to make sure we're on the right street," said the older boy.

"Yeah, once we cased a house in the Heights all fuckin' day," the nasally voice said. "Gonna boost this guy's car, but we figured we might as well see what he's got in his place, right? But we got fucked up, and when we came back at night, we broke into the wrong house. John-John just about shit. Was like his uncle's house."

Stevie Rich!

"Why'd he shit?"

Stevie Rich coughed.

"He, uh, he'd strangled his uncle's cat as soon as he'd crawled in through the window. Didn't recognize the cat."

"Sick fuck."

"You should see his dad."

"Worse?"

"Pees in jars and saves 'em in his shed."

"Nice."

"Right?"

Magdalene tried to remember what Franklin W. Dixon wrote about observation and memory. Her back was against whatever was wrapped in the trash bags in the back of the trunk. She didn't recall *The Hardy Boys Detective Handbook* mentioning what to do if one found a dead body while hiding in the trunk of a car.

"Hey, listen, you and John-John *ever* try to boost the Goat, I'll bust you down a notch."

"No, man, no. Listen, I owe…"

It smelled like a dead body—or what she thought a dead body should smell like: earth and old leaves and…

…her hands shook, and the metal latch on the inside of the trunk slipped from her sweaty palm.

"Hey, what's that—there?"

"Where?"

"I thought I saw something blink."

Magdalene reached up and slid her free hand along the roof of the trunk. There wasn't enough maneuvering room to reach into her back pocket for the Swiss Army Knife. When her fingers found the light bulb, she crushed it in her palm.

"Over here."

The voices grew closer. Behind them, Magdalene could hear distant shouts of joy. The Feast of the Baptist must be reaching its conclusion.

More footsteps.

"Well, little brother?"

"Yeah, this is the street. I swear to God." The younger voice was back, out of breath. She knew the voice (it sounded muffled from inside the trunk); the voice was warm, like an old blanket or a favorite book.

"Well, she ain't here."

The blood in her palm was warm too.

Michael's blanket. Too dark to see her hand in front of her face.

It was dead, whatever was wrapped in the trash bags.

That was where she'd learned to count. Under Michael's blanket. Count 'til it was over.

"Jesus Christ, the car! I should have recognized McAllister's Chevy."

Something pounded the left rear panel. It sounded to Magdalene like the end of the world.

"You were too busy gettin' busy to notice the car, right?"

"Watch it, big brother," the younger voice said.

That's where she'd learned to count her breaths.

It was Christina Fuller, of course. Preserved, mummified, shoved into the back of the trunk.

She used to be able to hold her breath forever. She could count to a million and not think about her brother, not pay any attention to the blows he methodically administered to the blanket: avalanche, volcano, cave collapse.

It was clear now: Frannie Five Fingers was trying to frame Mr. McAllister. It made sense. Frannie Tidwell thought Mr. McAllister was honing in on the widow Tidwell and making nice with Stevie Rich for the 9/11 insurance money. So Frannie Tidwell killed Christina and placed her in McAllister's trunk. That's why Stevie Rich was looking for her! He wasn't trying to help his father. Stevie Rich's fingerprints were all over the murder weapon, the gun Magdalene had taken from Frannie and given to Stevie, the gun Stevie had used to help her and Jerry escape the Lakes. Stevie Rich needed Magdalene to talk to the police about how he'd come into possession of the gun (like she needed him to talk to the police about the shooting of Henry Richard Cabot). Stevie Rich had found out it was *that* gun his father had used killing Christina (and who knows whom else). It was all making sense. Still, if the police *had* questioned Stevie Rich and if the lump behind her back *was* Christina, then the detectives hadn't made the connection between the gun and Christina Fuller yet. But if Stevie Rich knew of his father's plan, then he also knew the body would surface shortly. Maybe the police had hauled Stevie Rich in after she and Jerry had escaped, and now the police were in possession of the gun.

Unless…unless Mr. McAllister had killed Christina as a warm-up for killing Katie.

She'd been able to hold her breath and count her heartbeats. It was hard to stop—the counting—once she'd started: it was like her mother's lying or her father's drinking. But it had come in handy. Like when she'd pretended to drown in the Puddle. She'd cheated the dare. She'd broken the Rules. Michael had had to rescue her. Michael had had to prove his love back. It had been a handy little skill.

"Do you want to knock then?"

"No, if he's not home, then Valerie Plum's baby-sitting. She won't be any help."

"I could help her," Stevie Rich offered.

"Shut up."

"Knock it off, both of you," the older boy said. "She'd just call McAllister. We don't need that."

"Back to the carnivals?"

Counting was very handy indeed. Like when Michael had pretended to drown in…no, wait…

"Negative, dipshit," the older boy said. "Come on, where else?"

"The Puddle?" the younger boy asked. "Finch's Landing?"

"That's where what's-her-name was hiding."

"Stevie, you know the Puddle pretty well," the older boy said.

"Like the back of my hand."

"Alright, get in the Goat. We'll find her."

"Why don't we just case *her* house?" Stevie Rich asked.

The older boy spit.

"I don't think she's planning on coming home," the older boy said.

"Maybe someone should stay in case she does show up here," the younger voice suggested.

"Yeah, alright, I guess. Me and Stevie'll go to the Puddle. Don't fucking leave here, Jerry, okay?"

"I'll wait right here. If I see someone coming, I'll slip into the backyard."

"And if she shows her face?"

"I'll talk to her. I'll take care of it, Mick. She'll talk to me before she talks to either of you—especially Stevie. I'll just sit tight. If she comes up the street, I'll see her before she sees me."

"Alright, just sit here. No hero shit. Got it?"

"Clear as mud, Mick," Jerry said.

Pretend it's a game, Magdalene. Pretend it's just another blanket game.

THUNK.

The lid of the trunk CLICKED shut. Someone was sitting on it! The broken edges of the bulb cut into her face. She opened her mouth to scream, but it was filled with Puddle scum. The only word that came out was...

Chapter Fourteen

The Fire

…"MICHAEL!"

"What the fuck?" Stevie Rich yelled.

"You hear that?" Mick Eves asked.

The screen door squeaked open.

"Go, run, now!" Mick commanded. "Both of you, c'mon!"

Weight shifted on the trunk. Whomever had been sitting on it had dismounted.

Sneakers pounded the pavement.

"Hey, who's out here?" Valerie Plum asked. "That you, Paul?"

Car doors slammed.

"Hey, you can't—" Valerie Plum yelled.

Tires squealed.

"Paul?"

This was real: this pain. Blood trickled down Magdalene's cheek. She was truly out of numbers. This was what real life felt like.

It felt like hell.

Don't go losin' Lou's Head.

"It's not funny, Paul," Valerie Plum said, a tad nervously. "It's not even Halloween. Paul? You out here?"

Magdalene's hand found the trunk latch again. What if it didn't open from the inside? The thought of being rescued by Valerie Plum…

"Paul!"

"Hey, babe," Paul Stern said.

Jesus Christ.

"Were you trying to scare me?

"What? No, babe. I just came through the yards. Hopped fences and shrubs and stuff."

"There were some kids hanging around Mr. McAllister's car."

"Yeah, this piece of shit?"

Paul Stern POUNDED on the trunk.

"Old drunk don't even drive it anymore. Wonder if he'd sell it."

"Mr. McAllister's doesn't drink anymore," Valerie Plum said, a bit put out. "You comin' in?"

"Kid here?"

"Yeah, but she's upstairs. Fucking turtle escaped again."

"Turtle?"

"Yeah. C'mon, you comin' in?"

"What's in it for me?"

"Oh, Paul."

The air in the trunk seemed to have evaporated. If she didn't try the latch soon, she'd suffocate, her back against Christina Fuller's dead body. That was no way to go. But if Valerie saw her climbing out of the trunk...

"You know what I want, babe."

"What's that?"

"You."

"I'm only using my hand, Paul. Take it or leave it."

"I'll take it. I'm coming in."

The screen door slammed.

Voices faded: "You hear about that tramp Christina?"

Magdalene squeezed the latch.

Click, click...

Nothing.

She squeezed it again.

Click, click...

Shit.

Magdalene could smell it: Michael's blanket was nothing compared to this. Michael's blanket had smelled of Michael: of Michael going to bed sweaty after practice, skipping his shower, the smell of cells shedding themselves in the night. The trunk, bereft of air, smelled not of cells regenerating but of skin shriveling from the bone, blood sinking to the lowest levels of the body, eyes sinking inside their sockets.

No way.

Magdalene didn't realize she'd been screaming until the first puff of fresh air entered her lungs. She didn't realize both hands were ripped and bloody and that the bone of her left index finger was now peeking through the skin. Magdalene didn't realize any of these things until she'd punched the inside of the Chevy's trunk innumerable times, and it had popped open with a rusty squeak, and she'd run across the front lawn and dove into the basement window alcove.

"No, Paul—what was *that*?"

"Nothing, nothing. C'mon, Val. Just for a second, huh?"

Magdalene regarded her hands. The glass had gone deep into her right palm. Magdalene gingerly removed an inch long sliver. The index finger on her left hand hung at an odd angle from the rest of its brethren.

"Paul! No!"

Beneath Valerie's exhortations and Paul's heavy breathing—Magdalene could hear him huffing and puffing; it sounded like he was hyperventilating—the television rattled, and gunshots were fired, and vibrating, staccato strings insinuated a mandatory period of tension. Then: blaring synthetic horns, a series of call letters, a measured, serious tone:

"This news brief brought to you by Merriam-Webster..."

Magdalene climbed out of the alcove and peered in the front windows. Paul Stern's hand, up to his wrist, was down the front of Valerie's shorts. Valerie squirmed and shimmied this way and that on the sofa.

Merriam-Webster?

Paul was kneeling on the floor, his pants down around his ankles, and with his free hand, he appeared to be conducting a symphony orchestra with his penis.

"...the child, Christina Fuller, age twelve, reported missing by her parents, Doctor Samuel Fuller and his wife, Bernadette, head of Assumption of Our Lady's Faith Board ..."

Magdalene crept down the driveway and quietly closed the trunk.

"I'm sorry, Christina," Magdalene whispered. "I'll let them know you're in here."

She made her way to the backyard, on the lookout for Stevie Rich and the snipes (whose numbers included a possibly drugged or otherwise coerced Mick and Jerry Eves). Katie's bedroom windows were open and a light was on. Katie had lit the prayer candles along the window ledge facing the yard. Magdalene could hear Katie's radio, echoing the tones of the television report.

"...Father Dave Browne, the recently-named pastor..."

"Katie," Magdalene stage whispered. "Katie!"

"...released earlier today, and he had this to say to..."

She couldn't throw a penny at the window. If she hit a candle...

" '...and the entire parish will continue our prayers for the Fullers during this trying time...' "

Something rattled the trash cans alongside the house, and Magdalene retreated into the shadows of the dogwood tree.

"…we'll come back to this story as it develops, but right now…"

There was a scratching at the back door. Magdalene took a step away from the dogwood.

"Oscar Sceebers?"

The fat tabby clawed at the aluminum screen door.

"Come here, Oscar. Come here, boy."

The cat stood on his hind legs, and Magdalene saw his plump belly and his gray whiskers twinkling in the light, and inside her chest, her blown-glass heart shimmered and cracked, and she bent over, holding her stomach.

Somewhere, just east of Katie McAllister's house, a middle-aged black Labrador retriever was lying on his side in his own vomit, his shuddering stomach rising and falling, falling and rising as if trying to catch up with the slide show that zoomed between his ears of *SILK*: Monkey and Monien and Michael and football and belly rubs and cookies and sneaking into bed and Magdalene yelling at him to go away.

"Will you let the cat in already?" Valerie shouted.

From the second story window, a cheery: "Okay!"

Happy even.

Magdalene forced Raven's deathbed scene aside and crept towards the back stoop, reaching into her pocket for the dogwood petals. Oscar Sceebers rolled on his back for a belly rub, and Magdalene tickled him briefly then covered his belly with the wrinkled petals before retreating back to the shelter of the tree. Oscar Sceebers stayed on his back, carefully regarding a stray petal.

The porch light flickered, and Katie paused in the doorway. There was a halo of fuzzy light around her fair head. Oscar Sceebers shook off the dogwood petals and ran inside the house.

"Magdalene?" Katie whispered, her head peeking around the door. "Magdalene?"

"Will you go to bed already?" Valerie Plum screamed.

"I go to bed when *I* want to."

The screen door slammed shut over a rush of muffled voices.

When it flew open again, a little hand scooped up the dogwood petals.

"…what time does *Paul Stern* have to go to bed?"

Slam!

Magdalene stood beneath the dogwood tree. She couldn't see the stars; the pollution was too thick tonight. Faint tinkles of the dueling carnivals tickled her ears. The dogwood was in full bloom, about to begin a brief reign of the McAllister backyard before the inevitable indignities of fall. Everything gets to be beautiful once, Magdalene thought, sometimes even twice. If her time had truly come, then the jumping-off point was here, beneath the blooming dogwood tree in Katie McAllister's backyard. It wasn't all that different from Puddle Jumping; she could even hear the Dead Injun Tree whispering her name, releasing it like a broken dandelion wish in the early summer night breeze.

A penny hit Magdalene on the side of her head.

"*Psst!* Magdalene," Katie called from her window, carefully holding her hair away from the array of candles.

Katie pointed to the cellar storm doors and disappeared.

Magdalene rubbed her head, smearing blood across her forehead.

The cellar storm doors were built into the ground, *Wizard of Oz* style. But no matter how hard she pulled at the handles, the doors refused to give. The ground beneath her feet slipped away. The grass was cool against her face when she fell.

A few minutes, just a few minutes more. It was nice being buried beneath Michael's stinky blanket. It was nice and safe...

When she opened her eyes, the cellar doors were open. Magdalene crawled to her feet, holding on to the rusty doors for balance. A spider climbed up her arm. The stone steps were damp and cobwebs filled every corner. At the bottom of the steps, she reached out, and her hand caught a splinter on a short, wooden door. She swallowed a scream and pushed at the door with both hands. It swung open with a squeak borrowed from hundreds of horror movies. Something scurried over her foot. Magdalene reached back and eased the cellar storm doors closed.

Faint light from the moon finger-painted the cellar windows. The moth-eaten window treatments were intricate webs, festooned with the remains of former inhabitants, meals unfinished, and mouse excrement. Magdalene could make out a collection of tools hung on hooks above crudely made shelves. To her left were wooden steps leading to the first floor. In a cove beneath the steps, tall, shiny stacks (of what?) were stored against the wall. Ahead on the right, Magdalene could see the outline of an uneven doorway—it was more like an entrance to a cave. Her foot caught a dip in the stone floor—a drain. She could hear the faint gurgling of water. An old Nina Simone song floated through her head:

*"Old man sorrow's
Come to keep me company,
Whisperin' beside me
When I say my prayers,
When I say my prayers."*

"Your father doesn't want you in the basement."

"I don't think he wants Paul Stern lying on top of you on the sofa either."

"Paul's not here… he's—"

Magdalene crouched down in the cove beneath the stairs.

The television in the living room snapped off.

"I know he's here, Val. Now just you shut up or I'll tell."

Bass shuddered through the floorboards. Magdalene squeezed against the shiny stacks and tried to make herself small.

" '*…aw, keep your eyes on the road, your hands upon the whe-el…* '"

"Like the stereo just turned itself on, Val," Katie said as she opened the basement door.

Magdalene reached behind her back. *What the hell?* Trash bags. She was leaning against stacks and stacks of shiny new trash bags.

A metal rattle from the cave room competed with the bass from the stereo (and Paul Stern's off-key singing). The basement door slammed shut.

"Katie?" Magdalene whispered.

The air in the basement was tight, like a huge, living thing: thick and adverse to penetration. Magdalene's eyelids closed under the pressure.

" '*…let it roll, baby, roll…* '"

"…he just went to…"

" '*…give up your vows…* '" Paul Stern sang.

Hundreds and hundreds of trash bags.

" '*…save our city…save our city…* '"

"He's coming back. He's—"

"Why didn't you say so before? Jesus, Val, I'm outta here, babe."

The air in the basement was swampy, like the Puddle at the end of summer.

"It's not my fault!"

" '*…woke up this morning and I got myself a beer…* '" Paul Stern sang.

"Where are you going?"

Magdalene fought sleep. How long had it been since she'd really slept?

"Megan said there's a beer blast in the Basin."

Her father was drunk. He stumbled down the dock and fell into the water. There was a blanket over her head but it was thin; it didn't block the flashing police lights. Or mute her father's screaming.

"Paul!"

"Later."

There was a soft caress on Magdalene's cheek, and she awoke to Katie's smile. The little girl held a wilted dogwood petal between her fingers. Magdalene could barely see the scar on Katie's face.

"Come on, sleepyhead. I have to show you Minnie's new shell."

"Minnie?" Magdalene's mouth was sour and sticky.

"My turtle, silly!"

"New shell?"

"I painted it again—for the summer!"

The music ended. Magdalene shook her head. Cobwebs everywhere.

"What are all the trash bags for?"

Katie pulled on her arm.

"Magdalene! Come on! He'll be getting off the bus soon."

The floorboards above their heads creaked in rhythm. Magdalene yanked Katie beneath the stairs with her. Katie laughed.

"It's just ol' Val. Calling the whole wide world. 'Oh where, oh where is Paul? Oh, where's my Paul?' Plus I told her some boy called yesterday, but that it *wasn't* Paul. She always paces when she's yakking on the phone. Drives me bonkers! She'll be on the phone for a while. Come on!"

"The cat? That was—?"

"Oscar Sceebers! He's here all the time now, so I let him in and give him milk. He really likes it when I rub…what happened to your hand?"

"Listen," Magdalene said. "I have to get you—"

Katie lifted Magdalene's bloody hand. Magdalene turned her head away.

"Jumping fences. Fell off a carnival ride."

Katie ran her fingers over the little scrapes and cuts on Magdalene's cheek.

"You don't have to lie to me, Magdalene."

Rattle.

"You'll tell me when you feel like it."

Rattle.

It was coming from the cave.

"It's okay, Magdalene. You're my best friend."

RATTLE!

Magdalene screamed.

Katie's little hands covered Magdalene's mouth.

"Katie?" Valerie called from upstairs. "Paul?"

Katie shook her head.

"Paul? No, I guess it wasn't him. So that bitch, she says…"

"Once ol' Val gets on the phone," Katie said, slowly lowering her hands, "there's no end to it."

"What the hell *was* that?" Magdalene asked, pointing to the cave door.

Katie covered her own mouth.

"Tell me."

Who had Mr. McAllister imprisoned in his basement? How many bodies had he carted away in his trunk? Magdalene wondered how she could have been so wrong. It wasn't Stevie Rich or Frannie Five Fingers: *Mr. McAllister was the King of the Snipes!*

Magdalene shook Katie's shoulders.

"Tell me, who is it? Who's in there? We're leaving. We're getting out of—"

Katie spread her fingers and a giggle escaped. In the thick air of the basement, Magdalene thought she'd be able to watch the giggle float away. Katie's eyes went wide, and she smacked her hands firmly back over her mouth.

Don't go losin' Lou's Head.

"Katie…" Magdalene began softly, trying a different tact.

Katie lowered her hands, concern in her eyes.

"It's just the bunny," Katie said.

"The—?"

"I'm not supposed to know he's here. He's my birthday present."

Katie smiled, stood up, and walked through the cave door.

"Katie, no!"

Light—and Katie stood in the middle of a little room holding the balled end of a piece of string attached to an overhead light bulb. The cobwebs in the little cave room were less dense, more scattered. A washer and dryer stood along one wall, another gurgling drain in between, and in the middle of the floor, a large metal cage with a flop-eared rabbit blinking at the two of them. The bottom of the cage was mesh-like, so the bunny's droppings could fall into the sliding silver tray below.

"I haven't thought of a name yet. Echo maybe. 'Member that band your brother liked? You think that's good?"

"Echo," Magdalene repeated. Her head felt numb. The bunny nibbled at a pellet in an attempt to act casual, but Magdalene couldn't even muster that. "Echo and the Bunnymen."

"But I can't name him yet 'cause then my dad will know that I know."

Magdalene knelt down. A little piece of flesh clung precipitously to one knee, but both her knees were scraped raw. The pain lunged from her legs to her brain and then dove back down again.

"Katie, I came here tonight to—"

"Don't tell anyone I saw him, okay?" Katie said, as she pulled the string to switch off the light bulb.

Rattle.

Magdalene was kneeling in the dark. What if she just stayed and died right here? Being in the cave was like being under Michael's blanket—it was that dark and that stinky.

Katie took Magdalene's better hand. "If I squeeze too tight, lemme know," the little girl said, leading her out of the laundry room.

"Where—"

Katie stopped and put a finger to Magdalene's mouth.

"Shhh. Just follow me. Ol' Val'll be too busy gabbing away. We'll clean your hands up. I know where the Band-Aids are. We've only got a few minutes before my dad comes home. Then I'll show you Minnie."

Magdalene grabbed Katie's arm.

"Your dad is coming back?"

"Magdalene, you're hurting—"

Magdalene pulled her hand away. A wave of red fingerprints encircled Katie's wrists.

"I'm sorry."

"It's like a bracelet," Katie said, admiring the red fingerprints.

"But your dad—"

"Yeah, he's coming back," Katie said, her face growing red. "I know he—I know he yelled at you and that he wanted Valerie instead of you." Her volume increased. "But I didn't. I swear, Magdalene, I didn't."

Magdalene kissed Katie's forehead.

"I know you didn't."

"It just—"

"I know."

They stood on the wooden staircase, cobwebs dancing on their heads like halos.

"He was only going to be gone for a few minutes, he said."

"A few minutes?"

"He just went to get turtle food for Minnie."

"On a Sunday night?"

Katie shrugged.

"He took the bus to the shops."

"Right."

Katie picked at the crumbling basement wall, peeking up at Magdalene's face.

"Katie, what are all the trash bags for?"

"Trash, I'm guessin'," Katie giggled as she dragged Magdalene up the remaining steps. Magdalene pushed open the basement door a crack. Valerie Plum flew past her view.

"You *have* to see Minnie!" Katie whispered, yanking Magdalene through the door before Magdalene gathered her wits. "You just have to, and we'll clean you up, and then you can leave before my dad comes home, but you can come back tomorrow, and do you know a kid named Danny?"

Valerie was pacing back and forth in the dining room, sobbing into the phone between mouthfuls of food.

"...but, I don't want to!" Valerie declared into the phone. A half-eaten Hostess Twinkie greased her free hand. "So gross. It's funny looking."

Valerie marched into the living room and shoved the Twinkie into her mouth.

"What if I just spit it out?" the baby-sitter asked around the Twinkie.

"Go!" Magdalene whispered, and, crouching low, they ascended the stairs to the second floor. Valerie kept her back to them as she concentrated on the phone.

"The fourth step—" Katie began.

CREEEEAK!

Did every house in Mondauk Proper have a creaky fourth step?

"No, wait, hold on...Katie?" Valerie called. "Katie?"

Magdalene covered Katie with her body and listened to Katie's slow, steady heartbeat. If she could just force her pulse to match Katie's—

"You better not be eavesdropping, Katie McAllister," Valerie Plum said.

Magdalene could hear the radio from Katie's room, muffled and distant. *Calm, cool, collected: slow it down, be ready for anything.* Magdalene had once read that legendary magician Harry Blackstone had been able to stop his pulse by placing a tightly knotted handkerchief in his armpit. Magdalene was sure the trick had come in handy; it was the opposite of counting.

"This isn't funny, Katie," Valerie yelled, "this is my life!"

Valerie moaned a spooky, wounded animal moan and returned to the phone.

"No, just the spoiled brat. I told him, I'm not working Saturday *and* Sunday nights, but Mr. McAllister promised…"

Katie crawled out from under Magdalene, and Magdalene followed her up the stairs. The second floor hallway was warm.

"I figured in honor of the Summer Sky," Katie said, throwing open her bedroom door with a flourish, "I'd…Magdalene, where are you?…my room is…"

Magdalene knew the front room was *his* room. The door was always closed whenever Magdalene baby-sat, and Katie never extended her games or adventures into his domain. When Magdalene pushed the door open with her fingers (*gentle, gentle*), she was fully prepared for a horrific tableau: photographs of the victims on the walls, Biblical passages written in blood, notebooks full of scribbling, women's undergarments, and rope, lots of rope.

Magdalene took a breath. The scene was considerably more genteel than in her imagination.

The perfume was old. Its true scent had died with the wearer, but here, within Mr. McAllister's bedroom, it lingered, an Indian summer, a snow flurry in April, even with all the windows open. Magdalene closed the door behind her and turned the lock without looking— and he was *there*, his fingers just missing the goose bumps tattooing her skin. She turned around slowly.

A woman's dress swung from a hanger on the back of the door. The dress had a pattern of wine colored petals and faded green stems. Magdalene buried her nose in the flower pattern. It wasn't the scent of an old lady's perfume; it had the fading smell of Stargazer lilies. Magdalene wondered how long it would be before the perfume faded away completely. How many times had Mr. McAllister done the same thing—buried himself in the fading wisps of his dead wife. Before today, Magdalene wouldn't have thought it possible.

The tag on the inside of the dress was ragged from too many washings, but Mrs. McAllister had written her name in magic marker, an odd touch. Maybe Mrs. McAllister had been brought up in a large family.

Tap-tap-tap.

"Magdalene," Katie moaned into the keyhole. "No one's allowed in there. Daddy said…"

In faded black marker, across the front of the tag: *Patricia*.

Magdalene shook her head. That was *her* mother's name: Patricia. This couldn't be a coincidence. She tried hard to picture Nancy McAllister but couldn't. Had Katie's mother been friends with Patricia Archer Rumsey Barrows?

Magdalene turned the lock back and pulled the door open. Katie was on her knees holding Minnie the turtle. The little girl's eyes were huge crop circles.

"You're not allowed in there. If Daddy—"

"Katie, what was your mom's name?"

"Her name? Nancy. It means 'grace' in Hebrew."

"Her *full* name, Katie. What was her full name?"

Katie smiled.

"Patricia Nancy McAllister. But everyone called her Nancy."

Magdalene closed the door again, taking in the rest of the room. Surely Mr. McAllister kept a picture of his wife. The light had been just about drained from the early summer sky, and Magdalene squinted into the darkness and jumped when the streetlight blinked on.

"Magdalene," Katie whispered into the keyhole.

It was a woman's bedroom. The bedspread had pink roses and white lace. A gold trimmed, mirrored tray on the bureau held a variety of perfume bottles, but only one was near empty. Fans with Japanese writing hung on one wall, and on the nightstand was an old picture frame. The silver was almost green, and the picture inside was washed out. Mr. McAllister didn't look so mean in the photograph; he looked a little ridiculous and very happy. He wore a tight t-shirt, his muscles just about popping out. Mrs. McAllister—Patricia Nancy McAllister—wore a simple sundress, but her big, wide smile took the focus away from anything else.

Magdalene wondered if Mrs. McAllister had been a liar too.

"*Mag-da-lene*," Katie sang softly into the keyhole. "Minnie's here…"

Of course Nancy McAllister was a liar. She had been a mom and a wife and then had taken her own life as if those first two things hadn't amounted to a hill of beans. Being married to the King Snipe of Mondauk County wouldn't have contributed a whole hell of a lot to her marital bliss, but still…

Whistling.

With all the windows open, Magdalene knew Katie heard it too. She heard Katie scrambling to her feet.

Magdalene ran to the far left window and peeked out, careful to keep low. She didn't want to cast any shadows.

Three quick knocks.

"Um, Magdalene, I think…"

The street was empty, just the coda of a whistled tune drifting away and back, then a hint of a refrain, a change in key—and she saw him: the Big Bad Wolf, the Evil of Mondauk, walking with a purpose, a whistle on his eager lips, tossing a cigarette butt aside, licking his chops, his shadow long and distorted under the street lamps of Orchard Street.

"Magdalene," Katie whined. "I don't want you to get in any trouble. C'mon."

"Please," she added.

There was a shadow slinking next to Mr. McAllister's. One second it looked skinny, the next tall and broad. This shadow's footsteps weren't as sure or as eager as Mr. McAllister's. They were careful, reticent. Maybe the second shadow was about to do something it didn't want to do, or it had been forced into an arrangement not of its own choosing, or maybe—

A car swung around the corner, skidded to a stop at the front of the house, then peeled away. The smell of burnt rubber mixed nauseously with the late Patricia Nancy McAllister's perfume.

What if the second shadow was Stevie Rich?

Magdalene couldn't see either one in the smoky aftermath of the peel-out, but she knew they were there, perhaps waiting out the departure of the car in the berry bushes or stalking the McAllister house in slow, careful strides along the driveway.

What if Mr. McAllister was working in cahoots with Stevie Rich, and while the voices Magdalene had heard from inside the Chevy's trunk that she'd thought had been the Eves brothers searched the Puddle for her, Stevie Rich, having caught the scent himself, had now returned with Jack McAllister, the hidden daddy vampire of Mondauk?

A hand tugged at her sleeve and Magdalene screamed.

"AHHHHHHHHHHHHHHHHHHHHHHHHHHHHHHHHHHHH HHHHH!"

Katie McAllister looked ready to scream back.

"My turtle," Katie said weakly.

On Minnie's shell, Katie had painted the summer sky. Magdalene knew the triangle in the center was the Summer Triangle: Vega, Deneb, Altair, but in the streetlamp glow, the white drops of paint on Minnie's shell were as random as blood splatters or fingerprint whorls or raindrops—except that nothing was quite as random as it seemed. Not anymore. Everything was connected now.

"There's no time," Magdalene said.

Downstairs: a thud. The ding of a phone being jammed into the receiver and missing the cradle. Valerie yelled up the stairs: "Katie?"

Magdalene tucked Minnie under her arm (like a football) and pushed Katie down the hall towards her bedroom.

"What the hell? Katie?" Valerie called. "Are you okay, Katie?"

Magdalene hoped, among other things, that it was not Valerie's time either, that there was no profile in courage at the McAllister house tonight from the baby-sitter substitute.

"Katie?" Valerie was halfway up the stairs.

Magdalene grabbed Katie's arm and pulled her into her room and slammed the door shut. She fumbled with the knob, but there wasn't a lock. *Shit.* The radio was still on, and she knew that she should turn it off so she could hear anything that was happening on the other side of the door, but Magdalene couldn't ascertain its location over her kick drum heart.

"*...Cracklin' Rosie, make me smile / God, if it lasts for an hour, that's alright / We got all night / To set the world right...*"

Magdalene and Katie stared at each other as the song faded away. A man's voice shouted from the southeastern corner of the room.

"*...traffic and weather on the twos...!*"

Magdalene swung her fist and connected with a bedpost.

"*...brought to you by Strunk and White...*"

"It's...it's just the radio," Magdalene said as she rubbed her knuckles. "It's alright, Katie, it's okay."

" 'Cracklin' Rosie,' " Katie sniffled.

Strunk and White?

The candles along the south windowsill flickered in the breeze and threw crazy, unrecognizable shadows on the walls.

"Okay, there's only one way out: the window. You grab my wrists, and I'll lower you down," Magdalene instructed.

Katie rubbed her arm. "Why'd ya pull me?" Katie asked, her eyes beginning a long, slow drowning. She took the turtle from Magdalene and placed Minnie inside a little aquarium. "You hurt me again. Why'd ya hurt me, Magdalene?"

"*...we take you now to our roving reporter, Bess Bouvant, who's on the scene...*"

"Katie?" Valerie was closer.

"*...thanks, Howard. The mystery of Mondauk ended today when police discovered...*"

Magdalene crouched down in front of Katie. Katie flinched.

"I thought you were going to bully me," Katie said.

"Me? I don't—"

"Katie?" Valerie called from the second floor landing. The candle flames danced then shuddered.

"Look," Katie said, extending her arm. A second bracelet of red ovals glowed on her forearm.

"I'm sorry," Magdalene said, not realizing she was crying too until Katie wiped away the tears. "I really am. But I know what he's doing to you."

"Who?"

"Katie?" Valerie whispered at the door.

"Go away!" Magdalene shouted.

"Katie?" More urgent his time. "Are you okay? Do you want me to—?"

"Valerie, go the fuck away or I'll kill you, I swear!" Magdalene screamed.

"Your dad, Katie. I know, alright, I know what he's doing to you," Magdalene whispered quickly. "I know what he does. And I'm gonna get you outta here, get you on a bus to your Aunt Angela's. Maybe I can ride with you, but I don't know, I...Aunt Angela's your favorite aunt, right?"

"Daddy never hurt me," Katie said. The little girl's eyebrows were knitted in puzzlement.

Magdalene stood up. If that had really been Mr. McAllister

creeping along Orchard Street—Mr. McAllister and his shadow friend—then Valerie was the least of their worries. The drop to the backyard was maybe eight feet, she thought. If she dangled Katie, then it would be less, and Katie could drop and roll.

The reflection in the top half of the window made Magdalene jump back and blink: it was Mrs. Bochdan, distracted, pretending, serving tea. Magdalene blinked again and there was the widow Tidwell, mousy Beth Tidwell, flinching at the light, every flicker a reminder of her husband's fate.

When Magdalene blinked a third time, it was her own face she saw in the window, at first in pieces, innumerable pieces, tricks of the light, then slowly it came into focus—just another doomed face in Mondauk Proper's pantheon of doomed faces. A Goner. There were massive circles under her eyes; her hair was dirty; her face was damp but her lips were cracked.

It was her time.

Katie cried softly behind her, her fingers hooked into the loops of Magdalene's jeans. Magdalene patted Katie's head and lifted the tray of candles.

"Hold on to my wrists, and I'll lower you down," Magdalene said. "You won't get hurt, I promise. I'll be right behind you."

"*...although the DA's office hasn't commented yet, sources say they aren't planning to level any charges at the young girl...again, Howard, Christina Fuller is alive and well, discovered by police earlier today hiding in Pennypack Woods in the area known as Finch's Landing, sustaining herself on crackers and soda. Sources say the ruse was an attempt to hide what she believed to be a pregnancy from her parents...*"

She should have blown the candles out first. There were at least twenty little candles on the tray. And she had meant to: she had meant to extinguish the candles—but she'd blinked again and images of Father Demetrius had distracted her, Father Demetrius endlessly dousing and lighting candles in the basement chapel.

Christina faked her disappearance?

The radio spilled the truth.

"*...Father Dave Browne offered prayers for the family tonight, even as Dr. Fuller announced his wife's imminent resignation from Assumption's Faith Board in a press conference, offering his sincerest apologies to the priest...*"

"*Thank you, Bess...in other news, President Bush said today of Iraq, 'America must not ignore the threat gathering against us; facing clear evidence of peril, we cannot wait for the final proof'...*"

The heat from the candles was unbearable. The tray was scalding her injured hands. She had meant to lay the tray on Katie's desk. She had meant to set the tray aside, blow all the candles out, and lower Katie to safety. They'd have to hustle through the yards to escape Mr. McAllister and his shadow partner. Valerie Plum was merely a nuisance, a whiny wimp; the baby-sitter wouldn't be a hindrance to their escape.

Valerie slammed the door open and the wood connected with the wall like a gunshot.

Katie shrieked.

Valerie shrieked back.

Magdalene turned and dropped the tray of candles.

Chapter Fifteen

The Puddle

First he chants:
    "Divide, conjugate, bag o' stones;
    Next sound you'll hear is the rattling of bones.
    Diverge, gin mill, Daddy's dive bar;
    Next sound you'll hear is the falling of stars."
    Then Michael says: "It's a goddamn whirlpool."
    Then: "Cannonball!"
    Magdalene hears quite clearly the last thing he says before he jumps from the Dead Injun Tree a second time.
    He says: "Cannonball!"
    Legs tight, head bent, arms holding in his legs.
    She pulls Michael's hood tight so it covers almost her entire face. The rain hurts now, like pieces of hail, big fat drops. The drum patterns the rain makes on the Puddle drowns out the last vestiges of heavy metal from the Lakes. The thunder makes her grab her ears.
    Magdalene pulls the hood tighter and listens for her brother's splash: the biggest raindrop of all.
    The already swollen Puddle tangos in the wind, and little expeditionary currents tickle her feet. She should have waited on the dock, but she doesn't want any splinters.
    No splash: but so many ladybugs. They climb all over the refuse-ornaments of the shore.
    So many ladybugs—and each with dots, dots, dots.
    There isn't a splash—the thunderclaps hide Michael's entry into the Puddle—it's more like the sound a hand makes when it slaps the water.
    Bad boy, water—bad boy.
    And where is Michael? Oh where, oh where has Michael Barrows gone? Oh where, oh where could he be? There! *(Where else?) In the middle of the whirlpool, yelling. Yawping. Faking out the opposition. Getting revenge for Magdalene cheating the dare, evening the score for having been made to rescue her.*
    Magdalene cuts off her ears to spite her eyes. She's had enough yawping for one day. If your eyes offend thee, cut them out, right?
    What if your brother offends thee?

Michael yawps again—at least it sounds like a yawp—it's hard for her to tell with all of Thor's hammering and raindrops pounding like heaven's hailstones and the whirring of a thousand ladybug wings.

One, two, three,
Four, five, six,
Seven, eight, nine,
Ten, eleven, twelve
Ladybugs
Came to the ladybugs' picnic.

What if your brother tells everyone—everyone!—that you thought the gray line of the horizon was the far off coast of jolly ol' England? What if all your cousins and second cousins, the whole lot of them, the Clan of the Barrows, laughs—laughs!—and never mind the splinter from the lifeguard stand in your ass: you are the butt of the joke—AGAIN!

"That was *so* mean!" Danny Kildare would later declare. "Did you want to just kill your brother?"

What if your brother wants you to touch his penis? What if you want to and you don't really know why?

Okay, so it was her idea for Michael to bring her out to the Puddle today— and she did cheat the dare. Still, she loves him and isn't that the whole kit and caboodle, to quote Aunt Tiddy? But the bone marrow truth of the matter was this: she really can't swim. Never learned how. She is even a little afraid of water. (Not unlike Boo Raven.) Oh, she can dog paddle for a dog's age, but Michael's rescuing wasn't quite the sham he thought it to be.

Also can't forget this: Michael knows she can't swim—and there's the coast of England again, drifting, fading into a line of pollution.

"If you think like a bully thinks for a half a second," her father would say, "you can stay one step ahead."

But it was her idea to come here.
(Michael splashes about in the muck.)
But it was his dare.
(Michael flounders a bit.)
But she had cheated the dare.
(Michael goes down.)
One, two, three,
Four, five, six,
Seven, eight, nine,
Ten, eleven, twelve,
And they all played games
At the ladybugs' picnic.

Counting is easy to start and hard to stop, but with the rain and the thunder and the lightning and Michael's admittedly impressive dramatics, it's better to count than to think. Better to let something else—ladybugs, say—take over for her pulse. Better to count than to be had. Shakespeare said that.

The rain pelts her head until the hood is soaked, and the sound of water-kissing-water smack-on-the-mouth is like little yelps, little shouts from a distance: the raindrops yawping before they surrender themselves to a sea of sameness.

Don't look up, Magdalene, or you'll never stop counting.

Don't look directly into the rain.

One, two, three,

Four, five, six,

Seven, eight, nine,

Ten, eleven, twelve,

And they chatted away

At the ladybugs' picnic.

She pulls the hood from her head—the ladybugs are gone. Her hair is a dirty, wet mop in seconds. If she raises her head, she could count every single one of God's teardrops, she could...

(Ignore the yelling—the yawping. He'll swim underwater, his eyes open. He'll swim to the dock, crawl quietly up its side, and scare the bejesus out of her—she knows the script.)

$1 + 2 + 3 = 6$

(The yelling doesn't stop when Michael's head goes down a second time. Damn, he's good.)

$1 + 2 + 4 + 7 + 14 = 28$

He calls her Lil, he says, because he's big and doesn't want someone so lil to forget it.

Fuck perfect numbers.

The prime numbers less than 100 are: 2, 3, 5, 7, 11, 13, 17, 19, 23, 29, 31, 37, 41, 43, 47, 53, 59, 61, 67, 71, 73, 79, 83, and 97.

(The yelling doesn't stop when Michael's head goes down a second time?)

She can barely see them, just little dots jumping up and down, running on the old stone fishing bridge that connects Spring House to Mondauk Proper. Bullies, no doubt, catching her out, thrilled to have prey on such a downcast day.

Nothing biting today, John-John?

Not a nibble, Stevie, John-John answers, his words slurring around a pacifier.

They are pointing, yawping themselves, running towards her, pointing at the Puddle—ha! Michael's fooled them too!

Then Michael screams her name.

At least she thinks it's her name. She's so used to being called Lil.

Besides: "Cannonball" had been barely audible over the rain and thunder.

One, two, three,

Four, five, six,

Seven, eight, nine,

Ten, eleven, twelve,

And they all played games

At the ladybugs' picnic.

"One Michael two Michael three Michael four," Magdalene speaks into the rain.

They run towards her—those bullies on Olde Bridge—Paradise Lakes trailer trash, still wearing flannel over their black concert t-shirts, looking to cause trouble or steal their spare change or force her to tell the truth.

"Five Michael six Michael seven Michael eight," Magdalene whispers into her hands.

The bullies are almost upon her. And Michael is still fooling around, splashing about in the whirlpool—how long has he been in there: thirty seconds, sixty seconds?

"Oh my God, kid, are you alright?" the first bully asks, and Magdalene covers her head, for the reign of blows will come as surely as God's tears fall from the sky. The bully is wearing a fisherman's hat. Lures dangle dangerously.

"Go—go and call 911," he yells to one of his companions.

"Where?" a second voice screams back over the thunder. "I don't have a—"

"Anywhere—just go!" the first voice shouts back.

"Jesus Christ—is that Michael Barrows? Michael Barrows is drowning?" a third voice asks, and the thunder god rolls another split, and Magdalene finds herself on the edge of the dock.

It's a whirlpool—just like in the movies: hypnotic, tempting, utterly violent. A whirlpool lies—it seduces—it bullies.

Now—the dream within a dream:

Michael is screaming her name, or maybe it's the thunder, and the fishermen have a ladder on their truck, and she lies on her belly on the ladder, and one of the Olde Bridge fishermen holds her feet.

R—E—A—C—H.

It's fourth down, less than a yard to go, and Michael Barrows stretches out his arm.

Michael always says that to hold somebody by the wrists is to save a life.

Magdalene snatches his fingers and then feels his fingerprints sliding away from hers.

Yellow star, red star, white star, black.

Not shooting stars: falling.

Falling stars.

Michael goes under a third time.

"Goes down three times, only comes up twice," said one of the fisherman, as if this were common knowledge among anglers.

Magdalene stays on her stomach, her fingers outstretched, the fishermen holding the dream ladder, waiting, counting bubbles.

ONE.

TWO.

THREE.

FOUR.

FIVE.

SIX.

SEVEN.

EIGHT.

NINE.

TEN.

ELEVEN.

TWELVE.

"The police are coming," the first fisherman shouts. "They'll be here any minute. They called your dad too. You're Magdalene Barrows, right?"

"Lil," Magdalene says. "It's Lil."

+

For one brief, heart-stopping, movie moment, Magdalene thought Valerie Plum was on fire. The fallen candles enjoyed their freedom, all the little flames joining together, sharing their good fortune with the carpet glue, filling the doorframe with an audible *whoosh.*

Valerie stepped back, as surprised at the fire filling the doorway as at seeing Magdalene on the other side.

"Oh, you are in so much trouble, Magdalene Barrows," Valerie said.

The flames tasted the old wooden door and burst skyward, devouring it.

"Valerie?"

The voice came from the first floor. Mr. McAllister!

"Valerie? Why is the phone off the hook? Valerie?"

Anger swirled in his voice—anger and violence and booze maybe.

The bully was home.

Katie clung to Magdalene's leg.

"I won't let him hurt you, Katie," Magdalene said. "I won't let you die."

Mr. McAllister's voice was closer now, at the bottom of the stairs perhaps: "Valerie? I swear to God, if you're snoopin' 'round again…"

A second voice (female) shouted from the living room: "She's not in the basement, Jack."

"Jesus fucking Christ."

Valerie looked behind her—Magdalene knew ol' Val heard the bully in Mr. McAllister's voice too.

If this was a comic book blurb, it would read, "The Bully Was Most Definitely Home, and It Was Clobberin' Time."

"Listen, Katie, listen. I have the money—I can put you on a bus."

Valerie and Magdalene stared at each other through the flames. The doorway was completely engulfed, and in the flickering light, Magdalene saw Valerie's face, watched it change, shift, process, decide.

"Hand her over," Valerie Plum said, and Magdalene tossed a small blanket over Katie's head and lifted her up, then she stopped. Her time had come and gone again—Magdalene's time had come and gone. This was a brand new time.

Mr. McAllister's shoes were thunderclaps on the stairs.

Valerie thrust her arms through the flaming doorway, and Magdalene handed Katie to the replacement baby-sitter.

Magdalene could see a hulking shadow in the hallway. The shadow of a bully.

"Just run and jump!" Valerie Plum cried. "Take a running start and jump, Magdalene!"

"Minnie!" Katie screamed.

The bully finally had her. Magdalene was sure that if it wasn't for the fire, she'd be able to smell his cologne—but her nostrils were filled with the smell of burnt popcorn: Raven asleep (but not asleep) on his side, Monkey and Monien the mute panda by his head, his *SILK* Labby ears resting (but not resting) in a pool of vomit, his food bowl empty.

Magdalene lifted the turtle's aquarium and handed it through the flames to Valerie. Minnie stayed in her shell of stars.

There was another *whoosh* and the doorway was gone. Flames tickled the ceiling, and a hand—fat, hairy fingers, bruised knuckles, a white circle on one finger where his wedding band had been—grabbed the front of Magdalene's shirt, dragging her into the fire.

And somewhere, in the back of her head, Jerry Eves was yelling: "Tonto! Tonto!"

Not Lil, Magdalene thought.

Tonto.

A bell sounded in the night, and Magdalene closed her eyes.

+

This is how you let go of someone. This is how you let someone go. One finger at a time. One finger at a time.

Magdalene stays on her stomach on Finch's Landing, her hand outstretched, and the fishermen huddle over her until the first of the police cars arrives, its flashing lights dueling with the lightning, its sirens battling with the thunder. The ladder has vanished like Michael has. There are splinters in her belly.

Arms pick her up and set her against the Dead Injun Tree, facing away from the Puddle.

Sirens and lights multiply.

She sees him coming, stumbling like a penny does when it's thrown in the air and lands all willy-nilly; he runs to Finch's Landing like a confused penny.

Magdalene pulls the wet hood over her head.

He isn't wearing his glasses—it's raining too hard perhaps, or maybe they fell off. Magdalene smells the booze and cigarettes on his breath—like something has crawled into his mouth and died.

"Thank God, Michael, thank God!" her father says, and he reaches out and lifts her hood.

"Daddy?" Magdalene asks, and her father's face freezes, and when the lightning strikes the sky, the little red lines staining his jutting eyeballs threaten to burst wide open.

Here is a turtle without its shell, Magdalene thinks as she reaches for her father and her father reaches for her.

"Michael Michael Michael," he whispers.

"Daddy, it's me, it's Magdalene," she says. "Michael's sleeping. It's Maddie, Daddy, it's me," she says. "Maddie Monkey. Lil."

The drunk man lets her go.

The drunk man peels her fingers from his arm.

The drunk man reels towards the dock.

"*Oh God, no, no, no—not Michael! No!*" *the drunk man screams at the skies.* "*Michael, Michael!*"

Not Michael.

Magdalene.

+

His head was there for a flash, puffed and sour and hungry for blood.

The bell rang three times.

Magdalene dug her nails into Mr. McAllister's hand and jumped back when his hand did the same to hers. The skin on her arm was bubbling and smelled like bacon.

"Get Katie out of the house!" Mr. McAllister's head yelled at Valerie Plum.

"Call 911!" the head commanded. "Now!"

"Tonto!"

The head and the hand were gone.

Again the bell rang. But it wasn't a fire bell. It was coming from the backyard.

Magdalene stumbled to the window. Smoke choked her nostrils and stung her eyes. Jerry Eves was standing in the middle of Katie McAllister's backyard. His brother Mick, his head an inch above Jerry's, stood by his side.

Jerry was holding the Bell of the Yawp, banging on it with a stick.

"Jump!" Jerry shouted. "We'll catch you, me and Mick!"

"Eves!" a voice shouted from the driveway, and Stevie Rich burst through the shadows in the yard.

Mick stepped towards him.

"Did you—?"

"The baby-sitter already did," Stevie Rich answered.

"Run, Jerry, run!" was what she wanted to yell, but the back of her throat was sandpaper, and her voice shut down.

Jerry shook his head.

"He's with us, Tonto. We went to your house to tell you that Stevie told the police about what happened in school. With Joseph Bochdan and Henry. The door was open, so we went in. We saw the note to Michael, Magdalene. We've been looking for you all day."

Magdalene fingered the pills in her pocket, but there wasn't any time for pills. Something burst behind her. If she could just sit down for a spell, just think of Raven and Aunt Tiddy and her mother, then maybe it wouldn't hurt so much. Maybe she could just close her eyes and suck it all in and let the summarizing begin. Katie's bed looked small but oh-so comfortable.

She realized she couldn't stop coughing.

"Magdalene Barrows, now you listen to me!" Mr. McAllister boomed from the backyard over the crackle of the flames. "Can you hear me?"

She'd done it again: now Mick and Jerry would end up wrapped in trash bags in the trunk of Mr. McAllister's car. Magdalene struggled to open her eyes. Katie's bed was so soft, so...

One of the two rabbits screamed.

Magdalene leapt back and pulled the cage off the floor. The two rabbits were wild-eyed, almost foaming. The guinea pig was shivering in the corner, trying to appear inconsequential.

Approaching sirens competed with the scream of the rabbit. Mr. McAllister stood in the center of the yard, his chubby hands planted on either side of his puffy waist. Jerry, Mick, and Stevie Rich huddled to his right. The shadow partner Magdalene had seen tailing Mr. McAllister from the master bedroom window was there too, blending in with the shadow of the dogwood tree.

Frannie Five Fingers?

The cage just fit through the window frame.

"Jerry, Mick, catch this." Words scraped her throat. "Katie's rabbits and her guinea pig."

She pushed the cage through the window and watched the boys snatch it in the air.

"Jump, Magdalene, jump!" Mr. McAllister yelled. "Just jump. I'll catch you!"

"You'll hurt me."

"Magdalene," Mr. McAllister said, "there's no time!"

The rabbit cage had been turned on its side midair, and before the boys could set it down, the guinea pig and one of the rabbits fell out and took off for the high grass near the back of the yard. Mick took three strides, launched himself horizontally, and grabbed the rabbit mid-hop.

The sirens grew closer. Magdalene wondered if they would make it in time to rescue her. (*Did she even care?*) Surely, she couldn't trust Mr. McAllister not to stow her under the basement stairs or in the trunk of his Chevy, even with the Eves brothers looking on.

Who the hell was hiding under the dogwood tree?

Magdalene leaned her head out of the window. Stevie Rich was sitting on the grass, the guinea pig in his lap. Stevie Rich was petting the guinea pig and talking to it. With his free hand, he tickled the nose of the rabbit still in the cage through the metal mesh squares. The Bell of the Yawp lay forgotten next to him.

"Magdalene, jump now! There's no time!" Mr. McAllister yelled into cupped hands. The fire had grown loud as it snarled and chewed its way through wood and metal and siding.

The fish!

"The fish!" Magdalene cried.

"Forget the fish!" Mr. McAllister yelled back, but Magdalene knew that was just the kind of man he was: he'd leave his own daughter behind! He'd set fire to his own house.

Magdalene paused: *I started the fire. I almost killed Katie.*

The water in the aquarium was warm. Magdalene used the little net to scoop two catfish sharks. She could barely see them through the smoke. A third fish hid inside a pink pirate's skull until Magdalene lifted the skull out of the aquarium, and she scooped him up too.

"Jerry!" Magdalene yelled as she dropped the net out of the window.

"Get 'em in some water now!" she commanded.

The suckerfish!

Smoke stormed back into her nostrils. Her coughs tore her throat; her stomach burned. If she passed out now: barbecue. She bent over until the dizziness passed.

The suckerfish was stubborn: it clung to what it knew. She plunged both hands into the warm water and poked it with her fingers until it let go for half a second.

When she turned around, Katie's desk was gone, and the headboard and the wall behind it were painted in orange and black.

Mr. McAllister was still yelling. Jerry and Mick too—even Stevie Rich. Mr. McAllister's shadow partner remained huddled beneath the dogwood tree.

"Magdalene, please jump!" Mr. McAllister yelled. "Please!"

"You hurt Katie," Magdalene yelled back.

The sirens were close, but not close enough. The suckerfish flipped inside her closed palms, desperate to cling to something, *anything.*

"I never hurt Katie!" Mr. McAllister shouted.

"I saw her bruises!" Magdalene screamed.

Goddamn adult liars—LIARS!

"She fell out of the tree, Magdalene," Mr. McAllister said in a softer voice; she could barely hear him over the crackle of the fire eating the bed.

ALL OF THEM—EVERY SINGLE ONE OF THEM—PLAYING TRICKS ON HER—LIARS! THEY KNEW WHERE MICHAEL WAS! THEY *ALL* KNEW! EVERY SINGLE *FUCKING* ONE OF THEM!

"What's in the trunk of your car?" Magdalene screamed. Her back was hot and sweaty. She could barely see through the smoke as it escaped through the open window.

"The trunk? Pieces of a cage…I had leftover pieces from…never mind, just—"

"JUST WHAT?!" Magdalene screamed. The suckerfish felt the heat too, and its flipping had become both exhausting and urgent.

"…and I don't want you to—"

A hand—a woman's hand—left the shadows of the dogwood and rubbed Mr. McAllister's shoulder before disappearing.

Mr. McAllister cupped his hands together over his mouth again.

"Okay, okay. I bought Katie a new rabbit, one of those flop-eared ones she'd been wanting. I built the cage myself. Thought I could use the extra pieces to build some sort of lid for Minnie's aquarium. Damn turtle's always trying to run away. Have no idea how she gets out. Found her tonight on the pavement in front of the house. Also bought Katie a huge bag of cedar chips for the rabbits and the guinea pig. Wrapped it up in trash bags so it wouldn't spill out in the car."

A woman's voice said: "Keep talking to her, but be quick about it," and Magdalene leaned against the window frame. It was so hot. She held the suckerfish out of the window. Sirens screamed in her ears.

"I kept the new rabbit hidden in the basement. I was yelling at Katie, trying to keep her from going down there, and she ran away from me, up the tree. I went after her—I wasn't really mad—just didn't want her to see her present. She's been upset—upset about seeing…well, upset about seeing me and Beth holdin' hands outside. Beth and me, we wanted to do something special for…"

Magdalene couldn't keep her eyes open. Smoke draped her body.

The suckerfish flipped one final time, and Magdalene opened her hands and dropped it to where she hoped Jerry Eves was still standing.

"...just jump, oh God, Beth—she's gonna—Magdalene, the branch broke. That's it. I was trying to get Katie outta the tree. She'd just seen me and Beth the night before. She was upset and climbed really high. I climbed up after her, and when I reached her, the branch she was on broke. I grabbed her so she wouldn't fall. Oh God...Jesus...I'm sorry I didn't let you baby-sit. I was scared, okay? I was wrong. There was just so much at stake..."

Magdalene opened her eyes. She thought she could smell her hair burning. Her skin hurt. Her back felt like a river of blisters. She had murdered sweet Raven. She was no Sister Mary Magdalene de Rosa.

"You were the best baby-sitter, I swear. Jump, goddamn it!

"JUMP!" Mr. McAllister yawped to the little girl inside the fire that was eating his house.

The smoke poured out into the summer sky and crowded the stars, obscuring them even more than the pollution had—Magdalene could barely tell the tops of the blooming dogwood flowers from the remnants of the dead stars.

Mr. McAllister and Jerry Eves and Mick Eves and Stevie Rich: their shouts and yells and pleading merged into one voice, and the voice yawped its one dare.

JUMP!

And then it happened:

The shadow separated from the dogwood tree, and the shadow that was no longer a shadow approached the burning house, arms open wide, voice so soft and so quiet that Magdalene wasn't even sure the shadow had spoken until she heard the name it said, until the name *Bobby* fought its way through the choking smoke and the long-dead stars and the dormant numbers and the stinky blankets.

Mrs. Tidwell stood beneath the window and said her fallen husband's name again.

Magdalene climbed through the window frame, grabbed the curtain for a parachute, and released herself.

This is how you let go of someone. This is how you let someone go. One finger at a time. One finger at a time.

And the fire engines sounded like the Bell of the Yawp, and the arms of bullies and bell ringers and a firefighter's widow lifted her towards the sky like they were replacing a fallen star.

A Lab's Ears Are Made of *SILK*

Episode V

What Transpired after the Dance of the Dead Cats

"The Dance of the Dead Cats," Finn whispered to himself.

"Did you like it?" Coulda asked.

"We worked all summer on making it more modern," Shoulda said between giggles.

"I was the one spitting," Woulda said, wiping himself. "I played Rain."

Finn opened his mouth, but nothing came out.

"That was *D*eath, Huckleberry," Alley Cat said. "The last of the D words. Not very pretty, but still somehow beautiful."

Finn thanked Shoulda, Coulda, and Woulda, who backed away, bowing their heads.

"I don't pretend to know what happens when cats—or dogs or pigs or turtles—die," Alley Cat said. "Maybe one of the Good Books is right. Maybe there is a judgment day, and every little thing you've done, everything you've stolen, will be accounted for. But if there is, and you've lived a pretty good life, does it matter if you ate meat on Friday or forgot to bow to Mecca one afternoon?"

Coulda and Shoulda looked at one another and began emptying their pockets of all sorts of booty: soda pop bottles, a can opener they could never use because of their lack of opposable thumbs, a couple of tennis balls, half a bologna sandwich (an awkward grin crawled across Shoulda's puss), a pair of mice dressed like astronauts (who exited the scene hastily with the remains of the bologna sandwich), the soundtrack album to *West Side Story*, and last, from Coulda's deep pocket: Finn's orange and blue basketball! The basketball was glowing just the slightest bit, as if someone had lightly scattered Faerie dust over it.

Now, Finn's stomach had started growling at the mention of meat on Fridays—it had been a while since he'd eaten anything, and he'd caught a cold from sleeping on the air conditioning vent before his encounter with Pig—but when Finn caught sight of the basketball, Little White Tie's tempo doubled and drowned out his stomach.

"See, when you die—when any of us dies," Alley Cat continued, "all that happens is that we change. Change is scary. We like what is comfortable. If things change too much or too fast, we grow scared and jumpy. We cling to ideologies and religions to help us explain why things change. But change is the only thing that doesn't change."

Finn listened, but seeing his basketball again after his long Great Journey made Little White Tie hurt more than expected. Finn thought of the Boy and how the Boy would whisper to Finn before they both fell asleep. He remembered the Boy rubbing Finn's tummy and feeding him cookies, and the two of them shaking hands and playing basketball and snoozing under the warm, warm sun.

"When we die, we change," Alley Cat said. "What happens afterward is none of our business. We're no longer. That is the only truth. The Good Books go endlessly on about it, but they are too concerned with rules and regulations and rituals to address the simple fact: we, all of us as we know our ourselves, will one day be no more. All their rules won't change that. Religion concerns itself with the possible outcomes. If there's more than this, then..."

Alley Cat shrugged.

"But what if I didn't live a good life?" Finn asked. "The Boy and the Big Uns were so mad at me because I was bad."

"And your sin?" Alley Cat asked.

"Shoes," Finn sighed.

"You wore the Boy's shoes?" Alley Cat asked.

"No," Finn replied. "I ate them."

"I ate a pair of Converse once," Woulda said, "and the laces got all entangled inside my tummy, and when I pooped—"

"Is that all?" Alley Cat asked, speaking to Finn (but glaring at Woulda, who sulked away and put his Lone Ranger mask back on). "No more sins?"

Finn tapped into his Smart Bump. Gosh, there were so *many* sins—if sins were what bad behavior was called. Finn's whole life was one big sin! Bad dog!

"I bullied Turtle," Finn admitted.

"Bullied him?" Alley Cat asked.

"Yes. Turtle said all cats—begging your pardon, Count Bjørn— were bullies, and that's why he had to wage war on you. But I bullied Turtle into his shell!"

Alley Cat laughed. "That's a pretty grave sin there, Huckleberry, but you don't go around bullying turtles in general, do you?"

"He's a colonel—but no!" Finn barked.

"I only know one turtle," Finn added as an afterthought.

Alley Cat descended from the dogwood and sashayed over to Finn.

"We're all bullies once in a while," Alley Cat explained. "The Good Book has it wrong. *Bullying* is the original sin. The trick is to not do it quite so often if you can help it. We're all animals, Huckleberry. Some animals eat other animals. Some people stomp on ants. There's a difference. Lions and tigers and bears (oh my!) have to eat, and the antelope are aware of this, so the Lord or God or Whoever (the Is, if you will) gave the antelope strong, powerful legs so they can try to outrun its predators. The antelope, of course, are not particularly pleased with the situation, but they understand, in their Little White Ties, to borrow a phrase, that D word *Death* is inevitable and that lions and tigers and bears (oh my!) mean them no real harm—they're just being lions and tigers and bears (oh my!); they're just being true to their true nature. But if we try to remember to curtail the kind of bullying that hurts other animals for no reason—why then: when our time comes to change, we can ascend the pile of bones free from original sin (or least free enough)."

Alley Cat cleared his throat.

"All this speechifying has left my throat dry," Alley Cat rasped. "Could one of you please…?"

Coulda and Shoulda had paid no attention to Alley Cat's dissertation and were busying themselves bouncing Finn's basketball off Woulda's noggin.

"Never mind," Alley Cat said, making his way towards a puddle.

Finn watched the Realists playing basketball. He wondered if they'd let him join in.

"Which brings us to freedom," Alley Cat said when he finished quenching his thirst. "Your second question, I believe. Death, then freedom."

Finn tore his eyes from the game. If he could get his basketball back, then maybe…

No, better to not think about the Boy too much. The Boy probably thought Finn was dead.

"What is freedom?" Finn asked. "Turtle said that's why our country's better than other countries. Freedom."

"Been to many countries, have you?" Alley Cat asked. Woulda and Coulda leaned closer to hear Finn's answer. Coulda, in particular, being Siamese, felt that Wold travel was in his blood—and relayed this information to Finn. Shoulda chased the costumed mice around the backyard.

Alley Cat ignored the other Realists and paced in front of Finn.

"Freedom, Huckleberry, is tricky," Alley Cat began. "An absence of undue restrictions? Yes, yes. That's one way to describe freedom. Meaning what? Just this: no individual or government can inhibit what you say or think or write or express—unless you're on television or radio or write for a newspaper or magazine."

Finn never watched television; it took too much time away from snoozing or playing basketball—or at least it stole the Boy's attention away from the game. Finn didn't read either, but he enjoyed being read to.

"Why are those things not free?"

"Oh they are, they are," Alley Cat said. "But some have a very high cost. We have to protect the ears of our young uns, so no 'shit,' 'damn,' or 'hell.' We have to keep our young uns pure 'fore we send 'em off to war. And sometimes, we have to squash civil rights at home to fight the infidels abroad. Very high cost there. Then it becomes the game of 'can't'."

"And can't means won't," Coulda said, lowering his eye patch.

"Can't never could do anything," Shoulda said, shaking his head.

"Can't means won't," Woulda repeated quietly, "and won't means jail."

Finn was confused: "You said no one individual can stop me from expressing myself."

"True, true," Alley Cat replied. "Unless you want to take your clothes off or say dirty words or pass wind in a crowded room."

"Poof!" Coulda said.

"Cut the cheese," Shoulda added, gasping for air.

RRRRIP, went Woulda's heinie.

Woulda, who'd succeeded in trapping the astronaut mice in a corner of the backyard, waved his hand in front of his malodorous, fuzzy butt, and the two cornered mice fainted in exaggerated flourishes. Coulda approached on tiptoes and sprinkled something glittery over their comatose bodies.

"Censorship is but a minor bending of freedom done to save young uns from material that could make them bring a gun to school," Alley Cat explained, steadfastly holding his nose, for Woulda's fart smelled like cheese that had been kept under your bed, inside a dirty sweat sock, for a month or more. "Our country is surely great compared to countries where the citizenry are beaten or threatened or beheaded. Our country is great because of the central concept that all cats are created equal—which sounds better on paper, by the way, than it actually works in real life. Equality is a misunderstood concept. The rich have more options than those born poor. The antelope has certain freedoms never grasped by the lion, but in the end, the lion will lunch with the antelope, and in that dining experience (during which the antelope is the main course *and* the honored guest), all things *are* equal: two animals, lunch. Equality is the concept of all creatures having the same *opportunities*, which in our society is both true and a pile of horse hockey, but *true* freedom is something else altogether."

Coulda and Shoulda marched behind Alley Cat, Coulda banging a little drum, Shoulda blowing into a stick like a fife. Woulda busied himself fashioning what looked like a tiny noose for the condemned mice from a piece of fishing line.

Finn tried to follow Alley Cat's speech. He really, truly did. As best Finn could understand it, freedom required rules. Turtle had implied as much in a backward kind of way. But still—what *was* freedom?

"Freedom," Alley Cat began, "let me tell you what freedom *isn't*. Freedom isn't about addiction—to drink or catnip or a school of thought or endless dreaming about a cathouse…"

Coulda, Shoulda, and Woulda froze, then walked in a little circle, examined the sky, and whistled an old Irish sea shanty.

"…those things," Alley Cat continued, rolling his eyes, "will tie you down. Addiction is slavery. Can't be free if you're tied to a chemical substance or someone else or a set of ideas."

The mice took the opportunity to embrace freedom themselves. While Woulda feigned ignorance concerning certain Thursday night cathouse activities, the condemned astronaut mice ran off, fishing line nooses still around their scrawny necks. The mice were covered in Coulda's sparkles, and they glittered in the sunlight.

"Death is freedom in a way," Alley Cat said. "The final freedom."

Shoulda and Coulda fell over, clutching their chests. Woulda watched his fellow Realists, then did the same, landing in—you guessed it.

PLOP!

Alley Cat continued: "But our concern is about freedom right here, right now. The thing is, if you listen to the Big Uns (yours or someone else's), you'll hear all about Jesus or Mohammed or Yahweh or Buddha or the six-armed elephant or this political ideology or that. Or worse: existentialism, the catch-all-ism for pretending that not being tied to God or to your fellow man is the same as being free. But those Big Uns are tied to these ideas. Then we're back to the meat on Fridays scenario."

Coulda and Woulda used Finn's basketball as a pillow and watched Woulda scrape the poop from his chest—again.

"True freedom is this: don't hold on to anything and embrace everything. The Wold's my home, Huckleberry. No boundaries, no turf wars."

Alley Cat lowered his voice and whispered: "I grew out of all that Jets and Sharks stuff when I was but a wee kitten.

"Of course," Alley Cat mewed, "holding on to the theory of not holding on to anything is holding on to something, so it's a true enigma, this freedom. A riddle for the ages."

Finn scratched an ear. His head was filled and his stomach was empty and his Smart Bump didn't feel so smart.

"But Turtle said fingerprints make us unique," Finn said.

"Of course, you're unique," Alley Cat said. "Fingerprints have little to do with it. Hold on to something as tight as you can, but as soon as it's gone, you're still there. But you're different. Freedom is knowing that. (Doesn't make it hurt any less though, especially if you're responsible for the disappearance of the thing you'd clung to.) The little girl who's writing this book is tied to the skinny, freckled boy illustrating it. Take one away and everything is different, but the little girl still remains the little girl.

"Still confused?" Alley Cat asked. "It's all tied together. Everything is. Boys!" Alley Cat clapped his paws. Shoulda raised his arms to the sky. Coulda licked his paw, held it in the air, then jumped, landing on top of Shoulda's head. Woulda took a running start, tripped on the basketball (which rolled dangerously close to the pile of poop), and instead of jumping, scaled Shoulda and Coulda (scratching the latter's nose something terrible) until he stood on the top of Coulda's noggin. Woulda reached blindly above his head with his paw.

Nothing was there.

Shoulda belched from the strain on being on the bottom, and the belch smelled like Butterscotch Krimpets. Finn swore his stomach was going to start eating itself if he didn't fill it with food soon.

Woulda stood on his tippy-toes and stretched and took hold of a long cord Finn hadn't seen hanging from the sky before and pulled on it. The sky went dark again, and Woulda lost his footing, flapping his arms like a bird before falling backwards to the ground, right into...

SQUISH!

Coulda, dying to scratch his wounded nose, did so in a furious, violent manner that tickled his toes—which in turned tickled Shoulda on the bottom. Shoulda belched again, loud and hard.

Woulda cleaned his toes and sniffed the belch-infested air.

"Bologna?"

Finn tried not to laugh, but the Realists were a funny lot—like watching puppies.

"*Ahem!*"

Alley Cat cleared his throat and spit a hairball. The sparkly mice hugged each other and ran up the dogwood tree.

"If you will turn your attention once again to the skies..." Alley Cat instructed, and when Finn did, he forgot all about his Little White Tie and his orange and blue striped basketball and Woulda cleaning off excrement for the third time.

The sky was crowded with a thousand blinking diamonds, more precious than any stuffed animal or tennis ball Finn had ever owned.

"Stars," Alley Cat said.

Shoulda stretched himself on the ground, and Coulda leaned his head on his companion's stomach. Woulda lay in the grass and crossed his arms behind his fuzzy head a few feet away. Finn heard the sound of giggling mice coming from the sky.

"You've heard the expression: a blanket of stars?" Alley Cat asked. Finn hadn't, but it sounded nice. The stars twinkled and blinked and winked at him.

"They're as unique as fingerprints—even more so, because there's only one of each. Every Big Un has more than one fingerprint. Every animal has paw prints. That's how we identify one another—one way anyhow. (Besides smell.) We need to recognize one another. We need clues. The stars—they don't need anything. They're just stars, and that's enough. In fact, Huckleberry, most of them are already *d*ead."

Finn gasped and jumped back, sitting on Shoulda and Woulda.

"No, no. Don't worry. They're not going anywhere," Alley Cat said. "I don't know why or how, but every night, they're always here. A blanket of stars? Sure, but this blanket doesn't cover your eyes from the rest of the Wold, nor does it require the rest of the Wold to climb under there with you. Stars don't think they're better than you just 'cause they're up in the sky and burn real bright, so bright that we can still see 'em long after they're dead. Stars are concerned with being stars. Not isolationists, mind you. Just not tied to any one school of thought or Good Book. A bit altruistic actually, the stars, being dead and all but still leaving their light for us to enjoy. Hard to pry an almost empty can of tuna from a dead cat's hands."

Shoulda and Coulda crawled out from under Finn's behind and sat next to him on either side, rubbing against him.

"And Huckleberry?" Alley Cat said. "If there is a God, a Lord, an Is, then surely the first things created were the stars, for everything the first creatures needed to learn were in the skies."

Finn stared at the stars with Count Bjørn de Vagabond and the Realists. Even Woulda stopped cleaning himself to smile at the skies. Finn stared and stared, following one shooting star after another with his eyes until his lids grew heavy, and when he opened them, Alley Cat was sitting in front of him, nose to nose, but the skies were back to their late afternoon gray. Shoulda and Coulda snoozed beneath the dogwood tree, nestled among its fallen flowers. Coulda's eye patch had slipped down to his nose. Woulda rolled in the grass (and into a puddle) in a final attempt to wash up before joining the rest of the Realists for a nap. The glittery mice had lowered themselves to the ground and were untangling the fishing lines that dangled from the dogwood tree. They brushed the Faerie dust from each other's shoulders, removed their astronaut costumes, and took a bologna break.

"Understand?" Alley Cat asked, and Finn nodded his head. But there was one thing...

"Are my ears made of *SILK*?" Finn asked quietly. "The Boy told me they were a thousand times. And I want to know: what is *SILK* and are my ears made of it?"

Alley Cat kissed Finn on his big, black nose.

"You, my friend, have the gift of Absolute Love," Alley Cat said. "Not many of us get that gift, but it comes at a great cost. For anything we love can be gone in an instant. (I wish I could be as open as you with love.) To know your true nature and embrace it. That is a kind of freedom, I guess, and I envy you for it just a little, Huckleberry, and I pray for you too, for the worst pain of all is the pain of not being loved back. Nothing else even comes close."

Finn started to cry, and when he looked up, Alley Cat was crying too.

"Come here, my friend," Alley Cat said, leading him towards a puddle.

At the edge of the puddle, Alley Cat put both paws on Finn's noggin.

"What I'm going to show you, Huckleberry, is the Most Absolute Truth of All."

"The Most Absolute Truth," Finn repeated.

Alley Cat stepped back and sat next to Finn.

The puddle shimmered; a slight breeze tickled the water and made it laugh. Alley Cat leaned over so his face looked straight down into the puddle. Finn could hear the Realists snoring gently (except for Woulda, who sounded like an asthmatic tuba) beneath the dogwood tree.

The puddle settled down, current by current, until the late afternoon sky stared back at Finn and Alley Cat.

"Your answer is there," Alley Cat said, gesturing with his nose at the puddle, and Finn peered in.

Finn had seen his reflection in a puddle before, but he usually splashed around too much if he was playing or very thirsty. But it was different this time. Finn had never given his reflection much attention, but something caught his eye and refused to let go.

"Ask your question," Alley Cat said.

Finn leaned his muzzle as close to the water as he could; his runny, black nose was an inch away from the surface.

"Are my ears made of *SILK*?" Finn asked.

His breath stirred the water and everything went blurry. Finn's Little White Tie just about stopped.

"It's going away, Count," Finn cried. "It's leaving."

"Ask again," Alley Cat said.

"Are my ears made of *SILK*?" Finn breathed into the puddle.

Again, the surface of the puddle shimmied and drifted. The reflected sky lost its shape and returned.

"Once more," Alley Cat said and stepped back.

Finn held his breath, and the puddle fell still, and there, in the middle of the shiny puddle, was the most beautiful, the softest-looking, the most…well…*SILK*-like *things* he'd ever seen. When Finn tilted his noggin, the *SILK* flapped lazily. When Finn expressed surprise, the *SILK* rose up slightly, as if listening intently to a far off sound. And when Finn turned his noggin back and forth? Two of 'em! Two pieces of *SILK*!

Alley Cat's reflection appeared over Finn's shoulder.

"They're my ears?" Finn barked. "Count Bjørn, Count Bjørn—my ears *are* made of *SILK*!"

"Of course they are," Alley Cat said, sheathing his claws to pet Finn's ears. "You almost always know the answers."

"I feel…" Finn began. "I'm not sure *better* is the right word, but *different*. A good D word—Different. And *d*ifferent is better, right?"

"You would know," Alley Cat said.

The other Realists woke up and took turns petting his *SILK*.

"Look one more time, Huckleberry," Alley Cat said, and Finn leaned over to peer into the puddle. "See the gray muzzle? See the long eyebrows sprouting out? Change, Huckleberry. Change. Your skin gets tougher and looser, you run a little slower. Look at me. I'm all tufts. But tufts equal toughness."

Alley Cat knocked on Finn's noggin.

"Same for the brain," Alley Cat said. "Grows tougher, maybe a wee bit slower too, but still whip-smart."

"But this," Alley Cat said, touching his paw to Little White Tie. "This never stays tough long."

Alley Cat lowered his mews to a whisper.

"You will learn to love again, Huckleberry. The gang doesn't want to hear it sometimes. Ruins their image as street warriors."

Shoulda and Coulda had grown bored of petting Finn and had turned on Woulda, petting Woulda's ears with his own tail, a display of affection not entirely appreciated by the gray bundle of Woulda.

"Learn to love again," Alley Cat whispered. "That's the trick. That's the answer to both of your other questions too. Freedom? Just knowing you'll love again, that's freedom enough. Dying? Who knows? So love what you can while you can.

"Your ears, Huckleberry, aren't the only things you have made of *SILK*," Alley Cat said. "They're just the beginning."

Thunder rolled in the heavens, and Finn shivered. (He didn't much like thunder.) Shoulda and Coulda, who'd lifted Woulda off the ground for a game of catch, dropped him—you know where!

Alley Cat snapped his finger-knives to attention.

"The time has come to go home, Huckleberry Finn," Alley Cat said.

Finn looked up, his eyes and nostrils wide.

"Where is my home now?"

"You're adopted," Alley Cat said. "Home is wherever you lay your head—while you still have it."

Coulda, Shoulda, and Woulda surrounded Finn. Alley Cat flashed his finger knives, and the dying sun glinted from their sharp ends to Finn's eyes.

"I thought I was going to be a Realist," Finn said, looking from one cat to another. "Aren't I one of you?"

Alley Cat raised his claws in the air and the Realists did the same. *SWOOP!*

In one swift arc, the finger-knives came down and sliced the surface of the puddle. Finn watched his reflection wave goodbye. Finn lifted his paw too.

"You are family, Huckleberry," Alley Cat said. "You always were."

Coulda, Shoulda, and Woulda embraced Finn in a massive hug, promising to visit soon, writing down his jacket size, and showing him, as quick as possible, the secret Realist handshake. Woulda made sure to wipe away the little bit of poo he'd rubbed on Finn's fur, but Finn figured it was his own poo that Woulda was magnetically attracted to, so he smiled and barked hardy farewells. Even the mice came out from hiding to shake Finn's paw.

There exploded in the sky more thunder (the mice headed for the hills)—followed by the siren call of an intruder. Another dog? A Big Un? Turtle with his army or Pig with his congregation?

The Realists—save Alley Cat—disappeared over the wooden fence.

Then Alley Cat and Finn hugged goodbye in the din of the coming storm, and this hug became legendary. And although its importance in relations between dogs and cats can never be understated, the Legend of the Hug grew to such extremes that little kittens wrote careful letters in cursive to Finn and Bjørn, who never failed (with the help of the kittens' parental units) to deliver a present to each and every one of them on the anniversary of the embrace. Puppies were taught the hug as the symbolic end of a treaty, a treaty so long in coming that (according to the Legend) the heavens had rained down dog cookies upon its undertaking. So every year on the date of the hug, puppies and their parents sit down to share an extra cookie or two and give thanks and praise to two so wise, Bjørn and Finn, that the Lord or God or Whoever, had seen fit to rain down cookies. And then all the dogs hug and promise, at least for that day, not to chase cats, even if they climb into their backyards and dance on the fence tops.

And rain down it did on that very special day (but not cookies, not really), drenching both Alley Cat and Finn.

"I'm going to miss you, Count," Finn cried softly.

Footsteps on the patio. Shouts. A door slamming shut.

"I'll miss you too," Alley Cat said. "Maybe you can chase me around the backyard tomorrow if the weather breaks."

Finn ran in a circle.

"If I find a home, do you want me to see if you can move in too?" Finn asked, his tail wagging, Little White Tie thumping.

THUMP THUMP THUMP *BUMP!*

THUMP THUMP THUMP *BUMP!*

Alley Cat smiled and spread his arms as if to embrace the backyard.

"I'm already home," Alley Cat said.

Finn smiled back and let his long tongue hang out.

"You've taught me so much, Count. I'm so glad I'm in the gang and that you're the leader and—"

The footsteps were on the edge of the patio. They'd reach the grass any second now.

"Believe in yourself, Huckleberry," Alley Cat urged. "Don't believe in me. Besides: everything I said could be wrong."

And that was what Alley Cat said.

Alley Cat climbed the wooden fence, raised his paw (Finn did the same), and jumped out of this book and into the wide Wold.

The footsteps reached the grass.

"Finn!" the Boy cried, splashing through the mud towards Finn.

"Finn!" Mrs. Big Un cried, not minding the muddy Lab one bit.

"Get out of the rain, old man," Mr. Big Un said, quite cheerfully.

When the Boy hugged Finn, both of them soaked to the bones, it became the second most written about and discussed hug in history, just after the one between Finn and the Count. For the Boy loved Finn and thought of Finn as a brother. Growing into a man was hard work and required more time and effort than being a Boy did. Finn would learn to understand this in time: the Boy was growing older, but Finn wasn't. Oh sure, maybe in actual years (dog years or Big Un years, it doesn't matter), but Finn, like all dogs, remained little inside.

The Boy knelt in the mud and caressed Finn's ears.

"*SILK*," the Boy said.

Finn's Little White Tie almost broke free of its cage. The Great Journey had been long and hard on Finn's Little White Tie, but Little White Ties have ways of beating through even the worst storms.

Learn to love again, Alley Cat had whispered in Finn's *SILK* ears.

"Come home, Finn," the Boy said, and Finn bounded after him, shaking away the rain before he stepped through the sliding glass doors (careful not to wake the turtle), through the family room (ignoring the squeak of the guinea pig), up the stairs (where Mrs. Big Un rubbed him dry with a soft towel), and into the Boy's room. There he jumped into bed and waited for the Boy to finish brushing and flossing so Finn could tell him everything he'd learned and so the Boy could rub his belly and his ears and read to him from the Blue Books, and whisper…

Finn fell asleep.

+

A Few Minutes Later:

The orange and blue striped basketball rolled in the wind of the rainstorm and landed in the puddle. The backyard was deserted. Alley Cat climbed over the fence and, with much difficulty, stuffed the basketball into his pocket and became one with the night.

Chapter Sixteen

The Panda Sings

If this were a movie, a title card would be required here:
THREE MONTHS LATER.
Cue the music.
"Ain't no sunshine when she's gone…"
It was all there in the singer's voice, tripping out of the school loudspeaker; all the syrupy strings in the world couldn't hide the pain. The singer didn't know how to hide it, and he didn't want to. He knows, he knows, he knows, he knows, he knows…
(*"…I know I know I know I know I know I know I know…"*)
"Happy endings suck," Stevie Rich had said once, and maybe that was true. More likely, Magdalene thought, what he meant was that happy endings didn't happen in real life: only in books or movies and always on television.
But what if they did?
Well, for sure, they wouldn't be the neatly tied package so often presented in the movies. People who died in real life usually remained dead. The guy sometimes *never* got the girl. The missing, if found at all, are often found in pieces.
Aunt Tiddy had said more than once that the world was a scarier place now than it was when she was a child, and Magdalene had learned to agree with her. But right now, more than anything, Magdalene wanted to run to her aunt and tell her: no it's not, we just know more, we see more, nothing is ever completely hidden, and even Scrooge learned to love again. Surely, if Ebenezer Scrooge had learned this, the simplest of acts, then we too could rise above— maybe not better, but more experienced, battle scarred, ready for the final dare.
Magdalene hung back under the bleachers, the football helmet Aunt Tiddy had bought for her dangling at her side. She didn't know if she could face Aunt Tiddy—survivors were often found in pieces too.
"This is bad," Aunt Tiddy was saying to a woman stooped inside a tattered sweater in the bleachers above, the words little clouds floating above their heads like brief halos. Tiddy's wrinkled fingers

hugged her own bent shoulders in an effort to defeat the shivers. "I can't even see. And where's that damn dog? I can hear him. I'm telling you—stuff like this didn't happen in my day."

Aunt Tiddy's companion put an arm around the old woman.

"He had to go into the office, they said. He'll be back."

"But that was how long ago—and those two assistants!"

"Still, they won."

"The world is a different place now," Aunt Tiddy sniffed, and Magdalene knew Stevie Rich would agree in his own way.

"*...wonder if she's gone to stay...*"

But what if it's not the world that's different, Aunt Tiddy, what if it's us—Magdalene stopped herself: the world *was* different now. It wasn't just her. Happy endings didn't always suck.

"And the other one? I ask him to bring back hot chocolate, but, no, he says, you just need some soup," Aunt Tiddy said. "Soup? Can't put nothing in soup! Whoever heard of spiked soup?"

Mrs. Tidwell hid a smile and rubbed Aunt Tiddy's arms.

"It won't be long now," Mrs. Tidwell said.

"I'll be dead by the time it's wrapped up," Aunt Tiddy declared.

"They should be coming out soon," Mrs. Tidwell replied.

"Where's Katie?" Aunt Tiddy asked sharply.

"There—over there by the school. She's with—"

"That was a good thing you did for my family," Aunt Tiddy said.

Silence.

"They had it out in a heartbeat," Mrs. Tidwell said. "Didn't do a whole lot of damage. Just the hallway and Katie's room, part of the roof. The fire looked worse than it was."

"What you did for Magdalene..."

Aunt Tiddy started to cry.

Mrs. Tidwell reached into the purse at her feet and offered Aunt Tiddy a tissue. Tiddy shook her off and pulled one from her sleeve.

"Oh, Jack just wanted to go crazy at first," Mrs. Tidwell said, "even after the shock wore off. But I wouldn't let him give in to that. Jack—he was an angry man, but he's learning. Working with Big Brothers, helping me. I told him: if you want to be with me—and he does—then you need to start letting go. I learned the hard way. And you never *completely* let go. But just enough to breathe fresh air again, just enough to see the world's still in one piece, and you're still in it, and you've got some people who need you. Two now, in fact. Three counting..."

"And a whole lot of rabbits and critters, I hear tell," Aunt Tiddy said, her voice cracking like soft ice.

"Oh, we have those," Mrs. Tidwell replied, and she was crying now too.

Magdalene shirked back in case Mrs. Tidwell reached for another tissue; she'd see Magdalene standing beneath the bleachers for sure. Magdalene hadn't meant to eavesdrop, but the detective inside her couldn't help it. Bad habits, as the Bard said (or should have), are the hardest to break.

Aunt Tiddy freed another tissue from her sleeve and passed it to Mrs. Tidwell.

"Played almost the whole game," Aunt Tiddy said, shaking her head. "Never thought I'd see the day. Stevie did okay too."

"It's a whole new world for Stevie. It'll take some time for him to get used to everything. Going to Assumption was a leap, but living in the Heights—just getting him out of the Lakes—well, you understand."

Tiddy stuck her hand into her jacket, pulled out a flask, and offered it to Mrs. Tidwell.

"Something to keep you warm?" Tiddy asked.

"No, thank you," Mrs. Tidwell said, laughing. "Had enough of that stuff when my Bobby died. I just don't want to now. I don't ever want to see the inside of a tap room again."

"Just as well," Aunt Tiddy said between swallows, "not much left, and I can't wait for that butcher to return with the soup or whatever the hell he went to get."

"That's where I met Jack—at an AA meeting."

"I'm too old to worry about it, dear," Aunt Tiddy said, finishing off the flask.

"You been feeling alright?

"Oh, my old bones," Aunt Tiddy said, "they got quite a rattle, as Shakespeare would say. It's these modern cars—the brakes are for shite."

Aunt Tiddy turned the flask upside down over her mouth and shook out a few drops.

"Coming back from Bill's shop, I was. Had to get some chops," Aunt Tiddy said, glancing sideways. "I remembered the sporting goods shop in Spring House. I went out that way to buy shoulder pads and a helmet."

"Hmmm," Mrs. Tidwell said. "And cleats."

"*...ain't no sunshine when she's gone...*"

"I told Gregory: I'm done driving, but it looks like I ain't done living. Selling my apartment, selling my car. Gonna move in with Gregory and Magdalene permanent."

"What about Bill?" Mrs. Tidwell asked.

"Bill's got a house," Tiddy snapped, as if the question was indelicate.

"McAllister's house almost done, is it?" Tiddy asked, changing the subject.

"Almost. Jack's there now. The people your nephew hired work fast. Jack and I appreciate that."

"*Pisshaw*, it's the least," Aunt Tiddy said. "Are you—are you living there now?"

"I think I will be soon. Stevie too. But we're leaving it all up to Katie. We were supposed to meet, really meet, the night of the fire. She'd seen me and her dad...holding hands one night, but we hadn't met formally. So, it's really up to her, the moving in part. Whenever she's ready. We get along famously, Katie and I, and I think she understands that I'm not trying to replace her mother. I just want to be with Jack and her and Stevie."

"*...anytime she goes away...*"

"Happy endings suck," had been Stevie Rich's assessment once, but what about endings that were ambiguous? What about denouements where the characters had to create happy endings out of the ashes of tragedy—and not the grand tragedy of Shakespeare? Where was the tragic flaw? Magdalene knew some of the characters in Mondauk Proper had created their own hell, but a tragic flaw indicated something inherent rather than transient, something permanent rather than ephemeral, something congenital rather than situational.

What if, despite it all, Magdalene whispered to herself, we'd all *chosen* the final dare?

"*... anytime she goes away...*"

As she listened to Bill Withers' song shudder and vibrate to an end, Magdalene thought of Michael hunched over his crates of records, studying liner notes, still half-dressed in his football uniform. It was funny: she would have given anything to hear a little Neil Diamond right now.

Don't go losin' Lou's Head—too late!

"What light in yonder bleacher breaks!" a deep, funny voice

634 · *Saving Magdalene*

intoned, and Magdalene ducked behind a trash barrel. It was a voice hoarse from shouting over the *whack!* of the chopping block and the *swift!* of the meat slicer and the bustle of customers in a hurry.

Mr. Bard climbed the bleachers with a deftness hobbled by neither his considerable paunch nor his estimable age.

Aunt Tiddy shoved the flask up her sleeve.

"For you, m'lady," Bard the Butcher said, bowing his head towards Mrs. Tidwell and handing her a coffee.

Mr. Bard swiveled on his heels and offered a Styrofoam cup to Aunt Tiddy.

"This better not be soup," Tiddy said, eyeing the cup suspiciously.

" 'My mistress' eyes are *nothing* like the sun,' " Mr. Bard said.

"I don't think that's a compliment, Bill," Mrs. Tidwell laughed.

"*Principal* Tidwell, I presume," Mr. Bard said.

Mrs. Tidwell stood and curtseyed.

"Not quite yet, Sir William."

"You'll be a wonderful teacher, Beth," Aunt Tiddy said.

Mr. Bard bowed deeply.

"Bill the Butcher at your service."

"The Bard," Mrs. Tidwell said.

"I like to say I give out a little food for thought with my choicest cuts."

Magdalene knew Aunt Tiddy had just rolled her eyes.

"I met him at a funeral," Aunt Tiddy said.

"Turns out neither of us knew the guy," Mr. Bard added.

"The deceased?" Mrs. Tidwell asked.

"Yep, didn't know him, so I invited Tiberius here back to the shop for a pork chop."

"I'll bet."

"Here they come," Aunt Tiddy said, pointing towards the clubhouse door, and they poured out: the Assumption Knights. Most of the kids were still in uniform—they wanted their friends and family to see them in full gladiator gear. Magdalene fell in behind Stevie Rich.

"You look good in tights," Magdalene said.

"Bully," Stevie Rich said. He still had his helmet on.

"Guys! Up here!"

"Stevie—the sky is falling, the sky is falling?" Mr. Bard asked.

"I can't undo the strap," Stevie admitted.

Jerry Eves ran up behind Magdalene and Stevie. His hair stood on end and his freckles shined with sweat.

"Here," Jerry Eves offered, undoing the snap on Stevie's helmet.

"Ahh, Stick Man," Mr. Bard said by way of a greeting to Jerry.

"How'd I do?" Stevie Rich asked.

"You did good, real good," Jerry said. "Just don't be afraid to put the other guy on the ground, okay? Just *plow* right into him. Put him on his ass."

Jerry Eves grinned at Aunt Tiddy: "Begging your pardon."

"Horse hockey!" Aunt Tiddy sniffed, as she tried to look put out.

"Shakespeare *had* to have said that!" Bill Bard the Butcher said. " 'A rose by any other name…' "

Magdalene ignored the adults.

"You did great," Jerry Eves whispered, sneaking his hand into hers.

"I'll pretend I didn't see that," Aunt Tiddy said, covering her eyes.

Behind them, a swarm of relatives and friends surrounded Magdalene's teammates, all pieces of a bigger whole. Counting all of them, Magdalene realized, would have been an exercise in futility. There was no summarizing all the hearts beating in the brisk autumn air; there were too many stories, and none of them was finished.

Aunt Tiddy stood on her tippy-toes and waved. The flask slipped from her sleeve and *clanged* on the metal bleacher.

"I'll pretend I didn't see *that*," Magdalene said.

Jerry Eves squeezed her fingers.

She loved Jerry Eves. She always would. How was that for summarizing?

Above the circling clusters, her father's head made its way towards the bleachers. His sideburns were gray, and so was the hair near his temples. "Distinguished," was what Mrs. Tidwell called it. "Getting old," was what Aunt Tiddy said. The gray, ADA Barrows had explained to his daughter, was the survivor's souvenir. A summarizing of sorts.

The past was never past.

Still, just seeing her father filled Magdalene's head in a way numbers never could. It was odd to not want to count, but it was odder to still be breathing and to feel so alive. (And if the breath included the smell of her father's aftershave, then all the better.)

She had some gray of her own now. Her skin had healed quickly.

First degree burns mostly, they said. Her hair grew back. But on the sides, it had grown back gray.

The past was never past; it was just the summary of you—until the next chapter.

"Well, Gregory Barrows," Aunt Tiddy said, "what's your excuse?" She shook her head. "Leaving a game early, abandoning your team to work on a Saturday morning."

Her father eased his hand under Magdalene's hair, and his palm was cool on her neck. Jerry nervously let go of her hand.

"The judge called for an early Saturday session to wrap things up without the press swarming around. He agreed to counseling for Joseph Bochdan. There won't be a civil suit either. The Cabots were adamant about that. The judge says Mrs. Bochdan's free to sell the house—Sol's too—and move so long as Joseph receives counseling in the state. I think she might stay though. They're finishing up as we speak."

"Then why aren't you there now, Daddy?"

"I needed to be here," her father said. "I'm sorry I still ended up missing the end of the game, guys—and girl. Kudos to all for the win. Savor it, though remember the season is long, and there's a lot of hard work ahead of us.

"As far as the rest of it—Karl's taking care of putting this to bed. Our office is dropping all charges. We want the father. We want Andriy Bochdan. Our guys say they're close."

"Thank heavens," Aunt Tiddy said.

Jerry Eves punched Stevie Rich in the arm.

"Happy endings suck, right?" Jerry asked.

Steve Rich snarled.

"Boys!" Aunt Tiddy said sharply.

No, Stevie, Magdalene thought, *happy* endings don't suck—just *endings*. It's always hard to say goodbye.

And as if she was reading Magdalene's mind, Aunt Tiddy said: "Mrs. Bochdan and the Cabots—I only wish them our ending."

"Amen!" Mr. Bard said.

"Magdalene, Magdalene, Magdalene!"

"Katie!"

Katie's hair had grown back too, only without the gray (it had burned despite being beneath the blanket), and as she ran towards Magdalene from the far side of the Fields, a dark, lumbering shadow followed close behind her.

Magdalene paused to quickly go over her mental to-do list—it had changed significantly from the COUNTDOWN, and Magdalene had to keep reminding herself of the tasks. She was doing well in high school so far, but numbers remained a challenge. She thought a remedial math class would be humiliating, but bringing order to the chaos was a challenge fit for a detective.

Now then: THE LIST.

There were three items:

- Mail the invitation to Chloe. (Stevie Rich said he knew her address, and Jerry said that it was a damn good idea to invite Chloe to her birthday party. She hoped Chloe would be okay with nothing stronger than Aunt Tiddy's Fizzle Punch—Fresca and Hawaiian Punch—but Magdalene thought Chloe might actually enjoy being twelve after years of being older.)
- Finish Tiddy's scrapbook. (She was very close to being finished. After editing her own book and binding copies with yarn, she'd started on Tiddy's. Magdalene had horded away all of Tiddy's Polaroids, all the blurry photographs of Barrows' elbows and eyeballs and nostrils, and had started mounting them in an old photo book she'd found at a flea market. Magdalene planned on giving everyone a copy of *her* book, the one she'd written, but Magdalene wanted to give her great aunt something special. Magdalene had helped almost break Aunt Tiddy; she wanted to give Tiddy the pieces back.)

Katie ran into Magdalene's legs. The bulky shadow crashed into Katie.

"You threw for forty-four yards and only got sacked once!" Katie said.

"Yeah, but it was by someone on my own team!"

"Sorry!" Stevie Rich yelled through his mouth guard.

Jerry punched him in the shoulder again.

"I kept stats for the whole game!" Katie cried. "Danny Kildare was there, and he helped, and he said if this were a movie poster, it would read, 'Good Girl Goes Bad and Back Again.'"

"Here," Katie said, thrusting a piece of loose-leaf paper into Magdalene's hand. She cocked a thumb behind her. "There's slobber on it though."

The lumbering shadow behind Katie barked.

"Damn dog's getting fat, Gregory," Aunt Tiddy said.

Tiddy turned to Mrs. Tidwell: "Wouldn't eat a thing all summer."

"Dogs' know; they catch moods," Mr. Bard said.

"Food was going to waste. Had to switch brands. 'Course, when this one came home from the hospital," Tiddy said, looking over her glasses at Magdalene, "it was like he never ate before. Hasn't stopped since."

Okay, okay, the end of THE LIST:

- Read *A Lab's Ears Are Made of* SILK to Raven. (The hero was based on him, after all: a dog named Finn who learned to love again.) She'd had to make a few changes in the three months since the first draft. Experience will do that. It was less a children's book or a young adult fable than a…she didn't know. Rated PG according to Jerry. He had finished all the illustrations just a couple of weeks ago. Gone were the stick figures; turned out Jerry had more in reserve than just acts of heroism and jokes involving bodily emissions—the boy could draw! But before Magdalene gave the little handmade books to anybody else, she would read it to Raven. Then she would read it to her father, Assistant District Attorney Gregory Barrows, who, like herself and her dog, had learned how to love again.

Raven ran in a circle around Katie, and Katie spun in the opposite direction. She reached into her pocket and showered Raven with dogwood petals, the last of them before Deep Autumn devoured the rest. Raven shook his fur like he did after a bath. It looked like an explosion of petals—the dogwood's last gasp.

But that wasn't completely true, now was it, Magdalene thought. No, the dogwood got a second chance. "All the dogwood had to do was remain strong, and Jesus took care of it," was what Katie had said oh those many moons ago. Magdalene figured if Jesus took care of the dogwood it was because the dogwood took care of itself first.

Raven wore a little Assumption Knights football jersey, the one he'd wear to next year's dog parade (if he could stand the canine company). He smelled like popcorn. As Magdalene watched Raven shake off the last of the dogwood petals, with Katie running around him laughing, the little white and pink petals in their last flight, pieces, parts of a bigger whole, falling in the early autumn air like gently rocking baby cradles, she thought: what if we're many parts?

What if we're made up of pieces of everyone else, and we're responsible for giving a little bit of ourselves back? Wouldn't that make us a little more impervious to being splintered, knowing that we're part of a bigger whole? Yes. Does it make us less unique, less independent? No, Magdalene thought: no one else is made of exactly the same pieces of the blanket, but it covers us all, nonetheless. We all have the freedom to weave what we will from the experiences we've taken in. Experience is the blanket—and breathing is the dare. For to live, to really live, is the bravest dare of all.

It was like the way Michael heard music: it was more than *just* a song. It was a lifetime in three and a half minutes. It was momentary and possibly disposable and absolutely fraught with terror and beauty and everything in between. And Michael grabbed it with both hands like he was catching a Hail Mary pass.

And that's really the final dare, isn't it—to breathe and not count?

Raven snatched the panda from the grass and barreled towards her.

And when the panda finally sang, well, it was the most beautiful music in the world, and Magdalene knew that Michael heard it too. He was listening. Everybody loves a happy ending.

The stuffed panda's voice was creaky from misuse, off-key, more a dirge than a sound of joy, but the joy was inherent. The notes were jumbled and messy, confused and irritated one bar, harmonious and ethereal the next.

Of course, it was "Sea of Love," the First Song, their First Lullaby.

Magdalene hummed it under her breath.

Raven was running towards her, the panda singing in his mouth, closer, close, a million frames a second, and in variable focus: his wet nose, gray muzzle, stinky breath, flagrant whiskers, kind, brown eyes...

If this were a movie, Monien the panda would sing "Sea of Love" until the slow fade before the roll of the credits.

But "Sea of Love" was a Goodbye Song. What Magdalene thought her movie needed was a Hello Song.

And, come to think of it, as Raven chomped on Monien, the tempo seemed to pick up and the shaky notes sounded an awful lot like Neil Diamond.

"And when I hurt / Hurtin' runs off my shoulders / How can I hurt when I'm holding you?"

Raven was in her face now, seconds away from a sloppy kiss…
Eager…
Panting…
Happy endings.
Cue the music again so it ends the way it began.
Hmm-*hm*-hmm / *hmm*-*hm*-m-*hm*, *hm*-m-*hm*.
Hmm-*hm*-hmm / *hmm*-*hm*-m-*hm*, *hm*-m-*hm*.
Hmm-*hm*-hmm / *hm*-m-*hmmm*-*hmmm*-hmmm-*hmmm*.
And…
FADE TO BLACK.

A Lab's Ears Are Made of *SILK*

Episode VI

What Becomes *SILK*

Finn wasn't quite the Goner he'd thought. Mrs. Big Un said he'd caught cold from staying outside in the rain all day. His bones were weary, his nose runny, and his stomach rumbly. After a quick dinner and a couple of cookies, Finn was bundled into a blanket on the Boy's bed, and when the Big Uns closed the door, the Boy hugged him tight and read to him.

The books the Boy read to Finn that night (and many other nights after) weren't Blue Books. Finn didn't mind at all, but as both the Boy and Finn grew older, Finn noticed the Blue Books were growing beards of fine, gray dust. And in the middle of the front cover of *The Missing Chums*: a tiny fingerprint, surely too tiny for the Boy who looked bigger to Finn every day. And the smudge next to the little fingerprint? Why, that was Finn's nose print! He'd have recognized his nose print anywhere!

One rainy afternoon, while the Boy was in school, Mrs. Big Un charged into the room with what looked like a fluffy bird on a stick and attacked the Blue Books. Then she placed all the Blue Books in a big cardboard box. Finn stuck his nose in the box and cried a little. Finn knew the Blue Books were leaving.

"He's too old for the Hardy Boys, Finn." Mrs. Big Un said.

Mrs. Big Un lugged the box into the attic, and Finn never saw the Blue Books again.

Finn's days were spent much as they had been before his Great Journey. During the week, he'd help the Boy get ready for school. (Unless it was snowing; on those days, the Boy and Finn huddled beneath the blankets, feeling very much a team, and waited to hear their school number announced on the radio; if it was, Finn knew, the day could be spent building forts, throwing snowballs, and eating snow; Finn liked to eat snow.) Then Finn would spend the hours after lunch napping, moving from room to room to avoid the monster Mrs. Big Un used to vacuum the house. At night, the Boy and Finn would horse around with stuffed animals or play fetch with Finn's new green and black striped basketball. But the Boy had lots and lots of homework, and sometimes other loud boys came over to listen to music, and every once in a while, a girl would stop by and the Boy would blush.

Finn still went into the backyard to go to the bathroom, and when it was nice, he'd cruise the fence line, looking for Count Bjørn and the Realists, but they were gone, and no amount of hoping, it seemed, would bring them back.

Then there came the day when the Vicar Pig caught cold. He didn't last long—guinea pigs rarely do once they catch cold. Mrs. Big Un gave Pig orange liquid in an eyedropper, but the Vicar died anyway. Shortly before he did, Finn visited him in the family room.

"Mr. Vicar," Finn whispered, "are you awake?"

Pig lifted his head from his blanket of torn-up newspapers.

"Is that you, O Lord?" Pig asked. "Or are you an angel?"

"No," Finn said. "I'm a Lab. Huckleberry Finn. Remember me?"

"Huckle-who? Why are you taking me, Lord? I've been your faithful servant. I've spread your word. I've condemned your enemies and made new ones for you. I've—"

"Would you like me to get you a carrot or some celery?" Finn interrupted.

"The only thing I need is the Good Book," Pig said.

"I don't have one of those," Finn replied.

"Goddamn dog..." Pig said, and then he was gone.

Finn was sad for his passing and watched as Mr. Big Un dug Pig a little hole in the backyard.

The Colonel Turtle would soon be in a hole next to the Vicar Pig—a positioning that neither party would have much appreciated. The Colonel was old when he died. When the Boy first said Turtle was ill, Finn went to visit the Colonel on the other side of the family room, but Turtle wouldn't come out of his shell, which looked worn from age and battles past.

"How could they do this?" Turtle's shell asked.

"Who?" Finn asked. "What did they do?"

"*They*, soldier!" Turtle's shell thundered. "We tried to stop them. In my day, we'd have crushed them like we did the pinkos. Now— why, just look at the news! *They're* everywhere! Do the math! Look at the clues! Conjugate the verbs! We need a sneak attack. We need Special Ops. We need Black Ops. We need—"

Finn left. He never could figure out who *they* were. And soon enough, the war was over for the Colonel. Turtle was buried next to Pig in a ceremony attended by only Finn and Mr. Big Un. The Boy didn't like these kinds of ceremonies, Mr. Big Un said, and Finn understood. Finn didn't like these kinds of ceremonies either.

Then one day: the impossible happened.

One short whistle. One long. Another short.

Finn had been cruising the fence line, getting ready to poop, enjoying the sunshine and the cool breeze. He'd paid his respects to Pig and Turtle, as he did every time he went out to the backyard. Now he was just sauntering, barking at squirrels and birds, chasing dandelion wishes.

Again: one short whistle—one long—another short.

Finn stepped away from the fence, and there he was: a little ragged, a trifle skinny, but it was him, and Finn's Little White Tie pounded double time, then triple time.

"Count Bjørn!" Finn barked.

"It is I," Alley Cat said, spinning on his toes.

"And the Realists?" Finn asked, turning his head back and forth, his tongue hanging out.

There was a rustle on the other side of the fence, then Coulda appeared, looking *really* skinny, but still quite regal in his Siamese coat and eye patch, followed by Shoulda, still chunky, but missing patches of fur here and there. They all looked cool in their imaginary leather jackets.

"The Realists!" Finn cried, and the cats leapt from the fence, and they all danced and exchanged paw shakes.

"I thought you'd forgotten all about me," Finn said.

"Not at all, my brother," Alley Cat said. "But Woulda…"

Coulda and Shoulda bowed their heads.

"He's…Woulda's *dead*?" Finn asked. "Woulda's the D word?"

"No," Coulda, choking back tears.

"Adopted," Alley Cat explained.

"But wait," Finn said, "I'm adopted!"

And once the Realists digested this bit of realism, they hugged and danced once more, and they broke out the vitals and the vino and raised their imaginary glasses to Woulda.

"May he crack nuts," Alley Cat said, "forever!"

Coulda, Shoulda, and Finn shouted the customary response: "May he break the wind! May he cut the cheese! Forever! Forever!"

The Realists then gave Finn his imaginary leather gang jacket. (They'd been carrying it around for a long time, but the wear and tear gave it an appropriate toughness.) It didn't fit—cats were smaller than black Labrador retrievers, but Shoulda draped it from the top of Finn's noggin, and even though it wasn't really there, all four of them saw it and admired the way Finn looked in it.

"So, that's where we've been. We tried to break him out a dozen times," Coulda said.

"I think he likes it there," Alley Cat admitted. "Animals who are adopted learn to like living in houses."

Finn agreed and filled the Realists in on everything that had happened since they'd last met.

When Finn was done, Alley Cat winked at Coulda and Shoulda.

"Are you ready?" Alley Cat asked Finn.

Finn jumped up on all fours and wagged his tail.

"Sure!"

"Okay, rules are: there are no rules," Alley Cat said. "Just nothing real, okay?"

"Okay!" Coulda, Shoulda, and Finn shouted.

And so the Games began.

The Games took place every day at roughly noon (with the offspring of the astronaut mice acting as referees, cheerleaders, and, occasionally, quarry). Once in a while, they played at night, and sometimes they tried mornings, but the Big Uns always yelled at the noise. (Woulda joined them as often as he could escape, but he was quite comfortable in his new home, thank you very much.) When Shoulda died (he choked on a bologna sandwich that wasn't his, an unfortunate turn of events, but Shoulda liked to eat; Alley Cat buried him with what was left of the sandwich), the remaining Realists held a Memorial Game in his honor. When Coulda passed away at an old age, Finn and Alley Cat donned eye patches and dedicated a Game to their fallen comrade. Coulda, it turned out, had been a collector—of fallen stars. His pockets were full of them. Even as his breath took leave of his golden Siamese body, the stars in his pocket winked and shined. He'd strung them together with fishing wire to form a necklace, and they glittered and sputtered and looked nothing at all like Finn thought they would.

"The big picture, Huckleberry," Alley Cat said, "rarely looks anything like you think it does."

"But in the end," Alley Cat added, "everything is connected."

Woulda managed to sneak out for both burials. (Woulda had been so overcome with grief at Shoulda's funeral, he insisted on burying his portly pal with two pounds of old bologna.) But by the time of Coulda's interment, Woulda's flatulence had reached such extreme proportions that he was forced to attend the service from behind the wooden fence.

Alley Cat bowed his head and read from *The Book of Hardy*—*The Missing Chums* to be exact. This is the passage Alley Cat read:

" ' "Frank! Joe!" cried Chet, overjoyed. As soon as his hands were untied, the stout boy dragged his pals and hugged them in excitement.' "

"Amen," said the chorus of astronaut mice offspring.

"Amen," said Finn.

Nothing more needed to be said.

Woulda farted on the other side of the fence.

RRRIPPP!

"How does he look?" Woulda yelled.

"He looks dead," Alley Cat shouted back.

RRRIPPP!

"Sorry," Woulda said. "Excuse me."

"You don't want to see him," Alley Cat yelled. "It's better if you don't."

"Okay," Woulda yelled back. "Is he shining? The stars in his pocket. Are they shining?"

"Always," Alley Cat said, shoveling the last of the dirt over his old pal's body.

"So much for Realism," Alley Cat whispered to Finn.

"What?" Woulda shouted.

"Nothing," Alley Cat said.

RRRIPPP!

"Sorry," Woulda said. "Excuse me."

When Woulda died, he died farting. At least that was the word on the streets of the Wold. Woulda's adopted parents had tried to hide Woulda's demise from their Girl, but when the Girl found her parents burying Woulda, wrapped in an old Star Wars blanket, in a hastily dug hole, she squeezed the mangy, old cat so hard, he gave his last fart.

SQUEAK!

Legend in the neighborhood had it that you could still smell Woulda's final escaped wind. And, the legend continued, in deference to his old partner, Shoulda, it smelled very much like bologna.

Finn and Alley Cat met just about every morning and afternoon to relive the past. They tried to continue the Games, but even the astronaut mice's offspring had passed away, and *their* offspring had little time for two old Realists.

One afternoon, shortly before Finn caught a cold he wasn't able to shake (his legs ached, his breathing grew labored, and a lump developed on his side), the two friends lounged in a sunspot in the backyard.

"It's been an extraordinarily Great Journey," Finn said, watching a dandelion wish fall like a dying star.

Alley Cat yawned and snuggled closer to Finn.

"It's not over yet," Alley Cat said.

"I know," Finn said.

And he did know—in the way that dogs know their owners are sad or angry or happy. Finn wanted to see the Boy graduate from high school. But inside his Little White Tie, Finn knew his attendance wasn't a reality.

"Will I see you again, once—?" Finn couldn't finish.

"I love you," Alley Cat said. He didn't know the answer.

"I love you," Finn said.

"You saved me," Finn added.

"You saved you," Alley Cat mewed. "And then you saved me."

"It's a mystery," Finn concluded.

"No, not really," Alley Cat said after a long pause. "We all learned to love again. The only mystery is why we lost love in the first place. Go to sleep, Huckleberry. Go to sleep."

Finn slept even more than before. He tended his morning duties, made sure the Boy got off to school okay, ate a cookie with Mrs. Big Un, and then would spend the rest of the day sleeping. He went outside only when he had to use the bathroom or share a secret with Alley Cat. Mrs. Big Un didn't want Finn sleeping in the yard. She gave him medicine that tasted like rancid cherries, and Mr. Big Un rubbed the inside of Finn's old ears with ointment, and a gray-haired, kind doctor tended to Finn's lump.

And the Boy: the Boy grew into a young man, and Finn's Little White Tie beat a frantic tempo whenever he caught site of the Boy in the act of growing up: dressing up in funny suit for a Prom Dance, getting grounded for sharing a beer with a buddy behind the shed (Alley Cat filled Finn in on the details), kissing a girl named Mary Lou (who smelled like vanilla milkshakes!) over and over again on the sofa in the basement.

Finn knew he would leave the Boy soon, and he had to swallow a different kind of lump whenever he thought of this. Finn didn't know where he was going; Alley Cat didn't know either. But Finn knew this: it would be a Great Journey of a Different Sort. Finn was ready, whatever was next, but he was scared just the same, for he so loved the Boy and the Big Uns and Alley Cat. Not seeing them anymore—there was nothing scarier to Finn. Not even thunderstorms.

When the day came—it was a beautiful fall day—Finn lay in the Boy's bed trying to find his breath. He'd climbed into bed with it, but it was running away from him. Finn wanted to chase after his breath and retrieve it. He was good at retrieving. Finn imagined running after his breath, and he knew, inside his Little White Tie, that *this* was his Last Great Journey.

The Boy was crying, and Finn licked his face.

Mr. and Mrs. Big Un were crying too, but Finn couldn't reach them with his tongue. They rubbed his belly, which went up and down, up and down, up and down, as if trying to make up for Little White Tie. Finn's Little White Tie was coming undone.

"Good dog," Mr. Big Un said.

"Do you want a cookie, Finn?" Mrs. Big Un asked, but this one time, he didn't.

Maybe he'd see Coulda, Shoulda, and Woulda where he was going.

Maybe he'd see his mom.

Outside, a cat howled into the falling of the leaves.

The Boy leaned his face against Finn's. Finn wagged his tail and managed a little growl that said, "I love you." Finn hoped the Boy understood.

The Boy lowered his mouth against Finn's ear and whispered.

The Boy whispered in his ear.

"A Lab's ears are made of *SILK*," the Boy whispered, and Finn knew it was true.

Little White Tie beat once, twice, three times...

+

A Few Minutes Later:

Finn was buried in the backyard, beneath the dogwood tree. The Boy and Mr. Big Un had wrapped Finn in the Boy's blanket and had laid Finn's stuffed animals—monkey and frog and elephant and panda—next to him. When Mr. Big Un shoveled the first load of dirt upon the blanket and monkey and frog and elephant and panda, the Boy sobbed so loud, Finn could hear him from where he'd been watching, high above the clouds, nestled in between the stars. Coulda, Shoulda, and Woulda were there. Finn's mom too. And lots of mice in costumes. They were all stars, and when they fell, as stars do, they were only playing a game, dipping their light into the great big wide Wold below.

Once Finn learned how, he fell every night to whisper into the Boy's ear, and he rose again to shine light upon the Great Journeys the Boy had yet to take but one day would. Wherever the Boy went, a star of absolute *SILK* made his way a little brighter, for the paths would sometimes be thorny and dark, and Finn wanted the Boy to know they were all *SILK* and *SILK* they would all remain.

+

Too:

The last of the Realists waited on top of the fence until the Big Uns and the Boy had gone inside. The Boy went in last, sitting for a long time beside the mound of earth that marked the beginning of Finn's Last Great Journey. The Boy never stopped crying, and when he finally went in (it was growing dark and more than a little chilly), Alley Cat realized that what he had taken for rain were his own tears.

Alley Cat was old and felt every passing year. His fur was matted, and his eyesight wasn't what it used to be. The stars, on certain nights, threw enough light for him to get around. Alley Cat knew his own Last Great Journey would start soon. He was ready. He missed his friends. He missed the Games. He even missed Woulda's flatulence, although Alley Cat farted enough these last, long days for the whole gang. Alley Cat thought of it as gas to help him take off for the stars.

Alley Cat hoped the stars called soon.

He sat next to the mound of earth marking Finn's grave. He rolled in the dirt, rubbed his face in it, tried to snuggle next to it.

When he rose from the dirt, Alley Cat was every inch the regal Count Bjørn de Vagabond of legend, and he reached into the pocket of his imaginary leather jacket.

His paws shook, but he never dropped the ball.

"*SILK*," Alley Cat said.

Alley Cat kissed the orange and blue striped basketball and placed it on top of the mound of dirt.

"We are all *SILK*," Alley Cat said before falling asleep next to the basketball.

And that night and all his remaining nights, Alley Cat dreamed of the stars.

And when, soon after, the stars called him by his full name, Alley Cat ascended slowly, for he'd remembered to bring Finn's basketball at the last second.

Oh, the games we'll play, Alley Cat thought, and then Alley Cat was a Goner too.

Epilogue

A Postscripted Apology

Michael,

I'm scribbling in the flap, and I'm going to leave this for you. A belated farewell.

Dad comes here every week and cleans the area around your stone. Fresh flowers, new soil, a blanket, sometimes a little American flag.

I know Jerry leaves a football every year, just as the season begins.

I'm leaving you my words.

Remember how I used to believe nothing was connected? Well, everything is. *Everything*. Whether we want it to be so or not. And everything changes, disconnects, finds itself again.

We are all prime numbers, Michael. Divisible by one (someone else) and ourselves. And when the time comes, we are all shooting stars. Some of us disappear and others leave light that will burn for all time.

What will you do when your time comes?
What did I do?
Not enough.
Nothing.
I'm sorry, Michael. I will be sorry for the rest of my life.

But the rest of my life, Michael! I'm going to live it, like you said, with my head to the gun, only the gun is empty and my head is filled—not with numbers, but with words. Lou's Head had it right.
Sing until your lungs are bereft of air.
Sing every word you know.

And I do. I sing them and then I write them down.

This book: these are just the first words. There will be many, many more.

And they're all for you.

That's my final dare to myself, Michael. I whisper it every morning. I pretend you're tickling my ear and whispering to me:

Live, Lil. Live.

And each morning, I learn to love again, and each evening, I forgive myself. It's something I've had to learn to do: love again and forgive. Because, eventually, Michael, eventually the panda sings.

I still see you every night before I close my eyes and reach for sleep and watch the stars come together like they always do: you're running along the shore, shedding your shoes and socks and shirt, and when your feet hit the dock, they thunder like my heart, and when you jump, the dying sun catches you mid-flight, and then you shine so bright before you fade away, Michael. And you always fade away.

And when I open my eyes in the morning, you're there, ready to jump the Puddle another day, for this is how you learn to let go of someone, this is how you let someone go: you don't.

I love you so much.
Your sister,

Magdalene

About the Author's Dog.

Helium Raven Teardrop was a black Labrador retriever. He was born on November 1, 1997 in Bensalem, PA. Whether he was a pure bred is up for debate. If he wasn't, Raven never let on, although that was mostly because he was a dog and dogs don't talk.

Raven was adopted from the Brookline Labrador Retriever Rescue on October 26, 2003 and moved into the author's swingin' bachelor pad in Ambler, PA. Raven turned six on the same day that the author's first book, *Deep Autumn*, was released. It was a heady time.

Raven didn't read books, through no fault of his own (dogs just don't have the time, really), but, on occasion, he heard pieces of this work and other writings read aloud. Generally, he rejoiced, only falling asleep once in a while. He was tickled at having two roles in this novel (Finn and Magdalene's Raven) because that meant double the amount of cookies.

Raven's favorite inanimate objects in the world were his stuffed animal collection, among which numbered Monkey (the favorite by far), a pig, an elephant, a crab, a turquoise dog, a frog, but, sadly, no panda. He was the Basketball King and could dunk into the laundry basket. Raven enjoyed barking at neighbors, playing Frisbee, peeing in the grass, listening to Joni Mitchell, and napping roughly two-thirds of the day. He made no excuses for his cookie predilection and insisted that rubbing his tummy was good luck. Raven's girlfriend was a chocolate Lab named Emma Lou, and together they enjoyed many supervised sleepovers.

Helium Raven Teardrop passed away on November 2, 2011, the day after his fourteenth birthday. His ears were truly made of *SILK*. My heart is a poorer place without him.

www.ingramcontent.com/pod-product-compliance
Lightning Source LLC
Chambersburg PA
CBHW050118030726
47505CB00007B/1925